THE BIFROST GUARDIANS

VOLUME TWO

BOOK FOUR
Shadow's Realm

•

BOOK FIVE
By Chaos Cursed

Mickey Zucker Reichert

DAW BOOKS, INC.

DONALD A. WOLLHEIM, FOUNDER

375 Hudson Street, New York, NY 10014

ELIZABETH R. WOLLHEIM
SHEILA E. GILBERT
PUBLISHERS

www.dawbooks.com

First Paperback Printing, November 2000
2 3 4 5 6 7 8 9

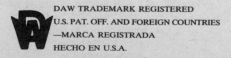

DAW TRADEMARK REGISTERED
U.S. PAT. OFF. AND FOREIGN COUNTRIES
—MARCA REGISTRADA
HECHO EN U.S.A.

PRINTED IN THE U.S.A.

**Be sure to read these other extraordinary
DAW Science Fiction and Fantasy Novels by
MICKEY ZUCKER REICHERT**

THE BIFROST GUARDIANS

VOLUME TWO

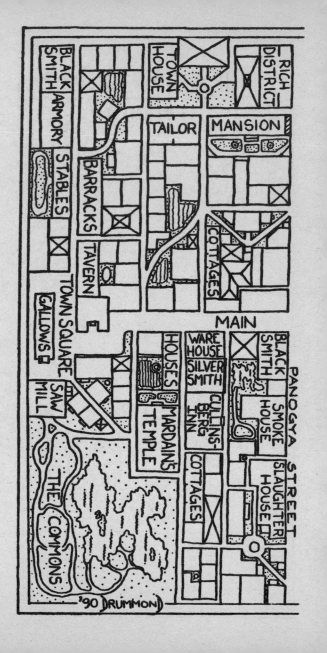

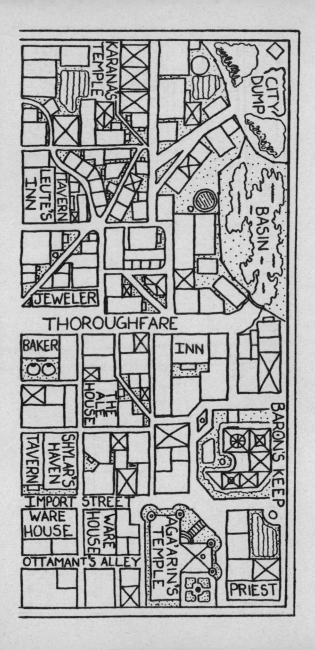

Shadow's Realm

For Dwight V. Swain
Who taught so many. So well.

ACKNOWLEDGMENTS

I would like to thank Dave Hartlage, Sheila Gilbert, Jonathan Matson, Richard Hescox, D. Allan Drummond, Joe Schaumburger, our parents, and SFLIS for their own special contributions.

Prologue

The sun rose over the eastern horizon, casting red highlights across the pastures and grain fields of Wilsberg until the land seemed crusted with rubies. Atop a grassy hillock overlooking the village, the Dragonmage, Bolverkr, sprawled casually across the doorstep of his mansion. A breeze ruffled hair white as bleached bone, carrying the mingled smells of clover and new-mown hay. Clouds bunched to towering shapes or drifted to lace in the mid-autumn sky.

Bolverkr stretched, attuned to the familiar noise of the town he had considered home for his last century and a half: the splash of clay pots dipped into the central fountain, the playful shrill of children chasing one another through narrow, cobbled lanes, the metallic rattle of pans at the hearth behind him. The latter sound brought a smile to his lips. He twisted his head, peering down the squat hallway of his home to its kitchen. His young wife, Magan, whisked from table to fireplace, black hair swirling around sturdy curves marred by the bulge of a womb heavy with child. She was dark in every way Bolverkr's Norse heritage made him light. *Beautiful. Sensitive to my needs as I am to hers. I picked a good one this time.* Bolverkr chuckled. *Two hundred seventeen years old, and I've finally learned how to select the right woman.*

The throaty low of a cow drew Bolverkr's attention to the southern paddock. A ribby herd of Cullinsbergen cattle chewed mouthfuls of alfalfa hay, browsing through the stacks with wide, wet noses. Chickens scurried to peck up dislodged seeds, muddied feathers matted to their breasts. Children, shirking chores, alternately tossed bread crumbs and pebbles to a flock of pullets, giggling whenever the birds flapped and fought over the rocks. From his world on the hill, Bolverkr studied the children's wrinkled homespun and their dirt-streaked faces, aware nearly all of them car-

13

ried his blood at some near or distant point in their heritage. *Seasons come and go. Cottages crumble and are rebuilt. My grandchildren have spawned grandchildren. And the only constant feature of the farming town of Wilsberg is an old sorcerer named Bolverkr.* Contented by his musings and cheered by the promise of a clear day, Bolverkr eased his back against the doorjamb.

The Chaos-storm struck with crazed and sudden violence. Without warning, the clouds wilted to black, smothering the autumn sky beneath a dark, unnatural curtain of threat. A half-grown calf bellowed in terror. A startled woman flung her jar into the fountain, throwing up her arms in a gesture to ward away evil. The clay smacked the basin stones, shattering into chips that swirled to the muddy bottom. Frightened children fled for shelter. Before Bolverkr could raise his withered frame from the doorway, Northern winds knifed through the town of Wilsberg.

Bolverkr gaped, horror-struck, as the force raged through threadlike walkways, scooped up a handful of children, and hurled their mangled bodies like flotsam on a beach. One crashed into the fountain, slamming a gale-lashed wave of water over the peasant woman. A wall tumbled into wreckage, and the squall tore through Wilsberg like a hungry demon. It shattered cottages to rubble, whirled stone and thatch into a tornado force of wind. The fountain tore free of its foundation; the gale scattered its boulders through homes, fields, and paddocks.

The dragonmark scar on Bolverkr's hand throbbed like a fresh wound. Desperately, he tapped his life energy, twining a shield of magic over a huddled cluster of frightened townsfolk. But his power was a mellow whisper against a raging torrent of Chaos-force. It shattered his ward, claiming sorcery, stone, and life with equal abandon. It swallowed friends, cows, and cobbles, the mayor's mansion and the basest hovel, leaving a sour trail of twisted corpses and crimson-splashed pebbles.

Bolverkr tossed an urgent command over his shoulder. "Magan, run!" Gritting his teeth until his jaw ached, he delved into the depths of his being, gathering life energy as another man might tap resolve. Holding back just enough to sustain consciousness, he fashioned a transparent, magical barrier of peerless thickness and strength. His spell snapped to existence, penning scores of townsfolk against the base of his hill. The effort cost all but a ragged shred of Bolverkr's stamina. Too weak to stand, he sank to one knee; a dancing curtain of black and white pressed his vision. Sick with frustration, he focused on shadows as panicked men and women bashed into the unseen shield, unaware they were safe from the onrushing winds.

Suddenly, sound thundered, pulsing through the village as if some wrathful god had ripped open the heavens. The gale-force burst through Bolverkr's shield. Once protected, the farmers now became prisoners of the spell. They ran for freedom, only to crash into its encumbering sides. Gusts heaved bodies against the solid remnants of Bolverkr's magic, smashing townsmen into gashed and battered corpses.

Bolverkr staggered to his feet, too weak to curse in outrage. Only one course remained to him, one power left to tap; but he knew it might claim a price equal to the otherworld storm he faced. He felt Magan's touch through the bunched cloth of his tunic. Ignoring his command to flee, she caught his arm, steadying him against the door frame with trembling hands. Raven-hued hair touched his cheek. Magan's abdomen brushed his hip, and he felt the baby's kick. In Bolverkr's mind, there was no longer any question. "Run," he whispered. "Please." He gouged his fingernails against the ledge for support, oblivious to wood slivering painfully into flesh. Head bowed, he fought down the natural barriers that shielded men's minds from the manipulations of sorcerers and began the sequence of mental exercises that would call unbridled Chaos to him.

Bolverkr knew nearly two hundred years had passed since any Dragonrank mage dared to draw power from a Chaos-source other than his own life energy. But, pressed to recklessness, Bolverkr drew the procedure from the cobwebbed depths of memory. His invocation began as a half-forgotten, disjointed mumble of spell words.

And Chaos answered Bolverkr. It seeped into his wasted sinews, restoring vigor and clarity of thought. The method of its summoning returned like remembrance of a lost love. His conjuration grew from a mental glimmer, to a verbal whisper, to a shout. Golden waves of chaos filled him, exultant and suffocating in their richness. Gorged with new power, Bolverkr laughed and raised his hand against the force that blasted grass from the hillside as it raced toward him like a living thing.

The storm, too, seemed to have gained intensity. It howled a song luxuriant with ancient evil, feeding off the same Chaos Bolverkr had mustered. Too late, the Dragonmage realized the reason, and he shouted his defeat to winds that hurled the cry back into his face. At last, he knew his enemy as a renegade mass of Chaos-force. His rally had accomplished nothing more than luring the tempest to his person and opening his protections to its mercy.

The Chaos-force speared through Bolverkr, cold as Helfrost. He staggered, catching his balance against the door frame as the storm pierced him, seeking the soul-focus of his very being, itself the primal essence of the elements. Fire and ice, wind and wave, earth and sky swirled through his blood, beyond his ability to divine an understanding. It entered every nerve, every thought, every fiber, and seemed to rack Bolverkr's soul apart. It promised ultimate power, the mastery of time and eternity, control of creation and destruction, of life and death. It played him without pity, no more trustworthy than the Northern winds whose form it took. It suffused him with pleasure, drove him to the peak of elation and held him there, tied to a blissful swell of power.

For all its thrill, the tension grew unbearable. Bolverkr felt as fragile as crystal, as if his spirit might shatter from the power which had become his. Ecstasy strengthened to pain. He screamed in agony, and the Chaos-force transformed his cry into a bellow of wild triumph. Sound echoed through the wreckage of Wilsberg. Then Bolverkr exchanged torment for oblivion.

Bolverkr awoke with numbed wits and a pounding headache. From habit, he tapped a trifle of life energy to counteract the pain. The throbbing ceased. His thoughts sharpened to faithful clarity, bringing memory of the previous morning, and realization drove him to his feet. The sun shone high over the ruins of the farm town that had been his home. Straw and boulders littered the ground. Bodies lay, smashed beneath the wreckage, half-buried in mud, or hanging from shattered foundations of stone like the broken puppets of an angered child.

Tears filled Bolverkr's eyes, blurring the carnage to vague patterns of light and dark. Grief dampened his spirit, leaving him feeling awkward and heavy. Faces paraded through his mind: Othomann, the old tailor who had spent more time weaving children's stories than cloth; Sigil, a plain-appearing woman whose gentleness and humor won her more suitors than the town beauties. One by one, Bolverkr pictured the townsfolk, and one by one he mourned them. The shadows slanted toward sunset before he gained the will to move. Only then did he realize he still clutched a piece of his door frame in fingers gone chalky white. Slowly, he turned toward his mansion, heart pounding, deathly afraid of what he might find.

Through water-glazed vision, Bolverkr stared at the rubble of the mansion. Magically warded rock and mortar had crumbled as completely as the mundane constructions of peasant cottages. Half the southern and western walls remained, clinging to a jagged corner of roof. Gray fragments covered the hillock, interspersed with the occasional glimmer of metal coins and gemstones. Only splinters and shards of wood remained of Bolverkr's furniture, much of which he had proudly carved with his own hands.

A pile of rubble blocked Bolverkr's view of the single standing corner. He sidled around it, suddenly confronted by Magan's corpse. She lay in an unnatural pose, mottled white and purple-red. Flying debris had flayed her, chest to abdomen, and blackflies feasted on piled organs. Bolverkr felt as if he had been suddenly plunged in ice water. Horror gripped him. Mesmerized, he shuffled forward. His foot slipped in a smear of blood and flesh, and he stumbled. Flies rose around him in a buzzing crowd. Bolverkr twisted to see what had tripped him. It was another corpse, no larger than his hands and still connected to its mother by a bloodless umbilical cord.

With a frenzied sob, Bolverkr turned and fled. After three running strides, his heel came down on a craggy hunk of granite. His leg bowed sideways. Pain shot through his ankle. He fell, arching to avoid sharp fragments of stone jutting from the grass. Off-balance, he crashed to the ground and rolled over the side of the hillock.

Bolverkr tumbled. Rock, wood, and bone bruised his skin. He clawed for a grounded rock or plant. Debris loos-

ened by his attempts skidded toward the ground for him
to bounce over a second time. Three quarters of the way
down the side, his hand looped over a root. It cut into the
joints of his fingers. Quickly, he released it, using the moment of stability to turn his crazed fall into a controlled
slide. He jarred to a halt, facedown, by a pile of bodies.
The air hung heavy with the salt reek of blood and death.

Bolverkr swept to a sitting position. His gaze flicked over
the ruins of Wilsberg, and his tears turned from the cold
sting of grief to the hot fury of anger. It had taken him
fifty years to find the peace of a lifetime. Half a century of
peasant distrust had elapsed in misery until one generation
passed to the next and the children accepted Bolverkr as a
kindly old man, a fixture on the hillock over their village.
The term "Dragonrank" meant nothing to them; they were
too far removed from the sorcerers' school in Norway to
have heard of its existence. *To them, I served as a timeless
oddity.* Bolverkr watched blood trickle across his palm, and
though it was his own, it seemed to him more like that
of the entire town. *So long to create the dream, and so
quickly shattered.*

Thoughts raced through Bolverkr's mind, age-old memories of the crimes of his peers. He recalled how Geirmagnus, a man from the future with no magical abilities of his
own, had discovered and taught the first Dragonrank mages
to channel Chaos-force into spell energy. Then, the sorcerers had called volumes of Chaos from external sources,
blithely ignorant of its cost. He remembered how the excess
Chaos had massed, taking the dragon-form that gave the
Dragonrank sorcerers their name, steadily growing, feeding
off the Chaos they summoned for spells more powerful
than any known before or since. One such feat gave Bolverkr and his peers the ability to age at a fraction of the
rate of normal men. Too late, they realized their mistake.
As the chaos-creature grew more powerful, nothing could
slay it but the strongest Dragonrank magic. And the calling
of Chaos for that magic served only to further strengthen
the beast until its presence threatened to disrupt the very
balance of the world.

Cruel remembrances fueled Bolverkr's rage. He blinked
away the beads of water clinging to his lashes. The mad
blur of corpses transformed in his mind to the faces of his

ancient friends. He recalled how, in desperation, the mages had forsaken external Chaos sources for their own life energies. The younger sorcerers never learned the techniques of mustering Chaos. Their elders tried to resist marshaling the great volumes of entropy they had used in earlier days; but, having tasted of ultimate power, they slipped back into the old ways. All except Bolverkr. He alone remained true to his promise, and he alone the dragon spared. Singly and in groups, he watched his friends die, clawed to death by the chaos-creature's fury until Geirmagnus trapped it, though he was mortally wounded by Chaos in the struggle. The quest for peace brought Bolverkr to Wilsberg while the pursuit of knowledge drove the younger mages to found the Dragonrank school that Bolverkr had never seen. As generations of sorcerers came and went, he was forgotten or presumed dead.

That storm was no work of nature. Bolverkr's hands clenched to fists, and he stared at the blood striping his knuckles scarlet. Tendrils of Chaos-force probed through the breach he had opened in his mental barriers; where it touched, its power corrupted. Rage boiled up inside the sorcerer, fueled and twisted by the Chaos that had ravaged Wilsberg and, now, found its master. The seam blurred between the meager remnants of Bolverkr's natural life aura and the seeming infinity of Chaos, and it quietly goaded him as if it was the master and he the source of its power. It twisted his thoughts, filling gaps in information, leading to one conclusion: *Someone loosed Chaos against me, and that someone is going to pay!*

Bolverkr leaped to his feet, bruises and aches forgotten. He waded through the wreckage of Wilsberg, the sight of each familiar corpse invoking his ire like physical pain. By the time he reached the town border, Chaos roiled through his veins. A small voice cried out from within him, *Why me? Why me? Why me?* Then, the last vestiges of Bolverkr's grief were crushed, replaced by a blind, howling fury more savage than any he had known. Once a separate entity, the Chaos-force remained, poisoning his life aura, all but merged with it. Chaos promised spell-energy to rival the gods: death, destruction, and vengeances beyond human comprehension. It showed him shattered human skeletons on a shore red with blood, skies dense with tarry smoke, its breath lethal to the men of Midgard.

Not yet fully swayed to Chaos' influence, Bolverkr shuddered at the image, and horror sapped his anger.

Quickly, the Chaos-force amended its simulation, instead showing Bolverkr a clear night speckled with stars. Two men lay chained to a block of granite, their faces twisted by fierce grimaces of evil. Prompted by the Chaos-force, Bolverkr knew these as the men responsible for the destruction of Wilsberg. Understanding whipped him to murderous frenzy. He struggled for a closer look, but the Chaos-force teased him, holding the perception just beyond his vision. Bolverkr shouted in frustration, forgetting, in his rage, that a simple spell could obtain the same information. Instead, he raced without goal into the afternoon, seeking a target for his fury.

Once beyond the borders of the town, Bolverkr ran along a well-traveled forest trail; wheel ruts and boot tracks from the spring thaw dimpled its surface. Branches of oak and maple rattled in a light, autumn breeze, its gentleness a mockery after the tempest that had gutted Wilsberg. Shortly, the creak of timbers and the clop of hooves on packed earth replaced the rasp of air through Bolverkr's lungs. He paused, breathless, as a half-dozen wooden horse carts appeared from around a bend in the pathway. A man marched at the fore of the procession, his chin encased in a crisp, golden beard and his face locked in an expression radiating kindness and demanding trust. The horses appeared gaunt. A layer of grime stained their coats, but their triangular heads remained proudly aloft, ears flicked forward in interest.

Bolverkr knew the commander as Harriman, Wilsberg's only diplomat. He wore briar-scratched leather leggings beneath the blue and white silks that proclaimed his title. Returning from their quarterly trading mission to the baron's city of Cullinsberg, the men aboard the wagons laughed and joked, glad to be nearing their journey's end. The odor of alcohol tinged the air around them.

The Chaos-force seethed within Bolverkr, and he stumbled forward in blind, convulsive rage. Greedily, he seized its power, shaping it to a spell he had not attempted for over a century. Ignorance and lack of practice cost him volumes in energy, but he tapped his new Chaos power with ease.

Harrimans's gaze fell across Bolverkr's tousled gray head and harried features. He signaled his men to a sudden stop. The wagons grated to a halt.

Grimly, Bolverkr dredged power through the self-made opening in his mind barriers. Chaos-force coursed through his body, wild as a storm-wracked tide. Driven by a once alien, Chaos-provoked need for destruction, he channeled its essence, calling forth a dragon the size of his ruined mansion. The beast materialized through a rent in the clouds. Sunlight refracted from scales the color of diamonds; yellow eyes glared through the afternoon mists. It struck with all the fury of its summoning. Unfurling leathery wings, it hurtled like an arrow for the wagons.

Harriman and his charges stood, wide-eyed, stunned by the vision of a monster from legend bearing down upon them. One screamed. The sound tore Harriman from his trance. Rushing forward, he drew his sword and thrust for the dragon's chest. It swerved. The blade opened a line of blood between scales. Its foreleg crashed against Harriman's ear. The blow sprawled the nobleman, and the dragon's wings buffeted him to oblivion.

Bolverkr quivered with malicious pleasure, hardened by the Chaos-force whose rage had become his own. A gesture sent the dragon banking with hawklike finesse. A horse reared, whinnying its terror to the graying heavens. Its harness snapped with a jolt, overturning the cart. Richly woven cloth was scattered in the mud, and the odor of spices perfumed the air. Another horse bolted, dragging a wagon that jounced sideways into a copse of trees where it shattered to splinters against tightly-packed trunks. Before the others could react, the dragon renewed its assault. Fire gouted from its jaws. The remaining wagons burst into flame, and the jumbled screams of men and horses wafted to Bolverkr like music. A man staggered from the inferno, his clothes alight, then collapsed after only two steps. At Bolverkr's order, the dragon whirled for another pass.

Again, the dragon swooped, spraying the burning wreckage with flame. Strengthened, the fire leaped skyward, an orange-red tower over the treetops, splattering cinders across a row of maples. A wave of heat curled the hand-shaped leaves. Branches sputtered. Wind streamed acrid smoke, stinging Bolverkr's eyes. The crackle of hungry flames replaced the pained howls of men and beasts. Soon, nothing remained but the diminishing blaze, unrecognizable, charred shapes, and the dragon circling the rubble, awaiting Bolverkr's next command.

Though no less potent, Bolverkr's Chaos-inspired rage became more directed. The identities of the men in his vision, the men responsible for his terrible loss, became as tantalizing as forbidden fruit. He dispelled the dragon with a casual wave. Turning on his heel, he left the fire to burn itself out on the forest trail.

Something stirred at the corner of Bolverkr's vision, and he went still with curiosity. His hard, blue eyes probed the brush, finding nothing unusual. The movement did not recur. Unused to the amount of power he now wielded, Bolverkr approached with the caution of a commoner. Raising a hand, he brushed aside hollow fronds. Stems rattled, parting to reveal Harriman, protected by distance from the dragon's flames. Blood splashed his short-cropped hair. The dust-rimed, blue silk of his tunic rose and fell with each shallow breath. Just beyond his clutched hand, his sword reflected highlights from the dying fire.

Bolverkr scowled. He hooked his fingers beneath Harriman's inert form and flipped the diplomat to his back.

Harriman loosed a low moan of protest, then went still.

Bolverkr's hand curled around Harriman's throat. A pulse drummed steady beats against his thumb, and he paused, uncertain. Despite his bold rampage against the trading party, Bolverkr was a stranger to murder. He explored the firm ridge of cartilage with his fingers, and the wild storm of Chaos eased enough to give him a chance to consider. *Surely I can find a use for a diplomat trusted by the highest leaders of our lands. Wilsberg was Harriman's home, too. No doubt, he will aid my vengeance.* Still influenced by the Chaos-force that had claimed him, Bolverkr did not deliberate over the unlikeliness of their association. Drawing on his new-found power, he wove enchantments over Harriman to dull pain and enrich sleep. Kneeling, he slung the nobleman's limp form over his bony shoulder, using Chaos magic to enhance his own strength and balance. As an afterthought, he retrieved the sword and jammed it, unsheathed, through his own belt.

Harriman's body thumped against Bolverkr's chest, and the sword slapped his leg painfully with every step. His journey along the pathway became a taxing hop-step that transformed blood-lust into annoyance and calculation. Plans spun through Bolverkr's mind. Absorbed with his task, he'd nearly reached the edge of the forest before he realized he had no destination. Wilsberg lay ahead, strewn with the bodies of relatives and friends. Carrying Harriman to any other village would invite interference from healers and noblemen, and the woods held no attraction for Bolverkr. He realized he had unconsciously chosen the most appropriate home base. Despite its ghosts, Wilsberg was his town, molded through centuries of effort, and now it would become his fortress. Enemies who could raise a Chaos-force as fierce as the one that had claimed him would need to be studied, their flaws and weaknesses discovered and made to work against them.

The sight of corpses littering the shattered cobbles of Wilsberg's streets set Bolverkr's teeth on edge. Gone was the gentle compassion of Wilsberg's aged Dragonmage; the soft-spoken patriarch who protected the village of his children's children had died with his people. No mercy remained in the heart of this sorcerer forced to view the destruction of the world and loves he had created and nurtured through a century and a half of mistrust. Chaos transformed from intruder to friend; its threats became promises. Their relationship was that of lord and vassal, though a friend who had known Bolverkr in happier times might not have been able to tell which was master and which slave.

Bolverkr shuffled toward the wreckage of his mansion. The familiar features of every dead face became another murder attributed to the men the Chaos-force had revealed in distant images. Bolverkr judged each crime, found every verdict guilty. And he fretted for the time when he might serve as executioner as well.

Once atop the hill, Bolverkr dumped Harriman down on a dirt floor polished by the unnatural winds. Beyond sight of Magan's corpse, he crouched and traced a triangle on the ground with the point of a jagged rock. Despite the expenditure of massive amounts of his own life energy,

Bolverkr's aura still gleamed, nourished by the Chaos. Power surged through him, vibrant as a tiger and every bit as deadly. He channeled a fraction to the shape cut in the soil. Red haze warped its form. Gradually, it muted to a pattern of alternating stripes of green and gray, resolving, at length, into a clear picture of Bolverkr's enemies.

A forest of pine filled the frame, every needle etched in vivid detail. Branches sagged beneath white blankets of snow. Stiff crests of undergrowth poked stubbornly through layers of powder, not quite ready to succumb to autumn gales. Four people tromped across the openings left by dying weeds. One towered over the others. A bitter, Northern wind lashed his white-blond locks into tangles, revealing angular features. Bolverkr stared, uncertain whether to believe what his magics displayed. Pale brows arched over eyes the stormy blue of the ocean. An ovoid face with high cheekbones drew attention from ears tapering to delicate points.

An elf? Have creatures of Faery returned to Midgard? Bolverkr tossed his head and answered his own question. *Not likely. The townsfolk of Wilsberg knew nothing more of elves than they did of sorcerers. If either had become commonplace, rumors would surely have reached us from the North.* Guarded disbelief goaded Bolverkr to take a closer look. The countenance appeared undeniably elven, but their owner paced with the stolid tread of a man. His simple features seemed incongruously careworn, stark contrast to the lighthearted play of elves in Alfheim.

Uncertain what to make of the paradox, Bolverkr turned his attention to the other enemy within the vision of his spell. The elf's only male companion stood a full head shorter. A black snarl of hair fringed pale eyes alive with mischief. Calluses scarred his small hands, positioned on fingerpads rather than the palms the way a warrior's would be. Despite this oddity, both he and the elf wore swords at their hips.

In silence, Bolverkr studied the reflections of enemies brought strangely close by his magic. His concentration grew fanatical, and he stared until his vision blurred. Every detail of appearance and movement etched indelibly upon his memory until hatred drove him to a frenzy. A fit of venomous passion nearly broke the link between Bolverkr and his spell. The scene wavered, like heat haze quivering from darkly-painted stone. He hissed, reclaiming control. The image grew more distinct.

For the first time, Bolverkr turned his attention to the woman at the elf's side. Once focused, he found himself unable to turn away. A heavy robe hugged curves as perfect as an artist's daydream. She sported the fair skin and features of most Scandinavian women. But, where years of labor normally turned them harsh and stout, this woman appeared slim, almost frail. A gust swirled strands of yellow hair around her shoulders. Bolverkr had always preferred the darker, healthier hue of Southerners, but the beauty of this woman held him spellbound.

The elf hooked an arm around the woman's back with casual affection. Bolverkr's hatred rose again, this time with a knifelike, jealous edge. He forced it away. Beyond the conscious portion of his mind, a plan was taking form, a means to cause these enemies the same torment they had inflicted upon him. Though not yet certain of the reason, Bolverkr knew this woman must die. And, with dispassionate efficiency, he rejected his own desire. Only then did he notice the staff she held in a carelessly loose grip. A meticulous artisan had gravel-sanded it smooth as timeworn driftwood. Darkly stained, it tapered to a wooden replica of a four-toed dragon's claw. A sapphire gleamed between black nails.

Dragonrank. Bolverkr leaned closer until his nose nearly touched his magics. His image reproduced reality with flawless definition. There was no mistaking the gemstone for one of lesser value. Bolverkr had followed the founding of the Dragonrank school closely enough to know the clawstones symbolized rank, the more costly the gem, the more skilled the sorcerer. A sapphire placed this woman just below master. Power even distantly approaching hers was almost singularly rare, but it did not surprise Bolverkr. *Behind any unnatural act of mass murder must stand a Dragonrank mage.*

Despite reckless squanderings of life energy, enough to have killed Bolverkr twice over without the added power of the Chaos-force, the edges of his aura scarcely felt dulled. He studied the woman more carefully. No longer fully absorbed by her beauty, he recognized the fierce glare of a vital, untapped life aura surrounding her. Nearby, a more sallow glow hugged the fourth member of this odd group. Though young and vibrant, her simple attractiveness paled beside her sapphire-rank companion. She stood shorter than any adult Bolverkr had ever seen, slighter even than her dark-haired consort. Her fine features swept into high, dimpled cheeks, and her mane of golden ringlets revealed a Northern heritage. She, too, held a dragonstaff, its ornament a garnet.

Bolverkr hesitated, his next course of action uncertain. Without the advance glimpse the Chaos-force had provided, he could not have centered his location spell on strangers. Even so, he could only visualize a limited range around them. A village sign within the area of his spell might have pinpointed their locale, but it would have been an improbable stroke of luck. Mid-autumn snow suggested Scandinavia. However, endless miles of pine forest covered Norway, far too much for Bolverkr to explore. *And I don't even know their names.*

For several seconds, Bolverkr wrestled with his quandary, the sustained sorcery draining Chaos energy like the endless trickle of water down a gutter spout. His gaze strayed to the wreckage of Wilsberg, and the sight of corpses piled where his own wards had trapped them against the hillock stirred guilt that raged to anger. He knew where to obtain the information he needed. *Somehow, I must enter one of their minds.* He pondered the idea, aware this plan must fail, but goaded by frustration. He knew that nature endowed every man of Midgard's era with mind barriers to protect them from sorcerers' intrusions. Only the minority of humans had enough cognizance of their own barricades to lower them for a dreamreader or mage to interpret nightmares or thought obsessions. *But one of my enemies is not a man.* Bolverkr explored this loophole with eager intent. *I've never heard of any mage breaking into or destroying mind barriers, but I've more power now than anyone before me. Sorcery always works best against other users and conceptions of its art, and the creatures of Faery are products of Dragonrank magic.*

Bolverkr grinned with morbid glee. He could not fathom the effect his attempt might have upon the elf. He had no previous experience to consider. He suspected it might plunge his victim into madness, perhaps kill him. At the very least, it would open his thoughts and memory to cruel manipulation. And the later possibility caused Bolverkr to smile. He harbored no wish to take his enemies' lives. Not yet. He wanted to return the anguish they had directed upon him, if possible, ten times over.

Bolverkr gathered vitality to him, unable to guess how much energy this spell would require, but certain it would demand more than any other spell he had ever known or used. Supplying too little would cause the spell to fail; too much would cost Bolverkr his life. Once properly cast, the spell would claim as much of the Chaos-force and of Bolverkr's life aura as it needed, draining power too fast for him to control. Like any untried magic, it held the risk of requiring more stamina than he could feed it, of sapping him to an empty, soulless core. But Bolverkr never doubted. The Chaos-force seemed infinite, and its vows of service drove him to impulsive courage.

The location triangle faded as Bolverkr reared to strike. Braced for pain, he smashed into the presumed area of the elf's mental barriers. His attack met no resistance. Alien surprise flowed around him as he skidded through a human tangle of thought processes and crashed into the side of an unwarded brain. The elf's involuntary cry of pain reverberated in his own mind. Bolverkr's confusion mimicked the elf's in perfect detail. *No mind barriers? Thor's blood, no mind barriers!*

Bolverkr actually heard the sorceress' words with the elf. "Allerum, are you well?"

Ideas tumbled through the elf's mind, some leaking through Bolverkr's contact, others fully his own. *Did some god or sorcerer invade my mind again? Or did I burst a goddamned blood vessel?* Bolverkr went still, holding his emotions in check. He watched in fascination as the elf probed his own mind, ungainly and haphazard as a hen in flight. *My enemies are dead, and I've gone paranoid. No need to worry Silme.* The elf shaped his reply. "I'm fine. Just a headache."

No mind barriers. Bolverkr kept the realization to himself, careful not to allow his surprise to slip into the elf's thoughts. Alert to the elf's defenses, he began a cautious exploration of the dense spirals of thought. Only one other person in Bolverkr's experience had lacked the natural, mental protections. Geirmagnus, the man who unlocked the secrets of Dragonrank magic, had come to Midgard from a future without sorcery or the necessity for defenses against it. Bolverkr held his breath. Already, he detected incongruities. The elf's mind was decidedly human and flawed as well. Trailing along thought pathways thick as the deepest strings of a harp, Bolverkr found evidence of tampering. Someone had cut and patched blind loops and inappropriate connections. Others remained, frayed and easily sparked by stress.

With effort, Bolverkr resisted the urge to incite painful memories to torture the elf. Instead, he tiptoed through the intricacies of thought, collecting the information he needed for a full-scale attack. Through the elf's perceptions, Bolverkr learned the identities of his enemies. The elf knew himself as Al Larson, though his companions called him Allerum. The sapphire-rank Dragonmage was Silme, and Larson's love for her rivaled Bolverkr's for his slaughtered wife. The garnet-rank sorceress, Astryd, served as Silme's apprentice. Larson knew his little accomplice by the alias "Shadow." Further probing revealed his true name as Taziar Medakan.

Uncertain of Larson's abilities to police his mind, Bolverkr delved deeper with guarded enthusiasm. He focused on the ideas that brought Larson pleasure. Should Bolverkr accidentally trigger a memory, he hoped Larson would pass it off as fancy, and discovery of the elf's devotions would supply Bolverkr targets for attack. Eagerly, Bolverkr selected a childhood remembrance:

Thirteen years old, Al Larson perched on the ledge of a tiny sailboat beside a girl he knew as his sister. His bare feet dangled into a square-cut hold, and brackish water swirled about his ankles. A triangle of gaily-colored canvas spilled summer winds. The seal-smooth construction of the boat's hull looked like no material Bolverkr had ever seen. The gauzy fabric of Larson's swimsuit and the violently brash colors of the sister's bikini seemed similarly alien.

Suddenly, another craft whipped by Larson's, sail drawn tight to the mast. A middle-aged man with close-cropped yellow hair waved as he passed, and Bolverkr knew him as

Larson's father. Behind the father. Larson's younger brother flung sunburned arms into the air with an excitement that caused the boat to rock dangerously. "Slowpokes!" he screamed.

Larson accepted the challenge. He hauled in the sheet, hugging winds into the shortened sail. The boat rocked to leeward as it sprang forward. The tip of the mast scraped the lake, then bounced upward, and icy water surged over the sides. With a short shriek of outrage, Larson's sister thumped to the opposite ledge to balance weight. The line bit into Larson's palms. Using his toes to anchor its knot, he hardened the sail to the mast. His boat caught and inched ahead of his father's heeling almost parallel to the water. Spray drenched Larson. He laughed at his sister's shrill admonishments to free the winds.

An unexpected gust tapped the slight craft, and its sail brushed the surface of the lake. Quickly, Larson eased the canvas. The sailboat hovered momentarily, then capsized into cedar-colored waters, the sister sputtering, the brother and father laughing until their sides ached.

Bolverkr disengaged from Larson's memory. The scene confirmed his worst suspicions. Like Geirmagnus, Al Larson came from a future time and place. Bolverkr knew Larson's family would have served as the perfect target for his vengeance, but, with ruined hope, he also realized they dwelt beyond the abilities of Dragonrank magic to harm them. He recoiled in dismay and felt Larson grow alarmed in response. Quickly, Bolverkr regained control, masking his emotions with necessary thoroughness. *It's not over yet. There are other things a man grows to love.*

Bolverkr renewed his search with a malice that knew no bounds. He pried information from Larson's mind, discovered deep affection for Silme as well as concern for his other two companions. Bolverkr's efforts also uncovered a pocket of bittersweet grief. He dug for its source to find the remembered image of a samurai named Kensei Gaelinar who had served as a ruthless swordmaster and a friend. Some teachings of this warrior had convinced Larson that a whisper of his mentor's soul still resided in the finely-crafted steel of the Japanese long sword he had taken from the dead man's hands and now wore at his side.

Uncovering no other objects of comparable fondness, Bolverkr turned his attention to Larson's fears and hatreds. These he prodded with meticulous care, not wanting to reveal his presence in a wild induction of rage. He found orange-red explosions of light, noises louder than the nearest thunder, a savage, crimson chaos of future war Larson called Vietnam. Gory corpses with eyes glazed in accusation intermingled freely with the memory of Larson's own mortality. An oddly-shaped parcel of metal chattered like a squirrel grazed by a hunter's arrow as Larson charged enemies with a final, desperate courage. Oblivion followed, a pause of indeterminate length before a rude awakening in a strange elven body and an ancient time.

Larson stiffened. The recognition of an intruder's presence flowed through his mind, and a conjured mental wall snapped over the exit. A tentative question followed. *Vidarr? Is that you?* Bolverkr froze. When no attack followed, he relaxed. For now, he harbored no desire to leave; he found the blockage of no significance. After the consideration of violating biological barriers, a wall manufactured from substance as ephemeral as thought seemed a pitiful substitute. Treading more lightly, he continued his search.

Bolverkr skimmed through Larson's memories, plucking tidbits with the graceful precision of an acrobat. He found divine allies. These he dismissed, aware gods' vows would not allow them to meddle in the affairs of mortals. And among the deities, Bolverkr also discovered enemies. He watched the elf's sword slice through the spine of Loki the Trickster, saw Larson hurl the god's body into the permanent oblivion of Hvergelmir's waterfall. The corpse toppled through the Helspring, destroyed, as all things, by the magical braid of rivers that plunged, roaring, from Midgard to Hel. No longer existent, even in Hel, Loki and the mass of Chaos he controlled were destroyed, tipping the world dangerously toward Order.

Attempting to restore the balance and free another god from more than a century in Hel, Larson and Taziar had traveled to Geirmagnus' ancient estate. Through Larson's memory, Bolverkr saw the ancient, imprisoned Chaos-force released, its dragon-form towering to the heavens. In horror, the sorcerer stared as Larson, Taziar, and Kensei Gaelinar slashed and stabbed at the creature. Bolverkr saw the Japa-

nese swordmaster dive through razor-honed wire, killed in a
desperate self-sacrifice that incapacitated the Chaos-creature
and bared its head to Larson's sword. And Larson seized
the opening, slaughtering the dragonform, apparently unaware that its now unbound Chaos must seek a living
master.

The personal tragedy of this finding burned anger through
Bolverkr. *Your stupidity destroyed me, and you'll pay with
everything you hold dear.* He imagined a teacher's long
sword, its shattered pieces strewn across a meadow stained
with Silme's blood. Shards protruded from the scarlet haft
Larson clutched to his chest, and his voice loosed the
screams of a dying animal. Through the nightmare visions
he created, Bolverkr relived his own grief. Yet, despite the
temptation, he held his fantasy back from Larson's perception. The Chaos-force and its seemingly limitless power
goaded him to recklessness and uncontrolled fury, but it
did not make him foolish. Even after a century and a half
of peace, he recalled two important rules of a sorcerer's
war: never sacrifice surprise, and, when an enemy proves
powerful, fight him on familiar territory.

Bolverkr retreated. He turned to the exit from Larson's
mind, pleased to see the wall had already faded. Patiently,
he waited until it disappeared completely. Stepping out, he
immediately attempted to gain access to the minds of Larson's companions. Each effort flung him against natural
mind barriers solid as stone. Briefly, he considered. To assault Taziar's mind here would violate both of the battle
tenets he had just uncovered from memory. Instead, he
slipped back into Larson's thoughts, digging for information
about the elf/man's small companion.

Bolverkr's toil exposed a stormy childhood in the city of
Cullinsberg. With effort, he dug out revealing shreds of
information, most lodged in the deeper, subconscious portion of Larson's mind. Here, Bolverkr uncovered a name.
There, he found an incident. In the end, he pieced together
a patchwork history of the only son of an honorable and
heroic guard captain, a son too slight in build to follow in
his father's footsteps. A prime minister's treason against
the elder Medakan had cost the captain his life and his
honor, turning Taziar's carefree youth into a life of running,
hiding, and living on the edges of society. It was this dishon-

orable stage of Taziar's life that gained him his closest friendships. Bolverkr seized every name he could glean from Taziar's revelations to Larson. And here, too, Bolverkr decided his plan of attack. *If I begin with the little thief's allies in Cullinsberg, I lure my enemies to the south. I have no measure of their true power, but it encompasses at least enough to challenge gods. Best to start my vengeance with something not currently in their possession.*

Something tugged at Bolverkr's hip. Engrossed in the mind-link, he slapped at it idly. To his surprise, a sharpened edge sliced his palm. Pain and the warm trickle of blood hurled him back into his own body on the hill over Wilsberg. Harriman stood before him, clutching the sword he had torn free from the belt lying, halved, at Bolverkr's ankles. The sorcerer rolled more from instinct than intent. The blade swept the ground, rasping off a rock shard. Bolverkr managed to work his way to one knee before Harriman lunged for another attack.

Bolverkr ducked, mouthing spell words with furious intensity. The blade whistled over his head, and Harriman's foot lanced toward his chest. Desperation made Bolverkr sloppy. His spell cost him more energy than necessary. But a shield snapped to life before him. Harriman's boot struck magics as firm and clear as glass. Impact jarred the nobleman to the ground. Surprise crossed his features, then they warped to murderous outrage. He sprang to his feet and charged the shielded Dragonmage.

Harriman's sword crashed against the unseen barrier. Bolverkr saw pain tighten the diplomat's mouth to a line. Undeterred, Harriman smashed at the magics again and again until his strokes became frenzied and undirected. "Why!" he screamed with every wasted blow.

Bolverkr waited with a stalking cat's patience.

At length, Harriman sheathed his sword, apparently tired of battering his frustration against a barrier he could not broach. "Why?" he shouted. His tone implied accusation rather than question.

Bolverkr rose, his sorceries still firmly in place. "Why what?" he demanded.

Harriman gripped his hilt in a bloodless fist, but did not waste the effort of drawing the blade again. "Why did you . . . ?" He trailed off and started again. "Why would you . . . ?" His broad gesture encompassed the wreckage of the farming town of Wilsberg.

Suddenly, Harriman's misconception became clear. *By the gods, the fool thinks I destroyed the town.* Bolverkr shook his head in aggravation. "Don't be an idiot, Harriman. I didn't do anything, but I know who did. I need your help . . ."

"No!" Harriman shuffled backward. "You're lying! I saw you laughing when your winged beast attacked me. What have you done with my friends? *Did you kill them, too?*"

"Stop!" Bolverkr hollered in defense. "I attacked you in the same grief-frenzy you just displayed. I apologize for your companions; they died without fair cause. But I want your help against the murderers who slaughtered our kin."

Harriman shrank away. His dark eyes gleamed with disbelief, and behind Harriman's expressionless pall, Bolverkr suspected fear warred with anger. His voice went comfortably soft, soothing without a trace of patronage. "We're not barbarians, Bolverkr. Justice will be done, but it's for the baron of Cullinsberg to decide guilt and punishment. Come with me. I'm certain he'll listen to your story."

Harriman slipped into the role of diplomat with ease, but Bolverkr was too cagey to be taken in by platitudes. He realized his displays of sorcery would work against him. South of the Kattegat, men knew nothing of magic beyond a few mother's stories that sifted to them from Scandinavia. *Common men revile what they cannot understand. No one in Cullinsberg would question my guilt.* "Don't trifle with me, Harriman. Look around you. All our friends have died, massacred by strangers. My wife and child were not spared, but you were. What possible reason could I have for working such evil? If I caused this, why would I slay Magan and leave you alive?"

"I believe you," Harriman said. Though his tone sounded convincing, his sudden change in loyalty did not. "Please. Talk to the baron. He'll believe you, too."

Harriman's deceit angered Bolverkr. "Damn it," he raged. "Listen to what I'm saying! Think, Harriman. I didn't ravage the town. I fought to the last shred of my life to save it."

Harriman opened his mouth to affirm his sincerity.

But Bolverkr made a curt gesture of dismissal. "Save

your sweet deceptions for the baron. I can call dragons from the bowels of the earth and shields from midair. Don't you think I can read your intentions?" Bolverkr glared to emphasize his lie. The mind barriers rendered emotions as impossible to tap as thoughts, but Bolverkr doubted that Harriman knew that fact.

Apparently fooled, Harriman dropped all pretenses. His cheeks flushed scarlet, and his expression went hard as chiseled stone. "Of course, I think you killed them. What else could I believe? You're no man; you're some sort of . . . of demon. You were old when my great-grandfather was born. You never caused us any harm before, so we learned to trust you, even love you. But nothing else could have done this." He gestured angrily at the ruins.

Harriman's words stung Bolverkr. In his rage, he forgot that his own insistence had inspired the nobleman to speak against him. "How dare you! I built this village, stone by precious stone. I lent my efforts to every labor, nursed the sick, brought prosperity to an insignificant dot on the landscape." He took a threatening step toward Harriman. "My wife and child lie dead! I'm pledged to avenge myself against their slayers. Are you with me or against me?"

Harriman cowered. He seemed about to speak, then went silent. He started again, and stopped. The inability to act as a negotiator seemed to unman him. Suddenly, he fled.

Caught off-guard by Harriman's unexpected flight, Bolverkr stood motionless for a startled moment. Dropping his shield, he followed the nobleman's course as he bounced and leaped over standing stones and corpses. "Stop!" Bolverkr shouted. "Harriman, stop. Don't force me to use magic." *If he reaches Cullinsberg, he'll turn the barony against me. He'll foil my vengeance!* The realization goaded Bolverkr to prompt action. And, though a more subtle spell might have sufficed, because of his success with Larson, an attack on mental protections came first to Bolverkr's mind. Gathering a spear of Chaos-power, he crashed into Harriman's mind barriers.

Bolverkr's probe met abrupt resistance. For a maddening second, nothing happened. Then Harriman's barrier shattered like an empty eggshell. The nobleman collapsed, face plowing into the dirt. Pain and surprise assailed Bolverkr. His screams matched Harriman's in timing and volume. He floundered in the fog of agony smothering Harriman's thoughts, shocked to inactivity by his own success. The nobleman's shrieks turned solo, but still Bolverkr stared in silent wonder. *How?* "How!" he shouted aloud. He had acted on a Chaos-stimulated impulse. In his centuries of life, he had never heard of anyone powerful enough to break through mind barriers, not even in the days when Dragonmages called on external Chaos sources.

Nonsentient, the Chaos-force did not speak in words. Instead, it drew upon the basest instincts of its master, allowing him to understand. *I wield more power, more Chaos, then any sorcerer or god before me. It's mine to tap freely, restored by the same rest that replenishes my own life aura vitality.* Bolverkr struggled with the concept, at once awed, excited, and frightened by it, irrevocably lusting for the same Chaos power that must ultimately corrupt him with its evil. Pain awoke when he attempted to contemplate the immensity of his newfound strength, and, in self-defense, Bolverkr held his goals to a comprehensible level. *Before I battle my enemies directly, I have to learn to handle my own power, to gain full mastery over this Chaos that has become my own. And I have to draw those enemies to me.*

Bolverkr surveyed the coils of memory composing Harriman's mind, now fully opened to him. Quietly, without further preamble, he set to his task.

CHAPTER 1
Shadows of Death

Cruel as death, and hungry as the grave.
—James Thomson
The Seasons. Winter

The tavernmaster of Kveldemar hurled wood, glossed with ice, onto the hearth fire. It struck with a hiss, and smoke swirled through the common room, shredded to lace by beer-stained tables. Taziar Medakan blinked, trying to clear the mist from his eyes. His three companions seemed content to sit, sharing wine-loosened conversation, but restlessness drove Taziar until he fidgeted like a child during a priest's belabored liturgy. His darting, blue eyes missed nothing. He watched the tavernmaster whisk across the room, pausing to collect bowls from a recently vacated table. Flipping a dirty rag across its surface, the tavernmaster ducked around the bar with the efficiency of a man accustomed to tending customers alone. Not a single movement was wasted.

Taziar turned his attention to the only other patrons; a giggling couple huddled in the farthest corner, their chairs touching as they shared bowls of ale and silent kisses. Larson launched into a tale about two-man sailboats and a red-water lake, just as the outer door creaked open. Evening light streamed through the gap, glazing the eddying smoke. A middle-aged man stepped across the threshold. Dark-haired and clean-shaven, he seemed a welcome change from Norway's endless sea of blonds. Blinded by the glare, the stranger squinted, sidling around a chair. His soiled, leather tunic scraped against Taziar's seat with a high-pitched sheeting sound. A broadsword balanced in a scabbard at his waist, its trappings time-worn like a weapon which had been passed down by at least one generation.

Depressions pocked its surface where jewels had once been set in fine adornment.

Taziar had long ago abandoned petty thievery, but boredom drove him to accept the challenge. With practiced dexterity, he flicked his fingers into the stranger's pocket. Rewarded by the frayed tickle of purse strings and a rush of exhilaration, he pulled his prize free. A subtle gesture masked the movement of placing it into a lap fold of his cloak. Taziar's gaze never left his companions. He saw no glimmer of horror or recognition on their faces, no indication that anyone had observed his heist. Apparently oblivious, the stranger marched deeper into the common room and took a seat at a table before the bar. The tavernmaster wandered over to attend to his new patron.

Taziar frowned in consideration. The stranger's money held no interest for him; having developed more than enough skill to supply necessities for his friends, he had lost all respect for gold. Only the thrill remained, and much of his enjoyment would, in this case, come from devising a clever plan to return the purse to its owner. Taziar regarded his companions. Larson's words had passed him, unheard. Patiently, Taziar waited until his friend finished. Taking a cue from Silme's and Astryd's laughter, Taziar chuckled and then claimed the conversation. "Allerum, do you see that man over there?" He inclined his head slightly.

Larson nodded without looking. Aside from the engrossed couple, the tavernmaster, and themselves, there was only one man in the barroom. "Sure. What about him?"

Taziar raked a perpetually sliding comma of hair from his eyes. "When I was a child, my friends and I used to play a game where we'd guess how much money some stranger was carrying."

"Yeah?" Larson met Taziar's gaze with mistrust. "Sounds pretty seedy. What's it got to do with that man?"

Taziar clasped his hands behind his head. "I'll bet you our bar tab I can guess how much he has within . . ." Unobtrusively, he massaged coins through the fabric of the stranger's purse. Some felt thinner, more defined than Scandinavian monies, unmistakably southern coinage. Having discovered familiar territory, Taziar suppressed a smile. ". . . within three coppers."

Larson's eyes narrowed until his thin brows nearly met. He shot a glance at the stranger. "From here?"

Taziar turned his head as if studying the common room. Ice melted, the hearth fire blazed, now drafting its smoke up the chimney. "Why not? I can see him well enough."

Still, Larson hesitated. Though accustomed to idle barroom boasts, he was also all too familiar with Taziar's love of impossible challenges. "All right," he said at length. "Make it within one copper, and I'll handle every beer between here and Forste-Mar."

Taziar stroked his chin with mock seriousness. "Agreed." He studied the olive-skinned stranger in the firelight. The man ate with methodical disinterest, occasionally pausing to look toward the door. "Hmmm. I'd say . . ." Taziar paused dramatically, defining coins with callused fingertips. "Four gold, seven silver, two copper. And the gold'll be barony ducats."

"Ducats?" Larson's gaze probed Silme and Astryd before settling on Taziar.

"Cullinsberg money." Under the table, Taziar hooked Astryd's ankle conspiratorially with booted toes. "The man looks like a Southerner to me."

Astryd answered Taziar's touch with a questioning hand on his knee.

Larson shrugged. "Very impressive. What do we do now? Ask the man?" He play-acted, catching Taziar's sleeve and yanking repeatedly on the fabric. "Excuse me, Mac. Excuse me. My friend and I have a bet going. You see, he thinks you've got four gold, seven silver, and three copper . . ."

"Two copper," Taziar corrected. "And that won't be necessary." He retrieved the purse and tossed it casually to the tabletop.

Larson made a strangled noise of surprise, masking it with a guileless slam of his hand over the purse that drew every eye in the tavern. Silme clapped a hand to her mouth, transforming a laugh into a snort. Astryd's fingers gouged warningly into Taziar's leg.

Apparently, Larson's crooked arm adequately covered the stranger's property. Within seconds, the tavernmaster and his other patrons returned to their business, but Taziar knew the matter was far from closed. Relishing his companion's consternation, Taziar drained his mug to the dregs.

Larson's voice dropped to a grating whisper. "You ignorant son of a bitch."

"Son of what?" Taziar repeated with mock incredulity. When angered, Larson had an amusing habit of slipping into a language he called English.

"Jerk," Larson muttered, though this word held no more meaning to Taziar than the one before. "You cheated."

"Cheated." Taziar smirked. "You mean there were rules?"

"Damn you!" Larson raised a fist to emphasize his point. He tensed to pound the table. Then, glancing surreptitiously around the barroom, he lowered it gently to his wine bowl instead. "You get insulted when I call you a thief, then you pull something stupid like this! We don't need more trouble than . . ."

Taziar interrupted. "I'm no thief," he insisted.

"Then why did you take this?" Larson lowered his eyes momentarily to indicate the purse still tucked beneath his palm.

"Sport." Taziar shrugged, his single word more question than statement.

"Sport!" Larson's voice rose a full tone. "Let me get this straight. We capture a god in the form of a wolf and battle a dragon the size of Chicag—" He caught himself. "— Norway. As an encore, we face off with a Dragonrank Master holding a bolt action rifle. You're still limping from a bullet wound, for god's sake! Forgive me if you find my life bland, but isn't that enough excitement for you?"

"That was more than a month ago." Taziar's voice sounded soft as a whisper in the wake of Larson's tirade.

Larson passed a long moment in silence before responding. "You're insane, aren't you?"

Taziar grinned wickedly.

The women exchanged glances across the table. Silme's lips twitched into a smile, and she bit her cheeks to hide her amusement.

"You think this is funny, don't you?" Larson's tone made it plain he did not share his companions' glee. "And even you may think it's funny." He jabbed a thumb at Silme who wore an unconvincing expression of bemused denial.

"But shortly, that man over there is going to try to pay for his meal. He'll find his money missing; and, if he's half as smart as a chimpanzee, he'll look here first."

"A chimp and Z?" Astryd repeated, but Larson silenced her with an exasperated wave.

"I doubt he's got an attorney. In your lawless world of barbarians, he'll talk with his sword. You're too damned small to bother with." Larson glared at Taziar. "So, I'm going to die because you're crazy. Or perhaps, my dying is your idea of sport. Well, forget it." Larson leaped to his feet. "I'm giving it back."

Before Larson could take a step, Taziar hooked his sleeve with a finger. Mimicking the elf's Bronx accent, he tugged at the fabric, reviving Larson's earlier play-acted scenario. "Excuse me, Mac. Excuse me. Your purse just happened to fall out of your pocket. I'd like to return it."

Larson hesitated. "What the hell am I doing?" He retook his seat and jammed the pouch into Taziar's hand. "You're the one who wanted sport. You took it. You put it back."

Taziar rose and bowed with mock servility. "Yes, my lord. At once." He twisted toward the stranger's table, and, despite his facetious reply, he examined the man with more than frivolous interest. The tavern contained too few patrons to hide the antics of one. But the inherent danger of Larson's dare made it even more attractive to Taziar, who had intended nothing different.

A hand tapped Taziar's shoulder. He whirled to face Larson. The elf's features bore an expression of somber concentration. "If you get caught, and he kills you before we can stop him, I just want you to know one thing."

Taziar nodded in acknowledgment, the possibility a particularly unpleasant consequence but one he could not afford to dismiss. "What's that?"

"I told you so."

Taziar snorted. "Jerk," he replied, borrowing Larson's insult. He shook the knotted lock of hair from his eyes and turned back to study the common room. No object passed his scrutiny unnoticed. Two tables, each with four chairs, stood between the stranger's seat and his own, the narrow lane they formed comfortably passable. Beyond the man, a table sat in the opposite corner from the door. Beside it, at a diagonal to the stranger, a cracked, oak table occupied a space beside the one with the engrossed couple near the hearth. Someone had crammed six chairs around the flawed table, though its area was constructed to support only four. The corner of one chair partially blocked the walkway, its legs jammed crookedly against its neighbors.

Taziar feigned a yawn. He stretched luxuriously, splaying callused fingers to work loose a cramp. Not wishing to draw attention by pausing overlong, he trotted farther into the barroom. Skirting the dark-haired stranger, he seized an extra chair from the overcrowded table and spun it toward the couple. His action knocked the misplaced chair further askew. Still standing, he leaned across the back of his seat and spoke to the boy in strident, congenial tones. "Ketil! Ketil Arnsson. I thought it was you." Framing a knowing smile, he tipped his chin subtly toward the girl. "Does your mother know you're here? And what are you doing this far from home?"

Startled, the youth released his partner's hand. "But— but I'm not . . ."

Taziar interrupted before he could finish. "How's the apprenticeship going? I saw your father yesterday, and he said . . ."

The youth pushed free of his girlfriend. "Please, sir, my name's Inghram. Kiollsson."

Taziar continued as if the boy had not spoken. "He said you'd been spending more time . . ." He stopped suddenly, as if the boy's words had finally registered and slouched further over the rail for a closer look. "Inghram?" he repeated.

"Kiollsson," the boy finished.

Taziar straightened, working embarrassment into his voice. "Oh. I'm sorry. I thought . . . I . . ." He backstepped. Though the movement appeared awkward, Taziar knew the precise location of every stick of furniture. "Not Ketil. How did I . . . ?"

Soothingly, the girl spoke in an obvious attempt to help Taziar save face. "A natural mistake. We don't mind."

But Taziar acted even more distressed by her comforting. He spun, taking a harried step toward his companions. Carefully executed to appear an accident, his foot hooked the leg of the displaced chair and his thigh struck its seat. The chair toppled, taking Taziar with it. He crashed to the floor, suffering real pain to keep his performance convincing. Momentum slid him and the chair across the polished floor. Gracelessly, he tried to rise. But still entangled in the chair, he lurched toward the stranger, wadding the purse into his fist.

Taziar slammed into the man. Berating his clumsiness with profanity, Taziar used his body to shield his actions from the other patrons. He flicked the pouch into the stranger's pocket. Too late, he realized he had chosen the wrong pocket. But, before he could correct the error, the stranger leaped up, catching Taziar by the wrist and opposite forearm. The purse fumbled, balanced precariously on the edge of the pocket. Taziar stared in horror; his heart rate doubled in an instant.

The stranger's grip tightened. He lowered his head and pulled Taziar to within a hand's breadth of his face, as if memorizing his features. Belted by the odor of onions and ale, Taziar resisted the urge to sneak a look at the teetering pouch of coins. He tried to read the man's intentions, but the blankness of expression did not quite fit the tenseness of the stranger's hold on Taziar. *Allerum, are you blind?* Suddenly, Taziar wished for Silme's and Astryd's abilities to contact Larson through his flawed mind barriers.

"You!" the stranger said, his voice devoid of malice. He used the language of Cullinsberg's barony with an odd mixture of accents. "You?" He blinked in the smoky half-lighting from the hearth. "Is your name Taziar Medakan?"

Taziar all but stopped breathing. Months had passed since he had escaped the tortures of the baron's dungeon, but a thousand gold weight price on his life might prove enough to keep bounty hunters on his trail for eternity. He knew someone would catch up with him eventually, yet he had always expected a direct attack rather than a questioning.

The stranger shifted his weight to the opposite leg. Coins clicked, muffled by linen, though to Taziar they sounded as loud as a drumbeat. "Well?" the man prodded.

Taziar sidled a glance toward his companions. Though too distant to hear words, they watched the exchange with concern. Larson's fingers curled into a fist on the table, his other grip lax against his hilt. Silme's hand rested on his arm, restraining. The bartender feigned disinterest, but his gaze flicked repeatedly to the stranger and his prisoner, awaiting trouble. Though Taziar knew of no other reason why this man should know his name, he answered truthfully in the same tongue. "I'm Taziar. How do you know me?"

The stranger's brown eyes lowered and rose. "You're even smaller than I expected. I have an eleven-year-old daughter bigger than you."

Taziar found the comment annoyingly snide, but familiar with such taunts, he resisted the urge to return a sarcastic comment. "I think I've got my equilibrium now. Could I have my hands back?" He twisted slightly in the man's grasp.

The man seemed surprised. He released Taziar and gestured at a chair across the table. Apparently realizing he had never answered Taziar's first question, he corrected the oversight. "I have a message for you."

"A message?" Taziar ignored the proffered seat. Instead, he caught the toppled chair, positioned it within reach of the stranger and sat. If the opportunity arose, he wanted to flip the purse safely into its pocket.

The stranger sat also, hitching his chair sideways and further from Taziar.

Recognizing an attempt to preserve personal space, Taziar suspected the man was city bred. "Who sent this message?"

"I was told to mention Shylar." The stranger examined Taziar for any sign of reaction.

Taziar gave him none, though the name held more significance than any other the stranger might have spoken. An image rose in Taziar's mind of a matronly woman, a handsome figure still evident beneath sagging skin, dark eyes shrewd and eclipsed by graying curls. She served as madam to Cullinsberg's whorehouse and mother to its beggars and thieves. An uncanny reader of intentions and loyalties, Shylar had recruited pickpockets and street orphans like Taziar, building a faction of the underground that had become not only the most powerful, but peculiarly benevolent as well. Once one of Shylar's favorites, Taziar knew most of his fellows catered to the semilegitimate vices of men: mind-hazing drugs, women, and gambling. Others acted as spies, scouting the city and its treasures until every corner of Cullinsberg belonged to the underground. Those attracted to politics bought guards and information.

"There's trouble in Cullinsberg," the stranger explained.

"Trouble?" Taziar gripped the edge of the table. "What sort of trouble?"

"Violence in the streets. Merchants robbed to their last ducat, and sometimes beaten and killed. Guards brutalized so badly they've taken to carrying weapons off-duty and using them at the slightest provocation. Daughters dragged away in broad daylight to be sold as slaves in distant ports." No trace of emotion entered the stranger's voice; he relayed information in the matter-of-fact tone of a teacher.

But the words stunned Taziar. He tried to picture his companions assaulting guardsmen in cobbled alleyways, but the image defied his experience. Shylar taught her lessons well. Taziar knew merchants expected to lose a small percentage of wares when they came to the baron's city, but huge profits absorbed the pilferings and encouraged the traders to return. Greedy thefts could only harm trade and, in the long run, destroy the thief's own livelihood. And Shylar's followers would never resort to violence. Taziar spoke, his mouth suddenly dry. "Anything more?"

The stranger shrugged. "I was told to tell you, Taziar Medakan, that the baron's fighting back. His men have infiltrated organized gangs. The guards arrested some of the strongest leaders. They're rotting in the baron's dungeons while he collects a few more before a mass execution on Aga'arin's High Holy Day." The stranger circled his own neck with his fingers, simulating a noose. He made a crude noise, then dropped his head to one side, eyes bulging and tongue dangling from a corner of his mouth.

Taziar scooted backward with a pained noise, the memory of his father's death on the gallows rising hot within him. He recalled the elder Medakan's quietly dignified acceptance of an execution based on betrayal, the convulsing throes of suffocation, and hard, gray eyes still steely after death. Visibly shaken, Taziar gulped down half the stranger's ale before he realized his mistake.

The stranger's face resumed its normal appearance, and he laughed at Taziar's discomfort. "Gruesome, eh, but no worse than they deserve."

Taziar nodded, not trusting himself to speak. He wondered whether the stranger's cruelty had been intentional. Taziar's father had led the baron's guards during the decades of the Barbarian Wars. And anyone in Cullinsberg who didn't know the captain from his years of service would certainly remember his public hanging. Then, too, Taziar's alias as Shadow Climber must have become common information. *He's setting me up for capture.* But something about the situation seemed jarringly amiss. *Only an insider would think to lure me with the name Shylar, but no professional would be stupid enough to send a Cullinsbergen with the message.* Taziar regathered his shattered composure. "You're from Cullinsberg?"

"Me?" The stranger shook his head and spoke with honest casualness. "Many years ago, right about the start of the wars. My father didn't want to make me an orphan, or a solider when my time came, so we moved away. I spent most of my life in Sverigehavn." He twitched, suddenly appearing uncomfortable. "You probably don't think much of war dodgers, not if you're related to the hero with your same name."

Taziar always prided himself on reading motivations; on the streets, his life depended on it. This man's replies came too effortlessly to be lies, unless they were exceedingly well-rehearsed. His explanations seemed appropriately fluent, his uneasiness heartfelt. He did not stumble over the term "hero," despite the fact that the citizenry had long ago exchanged the word for "traitor." Taziar dismissed the confession with a mild signal of good will. "Not everyone's meant for battle. I was more interested in how you came by the information you just gave me."

"Now that's odd." The stranger reclaimed his mug from Taziar, tracing its rim with a dirty finger. "I'm a dockhand. The ferry, *Amara,* came ashore a few weeks back. An old man approached me, picked me out because of my accent, I guess. He said he'd come on *Amara* from Cullinsberg and asked me to give you that message. I don't know how he knew where I'd find you. Didn't tell me his name, just told me you wouldn't know him and said to mention Shylar. Paid me well enough to make it worth my time finding you."

Taziar studied the stranger more carefully in light of this new information. He noticed a face chapped and windburned from exposure to elements, muscled arms, and hands callused like a laborer's. The last piece of the puzzle slid into place with smooth precision. Though a southerner residing in Sweden was rare, the stranger's story seemed plausible and circumstance supported it. The elderly man could have been any of a hundred street people aided by Taziar's charity; enamored with the thrill rather than the money, Taziar had always freely shared his spoils with hungry beggars. The payment explained why a dockhand carried gold, but a street person from Cullinsberg could only have gathered enough coinage for travel and ferry passage from one source. *Shylar. And if she went to this much expense and trouble to find me, not even knowing whether I'm still alive, she's in serious trouble.*

Taziar frowned, confused as well as concerned. The underground had long ago adopted a complex series of codes for positive identification of authenticity of messages. The stranger's method of delivery defied all correct procedure. *Maybe the signals have changed or Shylar thought I might have forgotten them. Perhaps she was too desperate to waste time with details.* Taziar fidgeted. *Could this be a trap, a trick of the baron's to draw me back to Cullinsberg?* He dismissed the thought from necessity. *If there's any chance Shylar's in trouble, I have to help. I'll just have to be careful.* Another realization jarred Taziar with sudden alarm. "Has the ferry made her last run until spring?"

The stranger bobbed his head in assent. "But she'll winter in the south, so she'll cast off early next week for the return to Calrmar Port."

Taziar laced his fingers on the tabletop, his thoughts distant. *If we leave tonight, we'll still have to travel hard to reach Sverigehavn Port in time. From there, if we push on just as hard, we should make Cullingsberg with a few days to spare before Aga'arin's High Holy Day.* "Could you describe the person who gave you the message?"

The stranger poked a thumb through a knothole in the tabletop. His face crinkled into a mask of consideration. "Tall, thin. He had that withered look of someone who'd weathered plagues that killed his young ones. Had a healthy amount of Norse blood in him, too, by his coloring. But his accent was full barony. In fact, he used that funny speech of the villages south of Cullinsberg." The stranger continued, clipping off final syllables with greatly exaggerated precision to demonstrate. "He migh' o' co' from Souberg or Wilsberg origina'." He laughed at his own mimicry.

"Never could figure out how they did that so easily. Always seemed like more effort than it was worth."

Taziar's answering chuckle was strained. "Thanks for the information." He tossed a pair of Northern gold coins, watched them skitter across the table and clink to a halt against the mug. "That should cover the drink, too." The payment had come from reflex. Abruptly, Taziar realized his mistake. He winced as the stranger reached for his purse to claim the money.

An elbow brushed the precariously balanced pouch. It overbalanced. Ducats and silvers clattered across the polished floor. The barroom went silent, except for the thin rasp of coins rolling on edge, followed by the sputter as they fell flat to the planks.

The stranger remained seated, blinking in silent wonderment. He glanced at Taziar, but addressed no one in particular. "Odd. Now how do you suppose that happened?"

Taziar rose, suddenly glad the stranger had positioned himself beyond reach while they chatted; it took the blame from him. "I couldn't begin to guess." He trotted back to his own table, leaving the stranger to collect his scattered coins.

Reclaiming his chair, Taziar gathered breath to convince his companions of the necessity of traveling quickly to Cullinsberg. Then, realizing it would take more than a few delicately chosen arguments, he sighed and addressed Larson. "You know those drinks you owe me?"

Larson nodded.

"Any chance I could have all of them right now?"

Taziar's concern heightened during the week of land and ocean travel that brought them from Norway's icy autumn to the barony of Cullinsberg. He spent many sleepless nights agonizing over a summons he believed had come from Shylar. *What do I know? What skill do I have that Shylar might need desperately enough to send a beggar to find me?* And always, Taziar discovered the same answers. He knew the city streets, but others closer and more recently familiar could supply her with the same information. Though a master thief, Taziar retained enough modesty to believe others with determination could accomplish anything he could. Only two skills seemed uniquely his. As a youth, Taziar had always loved to climb, practicing until his companions bragged, with little exaggeration, that he could scale a straight pane of glass.

Taziar hoped this was the ability Shylar sought, because the other filled him with dread. In the centuries of the barony's dominance, only Taziar had escaped its dungeons, and even he had needed the aid of a barbarian prince. Taziar had paid with seven days in coma and a beating that still striped his body with scars. It was an experience he would not wish even upon enemies, and, despite his love for impossible challenges, he harbored no desire to repeat it. *I doubt my knowledge will serve Shylar, yet I have no choice but to try.*

Two days before Aga'arin's High Holy Day, Taziar Medakan peered forth from between the huddled oaks and hickories of the Kielwald Forest. Across a fire-cleared plain, the chiseled stone walls enclosing the city of Cullinsberg stretched toward the sky, broad, dark, and unwelcoming. A crescent moon peeked above the colored rings of sunset, drawing glittering lines along the spires of the baron's keep in the northern quarter and the four thin towers of Aga'arin's temple to the east. The squat walls hid the remainder of the city, but Taziar knew every building and corner from memory.

Taziar crept closer. From habit, he sifted movement from the stagnant scene of the sleeping city. Sentries paced the flat summit of the walls, their gaits grown lazy in the decade of peace since the Barbarian Wars. Taziar knew their presence was a formality. The city gates stood open, and no one would question the entrance of Taziar and his friends. *Unless the guards recognize me.* The thought made Taziar frown. He turned and started toward the denser center of forest where his companions were camped.

An acrid whiff of fire halted Taziar in mid-stride. It seemed odd someone would choose to set a woodland camp so close to the comforts of a city. Taziar twisted back to face the walls. His blue eyes scanned the tangled copse of trees. Eventually, he discerned a sinuous thread of smoke shimmering between the trunks. Curious, he flitted toward it, his gray cloak and tunic nearly invisible in the evening haze. He pulled his hood over unruly, black hair, hiding his face in shadow.

Half a dozen paces brought Taziar to the edge of a small clearing. A campfire burned in a circle of gathered stones. The reflected light of its flickering flames danced across the trunks of oak defining the borders of the glade. A man slouched over the fire. Though his posture seemed relaxed, his gaze darted along the tree line. He wore a sword at his hip, a quiver across his back, and a strung bow lay within easy reach. Four other men occupied the clearing, in various stages of repose. Each wore a cloak of black, brown or green to protect against the autumn chill. Bunched or crouched against the trees, they appeared like wolves on the edge of sleep, and Taziar suspected the slightest noise would bring them fully awake.

Taziar considered returning to his own camp. He had no reason to believe these people meant Cullinsberg any harm, and the baron's soldiers could certainly handle an army of five men. Still, their presence this near the city seemed too odd for Taziar to pass without investigation. Noiselessly, he inched closer.

As Taziar narrowed the gap, the man before the fire shifted to a crouch. Flames sparked red highlights through a curled tangle of dark hair. The pocked features were familiar to Taziar. He recognized Faldrenk, a friend from his days among the underground. Though not above thievery, Faldrenk had specialized in political intrigue and espionage. Surprised and thrilled to discover an old ally, Taziar studied the other men in the scattered firelight. With time, he made out the thickly-muscled form and sallow features of Richmund, a bumbling pickpocket who scarcely obtained enough copper to feed his voracious appetite. In leaner times, he often joined the baron's guards and always knew which sentries could be bribed. The other three men were strangers.

Taziar tempered the urge to greet his long-unseen comrades with his knowledge of the changes in Cullinsberg and the realization that they might be performing a scam easily ruined by his interference. The evident weaponry seemed incongruous. Like most of the thieves, gamblers, and black marketeers of the underground, Faldrenk and Richmund were relatively harmless, catering to the greed and illegal vices of men rather than dealing in violence. Taziar stepped into the clearing. Avoiding names, he chose his words with care. "Nice night for hunting?"

Every head jerked up. Faldrenk shouted as if in warning. "Taz!" Bow in hand, he leaped to his feet, flicking an arrow from his quiver to the string. Faldrenk's companions scrambled to their feet.

Taziar's smile wilted. Shocked by his friends' reactions, he went still.

Faldrenk raised his bow and drew. Taziar dodged back into the forest. The arrow scraped an ancient oak, passed through the place where Taziar had stood, and grazed a furrow of flesh from his arm. Pain mobilized him. He charged through the forest, leaping deadfalls and brush with a speed born of desperation. He wasted a second regaining his bearings, aware he needed the aid of his companions to face this threat. An attack from men who had once been allies seemed nonsensical, but Taziar did not waste time pondering. He raced deeper into the forest. Branches tore his cloak. A twig whipped through his torn sleeve and across his wound, stinging nearly as much as the arrow.

Taziar careened around an autumn-brown copse of blackberry and nearly collided with a man, an instinctive side step all that saved him from impaling himself on the stranger's sword. The man followed, lunging for Taziar's chest. Taziar sprang backward, pawing for his own hilt. His heel mired in a puddle. He fell. The stranger's sword whisked over his head, then curled back and thrust for Taziar's neck. Taziar rolled into the wild snarl of brambles. The stranger's blade plowed through mud, splashing slime and water across the vines.

Taziar floundered free of the encumbering vines, heedless of the thorns that tore welts in his skin. He caught his swordgrip in both fists and wrenched. Vines snapped, and the sword lurched gracelessly from its sheath. The stranger swept for Taziar's head. Taziar spun aside. "Why?" he managed to ask before the stranger cut to Taziar's left side. This time, Taziar took the blow on his sword. The stranger's blade scratched down Taziar's, locked momentarily on the crossguard. Small and a scarcely adequate swordsman, Taziar realized, with alarm, he had little chance against his opponent's superior size and strength.

"Traitor!" the stranger screamed. A sudden push sent Taziar stumbling backward.

Taziar could hear the crash of his pursuers, growing closer. He dropped to his haunches, gaining balance with ease but feigning instability. The stranger pressed his advantage. He stabbed with bold commitment. Taziar skirted the thrust and dove between closely-spaced trunks. He hit the ground with head tucked, rolled, and ran, oblivious to the shouts behind him. His thoughts swirled past like the endless ranks of oaks. *Everyone's gone mad! What in Karana's deepest hell is going on?*

Taziar jammed his sword into his sheath as he tore through underbrush and wove between a copse of pine trees toward the clearing that sheltered his companions. The sweet wood odor of a campfire reaffirmed his bearings, the snap of its flames lost beneath the crash of bootfalls. Shouting a warning to his friends, Taziar cut across a deer path and skittered into the camp, the bandits on his heels.

Silme stood at the far end of the glade, her manner alert and her stance characteristically bold. Head low, but gaze twisted toward the new threat, Astryd muttered spell words in a furious incantation. Larson charged without question, his swordmaster's katana lit red by flame. Taziar ducked as Larson's sword blocked a strike intended for the Shadow Climber's head. Caught by surprise, the bandit missed his dodge. Larson's hilt crashed into his face, staggering him. The follow-through cut severed the bandit's head.

Taziar dodged past, Faldrenk and his companions in close pursuit. Taziar caught a glimpse of Astryd, abandoning a magical defense foiled by the proximity of battle. He pitched over the fire. Rolling to his feet, he used the moment this maneuver gained him to catch his breath and his balance. Larson thrust for the trailing bandit. The bandit whirled to tend to his own defense, and Richmund came to his aid. Faldrenk and his remaining ally advanced on Taziar from opposite sides of the campfire.

Taziar crouched. Desperate and uncertain, he swept a brand from the blaze and hurled it at Faldrenk's companion. Heat singed Taziar's fingers, the pain delayed by callus, but the bandit cried out in distress. Taziar scuttled backward. Faldrenk's blade missed Taziar's chest by a finger's breadth of air.

"Faldrenk!" Taziar seized his sword hilt as his old friend jabbed sharpened steel for the Climber's abdomen. Taziar lurched sideways, freeing his blade in the same motion. He caught Faldrenk's next sweep on his sword. "Stop! Don't! Faldrenk, we're friends . . ."

Steel chimed beyond the firelight as Larson returned strikes and parries with a ferocity that would have pleased his teacher. Faldrenk slashed. "Adal was your friend, too."

Taziar batted Faldrenk's blade aside, not daring to return the attack. "And that's not changed. Why . . . ?"

Faldrenk bore in, slicing for Taziar in an angry frenzy. Hard-pressed, Taziar gave ground freely. He kept his strokes short, intended only for defense. Sweat-matted hair fell, stinging, into his eyes. From the edge of his vision, he saw Faldrenk's companion closing from around the fire. "Faldrenk, why?"

Faldrenk's voice held a contempt once reserved for guards who abused peasants in the streets. "Because you're a foul, filthy, shit-stinking traitor." His blade whistled for Taziar's face. "Karana's pit, *treason runs in Medakan blood!*"

The gibe hurt worse than Faldrenk's betrayal. Taziar spun aside, but shock cost him his timing. Faldrenk's blade nicked Taziar's ear, and blood trickled down his collar in a warm stream. The remaining bandit charged into sword range. Taziar abandoned speech as he blocked the stranger's strike with his sword. The force of the blow jarred him to the shoulders. Before he could muster a riposte, the stranger's sword hammered against his again. Impact staggered Taziar. Driven to the edge of the clearing, he felt branches prickle into his back.

Again, Faldrenk lunged, blade sweeping. Taziar leaped backward. Twigs snapped, jabbing into his skin like knives. His spine struck an oak; breath whistled through his teeth. The stranger cut for Taziar's head. Taziar ducked, and the blade bit deeply into the trunk. Taziar seized the opening; he skirted beneath the stranger's arm as the sword came free in a shower of bark.

"Faldrenk, listen . . ." Taziar gasped, nearly breathless. The stranger paid the words no heed. His blade arced toward Taziar. The Climber spun to meet the charge. Their blades crashed together.

Silme's anxious voice rose above the din. "Shadow, behind you!" Astryd screamed a high-pitched, wordless noise. Taziar spun, slashing to counter Faldrenk's strike. But his friend had gone unnaturally still, sword poised for a blow. Instead of steel, Taziar's blade found flesh. It cleaved beneath Faldrenk's left arm and halfway through his chest. Blood splashed on Taziar and ran along his crossguard, but he noticed only Faldrenk's eyes. The pale orbs revealed fear and shock before they glazed in death. The corpse crumpled, wrenching the sword from Taziar's grip.

Instinctively, Taziar whirled to face his other opponent, dodging to evade an unseen strike. But the stranger, too, had noticed Faldrenk's sudden immobility. Wide-eyed, he backed away from Taziar signing a broad, religious gesture in the air. Once beyond sword range, he turned and ran.

Apparently, Larson's opponents also abandoned their assault; the world went eerily silent. Taziar stared at the lifeless body, once a friend, who had berated him with insults as cruel as murder. The scene glazed to red fog. Unable to discern Faldrenk's features, Taziar knelt. Only then did he recognize the tears in his own eyes. And the realization brought a rush of grief. He placed a hand on the shapeless blur of Faldrenk's corpse, felt life's last warmth fleeing beneath his touch.

Taziar lowered his head. He knew what would come next. In the past, the mere idea of killing had brought memories vivid as reality. Thoughts of his troubled childhood had remained quiescent since the familiar restless attraction to danger had driven him to chase down and slay his father's murderer, and seek adventure in the strange realms north of the Kattegat. Now, back on his home ground, steeped in a friend's blood, Taziar cringed beneath an onslaught of remembrance.

Images battered his conscience like physical blows. He saw his mother's frail form, withered by the accusations against his father. He heard her wine-slurred voice berating her only son with words heavy with reproach and accusation. He recalled how she had trapped him into promising to take her life and forced him to keep that vow, the jagged tear of the knife through flesh, the reek of blood like tidewrack on a summer beach. Taziar's stomach knotted with cramps. He dropped to his hands and knees, fighting the urge to retch.

A firm hand clamped on Taziar's shoulder and steered him beyond the sight and odor. Larson's tone was soft and nonjudgmental, but liberally tinged with surprise. "Your first?"

Taziar rubbed his vision clear. He shook his head, not yet trusting himself to speak. Despite heated battles fought at Larson's side against wolves and conjured dragons, Taziar had not killed a man since he slew the traitor in Sweden's forest. "Third," he confessed. He did not elaborate further. "It's a weakness."

Larson slapped Taziar's back with comradely force. "Ha! So you're not perfect after all. If you have to have a flaw, I can't think of one more normal than hating killing men."

Taziar smiled weakly. "Thanks." As the excitement of combat dissipated, his legs felt as flaccid as rubber. His arm throbbed where the arrow had nicked it, his fingers smarted, and his ear felt hot. Yet, despite pain and fatigue, Taziar dredged up the inner resolve to make a vow. *I'll take my own life before I cause another innocent death. And I'll not allow any other wrongful execution on the baron's gallows.*

Taziar turned his head, noticing for the first time that Astryd stood on shaky feet, her eyes slitted and most of her weight supported by Silme. Alarmed, he ran to her side, ashamed of the time wasted on his own inner turmoil. "What happened?"

Silme explained with composed practicality. "She tapped her life energy harder than she should have. She'll be all right." She added, her tone harsh with rebuke, "And she'll learn."

Taziar caught Astryd to him, relieving Silme of the burden. He knew the spell that weakened Astryd was the one that had frozen Faldrenk, preventing an attack that might otherwise have taken Taziar's life. Sick with guilt and concern, it did not occur to him to wonder why Silme had not aided in the battle.

CHAPTER 2
Shadows in the City

Beware lest you lose the substance by grasping
at the shadow.

—Aesop
The Dog and the Shadow

Sleep eluded Taziar, leaving him awash in pain. He lay on
his stomach to avoid aggravating the jabs and scratches in
his back. He tucked his arrow-slashed arm against his side;
the other rested across Astryd's abdomen, attuned to the
exhaustion-deep rise and fall of her every breath. His ear
throbbed, and he kept his head turned to the opposite side.
But the ache of superficial wounds dulled beneath the anguish and confusion inspired by Faldrenk's betrayal. *He
called me traitor. Why? I've not set foot near Cullinsberg in
months.* Taziar considered, seeking answers he lacked the
knowledge to deduce. *Maybe that's it. Perhaps Shylar
needed me, and I wasn't here.* He drummed his fingers in
the dirt, ignoring the flaring sting of his burns. *That makes
no sense. My friends know I fled with Cullinsberg's army at
my heels; how could they hold such a thing against me?*

Aware that Faldrenk would not deem ignorance nor inactivity a crime punishable by death, Taziar abandoned this
line of thought. *It wasn't mistaken identity either. Faldrenk
called me by name. Something strange is happening, a break
in loyalties that touched Faldrenk and Richmund.* Taziar felt
his taxed sinews cramp. Having already taken long, careful
moments to find a posture that did not incite the pain of his
injuries, he resisted the impulse to roll. *But Shylar knows I
still care about the underground. Otherwise, she would never
have expected me to answer her summons.* Taziar worked
tension from his muscles in groups. *She knows me too well
to suspect I would act against friends. And she'll have explanations. I have to see her. Until then, I can do nothing.*

Mind eased, Taziar surrendered to the urge to reposition his body. Pain flared, then died to a baseline chorus. Gradually, Taziar found sleep.

Dawn light washed, copper-pink, across the battlements of Cullinsberg. Huddled within the overlarge folds of Larson's spare cloak, Taziar felt a shiver of excitement traverse him. After months in the cold, barbaric lands north of the Kattegat, returning to the city of his childhood seemed like stepping into another world. He tried to map the cobbled streets from memory but found gaps that would require visual cues. The lapses reminded him of an ancient beggar who knew every street and alleyway in the city, but, unable to give verbal directions, would walk an inquirer to his destination.

"What about me?"

Larson's question startled Taziar. Lost in his past, he had nearly forgotten his companions. "What about you?"

As they neared the gateway and the uniformed guards before it, Larson kept his voice soft. "I hate to bring up the subject. I still find it hard to believe myself, but people tell me I'm an elf. In the North, no one seemed to care much for elves. Am I going to get attacked every time I step into a crowd?"

"Attacked?" Taziar chuckled. "You're approaching civilization. Draw steel in the streets and you'll get arrested." Recalling the report of the Sverigehavn dockhand in Kveldemar's tavern, Taziar hoped his description was still accurate. "Besides, no one in Cullinsberg will know what an elf is. They'll just assume you're human. Ugly, but human all the same."

"Gee, thanks." Larson caught Silme's arm and steered her beyond Taziar's reach. "You little creep."

"Cre-ep?" Astryd repeated, her light singsong adding a syllable to the English word. "Is that the same as 'jerk'?"

"Exactly," Larson said.

"And its meaning?" Silme showed an expression of genuine interest, but she still fought back a smile.

Larson shot a wicked glance at Taziar. "It's a term of endearment."

"Sure." Taziar worked sarcasm into the word. "Which explains why you're madly in love with that woman . . ."

He gestured at Silme. ". . . but you've only used the term to refer to me." Adopting a wide-eyed, femininely seductive expression, he grasped Larson's free hand and raised his voice to falsetto. "Sorry, hero, I'm already taken."

Astryd slapped Taziar's back playfully, which, because of the scratches, turned out to be more painful than she had intended. Taziar winced, released Larson, and resumed his normal walk toward the gateway with a final whispered warning. "Avoid my name. If the dockhand told the truth, the baron may have dropped my bounty to concentrate on closer, more formidable enemies. But no need to take a chance."

The four fell silent as they reached the opened, wrought iron gates and a pair of guards dressed in the barony's red-trimmed black linen. Taziar lowered his head, hiding his features beneath the supple creases of his hood. But the guardsmen seemed more interested in his blond companions and the women's oddly-crafted staves. They stared without questioning as Taziar and his companions entered the town.

Despite the early hour, men and women whisked through the main street, rushing to open shops, tend to jobs, or run errands. Merchants pulled night tarps from roadside stands, piling fruit in bins or setting merchandise in neat rows. They worked with the mechanical efficiency of routine. Yet, to Taziar, their manner seemed anything but normal. Mumbled conversations blended to indecipherable din, devoid of the shouted greetings between neighboring sellers who had known one another for years. Stands and merchants older than Taziar had disappeared, replaced by either strangers or glaring stretches of empty space. Others remained. But where women once tended their wares alone, now they shared stalls, hoping to find safety in being part of a group, or else they hired men to guard them. Despite laws against it, swords and daggers were boldly displayed. Many of the blades were crusted with dried blood, as if to warn predators that their owners had killed and would do so again if pressed.

Astryd gawked at the bustling crowds and towering buildings. The Dragonrank school required its students to remain on its grounds eleven months of every year, and

Astryd had never found time to visit the more civilized lands south of the Kattegat. "So this is Cullinsberg."

Larson watched Astryd's rural antics with wry amusement. "This is the great city you keep bragging about?"

"Sort of," Taziar admitted uncomfortably as he led his companions along the main thoroughfare. Concern leaked into his tone, and his friends went quiet as they followed. Though most of the passersby remained unarmed, they gave one another a wide berth, and Taziar was unable to make eye contact with any of Cullinsberg's citizens. The buildings, at least, seemed unchanged. Rows of stone dwellings and shops lined the streets behind the merchants. Still, something as yet unrecognized bothered Taziar; a piece of city life seemed awry. And, since it was missing rather than out of place, Taziar wandered three blocks before he realized what disturbed him. *Where are the beggars?*

Taziar turned a half-circle in the roadway, gazing across the sewage troughs in search of the ancient crones and lunatics who took sustenance from the discarded peels and cores that usually littered the roadside ditches. The maneuver uncovered neither vagrants nor scraps, but he did notice a scrawny boy dressed only in tattered britches who was huddled on the opposite street corner. The child sat with his head drooped into his lap, his hand outstretched as if from long habit.

Taziar's companions watched him with curiosity. "Shad—" Silme spoke softly, shortening his alias beyond recognition. "What's the problem? Maybe we can help."

"Is it the child?" Astryd asked, touching Taziar's hand. "We have more than enough money to feed him."

"No!" Taziar answered forcefully. "Something's not quite right. It's subtle, and I don't understand it yet." He spoke low and in Scandinavian, though his companions understood the barony's tongue. Astryd and Silme had learned several languages at the Dragonrank school, and Larson spoke it with the same unnatural ease and accent as he did Old Norse. "I was born and raised here. I've learned the laws of the barony and its streets. This is my river, and I know how to stay afloat." Taziar paused, trying to phrase his request without sounding demanding or insulting. "Please. Until I figure out what's bothering me, let me do the swimming. Just follow my lead." Taziar studied the boy. "Wait here." He crossed to the corner, relieved when his friends did not argue or follow.

The boy raised hollow, sunken eyes as Taziar approached. He climbed to skeletal legs and hesitated, as if uncertain whether to run or beg. At length, he stretched scarred fingers toward Taziar. "Please, sir?"

The sight cut pity through Taziar. Impressed by the child's fear, he fixed an unthreatening expression on his face and leaned forward. Unobtrusively, he reached into his pocket, emerging with a fistful of mixed northern coins. "I'm sorry." Taziar edged between the child and the next alleyway, surreptitiously pressing money into the beggar's tiny hand as he shielded the exchange from onlookers. "I have nothing for you today," he lied, gesturing toward Astryd in a matter-of-fact manner. "But my woman insisted I come over and tell you we feel for you, and we'll try to save something for you tomorrow."

The child accepted Taziar's offering into a sweating palm. A sparkle momentarily graced his dull, yellow eyes. Playing along like a seasoned actor, he spoke in a practiced monotone. "Aga'arin bless you, sir." Slowly, he wobbled toward the market square. His gaze fluttered along streets and windows, as if he expected someone to seize his new-found wealth before he could buy a decent meal.

Taziar returned to his companions. Incensed by the beggar's paranoia, he did not take time to properly phrase his question. "Have you ever seen anything like that?"

"No." Anger tingéd Astryd's reply. "When did you become stingy? You could have at least given him food."

Taziar laughed, realizing the trick intended to divert thieves had also confused his companions. "I gave him more money than he's seen in his life." A pair of uniformed guards walked by, eyeing the armed and huddled group with suspicion. Taziar waited until they'd passed before elaborating. "I meant the fear. Have you ever met a beggar too scared to beg? Worse, a starving beggar afraid to take money? Who in Karana's darkest hell would rob a beggar?"

"Easy target." Larson shrugged, his expression suddenly hard. "In New York City, the hoods'll rob their own mothers for dope money. There's too many to count how many

Vietnamese kids look like that one, and they'll take anything from anyone."

Little of Larson's speech made sense to Taziar. Finding the same perplexed look echoed on Silme's and Astryd's faces, Taziar pressed. "Interesting, Allerum. Now, could you repeat it in some known, human language?"

Larson gathered breath, then clamped his mouth shut and dismissed his own explanation. "Yes, I've seen it before. Leave it at that." He addressed Taziar. "Now, swimmer, what river do we take from here?"

"This way." Taziar chose a familiar alley which he knew would lead nearly to the porch steps of Cullinsberg's inn. Rain barrels stood at irregular intervals; old bones and rag scraps scattered between them. From habit, Taziar assessed the stonework of the closely-packed shops, dwellings, and warehouses hedging the walls of the lane. Moss covered the granite like a woolly blanket, its surface disturbed in slashes where a climber had torn through for hand and toe holds. Taziar glanced at the rooftop. A cloak-hooded gaze met his own briefly, then disappeared into the shadow of a chimney. A careful inspection revealed another small figure in the eaves. A third crouched on a building across the walkway.

Engrossed in his inspection of the rooftops, Taziar never saw the trip-rope that went suddenly taut at his feet. Hemp hissed against his boots, making him stumble forward. A muscled arm enwrapped his throat and whetted steel pricked the skin behind his left ear. A deep voice grated. "Give me your money."

Taziar rolled his eyes to see a blemished, teenaged face. He felt the warmth of the thief's body against his spine, and the realization of a daylight attack against an armed group shocked him beyond speech. It never occurred to Taziar to fear for his life; he knew street orphans and their motivations too well. Instead, he appraised the abilities of his assailant. The youth held Taziar overbalanced backward. The grip was professional. He could strangle Taziar with ease. If threatened, a spinning motion would sprawl Taziar and drag the blade across his throat.

The assessment took Taziar less than a heartbeat. Aware the setup would require one other accomplice to draw the rope straight, Taziar numbered the gang at five. *Whatever happened to peaceful begging and petty theft?* "Fine. I'll give you ten gold. Two for you and each of your friends," he said deliberately, intending to inform his companions as well as appease his assailant.

Taziar felt the bandit's muscles knot beneath his tunic. "No. I want all your money."

Apparently taking his cue from Taziar's calm acceptance of the situation, Larson loosed a loud snort of derision. "Are you swimming now, Shad? Upstream? Downstream? Backstroke?" His taunt echoed between the buildings.

Agitation entered the thief's tone. "Tell your friend to shut up. Now!" Sharp pain touched Taziar's skin. Blood beaded at the tip of the blade, and sweat stung the wound.

Larson's hand fell to his hilt, and he took a menacing step. "Who are you telling to shut up, asshole? I'll cut off your ears and shove them up your nose."

"Calm down." Taziar tried to keep his voice level. He had never seen Larson so hostile, and the thief's greed alarmed him. Ten gold was more than a common laborer might make in a year, and the northern mintage would make it no less valuable. If Taziar had been alone, he would have felt certain that the thug would not harm him; but, challenged by Larson, the youth might be driven to murder. "You're not the one with a knife at your throat." Reminded of what he might have become at the same age, Taziar grew careless of risk. "Friend, you're doing this dumb."

The thief's fingers shivered against the dagger's hilt. He, too, seemed out of his element, unaccustomed to getting lectured by victims. "I'm doing this dumb? Which of us is jabbering on the blade end of the knife? If one of us is stupid, I'm not guessing it's me. Now give me your money and I may not kill you. Everyone else can just drop their purses, turn around, and leave."

Taziar cursed the loose hood that slid over his eyes and made it impossible to meet his assailant's gaze. "Look, friend, you can't have all our money. I offered you some. I'd have given the same to you if you'd asked nicely. Anything more than we're willing to give freely, you'll have to take. You've got four companions. See that man there." He tensed a hand to indicate Larson.

Immediately, the arm clamped tighter around Taziar's neck, neatly closing off his airway.

Taziar fought rising panic. Blackness swam down on him, but even vulnerability could not shake resolve. Given slightly different circumstances, he could have been this teen.

Gradually, the thief's grip relaxed. Taziar gasped gratefully for breath, then forced himself to continue. "If you want to take money from my friend, you'll need at least six more of you. Then, the one survivor can gather the money into a pile and spend it." Taziar measured the thief by his actions, sensed uncertainty beneath forced defiance. "Ten gold could feed you all for a month and more. Are you going to take the ten I offered you, or will you get all your friends slaughtered for the chance to get a few more? I can't compromise. My friends have to eat, too. And you won't live long on the street acting stupid."

"Stop. It's all right." Silme spoke in the rapid, high-pitched manner of a frightened woman, but Taziar knew the sorceress too well not to recognize a performance. She passed her dragonstaff to Larson who accepted it grudgingly in his off hand. "I'll give you my purse. I don't care. Money doesn't mean anything. Just don't hurt him." Reaching into her side pocket, she removed a thin pouch of coins. She approached the thief, flicking her hands in contrived, nervous gestures. "Let him go. You got his ten and mine. That's more than half of it. It's better than the deal he gave you. Just let him go." She pushed her purse at the thief's free hand. "Here. Take it. Take it."

Instinctively, the thief glanced at the purse.

Quick as thought, Silme grasped the youngster's knife hand. Positioning her thumb on his littlest knuckle and her fingers around and over his thumb, she gained the leverage to twist. The blade carved skin from Taziar's cheek. He dodged aside as Silme used her other hand to wrench the dagger from the youth's surprised grasp. A sudden punch beneath his elbow finished him. The thief tumbled, flat on his back, in the street.

A rock sailed from the rooftop.

Larson dropped Silme's staff. His sword met the stone in midair and knocked it aside. He completed his stroke, stopping with the blade against the thief's neck. "One more rock and the next thing in the street's your friend's head."

The gang went still.

Taziar pressed a palm to his gashed face to stop the bleeding. Silme's maneuver had jarred his hood aside, and black hair was plastered to the wound. He watched as Astryd whispered to herself, casting a spell. Hunched behind a rain barrel, the thief's partner suddenly became as immobile as a statue. Taziar knew from the strategies of his own childhood gang that the thief beneath Larson's blade was undoubtedly their leader.

Larson caught the thief by stringy, sand-colored hair and hoisted the youth to his feet. "Bend over."

The thief hesitated, then complied.

Larson raised his katana and yelled to the accomplices on the roof. "One move and your buddy's head comes off." He lowered his voice. "This is how you stop someone in the street, you little jackass."

Taziar stepped around the thief, met eyes dark with hatred. He winced, fearing Larson had taken things too far. Humiliation might force the thief to kill an innocent or a follower to maintain his position as leader. At the least, the youth would have to defy Larson, perhaps at the cost of his own life.

The leader howled. "Idiots! Don't let them get away with this. Throw rocks. Attack! Do something."

"Quiet!" Taziar seized a handful of gold from his pocket, trying to maintain the thief's self-respect by creating an illusion of partial success. "Here's your money." Seeking answers, he dropped the gold at the boy's feet and continued. "This isn't how things work here. I don't care about me. I wasn't in any trouble. I knew you wouldn't hurt me. You were in more danger than I was because there was a good chance the man with the sword would kill the whole damn bunch of you. What, in Karana's hell, is going on here?"

The youth stared, as if noticing Taziar for the first time. "Wait! I know you. You're that filthy Medakan worm. We don't want your blood-tainted money."

Shocked, Taziar searched for a reply.

Larson spoke first. "Uh, could you repeat that for the

benefit of the person holding the sword ready to decapitate you?"

"I don't care!" Still hunched, the leader screamed, "I'll die before I'll be humiliated by some traitor."

Larson hollered back, apparently as confused as Taziar. "What's this traitor bullshit?"

The youth refused to elaborate.

Taziar used a soothing tone. "Speak up, friend. Please. Were I you, I'd want to befriend the man holding the sword."

The youth remained stalwartly silent.

Behind the thief, Larson raised a threatening foot.

Afraid for the leader's dignity, Taziar waved Larson off. "Don't kick him."

Larson lowered his foot, but he went on speaking in a voice deep with rage. "What do you mean 'don't'? He put a knife to your throat. I ought to cut his goddamned head off. He's a threat. I can remove a threat in an instant. Want to see?"

"No." Taziar winced, his loyalties suddenly shifted. "Look, Allerum, he's a street orphan. He's got enough problems without you making things worse. I grew up like that, damn it!"

A stone bounced from Astryd's magical shield, unnoticed by anyone but its thrower. Larson relented. "Fine, street scum. Pick up the money and go. Right now!"

The youth did hot hesitate. He scooped up the coins and ran. Astryd scarcely found time to dismantle her sorceries before the leader and his smaller companion raced deeper into the alleyway.

Taziar watched the teens' retreating figures. Bleeding stanched, he flicked his hood back over his head and chastised Larson. "Allerum, you can't treat these people like that. He's got enough problems, more than you could ever imagine."

Larson sheathed his sword, breaking the tension, but his expression did not soften. He glared after the gang. "Yeah, well. I've got problems, too. But you don't see me inflicting them on the weak and helpless."

"Weak and helpless?" Silme mouthed, but it was the Shadow Climber who spoke aloud.

"They're just hungry children!" Taziar's hands balled at

his sides in frustration as he tried to stifle the flood of memories welling within him: the pain of a week's starvation tearing at his gut; the restless, animal-light naps necessary to protect the few rags he owned. "What's wrong with you? I've never seen you like this." Taziar stared, concerned by Larson's uncharacteristic callousness and aware that his friend's manner had grown more cynical and confident in the month since Kensei Gaelinar's death. It seemed as if Larson felt he needed to fill the void his mentor had left. Yet Larson had never before lost the gentle morality that had driven him to put an elderly stranger's life before his own and had so impressed Taziar at their first meeting. "You've risked your life to protect innocents and children too many times to start hating them now."

"Innocents," Larson repeated forcefully. "And children? Those boys are neither. They get down on their luck, hit a few hard times. Then, instead of trying to better their lives, they take the rest of us down with them." The elf's eyes narrowed, making his face appear even more angular. "Give a kid like that a knife and a little muscle, and he thinks he has the god-given right to prey on people weaker than himself. Anyone with that kind of attitude deserves what he gets when he tries to intimidate some little man and finds out his victim's got a big friend with a howitzer." He slapped a hand to the katana's hilt.

Not all of Larson's speech made sense to Taziar, but the meaning came through despite the strange, English words. The Cullinsbergen pursed his lips, glancing at Silme and Astryd. The women whispered quietly, apparently trying to decide whether to interfere or let the men argue the issue out between themselves. "That's not right. What you saw here today isn't normal."

Larson snorted. "That gang was the most 'normal' thing I've seen since Freyr brought me to your world. For a punk, you're awfully naive."

The insult rolled right past Taziar; he knew Cullinsberg and its streets too well to take offense. But something in Larson's voice made the Climber push aside his anxiety for Shylar and his friends long enough for realization to take its place. Taziar had never heard of or conceived of a city larger than Cullinsberg, yet Larson had once claimed to come from a metropolis called New York, with a population four times that of the entire world. "This is personal, isn't it?"

Larson's frown deepened. "Yeah, you could say that." He nodded, as if to himself. His gaze met Taziar's, but his attention seemed internally focused. "A street gang beat up my grandfather for the thirteen dollars and sixty-seven cents he had in his pocket. That's the rough equivalent of two medium-sized, Northern coppers."

Taziar closed his lids, his mind gorged with the image of a white-haired elder with swollen eyes and abraded, purple cheeks. Larson's distrust and remembrances of his grandfather's misfortune had become one more obstacle to Taziar's already difficult task. Though he knew it was folly, he tried to explain. "Allerum, you don't understand. I probably put that gang together. All Shylar's people had ways of helping the homeless. Waldmunt paid them handsomely to keep quiet or create alibis. Mandel hired them to know every building and road in Cullinsberg or to study the patterns of changing guards. Shylar just gave freely." Taziar scanned the rooftops, making certain the gang youths had departed with their leader. "I shared food and money, too. But, I also taught the younger ones how to survive on the street. I organized them. Alone, a few bad days without food might weaken a child enough to drag misfortune into weeks of starvation, perhaps even death. As part of a group, someone always does well enough to share. And there's companionship. But I never intended them to band together against passersby and threaten lives."

"You're not thinking about *that* street orphan." Larson pointed down the alleyway. "You're thinking about *this* one." He tapped Taziar's scalp to indicate childhood memories.

"Exactly." Under ordinary circumstances, Taziar would have smiled at how neatly Larson had fallen into his trap; but now, weighed down by concern and confusion, he continued without expression. "And you're thinking about New York. Every issue, every action, every motivation has two sides. These children didn't hurt your grandfather." He waved in the general direction the gang had taken. "How can you condemn them until you've seen the streets from their point of view?"

Larson did not let up. "I don't need to know an enemy's life history. When we've got guns pointed at one another,

I haven't got time to ask his name before pulling the trigger. You can tell me Cullinsberg gangs are different until you're blue in the face, but I know a hood is a hood. Notice how the scum grabbed the smallest guy in the group."

Taziar sighed, cursing the time he was wasting bickering with Larson. *I have a summons to answer. And how can I hope to defend myself against a charge of betrayal when I don't even know what I'm accused of doing?* "Look, Allerum. Cullinsberg isn't New York. You're just going to have to trust me that what you saw here isn't normal. My friends are in trouble, and I stand by my friends."

"I stand by my friends, too," Larson started. "When punks threaten them in an alley . . ."

Worried about losing time, Taziar talked over Larson. "If you continue down this alley, it'll bring you to Cullinsberg's inn. Get some food and take a room on the top floor. That's the third story. See if you can rent the one on the south side. I'll meet you there."

"Meet us?" Astryd shifted her garnet-tipped staff from hand to hand, finally goaded to speak. "Where are you going?"

Taziar studied the side of a building. The uneven surface of stone would make an easy climb. "I have to meet with someone who can explain what's happening."

Astryd glanced from Larson to Silme, as if wondering why she seemed to be the only one voicing objections. "You can't go off alone. You might get killed. Take us with you."

Taziar edged toward the wall, amused by Astryd's concern. "I can't take you with me. If I brought strangers to the underground's haven, I really would be a traitor." The subject of safety turned his thoughts to his companions. "And if anyone asks for any reason, none of you knows me."

"Wait." Astryd grounded her dragonstaff. "Silme and I can handle room renting. At least let Allerum walk you part way. He can fight."

Taziar ignored the backhanded insult to his swordsmanship. In his current mood, Larson would prove worse than a hindrance.

To Taziar's relief. Larson took his side. "I'll be more trouble to Shadow than I'm worth. He had that situation under control. The boy had no reason to kill him, and they both knew it. Shadow's not threatening. I am. If someone robs Shadow, they'll put a knife to his throat. Someone robs me and Shadow, they'll have to frag us and go through the pieces."

"They'll what?" Astryd rounded on Larson, and Taziar seized the opening to steal a few steps closer to the wall.

"I won't be any protection," Larson clarified. "My presence will mean people have to kill us from a distance to handle us."

Astryd stomped a foot in anger. "You're going with him!"

"I am not going with him," Larson hollered back. "Nobody's going with him. He's safer by himself."

Taziar studied his companions and discovered that only Silme was actually looking at him. He winked conspiratorially and pressed a finger to his lips in a plea for silence.

Silme returned a smile.

"He's not safer by himself!" Astryd challenged Larson. "You can protect him. You're bigger and better with a sword. People are afraid of you. Nobody's afraid of him. He'll get himself killed." Without looking, she gestured at the place where Taziar had been standing.

But Taziar was no longer there. He positioned his fingers and toes in cracks between the wall stones and shinnied to the rooftop. Still, Larson's voice wafted clearly to him.

"Look, I'll settle this. There's one way he can be perfectly fucking safe . . ."

Taziar crept silently across the tiles pausing to assess a parallel thoroughfare.

". . . He can stay the hell here." A restless pause followed, then Larson's voice echoed through the alley. *"Where is he?"*

Harriman paced with the deadly patience of a caged lion. Floorboards creaked beneath heavy bootfalls, betraying his rage to the women in the whorehouse rooms below. Light streamed through the warped, purple glass of the window, striping the desk, and twisting Harriman's shadow into a hulking, animallike shape. "I don't give a damn what you say! I know those little weasels down on the north side are making more money than that. Either you or they are holding out." Harriman stopped, gaze boring into Harti's lean face. He read fear in the smaller man's features, and it

pleased him. "You had *damn* well better tell me it's them.
If it's you, they're going to be picking the meat off your
bones in the street next week!"

Cowed, Harti avoided Harriman's dark eyes, glancing
nervously at the other two men in the room. On either
side of the door, Harriman's Norse bodyguards, Halden
and Skereye, awaited their master's command.

Warped and controlled by an angered mage, Harriman
knew no mercy. "So who is it? Who's holding out, you
or them?"

"Well." Harti licked his lips with tense hesitation. "Of
course, they are, lord. I—I wouldn't hold out on you. I
trust . . . I wouldn't. I would never . . ."

"Well, you damn well better never!" Harriman resumed
his walk. "Tomorrow, I want double what you brought me
here!" He whirled suddenly, jabbing a finger at Harti. "I
don't care whether it comes from them. I don't care
whether it comes out of your pocket. I don't care if you
have to go terrorize some merchant. I don't care what you
have to do. Double!"

Harti shrank away.

". . . If you can get it from them, good. That's where it's
supposed to come from because I know they've got it. If
they're that much smarter than you and strong enough to
hold out on you, you better find somebody else to extort.
I'm getting double, or they'll find your organs scattered
through the alleys. Do you understand that?"

Harti's skin went pale as bleached linen. "Yes, please,
lord. I've got a wife and six children . . ."

"Widow and orphans." Harriman raised a threatening
hand to strike Harti. For an instant, a flaw in Bolverkr's
thought-splicing let Harriman's basic nature free. Thoughts
jumbled through his mind, liberally sprinkled with confusion. All notions of violence fled him, replaced by guilt,
and he turned the movement into a gesture toward the
door. Momentarily, he had no idea where he was; then
Bolverkr's handiwork regained control. Fury flared anew,
and Harriman continued as if he had never paused. "If you
stop whining and use some force, maybe you can get money
out of those children. Go do it now. Right now! If you
don't have that gold in my hands by sundown tomorrow,

you're going to be racing the men I'll be paying twice as much in bounty to bring me your head."

Struck by Harriman's inconsistent behavior as well as his irrational anger, Harti backed to the door, caught the knob, and twisted. The portal inched open. Immediately, an anxious voice floated through the crack. "Harriman! I have something to tell you."

Infuriated by personality lapses he could not explain and which might anger Bolverkr and weaken his command, Harriman responded more aggressively than he intended. "What!"

Halfway through the entryway, Harti froze.

Harriman waved Harti away. "You, get the hell out of here and go do what you're supposed to do."

Harriman waited until Harti darted down the hall, then returned to his desk and waited for the speaker to enter the room.

Almost immediately, a portly thief in clean but rumpled silk burst into Harriman's office. Unfastened cuffs flapped at his wrists, and mouse brown hair fringed plump cheeks in harried disarray. "Taz is in town."

Harriman went suddenly still. A long silence followed.

The thief waited, pale eyes interested.

"Who's in town?" Harriman asked carefully, earlier anger forgotten.

"Taziar Medakan. The little worm you told us to wait for. He's in Cullinsberg. Headed this way, too."

Harriman suppressed a smile, holding his expression unreadable instead. Bolverkr had carefully severed from Harriman's mind all memory of the dragon's attack and the hostilities between them. But the Dragonmage had left Harriman's diplomatic skills intact. "Are you sure? If you're wrong, you're in bigger trouble than the last idiot I was talking to."

The thief stood his ground. Apparently more accustomed to Harriman's brusque manner than Harti was, he remained unintimidated. "I'm certain. Absolutely reliable sources."

Harriman needed to be sure. "Would you put your life on it?" *You realize you are, don't you?*

The thief avoided the question. "It's him. Fits the description. Fits the characteristics. It has to be him. Can't be anyone else."

Harriman knew the time had come to consult Bolverkr directly. "Stand here. Don't move. I'll be back." Rising, Harriman pushed past the thief and his own bodyguards, trotted down the hall to his bedroom, and sat on a hard, wooden chair beside his pallet. Head low, he put mental effort into contacting his master. *Bolverkr?*

For some time, Harriman received no answer. Then a presence slid through his shattered defenses and Bolverkr's thoughts filled the diplomat's mauled mind. *I'm here.*

Taziar's in Cullinsberg.

Harriman felt Bolverkr's vengeance-twisted joy as his own. *Good. I've got plans for him and his companions. I want him to watch his girlfriend murdered and his friends hanged. Hurt him. But keep him alive, at least until the day past tomorrow.* Bolverkr broke contact.

Fine. Misplaced hatred sparked through the refashioned and tangled tapestry of Harriman's thoughts, sparking ideas far beyond Bolverkr's intentions. The sorcerer's meddling had created more than a simple puppet. Though guided, with motivations bent to Bolverkr's will, Harriman had not lost the ability to conspire. Awash in bitterness, he shuffled back to the workroom where the thief stood with obedient forbearance. "You're certain it's Taziar Medakan?"

"No question," the thief replied.

Taziar's no amateur. If I tell my people to abuse him, Taziar will play them like children. Besides, I'm not accountable for my lackeys' mistakes. Harriman met the thief's questioning gaze with a smile, then tossed a command to Halden and Skereye. "Kill Medakan."

CHAPTER 3
Shadows of the Truth

The treason past, the traitor is no longer needed.
—Pedro Calderon de la Barca
Life Is a Dream

Sunlight gleamed from the crisp, new hoops of rain barrels, slivering rainbows through a nameless alley off Panogya Street onto which the rear entry to Shylar's whorehouse opened. Crouched atop a neighboring warehouse, Taziar studied the walkway. Like most of the less well-traveled thoroughfares, it sported a packed earth floor that mired to mud with every rainstorm. The elements had hammered the black door, chipping away paint to reveal oak maintained in excellent repair.

Despite the closely-packed stonework of the warehouse and an artisan's attention to mortaring chinks, Taziar descended effortlessly into the vacant alleyway. He ducked into the rift between a barrel and the wall, where the shadows of both converged, and hesitated before the familiar doorway. The back entry was reserved for the underground; even they used it only in dire need and with gravest caution. Summoned from a distant land and uncertain of enemies and alliances, Taziar considered his situation urgent enough; but the attack by his former friends outside the city gates made him cautious. *I have to talk to Shylar. I don't dare trust anyone else. No matter how strong the evidence, Shylar knows me too well to consider me an enemy. At the least, she'll give me a chance to explain. And, if there are reasons and answers, she'll know them.*

Shylar's whorehouse had always served as a safe house and gathering place for Cullinsberg's male citizens, criminals and guards alike. Taziar had never found reason to enter by any means except the front door and once, after his escape from the baron's dungeons, through the emer-

gency, black portal set apart from the regular client areas
of the whorehouse. *I hate to break in, but, under the circumstances, Shylar could hardly blame me for being careful.*

Taziar glanced up the wall to the rows of windows lining
the second floor. Dark shutters covered many. Others had
their shutters flung wide, and filmy curtains in soft pinks
and blues rode the autumn breezes. Taziar knew each window opened into a bedroom; the only sleeping quarters in
the whorehouse without one belonged to Shylar. Next door,
the madam's study did have a window, but it overlooked the
crowded main street rather than the alleyway. Taziar frowned.
The idea of sneaking into a building in broad daylight, even
from a deserted throughway, did not appeal to him; but he
dared not waste the hours until night in ignorance.

*How much trouble is Shylar in? How long did it take her
messenger to find me, and what might that delay have cost
her?* Taziar shivered. His shoulder jarred the empty water
barrel, tipping it precariously. Quickly, Taziar caught it by
the base, steadying it and averting the noise that would
certainly have drawn guardsmen or curious passersby. He
cursed, aware his concern for Shylar was making him
sloppy. He knew he would perform better by suppressing
the myriad worries and questions that plagued him; he had
always managed to do so in the past. But now an image of
Shylar's kindly features was rooted in his mind, unable to
be dismissed. The darker portions of Taziar's consciousness
conjured a nebulous, nameless threat against her, pressing
him to a restless panic he had not known since the day he
had helplessly watched his father hanged and then taken
his mother's life.

Madness pressed Taziar. He rose to his knees, goaded to
an action he had not yet planned. It was not his way to act
without intense and meticulous research, but the idea of
Shylar endangered drove him to do something, anything,
no matter how severe the consequences. *The baron's "justice" took my parents from me. No one is going to hurt
Shylar without a fight!*

Calm. Calm. Taziar eased back into a crouch, trying to
temper need with reason. The inability to picture a specific
threat against Shylar gave him pause to think. *Who would
want to harm Shylar?* No answers came. She was the one
constant feature in a town that had little of permanence to

offer its street orphans and beggars. Her position as madam gained her no enemies. She treated her girls like daughters. Well-paid and fed, they came to her as a reasonable alternative to living hand to mouth on the streets. She kept the underground informed, gave shelter and money or jobs to those down on their luck. And, for every guardsman who suspected and felt obligated to report her connection to Cullinsberg's criminal element, three superiors were bribed or loyal clients.

This is getting me nowhere. There's too many things I don't know. I'll just have to talk to Shylar. Having made the decision, Taziar slipped into his calmer, competent routine. He turned to the wall, nestling his fingers into chinks between the stones, and scaled it with the ease of long habit. Drawing himself up to the first unshuttered window, he hesitated. Most of the whorehouse's bedroom business occurred at night, but it was not unusual for the guards on evening shift or night-stalking thieves to bed Shylar's prostitutes during the daylight hours. Quietly, ears tuned for any sounds from within, Taziar peeked through the window.

Pale blue curtains tickled his face. Through fabric gauzy as a veil, Taziar studied the room. A bed lay flush with the wall, covered by a disheveled heap of sheets and blankets. Near its foot, a multidrawered dressing table occupied most of the left-hand wall; a crack wound like a spider's web through a mirror bolted to its surface. Directly across from the window, the door to the hallway stood ajar. Seeing no one in the room, Taziar scrambled inside. Silently, he crept across the floorboards. Pressing his back to the wall that separated the room from the hallway, he listened for footsteps. Hearing none, he peered through the gap.

The unadorned hallway lay empty. Doors on either side led into bedrooms, some shut, some open and some, like the one Taziar peeked out from, ajar. Familiar with the signals, Taziar knew the closed doors indicated active business, the open doors empty rooms ready for use, and the ajar panels tagged dirtied rooms for the cleaning staff. To Taziar's right, the hallway ended in a staircase leading to the lower floor. At the opposite end of the hallway, a pair of plain, oak doors closed off the storage areas. Kept in perpetual darkness, these closets could be used to spy on the bargaining rooms below. Across the hall and to Taziar's left, the doors to Shylar's bedroom and study lay closed. Slipping into the hallway, he crept toward the madam's office.

Taziar had taken only a few steps when a doorknob clicked. A sandal rasped lightly across the wooden floor. Caught between two closed doors, he whirled, tensed for a wild dash back to the bedroom through which he had entered. He found himself facing Varin, a willowy brunette in her twenties. A purple-black bruise circled her left eye, abrasions striped her calves, and several fingers appeared swollen.

Taziar stared, shocked by Varin's wounds. Shylar's rules were strict, protective of her girls almost to a fault. "Varin?" he whispered. Gently, without threat, he shuffled a step toward her.

Varin's mouth gasped. Surprise crossed her features, and she raised whitened knuckles to her lips. Yet Taziar also read a more welcoming expression in her dark eyes, a sparkle of hope. "Taz?" Her voice emerged softer than his own. Her face lapsed into terrified creases. "You've got to get out of here. Go. Go. Quickly." She jerked her head about, as if seeking an escape, and her hands fluttered frantically. "Get away. Go!"

"Varin, please." Concerned for the woman, Taziar ignored the question of his own safety. "Calm down. Just tell me what's going on. Who . . . ?"

Varin's gaze drifted beyond Taziar. Her eyes flared wide, and she screamed. Fixing her stare directly on the Shadow Climber, she screamed again and again, then whirled and raced toward the staircase.

Taziar's every muscle tightened. He spun to face a burly, dark-haired strong-arm man he knew by sight but not by name. Before the Climber could speak, the larger man lunged for him. Taziar leaped backward, reeling toward the stairs. The man's hands closed on air, and he lurched after Taziar.

Taziar charged down the hallway, not daring to slow long enough to negotiate a corner into one of the rooms. *If I pause to climb through a window, he's got me. Have to get downstairs to the doors.*

The strong-arm man's cry rang through the whorehouse.

"It's Taz! The traitor's in the house!" His bootfalls crashed after the fleeing Climber.

Taziar's memory sprang to action, mapping the route through the kitchen to the emergency exit. *The open meeting area's just before the front door. Too many people there. Got to get out the back.* He skidded onto the landing, trying to catch a glimpse of the layout below, prepared to dodge whoever blocked his path to the exit. Below and to his right, a crowd of prostitutes sat bolt upright on gathered couches, benches, and chests. The half dozen men interspersed between them mobilized slowly. Beyond Varin, now nearly down to the lower landing, Taziar saw no one between himself and the door to the kitchen.

The strong-arm man sprang forward, catching a streaming fold of Taziar's cloak.

Yanked suddenly backward, Taziar lost his footing. He twisted. Cloth tore. He pitched into empty air. His shoulder crashed into the hard edge of steps, and momentum flung him, tumbling, down the stairs. Wildly, he flailed for a handhold, but the cloak tangled about his hands, the soft fabric slipping from the wood as if greased. His head struck the banister, ringing. Each step jolted the breath out of him, stamping bruises into his flesh.

Taziar landed, sprawled, at the foot of the flight. Dazed, he staggered to his feet. A wave of rising enemies filled his vision. Cursing the pain, but glad for the seconds his fall had gained him, he burst through the door into the kitchen.

A middle-aged man sat, composed and alone, at the huge dining table across from the cooking fire. At the far side of the room, the exit stood, slightly ajar, and Taziar knew it led into a small food storage room where Shylar screened whoever pounded on the black door, ignoring anyone who did not use one of the assigned, personal codes of the underground. Relief washed over Taziar. If it came to a race, he knew he could beat the stranger to the door. *Once in the entryway, I'm free.* He quickened his pace.

The stranger did not move. An odd smile graced his features, and he made a loud but wordless noise as Taziar caught the doorknob.

Before Taziar could pull it, the door wrenched open violently. For a startled instant, Taziar stared at a leather tunic stretched taut across a muscled chest. He glanced up to fair features so badly scarred that bands of tissue disrupted golden hair in patches. Pale eyes swiveled, unmistakably glazed from the berserker mushrooms some Vikings took to enhance ferocity in battle. Hands large as melons seized Taziar's arms. The Norseman dragged Taziar off his feet and through the doorway, then spun and hurled the Climber into the far wall.

Taziar's shoulder blades crashed into stone. Impact jolted pain along his spine. He heard the door slam shut as he stumbled forward and caught a glimpse of a second Norseman, larger than the first. Then, clenched fists slammed into Taziar's lower chest with the speed of a galloping horse. Something cracked. Pain jabbed Taziar's lungs, and momentum reeled him into the wall. His head smacked granite. His vision blurred and spun, and it required a struggle of will to keep from sinking limply to the floor.

A tottering side step regained Taziar his balance. He raised an arm in defense, his other hand pawing desperately for his sword. The scarred Norseman seized him by the wrists and ripped both arms behind him. Taziar struggled madly, but the larger man pinned him as easily as an infant. Through a whirling fog of anguish, Taziar watched the Norseman's partner approach and recognized the same drug-crazed expression on this man's features. "Wait!" he gasped. Doubled fists exploded into his abraded cheek. Taziar's neck snapped sideways. There was a sudden flash of brilliant white; blindness descended on him. For a second, he thought he was dead. Then the huge hands smashed his other cheek, sparking pain that made him scream.

"My turn." The man holding Taziar used the Scandinavian tongue with selfish eagerness, his grip pinching cruelly. "You'll kill him before I get a chance." Suddenly, he let go.

Drained of vigor and direction, Taziar collapsed. Weakly, he struggled to hands and knees, regaining clouded vision just in time to watch the scarred man's hand speeding for his face. He lurched backward clumsily. Curled fingers caught a glancing blow across the bridge of his nose with a blaze of pain. The follow up from the opposite fist pounded Taziar's lips against his teeth. Jarred half senseless, he sank to the floor.

"Skereye, enough!" A stranger's voice scarcely penetrated Taziar's mental fog. Through bleary, blood-striped vision, he examined the man who had been sitting at the kitchen table and had now entered the room. Dressed in blue and white silks and leather leggings, he stood with a quiet dignity that seemed out of place amidst the Norsemen's rabid violence. Despite his commanding manner, his eyes revealed gentle confusion, as if he had just escaped from a nightmare and had not quite reoriented to waking reality.

Skereye enwrapped his fingers in Taziar's hair and hefted the Climber to his feet. The Norseman's gaze jumped from Taziar to his master and back to Taziar. Robbed of control by the berserker drug, Skereye buried a fist in Taziar's stomach. The force sprawled the Climber. Air rushed from his lungs, leaving him no breath for a scream. Skereye pressed, hammering wild punches into Taziar's face until blood splotched his knuckles and Taziar fought for each ragged breath.

Even then, the beating might have continued had the leader not seized Skereye's wrist on a backswing. "I said enough!" He wrenched with a strength out of proportion to his average build.

Skereye stumbled free of his victim, and, with a bellow of outrage, turned on his master. Blood-slicked fists cocked in threat. Skereye's drug-mad gaze locked on his leader, but it was the Norseman who backed down. Skereye lowered his hands with a harsh oath. "You said we could kill him," he accused.

Unable to speak, Taziar raised a hand that shook so intensely he could scarcely control it. He wiped dirt from his eyes, and scarlet rivulets twined between his fingers.

Nonplussed, the silk-clad leader stepped around Skereye, his manner fiercely coiled. "My mind's been changed." Momentarily, he cocked his head, as if listening to something no one else could hear. His expression went strained, and he mumbled so softly Taziar was uncertain whether he heard correctly. "No one deserves to die like this." Then, catching a sleeve, the leader hoisted Taziar to his feet and shoved him into the other bodyguard's arms. "Halden, let him go. Skereye, disobey me again, and you'll know worse than death." Without bothering to clarify his threat, he stormed through the doorway into the whorehouse.

Taziar caught a misty glimpse of curious, female eyes peering through the crack before the leader's snarl sent them scurrying away. The door whacked shut behind him. Skereye opened the rear entry while Halden hefted Taziar by the hair and a fold of his cloak. Halden tossed a glance over his shoulder, apparently to ascertain that his master had not returned. Satisfied, he hurled Taziar's battered form, headfirst, into the warehouse wall across the thoroughfare.

Taziar's skull slammed against stone. Darkness closed over him, and he crumpled gracelessly to the dirt.

Taziar awoke to a foul liquid that tasted distressingly similar to urine. He choked. The drink burned his windpipe and sent him into a spasm of coughing. Agony jagged through his chest. He splinted breaths, moving air in a rapid, shallow manner that minimized the pain. The cold edge of a mug touched his mouth. A drop splashed the lacerated skin of his lip, stinging. "No more," he managed hoarsely.

Mercifully, the mug withdrew, and a tentative male voice spoke. "Taz?"

Taziar rubbed crusted blood from his lids. He lay in a narrow alley. Overhanging ledges blocked the midday sun into spindly stripes. Eyes green as a cat's stared back at him from a face a few years younger than his own. Other teens hung back, unwilling to meet Taziar's gaze.

"Taz," the youth repeated with more certainty. He lowered the mug to the street.

The boy's features seemed familiar, but it took Taziar's dazed mind unreasonably long to connect them with a name. He recalled a winter several years past when he had formed a team from a ragged series of street-hardened children. "Ruodger?"

The boy's dirt-smeared cheeks flushed. "They call me 'Rascal' now, Taz." He turned to address someone behind him. "I told you it was him."

A girl crept forward and sneaked a look. Barely twelve, she already matched Taziar in height and breadth.

Dizzily, Taziar worked to a sitting position, back pressed to the wall for support. He knew the girl at once. "Hello, Ida."

"Hi, Taz," she returned shyly. Beyond her, four boys

watched with mistrust. He recognized two, a lanky runner known as the Weasel and a portly dropman they called Bag. A child several years shy of his teens twisted a corner of his baggy, tattered shirt. The last was a sandy-haired adolescent with angry, dark eyes and a knife clearly evident at his hip.

Taziar turned his attention to the deep amber drink Rascal had forced upon him. "Did you dredge that stuff from a trough?"

"The alehouse actually." Rascal waved his companions closer, and they obeyed with obvious reluctance. "A lot of dregs and water, but it's the only stuff we can afford."

Taziar wrinkled his mouth in disgust. "I think I'd rather go without."

Ida nodded silent agreement. She shifted closer. Examining Taziar's punished face, she made a childishly blunt noise of repugnance. Rising, she produced a mangled tankard from a cranny and filled it from a rain barrel. Tearing a rag from the hem of her shift, she soaked it with water and dabbed at Taziar's bruised cheek.

Her touch raised a wave of pain. Taziar winced.

The armed stranger gripped Ida's arm and pulled her from her task. "Quit babyin' the traitor. Stick a knife in 'im, take 'is money, and get the corpse the hell outa our alley."

Rascal slapped the other youth's hand away. "Put your fire out, Slasher. Taz ain't no traitor."

"Is too," Slasher hollered.

"Ain't," Rascal insisted.

Slasher shoved Ida away with a violence that sprawled her onto Taziar. Agony sparked through Taziar's broken ribs, and he loosed an involuntary gasp.

"Harriman says 'e is, and 'e'll 'ave our hearts cut out if'n 'e finds us helpin' Taziar Medakan."

Rascal rose and stepped between Slasher and Taziar. Though slightly taller than the ruffian, he had not yet filled into his adult musculature. "I don't care. Taz ain't a traitor. If it weren't for him, we wouldn't have the group. Early on, we would've starved anyway if he hadn't given us money and facts."

Ida disentangled from Taziar, trying not to hurt him. "You say he's a traitor." She brushed Slasher's arm. "You say he's not." She tapped Rascal's foot with her toes. "Why not just ask him?"

The simple logic of Ida's suggestion stopped Slasher in mid-denial. All eyes turned to Taziar, though no one voiced the question.

The Shadow Climber fought a wave of nausea. "I don't think I betrayed anyone. Maybe you'd better tell me what I'm supposed to have done. And who's this Harriman who would kill children for helping a friend?"

Rascal answered the last question first. "Harriman's head of the underground, of course. Been that way more than a month since Shylar's gone."

Shylar's gone! Horror stole over Taziar. He struggled, aching, to one knee. His vision disappeared, replaced by white swirls and shadows. Weakness washed across his limbs, and he settled back against the wall, head low, until he no longer felt pressed to the edge of unconsciousness. "What do you mean gone? Where did she go?"

Slasher kicked a pebble into the air amid a shower of dirt. The stone bounced from the wall behind Taziar and dropped back to the roadway. "Taz knows. 'e's actin'."

"Is not." Rascal glared. "He really doesn't know. Does that look like the face of someone who's lying?"

Obligingly, Slasher studied Taziar. "No," he admitted. "It looks like a face what got kicked by an 'orse."

Weasel and Bag snickered. The waif between them twisted his shirt tighter, stretching it farther out of shape. Ida turned Slasher a disgusted look before replying. "Shylar's arrested."

"No." Taziar shivered, set upon by a strange merger of grief and doubt. Shylar had lived too long among thieves and deception to be taken easily. It was common knowledge that the prostitutes would work for no one else, and the whorehouse would collapse without Shylar to run it. Yet, apparently, miraculously, it had not. "How?" Taziar shook his head, aware this gang of street orphans could not have the political knowledge needed to explain. "Where did this Harriman come from? I can think of half a dozen trustworthy men who served the underground for years. Why would anyone submit to a stranger?"

The youths exchanged uneasy glances. "Half a dozen?" Rascal repeated. "More like eight, Taz. All grabbed by the baron's guards and tossed in the dungeons." Rascal ran down the list with a facility that could only come from repetition. "Waldmunt and Amalric first. Then Mandel, Fridurik, Odwulf, Asril the Procurer, Adal, and Waldhram, in that order. Anyone who could serve as leader was taken even before Shylar."

The Weasel added, "Harriman come along just 'fore the confusion. Ain't 'fraid ta kill or terrize no one, not even guards. 'e put th'unnerground back together."

Taziar sat in silent awe, certain he had slipped beyond consciousness and was now mired in nightmare. He rubbed a hand across his face, felt the cold reality of lacerated skin and dried blood. Tears of grief welled in hardened, blue eyes, and he banished them with resolve. Suddenly, the plight of the beggars became clear. The arrests cut them off from Shylar's charity and the money from members of the underground who paid them as witnesses or hired them to aid in scams and thefts. *Starvation must have killed some and driven others to prey upon one another.*

An image came vividly to Taziar's mind, the remembered visage of the dockhand in Kveldemar's tavern, neck twisted in an illusory noose. Dread prickled the skin at the nape of his neck. "What does the baron plan to do with my friends in the dungeons?"

Eternity seemed to pass twice before Rascal responded. "Hanging. Day after tomorrow on Aga'arin's High Holy Day."

"Except Adal," Ida clarified.

Rascal flinched. "Except Adal," he confirmed, and his tone went harsh with rising anger. "A blacksmith found his beaten corpse stuffed in a rain barrel."

Taziar lowered his head, distressed but not surprised. Until his battering at the hands of drug-inspired berserks, he had considered the baron's dungeon guards the most cruelly savage men alive. Grief turned swiftly to rage. He clamped his hand over his sword hilt until his fingers blanched; tension incited his injuries, and he felt lightheaded. His awareness wavered, tipped dangerously toward oblivion. "How?" The word emerged as a grating whisper. "How did the baron know who to arrest?"

Strained stillness fell. Every orphan evaded Taziar's gaze, except Rascal. A wild mixture of emotions filled the leader's green eyes, and misery touched his words. "Clearly, some trusted member of the underground betrayed them." He blotted his brow with a grimy sleeve. "Taz, aside from us, no criminal, guard, or beggar harbors any doubt that traitor is you."

"Me?" Startled, Taziar found no time to construct a coherent defense. "That's madness."

"Is it?" Slasher's finger traced the haft of his dagger. "Odd someone informed on ever' leader, 'ceptin' you and th' ones what joined after you left Cullinsberg. Ever' guard questioned, by bribe or threat, has guv your name."

"That's madness," Taziar repeated.

Before he could raise further argument, a long-legged, young woman skittered into the alleyway. "Rascal, Harriman's coming!"

Slasher muttered a string of wicked obscenities. Rascal delegated responsibility with admirable skill. "Ragin, tell the other scouts to stay where they are. Taz, put that hood up. Keep still, and don't say a word. The rest of you, act like normal. Slasher, don't do anything stupid."

Ragin trotted off to obey. The Weasel edged in front of Taziar.

"How can Slasher act normal if he's not doing something stupid?" Ida's quip shattered the brooding strain, and even Slasher snickered.

Moments later, Harriman and his bodyguards entered the alleyway, and the laughter died to nervous coughs. Studying the newcomers from the corner of his vision, Taziar recognized the Norsemen whose malicious pleasure had nearly resulted in his death. Skereye appeared uglier in daylight. Furrows of scar tissue marred his scalp where some sword or axe had cleaved his skull. Thin, white-blond hair veiled his head in a scraggly, nearly invisible layer. A film covered pallid eyes, as if years of the berserker drug had burned him to a soulless shell. Halden, too, appeared marked by battle. One hand sported three fingers. A swirl of flesh replaced a nose once hacked away. But his eyes remained fiercely alert.

A half-step behind the bodyguards, Taziar recognized Harriman as the man who had called his beating to a halt. In Shylar's whorehouse, the new leader of the underground had seemed out of his element. In a rogue-filled alleyway, he appeared even more the piece that jarred. He carried his swarthy frame with a nobleman's dignity, and his trust-inspiring features seemed more suited to a merchant. Only a dangerously fierce gleam in his eyes marred the picture. His gaze traveled over every member of the gang to rest, briefly, on Taziar.

Taziar stiffened. Aware the children's lives would be at stake if Harriman noticed him, Taziar hunched deeper within the folds and hoped the nobleman would not recognize his cloak.

A thin smile etched Harriman's lips and quickly disappeared. Otherwise, he paid Taziar no regard. Brushing aside the towering Norsemen, Harriman approached Rascal. "Only six coppers?"

Rascal swallowed hard. "The rest was food. We had a bad day."

Harriman pressed. "You have more."

Rascal moved his head stiltedly from side to side. Taziar read fear in the youth's demeanor, but his voice remained steady. "I'm sorry, Harriman. Ragin gave you all of it."

Harriman stood unmoving, leaving the children in a silence etched with threat. The unremitting quiet grew nearly unbearable. Suddenly, Harriman whirled to his guards. "Search them. *All* of them."

Taziar jerked backward as if struck. Horror crossed every orphan's face, and Ida hissed in terror. Taziar groped through the creases of his cloak for his sword hilt. He knew he would not last long against the Norsemen; he had barely regained enough strength to stand. But he hoped his interference might give the children a chance to run.

Before Taziar could move, Slasher stepped between Skereye and the remainder of the street gang. "Karana damn you ta hell! Rascal's told you we ain't got more."

Without warning, Skereye jabbed a punch. Slasher threw up an arm in protection. The Norseman's huge fist knocked the youth's guard aside and crashed into the side of his head. Slasher sank to one knee in agony, then scrambled backward to forestall another blow.

Arm cocked, Skereye took a menacing shuffle-step forward. But Harriman caught his wrist. "Enough. Don't hurt the children. They're family."

Harriman's voice and manner revealed genuine concern, but Taziar watched Harriman's eyes and the fleeting upward twitch at one corner of his mouth. By these signs, Taziar recognized a masterful performance. No doubt, Harriman savored the children's discomfort every bit as much as his guards. Abruptly, Taziar realized Harriman had met his gaze. The nobleman gave no indication of recognition, yet the icy lack of reaction failed to soothe. Identified or not, Taziar expected no clues from Harriman. Cursing his helplessness, the Shadow Climber turned his face toward the wall, clasped his hands to his knees, and waited.

"Fine." Harriman used a voice devoid of emotion. "Tomorrow, you'll make up for today. I'll expect a full gold. Whatever you have to do, get it."

Taziar sneaked a peek from beneath his hood. Rascal returned Harriman's stare with no trembling or uncertainty. For a moment, Taziar thought the youth would protest; a full gold would require an extraordinary stroke of luck in addition to the best efforts of every gang member. But Rascal responded with the bland good sense that explained why he, not the tougher but more impulsive Slasher, served as leader. "You'll have it," he said simply.

The matter settled, Harriman nodded. "One thing more. The traitor, Taziar Medakan, is back in town. If you see him, turn him in to me and it'll be worth twenty gold ducats, free and clear." Harriman's gaze roved beyond Rascal to settle, unnervingly, on Taziar. "It's another twenty if you give me the names of anyone who aids him." His voice went soft and dangerous as a serpent's hiss. "Because anyone caught helping him will die." Without another word, he spun on his heel and walked back the way he had come, the Norsemen at his heels. In the ensuing silence their receding footsteps thundered through the alleyway.

Taziar clambered to his feet, glad to find he could stand without reeling; his mind remained clear.

Rascal seized Taziar's arm with such sudden violence, he nearly knocked the little Climber back to the ground. Though eighteen, three years younger than Taziar, he stood a forearm's length taller. "What's going on here? Harriman recognized you."

"He did not," Ida chimed in to defend Taziar. "If he did, he would have taken Taz."

For once, Slasher remained silent, rubbing his aching cheek.

Taziar winced in sympathy, familiar with the Norsemen's power. "I don't know whether he knew me or not. But if he wanted me, he already had me." Reaching into the pocket of his britches, he emerged with his depleted purse. He dumped the contents into his hand, counting seven gold coins and as many coppers and silvers. He offered the money to Rascal. "Buy horses and traveling rations. All of you, leave town. You're not safe here."

Rascal stared at the assortment of Northern coins without moving. "We can't take all that." He said nothing further, but his tone implied he would refuse to leave Cullinsberg as well.

Taziar pried Rascal's fingers from his sleeve, slapped the coins into the youth's palm, and curled the grip closed. "I owe you that and more. Take it." He released Rascal's hand, stuffing the empty pouch back into his pocket. "Believe me, Rascal. I understand how difficult it is deserting the only home you've ever known." Taziar recalled how his own loyalty to the city of his birth kept him from moving to the farm of an uncle after his parents' deaths. "There's a world outside Cullinsberg. It's a lot less civilized but definitely worth seeing." He broke off there, too familiar with street mentality to lecture. *Sometimes even certain death seems easier to face than the unknown.*

"I'm sorry about what happened, Taz," Rascal said softly, though whether he referred to the incident in the alleyway or his refusal to abandon Cullinsberg was unclear.

"I'm the one who should apologize. I never meant you any trouble." Taziar's hands balled to fists, and, though he addressed himself, he expressed the words aloud. "No more innocent deaths; I can't allow it. The baron's gallows will lie idle if I have to unravel every rope in Cullinsberg with my own hands." He turned to leave amid a tense stillness, the promise a burden that lay, aching, within him. And he had no idea whether he could keep it.

CHAPTER 4
Shadows of Magic

A man cannot be too careful in the choice of his enemies.
　　　　　　　　　　　　—Oscar Wilde
　　　　　　　　　　　　　The Picture of Dorian Gray

Al Larson crouched in the deepest corner of the third-story inn room, his spine pressed to the wall. The last dim glare of the day trickled through the single window, casting a watery sheen over the only piece of furniture. A table stood in the center of the room, carved into lopsided patterns by an unskilled craftsman. Atop it, a pewter pitcher and a stack of wooden bowls stood in stately array. A fire burned in the hearth. Earlier, sunlight through the open window had eclipsed the hearth fire to a flicker of gold and red. Now, the flames cast fluttering patterns on the wall, plainly illuminating Astryd and Silme where they perched on the stacked logs, but knifing Larson's half of the room into shadow.

Larson flicked open his left cuff and glanced at his naked wrist. In the last four months, since the god, Freyr, had torn him from certain death in Vietnam and placed him in the body of an elf, Larson had spent nearly all his nights in evergreen forests. The inn did not seem much different. *It's not as if we'll find mints on our pillows; there aren't any pillows. Sleeping on floorboards and spare clothes can't be much better than sleeping on pine needles and spare clothes. There's the fire, of course. But if I don't shutter the window, it won't provide any more warmth than a campfire in a drafty wood.*

The thought turned Larson's attention to the only window, cut in the southern wall and directly opposite the door. From his hunkered position in the southeastern corner, he gleaned a slanted impression of mortared stone buildings on the other side of the thoroughfare. Rambling, narrow, and discolored by mud, moss, and dying vines, they reminded Larson of row houses in New York City, with the graffiti conspicuously absent. From a more detailed study a few hours earlier, he knew ashes, rotted vegetables, and broken wood littered the dirt floor. Now, he heard the crunch of bones as a cat or rat feasted on the garbage. Every other side of the inn overlooked a cobbled roadway, and Larson could not fathom why Taziar had suggested this particular room. *Whatever his reason, it wasn't for the view.*

Astryd tapped the brass-bound base of her staff on the stacked logs. Metal thumped against wood. "Allerum, why do you keep staring at the back of your hand? Are you hurt?"

Self-consciously, Larson rubbed his wrist, unaware that concern over Taziar's absence had driven him to consult his nonexistent watch often enough for his companions to notice. Explaining the conventions of his era always seemed more trouble than it was worth. Freyr had bridged time in order to fetch a man from a century without magic or its accompanying natural mental defenses to serve as a means of telepathic communication for a god trapped within the forged steel of a sword. Once, while Silme attempted to contact the imprisoned god through Larson's mind, a way-ward memory had pulled them all into the deadly light show of the Vietnam war. Since then, Silme never doubted Larson came from another place and time. But unfamiliar with faery folk and never having accessed his thoughts, As-tryd and Taziar attributed Larson's peculiarities to the fact that he was an elf.

"Old habit," Larson replied simply, surprised by the sur-liness that entered his tone. Though inadvertent, Astryd's curiosity had returned his contemplations to the one topic he wished to avoid: Taziar's absence. The conversation in Cullinsberg's alley returned in detail, replaying through his mind for what seemed like the twentieth time. In Vietnam, a competent, reliable companion was forgiven even the most callous insults once the fire action started. Yet Larson could not forget his own unyielding manner, cruel words, and the stricken look on Taziar's face when the Climber found his loyalties torn. *I shouldn't have called those street kids "scum." Shadow's sensitive, and he identifies with them. The punks may be thieves and hoods, but buddies do for*

*each other. I owe it to the little slimeball to watch his back.
He'd do the same for me.*

Frustrated by guilt, Larson slammed a fist into his palm.
Astryd was right. I should have gone with Shadow. He knew
his thought was foolish, but it would not be banished. An
image filled his mind. As vividly as though it had happened
yesterday, he recalled Taziar's wiry frame, clothed in black
linen and clinging, naturally as a squirrel, to the "unscalable" wall of the Dragonrank school, returning from an
unannounced visit to its "impenetrable" grounds. Again, he
glimpsed a flash of steel as Gaelinar, his ronin swordmaster,
slashed for Taziar's hands. And, though severely outmatched, Taziar had accepted the challenge, turning Gaelinar's hatred and attempts at murder into a dangerous game
of wits. *All it would take is one person to call something
impossible, and that jackass, Cullinsbergen friend of mine
would go off, half-cocked, to prove he could do it.*

Larson sprang to his feet, his decision made. "I'm going
after Shadow. He's in trouble."

"No." Silme's voice scarcely rose above the crackle of
flame, but it held the inviolate authority of a general's command. "Allerum, don't be a fool. Shadow knows the city.
You don't. If he's in trouble, you're not going to find him.
Your leaving can only divide us further and put us all in
danger."

Larson could not deny the sense of Silme's logic, yet the
thought of waiting in ignorance seemed equally distasteful.
"Don't you have some sort of magic that could tell us
where he is?"

The women exchanged knowing looks; apparently they
had already discussed this possibility. Astryd allowed her
staff to slide gently to the floor. "I could cast a location
triangle, but it's not in my repertoire. It would cost a lot
of life energy for little gain. I'd have to center it on
Shadow. We'd get a glimpse of his surroundings, perhaps
enough for him to know where he was, but not for people
who don't know the city."

Silme elaborated. "If Shadow's fine, we would have
wasted Astryd's efforts. If he's in trouble, we won't know
where to go, and Astryd won't have enough life force left
to cast spells to help him."

Larson lashed out in restless resentment. "Let me get

this straight. You can conjure dragons from nothing." He stabbed a gesture at Astryd, then made a similar motion to indicate Silme. "And I've seen you design defenses I couldn't even see that were strong enough to burn a man's hand. Both of you want me to believe neither of you could make Shadow unrecognizable to the guards or figure out where the hell he is? That makes no sense."

Astryd's brow knotted in surprise. "Why not?"

"Why not?" To Larson, Astryd's confusion seemed ludicrous beyond words. "Because making disguises and finding people seem like they ought to be simple." He raised his voice, waving his arms with the grandeur of a symphony conductor. "Calling dragons and split-second appearances are incredibly dramatic." He dropped his hands to his side. "How come you can do the hard stuff and not the easy stuff?"

Idly, Silme rolled Astryd's staff with her foot. "You're just looking at it the wrong way. Dragonrank magic comes from summoning and shaping the chaos of life energy using mental discipline. By nature, it works best when used for or against users and products of magic." She glanced up to determine whether Larson was following her explanation.

"So?" Larson prompted.

"So," Silme continued. "Large volumes of masterless chaos take dragon form routinely; that's why we're called Dragonrank. Think of calling dragons as summoning the same chaos we need for any spell. How difficult can it be to work that force into its inherent shape? Then, think of a transport escape as moving a user of magic with magic."

"O-kay." Larson spoke carefully, still not certain where Silme was leading, but glad to find a topic other than Taziar. He spun a log from the stack with the upper surface of his boot and sat across from the women.

"But," Silme said. "A disguising spell would require not just moving, but actually changing a human being. Location triangles have to be focused on a person, in this case, one who is not a sorcerer. Understand?"

Larson shrugged, not fully convinced. "And if you cast this location thing to find a sorcerer? It would be easier?"

"Much." Astryd smiled pleasantly. "As long as I knew the sorcerer. If I only had a name and a detailed description, it would cost nearly all my energy. Anything less would prove impossible." She added belatedly, "Yet."

"Yet?" Larson echoed before he found time to consider. Magic made little sense to him. Despite the Connecticut Yankee, Larson doubted a lit match or a predicted eclipse would impress his Dragonrank friends, even if he held enough knowledge of their era to prophesy. One thing appeared certain. *Magic and technology are not the same here.*

Larson did not expect an answer, but Silme gave one. "With enough life force, a Dragonmage could do virtually anything. The problem with creating new spells is that there's no way to know how much energy it'll cost in advance, and no one can have practiced it to divulge shortcuts. Once the spell is cast, it drains as much energy as it needs. If that's more than the caster has, he dies."

Astryd cut in. "You have to realize, Dragonrank mages don't become more powerful by gaining life force. We're born with all the life force we'll ever have. We have to rehearse spells to improve at them. Even though Silme and I are nearly the same age, she discovered her dragonmark much younger. She's had a lot more time to practice and more desperate opportunity."

Larson nodded, having experienced much of that desperate opportunity.

Astryd reclaimed her staff, bracing it against the woodpile. "Magical skill is different than sword skill. You get better by making the physical patterns routine and learning to anticipate enemies. Sorcery is a fully mental discipline. We learn new spells by comparing them with old spells, if possible, and explanations from more experienced mages. Proficiency means using less life energy to cast the same spell. That can only come from mental 'shortcuts,' that is, looking at the techniques in my own unique way."

Larson said nothing, bewildered by Astryd's final disclosure.

Silme attempted to elucidate. "Did you ever have some intellectual problem you needed to solve, but it didn't make any sense no matter how many friends tried to explain it in how many different ways? Then, all of a sudden, you think about it from your own angle and everything becomes instantly clear. You feel stupid and wonder why it used to seem so hard."

Sounds like ninth grade algebra. Only I still feel stupid.
Larson shrugged noncommittally. "I guess so." He imagined a cartoon with a mad scientist and a light bulb appearing over the character's head as he composed a
wickedly interesting idea.

"Each time one of those personal revelations arises, the
spell gets easier . . ." Silme clarified, ". . . for me. But it's
hard for me to turn around and teach what made the spell
simpler. I can help steer, but eventually Astryd has to find
her own shortcuts. Anyway, I can only practice so many
spells to this high degree, so I have to limit my repertoire
to a fraction of the available spells. Why waste time and
energy risking my life to create new ones? Of course, most
Dragonranks specialize in those magics most useful to them
or the ones they seem to have a natural bent for. Like
Astryd's dragon summonings. The larger the repertoire, the
less practice time I can give to any particular spell and the
more energy it takes to cast."

"It's a trade-off," Astryd added. "It would be as if Gaelinar taught you sword and bow skills. You could spend all
your time practicing footwork and strokes and become a
superior swordsman and a mediocre archer. Or you could
do the opposite. Then again, you could work on both
equally and become reasonably competent in two areas, but
you'd probably lose a sword duel against an opponent who
put as much time into blade drills as you did into both.
Most Dragonrank mages know the basic discipline of a
large number of spells, yet they understand only a handful
well enough to . . ."

A sudden premonition of danger swept through Larson.
He stiffened, interrupting Astryd with a cutting motion of
his hand. Rising, he slipped back into the darkened portion
of the room and crept to the window.

Abruptly, Taziar's head and fingers appeared over the
sill. Wounds marred his familiar features, discolored red-
purple from bruises. Concerned about pursuit, Larson
caught Taziar's wrists, yanked him through the window,
and sprawled him to safety. In the same motion, Larson
drew his sword and flattened to the wall beside the opening, waiting.

A moment passed in awkward silence. Taziar clambered
painfully to his hands and knees. "Ummm, Allerum. I could

have gotten in by myself without you throwing me on the floor.''

Cued by Taziar's composure, Larson inched to the window and peered out. The alley lay in a quiet, gray haze, interrupted only by a ragged calico perched on the shattered remains of a crate.

Larson heard movement from his friends behind him. Astryd's horrified question followed. "What happened?"

Larson seized the shutters, pulled them closed, and bolted them against autumn wind and darkness. Turning, he saw that Taziar had taken a seat on the floor before Astryd, his head cradled against her thigh while she tousled blood-matted, black hair with sympathetic concern.

Eyes closed and smiling ever so slightly, Taziar exploited Astryd's pity.

Milking it for all it's worth. Accustomed to boxing, Larson assessed the damage quickly. He knew most facial bones lay shallow and sharp beneath skin easily damaged on their surfaces. *Broken nose and, from the way he's breathing, snapped a few ribs, too.* "What happened?" he demanded. Urgency made his tone harsh.

Taziar's eyes flared open, the keen blue of his irises contrasting starkly with blotches of scarlet against the whites. Silme and Astryd glanced at Larson in surprise as if to remind him the question had already been asked and far more gently.

Taziar responded vaguely. "I got hit a few times."

Larson squatted, hand braced on the firewood that served as Silme's seat. He dismissed Taziar's reply with an impatient wave. "Obviously. Now I need to know who and why."

Astryd removed Taziar's cloak and tunic, surveying injuries more slowly and carefully than Larson had. Robbed of dignity, Taziar caught her hand before she could strip him fully naked. "Take off anything more and be prepared to enjoy the consequences." He twisted his abraded lips into a leer.

"Shadow!" Astryd reprimanded.

Taziar went appropriately serious. "Honestly, Astryd. You've seen all there is. Anything else would be for fun." He addressed Larson. *"Who* is a pair of berserks working for the new leader of the underground. Having mangled

their brains with mushrooms, they now exist only to pound
the life from men smaller than themselves." He added beneath his breath, "And not a lot of men are larger." He
continued, returning to his normal volume. "*Why* is because someone has convinced the street people I betrayed
the underground." He considered briefly. "Which is amaz-
ing given it's almost impossible to talk the entire underground into believing anything. And my friends are in
trouble. Does that answer your questions?"

"Yes," Larson admitted. "But now I have more. Define
'trouble.' Do your friends owe someone money?"

Astryd ran her hands along Taziar's chest, singing crisp
syllables of sorcery while the others talked.

Shortly, the bruises mottling the flesh over Taziar's ribs
faded, and he breathed more comfortably. "My friends are
in the baron's dungeons, set to be hanged the day after
tomorrow."

Larson winced, recalling Taziar's tales of the prison in
the towers of the baron's keep, his vivid descriptions of
torture. Taziar had told him most guards hated dungeon
duties, but some chose it as a means to satisfy aggression
by threatening and battering its prisoners to death. "Uh,
Shadow. Just how close are these friends?"

"Close enough that I have to rescue them." Apparently
misinterpreting Larson's alarm as reluctance, Taziar turned
defensive. "They're thieves and spies and con men. Damn
it, I know that! You may not believe me, but they're all
harmless and good people nonetheless. I once saw Mandel
pay hungry orphans to scout territory he knew by heart.
Amalric ran a lottery. He'd collect coppers, remove his
share, then award the remainder to a 'random' winner who,
somehow, always turned out to be the family most down
on its luck." Taziar cringed beneath Astryd's touch. "But
no need for you to risk your lives. The three of you go
back to Norway. I'll meet you at Kveldemar's tavern."

"Nonsense." Silme's single word left no room for
argument.

Still, Larson felt duty-bound to clarify. "What are you,
stupid? Of course, we stick together." *Without Shadow's
aid, the Chaos-force would have killed me as well as Gaelinar, and the rest of the world with us. I owe him this and
much more.* "Besides, we all know the ferry doesn't leave

for Norway until spring. Did you expect us to swim the Kattegat?"

Astryd added nothing to the exchange. A light sheen of sweat glazed features drawn with effort. The healing magics had cost her a heavy toll in life energy.

Larson dragged his fingers along the rough surface of bark. "So who are these friends, anyway? Shylar? Adal? Asril?"

Taziar stared. "How did you know?"

Astryd turned her sorceries to repairing Taziar's nose, and the Climber suffixed his query with a gasp of pain.

Larson shrugged. "You told me stories. Occasionally you mentioned names, mostly just in passing. I thought I'd forgotten most of them. They must have registered somewhere, though, because something's dredged those memories back up."

Silme went stiff as a spear shaft. Taziar tilted his head, confronting Larson from between Astryd's fingers. By the alarmed expressions on their faces, Larson could tell they had simultaneously come to a desperate conclusion. He glanced rapidly between them. "What?"

"Allerum." Silme's voice scraped like bare skin against stone. "Have you noticed anyone meddling with your thoughts."

"Meddling? I . . ." Larson trailed off, suddenly uncertain. He recalled a recent rash of mild pressure headaches, but he'd noticed no malicious entity triggering memories to goad or harm him. None of his thoughts felt alien, although he had become dimly aware of the reemergence of seemingly useless recollections in the last month. "I don't believe so. I'm still not used to people mucking around in my brain. I'm not sure I could tell."

"Gods." Taziar made a soft sound of anguish. "I really am the traitor."

They think someone read my mind to get those names. Guilt rose, leaving a sour taste in Larson's mouth. Anger followed swiftly. Since arriving in Old Scandinavia, his thoughts had caused more trouble than any differences in culture. Flashbacks of Vietnam had plagued him unmercifully; his mind lapsed and backtracked at the slightest provocation. His enemies had taken advantage of his weakness, provoking memories of war crimes and dishonor until he teetered on the brink of insanity. Later, they sifted plans from his mind, forcing his companions to leave him ignorant or use him as bait to trap those enemies, a warped cycle of betrayal within betrayal. *But Loki and Bramin are dead, and the world has only a handful of wizards and deities. What are the odds we just happened upon another?* He voiced the thought aloud. "You're suggesting the baron hired a Dragonrank mage to ferret out criminals? Seems extreme and expensive, not to mention farfetched."

"But remotely possible." Taziar's reply emerged muffled beneath Astryd's hands. "More likely, the baron captured one underground leader and beat the information from him. But, in all honesty, that's not a lot more likely. I'd die in agony before I'd intentionally inform against Shylar. And I don't think any of my friends would reveal *every* other peer; at most, the guards could jar loose a name or two."

Silme spoke with calm practicality. "I think you'll find the informant at the source of the lie. Who's calling you traitor?"

Weakly, Astryd sank to the log pile. Taziar placed a supportive arm around her waist and whispered something soothing which Larson could not hear. In response, Astryd nodded. Having ascertained that Astryd was all right, Taziar addressed Silme from a face vastly improved by Astryd's efforts, but by no means fully healed. "I don't know. I've been told several of the guards named me. I doubt anyone but the baron could get them to agree so consistently."

"Unless the same person interrogated the guards." Silme grasped the situation from the other side. "Then it wouldn't matter what the guards actually said."

Taziar drew Astryd closer. "That would be the new leader. Harriman. Of course, others in the underground would probably corroborate the story." He hesitated, addressing his own thought before it became an issue. "They'd corroborate by questioning other guards, guards paid by the underground . . . specifically, paid by Harriman. And Harriman seemed awfully quick to tell the street gangs I'm a traitor and to put a bounty on me. Odd thing though, he seemed intent on keeping people from talking to me, but he didn't kill me." He massaged a faded welt on his cheek. "And if he had wanted to, he sure could have."

"Methinks Harriman doth insist too much," Larson contributed, and even Astryd stared. "Shakespeare, sort of," he qualified sheepishly. *My god, now I'm misquoting a man who's not even born yet.* "I just mean if Harriman's making so much effort against you, it's probably to divert suspicion. You're right, he's the stool pigeon." When no one challenged his conclusion or his use of English slang, Larson continued. "Do you think Harriman would interfere with rescuing your friends?"

"No doubt."

"Then our course is clear." Silme reached across the log and took Larson's hand. "One way or another, we have to get rid of Harriman and break Shadow's friends out of prison."

"Oh. Is that all?" Larson tossed his free hand in a gesture of mock assurance. "You make it sound easy. Do you have an 'organized crime boss influencing' spell?"

"Obviously not." Silme ignored the apparent sarcasm. "The mind barriers keep us from altering moods and loyalties as well as thoughts. However, if it was *you* I was trying to manipulate . . ."

Larson interrupted, not wishing to be reminded of his handicap. "You wouldn't have to." Briefly, he leaned his head against her shoulder. "I'm putty in your hands."

Misunderstanding the comment, Taziar gibed. "You're not pretty in anyone's hands."

"You're not particularly pretty right now either," Larson shot back. He rose, attempting to reestablish a semblance of order. "We have a goal, and we have an enemy. Unfortunately, Shadow's the only one who's seen the inside of the prison or knows anything about Harriman." He whirled toward Taziar. "What can you tell us about this Harriman?"

Taziar released Astryd and knotted his hands on his knee. "Not much. I never saw or heard of him before today, but I didn't take much interest in politics either. The street orphans said Harriman used to be a diplomat of some sort from one of the smaller, southern towns. Apparently, some disaster killed everyone in his village, and he blames it on the baron. Harriman came just before the violence started in Cullinsberg." Taziar opened laced fingers. "Not surprising. I'll bet he caused it. He took command of the underground when the leaders got arrested. He had no previous dealings with criminals. He just seemed to appear from nowhere."

Larson settled back on his haunches. "Just seemed to appear, you say? Like magic? Does he happen to look Norse?"

Taziar leaned against the woodpile and drew his knees to his chest. "Maybe." He considered further. "Not really. He could be a half-breed. Why do you ask?"

Larson shrugged. "Before, you all seemed concerned we might be dealing with a Dragonrank mage. Did Harriman do anything you might consider magic?"

"Not unless you consider dragging a crazed berserk off his victim in mid-punch magic. It's impressive, at least."

"A good thought though," Silme encouraged Larson. "If Harriman's a sorcerer and of any significant rank, likely either Astryd or I know him. Can you describe him?"

Taziar launched into a detailed description, filled with stiff, golden curls and swarthy features while Silme and Astryd prompted with questions. A half-hour discussion brought no glimmer of recognition. The fire dropped to ash, and Larson restocked the hearth from the stray logs that were not being used as chairs.

Finally, Silme threw up her arms in defeat. "We'll just have to see him ourselves. I hate to use the power, but we have to know what we're up against." She stood, wandering toward the packed clothes and supplies. "Get some sleep. In the morning, Astryd can attempt a location triangle."

Taziar contested Silme's plan. "Who has time for sleep?"

"You do," Silme insisted. "We're of no use to your friends too tired to think or act quickly."

"Which is why I can't fathom why you'd want Astryd to cast a spell we know will drain her life energy nearly to nothing." Larson usually avoided decisions involving magic, but strategy would require coordination of all available forces. "And you want her to do it first thing in the morning. She'll be useless the rest of the day."

"Useless?" Astryd protested feebly.

"What choice do we have?" Ignoring Astryd, Silme sat amidst the packs. The fire colored her cheeks an angry red. "If Harriman's a sorcerer, we'd better know it. We can let Astryd sleep after the casting."

Something about Silme's explanation jarred Larson. "You have twice Astryd's experience. Can't you pitch this location spell triangle thing tonight before you sleep?" It suddenly occurred to him that more than a month had passed since he had seen Silme cast any spell, even one as simple as a ward. *Of course, things have gone relatively calmly until now. We haven't had much need of magic.* Uninvited to Silme's and Astryd's practices, Larson had no idea how much sorcery they expended. *But Astryd has taken over our nightly protections, too.*

Silme dodged the question. "Good night."

"Wait." Larson refused to let Silme off that easily. "Is something wrong? Did you lose your magic?" Sudden concern drew Larson to Silme's side, and he realized his question must seem foolish. Dragonrank sorcery required only that its caster remain alive. *And well.* Terror gripped him at the thought. "Are you sick?"

"No," Silme replied. "No to all your questions."

Astryd spoke softly. "Better tell them."

Silme hugged her pack to her chest. "No to that, too."

Thoughts swirled through Larson's mind, each worse than the one before. *She's ill. That's it. With all the diseases they had back then . . . back now. And no penicillin. Shit. But can't she cure herself? Cancer. My god, that's it. She's got cancer.* Abruptly racked with nausea, Larson swept Silme into a violent embrace. *I lost her once and spent Gaelinar's life retrieving her. All the forces on heaven and earth would prevent me from doing it again.*

Silme shuddered at the force of Larson's hold. Grim-faced, she fought free. "Allerum, calm down. I'll tell you. It can't possibly be as bad as what you must be thinking." She pressed wrinkles from her cloak with her hands. "I'm going to have a baby."

The announcement struck Larson dumb. *A baby? A baby!* "M-mine?" he stammered stupidly.

Astryd snickered.

The twentieth century, adolescent college freshman who had been Al Larson reacted first. Panic swept his thoughts clean. "Didn't you . . . couldn't you have *prevented* . . ." Then the combat-trained man returned, and sense seeped back into his numbed brain. *What did I expect her to do? Use the pill?*

Silme accepted Larson's reaction with her usual graceful composure. "Certainly, I could have prevented it. But why would I do that?"

Christ, the last thing we need now is a baby. Larson glanced across the room. The growing expression of terror on Taziar's features soothed him. He watched the Climber train a probing gaze on Astryd, saw her let him sweat before responding. "I don't think we're ready." She added wickedly, "Yet."

A host of emotions were descending on Larson. He knew pride at the accomplishment and shocked self-doubt that a woman of Silme's strength and beauty would choose to carry his child. He knew fear for the unborn baby, for his abilities as a father, unable to control his memories and trained only to fight and kill. The impulse to protect nearly overwhelmed him before he recalled Silme had more than enough capabilities of her own. Confusion touched him. "It's wonderful, of course," he said, not yet ready to contemplate the significance or sincerity of his words. "But what does it have to do with your magic?"

Silme took Larson's palm, tracing calluses with a fingertip. "Spells cost life energy. The baby is an integral part of me; I can't separate its tiny aura from my own. I wouldn't have to drain much to kill it."

Larson closed his grip over Silme's hand. "So you can't cast anything without . . ." He stopped, letting his observation hang.

Silme reached for her staff. "I stored just enough energy for a transport escape." She tapped the sapphire to indicate its location. "That's one of the first spells Dragonrank mages learn. It doesn't take me much life force anymore. Essentially, I have enough to cast a single, simple spell without risk."

Larson hesitated. The urge to keep Silme away from the conflict was strong, but he knew the suggestion would infuriate her. *She'd think I didn't trust her judgment or abilities, both of which are beyond question. But it's my baby, too. I have to say something.* Larson phrased his words delicately. Consequently, they emerged tediously slow. "I . . . love you, Silme. And I'll love the child, too. Don't . . ." He tried to keep from sounding patronizing. "If you must . . ." He gave up, tired of wrestling with parlance.

Silme smiled at his clumsy attempts at speech. "I won't take unnecessary chances. But Shadow needs us all, and even we may not be enough. With or without spells, I'm hardly helpless. I traveled with the greatest warrior in the world for years before you joined us. Do you think he taught me nothing?"

Larson remembered Silme's maneuver against the mugger in the alleyway. When he had happened upon Silme and Kensei Gaelinar as a misplaced stranger in the forests of eleventh century Norway, Silme had rebuffed Larson's initial advance with admirable martial skill. He recalled the sharp sting of Silme's blow and the glib death threat that had followed it. "Gaelinar surrender an opportunity to teach?" He tapped the hilt of the Kensei's katana. "Not a chance in hell."

Despite his casual response, Larson could not dispel the fear that gripped him as tightly as a vise. Concern for Silme allowed him to postpone his many worries and doubts about fatherhood. He knew any lessons Silme had received from Gaelinar had been informal. The focus of her strength lay in magic so advanced as to make her one of the most powerful beings in the universe. *Without it, she might be capable of handling street kids and my romantic advances. But berserks?* Larson glanced at Taziar, the image of bruises and abrasions still vivid in his mind despite Astryd's sorceries. *Shadow's river or not, only one of us has the fighting skills to handle this.* He clutched at the hilt of Gaelinar's katana. *I can't sit back while enemies threaten Silme and Astryd, and Shadow risks his life, alone, on the streets.*

Larson watched his companions prepare for bed, resigned to the fact that, as badly as he needed sleep, it would elude him for much of the night.

The Dragonmage, Bolverkr, had buried his neighbors and loved ones, each in his or her own marked grave, and, for every one of them he'd made a grisly promise of vengeance. Now, perched on the ruins of the fountain in Wilsberg, he frowned as he surveyed his partially-completed fortress. Much of the rubble still remained. But on the hill, at the site of his demolished home, now stood a castle of magnificent proportions. The curtain wall towered, shimmering with the protective magics Chaos had inspired him to create. He alone knew the winding sequence of pathways that would lead a man safely between the clustered spells. Even sorcerers versed in viewing magic would find themselves hard-pressed not to blunder into the jagged arrangement of alarms and wards. No guards would patrol Bolverkr's stronghold; he had no need of armies or mundane defenses. Yet the memory of his dead wife, Magan, staring in awe at the gaudy masonry of the baron of Cullinsberg's keep goaded Bolverkr to decorate his catwalk with magically-crafted gargoyles and crenellated spires.

Bolverkr rose, his tread as hard and unforgiving as it had been ever since the tragedy. His path to the fortress was arrow-straight, and, within a few paces, a boulder blocked his way. The Chaos-force seethed, creeping into the soul-focus that was Bolverkr, some mingling inseparably with the gentler chaos of his life aura. Its rage boiled up within him. For an instant, Bolverkr's mind etched Larson's face on the lump of granite that dared stand between him and the world he had built with his own hands and magic. Hungrily, he dredged up the power of Chaos as if it was wholly his own. He shouted a magical syllable, and a stab of his fingers lanced a sun-bright beam of sorceries into the stone.

The boulder shuddered backward. It shattered, flinging fragments in crazed arcs. A chip gashed Bolverkr's arm, and pain dulled Chaos-fueled anger. Confusion wracked him, admitting a pale glimmer of self. *Who am I?* Nameless fear welled up within him, sharpening to panic. The shy, young Dragonmage discovered and trained by Geirmagnus, the years of learning to focus his skills, the decades of gaining peasants' trust all seemed unimportant and distant to Bolverkr. Even his memories of Magan had faded to obscure descriptions of a stranger's life.

Bolverkr's fists clenched. He dropped to his haunches, arms clamped to his chest, calling forth an anger of his own to combat his undirected terror. He threw back his head, howling at the heavens. "Who am I?"

Chaos retreated across the contact, unable to comprehend, but naturally in tune with Bolverkr's need for self-identity. His fear died, replaced by understanding. *It's the Chaos.* Thoughts flashed through his mind in rapid succession, small things deftly underscored by his battle for identity. Again, he became aware of the poisoning that must accompany the near-infinite power Chaos promised. And as his underlying personality emerged, he realized something else. *I have to jettison some of this Chaos before I become nothing but a vehicle for its power.*

Now Chaos struck back, calmly, insidiously using Bolverkr's own natural, life aura Chaos against him. It probed his weakness, and finding it, incited Bolverkr's need for vengeance, drawing the image of Taziar Medakan, a shattered child curled at Bolverkr's feet and begging for the quiet mercy of death. He saw Al Larson driven to a reckless, destructive madness as ugly and chaotic as the war that spawned him. The Chaos-force sparked Bolverkr to remember that his enemies were far from helpless. The men had bested the same Chaos Bolverkr now possessed; as Dragonrank mages, the women should wield more and different power than their consorts. And Bolverkr came to a conclusion he wrongly believed was his own. *I need the power to destroy my enemies. The Chaos storm came to me because I am the strongest being in existence. I can handle this power. I can shape it to my will. I am the Master!*

And Chaos seeped inward with the patience of eternity.

CHAPTER 5
Shadows on the Temple Wall

Respect was mingled with surprise,
And the stern joy which warriors feel
In foemen worthy of their steel.
   —Sir Walter Scott
    The Lady of the Lake

Sadness enfolded Taziar Medakan as he sat, crosslegged, on the bare wood of the inn room floor. His cloak seemed a burden, as if it had trebled in weight during the few troubled hours he'd rested. Heedless of his sleeping companions, sprawled or tucked between packs and blankets, Taziar watched the play of light and shadow on the temple wall across the alleyway. Cold ash filled the hearth. The open window admitted autumn breezes that chilled Taziar to his core.

Taziar had grown familiar with the false dawn; the loyal dance of silver and black on Mardain's church served both as old friend and enemy. He could not recall how many hundred times he had perched on the rotting remains of the apple-seller's abandoned cart in this same alleyway at this same time of the morning watching this same pattern take shape upon the stonework.

A floorboard shifted with a faint creak. Taziar guessed its source without turning. Silme was the lightest sleeper, and the graceful precision of her movements was unmistakable. She approached, knelt at Taziar's side, and, apparently misinterpreting the unshuttered window, whispered, "I hope you're not thinking of running off alone again. You're of no use to your friends dead."

Taziar kept his gaze locked on the wall stones as forms emerged from the meeting of glare and darkness. He dismissed Silme's words and the subtle threat underlying them. "See that building across the alleyway?"

Silme touched her fingers to the floor for balance. She followed Taziar's stare. "Yes. It's big."

Taziar nodded assent. "Seven stories. Aside from the baron's keep and Aga'arin's temple, both of which are carefully guarded, it's the tallest building in Cullinsberg."

Silme said nothing.

Encouraged by her silence, Taziar went on. "It's Mardain's temple."

"Mardain?"

Taziar remained still as the light shifted, subtly changing the patterns on the wall. "God of life and death." He paused, then added, "Karana is goddess of the same, but Mardain's yonderworld is the stars, and Karana's the pits of hell. After death, Mardain claims the just and honest souls, and Karana gets the rest. Either treats his or her followers well. So long as a person worshiped the right god, he's assured a happy afterlife. Mardain's known for mercy. He forgives the worshipers of Karana whose souls find his star. But if they earn her realm, Karana tortures the followers of Mardain with heat or cold and darkness."

Silme considered several moments before replying. "Sounds like the intelligent thing to do would be to worship Karana. Then you can't lose either way."

"Sure." Taziar remembered the raid on Karana's temple that had resulted in the execution of his young gang companions. Atheism had spared his life; otherwise, he might have been at the temple and died with his friends. "If you're willing to admit to being conniving and untrustworthy. Karana's also the mistress of lies and sinners."

"But . . ." Silme began.

Taziar cut Silme's protestations short as the light assumed its final sequence before the world faded back into the blackness before true dawn. "There. Do you see that?" He pointed across the alleyway.

Silme leaned forward, eyes pinched in question. "What?"

Familiar with the dappled sequences, Taziar discerned them with ease. And, never having shared his discovery, he did not realize how difficult they might prove for a stranger to see. The memory was painful. But, since he had begun, he continued. "Straight ahead. Do you see that shadow?"

Many dark shapes paraded across the masonry. "Yes,"

Silme said, but whether from actual observation or simple courtesy, Taziar did not know.

"That's the baron's gallows. You can only see it on a clear day when the light hits just so." Grief bore down on Taziar, and he heard his own words as if from a distance and someone else's throat. "I noticed it the morning after they hanged my father." He recalled the restless need the vision had driven through him. "Then, though no one had succeeded before, I tried to climb that wall. At first, I just wanted to get high enough so if I fell, I'd die rather than lie wounded among the garbage. Once there, it seemed silly not to go all the way to the roof. And on top, I discovered another world."

The foredawn dwindled, plunging the thoroughfare into gloom. Finally, Taziar glanced at his companion. Folds and straps from her pack had left impressions on her jaw, and her golden hair was swept into fuzzy disarray. But her cheeks flushed pink beneath eyes bright with interest, and her cloak rumpled tight to a delicate frame. She was one of the few people Taziar knew who looked beautiful even upon awakening. "Another world?" she encouraged softly.

"Quiet. Alone with thoughts and memories and the souls of the dead." He clarified quickly, "I mean the stars, of course. This may sound strange . . ." Suddenly self-conscious, Taziar banished the description. "Forget it."

"Tell me," Silme prodded.

Embarrassed by his reminiscences, Taziar shook his head.

"Come on," she encouraged, her voice honey smooth.

Taziar blushed. "Never mind. It was stupid."

Instantly, Silme's tone turned curt. "Finish your sentence, Shadow, or I'll throw you out the window."

The abrupt change in Silme's manner broke the tension. Taziar laughed. "When you put it that way, how can I refuse your kind request? My first morning on the temple roof, I discovered a star I'd never noticed before. I'm certain it was always there, but, to me, it became my father's soul. It hovers in the sky from the harvest time to the month of long nights." Once his secret was breached, Taziar loosed the tide of memory. "It's small, a pale ghost, a pinprick in the fabric of night. Nothing like my father. He was huge in body and mind, and everything he did, he did in the biggest possible way. Moderating soldiers' disputes, leading the baron's troops, fighting for the barony, even conversation, he did it all in a wild blaze of glory. And only death came in a small way. He was deceived and condemned by the very warriors and citizens who'd loved him."

A rush of sorrow garbled Taziar's words, and he went silent. For the first time in nearly a decade, he felt defenseless and vulnerable. "Shylar and the others are family to me. If Harriman is a sorcerer, if my betrayal results in Shylar's hanging, I couldn't stand it." Taziar lowered his head, but his lapse was momentary. Shortly, his fierce resolve returned, and he felt prepared to face and revise any disaster fate threw at him. Dawn light traced past the window ledge, strengthening his reckless love of danger, and with it came understanding. With his own life at stake, every challenge beckoned. But the excitement of a jailbreak paled to fear when a mistake might cause the death of friends. *And I'm risking Silme, Allerum, their child, and my beloved Astryd for a cause that Allerum, at least, is firmly against.*

This time, Silme guessed Taziar's thoughts with uncanny accuracy. "I know you're concerned for us, too. But we chose to help because we care. If you go off alone, we won't wait around for you. Without your knowledge, I imagine we could get ourselves in more trouble than you could ever lead us into."

Taziar realized Silme spoke the truth. The urge to work alone was strong, but refusing his friends' aid would make his own task more difficult and endanger them as well. "Is mind-reading a Dragonrank skill?"

"A woman's skill, actually," Silme corrected. She smiled. "Shadow, you're just going to have to find some new friends. We know you too well." Silme raised her voice; and, after the exchanged whispers, it sounded like a shout. "Speaking of women, if you'll kick Astryd awake, I'll take care of Allerum."

"I'm up!" Larson said quickly. To demonstrate, he leaped to his feet, scattering blankets and sending the pack he used as a pillow sliding across the planks.

His antics awakened Astryd who groaned. Her eyes flicked open. Finding all her companions awake, she swept to a sitting position, cloak pulled tight against the chill. "No fire?"

"I'll take care of it." Glad for the distraction, Taziar trotted to the woodpile and began arranging logs in the hearth.

Larson pulled on his boots. "I don't suppose we can get room service around here."

Taziar cast a curious glance over his shoulder.

Larson laughed good-naturedly. "I didn't think so." He maneuvered on his boot with a final twist. "I'm going to the kitchen to get breakfast. Any requests?"

Taziar knew the question was polite formality. The fare would depend on the supplies and the inclination of the cook. "Anything not jerked, smoked, or dried for travel." He piled another row of logs, perpendicular to the first.

"Fine choice, sir." Larson assumed a throaty accent Taziar did not recognize. "Anyone else?"

Silme thrust the empty, pewter pitcher into Larson's hand. "More water so we can wash up this morning."

Taziar added a third layer to the stack. "And a brand to get this fire going." He rose, brushing ash from his knees as Larson slipped through the door, pitcher in hand.

Silme slammed the shutters closed and threw the latch. "Hand me three or four logs." She stretched out her arm for them.

Taziar selected four narrow branches and tucked them beneath his arm. He carried them to where Silme waited on a bare area of floor between the window and the table. One by one, he set the wood on the floor beside her. "What's this for?"

Silme knelt, settling the logs into a crooked rectangle. "Astryd's spell requires a boundary. No need to waste time. Once we know what we're up against, we can make a plan of action." Silme summoned Astryd with a brisk wave. "Besides, if Harriman is a sorcerer, best if he doesn't know we've discovered his secret. And we don't want to give him access to our plot."

Though not spoken directly, Silme's meaning was clear to Taziar. *She wants to take advantage of Allerum's absence. Should Harriman turn out to be a sorcerer, he could dredge any information we give Allerum from his mind.*

Astryd walked to Silme's side. Taziar touched her encouragingly as she passed, and the warmth of that simple gesture sent a shiver of passion through him. Everything about Astryd seemed functional, from her close-cut, golden ringlets to the dancer's grace of her movements and the plain styling of her dress and cloak. And, where Silme's beauty could transform a man into a tongue-tied fool, Astryd had a lithe, homespun quality that made her more real and more desirable to Taziar.

Astryd crouched before the lopsided outline of wood.

Taziar scooted the table closer; the screech of its legs against the floorboards made him wince. Hopping onto its surface, he let his legs dangle, allowing him a bird's-eye view of the proceedings.

Silme traced the outline of the rectangle, patting logs securely into place. "Ready?"

Astryd lowered and raised her head once. "I've been considering shortcuts all night."

Silme appeared outwardly calm, but her attempts at delay revealed hidden anxiety. "Any more questions for the man who met Harriman?"

"No." Astryd continued to stare at the rectangle.

Silme glanced questioningly at Taziar who shrugged. The grueling inquiry of the previous night had tapped his memory and powers of observation to their limits.

Astryd closed her eyes. Her lips moved, but no sound emerged. She stirred a finger through the confines of the rectangle. For several moments, nothing happened. Then, white light swirled between the logs on a shimmering background of yellow. Lines of black and gray skipped across the picture. Colors appeared, erratic splashes of amber, red, and brown that melted together and separated into a blurred, featureless man and woman lying close upon a pallet of straw.

Astryd made a high-pitched sound of effort. She sank to her knees, and the image within the rectangle smeared beyond even vague recognition.

Alarmed for Astryd, Taziar gripped the ledge of the table.

"Concentrate," Silme insisted with a casual authority echoing none of Taziar's concern. Her composure eased Taziar's tension, and, apparently Astryd's as well. The picture reformed, strengthened, and became discernible as the stiff-bearded figure of Harriman. Back propped against the wall, he reclined with bed covers drawn halfway up his abdomen. A tangle of golden hair enveloped a well-defined chest. A thickly-muscled neck supported features that might have appeared handsome if not for the unmistakable glaze of madness in his eyes. One arm was draped across the breasts of a slender woman. She lay, wooden with fear, trembling and half-exposed by the turned back blanket.

"That's Harriman," Taziar confirmed. He leaned forward for a better look, holding his balance with his hands on the lip of the table. "That's Galiana with him." Overgenerous to Shylar with his money, Taziar had always found her prostitutes eager to take him to bed.

Despite fatigue, Astryd gave Taziar a sharp look.

Immediately realizing his error, Taziar tried to save face. "I knew a lot of Shylar's girls." He clarified, "I mean I *met* a lot of Shylar's girls." Fearing to offend his companions, he amended again, "Women." Then, not wishing to over-emphasize the prostitutes' maturity, he returned to his original description. "Girls." Suddenly aware his antics were only driving him deeper into trouble, he changed the subject. "That hand at the edge of the picture. I think it's Skereye's. Can you focus in on him?"

"Astryd centered the spell on Harriman," Silme explained. "Anyone else in the image is coincidently within range. To see another, she'd have to recast."

"I don't see an aura." Astryd slouched on the floor, her hands trembling and her expression strained. "Harriman can't be a sorcerer."

Silme bent forward until her head blocked the patch of magics from Taziar's view. She gasped in alarm. "Astryd, look again."

Astryd shifted to her hands and knees and tilted her face closer. Silme's thick cascade of hair distorted her reply. "There is something there. Fine and almost transparent. He looks awfully alert for someone who's drained life energy that low."

Silme's words scarcely wafted to Taziar. "We've seen what we need. Don't waste your energy."

The women sat up, and Astryd dismissed her magics. The image disappeared immediately, and the polished wood floor replaced Taziar's glimpse of Harriman's room.

Taziar propped a foot on the table. "What's an aura?"

Engrossed in thought, Silme said nothing.

Astryd's head lolled; her eyes narrowed to haggard slits. Distracted by Silme's intensity, she answered without emotion. "It's a gross, visual measure of Dragonrank strength. It looks sort of like a halo of light. The color and magnitude change depending on fatigue and mental state." She rolled a bleary gaze. "Mine looks like porridge right now. But Harriman's is worse. The last time I saw an aura that weak, its master was in a coma."

Silme seized Astryd's arm in a grip so fierce that Astryd snapped to attention despite her exhaustion. "What's wrong?"

"You didn't recognize that aura?"

Astryd met Silme's intent stare. "No. Should I?"

"You may never have seen it." Silme released Astryd and swept the logs into a pile. "Harriman's not a sorcerer, but he is a product of sorcery. I've seen the spell used before. It requires a Dragonrank mage to kill its victim, body and soul. Then, the corpse can be animated to act as the mage commands, without knowledge, memory, or will. It can only obey simple directions; it can't speak or initiate actions."

The description contradicted Taziar's experience. "Silme?" He cleared his throat, choosing his phrasing to correct rather than confront. "I saw Harriman interact, and speak, too."

"That's impossible." Silme's words implied certainty, but her tone betrayed her doubt.

Taziar persisted. "I watched him extort money from a group of children. He's an expert."

Silme went silent in thought, as if deciding whether to challenge her experience or Taziar's observations. Her chin sank to her chest. Her blue eyes dulled, then went vacant as a corpse's.

"Silme!" Taziar jumped down from the table and skidded to the sorceress' side. "What's wrong?"

Astryd answered in Silme's stead. "She's channeling thought. I have no idea where."

Taziar stepped behind Astryd, massaging her knotted shoulders through the fabric of her cloak. Her muscles quivered, as if from a grueling physical battle. "Is it safe? What about the baby?"

Astryd's voice sounded thin. "Thought extension doesn't cost life energy the way spells do. Just concentration."

"Oh." Taziar accepted the information easily, but his concern for Silme lessened only slightly. Unless she had chosen to contact Larson, she could only have attempted to gain access to Harriman's mind. If so, she had disobeyed her own tenet. *After threatening me not to go off alone, why would she try something like this?*

Suddenly, Taziar found Silme returning his gaze. Her face was slack, and her fists clenched and loosened repeatedly, as if of their own accord.

Unable to read her emotion, Taziar prodded. "Silme, are you well?"

"Shattered," she replied, her voice strained. "Shattered like winter leaves beneath bootfalls, like a castle door beneath a battering ram." She cleared her throat and addressed Astryd in her normal tone. "I'm supposed to be one of the most powerful mages in existence, second only to the Dragonrank schoolmaster. But what I saw was the result of magic beyond my imagining. Someone smashed a hole through Harriman's mind barriers, accessed his thoughts, then rearranged them to the pattern and purposes he wanted."

"Are you certain?" Astryd's words emerged more like a statement than a question; she had asked from convention rather than disbelief.

"There's a hole, and pieces of the barrier still cling like shards of glass to a window frame. Thought pathways are looped, cut, and tied."

Taziar's hands went still on Astryd's shoulders. "Who?"

Silme ran her hands along her face. "I don't know. I didn't dare to delve too deeply. Surely, the person or thing who damaged Harriman is in frequent contact. If I used anything stronger than a shallow probe, he might have noticed me. At the least, Harriman would have detected my presence and called on his master. Alone and without magic, I couldn't hope to stand against a sorcerer with the power to break through mind barriers." She pressed her palms together, lacing her fingers with enough force to blanch them. Her manner clearly revealed the extent of her fear to Taziar. Even with spells and her companions' aid,

Silme obviously harbored no illusions she could win a battle against Harriman's master.

"But I did discover Harriman's basic purposes." Silme stared at her fingers. "He's been instructed to see Shylar and your friends hanged, to destroy the underground, and . . ." She paused, avoiding Taziar's curious stare. ". . . to cause you as much physical and emotional pain as possible."

"Me?" Taziar blinked, stunned.

"Shadow?" Surprise and distress etched Astryd's voice, to be instantly replaced by accusation. "What did you do? Who did you offend who has enough power to do this?"

Taziar considered. His reckless drive to accomplish the impossible might have gained him enemies. But he could only recall two instances where his antics could have angered sorcerers. He had once robbed a jade-rank Dragonmage, but that sorcerer's powers were weaker than Astryd's. He spoke the second circumstance aloud. "I did scale the walls of the Dragonrank school and bypass its protections."

Astryd shook her head. "You didn't steal anything or hurt anyone. Even if the Dragonrank mages wanted to make an example of you. If they could locate you, even the diamond-rank archmaster would not have the power to destroy mind barriers." She snapped to sudden attentiveness. "Unless . . . Silme, what about a merger?"

Silme dismissed Astryd's suggestion. "It would require every mage at the school to cooperate, an impossible feat in itself." She explained for Taziar's benefit. "It's supposedly possible for Dragonrank mages to combine life force. It's a lot like seventeen artists carving a masterpiece with only one allowed to make the actual cuts and every life hanging on the king's approval of the final project. I've never known any mage willing to entrust his life energy to another. I've been told the magics that ward the Dragonrank school were a result of such a merger. One was slain, drained of life force. Three others fell into coma. Later, two of those died and the third became a babbling idiot. The mage responsible, the one entrusted with channeling life force, eventually killed himself out of guilt."

"Besides," Astryd added. "There are easier ways to kill a man than risking forty-three lives to create a monster. If the Dragonrank mages wanted Taziar, they'd simply kill him or take him back and hang him from the gates."

Taziar stiffened, displeased by the turn of the conversation. "So, whoever Harriman's master is, he wants me to suffer. And we have no idea what we're dealing with."

"Not no idea," Silme's tone went calculating. She stood, rubbing her hands together for warmth. "We know he wants to torture you rather than kill you, or at least before he kills you . . ."

Taziar twined a finger through Astryd's hair. "Thanks for clarifying that."

". . . his delay might work to our advantage. And, we know he or she is intelligent. Notice, he hasn't come after us himself. He sent a pawn. My guess is he found some interesting and frightening things in Allerum's mind, and he's not excited by the prospect of taking us on personally. Ignorant and weakened as we are, I don't think we could stand against him. We need to keep the master away, to reinforce his reluctance by making him even more certain we're powerful. We have to encourage him to send lackeys we can use to assess his abilities."

"Fine." The explanation sounded logical to Taziar. "How do you suggest we do that?"

"By removing Harriman, either by capture or death. It'll get rid of one obstacle to freeing your friends. It'll remove our real enemy's means of keeping watch on you. And it will give us time to organize while Harriman's master decides his next plan of attack."

"I don't know," Taziar started. The idea of killing an innocent pawn repulsed him. But he also realized that Harriman's command of the underground might put his friends, once released, in greater danger from old companions than from the baron's guards. *Besides, Harriman's mind has been ruined. He's no longer truly a man, just a sorcerer's weapon.*

Before Taziar could protest further, the door swung open and Larson appeared in the entryway. He held a loaf of bread tucked beneath his arm, and the pitcher in the same hand. Spilled water slicked his fingers. His other hand balanced a bowl of butter and the flaming brand. Steam rose from the bread, gray-white against Larson's sleeve. The aroma of fresh dough twined through the room.

Silme tensed, casting a warning glance at Astryd and Taziar who went stiff and silent.

Larson caught at the corner of the door with the tip of his boot. "Are you all going to sit there watching me struggle, or will someone give me a hand?"

Leaving Silme to decide what information to share with Larson, Taziar crossed the room and accepted the brand and bowl.

Larson closed the door, shifted the loaf to his hand, and set pitcher and bread on the table. "So, is Harriman a sorcerer?"

Returning to the logs, Taziar placed the bowl on the floor and feigned engrossment in the fire.

"No," Silme replied truthfully.

Larson sighed in relief. "Good. Worrying about some stranger reading my mind, I was beginning to wish you hadn't told me about the baby."

Taziar cringed. The brand tumbled into the hearth, and the Climber felt certain he was not the only one holding his breath.

Larson did not seem to notice the sudden change in his companions' attitudes. He rapped his knuckles on the table-top. "So what now? We go to the baron, tell him who's causing all the trouble in his city and talk him into letting your buddies out of jail while the guards round up the crime lord and his cronies?"

Just the mention of the baron sent horror crawling through Taziar. "No!" Retrieving the brand, he jabbed it between the lowest layers of kindling. "We take care of the problem ourselves. The baron is a crooked, self-indulgent idiot who thinks loyalty is measured in moments. I'm not going to let my friends take chances with his depraved idea of justice." Taziar looked up to find every eye fixed on him above expressions of shock at his abrupt and seemingly misplaced hostility. Not wanting to deal with his friends' concern, Taziar returned his attention to the fire.

A brief silence followed. Then Larson spoke in the direct manner he used whenever he felt his otherworld perspective gave him a clearer, more levelheaded grasp on a problem. "Look, Shadow, you're being stupid here. I understand you don't like the baron. That only makes sense, and it really doesn't bother me. But the baron knows this town. We can use him. Hell, you ought to get a perverse joy out of using him. He makes the laws, for god's sake. I mean, he basically runs the town, doesn't he?"

"Yes," Taziar admitted without looking up. "Yes, he does."

"Well, I don't have any great, fond respect for authority, and I've been a victim of politicians myself." A floorboard squeaked as Larson shifted position. "But if something big and bad happened, I'd still go to the police." He clarified. "My world's guard force."

Taziar shrugged, not bothering to respond. As much as Larson claimed to understand, Taziar knew his companion could never know the agony of watching his father publicly hanged, murdered and humiliated by the leader he had served faithfully for a decade. Water glazed Taziar's vision. Angered by his lapse, he fought the tears, smearing ash across his lids with the back of his hand. He lowered his head, not trusting himself to speak.

Larson continued, apparently accepting Taziar's silence as a sign that he was wavering. "The guards see the city from a different side than your friends. We don't have much time. It makes sense to explore every possible source of information."

"No!" Gaining control of his grief, but not his resentment, Taziar whirled to face Larson, still at a crouch. "You don't know Baron Dietrich. I do. Ever since he claimed the title from his father, he's been dependent on advisers. First Aga'arin's temple turned him into a faith-blinded disciple to the point where the church gets a deciding vote in all matters of import. Then, some devious, power-mad worm of a prime minister convinced him to hang his guard captain and torture me to death. Does that sound like a just leader willing to listen to reason?"

"Well," Larson started. As the hearth fire licked to life, a red glow crossed his angular features. "Actually, he sounds pretty easy to manipulate."

"Sure," Taziar shot back. The image of his friends dealing with a petty, unpredictable tyrant off-balanced him. "If you're an Aga'arian priest or a scheming politician. Karana's hell, Harriman's probably already got the baron on his side."

"Well, if he does, don't you think we might want to know

that?" Larson snorted viciously, obviously on the verge of anger himself. "Now who's acting stupid because of a personal experience? I don't care how dumb this baron of yours is. He's not going to support some stranger undermining his authority and tearing apart his town."

Silme spoke up, as always the voice of reason. "Shadow, Allerum, listen . . ."

Taziar leaped to his feet, not pausing to let either of his companions speak. His heel cracked against the bowl, sending the butter skidding across his boots, and his unnatural clumsiness only fueled his rage. "I'm upset enough without you babbling about putting yourself in an enemy's hands. I know this town. I know what will work and what won't. No one goes near the baron! Is that clear?"

"I was just going to say . . ." Silme started, but Taziar never let her finish.

"This subject is closed."

"Closed, is it?" Larson shouted.

Taziar glared.

"Very well." Larson spun toward the door. "It's closed. If you want your conniving friends to hang while you drown alone in your own river, it's not my goddamned problem. I need a moment by myself, and I need to take a leak. Do I have your permission, O great and all-knowing god of Cullinsberg?"

Taziar waved Larson off, too enraged to deal with sarcasm and as appreciative of the chance to think without the elf's badgering. *He needs some time by himself to calm down, and so do I.*

Larson stormed through the portal, slamming the panel harder than necessary behind him. The door slapped against its frame, bouncing awkwardly ajar.

Taziar returned to the fire, trying to find direction and solace in the dancing flames. *Allerum's only trying to help.* The Climber would never have believed any cause could drive him to incaution and irrational rage, but the combination of ignorance, helplessness, and concern had done just that.

Silme rose, her manner casual, seeming out of place after Larson's and Taziar's savage display. "You two stay here. I'm going to talk to Allerum."

Taziar nodded absently as Silme slipped through the crack. The door clicked closed behind her.

Outside the inn room, Al Larson dropped all pretense of rage. He moved to the end of the hallway at a brisk, stomping walk consistent with the mood he had tried to create, down the staircase, and out the weathered back door into the alley. There, he slowed, pressing his chest to the spongy moss that coated the wall in patches. Not wanting his companions to spot him through the window, he clung to the stone, edging toward the southwest corner of the building. A loam smell filled his nostrils, and dislodged moss clung to his tunic like hair.

Inches from the turn, Larson back-stepped. He patted dirt and clinging plant matter from his clothing before stepping into the morning traffic of Cullinsberg's main street. A pair of elderly women shied from the tall, oddly-featured stranger who appeared suddenly from an alleyway; they skittered to the opposite curb and quickened their pace. Otherwise, the sparse groups of passersby seemed to take little notice of Larson.

Once on the cobbled roadway, Larson paused to get his bearings. Buildings of varying shapes and sizes surrounded him, a miniature panorama of New York City's colossal skyline. To the south, cottages dotted the landscape, gray and faceless, a monotonous series of identical dwellings. Larson turned. Eastward, the towering structures of the inn and Mardain's temple blocked his view; far to the north, a forbidding wall enclosed a structure with several proud, crenellated spires. It reminded Larson of the chipped, wooden rooks of his grandfather's ancient chess set. *That's got to be the baron's castle.* He headed toward it.

Instinctively, Larson adopted the natural protections born city dwellers learn. Though the streets were unfamiliar, he kept his attention fixed straight ahead, never glancing directly to either side nor meeting any person's gaze. He avoided alleys and darkened side streets, favoring the central areas of the main thoroughfares where the crowds tended to cluster. He kept his gait striding and purposeful, trying to indicate to would-be muggers that he had a specific destination and was more than willing to fight to get there.

In truth, the dangerous posture came easily to Larson. His failure to make a point to Taziar that seemed ridiculously obvious annoyed him. As much as he tried to convince himself otherwise, he felt responsible for Taziar's beating. *My unyielding cruelty, my insistence on humiliating street kids whom Shadow identifies with distracted him.* The image of Larson's grandfather rose unbidden, his kindly features swollen around a frown, his eyes moist, as if the city he loved, the one that had welcomed him from war-torn Europe, had betrayed him.

Larson caught himself grinding his teeth, and realized his jaw had begun to ache. He banished the memory, concentrating on keeping his facial muscles loose, forcing his thoughts to other matters. He remembered a day from distant childhood when he was barely five years old. The recollection came in vague and hazy detail, a day with his parents on the beach in Coney Island. High-pitched shrieks and giggles drowned the lazy lap of surf, and the ocean faded to an infinity of fog and water. As before, he heard his mother screaming his two-year-old sister's name again and again, first in question, then in abject panic. He recalled how his father had gone off to search while his mother clutched her son's arm with a grip so tight it pinched, terrified she might lose her other child as well.

Larson's reflection softened his manner. He recalled the husky, uniformed policeman who had returned with his sister, Pam, the child happily licking at an ice cream cone while his mother laughed and cried and wet her pants, too relieved to care who saw. There followed years of lectures on "your friend, the policeman," a concept pounded and etched so deeply that even years of unjust war could not make Larson forget. *Shadow's too much a hero for his own good. He's so afraid of risking any life but his own, he's not thinking straight. He can't go to the baron himself, not with a bounty on his head. But I can. I've finally found something I can do to help, and I'm not going to let Shadow's bias and paranoia take it from me.*

The intensity of Larson's thoughts caused him to drop the city manner he had not needed in the evergreen forests and tiny towns that dotted Norway. Jarred back to reality, he found himself glancing down a narrow, crooked alleyway, a more direct route to the wall-enclosed structure he believed was the baron's keep. For an instant, he hesitated, torn between the desire for safety and a natural urge to shorten his course. Then his sense of fairness prevailed. *I'd like to believe that Shadow uses as much discretion as possible when he's off by himself. I have a wife and a child coming. It's not fair for me to take unnecessary chances.* Responsibility crushed in on Larson, but he forced deep contemplations away. Delay of even a few hours might cost Taziar his friends' lives, and, on the wild streets of Cullinsberg, Larson did not want to get caught daydreaming.

Larson started to turn back toward the main street. Before he could pivot, the sound of footsteps reached his ears, and three men appeared from around a curve in the alleyway. Larson went still. Learned caution immediately set him to assessing the group of people emerging from a side road behind him. He stared at a trio of men, two portly and muscularly robust, the third lean and hard as a special forces ranger. Each wore the black and red uniform of Cullinsberg's guardsmen. Swords hung at their hips, and the thinner one clutched a spear.

Larson smiled in relief. *If the cops just swept through there, the alley's probably safe.* He remembered Taziar's stories of torture at the hands of the baron's soldiers, but his current thoughts of policemen and their ancient equivalents were positive. *Besides, Shadow was a criminal, a prisoner, and, to their minds, a traitor's son. And Shadow said the cruelest guards take prison duties. These are just normal sentries, pacing a beat.*

Still, Taziar's warnings of corruption and brutality rang clear. Not fully convinced by his own logic, Larson slipped into the alley but kept his attention locked on the guardsmen.

The guards watched Larson, too. Their conversation dropped to silence. But when he passed them, halfway between the main thoroughfare and the bend in the alleyway, they made no hostile gestures. The heaviest of the three nodded in wordless warning or greeting, Larson could not tell which, but no one challenged him.

Not wanting to arouse the guards' suspicions, Larson resisted the urge to glance over his shoulder and watch their progress. He continued onward, trusting his jungle-inspired instincts to alert him to any sudden movements behind him. When nothing untoward happened, Larson relaxed. *Great.*

Now the little thief's got me jumping at shadows, too. He groaned at his unintentional pun.

Shortly after the curve, the alleyway ended in another large, cobbled street. Larson stepped out into it, glancing to his right, and the sight of a walled-in structure with four, thin towers froze him in his tracks. *Shit! Is that the baron's castle?* He looked back to the multispired hulk he had been steering toward for the last ten minutes. *Or that?* Frustration sent him into another a cycle of teeth grinding, and thoughts rose of his high school girlfriend chastising him for the "male character flaw of driving in random circles in the hope that sometime in the next bazillion years you'll just happen to run into wherever you're trying to go." Larson could not help smiling at the memory. He studied the passing crowds, seeking someone harmless-looking to stop for directions.

While Larson stood in silent indecision, male voices wafted to him from the alleyway. The neighboring buildings muffled their words to echoes, but their tone came through clearly, the mocking, half-shouted taunts of construction workers ogling a pretty woman.

Larson whirled, tensing. *It's none of my business. Let the cops handle it.* Even as the thought surfaced, he knew the guardsmen were the cause, not the solution. The brief realization that Taziar did, indeed, know his city well flashed through Larson's mind, raising an irritation that blazed to anger. His jaw clenched. *Calm. A little teasing never hurt anyone. This is civilization. A real city with real laws. I can't go off half-cocked over nothing.*

The guards' exhortations rose in volume, indecipherable, but goading.

Larson imagined some wide-eyed, teenaged girl who had chosen to walk through the alley, reassured by the presence of the guardsmen, only to have them leer and slobber at her. *Jerks.* He waited, wondering why the woman had not just fled.

Then, the voice of one man rang over the din. "Hey, wench. How'd you like to be stracked by a guard?" He used a crude, local euphemism for sex that Larson had never heard, but its meaning came through clearly enough.

Though soft, the woman's reply cut distinctly above the

chaos. "No, thank you," she said simply, and her voice sounded too familiar.

Silme? Larson's heart quickened. *It can't be. Why would she follow me? How could she risk the baby?* Realization tightened his muscles to knots. *She's got no magic!* Outrage cut through him. *If they so much as touch her, I'll rip their goddamned lungs out!* He tensed to charge, delayed by another thought. *Back in the alley with the street gang, Shadow had the situation under control, and I almost turned it into a slaughter. If I go bounding in there like some rabid knight in shining armor, I might get Silme killed.* With caution befitting his combat training, Larson crept toward the bend in the alleyway.

"You don't understand," the same man said, his voice gaining a dangerous edge that made it obvious he no longer considered it a game. "We run this town. We don't have to ask, we take what we want."

Larson's hand crushed down on his sword hilt. He whipped around the curve just in time to see the guards separate and move to the walls, as if to let Silme pass unmolested. As far as he could tell, Silme had done or said nothing to defuse the situation, yet the guards appeared to have decided to let the matter drop. *What the hell?*

Despite the danger, Larson could not help but notice how the morning sun glazed Silme's hair like metallic gold, and her stance as she moved between the guards seemed regal and menacing. She held her dragonstaff in whitened knuckles, with the security of a king's scepter in his own court. Her gaze found Larson, and her frown deepened, warning him not to start trouble where it did not yet exist. But she must have taken some comfort from his presence because her manner relaxed slightly and the blood returned to her fingers.

Larson hesitated, wrestling his anger.

Attentive to Silme and partially turned away from the elf, the guards apparently did not notice Larson waiting deeper in the thoroughfare. Even as she strode past the two portly soldiers, the spear-wielder tossed back a shock of frizzled, dark hair and stepped into the center of the alley, blocking her path. "You might want to stay here where we can protect you from the unsavories out there."

He jerked a thumb over his shoulder blindly indicating Larson.

Silme stopped. Her expression did not change. "I can take care of myself."

Suddenly, the man leaped for Silme. She back-stepped. Catching his hand against her arm, she snapped her staff upward. The brass-bound base slammed into his groin.

The guard pitched forward amid his companions' howls of laughter. His knees buckled. The spear thumped to the dirt. His hands clenched to his genitals, but he managed to keep his feet.

Her pathway still blocked by the guard, Silme waited with patient composure.

That should cool his lust a bit. Larson indulged in a smile, but familiar with violent men who became enraged rather than muddled by pain, he silently edged closer.

Gradually, the injured man straightened. Several more seconds passed before he managed to speak beneath his friends' snickers. When he did, rage deepened his tone. "I was going to make it nice for you. Now I'll pin you down, and we'll all rape you till you scream."

The laughter stopped as if cut. Encouraged by their companion, the other three guards closed in on Silme at once.

Now, nothing could stay Larson. He sprang at the guard's back.

One of the others shouted a warning, but it came too late. Larson grabbed the spearman's right wrist, yanking the arm behind the man's back. His free hand crashed against the base of the guard's skull. Larson pivoted. Drawing up on the arm and shoving down on the head, he whipped the guard off his feet, driving his face into the packed earth roadway.

The guard screamed. Twisting from Larson's grip, he rolled beyond reach. He pawed at his face, blood from abrasions staining his fingers. Luck alone had saved his nose and cheekbones.

The other sentries froze. Larson crouched. Sidestepping the Cullinsbergens with dignified composure, Silme started toward Larson.

But the frizzle-haired guard regained his feet and bullied between them. "You stay out of this, stranger." He jabbed a finger at Larson, keeping his distance and apparently trusting to his companions to guard his back from Silme. "You don't know what you're getting into."

One of us doesn't know. Fury boiled through Larson. His hand fell to his sword, and he kneaded the hilt.

Despite the violence and the guard between them, Silme spoke gently. "Calm down, Allerum. It's not worth it."

Larson settled into a fighting stance, his eyes locked on the man before him. "I'll calm down when they're all dead."

The guard's hand dropped to his own hilt, and blood smeared the split leather grip. The other two pressed forward, copying their leader's martial gesture.

Silme pressed. "Allerum, we're doing something important. Don't let this get in the way. Let's just leave. It's under control now."

Understanding penetrated Larson's mental fog. *She's not going to stop me from seeing the baron. And, as always, she's right. It's over, and no one got hurt.* He studied the guard's scraped face. *No one important, at least.* The idea of leaving these guards to rape other, less capable women bothered him, but, for now, Taziar's friends had to take precedence. Reluctantly, Larson let his fist fall away from his belt, though his rage would disperse far more slowly. "You're right. Let's go. The baron'll be pissed if I tell him I just had to kill three of his guards . . ." He could not help adding, ". . . because they were *stupid*."

The guards exchanged glances. Their hands still hovered near their hilts, but they did not draw their weapons. "What do you mean, 'talk to the baron?' "

"That's where I was going!" Larson shouted. "You're goddamned lucky I have to see the baron. Otherwise I'd have left you all bleeding in the alley!"

From behind the leader, Silme made a sudden gesture of disapproval.

One of the heavier guards shifted restlessly, his eyes dark with malice. The leaner guard spoke. "What were you going to tell the baron?"

Ignoring Silme's plea for tolerance, Larson snorted. "None of your goddamned business. I'm not going to tell something this important to some jerk who's supposed to be upholding the law but is breaking it instead."

Silme chimed in. "It's urgent. It involves the criminals who are causing problems in the streets."

After the guards' attack on Silme, Larson doubted they would care about crime. But their hands slid away from their sheaths. The sentries exchanged interested, if skeptical, glances. Only then, did it dawn on Larson that, regardless of their own brutality, it still fell to the guards to police the streets. Until Harriman inspired the underground, violence was the sole reign of the guard force, and they sublimated their crueler tendencies by intimidating peasants or battering prisoners. As the city turned fiercer, so did the guards. *If we can get the crime element under control, the guards will follow naturally. And it's at least as much in their interest as our own to make the streets safe.*

"Fine." The leader used his handkerchief to staunch the bleeding on his face, his lips twitching into an angry frown. "You want to talk to the baron about that, we'll escort you personally. We'll just make sure nothing happens to you on the way." He smiled wickedly. "Afterward . . ." He glared, meeting Larson's gaze with fiery, green eyes. ". . . you and I are going to have a talk. What just happened here is between us. We'll settle it later."

Larson returned the stare without flinching, and the two stood, unmoving, neither willing to glance away first. "Sounds just fine to me."

In the northern quarter of the city of Cullinsberg, the baron's keep nestled between walls twice the height of a tall man. Standing at the gate with Silme, Larson studied the castle's seven stories of blocked granite, its corner spires rising to the heavens like dragons' tails. In the courtyard, peasants sat in huddled groups while uniformed guards threaded watches between them. A moat slicked with algae reflected the morning light, murky green beneath the lowered drawbridge that jutted from the dark depths of the keep. Two sentries stood before the walkway and rebuffed citizens with words or shoves of their spear shafts. A matching pair of guardsmen met Larson, Silme, and their three guard escort at the open gate.

The larger of the sentries regarded Larson and Silme from beneath a curled mat of blond hair. "Who are you?

Do you have an appointment?" He used a condescending tone that denied the possibility. "Does the baron know you?"

Still seething from his confrontation in the alley, Larson found the guard's brusque manner and formality a challenge. He opened his mouth, but before he could speak, one of the robust escorts piped in from behind him.

"It's all right. They're with us."

The sentry regarded the leader of the trio curiously. "Haimfrid?"

The frizzle-haired guard nodded, a single, curt gesture emphasized by the thud of his spear butt against the ground. "They need to talk to Baron Dietrich. We'll take them personally."

The sentries exchanged glances. Apparently, this went against accepted procedure, but Haimfrid must have outranked them because they stepped aside to let Silme, Larson, and their accompanying guardsmen through the gate.

Haimfrid led his charges past waiting clusters of townsfolk, across the drawbridge over the moat, and into the mouth of the keep. Braziers lit the hallway in evenly-spaced hemispheres. Though scrubbed clean, the stone walls supported no finery, and Larson suspected that the baron displayed his wealth and artifacts only in places where visiting peasants could not enjoy or steal them. A short distance down the corridor, they came upon an oak door and a hard, wooden bench across from it. "Sit," Haimfrid growled.

The two heavyset guards trotted off to make arrangements.

Larson and Silme sat. Haimfrid stood, stiff as his spear, directly before them. Only his eyes moved, as he studied Silme, taunting Larson with a hungry leer of anticipation.

Silme leaned against her dragonstaff with calm detachment, pretending to take no notice of Haimfrid's stare. Larson chewed at his lip, trying to rein his temper with little success. He latched his fingers onto the edges of the bench, rocking to waste pent-up energy, reminding himself repeatedly that he could never hope to win a battle against guards while in the baron's keep, *Take care of business first. Then I'll rip off the bastard's head.*

Minutes stretched into an hour. Stubbornly refusing to be intimidated, Haimfrid remained standing and gawking long after the position must have grown uncomfortable.

Silme dropped into a shallow catnap, and Larson's mood grew progressively uglier. Finally, he leaped to his feet to protest.

At that precise moment, the door edged open, and one of the heavyset guardsmen poked his head through the crack. "Haimfrid?"

"Come with me." Haimfrid beckoned as if no time had elapsed. Walking with the limp of cramped muscles, he led Larson and Silme through the door and into the baron's audience chamber.

A frayed carpet of multicolored squares formed a pathway to the baron's dais. Dressed in a gaudy costume of leather and silk, a finely-etched and jeweled medallion around his throat, the baron perched in a chair carved into the shape of a lion. The maned head topped its back, its mouth opened. Though intended to appear formidable, in Larson's current mood, it looked more as if the creature might swallow the baron's head. The fourteen guards positioned around the courtroom wore red-trimmed black uniforms, but the baron sported gold and silver, the colors of Aga'arin's priests.

As Larson traversed the carpet at Haimfrid's side, it became instantly apparent that the room contained no other exits. During his interminable wait on the bench no one had left by the main doors. *The baron saw no one before us. He made us wait for no good reason.* The realization deepened Larson's rage. *I won't be bullied.*

As if to prove him wrong, Haimfrid slammed the base of his spear into Larson's shin. "That's far enough. Now kneel and kiss the floor."

Pain flared through Larson's ankle. He hissed in fury. "Fuck you. I'm not putting my lips on any floor."

Haimfrid raised his voice so the others in the room could hear. "Insolent fool, you're in the presence of the most high, noble baron of Cullinsberg. What do you mean you won't bow?"

Born and raised in the king's city of Forste-Mar, Silme curtsied with practiced elegance.

Bow? Larson fought the urge to leap bodily upon Haimfrid. "You bastard," he whispered. More accustomed to saluting as a show of respect, he executed a rigid, clumsy bow.

Haimfrid sneered. "Now do it right, or I'll take this spear to you." He brandished the weapon in warning.

As the pain in his ankle subsided, Larson dismissed Haimfrid's threat softly, as if he were nothing more than a bothersome fly at a picnic. "You go back in the corner and play with your stick like a nice, little boy and you won't get hurt."

"Hold." The baron's voice thundered through the room. "There's time enough for violence if it's necessary. Right now, Haimfrid, you stand off."

Haimfrid couched his spear with obvious reluctance.

Baron Dietrich fondled a paw adorning his handrest. "You come into my presence. You show an appalling lack of proper regard. This had better be important."

In an obvious attempt to restore order, Silme broke in before Larson could gather breath. "You'll have to excuse him, lord. He comes from another realm where this sort of circumstance is unusual. He's a bit out of sorts, and the information we bring is of such great importance I didn't have time to brief him on all the appropriate courtesy and decorum someone of your mighty stature deserves."

"Fine. Fine." The baron waved a hand with impatience. "Proceed. If your news is truly important enough to bring to my attention, I can forgive a lapse of respect this once."

Silme curtsied again. "As I'm sure you know, the incidence of crime in Cullinsberg has recently increased and its nature has become more violent."

Forcing himself to remain collected, Larson avoided Haimfrid's stare.

"Yes, that's so," said the baron. "But we have taken what we feel to be the appropriate measures and have the situation under control."

Larson opened his mouth to disagree, but Silme tapped his other shin with her staff and seized his moment of surprise to continue. "This is in no way intended to be disrespectful, lord. The measures taken may eventually bring crime under control. As yet, they haven't been successful. The streets remain unsafe. But we have information regarding a leader of the organized underground who is causing the problems. It might be prudent for you to use the facilities at your disposal to remove this leader, thereby weakening the underground."

Impressed by Silme's eloquence, Larson awaited the baron's reply with the same quiet eagerness as his soldiers.

"Fine," the baron said agreeably. "I don't believe we still have an organized underground, just a bunch of thugs. But it might prove interesting to question whoever you name. Maybe he does know some useful information. We've already made a sweep of the leaders, but if we missed one, tell us. I'll be grateful, and you'll be handsomely rewarded."

This is almost too easy. Larson's spirits lifted, and even Haimfrid's persistent glare no longer disturbed him.

"The leader's name is Harriman," Silme said.

The baron leaned forward, hands clenched on the lion's paws. "Who? Repeat that."

Silme obliged. "The leader's name is Harriman."

"Do you have a description of this Harriman?"

Silme repeated the features Taziar had highlighted the previous night. "Over thirty. Average height but well-muscled. Curly blond hair and beard. Dark, shrewd eyes."

The baron slumped back into his chair. "Guards, show them out. I don't want to waste any more time."

Surprised by the sudden turn of events, Larson shouted. "Wait! What's going on here? What the hell are you doing?" As Haimfrid closed in, Larson hollered. "Idiot!" He intended the insult for the guard, but the baron took offense.

"Idiot?" Dietrich screeched in rage, and every soldier tensed. "Who are you calling idiot, you insignificant peon? Harriman happens to be one of my men, a nobleman in his own right, and not a criminal. You come to me. You make all kinds of demands. You burst into my presence without the proper respect or so much as a vague semblance of courtesy. Then you have the nerve to call me an idiot? Get out of my sight right now or you'll be hanging tomorrow with the rest of the vermin." He pounded a fist on the armrest. "Men, escort them out!"

Larson went rigid. *Baron's court or not, if Haimfrid touches me or Silme, I'll kill him.*

But Haimfrid seemed content to let the court guards do their jobs. He stepped aside as the others pressed in. One reached for Larson's arm. Larson dodged aside, unwilling to lose his freedom of movement. Spears rattled behind him. Concerned for Silme, Larson edged his hand toward the hilt of Gaelinar's katana. Then, realization froze him mid-movement. *If I fight, Silme may get killed. At best, they'd take her prisoner.* Images boiled up within him, of guards like Haimfrid defiling Silme with filthy hands, raping her, beating her, perhaps killing her before the birth of the child she endured their torture to save. *She has that one spell stored. But a transport escape only works on herself, and I don't think she'd leave me.* Hoping to avoid violence, he kept his hands high in a gesture of surrender and moved toward the door. Silme followed.

Haimfrid, his two companions, and a handful of court guards accompanied Larson and Silme from the audience room and down the hallway to the outer door. Then, apparently convinced the pair did not intend to cause any more trouble, one of the guards addressed them stiffly. "Thank you for your interest in the affairs of the barony. We greatly appreciate all assistance that can be given by dedicated citizens such as yourself." The guard paused in his rehearsed monologue, as if noticing Larson's foreign features for the first time. "I'm sure the baron has this under consideration and is currently looking into the matter. Thank you."

"Wait, no." Larson spun to the guards, not daring to believe Taziar had predicted the situation so closely based only on personal prejudice and mistrust. *It doesn't make any sense. An official bribed by a quiet crime lord is one thing. But why would the baron publicly scream about fighting crime while just as vocally supporting the criminals' violent leader?* Larson found himself facing a sneering Haimfrid and four lowering spears.

Silme gave him a warning kick.

"But . . ." Larson started. Then, recognizing the futility of protestation, he finished lamely. "Fine. Okay, fine. Let's go." Whirling back toward the courtyard, he seized Silme's arm. "This is insane."

"We can take it from here," Haimfrid said.

Larson heard the rustle of uniforms as the court guards returned to their posts in the baron's audience chamber, leaving Haimfrid and his two companions to escort them from the yard.

In the wake of Larson's failure with the baron, Haimfrid's threats in the alleyway seemed to lose all significance. *Maybe we can talk this damned thing out,* Larson thought, seeing the need to parley, but in no mood to try. He tromped over the drawbridge, footsteps echoing along the moat and shoved through the milling crowds. The same sentries stood aside to let Larson, Silme, and their accompanying guards through the gates in the enclosing walls.

Once in the main street, Larson considered the best arguments to defuse a situation that had grown beyond all proportion.

But Haimfrid prodded Larson's spine with his spear. "All right, hero . . ."

The touch rekindled Larson's rage, but Haimfrid's words sent him over the edge. Kensei Gaelinar had always referred to Larson as "hero," and, from Haimfrid, the taunt mocked not only Larson, but the only man who had ever fully gained his respect.

Oblivious to the depth of his harassment, Haimfrid continued, ". . . you delivered your message. Let's the five of us go for a little walk. We'll take care of you first and save her for dessert."

Larson's control snapped. His vision washed red. "Fine," he screamed. "You want to go someplace. Let's go, right now!" He took two striding steps forward, no destination in mind.

Silme gripped his forearm. "Calm down, Allerum." Her touched radiated concern as well as warning." She addressed Haimfrid. "You're making a big mistake."

One of the two robust guards behind Silme whispered, "Nice, very pretty. This won't be so bad."

Larson shook free of Silme's hand. "They started it. By damn, I'm going to finish it."

Haimfrid laughed. "Go ahead, talk loud. We'll see how loud you scream." He chuckled again. "We'll see how loud *she* screams." He poked Larson a few more times to hurry him away from the baron's keep. "Let's go. Let's go."

Larson whirled to face Haimfrid, glaring, his hands tensed on his hips. The other two guards were giving Silme as much space, though they held no spears.

Haimfrid back-stepped, spear readied.

Shaking his head with contempt, Larson turned to face forward again. He waited only until Haimfrid stepped in and jabbed him one more time. The instant the point touched him, Larson spun. He batted the spear aside with his left hand, pivoted along the shaft, and smashed his right fist into Haimfrid's temple. Haimfrid crumpled without a cry. His spear clattered to the cobbles.

It was a sucker punch, but, accustomed to street fighting, Larson did not trouble himself with ethics. The speed of his strike pooled the blood into his hand until it ached. Ignoring the pain, he sprang between Silme and Haimfrid's startled companions. One reached for his sword hilt, but too slowly. The sword had come only halfway free when Larson snapped a kick that struck the man's fingers. The sword fell back into its sheath.

Larson saw his own anger mirrored on his opponent's face. Again, the fat guard reached for his sword. Quick as thought, Larson knocked the hand away and slapped the ruddy cheeks. The other guard leaped for Silme. Larson hesitated, and his own opponent lunged for his throat. Larson responded naturally. He drove his hands between the guard's arms, back-stepping to draw the guard forward. Seizing a handful of greasy, sand-colored hair, Larson used the guard's momentum to drive his knee into the jowly face. Cartilage crumbled. Blood trickled, warm on Larson's skin, and the man crumpled, moaning, to the cobbles.

Larson looked over in time to see Silme tear the last guard's grip from her sleeve and bar his arm behind him. Larson charged, shoving between them. Before he could raise a fist, Silme hissed a warning from between gritted teeth. "Allerum, hold. Look up. Please, look up now."

Shoving the guard aside, Larson followed the direction of Silme's gaze. A half dozen crossbowmen perched on the curtain wall of the baron's keep, every bow drawn and aimed at Larson.

Silme made a wordless sound of outrage. The sapphire in her staff flared, staining the masonry inky blue. A column of flame sprang to life at the crossbowmen's feet. Flickers of blue and white danced like ghosts through the fire.

Shouts of surprise wafted from the wall top. The crossbowmen scattered. Three loosed bolts that went wild, their metal tips clicking on the cobbles.

Silme grasped Larson's arm. "Run!" She whirled, dragging Larson through the startled crowd and down the stand-lined street.

Muddled by a wash of rising and dispersing emotions, Larson followed without comprehension. Only after they had ducked beyond sight and sound of the baron's keep did he dare to question. "That spell you used. It didn't tap you?"

Silme brushed aside a man hawking jewelry. "I used the sapphire."

Larson pressed. "I thought you only stored a small amount of energy. That spell seemed so powerful."

"A light show." Silme ducked down a side street to avoid a milling crowd. "Harmless. Those flames had no heat. The guards were just too stupid to notice."

Larson frowned, thinking that in the crossbowmen's position, he might make the same assumptions. He studied the roadways to get his bearings. "You followed me from the inn, didn't you?"

Silme nodded.

"Why?"

"I wanted . . ." Silme started. She grinned, the humor striking her even before she spoke the words. "I wanted to keep you out of trouble."

"To keep me out of trouble, huh?" Larson thought about the guard's taunts in the alleyway and how much more easily his audience with the baron could have gone without Haimfrid's interference. "Well, thank God for that."

CHAPTER 6
Shadowed Alleys

Death is always and under all circumstances a tragedy,
for if it is not, then it means that life itself has
become one.

—Theodore Roosevelt
Letter

Lantern light gleamed from the upper room of the baron's
southern tower. Amidst midmorning sunshine, the glow dif-
fused to pale invisibility; but, from his study in Shylar's
whorehouse, Harriman recognized the summons. *Meet
now? The old fool.* Harriman slammed his ledger closed,
and dust swam through sun rays in a crazy pattern. Not a
number in his book was fact; it served only for show and,
eventually, for the baron's eyes. The true tallies remained
recorded only in Harriman's head.

Slouched near the door of Harriman's workroom, Halden
and Skereye had been arguing sword-sharpening techniques
since daybreak, their exchange gradually rising in volume
and intensity. Harriman interrupted their discussion before
it turned to violence. "We need to make another trip to
Wilsberg." Without further explanation, he opened the
door to the hallway and executed a broad, silent gesture.
Skereye abandoned his point with obvious reluctance. Obediently, he trotted off toward the eastern storage chamber
to light a lantern in answer to the baron's signal.

Halden flung a whetstone at his companion's retreating
back. It bounced from Skereye's thick shoulder and struck
the floor with a sharp click. Skereye turned, but Halden
pulled the door shut before his companion could retaliate.

Ignoring his guards' antics, Harriman fingered the silks
stretched over the back of his chair, gaze focused on the
light burning steadily through the baron's window. Shortly,
the flare winked out, acknowledging receipt of Harriman's

135

consent. "The old fool," Harriman repeated, this time aloud. Turning, he peeled his plain woolen shirt off over his head and exchanged it for the frayed blue and white silk of his diplomatic uniform. Before Harriman had fully laced his collar, Skereye returned.

Harriman pulled the knots into place and strapped on his sword belt, its buckle and scabbard crusted with diamonds. "Let's go."

Harriman and his Norse entourage wandered past rows of bedrooms. This early, most of the doors lay propped open to indicate vacancy; the few clients would be night thieves, off-duty guardsmen, and men of leisure. At the end of the hallway, a staircase led to the meeting and bargaining areas as well as the kitchen, bath, and living quarters that kept this house as much a home as a workplace for the women.

One of Harriman's three privileged officers stood, partway up the stairs, but Harriman made no allowances. He trotted down the steps, flanked by Halden and Skereye. The thief hesitated briefly. With an exaggerated flourish of respect, he gave ground, waiting for Harriman to pass at the base of the stairs.

Harriman acknowledged the sacrifice with a gruff, partial explanation. "We'll return shortly."

The thief nodded once. He made an undulating motion with his fingers to indicate he would see to it things ran smoothly in Harriman's absence, then continued his climb to the upper level.

The staircase ended in an open assembly chamber where seven well-groomed prostitutes reclined on chests, padded benches, or the floor. The instant Harriman appeared, all conversation ceased. Disinterested in the girls' discomfort, he wandered between them to the door. One shrank away from Halden's disfigured, leering face, and Harriman smiled in amusement. He caught the knob, wrenched the door open, and led his bodyguards through the entry hall to the outer door. Unfastening the lock, he pulled the panel ajar, and they emerged into the sunlight. He slammed the door behind them.

Harriman received little attention as he threaded through the thoroughfares of Cullinsberg, but the citizens gawked at his scarred and lumbering bodyguards. He knew that the underground and the street urchins on its fringes would ignore him. It had become common knowledge that Harriman visited the ruins of Wilsberg on occasion or knelt in the forests facing south to mourn family and friends. And, though accepted as truth, the information was spurious, its distribution well-planned. Early on, before he had gained the trust of the underground, he had led their spies to the devastated farm town. Later, as Bolverkr wore himself down constructing his fortress, Harriman steered his curious pursuers into the Kielwald Forest for a phony session of laments and vowed vengeance against Cullinsberg's baron.

The remembrance lasted until Harriman passed through the opened front gates of Cullinsberg. He crossed the fire-cleared plain without a backward glance and guided Halden and Skereye into the forest. Once lost between the trees, he waited. Whenever the baron called a meeting, he stationed one of his most trusted guards on the parapets. If anyone followed Harriman from the city, the sentry would signal by simulating the call of a fox. Harriman frowned at the thought. The majority of these conferences occurred at night or in the early morning when foxes normally prowled the woods. Now, the whirring imitation would sound nearly as suspicious as a shouted warning. But neither noise disturbed the stillness, and Harriman slipped deeper between the trees, certain no one had bothered to trail him.

Sun rays filtered through branches heavy with multicolored leaves; thick overgrowth trapped the light into a glow, revealing landmarks Harriman knew blind. He traversed the route without even thinking about it, fallen leaves crunching beneath his boots. Behind him, Skereye and Halden crashed like oxen through boughs, scurrying over deadfalls with an ease that belied their bulk. At length, Harriman brushed through a line of towering pines into a clearing blotted gray by overhanging branches. There Baron Dietrich waited, perched upon a stump. The gold medallion of office at his throat contrasted starkly with a tunic and breeks of untooled leather. At either hand, a sword- and spear-armed guard stood, proudly dressed in a uniform of red and black. A scrap of linen hung from one's knee where a briar had torn the fabric, exposing scratched flesh.

Though large, the baron's faithful sentries were dwarfed by
Harriman's berserks.

Harriman executed a flawless bow of respect. "My lord,
you summoned me?" His intended question remained unspoken. *What did you find of such urgency to risk a daylight meeting?*

The baron shifted on the stump. "Two strangers came to
my court this morning. They named you as head of the
criminals."

Harriman hid exasperation beneath an expression of interest. He spoke soothingly, never losing the tone of deference though he was fully in control of the situation. "Not
unexpected, lord. In order to help you destroy the organized underground and bring you the names of their leaders, I necessarily had to win their trust, to make them think
I was one of them. We knew this might happen. It's still
important that you pretend to see me as Wilsberg's diplomat and dismiss such a suggestion as nonsense."

"I thought I hired you to put an end to the violence."
The baron met Harriman's gaze, steely eyes flashing, de-
manding explanation. "The strangers reminded me that
Cullinsberg's streets are still unsafe."

Harriman banished rising anger with professional skill.
"Not unexpected either, as you must know, lord." The lies
came easily, without a twitch or furtive glance to betray
them. "The leaders are in your custody. What you're seeing
now is reaction to their capture." His gaze remained locked
and steady. Once the executions have concluded, the violence will die away. Meanwhile, I need to stay to watch for
upstart leaders."

The baron fidgeted. Harriman stood, unmoving, aware
something as yet unaddressed disturbed Dietrich. The medallion's chain clinked beneath the sough of wind as the
baron squirmed. At length, he spoke. "Those strangers.
They lacked common courtesy. They badgered my guards
into a fight. They insulted me. And . . ."

By the baron's sudden reluctance, Harriman guessed they
had come to the root of his discomfort. "And, lord?" he
encouraged gently.

"And," Dietrich continued. He leaned forward, his face
red in the gloom. "They fought free of three guards, injur-
ing one and humiliating another so badly I had to put him

on suspension until he calms down. And if the Norse woman who tried to kill my bowmen with fire isn't a Dragon-rank sorceress straight out of fairy tale . . ." He stopped, not bothering to complete the statement, and cast a nervous look at Halden and Skereye.

Harriman resisted the compulsion to swear. He knew Taziar's companions from Bolverkr's descriptions. And, though Bolverkr had never directly told Harriman, the noble-man knew his master planned to destroy Larson as person-ally and cruelly as he would Taziar. "These strangers you speak of. A willowy, blond man and a beautiful woman with a sapphire-tipped staff?"

Surprise crossed the baron's coarse features. "How did you know?"

So the little thief wants to bring outsiders into our feud. In his annoyance, Harriman conveniently forgot he had done precisely the same thing, and that the quarrel was Bol-verkr's, not his own. Instantly, the rules of his game changed. *Anyone who interferes will pay, beginning with those urchins who harbored him.* Harriman regained his composure masterfully and dispatched Baron Dietrich's query without answering it directly. "You'll get no more trouble from them, lord. I'll see to it. And there's some-thing I need to tell you." He met the baron's gaze again. "Taziar Medakan's in town."

The baron's face collapsed into wrinkles, and Harriman attributed his confusion to more than a decade spent work-ing with the guard captain of the same name. Then, the baron's eyes fell to slits and his nostrils flared. "The Shadow Climber?"

Harriman nodded confirmation.

Baron Dietrich drummed his fingers on his breeks, his manner calculating. "That weasel stole an artifact from Aga'arin's temple, escaped my dungeons, and led a faction of my men across the Kattegat *against my orders!*"

Harriman lowered his head and waited.

"Not one of my soldiers made it back, Harriman! Did you know that?"

"Of course, lord," Harriman reminded without offense. In his eighteen years as Wilsberg's diplomat, he had worked well and closely with the baron, cheerfully paying taxes to the last copper and supplying the baron with the best of the traders' crops and wares. Wilsberg's farmers had served their time among the baron's conscription forces in the years of the Barbarian Wars.

The baron went rigid. "I'll send every guard in Cullinsberg after the thief."

Harriman cringed, aware such an arrangement would destroy every trap he and Bolverkr had constructed. "I wish you wouldn't, lord."

The baron went silent, still shaking with anger.

Harriman seized the baron's quiet to continue. "Every criminal in town believes Taziar informed on the leaders. If you arrest him, it'll prove his innocence. The underground will look for another informant, and I'll be exposed as a liar at the least. So will the guards you commanded to name Taziar if questioned. And since nearly all your guards actually believe Taziar *is* the informant, you'll seem like a . . ." Harriman softened the accusation. "Your guards will know you fed them misinformation and wonder why you trusted these men and not them." He indicated the sentries beside the baron. "Criminals are unforgiving by necessity. If your men arrest Taziar, my life and those of several of your guards will become as worthless to the ruffians and assassins on your streets as Taziar's is now. Believe me, lord. They can do worse to the Shadow Climber than even your dungeon guards could." *And we will.*

"Very well," the baron agreed. "For your sake, I'll order my sentries to leave Taziar at liberty."

"Thank you, my lord," Harriman said respectfully, though he never doubted Baron Dietrich would take his advice. Despite maintaining courtly formality, Harriman had grasped control of this operation some time ago. *I may have lost some of that power thanks to Taziar's meddling friends, but I'll get it back.* Harriman harbored no doubt. *I have some lessons to teach, some warnings to give, and I'll need to get Taziar back into my custody.* He smiled wickedly, and, for the first time, a trace of true emotion slipped through.

Taziar Medakan pitched another log onto the already well-stocked hearth and watched flames lick around the cooler bark without catching. The firelight struck red and gold highlights through hair the color of coal and swept

across fine features ashen with concern. He took a seat on
the dwindling woodpile. Shortly, he grew restless and chose
to sit on the table instead. His back to the fire, he stared
at Astryd, asleep between the packs. An instant later, he
was up again, pacing the length of the inn room.

*I can't believe I let Allerum go off alone, knowing he
wanted to see the baron. What was I thinking?* Taziar
pounded his fist into his palm, aware the problem did not
come from a specific thought, but from no thought at all.
*That headstrong elf can get himself into more trouble eating
breakfast than I did breaking into the Dragonrank school
grounds. I'm just glad Silme was paying more attention to
Allerum's intentions than I was.* Now Taziar frowned, aware
more than enough time had passed for Silme to catch up
with Larson, convince him of the foolishness of running off
alone, and return with him to the inn room. *Unless he per-
suaded her to help him. Gods! Silme has to know you just
don't handle underground affairs through legal channels.*
Taziar cringed, familiar with Larson's single-mindedness
that often transcended common sense, a trait inspired and
nurtured by Kensei Gaelinar. *Silme might have found it
safer and simpler to give in to Allerum's obsession. But
we're wasting valuable time.*

Taziar's ambling brought him to the window over the
alleyway. He stopped, feeling the chill, autumn breezes on
his face, sharp contrast to the warmth of the fire at his
back. From habit, he measured the distance to the ground,
sought minuscule ledges in the featureless stretch of stonework. *They might need my help. I'll stay out of sight. How
much trouble can I get into just gathering facts?* Memory of
the beating in Shylar's whorehouse that still left his cheeks
and ribs swollen and splotched with bruises made him
wince. His lapse admitted Silme's warning:" "You're of no
use to your friends dead." Taziar wrapped his fingers
around the sill. *But I'm even more useless if they're dead.
My one life is worth little compared with their eight. How
many others may die for me?*

Taziar had climbed halfway across the window ledge before he realized it. Astryd rolled in her sleep, and her
movement froze him, dangling from the sill. *What in Karana's hell is wrong with me? I can't leave Astryd alone.* He
sprang back into the chamber, landing lightly as a cat on

the planking. He crossed to Astryd and perched on a pack near her head. Idly, he stroked the soft, blonde locks, pulling free strands that had caught at the corner of her mouth. Since Larson and Silme had departed, every position seemed uncomfortable to Taziar, and he found himself unable to sit still. Urgency spiraled through him, and he fought the impulse to return to the window.

Harriman doesn't know where we're staying; otherwise, he would have found us already. No one will disturb Astryd. Besides, she's hardly helpless. Taziar recalled his first encounter with Astryd. He had discovered her locked in a berth aboard the summer ferry. Then, mistaking him for a captor, she had evaded him faster than he could think to stop her. Once he managed to catch her, she had clawed and kicked him like a tiger. *She's slept long enough to restore most of her used energy, so she'll have magic, too.* Taziar kissed Astrryd's cheek, felt her settle more snugly beneath her spread cloak. Sliding his sword from its sheath, he placed it near her hand. *You won't need it, but neither will I. I'll feel more comfortable if you keep it.*

Having rationalized leaving, Taziar bounded across the room before he could change his mind again. He paused only long enough to ascertain that the alley stood empty, then lowered his legs through the opening and scrambled to the ground.

Again, Taziar peered the length of the thoroughfare. Satisfied no one had seen him, he turned his attention to the back wall of Mardain's temple. Having grown accustomed to longhouses, and simple cottages, the building appeared awesome, taller than any man-made structure in Norway. Taziar accepted the challenge with glee. Recalling the lack of hand and toe holds on the stones that formed the first story, Taziar took a running start. Fingers scraping granite, he sprinted the length of the alleyway, then flung himself at the wall. Momentum took him to the coarse areas of mortar at the second story. From there, he skittered to the roof.

Wind dried beads of sweat from Taziar's forehead as he stared out over the city of Cullinsberg. Shops and dwellings stood in stately rows between the confining square of the city's outer walls. Roads striped, curled, and crisscrossed through the business district, and people traversed the main thoroughfares in crowds. Taziar craned his neck to glance into the alleyway where Rascal's gang had tended his injuries and discussed the changes in the structure of the underground. A lone figure paced the earthen floor. Though distant and at too peculiar an angle to be certain, it looked like a child. Taziar read agitation in the movements.

The muscles of Taziar's chest bunched in worry, and he felt flushed. He found niches in the wall stones and clambered downward, jumping the last story back into the alley. He slunk close to the walls through the dappled shadows of the buildings until he came to a threadlike crossroad. He studied the alley quickly before darting across and into a throughway parallel to the first. Once there, he shinnied up a warehouse. His footfalls made no sound on the roof, and he scrambled to the opposite side. Flattened to the tiles, he peered over the edge.

Far beneath Taziar, Ida scuffed her sandals on the packed dirt floor of the roadway. A dress designed for an adult hung in loose bulges, its hem frayed and filthy. She clutched a tattered cloak tightly over it to protect her from the cold. Her head hung low, and she flung her hand outward on occasion, as if carrying on a conversation with herself.

Taziar examined the pathway; his aerial position accorded him a safe view over the rain barrels and garbage. Finding Ida alone, he descended the wall stones and slipped into the alley beside her. "Ida?"

At the sound of Taziar's voice, Ida jerked her head up. Her limbs went rigid. Tears traced meandering lines through dirt on her cheeks, and her eyes appeared swollen. A crimson bruise marred the soft arc of her jaw.

"Ida?" Cut to the heart, Taziar reached out to comfort her. *What kind of heartless madman would hit a little girl?*

Ida dodged Taziar's embrace, back-stepping until her shoulder touched the wall. Her voice sounded as scratchy as an elderly man's. "Harriman's men trapped Rascal and the others in an old warehouse in Ottamant's Alley."

Taziar cringed, his fear for the children intermingled with his memory of his own arrest in that same alley a few months earlier. "You escaped?"

Ida shook her head, avoiding Taziar's gaze. "They let me

go. I'm supposed to tell you . . ." Her breath came in sobs from crying. ". . . they'll kill anyone caught talking to you."

Aware how difficult Ida found her words, Taziar shared her grief. Slowly, without threat, he reached for her again.

Ida shrank away. She blurted, "I don't want anyone else to get hurt." Finally, she met Taziar's stare. "I don't want you to get hurt either."

"Ida, please." Taziar approached. "Rascal and the others . . ."

Ida shuffled backward for every step Taziar took toward her.

Taziar stopped, and Ida stood in miserable, quaking silence. "I'll get them free." Lacking any other way to soothe, Taziar promised without any knowledge of what his vow might entail. "You'll see. I'll release them and get you all safely out of the city."

All color drained from Ida except the angry splotch of the contusion. "Taz. The warehouse . . . Harriman . . ." Sudden panic made her stiffen. Her eyes rolled, revealing the whites like a frightened cart horse. Abruptly, she whirled and ran, the slap of her sandals echoing between the buildings.

For some time, Taziar stood in quiet uncertainty, senses dulled by a heavy barrage of emotion. Grief and guilt weighed heavily upon him, and he knew he had brought disaster to the only Cullinsbergens who dared to trust him. *They're only children.* Taziar wrestled between decisions. *Do I go after Rascal or try to comfort Ida?* The girl's sorrow and fear haunted him, and he made his choice quickly. The sound of her footsteps had already grown faint. Abandoning caution, he chased after her.

Ida had run straight to the alley's end, then turned into a zigzagging branchway. Taziar followed. Aware this lane had no outlet, he was not surprised when her footfalls fell silent. He jogged past rain barrels, skirted a shabby, abandoned cart, and dodged the bones and rotted fruit littering the ground. He saw where one of Ida's footsteps had smashed an ancient apple to brown mush. Ducking around the final corner, Taziar found her slumped between a stack of crates and a pair of barrels. An overhanging ledge hid her in shadow, her form barely discernible in the gloom.

"Ida?" Taziar freed his ankle from a discarded scrap of parchment, approaching slowly so as not to startle her.

"Ida?" Concern made Taziar careless. As he moved closer, he noticed that her back was not heaving, though he would have expected to find her crying. She did not stir as he reached out and gently grasped her shoulder.

Taziar's touch dislodged Ida, and she fell limply into his arms. Warm liquid coursed through his fingers. He cried out in shock and alarm. Catching her chin between his hands, he met sightless, unblinking eyes; and his grip glazed blood across her cheek. *Dead. How?* Taziar wrapped his arms around Ida, cradling her to his chest. He explored her lower back with his fingers, found the sticky slit where the knife had penetrated her dress at the level of a kidney. His grip tightened protectively, and tears stung his eyes. *Gods, no! She's just a child.* Silently, he rocked her like an infant in a crib.

"Freeze, Medakan *weasel!*" The voice came from directly behind Taziar, accompanied by wild scramblings amidst the crates.

Taziar's heart missed a beat. Ida's corpse slipped from his grip, smearing blood the length of his sleeves. He berated himself with every profanity he could muster. *I walked into their trap like an ignorant barbarian who never set foot in a city before and paid with Ida's life and probably my own.* It occurred to Taziar he might deserve whatever cruelties these men inflicted on him. But his survival instinct remained strong, fueled by the fact that he alone knew about the capture of Rascal's gang. Driven by the need to help them, he glanced up to meet the three men who threatened him with swords.

"I'm unarmed," Taziar said, the disclosure intended to make Harriman's men overconfident rather than as a plea for mercy. He rose, holding scarlet-slicked hands away from his empty sword sheath. He backed toward the wall, and the men closed into a semicircle around him. They all looked vaguely familiar to Taziar, strongarm men and cutthroats from the fringes of the underground.

The one directly before Taziar spoke again. "I said 'freeze,' Taziar. You forget the language?"

Taziar stole a glance at the stonework behind him, not bothering to reply.

The man continued. "Don't move, and you won't get hurt."

Keep them talking, Taziar reminded himself, aware he had to distract them before he could make a move. "That's not reassuring coming from someone who just knifed a twelve-year-old girl." The words emerged not at all as Taziar had planned. He winced. *That's right, Taz, you idiot. Antagonize the brute with his sword at your chest.*

"We didn't kill her." The man to the right spoke, revealing teeth darkly-stained and rotting. "You did. Murderer!" He spat. "Child killer."

Guilt stabbed through Taziar, sharper than the hovering swords. He back-stepped, feeling cold granite against his spine.

The center man gestured to the companion to his left who turned and started rooting through the crate wood. "Taziar Medakan, you're under arrest."

"Under arrest?" Taziar glanced between the swords, seeking an opening. But the central man took a side step, neatly closing the gap created by his companion's absence. "You can't arrest me. You're criminals, too."

The third ruffian returned. He had sheathed his sword and was clutching a sturdy board of the same length. "Then we'll beat you senseless, drag you to the baron's keep, and leave you on his doorstep as a present." He brandished the plank. "You'll wake up in the dungeon."

I've escaped before. And there might be some advantage to helping my friends from the inside. Taziar banished the thought immediately. *A lot of luck and an inhumanly strong barbarian aided that breakout. If I try something that crazy, I'll need at least Astryd's aid. And thanks to my impulsiveness, my friends have no idea where I am.* He studied the group before him, realizing from their sneers they had no real intention of surrendering him to the baron. *They're lying. Playing me. Probably preparing to take me back to Harriman for another pounding by his berserks.* "What's happened to the underground? We used to take care of each other. We settled differences among ourselves. We never hurt one another, never harmed the children."

The center man snorted. "So the traitor wants to give lectures on loyalty." He inclined his head toward his board-wielding companion. "Take him."

The instant the leader's attention turned, Taziar twisted, leaping for the wall stones. His fingers settled naturally into irregularities, and he scrambled upward. He had nearly reached the level of the ruffians' heads when his blood-wet fingers slipped. He tottered, catching his balance with effort. A hand skimmed the fabric of his pants leg, and he knew the men had him. If that grip closed, they would rip him from the wall and probably beat him in anger and frustration.

Desperate, Taziar sprang backward. Momentum knocked the fingers aside. He sailed over the men's heads, landed awkwardly on a mangled cartwheel, and rolled. He gained his feet as the men whirled toward him. "Get him!" the leader screamed.

Taziar ran. He swerved through the jagged alleyway, the pounding of his pursuers too loud and close for him to pause long enough to get a grip and climb. He charged back into the lane where he had met Ida, sprinted its length, and dodged into a branchway. Uncertain which way to go, he hoped to lose the ruffians in the crowded market streets. He had no goal. He only knew places where he did not dare lead Harriman's lackeys: the inn room that lodged his friends and the warehouse in Ottamant's Alley. *And the back roads are ruled by the underground.*

Taziar careened through the threadlike network of lanes, turned a corner, and slid into the bustling main street. Behind him, the leader's voice rose above the clamor. "Catch him! Murderer! That man killed my daughter!"

Damn! Taziar plunged into the masses, elbowing through tiny gaps, smearing blood across the passersby. A woman screamed. The crowd parted before him, most too afraid to get involved. A hand seized Taziar's cloak, jolting him backward. He slipped to one knee. Pulling his arms free, he let the fabric slide from his back. The resistance disappeared, and Taziar lunged forward. Women skittered, screeching, from his path.

"Murderer! Murderer! He killed someone! He stabbed a little girl!" The cries emanating from the thugs were picked up and echoed by the crowd. Blows rained down on Taziar. He ducked his head, using his arms to shield his face. No longer certain how close his pursuers were, he dared not glance back. A foot snagged his ankle, sprawling him into a tight knot of citizens. They scattered. A boot thumped painfully against his back and another crashed into his scalp. Dizzy, he staggered to his feet. Catching a glimpse of the gray mouth of an alley, he ran for it, no longer concerned about street toughs and thieves.

Most of the citizens feared the back streets, and the footfalls and shouts faded to those of half a dozen dogged pursuers. From the voices, Taziar recognized at least one of the ruffians among the group. The alley looked unfamiliar, which made Taziar uneasy. He knew the entire city to some extent, but this side of town least of all, and he harbored no wish to corner himself in some dead end. *Have to think. Plan my course. Climb?* Each breath came with a burning gasp. Cold, autumn air dried sweat from his limbs, and he felt simultaneously chilled and overheated. *Can't climb here. Enemies too close. Hands sticky. Buildings too far apart. They'll surround me.* He raked hair from his eyes, smearing blood across his brow. *A ruse. Something to gain me time and space, a moment out of sight.*

Taziar came to a four-way intersection. Recalling a rear door viewed from one of the alleyways, he chose the left pathway, grimly knowing it would again lead him to the main streets. A dozen strides brought him into the market area, and he plunged into the masses from necessity. Behind him, the leader of the ruffians hollered again. "Murderer! Catch him! He killed my daughter!"

Taziar counted shops as he ran. He leaped over a foot intended to trip him and deflected a punch with his elbow. Suddenly, he swerved, swinging wildly. Startled citizens shied from his path, leaving him a lane to the jewelry store. Catching the knob, he sprinted through the doorway. The panel slammed against the wall and bounced closed. A wizened jeweler glanced up from a project. Before a counter covered with tiny gemstones, a patron screamed. Taziar vaulted to the countertop, knocking a colored wash of precious stones to the floor. They scattered, rattling across the granite. The jeweler cursed Taziar with steamy epithets as the Climber sprang to the ground. Unable to gather enough breath for an apology, he struck the back door with his shoulder and emerged into the alley.

Aware his maneuver would only delay his pursuers, Taziar fled. He swung into the first byway, and there discovered a dark crack between buildings scarcely wide enough for the scraggly tomcats that prowled the streets. Skilled in squeezing into tight spaces, Taziar pressed his back to the opening and wriggled inside. Rats scratched and scuttled deeper in behind him. Stonework abraded skin from Taziar's shoulders. He heard the slap of the jeweler's back door followed by a gruff voice. "Which way?"

"This way!" the ruffians' leader called breathlessly. "The other way leads back to the street."

Footsteps pounded toward Taziar. He fought the urge to pant, holding his breath until he thought his lungs would burst. The noises passed, and he gasped gratefully for air. He grasped the edges of the fissure, dragging himself painfully toward the opening. For an instant, he writhed forward. Then he wedged tight, arms straining, the pressure aching through his shoulders. *I'm stuck.* A rat screeched, and Taziar's mind turned the sound into an echoing cry of hunger. He forced down panic. By degrees, he shifted, sucking in a deep breath and exhaling fully before making another attempt at freedom. This time, he edged back into the alley.

Aware his pursuers might return, Taziar took only enough time to wipe the drying blood from his fingers with his shirt. Then, catching handholds in a stone and mud wall, he clambered to the roof. He crept to the opposite side in time to watch the ruffians disappear around the corner of a parallel alleyway. Carefully, he braced his hands on the ledge of a neighboring roof and pulled himself across to it. He slithered down into the roadway they had abandoned and climbed another wall. In this manner, he gradually worked his way toward Cullinsberg's east side and Ottamant's Alley.

Crushed, winded, and alone, Taziar knew he could never hope to save Rascal's gang. *But I have to assess the situation so Astryd, Silme, and Larson have a clear idea of where we're going and what we're against.* He continued toward his goal, springing, climbing, and descending, concentrating on every back street, hidey-hole, and handhold to keep him from the pain of other contemplations. Ida's death, his imprisoned friends, Allerum and Silme facing off with a corrupt baron, Astryd asleep and by herself, he pushed all these thoughts to the back of his mind, not yet able to deal with the grief. Just as after his father's death, the excitement of evading enemies and performing a difficult task channeled aside what he could not face. He threw himself into his task with a fanatical thoroughness.

As Taziar drew closer to Ottamant's Alley, he grew even more absolute in his attention to details. Several blocks from the warehouse, he discovered lone men and women pacing around buildings with an idleness uncharacteristic of citizens or thieves. By establishing patterns and waiting for these guards to turn corners, he avoided them with ease. Closer to the warehouse, he noticed the singles had become groups, their patrols more erratic. With more difficulty, he dodged these, too.

Still two blocks from his goal, Taziar ascended the five stories of the alehouse and studied the layout from above. His vantage allowed him to view three of the warehouse's four sides. Windows were cut into the western and northern walls, with entryways to the north and south. Three men guarded each alleyway around the warehouse, their backs pressed to its walls. Another lay on the roof tiles, watching over the northern side, a crossbow and quiver of quarrels beside him. Acutely aware of the small number of people capable of climbing buildings, Taziar knew the crossbowman would prove quick and agile.

Taziar considered returning to his friends, but he wanted to make certain the children were inside before risking any more lives. A plan took shape in his mind. In the same manner as before, he worked his way to the south side of the alehouse. Locating an alley currently vacant of its guard, he secured a long, narrow board. Pulling off his bloodstained shirt, he wrapped the wood to muffle sound. He hauled the board to the back side of the warehouse across from the one in Ottamant's Alley and cautiously, grip by grip, dragged it to the roof.

Taziar's position gave him a perfect view of the bowman's feet and the three guards in the throughway below. He freed his shirt and tied it to one end of the plank. Secure in the knowledge that people rarely think to look over their heads, Taziar inched the board across the space between his rooftop and the bowman's. The cloth slid soundlessly across tile. He waited, heart pounding. But the man on the rooftop did not turn. Below, the thieves chatted, apparently oblivious to the events directly above their heads.

Taziar continued, the familiar euphoria of fighting against steep odds tainted by the realization that success would require nearly as much luck as skill. Quick efficiency would decrease the chance of a random glance in his direction, so Taziar did not hesitate. He stepped onto the board, felt it sag beneath his weight, and was glad for the slight stature that had served as both blessing and curse in the past. He crossed silently and without incident. The midday sun struck Taziar's shadow immediately beneath him, and he was careful not to let its edge fall near the bowman as he approached.

Reaching the western edge of the warehouse, Taziar flattened to the roof tiles and examined the wall below. The guards pitched stones at pieces of rotting fruit, laughing as a direct hit sent feasting yellow jackets into flight. Halfway between Taziar and the guards, the window lay flat and featureless beneath him. Taking advantage of the thieves' preoccupation, Taziar descended the wall above their heads, balancing speed against the risk of dislodging dirt and vines and thus revealing his location. The alley guards continued their sport as Taziar caught the window ledge and peered inside.

Men filled the room, perched on crates or on the floor, most huddled near the doors. A brief examination of the storage area revealed no sign of the children, and Taziar realized he had been set up. No doubt, the urchins' bodies lay, dismembered, in some back street, labeled with a warning of the consequences of helping Taziar Medakan. Few of the street people could read, but it would only take one man to interpret the writing and spread the news. Taziar froze, half-naked and shivering from cold that pierced deeper than the autumn weather. He watched in horror as a thief's gaze found him. A finger stretched toward the window, accompanied by a shout that mobilized everyone.

Taziar scurried up the granite, catching new handholds as fast as he could loose the ones below. An arrow sailed past his ear as he hurled himself over the ledge to the roof. His head slammed into the crossbowman's face hard enough to set Taziar's skull ringing. Impact knocked him to his side, and he caught a dizzy glimpse of criminals gathering far below him. He reacted instinctively, wrenching himself sideways to change the direction of his momentum.

Catching his balance, he charged across the rooftop to the board, realizing as he did that the bowman lay, moaning on the tiles, holding his nose. Taziar raced across the plank, too pained by the children's certain deaths to laugh.

Harriman's men poured into the alleyways, but Taziar had gained distance through his ploy. Dodging, ducking, and climbing, Taziar knew this sector of the city too well to get caught. But despite the excitement of the chase, he was unable to keep the tears from his eyes.

CHAPTER 7
Ladies of the Shadows

I like not fair terms and a villain's mind.
                              —William Shakespeare
                              The Merchant of Venice

Back in the inn room, Taziar Medakan huddled on the stacked logs, feeling weak and as tattered as an old rag. Everything he had done since arriving in Cullinsberg replayed through his mind in an endless loop of accusation. He had not asked Rascal to drag him, unconscious and bleeding, from the whorehouse alley. Even if Taziar had been coherent enough to warn the children, he had not known the danger. No one could have guessed that Harriman would choose that moment to demand his share of the day's take, nor just how cruel and warped his anger would become. Still, Taziar could not help feeling responsible for the children's deaths. And after he revealed the information to his friends, the fact that Larson, Silme, and Astryd sat watching him in silent sympathy only strengthened his guilt. Taziar wished just one of his companions would chastise him for running off alone.

Larson crouched in a corner near the window, saying nothing. Astryd sat among the packs, tracing a pattern on the hilt of Taziar's sword. It was Silme who finally broke the silence. "What time of day is the baron planning to hang Shylar and the others?"

Taziar stared at his hands. "Tomorrow sundown, almost certainly. Aga'arin's High Holy Day is the most sacred day of the year. His followers, including the baron, will spend most of daylight on the temple grounds." Taziar looked up, plotting diverting his thoughts from the orphans. "The number of guards on duty won't change. Atheists and worshipers of Mardain will work. But many of the shops will close early or won't open at all, and the streets will be nearly empty." Taziar sat straighter, touched by the first familiar stirrings of excitement that accompanied planning the impossible. "The holiday won't make the escape any simpler, but once we've freed them, we should be able to move through town without much difficulty." Uncomfortable with leaving his friends in prison any longer than necessary, Taziar frowned. "Assuming we wait until tomorrow to release them."

"Which gives us tonight to remove Harriman," Silme spoke gently, but her suggestion inspired a flare of guilt that made Taziar squirm.

"Forget Harriman for now." Taziar's words did not come easily. "We can kill him any time, but my friends could die tomorrow."

Larson looked pensive. "Silme's right, Shadow. Breaking your friends out won't do us any good if we leave an enemy at our backs. Harriman got them thrown in prison once. He can do it again."

Silme continued. "You couldn't talk a gang of frightened children into leaving Cullinsberg. Do you expect Shylar and the others to run away from the only home they know, passively waiting while Harriman destroys the part of city life they created?"

"Of course not." Mercifully, Taziar's remorse and the burden of blame retreated behind this new concern. "At the least, we have to know just how much control Harriman has over the remainder of the underground. We have to define friends and enemies. And that's never an easy thing to do with criminals. When . . ." Taziar avoided the uncertainty implied by the word "if." "When we free the leaders, we have to know who will stand with and who will stand against them. But . . ." He trailed off, licking his lips as he tried to frame the concept distressing him.

Three pairs of eyes confronted Taziar in interested silence, and he met them all in turn. "Harriman knew those children helped me yesterday, but he waited until we raised a hand against him. He killed Rascal and the others only after you went to the baron. I don't think that was coincidence. It was a warning. If we try to kill Harriman and fail, *which of my friends will he destroy next?*"

A hush fell over the room as Astryd, Silme, and Larson considered. Larson spoke first, with the guileless moral insight he had openly displayed before Gaelinar's death had driven him to emulate his swordmaster's gruffer manner. "This is war, Shadow. In war, innocents die. You can't feel responsible for every sin your enemy commits. The most you can do is limit your own killing to enemies and protect your buddies to the best of your ability. You try. You may fail. Everyone makes mistakes, and, sometimes, the wrong people pay. But there's no excuse for not trying at all."

Taziar lowered his head. It was against his nature to fear a challenge, but it went against all his experience to weigh children's lives in the balance.

Silme returned the conversation to practical matters. "Who would have the information we need about the underground's loyalties?"

"I'm not certain." Taziar wandered through the list of informants in his mind. "Of course, the people who always knew the most about the goings on in the underground are the ones in prison. I got most of my facts from Shylar." Frustrated, he shook his head. The gesture flung hair into his eyes, and he raked it back in place. "No one will talk to me. They all either hate or fear me, and I won't endanger any more innocents. Certainly, no one will talk to any of you. It took me eight years to gain enough trust to establish the connections I have. You can't accomplish the same thing in a day." Another desperate thought pushed through his disillusionment. "Unless . . ." he started before he could dismiss the idea as too dangerous.

"Unless what?" Silme's tone made it clear she would not accept denial or argument. "Speak up."

Taziar knew better than to try to hide knowledge from Silme. She had an uncanny ability to read people, and she never brooked nonsense. "Apparently, Harriman's working out of Shylar's whorehouse. That's not surprising. A lot of information goes through that house, and it's built for meeting and spying. For some reason, men tend to talk to Shylar's girls, and they share disclosures amongst themselves."

Silme picked up the thread of Taziar's thought. "And possibly would talk with another girl who joined them."

Unnerved by the course Silme's mind seemed to be taking, Taziar attempted to redirect the suggestion. "The girls know and trust Shylar like a mother. Harriman's sly, but I doubt even he could turn them against Shylar. In fact, I can't fathom how the whorehouse is running at all without her. If I could sneak in again and speak with one of the girls . . ."

Larson broke in with a loud snort of disgust. "Sure, Shadow. You're going to slip past Harriman, his drug-crazed Vikings, forty thieves, guards, and other assorted male citizenry out to kill you so you can talk to a hooker who might just as easily turn you in as talk to you. You'd have about as much chance as a frog on a freeway."

Larson's last sentence held no meaning for Taziar, but the skepticism came through with expressive distinctness. And having failed once, Taziar could understand his companion's doubt. "Are you trying to say it's impossible?" Taziar left his intention unspoken, aware his friends knew that naming a task impossible was to Taziar like dangling raw steak before a guard lion.

Obviously undaunted, Larson rose. "You're good, Shadow, but not that good. Besides, even if you made it through, you would force Harriman to kill whichever woman you spoke with."

Silme nodded agreement. "You're staying if I have to tie you to the door. Harriman may know you, but he's never seen any of us. There's only one logical choice as to who we send for information." She looked pointedly at Astryd.

Dread crept through Taziar, a wave of cold foreboding that left him frozen like a carving in ice. "No," he croaked. Then, louder, "No!" *I won't blithely deliver the only woman I've ever loved directly into Harriman's hands.*

Astryd responded with calm determination. "It's not your decision, Shadow. It's mine. And I choose to go."

"No!" Taziar sprang to his feet. He measured the distance to the window.

Apparently alert to Taziar's intention, Larson blocked his escape.

"But Harriman will know . . ." Taziar started. He stopped, realizing he was about to reveal information about Harriman's master that Silme had intentionally hidden from Larson. "Silme, I need to talk with you alone." To divert Larson's suspicions, Taziar glanced at Astryd as he spoke.

"Fine." Silme stood, walked to the door, opened it, and gazed into the hallway. "It's clear."

Taziar drew the hood of his spare cloak over his head and followed Silme into the passageway. She closed the door, and he kept his back to the hall so that anyone who passed would not recognize him. "Harriman's master can access Allerum's thoughts. Surely, he knows what we all look like."

"Certainly," Silme agreed. "But Harriman knows only what his master chooses to tell him. That could be nothing. Unlikely, but possible. Even then, it takes time to memorize features well enough to send images. The master wouldn't be able to show Harriman what we look like. That would be like an artist trying to draw a detailed picture of a stranger after only a few brief glimpses. He'd have to give Harriman a verbal description. You gave one of the best I've ever heard when you described Harriman, but I wouldn't have slain the first person on Cullinsberg's streets who fit the description. How would you portray Astryd?"

Taziar shrugged. "Small, short blonde hair, beautiful, female. Carries a staff with a garnet in it."

"Exactly." Silme smiled. "Take away the staff and that fits an eighth of Norway's population."

"Norway's population," Taziar repeated forcefully. "Not Cullinsberg's. Mardain's mercy, Silme, she's got an unmistakable accent. Isn't there something you can do to disguise her?"

Silme leaned against the door to their room. "I suppose. But do you think we have time to shop now? And do you really believe it would matter? New clothes and some makeup isn't going to do much to change a description Harriman only knows from vague reports anyway, other than to draw suspicion if it's noticed."

"I meant some sort of magical disguise." Taziar had never seen any Dragonrank mage change his appearance, even the ugly or elderly ones. But his contact with the rare sorcerers was limited to Silme, Astryd, and the few meetings they led him into, most notably his excursion to the Dragonrank school; and the situation seemed too dangerous not to ask. "Isn't there some way she could make herself look different, even if just to Harriman?"

Silme shook her head. "The mind barriers keep sorcerers from casting anything that works by modifying other people's perceptions or intentions, like dreams or illusions.

That's what makes Allerum's lack of mind barriers so dangerous. When he first came here, we couldn't trust anything he saw or heard. His every mood was suspect. Luckily, he learned how to tell when sorcerers tried to manipulate him and even how to fight back a bit.''

Taziar listened carefully. Though quick to revert to English words and a strange, distant morality, Larson doggedly avoided talking about the more serious aspects of his past.

Silme continued, "I might be able to enter Harriman's mind, but not without risking a confrontation with his master." She frowned, and fear touched her expression briefly.

Taziar stared. Never before had he seen Silme appear any way except in complete control of a situation.

Silme recovered quickly. "To actually alter Astryd would take phenomenal amounts of magic, certainly more than she has or can afford to waste. Even if she managed it, she'd never get herself back to looking exactly the way she does now."

Taziar shivered at the thought. It was Astryd he loved, not her appearance, but he wondered if he could still consider her the same person with unrecognizable features on a face he had come to use as the standard for beauty. *And even if Harriman doesn't recognize her, what if he finds her as attractive as I do?* The image returned, of the nobleman calmly blocking a berserk's punch, tearing Skereye away from his victim like a starved lion from its kill. *Harriman's strong, bold to the point of insanity, and Astryd's never had to physically defend herself against any man larger than me.* "It's too dangerous."

Silme sighed in exasperation, naturally assuming Taziar was still concerned about Harriman identifying Astryd. "She can leave the staff and take another name. This is a huge city. She can't be the only Norse woman in Cullinsberg. Besides, Shadow, everyone in the town would recognize you. Only Harriman might know Astryd. She may even be able to avoid him completely. Harriman may leave the simple chores, like hiring new girls, to his underlings. And you're forgetting the most important thing. If she gets into trouble, Astryd can transport back to us almost instantly. Can you do that?" Her gray eyes probed in question.

Taziar's rebuttal died in his throat. *That's true. As long as Astryd can transport, she's in no danger.* He managed a grimace of acceptance. "You're right, as always. But before she goes, I want to talk to her. I need to describe the layout of the whorehouse, to name some of the people, and give her some directions."

Silme clapped a hand to Taziar's shoulder, too relieved to quibble. "Take all the time you need."

Astryd threaded through the maze of city streets, concentrating on Taziar's complicated series of directions designed, it seemed, to keep her clear of back roads and shadowed alleys. Though still touched by fatigue, nervous energy drove her to shy at every sudden movement. Her edginess drew unwanted attention. The afternoon crowds eyed her with pity, questioning her intelligence or passing whispered comments about the tiny, young woman with no man to protect her from thieves. Under ordinary circumstances, Astryd would have found the citizens' concern amusing, but two days of draining her life energy nearly to nothing had left her more exhausted than a morning nap could overcome. Her aura spread around her, its usual brilliant white sheen dulled by weariness, its edges dark. Anxiety kept her hyperalert; each movement claimed more vitality than normal, fraying the fringes of her aura.

Astryd took slow, deep breaths. Gradually, the rapid hammering of her heart slackened, and she was able to pay closer attention to the shops and landmarks Taziar had detailed. She tried to recall the list of names and descriptions of people she might encounter in Shylar's whorehouse, but it all blended into a verbal lump of colors and shapes; the odd, Cullinsbergen names all sounded alike to her. The realization triggered another burst of stress. She calmed herself using the mental techniques taught in the Dragonrank school.

Astryd turned another corner, and, by means of a rotting signpost, identified her new location as Panogya Street. *Magic or not, I'm the most ill-suited for this task. What does a shipbuilder's daughter know of espionage?* Until Astryd's dragonmark had appeared seven years ago, she had spent a carefree childhood helping her mother and sisters sew clothes and prepare meals or skipping across the timbers her father and brothers used to construct the fishing boats. Every spring, as ice dissolved from the harbors, the thaw turned men restless. Many sailed off, in dragon-prowed ships crafted or patched by her father, to seek war and win treasures in distant lands. They returned, scarred but wealthy, sharing their spoils with a rowdy generosity. But Astryd's father and brothers never joined them. She had come by her slight stature honestly, by breeding, and her menfolk's small hands were unfit for wielding their heavy-bladed axes in wild battles. The most exciting ventures of her town she knew of only distantly and vicariously, from stories leaked thirdhand after drunken boasts in the village tavern.

Spending eleven months of each year at the Dragonrank school, Astryd had learned much of strength, meditation, and magic, but little of human nature. She spent her one month vacations with her family. But the fisherfolk treated her with uncharacteristic reverence. The boys she grew up with had married during her absence, and her relationships with people were as stilted and ungainly as those of a child playing at being an adult.

Astryd's reminiscences brought her to the polished wooden door of Shylar's whorehouse. She wiped sweating palms on her cloak, and smoothed the skirts beneath it, and tried, again, to remain composed. Only minimally successful, she hoped the men would attribute her discomfort to the understandable nervousness of a woman requesting employment in a whorehouse. *It may appear appropriate, but it won't help my powers of observation or make my task any easier.* Resigned, Astryd tapped a fist against the door.

Several seconds went by while Astryd feigned engrossment in the panel, avoiding the smug glances of passersby. Then, the door swung open and a male face peered out. "Yes?"

"I'm looking for a job," Astryd said, wishing she sounded less timid.

The man studied Astryd in the afternoon sunlight. Frowning, he gestured her into the entryway. When she stepped through, he closed the door behind her.

"Cooking and cleaning," Astryd clarified. "And running errands."

The man shook his head. "We have someone who cooks, and the girls pitch in with the other jobs. But I'll ask the master." He marched forward. The hallway ended in a door. Pulling it open, he gestured Astryd through it.

Astryd found herself in a huge, open room where women lounged in brightly-colored dresses styled to accentuate the bulges of breasts and thighs. A smaller number of men sat, mixed in with the girls. All discussion ceased as Astryd appeared, and every eye turned toward her. She met their gazes without flinching, making no judgments. Discovering the woman she had seen in her location spell, she smiled.

"Wait here." The man's tone seemed more suited to a threat than a suggestion. He trotted past the base of a staircase and through a door just beyond it.

As the conversations resumed, Astryd turned her attention to the layout of the whorehouse. The walls of the meeting room were painted a soft, baby blue, interrupted by a pair of doors in the farthest corner of the left wall that Taziar had explained led to matched bargaining rooms. The chambers above them remained in perpetual darkness, and knotholes in the floor allowed their occupants to hear and observe any business being conducted in the rooms below. To Astryd's right, the staircase led to the bedrooms, and the door the man had gone through opened onto the kitchen and private rooms of the women who lived here.

Shortly, the kitchen door was wrenched open. The man who had met Astryd emerged first, followed by Harriman and his bodyguards. Harriman was wiping his hands on a rag. His gaze roved up and down Astryd with the intensity of a man purchasing expensive merchandise. His expression never changed, but the movement of his fingers on the cloth slowed and became mechanical.

Astryd shivered. *Does he look at everyone this way? Does he like my appearance? Does he recognize me?* Harriman stepped around the man in front of him and tossed the rag at him. The other man fumbled it, then caught it in a two-handed grip. He sidled out of the way to give Halden and Skereye room to pass.

Astryd looked up at Harriman, studying bland features that appeared more kindly than she'd expected. Taziar's warning rose from memory. *"You're gathering information, Astryd. Don't try anything recklessly heroic. If you get Harriman alone in a position where you can easily kill him and escape, try it. But don't risk your life and destroy your cover for vague possibilities."* The thought of Taziar condemning headstrong courage made her grin.

Apparently thinking Astryd's expression was intended for him, Harriman returned the smile. "Fine. You can start today. Keep the dust off the walls and furnishings and make sure the beds are made. In return, we'll give you room and board. Don't take anything that doesn't belong to you. I'll expect you to run errands for anyone here who asks, but you take your final commands from me. Whatever I say, you do. Understand?"

Astryd nodded. Her glance strayed beyond Harriman to his bodyguards. They towered nearly half again her height; a layer of fat fleshed out their muscles, sacrificing definition for girth. Their scarred features and glazed eyes looked familiar. Astryd had known men addicted to the berserker mushrooms and the blood-frenzy of Viking raids who lived in desperate misery between sessions of pirating. She knew they would prove ferocious and unpredictable warriors, undaunted by pain.

Harriman gestured toward the staircase. "Get to work." He looked beyond Astryd. "Mat-hilde, you come with me. We need to talk." He spun on a heel and trotted up the steps, Halden and Skereye directly behind him.

The woman Harriman had indicated swallowed hard, and several others flinched in sympathy. With a slowness indicating reluctance, Mat-hilde uncrossed her ankles, rose from a stool, and yanked at the clinging fabric of her dress. Astryd read fear in Mat-hilde's eyes, and saw the woman shiver as she climbed the stairs.

Astryd seized the rag from the man's hands and followed, certain of two things. *The exchange won't be pleasant, and I'm going to know why.* She watched as Mat-hilde entered a room. Astryd caught a glimpse of Skereye's back and the corner of a bed before the door slammed shut.

Astryd scurried past rows of bedrooms. The door before the room Harriman had chosen for his conference was closed, but the panel of the next chamber stood ajar. Astryd peeked through the crack into a cramped, pink-walled room with no windows. The bed sheets and coverlet lay rumpled, and a nightstand held a flickering lantern. *Perfect.* Astryd slipped within, pulling the door closed behind her. Aware that the walls would have been built thick enough to block out sounds from neighboring rooms, Astryd tapped her life energy to accentuate her hearing. She pressed an ear to the partition, but Mat-hilde's voice wafted to her as an incomprehensible whisper.

Astryd drew more life force to her, channeling it into her spell. Her aura dimmed, then flared back to blend in tone with the half-lit room.

". . . and Shylar always said we don't have to do anything we don't feel comfortable doing."

Astryd heard the unmistakable sound of a slap, followed by a shrill gasp and a stumbling step. Harriman's voice sounded as loud as a scream. "Shylar's gone, damn it! I'm in charge now, and I say you do whatever the customer wants. Do you understand that?"

Harriman's words pounded Astryd's magically acute hearing, causing pain. She back-stepped, clamping a hand to her ringing ear. Turning, she pressed her other ear to the wall, felt the surface cold against her cheek.

Astryd heard no reply from Mat-hilde. Another slap reverberated through the room, and some piece of furniture scraped across the floor. "I asked if you understand."

Mat-hilde's voice held the hesitant, breathy quality of tears withheld. "I . . . understand."

"Good girl." Harriman spoke condescendingly, the way a man might praise a dog. A moment later, the door opened.

Astryd backed away from the wall, furiously pretending to dust. She heard the heightened stomp of footsteps as Harriman and his guards retreated down the hallway and the clomp as they descended the stairs. Quickly, Astryd dismissed her spell, pocketed the rag, and entered the room Harriman had vacated. Mat-hilde perched on the edge of the bed. The corners of her mouth quivered downward as she fought to keep from crying.

Astryd let the door click shut behind her. Without a word, she crossed the chamber, sat beside Mat-hilde, and wrapped her arms around the prostitute's shoulders.

Mat-hilde stiffened, resisting Astryd even as she struggled to contain her tears. Then, apparently reading sincere concern in Astryd's touch, Mat-hilde softened. Her sinews uncoiled, and her tears fell, warm and moist, on Astryd's neck. Astryd drew Mat-hilde closer; each sob made the

sorceress ache with sympathy. Finally Mat-hilde pulled
away, and the crying jag died to sniffles.

Astryd hesitated, torn between urgency and the need to
take the time to gain Mat-hilde's trust. The thought of taking advantage of Mat-hilde's vulnerability repulsed Astryd,
but she saw no other way. "Why do you stay with Harriman
if he treats you so badly?"

Mat-hilde looked up sharply. Tears clung to her lashes,
but she squinted in suspicion. "Who are you?"

Caught off-guard by Mat-hilde's sudden change in manner, Astryd stammered. "I—I'm a friend of Shylar's."

The creases in Mat-hilde's rounded face deepened. She
studied Astryd with the same intensity as Harriman had
used downstairs.

Knowing that any simple question would reveal her lie,
Astryd amended in the only way that occurred to her. "I'm
the friend of a friend, really. I've never actually met Shylar,
but we're going to free her." Astryd held her breath, aware
all chance of success now depended on Taziar being right
about the prostitutes retaining loyalty to Shylar. *And Mat-
hilde's use of the madam's name when Harriman confronted
her suggests the probability.*

Mat-hilde continued to stare. The hem of her dress had
balled up so it now revealed the edges of a gauzy undergar-
ment, but she made no move to straighten it. "You're with
Taz Medakan, aren't you?"

Startled by the directness of the question, Astryd answered too quickly. "Who?" She tried to sound confused,
but managed only to appear nervous.

"Honey." Mat-hilde brushed moisture from her eyes, revealing irises the color of oak. "If you're not going to trust
me, how can you expect me to trust you?"

Aware she was outclassed in affairs of subterfuge, Astryd
dropped all pretenses and relied on her instincts. Mat-hilde
seemed kindly and forthright. "Yes, I'm with Shadow . . .
I mean, Taz." She tensed, waiting for a shout or an attack.
When none came, curiosity overcame apprehension. "But
how could you possibly know that?"

Mat-hilde smiled. "You live among the underground, you
learn to pay attention. Taz came back here and got a greeting he didn't expect." The grin vanished, and she cringed
in remembrance. "We all know he escaped the baron's

guards by crossing the Kattegat. Then a Norse woman shows up here asking for work at a time when most girls would rather take their chances on the street. When you claimed to be a friend of Shylar's friend, it seemed the only answer."

Astryd frowned, displeased by the ease with which Mat-hilde had targeted her. "I just hope Harriman doesn't put the clues together."

"Men are stupid," Mat-hilde said in a voice that implied she used the phrase with such frequency it had become habit.

"Some," Astryd agreed. "But I can't count on my enemies being the feebleminded ones." Astryd pulled her knees to her chest, watching lantern light flicker through the misty-gray remnants of her life aura. "Don't you believe Taziar is a traitor? No one else we've met seems to have the slightest doubt."

Mat-hilde snorted. "Taziar Medakan a traitor?" She snorted again. "Men are stupid," she repeated in the same tone as before. "Taz has got more morality in him than any ten people together. The men in the underground get so used to constructing evidence and changing circumstance that they fall prey to it if someone does it better than they can. I think it's pride." Mat-hilde straightened, finally tugging her dress back into its proper position. "Besides, men say things and show sides of themselves to women they wouldn't ever let anyone else see. And they brag." Mat-hilde rolled her eyes. "When we girls put enough stories together, we learn a lot. Sure, the evidence against Taz is overwhelming, but there's other things besides evidence to consider. Instead of ten percent, Taz used to donate fifty, sometimes ninety percent of his paid heists to Shylar. Then he'd go out on the streets and hand most of the remainder to street orphans and beggars. Does that sound like the kind of person who would turn traitor?"

"Of course not." Astryd savored her rising excitement. *I've found a friend.* "But I'm biased."

Mat-hilde gave Astryd a knowing look that implied she guessed more than Astryd had revealed. "I don't think you came to listen to me ramble on about men. What do you need?"

"Mostly information. First, you never told me why you're

still working for Harriman. Second, I need to know which people are loyal to Harriman and which ones would forsake him if the old leaders returned."

All sadness seemed to have left Mat-hilde's face. Only a fading red mark on her cheek remained as a reminder of the ordeal. "We stayed because Shylar told us to follow Harriman just before they arrested her. We assumed it would be temporary. Shylar's got a lot of connections. As for loyalty . . ." Mat-hilde considered. "Harriman brought those two ugly, blond monsters with him. They follow his every command, and they're always at his side."

"Always?" Astryd prodded.

Mat-hilde loosed a short laugh. "Always," she confirmed. "They eat with him. They sleep in his room. When he goes off to relieve himself . . ." She trailed off.

Astryd crinkled her mouth in disgust. "They go off with him?"

"Always," Mat-hilde confirmed.

Astryd made a mild noise of revulsion. *So much for an easy opportunity to kill Harriman and escape.* "What about the rest of the underground?"

"Harriman pulled in some of the 'fringe guard.' Shylar kept in contact with a few strong-arm men she called on when some rare circumstance required violence. Harriman brought those men to the forefront of the underground. They've got more power and money than they used to, so they'll probably remain loyal to Harriman." Mat-hilde traced a floorboard with her cloth shoe. "There's twelve or fourteen of them. Taz should know who they are. As for the others, they'd be thrilled to abandon Harriman for Shylar and the imprisoned leaders. Careful, though," Mat-hilde warned. "I have no doubt they'll welcome Shylar back, but they still believe Taz informed on her. If they see him, they'll turn him over to Harriman or kill him. And, honey, it's possible even Shylar believes Taziar is the traitor."

Relief flooded Astryd, despite the fact that she wasn't out of danger yet. *I've got the information I came for, and it was easier than I expected.* "Thanks, Mat-hilde, for your trust and the facts. We'll do all we can to free Shylar and the others, I promise."

"I'm not certain it's possible," Mat-hilde admitted. "Then again, Taz had done a number of things I didn't think possible." She took Astryd's hand and squeezed encouragingly.

Astryd felt the warm flush of jealousy. Surprised by her own reaction, she tried to override emotion with rationalization. *She knew Shadow for years before I met him. She's a friend; she's not trying to take him from me. We're on the same side.* Astryd returned the handclasp.

Mat-hilde released Astryd. "When do you expect to try this prison break?"

"Tomorrow morning."

"More specifically?" Mat-hilde pressed.

"I don't know." Interest replaced rivalry. "Why?"

Mat-hilde shook back a mane of dark hair. "Because, if I'm careful, I should be able to send information about the escape to the right people and have them here to help depose Harriman. But he'll get suspicious if I have a large group of people sitting around all day."

Though short a significant amount of life energy, exhilaration lent Astryd a second wind. *Information and allies. What more could we ask for?* "I need to take what I know back to Taziar and try to find out a time for you." *That means I need the freedom to come and go from here as I please, hopefully without having to resort to magic each time.*

"Go," Mat-hilde encouraged. "Tell Harriman I sent you out for combs and food. He'll believe that, and I'll back it up."

A sudden knock on the door startled Astryd. A muffled female shout followed. "Mat-hilde?"

"Go on." Mat-hilde indicated the door. "Let them in on your way out. I'll take care of things."

Astryd rose. She pulled the panel open, and was immediately confronted by five prostitutes with worried faces. They stared as she slipped past, then entered the room in response to some gesture from Mat-hilde that Astryd did not see. As she reached the top of the stairwell, the sorceress heard the door snap closed behind her.

Astryd took the steps two at a time. Her mission had turned out more successfully than she'd ever expected. Though dingy and partially spent, her life aura remained strong enough for a few spells at least, more than enough for an emergency transport escape. Still, a sense of foreboding tempered Astryd's joy. In spite of greater numbers, the peaceful members of the underground might not hold out against Harriman and his warriors. The prison break would require a skill even Taziar might not possess, despite the help of a garnet-rank sorceress. And when it was all over, they might still have to face Harriman's master.

Engrossed in thought, Astryd nearly collided with Skereye at the base of the stairs. Startled, she skittered sideways and stumbled over the last step. A hand seized her forearm, steadying her. She glanced up at her benefactor, recognized Harriman's placid features, and a shiver racked her. A burst of surprise nearly caused her to trigger the transport escape, but Astryd held her magics. A spell cast in panic always cost more energy, and the need to break Harriman's grip would have increased the toll on her life force. *Besides, using sorcery now would certainly reveal me and destroy any chance of returning.* Instead, Astryd showed Harriman a weak smile. "Forgive my clumsiness." She tossed a glance around the conference room, noticed six large men with callused hands and scarred faces, and felt even more certain of her decision not to depart with magic. *Something's going on. I think I'd better know what.*

Attentive to the gathered warriors, Astryd missed the nonverbal exchange between Harriman and a stout, greasy man who stood before the door to the entry hall. Harriman's grip tightened, and Astryd twisted back to face him. "What's your name, Missy?"

"Linnea," Astryd replied, choosing the name of one of her sisters for convenience. She trained her gaze on Harriman's hand on her sleeve as an obvious suggestion that he remove his grasp.

To Astryd's surprise, Harriman released her. "Well, Linnea. This is Saerle." He beckoned to the man by the door who trotted forward. "Take him upstairs and do *anything* he asks."

Dread tightened Astryd's throat. She knew better than to protest; that could only earn her Harriman's wrath. *Casting an escape before one man must be safer and less conspicuous than in a crowd.* She maintained her composure. *I may even have enough life energy to evade Saerle and still listen in on Harriman's meeting. So long as I keep enough for a transport, I'm in no danger.*

Astryd studied Saerle. His round face sported a day's

growth of beard. A receding semicircle of sand-colored hair revealed a moist forehead, and his green-gray eyes regressed into sockets deep as a skull's. Three bottles of wine swung from between his fingers, the color of the vintage obscured by the thickness of the glass. "Come on," Astryd said. Though revolted by the thought of touching Saerle, she caught his wrist and pattered up the staircase.

Plans swirled through Astryd's mind as they ascended the steps. A natural ability to conjure dragons had biased her repertoire toward summonings. Most of her other spells were basic shields, wards, and defenses against magic, none of which would serve in this situation. But as Saerle and Astryd crested the landing, a distant memory drifted into focus. She recalled her early years as a glass-rank sorceress when she and her peers had spent half the day fashioning wards for the outer walls of the Dragonrank school. Then, boredom had driven her to seek entertainment. By shorting the Dragonrank defenses a few spells each day, she retained enough energy at night to pull pranks on the glass-rank mages who shared her quarters. She recalled a friend sputtering over ale laced with salt and another awakening in the middle of the night, tripping and stumbling over furniture silently rearranged with magic. The remembrance made her smile. *This might prove the most amusing challenge I've ever faced.* The idea made her laugh aloud. *Amusing challenge? Thor's hammer, now I'm starting to* think *like Shadow.*

Apparently believing Astryd's pleasure was directed at him, Saerle shuffled all three bottles into his opposite hand. He ran his fingers up her arm, caressing her shoulder briefly before dropping to her breast.

The touch made Astryd's skin crawl. She shivered free, then, realizing her mistake, covered neatly. "Not so eager, handsome. We have all night." It required strength of will not to follow the words with a grunt of abhorrence. She selected an open bedchamber at random and gestured him through the portal.

The room contained a cot with a straw mattress softened with coverlets and fluffed pillows. A tall chair framed of wood stood in the farther corner, pulled away from the wall. Dark green linen stuffed with down stretched over its seat and back. A sturdy end table sat at the opposite side of the bed. Above it, a lantern hung from a ring in the ceiling, its flame flapping light through the windowless confines.

Saerle set the wine bottles on the table. Stepping around the bed to face Astryd, he poised to sit on the edge of the mattress.

Astryd closed the door. She whirled suddenly, causing her skirt to flip partially up her thigh. Having captured Saerle's attention, she invoked her life energy for a spell. Silently, the bed swung around so its side was flush with the wall. "Sit," Astryd purred.

Eyes locked on Astryd, Saerle sat where the bed had stood a moment before. He crashed to the floor, sprawling beside the mattress.

Astryd ran to his side, suppressing a snicker behind an expression of concern. It lacked the sincerity she intended to convey, but Saerle seemed too shocked to notice. His head flicked from side to side as the new location of the bed registered and he tried to figure out what had happened. Catching his forearm, Astryd helped him to his feet. "I know you're eager, handsome, but let's do this on the bed, shall we?"

Saerle nodded absently. Seizing on his confusion, Astryd unobtrusively used her magic to slide the wine-laden table out of sight behind the chair.

"How?" Saerle started. He broke off, apparently realizing there was no way to ask the question without appearing insane. His gaze wandered to the site where the table had stood and froze there. He looked at Astryd, then suddenly back at the empty space where the table should have stood.

"Is something wrong?" Astryd reached out, massaging his shoulders seductively. "You feel tense."

"I . . ." Saerle went even more rigid beneath her touch. "No-o," he said, voice cracking halfway through the word. He cleared his throat. "I'm fine." He emphasized each syllable, as if to convince himself as well as Astryd.

"Here, let me help." Astryd sat beside Saerle, her side touching his. *I hope Shadow appreciates what I'm doing for him.* She seized the lacing at Saerle's throat and gently tugged it free. Using two fingers, she loosed the tie at each eyelet. While his attention focused on her, she quietly slid the table to the end of the bed, behind him. Her life aura flickered dangerously, and she knew she could only afford one more spell if she wanted to save enough energy for a transport. Catching the hem of Saerle's shirt, she pulled it over his head and flung it over her shoulder. At her command, the homespun hovered.

Saerle jerked backward with a startled noise. "My shirt!"

Astryd stared into Saerle's widened eyes. She wrapped her fingers around his ribs, trying to draw him closer.

Saerle resisted. "My shirt. Look at my shirt!"

"What's the matter? Did I tear it?" Astryd released her magics, saw Saerle's gaze fall as she turned. The fabric lay in a rumpled pile on the floor. "It looks fine to me." She twisted back to Saerle, clamping her hands to her hips in mock offense. "Are you trying to avoid me?"

Saerle groaned.

"Here." Astryd pushed him to the coverlet. "Have some wine. It'll calm you."

"Wine?" Saerle's voice had fallen to a whisper of its former resonance.

Astryd allowed herself a giggle, and it was only the weakness of having tapped most of her life energy that saved her from breaking into a torrent of laughter. "The wine you brought."

"Where?"

Hiding a grimace, Astryd caressed Saerle's damp forehead. She smothered the urge to wipe oily sweat from her hand. "On the table where you put it, handsome."

Saerle glanced wildly toward the end of the bed, and the sight of the table with its three bottles of wine induced a guttural moan.

"I'll get it," Astryd said helpfully. She leaned across Saerle's prone form, watching the dark glow of her remaining life aura wash across him, making his olive-skinned features appear more ashen. In the flickering light of the lantern, her aura seemed to disappear into the shadows. Frowning, she grabbed the bottles with both hands and dragged them onto the bed. Fumbling the knife she used for eating and odd tasks from her pocket, she jabbed it into a cork and twisted it free. She offered the opened bottle.

Saerle accepted the wine eagerly. Without bothering to sit up, he poured. Liquid sloshed into his mouth, across his naked chest, and trickled into the mattress. He drained a third of the bottle before offering it to Astryd.

Astryd shook her head. "You need it more than I do."

Obligingly, Saerle reclaimed the bottle. Three more gulps emptied it, and Astryd handed him the next. She waited while he drank, her patience thinning. *That meeting could have started already. I can't waste all my time with this idiot.* She clamped a hand to the crotch of his breeks, felt him soft and unresponsive against her palm.

Restlessness made her movement more sudden than intended. Saerle jumped in surprise, the bottle startled from his grip. Purple wine splashed across Astryd, Saerle, and the coverlet, and the bottle thunked to the floor. The room went silent except for the steady trickle of liquid on the planks.

Gracefully, Astryd rescued the remainder of the wine, returning the bottle to Saerle. She raised a hand, making certain he noticed it before replacing it on his genitals. She fondled more carefully, felt the first hint of reaction as the wine relaxed him. Her antics had rattled him, put her fully in control, and Astryd felt reasonably sure he would agree to anything she suggested. "Ever been conquered by a woman?"

Saerle shook his head, whiskers sticky with wine. "No. How does that work?"

Astryd caught interest in Saerle's tone that went beyond sexual desire. *I wonder if he hopes I'll say it involves a third person rearranging the furniture.* "I'll show you." Astryd unbuckled Saerle's belt. Pulling it from around his waist, she looped it around his wrist and lashed it securely to the leg of the cot beneath the mattress.

Saerle finished the last mouthful of wine from the second bottle. "I'm not sure about—"

Astryd cut him off with a finger to his lips. "Relax. Enjoy it." She uncorked the last bottle and pressed it into his free palm. "Drink."

Saerle obeyed while Astryd cut her own sash in two, using the pieces to tie his ankles. She pulled the lacing from his shirt and returned to the bed. Taking the now empty wine bottle from Saerle, she bound his other hand, wincing at what she was about to do. She knelt at the bedside. Softly, she turned his face toward her. "That's not so bad, is it?'' Before Saerle could reply, she swung the bottle down, as hard as she could, against his temple.

Saerle went limp instantly, and Astryd hoped he hadn't seen the blow. A sudden thought ground fear through her. *I hope I didn't kill him.* Until that moment, it had never occurred to her that she might have the strength to take a life. She had never killed before, and the idea of doing so as a punishment for seeking paid sexual favors repulsed her. She watched Saerle, and the deep rise and fall of his breathing relieved her conscience.

"Sorry," Astryd whispered. She spread the coverlet over Saerle, carefully hiding his bindings from anyone who might peek into the room. Crossing the room with as little sound as possible, she opened the door a crack. Footsteps filled her ears. She heard a gruff male voice, his words indecipherable, followed by a high-pitched giggle. Then a door slammed and the hallway fell silent.

Astryd slipped from the room. Most of the doors were closed. At the far end of the hall, the storage chamber doors overlooking the bargaining rooms stood ajar. *It must be approaching sundown.* Astryd winced, aware her friends would soon begin to worry about her. *Where would Harriman hold a meeting? Probably not up here; he'll need these rooms for business.*

She edged toward the stairs. At the top, she took a surreptitious glance into the main conference area. Three women and a man sat in discussion. Beyond them, Astryd caught a glimpse of one of Harriman's Norse bodyguards disappearing into a bargaining chamber. The door slammed shut behind him.

Astryd retreated, scarcely daring to believe her luck. Everything was falling into place. She still had enough life energy for a transport, should it become necessary. And Harriman had chosen to hold his assembly in the one place Astryd knew she could observe without being seen. She scrambled to the end of the upstairs hallway, and slipped through the gap into the room above the one the Norseman had entered.

A bar of light from the hallway penetrated a room devoid of furnishings. Astryd stepped into the center where knotholes and cracks between the floorboards gave her a view of activity below. Her aura was nearly lost in the darkness, no brighter than the light leeching through the doorway. Alone, without the nervous enthusiasm of Saerle's challenge, her head buzzed and her limbs felt heavy. She sat, cross-legged, on the paneling, hunched forward for a complete view of the chamber beneath her.

The six grim-faced warriors perched on chairs and stools. Before them, Harriman stood with his arms folded across his chest, flanked by Halden and Skereye. Astryd had to strain to hear his words. "I know . . . location of that . . . traitor . . . Medakan." Every few syllables, his voice fell too low for her to comprehend.

Suddenly alert, Astryd realized the importance of catching every word. A choice confronted her, and she felt too tired to make it. *If I enhance my hearing, I won't have enough energy left for an emergency escape.* The word "murder" wafted clearly to her, and she made her decision. She shaped her magics to listen, feeling dizzy and emptied as the spell wrung vigor from her. She waited until her head stopped spinning, and Harriman's speech became clear.

". . . female, so he has only one fighting friend to help him. A team of women should be able to handle that." Harriman's gaze traveled over each of the men before him. Briefly, he glanced upward.

Astryd went utterly still.

Harriman's eyes never stopped to fully focus, and he continued without a pause or signal to indicate he had seen anything. "Bring him in alive, it's worth a thousand weight in gold. Dead, it's a hundred." He hesitated, allowing time for the mentioned fortunes to register in every mind. "If you don't bring him back, I'd better find out he killed you all. And if he can do that, you've gone softer than my mother."

The warriors met Harriman's statement with grunts of amusement or denial. One cursed Harriman beneath his breath, and his words floated, garbled even to Astryd's heightened hearing.

"I'll get to the plan in a moment," Harriman continued. "But first, I've had a couple too many beers." He made a gesture Astryd could not see, and the men laughed. She watched him open the door, slip through with Halden and Skereye, and close the panel behind them.

Astryd leaned forward with a sigh. Every moment she held the spell cost her life force, but it was still far less than recasting. She waited, not bothering to focus on the warriors' conversations about weaponry. Shortly, she heard the pounding of footfalls on the steps, and terror drove her to her feet. She measured the distance to the door, aware she could never make it back to Saerle in time. *Loki's evil children!* The words seemed as much description as blasphemy. Rummaging through her pockets, she discovered the cleaning rag she had stuffed there. She wrenched it free. The movement flung her knife into the air. Desperately, she grabbed for it, juggled it once, then crammed it back in place. Hurriedly, she went to work dusting a corner as the door creaked fully open.

Astryd whirled, not having to feign her startlement. Harriman and his bodyguards stood in the doorway. The hall lantern threw their shadows across Astryd. "What are you doing here?"

"Cleaning," Astryd replied sweetly.

"Cleaning?" Harriman repeated without accusation. "In the dark?"

"There's no lantern in here. And there was enough light from the hall—" Astryd broke off, abruptly realizing her mistake. Taziar had told her the spying rooms were left dark. With the bargaining rooms lit, it accorded a perfect view from the upper room down, but did not allow the people in the lower room to see up between the boards. *But I left the door partway open. Apparently, Harriman saw. I've used my last spell, and now I'm in trouble.* She covered quickly. She reached for the knife in her pocket, closing her hand over the hilt. "The door was ajar. That means I'm supposed to clean it, right?"

"Usually," Harriman agreed. "But right now you're supposed to be with a client."

Astryd hesitated, exhausted. She knew too little of warfare to dream of killing a man with a single stroke of a knife. Even a lucky stab at Harriman would not rescue her from the berserks. "He's asleep. So I went back to work."

"He paid for the night." Harriman's tone betrayed no anger or suspicion. "Asleep or not, you stay with him."

Astryd nodded, not daring to believe she would get off this easily. Once Harriman returned to the meeting, she could still sneak away and warn Taziar, Larson, and Silme. "All right. I didn't know. I'm sorry."

Harriman stepped aside. Astryd wandered around him, tensed for an attack, but he made no movement toward her. Instead, he watched her stagger to Saerle's room.

Astryd released pent up breath in a ragged sigh. Catching the handle, she pulled open the door, unable to recall the panel feeling so heavy before. From the corner of her eye, she glimpsed Harriman's gesture, and his harsh voice followed. "Skereye, stay right by the door and make certain she doesn't leave until morning."

Horror crushed down on Astryd, and she tottered awkwardly into the room. The door crashed shut, leaving her with a comatose client tied to the bed and awash in panic that drained life energy nearly as fast as a spell. *Harriman must know who I am. Why else would he trap me in this room?*

Astryd's life aura faded, its edges invisible, and need alone kept her conscious. Her eyes dropped closed, and rational thoughts scattered or disappeared. *Got to warn Shadow. Enemy trap. Can't go through the door. Window. Window?* Blindly, she stumbled toward the window. She dragged her limbs onward, her mind and movements thick, as if wading through water. After what seemed like an eternity, her hand struck wall. She forced her lids apart and only then realized she was crawling.

Reaching up, Astryd caught the sill. Movement drove her to the edge of oblivion. Curtains fluttered into her face, filmy and clinging. Unwilling to waste a gesture removing them, she peered through. A full story below her, a packed earth alleyway reflected the red rays of sunset in a glow that put her life aura to shame. The black shapes of rain barrels and garbage filled her vision, then spread to engulf her sight in darkness. Astryd collapsed on the whorehouse floor.

CHAPTER 8
Dim Shadows of Vengeance

The land of darkness and the shadow of death.
—Job 10:21

The last rays of sunlight slipped past the inn room window, leaving the chamber awash in the red glow of the fire. Half-sitting, half-crouched on his pack, Al Larson wondered what it would be like to be a father. The oldest of three children, he tried to recall his siblings' infancies. His sister was scarcely two years younger, and his brother's babyhood faded into a muddled remembrance of wet burps and diapers. *I doubt Silme and I will have plastic bottles and jars of mashed peas.* The thought made Larson smile. He glanced at Silme, perched on the logs by the hearth, eyelids half-closed as she rehearsed some meditative technique too softly for him to hear. The hearth fire accentuated rosy cheeks and unlined features. Hair swept around her shoulders in thick, golden waves. The firelight carved a spindly imitation of perfect curves in a shadow on the floor beside her.

Larson looked away. Memories swept down on him then; though they lacked the nightmarish reality of the flashbacks, they seemed every bit as cruel. He pictured Silme's bumbling, raven-haired apprentice, Brendor, and recalled how he and Silme had planned to raise the boy as a son, until an enemy's magic had turned Brendor into a soulless killing machine. Larson could still feel the pressure and warmth of the boy against him as Brendor wrenched him to the ground with the inhuman strength of the sorcerer who controlled him. The child's grip seemed permanently impressed on Larson's flesh, the knife the boy plunged for his throat a constant in his mind's eye.

Remembrance of Silme's magic tearing apart the body that had once housed Brendor's spirit still brought tears to

177

Larson's eyes, and the image of the child's glazed blue eyes and blood-splattered features drove him nearly to the madness that had engulfed him at the time. Then the incident had sent him flashing back to Ti Sun, a Vietnamese boy with whom he had shared conversation and chocolate. Now, it came to him in fragments: the hidden grenade in the boy's hand that Larson had not seen, his buddy's gun howling, bullets tearing through the child, one moment so alive, the next as empty as his stained and tattered clothes, the rage that had churned up inside Larson and spurred him to batter his companion in a wild, irrational frenzy.

Larson winced, gritting his teeth against a memory too deeply engraved to keep from sliding into his mind next. Again, he saw Silme, blood trickling from a corner of her mouth, driven to her knees by his blind and misdirected attack, out of time and place. *And all of it because we dared to subject a child to my insanity and our enemies.*

One more boy entered Larson's thoughts, his younger brother, Timmy. Larson had enlisted in the army to ease the hardships on his family after his father's untimely death in an automobile accident with a drunken driver. *Timmy always felt betrayed, that Dad "abandoned" us. Eventually, he'll be old enough to stop blaming Dad for his death. But I promised Timmy we'd always be together, then ran off to a foreign land . . . and died there.* Guilt hammered Larson. When he had left for Vietnam, he was too concerned about grappling with his own mixture of fear and excitement to notice the expression of hostility and grief on Timmy's face. *Then and there, I could have comforted him, put things right. But I didn't. I was too goddamned worried about my own pain.* Only much later did the vision haunt Al Larson. And, by then, there was nothing left to say or do. *The same magical thinking that allows a child to believe his father died to punish him might force Timmy to think his bitterness killed his brother.* Remorse balled in Larson's gut, making him feel ill. *What a burden for a child to have to live with.*

Larson lowered his head. *Barely twenty, one semester of college, a war, and now I have a wife and almost a child.* Panic touched him. He glanced at Silme again, saw a woman more beautiful than any model or actress he could recall. *I'm not even old enough to drink yet. I never got to vote for a president, but I was old enough to die for him.*

Larson stared at Silme until his vision blurred and her form went as hazy and unrecognizable as her shadow. Still, the sight of her filled him with joy, and the thought of losing her inspired a wild urge to sweep her into his arms. *I love her more than anything before in my life.* Doubts smothered devotion in a rush. *But I'm not fit to be a father. I'm too young. I'm too inexperienced. And I've lost decency, sanity, and all sense of fairness in a mindless war. What sort of warped morality could I give to a son or daughter? Silme and the baby deserve better than I can offer.*

Seeking a replacement, Larson turned his attention to Taziar. The Climber had been pacing from door to window for the last hour. Now, Larson noticed a change in Taziar's patter, and curiosity dove self-deprecation and fear from his thoughts. Taziar's course was becoming shorter. He was turning farther from the door and pausing at the window with each pass. And Larson felt fairly certain Taziar had no idea what he was doing. *But I know. Any second now, that little thief is going out the window.*

Feigning indifference, Larson rose and stretched. He watched Taziar stare out the window at the grimy walls across the alleyway for some time before he whirled and started back toward the table. Quickly, Larson crossed the room to the window, not surprised to see Taziar spin back even before the Climber reached the center of the chamber. Casually, Larson placed a hand on each shutter and waited.

Five steps brought Taziar to the window again. He stopped there, palms pressed to the sill, blue eyes focused distantly, seemingly oblivious to Larson's presence. He shifted his grip, leaving a sweaty print on the ledge. Suddenly, he tensed.

Larson slammed the shutters closed. Wood thunked against flesh, and the panels rebounded open. Taziar sprang backward with a startled cry. He nursed the fingers of his left hand, eyes wide and turned on Larson in shocked accusation. "Why did you do that?"

Larson caught the swinging shutters and nudged them closed more gently. "That's 'why the *hell* did I do that?' Don't you people know how to swear?"

Taziar rubbed his pinched fingers. "You *jerk!*" he said in stilted, heavily-accented English. "Why in *Karana's deepest, darkest, frozen pits of hell* would you do something like that?"

Larson resisted the impulse to answer "sport." "You were about to climb through that window, weren't you?"

"No!" Taziar responded instantly, then paused in consideration.

"Admit it."

"No," Taziar repeated less forcefully. "But now that you raised the subject, Astryd's been gone far too long."

"I didn't raise the subject, you just did." Larson leaned against the shutters. "But you're right. That's why I'm going after her."

"You?" Taziar and Silme spoke simultaneously, in the same incredulous tone.

"Me?" Larson mimicked. "Yes, me. Of course, me. I am, in fact, the only logical choice. Astryd can transport. If she's not back, it's because someone's holding her. That someone has to be defeated. I may not be the best swordsman in the world, but I'd venture to guess I could beat either of you."

"I can think of other reasons Astryd might not have returned yet," Taziar shot back, his injured hand forgotten. "She may still be gathering information. She could have gotten lost. We can't all go. Someone has to stay here in case she returns. Rescuing her may require stealth and knowledge of the city, so I'm the one to go."

Larson glanced past Taziar, saw Silme shaking her head in disagreement. "I can handle 'stealth,' and I know Cullinsberg as well as Astryd." Though irrelevant, Larson made the latter statement sound as if it held some grand significance. "Besides, even lost, she could still transport. If she's gathering information and you show up, everyone will try to kill you. Plus, they'll know Astryd's with you and try to kill her, too. But no one knows me."

Taziar tossed a meaningful look at Silme who became suddenly engrossed in the fire.

Lacking the knowledge to make sense of the exchange, Larson dismissed it. "Then it's settled. I go. You stay with Silme." Larson hated to use guilt as a tool against Taziar, but he saw no other way to keep the Climber from taking off on his own. "If anything happens to her or my baby while I'm gone, I'm holding you responsible." Larson winced, not liking the sound of his own threat. Ignoring Silme's glare, he crossed the room, opened the door, and slipped into the hallway.

The panel clicked closed behind Larson. Through it, he heard Taziar's muffled shout of protest and Silme's curt reply distorted beyond understanding. Larson trotted down the corridor. Soon his companions' voices faded into the obscurity of a dirty passage, its chipped, indigo paint revealing a previous layer of white. Blue flakes crunched beneath Larson's boots, and he trod carefully across boards, warped by water, to the staircase at the farther end. In the center of the steps, the passage of countless feet had worn down its carpet to the planks. But at the corners, the dark brown wool appeared new. Larson passed no one as he shuffled down the three flights into a back room grimier than the halls. A door to his left led to the common room; a wild clamor of voices drifted from beneath it. Choosing the opposite door, he emerged into the alley beneath the chamber window.

The wind felt comfortably cool to Larson after hours sitting idle before the hearth fire. He had grown accustomed to the smoke; the crisp air made his eyes water and the night seemed unusually clear. Around the spires of the baron's keep, he caught a vivid view of stars, like pinholes in black velvet, and picked out the constellation of Orion. Then his instincts took over. He discarded the beauty of the night sky as insignificant background. Alert for movement, he abandoned the alley for a cobbled main street and delved Taziar's directions to Astryd from his memory.

The street stood deserted, the shops closed and dark, the sidewalk stands vacated for the night. The merchants had hauled away their wares, leaving wooden skeletons or empty wagons, some protected from the elements with tarps. Larson moved quickly and smoothly, keeping to the edges where the walkways met the streets and away from the yawning darkness of alleys and smaller thoroughfares. A noise snapped through the darkness. Larson flattened against a cart, eyes probing. Across the road, a gray sheet of canvas fluttered like a ghost in the breeze. Larson loosed a pent up breath and continued.

Thoughts of survival channeled aside Larson's concerns and self-doubts. His abilities as a father paled before the more urgent matter of Astryd's safety. Lacking information, he had made no plan, and Kensei Gaelinar's words emerged from memory, equally as alarming as they were comforting: "A warrior makes his plans in the instant between sword strokes." But Gaelinar had been capable of split second strategies and instantaneous wisdom. As much as Larson tried to emulate the Kensei, he doubted he would ever learn such a skill. *My mind doesn't work that fast.* But, this time, Larson knew his life and Astryd's might depend on it.

Larson turned a corner onto another main street and immediately realized he was no longer alone. Half a dozen men stood in a cluster. Their breath emerged as white puffs in the cold. Their conversation wafted indistinctly to Larson. Darkness robbed him of his color vision, making them appear as caricatures in black and gray. Trained to mistrust groups in towns, Larson backpedaled. Before he could duck back around the turn, he saw an arm rise and a finger aimed in his direction. Every head turned toward him.

Something seemed vaguely familiar about the men, but Larson did not take time to ponder. He dodged around the corner and broke into a hunched run. The men gave chase. Their footfalls clattered along the empty streets. Larson quickened his pace. Realizing he was on a straightaway, he skittered into an alley, then sprinted around the first narrow branchway. His boot came down on something soft. A screech rent the air. A claw swished across leather, and a cat raced deeper into the shadows. Off-balanced, Larson careened into a rain barrel. Icy water sloshed on his chest and abdomen. He tried to compensate, but the barrel crashed into his hip with bruising force. He fought for equilibrium, lost it, tumbled and rolled. Heavy wood slammed against his foot, followed by the slap as the barrel struck the earthen floor of the alleyway.

Moisture penetrated to Larson's skin. He tensed to rise, found himself staring into a semicircle of drawn spears, and sank back to his knees. Slowly, nonthreateningly, he raised his hands. *Who are these people? What do they want?* Suddenly realizing lifted hands might not serve as a gesture of surrender in this world, he lowered them to his thighs.

"Don't move." The man directly before Larson let his spear sag and hefted a lantern. Light played over the group, revealing an array of male faces and muscled torsos clothed in black and red linen. A seventh man stood behind the others, his face a dark blur. He wore a tunic, breeks, and cloak. He carried no spear, but a sword dangled at his hip.

Uniforms of red and black. Larson relaxed and allowed himself a crooked smile. *Smart move. I just ran from the cops.*

The man with the lantern wore a silver badge on his left breast; apparently he was their leader. "What are you doing out after curfew?"

Curfew? Shadow didn't say anything about a curfew. Larson looked into the leader's round face, met eyes deep brown and demanding. *The curfew probably came as a result of the violence. Shadow wouldn't even know about it.* Larson cleared his throat. "Sorry. I'm a foreigner, and I didn't know about the curfew. A young woman friend went out this afternoon and hasn't returned. I was worried and came looking for her." Having spoken the truth, Larson had no difficulty adopting a sincere expression.

Spears bobbed as the guards shifted position. The leader seemed unimpressed. "What did you take, *thief?*" His inflection made the last term sound like the most repugnant word in Cullinsberg's language.

"Thief?" Larson repeated, his tone colored with genuine incredulity. "Don't be absurd. Do I look like the type who would steal?" Realizing he very well might, Larson tried another tactic. "If I was a thief, I wouldn't have lived this long by being inept. You never would have seen me, and you certainly wouldn't have caught me." Larson winced. Though unintentional, his comment could be taken as a backhanded insult to the guards' abilities. *And the way things are going today, that's exactly how he's going to take it.*

The leader balanced his spear with the hand he held the lantern in. Light disrupted shadow in crazed arcs. He caught a tighter one-handed grip on the shaft and raised the lantern again. "If you're not a thief, why did you run?"

Blinded by the glare, Larson blinked. "I was attacked my first day here. I saw a gang of men in the dark and mistook you for criminals." He fidgeted with impatience, and the arc of spears tightened. "Look, I didn't take anything. You're welcome to search me. Just do it quickly."

The man standing behind the guards spoke. "He took

something." The voice was dry with contempt and familiar to Larson.

The idiot I decked outside the baron's castle. Larson's skin prickled to gooseflesh. He dredged the man's name from memory. *Haimfrid.*

The leader responded without turning. "What did he take?"

"I don't know." Haimfrid shifted closer, and his features became discernible in the light. His dark hair had become even more frizzled, dried blood speckled the abrasions on his cheek and he sported a day's growth of beard. The combination gave him the look of a madman. "I'll think of something." Purposefully, his hand clamped around his sword hilt.

Larson resisted the instinct to reach for his own weapon. He already knew he could best Haimfrid in a fair fight, but the six guards would tip those odds far into Haimfrid's favor. "Haimfrid, please. What happened before was between you and me. You shouldn't drag your friends into a personal matter they know nothing about. I don't have time to fight with you."

"Is this the man . . ." the leader started.

But Haimfrid's attention was fully on Larson. "How appropriate. The worm's on his knees begging for mercy."

Anger rose in Larson, hot contrast to the damp chill of his soaked cloak. He reined his temper in easily, aware Astryd's safety depended on his dispatching this matter peacefully and with haste. "If you insist, we'll settle our differences later. Right now, a woman's life is at stake."

"What a coincidence." Haimfrid's sword jolted from its sheath with a rasp of metal. "Right now, a man's life is at stake, too. Get up and draw your weapon!"

It took every bit of self-control for Larson to remain immobile. "No, Haimfrid. I won't kill without good cause, and that incident outside the baron's castle is not good cause." *Threatening Silme was, but I can't afford to let my temper get me into trouble now.*

Haimfrid made a wild gesture with his sword, and the spearmen retreated slightly. "Get up!" he screamed.

Larson shook his head. Aware a certain amount of morality must go into the decision to become a guard and uphold the law, Larson appealed to what little sense of decency Haimfrid and his companions might harbor. "I'm not fighting. If you kill me, it's going to have to be cold-blooded murder." Despite Larson's bold pronouncement, his hand slipped unconsciously toward his hilt.

Haimfrid's left cheek turned crimson; the right twitched, lost in shadow. "Just as well. I'll butcher you like the pig you are."

The guards stepped back, closing the circle around Haimfrid and Larson. Haimfrid raised his sword to strike.

Appalled again by the guards' complete lack of respect for life and law, Larson reacted with the instinct of long practice. In a single motion, he wrenched his sword free and slashed for Haimfrid's neck. Surprised, Haimfrid sprang backward. Larson seized the opening to surge to his feet. Haimfrid swept for Larson's chest as Larson continued his maneuver with a downstroke. Haimfrid's blow fell short, but Larson's katana cleaved Haimfrid's scalp. Larson ripped the sword free and finished the pattern. He flicked the blade in a loop and splattered the startled onlookers with blood, then slid it neatly back into its sheath. Haimfrid's corpse flopped to the ground.

The lantern toppled to the dirt, splashing Larson and the guards with glass shards and burning oil. The six spears snapped into battle position in an awkward chaos of ones and twos. Though bothered by the senseless loss of life, Larson prepared to meet this new threat. He kept his hand clamped to his haft. "I'm sorry. He left me no choice. You all saw that it was self-defense. Give me some space, and we can all go in peace."

The points remained, unmoving. Larson drew his sword again, his stance light as he tried to assess all his enemies at once. The sword had scarcely left the sheath when the leader jabbed for Larson's chest. Larson parried, then ducked beneath the opening and spun past. He attempted a parting slash, but his blade skimmed across the linen covering the leader's hamstring. Afraid to turn his back to run, he completed the maneuver with a pivot that brought him around to face the guards. A spear plunged for Larson's abdomen. He deflected it with his sword, caught a glimpse of movement to his left and dodged. A spear tip tore his breeks, slashing a line of skin from his leg. Another guard thrust for him. An awkward lurch back to his left was all that saved Larson. Hard pressed by the three men before him, he was unable to guard his sides. The others slipped by him, hemming him into a circle once more.

Larson took the offensive. He sprang for the leader. A spear pierced the darkness to his left, and he redirected his strike to meet it. Steel crashed against wood. The spear retreated, and another pitched toward him from behind. Larson whirled to meet the attack. A spear butt cracked across the base of his neck. Pain shocked through him, then Larson's world exploded into darkness.

Astryd dreamed of ocean surf. She sprawled, facedown, on the rocks of a beach familiar from her childhood. Waves splashed over her, strangely warm and soothing, the wash revitalizing her where it touched. A seagull shrilled, gliding zigzags through the darkness.

Astryd's hand twitched, banging painfully against wood. She awoke with a suddenness that strained every sinew; her heart hammered in her chest. The shore became a hard, oaken floor, and the noises of the gull dissolved into Saerle's steady snores, each ending with an exhaled whistle. A band of moonlight glazed the planks.

It has to be almost morning. Astryd sprang to her feet. *I've got to get out of here before Harriman comes to check on me.* Her aura blazed around her, restored by the length and depth of her sleep. Despite concern for her companions, Astryd took some satisfaction from the strength of her life energy. *At least one good thing came out of this.* She raised a hand to cast a transport escape when a thought froze her. *Shadow's friends are due to hang tonight. He's going to need all the help I can give him, and a speck of life energy might mean the difference between life and death for all of us. I can't afford to waste it on unnecessary spells.* She studied Saerle one more time. Spread-eagled beneath the bed covers like some warped god's sacrifice, he looked as innocent as a child, and Astryd felt a pang of remorse. *I couldn't possibly have hit him hard enough to keep him out this long; it has to be the wine.* At the time, need had made her too impatient to wait for the alcohol to do its job. Now, she thanked any god who would listen that Saerle had brought it and that she had managed to force it upon him.

Turning her head, Astryd glanced out the window. Wind

plucked at a pile of scraps that had once been a child's doll, unable to blow it completely away, but sending the tatters into a wild dance. Placing her fingers on the sill, she brushed aside the curtains and glanced down. A rain barrel sat by the gutter at the corner of the building. Another stood, upended, beneath the window, moss striping the cracks between closely-spaced planks.

The irony was not lost on Astryd. *Now Shadow's got me climbing out windows. What's next? Scaling buildings? Accepting every challenge anyone calls impossible?* Recognizing her contemplations as a delaying tactic, Astryd forced herself to stop thinking and start acting. She clambered onto the windowsill, hunching to keep from banging her head. Though accustomed to ascending riggings and balancing on timbers, slipping through a window was new to her. *At least ropes offer handholds.* She gripped the sill and swung her legs over it. Dangling, she looked down. The barrel lay farther below her than she had guessed it would, and an idea that seemed so natural before suddenly transformed into a crazed notion. *I should have gone out the front door. Caught by Harriman, I could always transport. If I kill myself, I'm just dead.*

Astryd's grip tightened, and she knew she could still change her mind. But the thought of dealing with Harriman and his beserks sent a shiver of dread through her. *It's not as far down as it seems. Better to just get out as quickly and quietly as I can.* She edged along the sill until the barrel stood immediately beneath her. Whispering a word for luck, she released her hold.

Astryd plummeted, her muscles knotting in anticipation. Her feet struck the barrel with a hollow thud, her bent knees absorbing the impact. For an instant, she basked in triumph. Then the barrel teetered dangerously on one edge. Instinctively, she threw her weight in the other direction to counter, too hard. The barrel overbalanced. Astryd tumbled, headfirst, twisting as she fell. She landed on her shoulder and rolled. Pain shot through her back, and the barrel slammed against her shin.

For a moment, pain immobilized Astryd. *Too much noise. I have to get out of here.* She staggered to her feet, limping into a side street, down the darkened pathway and into another alley. Youthful voices wafted to her from a cross

path, soft but growing louder. She ducked back into the
side street, massaging her bruised ankle. And she listened.

For Taziar Medakan, every second of Larson's absence
passed like an eternity. Early on, he had tried to converse
with Silme, but his thoughts strayed continuously to Astryd
and Larson. The need to concentrate on each word stilted
his speech, and even simple discussion became a chore.
Now they waited in silent contemplation, Silme seated on
the stack of logs between the hearth and the door, Taziar
on the floor beneath the shuttered window.

Suddenly, Silme snapped to attention with a gasp of horror. "No. By Thor, no!"

Silme's distress drove Taziar to his feet, every muscle
coiled for action. "What happened? What's wrong?"

Silme glanced at Taziar. She kept a hand clamped over
her mouth, making her reply sound distant. "They got
Allerum."

Taziar crossed the room to Silme and grasped her other
hand, where it wrapped around her dragonstaff. "Who's
got Allerum? How?"

"The guards." Silme's voice was pained.

"The guards? Why would the guards . . . ?" Confusion
beat aside urgency, and Taziar dropped to his haunches.
"Silme, I don't understand. What happened? How do you
know? What can we do to help him?"

"I probed his mind," Silme confessed.

Taziar nodded, careful to pass no judgments on her decision. Tortured by enemies twisting his thoughts and accessing intimate and painful memories, Larson tolerated no
intruders in his mind. Taziar knew Silme had long ago
promised never to take advantage of Larson's lack of mind
barriers; until now, she had respected his privacy. Now,
Taziar realized her concern had driven her to forsake her
vow, just as his had goaded him to sneak through the window and try to aid Shylar without risking his new friends.
"And . . ." he prodded.

"I found nothing. No thoughts, only darkness."

Taziar removed his hand from Silme's clenched knuckles.
"Nothing?" The word strangled in his throat. *By the gods,
no. He can't be dead. I should never have let him go. I*

should have protested harder. "He's not . . . ?" Taziar found himself unable to speak the last word.

"Dead?" Silme finished for him. "No. I dug deeper and found images of men in red and black harassing him with spears. Dead, he would have no memories at all."

The fire felt uncomfortably warm on Taziar's back. The flickering, scarlet glow splashing the walls reminded him of the blood spilled, and a shiver wrung through him. *How many more must die?* "Why would the guards want Allerum?"

Silme flipped her staff so that it rested across her knees. Though understandably pained and concerned, she apparently realized the need to inform Taziar. "One held a grudge from an incident near the baron's keep. According to Allerum's memories, he killed that guard but couldn't fathom why the others allowed the fight nor why they banded against him once the fight was finished." She glanced down to meet Taziar's gaze.

"I can." Taziar rose, reminded of the angry ramblings of an old soldier who had served under his father: "Most of the guards live off the so-called glory of the previous generation. They wear their free uniforms like medals of courage. They hold themselves above their families and display their competence against the helpless: prisoners, beggars, and street orphans." *In the wake of Harriman's violence, the baron has probably given his men free rein to prey on the innocent. No matter the cause, if Allerum killed one, the others would take vengeance against him.* Taziar explained simply. "Harassment is their idea of sport." *What now?* The thoughts that answered his own question seemed foreign and unreal. *They might torture him to death in the streets. More likely, they'll drag him back to the dungeon where they can shackle and control him.* Taziar kept his thoughts from Silme, but hysteria edged his voice. "We're wasting time. Do you know where the incident took place? How long ago?"

"I have no way to judge time. He's unconscious and—"

Something heavy crashed against the door with a groan of timbers. Taziar scarcely found time to rip his sword from its sheath before the panel slammed open. Two pairs of men rushed to the threshold, their drawn swords scattering red highlights through the chamber.

Silme reacted first. Without bothering to stand, she whipped her staff sideways. Wood cracked against the leading man's shins. Tripped, he staggered forward. Taziar's harried sword slash tore open the stranger's abdomen. Taziar curled the sword back into a defensive position.

Caught off-guard by Taziar and Slime's closeness to the door, the injured man's partner attempted to backpedal. But momentum from the companions behind him drove the man onto Taziar's blade. Impact jarred Taziar over backward. His spine struck the floor with a force that dashed the breath from his lungs. His head thunked against wood, and the corpse landed atop him, pinning him to the planks.

Through the ringing in his ears, Taziar scarcely heard the door slap closed and the bolt jarred hurriedly into place. Abandoning his sword, he wriggled from beneath the dead stranger, blood warm and sticky on his hands and face. The groans of the gut-slit bandit and the thick odor of bowel and blood made Taziar's stomach churn. He tasted bile. Fighting nausea with desperation, he took in the scene at a dizzy glance. Silme stood with her back pressed to the door, adding her meager weight to support the panel that shivered under the force of a battering from the opposite side. Apparently, the sorceress' quick reflexes had allowed her to latch the door against the last two assailants. *But for how long?*

Urgency allowed Taziar to gain control of his impulse to be sick. "Stay there," he whispered. "Don't move." Scampering across the room, he wrenched open the shutters. In the darkened alley below, two men looked up, returning his stare. Both wore swords, and one clutched a crossbow, a quarrel readied against the string. He recognized them now, strong-arm men on the fringes of the underground. *Harriman's men.* Taziar swore, aware he would have to act quickly. He shot Silme a look intended to reinforce his command, then shouted for the benefit of the men pounding on the door. "Quick! He's going out the window!" He hesitated just long enough to ascertain that the would-be assassins had abandoned their attack on the door. "I'll be back," he reassured Silme and climbed out on the sill.

Beneath him in the alleyway, Taziar heard a wordless shout of recognition. Hurriedly, he hooked his fingers in irregularities in the wall stones and scurried upward. A fin-

ger's breadth from his hand, a quarrel glanced off the granite. Reflexively, he jerked away. The sudden movement lost
him his toe hold. Dislodged mud chinking pattered to the
dirt. Taziar shifted his weight and clung with one hand, pawing blindly for a new grip. Mentally, he counted the moments
it would take to reload the crossbow. Then his fingers looped
over the edge of the roof. He dragged his body upward,
hearing the twang of the bowstring through heightened
senses. The arrowhead smacked into hardened mud. He
felt no pain, but, as he made a dive to the rooftop, something jolted him so hard he nearly fell. The arrow had
pierced his boot, pinning it to the wall but missing his foot
with an uncanny stroke of luck. Ripping his leg free of the
boot, he rolled to the rooftop.

Once there, Taziar wasted a moment pulling off his other
boot while he gazed out over the city. Below him, the men
scattered, ready to catch him no matter which wall he chose
to descend. To the south, Mardain's temple rose over the
inn. To the north, a cobbled roadway gaped between Taziar
and a single story dwelling. Some distance beyond it, lantern lights glimmered like stars in the windows of the baron's towers. To the east, Taziar knew he would find another
wide street separating him from a cottage. Westward, across
a narrower thoroughfare, the roof tiles of the silversmith's
combination of shop and home beckoned, one story beneath Taziar. Beyond it, moonlight revealed the irregular
stonework of a building roof under repair.

Fearing the strangers might attack Silme if he waited too
long, Taziar made his decision quickly. He hurled his boot
at the crossbowman in the eastern alley. It struck the
ground, a distant miss from its target. But the bowman's
shout drew his companions, and Taziar seized the precious
seconds this gained him. He sprinted toward the western
lip of the rooftop. Doubts poured forth as he reached the
edge. The roadway was wider then he had estimated; even
a running start might not provide the momentum needed
to clear it. For an instant, he imagined himself falling, air
hissing through his tunic, until he crashed, broken and
bleeding, on the cobbles below. Committed to action, he
turned a jump into a reckless dive for the silversmith's roof.

A distant shout wafted from below. Wind whipped the
hair back from Taziar's eyes, revealing the ledge silhouet-

ted by starlight. *I'm going to miss that roof by a full arm's length.* The realization upended Taziar's senses, but he clung to life with stubborn determination. The arc of his descent straightened. He slashed crazily through air. The knuckles of his left hand banged painfully against wood. Redirecting instantly, he caught the rim with the fingers of his right hand. He jerked to an abrupt halt, wrenching every tendon in his forearm. Ignoring the shrill ache of his muscles, he clawed his way to the rooftop.

Taziar lay on the tiles, trembling. In spite of bare feet and biting autumn cold, sweat plastered the Climber's tunic to his skin. He climbed to his feet, aware delay would sacrifice the time his maneuver had gained him. He dashed across the rooftop, the tiles chill and coarse against his soles. The shouted exchanges of his pursuers wafted to him, distant, incomprehensible echoes in the night. As Taziar ran, he studied the building ahead. A wind or rainstorm had toppled the chimney near its base, leaving a jagged edging of flagstone. Stone blocks and dirty tiles littered the roadway between it and the silversmith's shop. Boulders stood neatly arrayed on the rooftop in preparation for restoration. Nearby lay stacks of tiles. A ladder angled from the alleyway to the roof, and Taziar could just make out the top of a second ladder on the opposite side.

At the end of the silversmith's roof, Taziar spun and lowered his feet over the side. He wedged his toes into mossy clefts, caught handholds on the ledge, and clambered down the wall with the ease of long practice. Still, his movements seemed clumsy to him. His muscles quivered, and each hold required concentration. He jumped the last half story, careful to avoid the shattered pieces of chimney scattered across the walkway. The footsteps of his pursuers rang through the streets. Taziar forced himself to remain still, sifting and interpreting the sounds. His crazed dive had placed Harriman's men behind him. They rushed toward him from opposite sides of the silversmith's shop.

The instinct to run nearly overpowered Taziar, but he held his ground. *I have to make them think they have me. I can't give them time to think. Otherwise, they'll surround me.* The first pair of ruffians appeared around the corner to Taziar's left. Too restless to wait any longer, Taziar started toward the ladder, feigning the choppy desperation of panic. A contrived limp slowed his escape. Harriman's men rapidly closed in on him. By the time Taziar reached the base of the ladder, they had narrowed the distance to two arms' lengths. *I can't let them get too close, either, or they'll just knock the ladder down with me on it.*

Taziar scurried up the ladder, his quicker reflexes enabling him to regain several steps of his lead. At the top, he whirled, pleased to find that all four of the men had followed him. *Child's play.* Taziar's overtaxed muscles belied his thought. Despite the need for fast action and strategy, his mind groped through a fog of fatigue, and the ache of his injuries could not be ignored. Avoiding the holes and alert for loose tiles, he skittered across the roof to the opposite side. Behind him, the heavier, shod feet of his pursuers sounded thunderous. Apparently unused to rooftops, the rhythm of their movements was broken and uncertain.

Taziar never hesitated. He caught the top of the ladder, scrambled halfway down it, then kicked it loose from the wall. It fell, carrying him in a shallow curve. As he neared the roadway, he leaped free. He struck the ground, cobbles jabbing his bare feet, dropped, and rolled. Pain speared through his legs, and stone bruised his side. The ladder crashed to the stone behind him.

Taziar sprang to his feet and ran, aware he had turned the hunt into a race for the remaining ladder. Taziar knew his jump from the ladder must have seemed madness to Harriman's men. *A leap from the rooftop would be sure suicide.* Necessity lent him speed. He circled the building, not daring to waste a second looking up. *They might shoot quarrels or throw rocks, but I doubt it. They'll be more concerned with their own escape. They know as well as I do they're trapped if they don't reach that ladder first.*

Taziar rounded the final corner at a run and hit the ladder with his shoulder. Momentarily, he met resistance. Then the ladder overbalanced. He heard a short scream of fright followed by the rapid scramble of fingernails against stone as a man who had started down the ladder pawed and caught a hold on the ledge. A frustrated blasphemy rebounded through the roadway. Taziar ducked into a shadowed alley. Angry curses chased him as he raced through the maze of thoroughfares, but they soon faded beneath the mingled cries of night birds and foxes.

When he could no longer hear the men, Taziar paused to catch his breath. For the first time in days, he allowed himself a laugh.

The predawn found Bolverkr astride the curtain wall of his fortress, his legs dangling inches from the glitters of sorcery as if to challenge his own magic. The constant construction, the movement of stone and the setting of complicated defenses had drained his life aura to a wisp of gray. He felt weak, more tired than he had in years, but it was the comfortable, sated exhaustion that comes of honest labor. Ordinarily, fatigue would have frustrated him, but now he gained a strange satisfaction from the knowledge that even his mass of borrowed Chaos-force had its limits. Secure in the knowledge that Harriman would continue his vengeance, at least against Taziar, Bolverkr rose and headed for the steps cut into the stone.

Thoughts of Harriman made Bolverkr grin. The arrangement had become more convenient than he'd ever hoped, freeing him to build until exhaustion while his enemies tangled with his marionette. Bolverkr's contacts with Al Larson's thoughts confirmed that his enemies were blithely unaware of the master pulling Harriman's strings. *Practical, simple, a fine arrangement.* Bolverkr's smile widened. *Once I've killed Taziar, I'll need to make another puppet for the elf.* Even perilously low on Chaos energy, Bolverkr felt the permanent effects of its poisoning. *Or perhaps Taziar could serve that purpose. Who would know better how to torture Allerum?* The answer came in an instant. *Silme.*

Having reached the steps, Bolverkr hesitated before descending into his partially-enclosed courtyard. He turned, looking out over the wreckage of Wilsberg. Mentally, he replaced each buried corpse, unable to keep from seeing beauty in the natural asymmetry of Chaos' flagrant denial of pattern. Again, he relived the scattered panic of the townsfolk he had loved, watched his protecting magics wall them into a cage of death. Always before, the memory had faded to grief before blossoming into anger. But this time his emotions skipped the pivotal step. Rage warmed him, but it drained life aura, too, and he quickly quelled the mood. *What if I had died with my people?*

It was the first time Bolverkr dared to ask the question,

yet the answer came without need for thought. *The Chaos-force would have gone to the next most powerful sorcerer. Silme perhaps? Or some master at the Dragonrank School?* He recalled the blissful agony of Chaos' arrival, the power it promised that he could not have resisted, the transfer that would have killed a lesser man. *I'm of the original Dragonrank. No other mage could have survived it.* He imagined the Chaos-force seeking a master, tearing through cities, claiming lives with the unthinking nonchalance of a child picking wildflowers. Every slaughtered servant of Law would weaken the Chaos-force as part of the natural balance. Every Chaos death would strengthen it.

Bolverkr's vision filled with lines of corpses, and a nameless joy welled within him. He raised his head, howling his laughter, and the sight of the turreted towers, built in memoriam to his beloved, jarred him into silence. *Magan.* The image of his sweet, unassuming wife wound a crack through Chaos' control that admitted a ray of the Dragon-mage that had once been Bolverkr, a sorcerer who had sought and found the quiet solace and anonymity of a farm town. He recoiled from the same death-visions he had welcomed moments earlier.

I thought I could handle Chaos, but I was wrong. There's too much here for one sorcerer. I have to share it with someone strong enough to wield it. Bolverkr gazed at his citadel. Pictures of Magan made him realize how much he missed her beauty, her calm steadiness and logic and the way she supported him no matter how gloomy or ugly his mood. Then, he remembered his first sight of Silme, the way her radiance had driven him to breathlessness, the lust a single glimpse had raised in him. *Allerum took my woman from me. It's only fair that he should pay with his.*

Chaos seeped slowly back into Bolverkr's wasted sinews as he started down the steps.

CHAPTER 9
Shadows of Justice

So long as governments set the example of killing their enemies, private individuals will occasionally kill theirs.
—Elbert Hubbard
Contemplations

By the time Taziar Medakan returned to the inn, dawn was tracing streaks of yellow and pink across the horizon, etching the Cullinsberg skyline dark against the rising sun. The scene was familiar to Taziar; he knew every ledge, angle, and distant spire. But now his concern and fatigue gave the city an alien cast, like the first stirrings of dementia in a loved one or a favorite recipe with an ingredient missing. A week of restless nights followed by a full day of plotting and a run through the roadways had tired him. His thoughts stirred through an encumbering blanket of exhaustion, and he felt certain his movements were equally dulled.

Harriman's master has what he wanted. Anger pierced Taziar's mental haze. *He's got me in pain and torn with guilt, desperate to save my friends from the gallows, and aware I might fail despite my best efforts.* Taziar delved for resolve, shouldering aside fatigue and the heavy burden of mixed and mangled emotions. *Like Silme said, Allerum knows me too well, and through him, so does Harriman's master. I've walked into every trap he's set for me, delivered myself, the children, and Astryd into his hands. He's even forced me to kill.* An image of the corpses in the inn room filled Taziar's mind, but he banished it with rising will. *I'm not going to mourn them. I won't take blame for the deaths of vicious men who lived and, appropriately, died by violence.* Despite his decision, guilt swam down on Taziar, his conscience an accuser too terrible to ignore. *This must be what it's like to be a soldier: killing out of necessity, at first forcing oneself to forget, until each corpse blends into the nameless infinity of murder.*

Taziar poised against the cold granite of the inn wall while he fought a battle inside himself. *Harriman's preying on my weaknesses: my loves and loyalties, the ethics that my father had no right to embrace as a guard captain nor to teach to his only son. Again and again, Harriman has used my emotions as a weapon against me. The only way I can escape Harriman's master is to become someone else.* The idea rankled. The thought of abandoning the tenets he had held since childhood pained Taziar to the core of his being, and the words of his father's underling came unbidden. "You have none of your father's size nor strength, yet you inherited the very things that killed him: his insane sense of morality and his damnable courage." *The time has come to dump the morality and focus on the courage. The urchins are dead; nothing I can do will bring them back. I've killed three times, but men have done worse for baser reasons. If Astryd lives, I'll rescue her; if she's dead, there's nothing I can do for her. I can't be driven to carelessness by sentiment. My cause is to free my friends with as few casualties as possible. Nothing more, nothing less.*

Grimly, Taziar channeled to a single goal, building a wall of determination to hold guilt and sorrow at bay. Weariness retreated, but deep within him, something mourned the price. Taziar started toward the back entry.

A movement froze Taziar in mid-stride. He pressed back into the shadows of the wall as a slight figure flitted toward the door. The first rays of morning sun sparked gold highlights through feathered locks the yellow of new flames. *Astryd?* Joy flooded Taziar, but for the sake of his vow, he crushed passion ruthlessly. Instead, he scanned the dwindling darkness for evidence of someone watching or trailing Astryd. Discovering no one, he caught her arm as he reached out to trip the latch.

Astryd whirled with a gasp of startled rage. Only a reflexive leap backward saved Taziar from an elbow in his gut and a knee in his groin. "It's me," he whispered.

Astryd's expression softened as she recognized Taziar. "Shadow. Thor's justice, it's you." She enwrapped him in an exuberant embrace.

Relief and elation chipped at Taziar's self-erected barriers. Unwilling to abandon the persona thwarting Harriman would require, he hugged Astryd briskly. Pulling the panel open, he found the entry chamber empty; this early, no sound drifted through the cross door from the common room. Gesturing Astryd to the stairs, Taziar yanked the outer door closed. "What happened? Are you well?" He kept his tone businesslike.

Astryd hesitated, struck by Taziar's manner. When she spoke, her voice was frenzied. "I think Allerum's in the dungeon. And Harriman knows you're here. He paid men to capture you!"

Capture? Taziar started up the stairs, taking note of Astryd's choice of words. *So Harriman's not ready to kill me yet. His delay can only work to my advantage.* "Silme and I handled Harriman's men, and we knew about Allerum. What detained you? Did Harriman recognize you?"

Astryd followed. "I don't know if Harriman recognized me or not. He gave no indication that he did, but he certainly made things hard for me."

Subtlety is Harriman's style. Taziar kept the thought to himself as he rounded the second story landing and climbed toward the third, cautious and alert for movement.

"I drained my life energy on a lot of small but necessary spells," Astryd continued. "Then Harriman locked me in a room overnight with a client and a guard at the door."

A client? Not wishing to contend with his emotions, Taziar did not request further information and was pleased when Astryd offered none. "How did you get free?"

Astryd's shod footfalls made no more sound on the stairs than Taziar's bare feet. "The same way you would have. Out the window." She smiled up at him, apparently expecting shock or at least a glimmer of curiosity. When Taziar did not question her, she finished in a disappointed mumble. "So here I am, well-rested, untapped, and ready to assist in any way I can."

Resourceful. Astryd's attitude is precisely what we need to defeat Harriman. Taziar did not voice the praise aloud. *Well, I can be resourceful, too.* He crested the steps and headed down the hallway toward their room. "Did you find out anything?"

"I got the information you wanted." Astryd trotted around Taziar, then stopped to stare at the twisted piece

of painted black metal that had served as the latch to the
inn room door. "Harriman's men?"

Taziar nodded, not bothering to clarify. An explanation
would only waste time. "Silme?" he whispered.

Silme's voice wafted through the crack in answer. "It's
safe."

Taziar pushed open the door, escorted Astryd through
it, and closed it behind them. Apparently, Silme had
cleaned up in his absence. She had bolted the shutters
against the wind. The corpses were gone. *Out the window,*
Taziar surmised, but he did not bother to ask. Silme had
stuffed the jumble of traveling gear and blankets back into
the packs which lay in a neat stack, ready for travel.

At the sight of Astryd, Silme smiled. She pressed forward, but Taziar interrupted before she could question her
friend. "We need to make some fast plans and get out of
this inn. First, Astryd, what did you find out?"

Startled by Taziar's brusqueness, Silme abandoned her
greeting. Her smile wilted.

Astryd smoothed her skirt with her hands, ignoring Taziar's intent stare. "Harriman's followers include the berserks
and twelve to fourteen warriors Mat-hilde claimed you
would know." She glanced sharply at Taziar as if to confirm
this, but he was deep in thought. "She called them the
'fringe guard.' If I can give her some idea of when we're
going to free the leaders, she promised to fill the whorehouse with men who would take their side." She winced,
studying Taziar as if to look deep enough into him to understand the change in his usually gentle and caring manner. "Mat-hilde warned, though, that those same men who
would help the leaders might kill you."

Taziar ignored Astryd's final statement. Right now, his
friends' lives mattered more than his own. "Good. Then we
can concentrate on the jailbreak and worry about defeating
Harriman afterward." Taziar skirted the women and knelt
before his pack. "This is my plan." He emulated Silme's
no-nonsense manner, aware his idea would meet with stren-
uous objections.*Yesterday, I rejected it myself.* "I'll have to
get into the prison and work with my friends from the
inside."

Silme settled back on the wood pile near the fire. "A
breakout from inside the dungeon. Ingenious," she said

with a trace of sarcasm. "How do you propose to do such a thing?"

Avoiding Astryd's gaze, Taziar rummaged through his gear. He tried to sound matter-of-fact. "I'll get myself arrested, and—"

"No!" Astryd denied the possibility, achieving the no-nonsense delivery with far more success than Taziar. "The guards might kill you."

"They might," Taziar admitted, keeping his tone level. "But I doubt it. You said Harriman sent those men to capture me. He still wants me alive, for a while at least. Harriman apparently has some influence over the baron on the matter of the underground and its members." Taziar felt leather beneath his fingers and jerked his boots free with a suddenness that sent his spare breeks sliding across the floor. "Besides, there's a mass criminal hanging today. No doubt, the baron would want to make a public example out of the man who robbed Aga'arin's temple and escaped the dungeons. What better way than a hanging on Aga'arin's own High Holy Day?"

"No," Astryd repeated. "What possible good can it do to make you one more person we have to free from the baron's prison?"

Taziar indulged in a smile, pleased Astryd would give him a chance to explain rather than dismissing his plan out of hand. "I've been jailed before. I know the kind of locks the dungeon has and what supplies I'd need to trip them. I can free Shylar and the others from their cells and rally them against the guards. A rope will get us all out the window to safety." He pulled the boots onto his feet, awaiting the inevitable question.

"Rope? A locksmith's tools?" Silme sat and drew her knees to her chest. "After they catch you, the guards will let you keep such things? And I suppose the underground leaders will battle swords and crossbows with their fists."

"I suspect the guards will take everything I have." Taziar recalled his previous arrest. Then, blood loss from an arrow wound had drained him to unconsciousness, and he had no remembrance of being searched. Still, when he had awakened in his cell, he had nothing except his clothes. "But they can't stop Astryd from bringing anything I need."

Surprise creased Astryd's features.

Taziar grasped the opportunity to elaborate. "While I'm getting myself in trouble, the two of you can purchase the tools I'll describe, the longest piece of rope you can find, and as many knives and swords as Astryd can handle. Once I'm imprisoned, Astryd can transport in with supplies." Taziar glanced at his companions in triumph, the comfort of a plausible plan tempered by his new attitude and the growing look of skepticism on Silme's face.

Silme cleared her throat. "It won't work."

The certainty in Silme's voice mangled Taziar's hopes. "Why not?" he challenged her.

"Because Astryd can only transport to a place she's seen before."

The revelation stunned Taziar. "Really?"

"Really," Astryd confirmed.

Taziar recalled an incident that had occurred soon after he'd met Astryd. "But when Mordath held me prisoner on a dinghy, you transported onto it. You couldn't have boarded his boat before."

"No." Astryd shuffled from foot to foot. "But I could see it from the rail of the ship I was on. I knew exactly where to go. Even so, it was my clumsiest transport since glass-rank. I nearly capsized the boat."

Still clinging to his idea, Taziar pressed. "What if I describe the interior of the prison for you? In detail."

The women shook their heads. "Not good enough," Silme said. "She'd have to actually see it, with magic at least."

Silme's clarification raised another possibility. "A location . . ." Taziar started.

Astryd kicked at a loose nail in the floorboards. "A location triangle has to be centered on a familiar person. Background is revealed incidentally. If I centered the spell on Allerum, I could only see the inside of his cell, and my transporting into a locked cage won't help you. If the dungeon is dark, I wouldn't even see that much."

Sarcasm returned to Silme's voice. "Despite the practice Astryd's been getting the last few days . . ." She continued in her normal tone. ". . . she still expends too much energy casting location triangles. After a location and a transport into the prison, she might not have enough life force to transport back out. She certainly won't have enough to help you and your friends escape."

It finally occurred to Taziar to question Astryd's knowledge. "How did you know about Allerum's capture?"

"I heard some children talking about it in an alley. Apparently, a street gang saw the guards' attack and watched them drag their victim off toward the baron's keep. The description fit Allerum. Then I heard Harriman paid the guards well for the victim's sword, and there was no longer any doubt in my mind."

Silme spoke, her voice painfully calm. "Shadow, your plan may still work."

Taziar swung his head toward Silme in expectation; his discussion with Astryd became dim background.

Silme rose. "Anything Allerum knows, Astryd or I can access. Apparently, the guards dragged Allerum into the dungeon while he was unconscious. Once he wakes up and looks around, Astryd can get her visual image of the prison and transport inside."

"Perfect." Taziar quelled rising excitement. "Allerum has to wake up eventually. Once I get in, I can tell him the plan. By following his thoughts, you'll know the best time to transport, and it won't even cost a significant amount of life energy." Taziar straightened. "No need to delay any longer. You'll have to carry our packs. The guards will only take them from me. There's another inn at the other end of town run by a woman named Leute. Get a room on the second floor. The north side, if possible. It'll give Silme a place to stay, Astryd a place to transport to, and all of us a place to regroup if something goes wrong."

Astryd and Silme had gathered up the packs before Taziar finished speaking. Briefly, he described the required locksmith's instruments in layman's terms. "After you get the supplies, try to find time to give Mat-hilde some idea of when the prison break will happen." Taziar tensed, awaiting more criticisms of his plot. When none came, he rose, crossed the room and peered out the window. Dawn light drew familiar shadows on the walls of Mardain's temple, but, mired in his forced emotionlessness, Taziar did not allow himself to study them. Instead, he stared at the alleyway below. Finding it empty, he climbed to the sill. "Best if you're not seen with me, if possible. We'll be back together soon." He did not allow the vaguest trace of doubt to enter his voice, but an image of Astryd's ashen features haunted him as he shinnied down the wall into the alley.

Once solidly on the dirt pathway, concerns, fears, and fatigue closed in on Taziar. He held his worries at bay, turning the thought and energy they might cost him to the matter at hand. Brushing dust from his cloak, he headed from the back street onto the main market roadway leading to Cullinsberg's entrance.

The bang and clatter of opening shops and stands assailed Taziar. Merchants and their apprentices scurried through the city in huddled knots, some guiding cart horses down the cobbled streets. Attentive to their wares, the merchants seemed to take no notice of Taziar threading cautiously around them. Unchallenged, he kept to the sidewalks, moving into the roadway whenever displayed wares made the walkways impassable. At length, he discovered a guard in the familiar black and red uniform stationed on the opposite side of the road at the mouth of an alleyway. He seemed to Taz to be the type who would respond with reasoning before threat and threat before violence. He was lean and tall and held a spear in a lax grip as he watched the flow of traffic through slitted eyes.

He'll do fine. With exaggerated casualness, Taziar turned his back to the wall of a butcher's shop and rested his shoulder blades against the granite. Bending his knee, he propped a foot against the wall behind him. The position placed him directly across from the guard.

A cart brimming with hearth logs creaked along the roadway, pulled by a burly chestnut gelding. The topmost layer of wood rocked with each movement, threatening to crash to the street at any moment. Taziar waited until it passed and the lane between him and the guard had cleared once again. The guard visually followed the wagon until it rounded a corner. Then his dark gaze flicked forward. Briefly, the guard inspected Taziar and, apparently finding nothing of interest, he moved on to a middle-aged couple ambling toward the Climber.

Taziar assessed the couple. The man sported the heavily callused hands of a smith or builder, and well-muscled arms completed the picture. A receding line of brown hair dusted with gray revealed a scalp freckled from exposure to the sun. The plump woman at his side wore her locks swept back into a tight bun. Clothes of unsoiled linen suggested a comfortable living. Taziar located their purses by the play of dawn shadow on pocket fabric. He guessed that the woman carried the bulk of their money in a recess in her shift, while the left pocket of the man's tunic held a smaller amount. Taziar suspected they'd chosen the arrangement to confuse thieves, but he doubted it would succeed against any except a young amateur. *Or maybe I'm overestimating the average pickpocket.*

Since Taziar sought attention rather than money, he went after the bait. As the couple wandered by, he slipped his fingers into the man's pocket, seized the pouch of coins, and ripped it free. Taziar fumbled it intentionally, catching the bag with a dull clink of coins. Through the fabric, he identified six copper barony ducats before whisking it into the folds of his own cloak. He awaited the woman's scream, the man's bellow of outrage, the guard's shouted command above the irregular clamor of the merchants.

But none of those sounds came. Apparently oblivious, the couple continued down the walkway without so much as a break in stride. Dumbfounded, Taziar turned his attention to the guard. The man chewed a fingernail, stopped, and studied the tattered edge. He picked at it with his thumb, then bit at it again.

Irony struck Taziar a staggering blow. *Aga-arin's almighty ass, I can't be that good.* Stunned by the revelation, Taziar allowed a young man carrying a crate of chickens on his shoulder to pass unmolested. Taziar's hand closed over his spoils. *I have to give this back.* He glanced in the direction the couple had taken, but they had disappeared around a corner. Weighing the time the return would cost him against the couple's affluence, Taziar accepted his new-found money reluctantly. *I'm just going to have to learn to be more inept.* He settled back into his position against the wall.

Within seconds, a young man trotted along the sidewalk, his expression harried. He wore a patched, woolen cloak, sported a blotchy beard, and carried a stand sign tucked beneath his armpit. From a glance, Taziar discovered a pouch of coins in the man's hip pocket. He closed, every movement deliberately awkward. Jamming his hand into the pocket, Taziar meticulously gouged his fingers into the man's pelvic bone before scooping the purse free. It flew in a wild arc, and Taziar caught it with a dexterity that belied his earlier clumsiness. He shoved it into his cloak with the other purse.

The stranger spun with a yell of outrage. "Help! Thief!" The lettered board thunked to the cobbles. He swung a punch at Taziar who dodged easily. The guard rushed toward them from across the street. Locking his gaze on the stranger's hands and seeing that the man intended to grab rather than hit, Taziar suppressed his natural urge to dodge. Thick hands seized the collar of Taziar's cloak and crossed, neatly closing off his windpipe. He gasped and struggled, suddenly wishing he had not made it so simple for the stranger to catch him.

"Stop!" The guard's spear jolted against the stranger's arms. The hands fell away, and Taziar staggered free with a dry rasp of breath. "What's going on here?"

The stranger answered before Taziar could regain enough air to speak. "He stole my money. Guard, that man is a thief."

Taziar cringed, aware most of the baron's guards would seize the opportunity to batter him to unconsciousness.

The guard whirled, his forehead creased. He studied Taziar in the thin light of morning, and his eyebrows arched abruptly in question. His expression went bland as he turned back to face the stranger. "I'm sorry, sir. You've made a mistake. This man took nothing."

Taziar went slack-jawed with surprise, and his victim's face echoed his like a mirror. "He's a thief," the man insisted. "He stole my purse. I demand justice. Are you going to let the little weasel go prey on someone else?"

"I'm sorry," the guard said with finality. "I was standing here, and I didn't see him take anything." He winked at Taziar. "It's your word against his word."

"No, it's not." Desperate, Taziar abandoned subtlety. "I took his purse I admit it." To demonstrate, he retrieved the pouch and dangled it before the guard.

The stranger's eyes went so wide, the whites showed in a circle around the irises, and he made only a feeble gesture to retrieve his property. As the stranger's fingers touched the strings, Taziar released it. The pouch plummeted to the walkway. A coin bounced free, wound a wobbly course around a cobblestone, and dropped to its side. The guard recovered first. "You've got your money back." He jabbed a finger into the stranger's arm, then waved curtly at Taziar. "You, be on your way, and don't cause any more trouble." Using his spear like a walking stick, the guard returned to his post before the alleyway.

Bending, the stranger rescued his money and his sign and continued silently down the sidewalk as if in a trance. Taziar hurried off in the opposite direction, equally confused. The guard's reaction made no sense to him. A decade without war had driven Cullinsberg's soldiers to turn any violent tendencies they might harbor against criminals, orphans, and beggars. Many disdained the justice system, abandoning law for the right price. Taziar shook his head, floored by the idea that he had discovered a guard not only mercifully peaceful, but who disregarded pickpockets without so much as a hint of a bribe. *It was an accident, a bizarre coincidence I'll probably never understand. How hard can it be to find a normal guard?*

Taziar wandered by the stands, noting as he passed that many had not opened because of the holiday. The others would close by midday, and Taziar knew he would need to work fast or lose any chance of getting himself arrested. *Who would have imagined I would find it difficult to get thrown in prison?* He chuckled as he wandered by a barefoot girl in tattered homespun selling flowers. Across the road on the opposite walkway, Taziar saw a guard, eyes glinting from beneath a disorderly mop of hair. One meaty hand prodded an unkempt, young woman who cursed him with oaths vicious as a dockhand's.

Seizing the opportunity, Taziar darted across the street, narrowly missing a trampling by a pair of mules hauling a groaning wagon. The team pulled up reflexively, with the calm indulgence of habit, but the driver's blasphemies paled beneath the girl's coarse profanities.

Oblivious, Taziar skidded across the walkway and caught the guard's forearm. "Wait! She didn't do it. I did."

Startled, the guard and his prisoner stared with perfect expressions of surprise. Gradually, the guard's features lapsed into the same complacent smirk Taziar had seen on the face of the other sentry. "Did what?" the guard challenged.

Taziar tugged at the guard's sleeve. "Whatever she did. What are you arresting her for?"

The guard rolled his tongue around his mouth, then spat on the cobbles. "Freelance prostitution."

I can't get a break. Taziar changed his tactics instantly. "You can't take her in. She's . . . my sister."

The guard glanced from Taziar's fair skin and light eyes to the girl's olive-toned countenance. "Sure." He brushed off Taziar's grip. "Go bother someone else."

"Really. She's my sister." He seized the guard's hand in a grip tight enough to pinch, watched the man's cheeks redden in annoyance. "You're my sister. Aren't you my sister?"

Eager to grasp any chance at freedom, the woman nodded. "I'm his sister." A harsh Western accent made her claim sound even more ludicrous.

The guard made no attempt to free his hand. "Do I look stupid to you? She's not your sister, and I wouldn't let her go if she was your sister."

Taziar met the guard's gaze, followed the pursed lines around the stranger's mouth and read waning tolerance. Carefully, Taziar's hand skittered across the woven linen of the guard's uniform. Discovering a pocket in the lining, Taziar dipped his fingers inside. He was rewarded by the grayed, leather braid of a purse's strings. Seizing it, he pulled it out, released the guard, and slipped the pouch into his own hip pocket. "I'll bribe you to let her go."

The guard kept a firm hold on the prostitute's bony wrists. "How much?"

Taziar groped the contents of the guard's purse. "Four silver."

The guard's grip relaxed. "Fair enough."

Taziar produced the guard's pouch, little finger hooked through the braid.

The guard sucked breath through his teeth. The plump face creased into a mixture of emotions Taziar could not begin to decipher. "You little bastard! That's mine." He reached for it.

Exploiting the guard's consternation, the prostitute

twisted free and ran. The guard lunged for her, missed, and tensed to give chase.

Taziar shot a foot between the guard's ankles. The man crashed to the cobbles as the woman sprinted around a bend in the road and was lost to sight.

The guard scrambled to his feet with the natural grace of a warrior. "Why!" he sputtered. His fists clenched to blanched knots, and his cheeks twitched involuntarily. "What in hell . . . ? Why did you . . . ?" Apparently realizing something more important was at stake, he changed the focus of his verbal attack. "Give me back my purse!"

"No." Glibly calm, Taziar tucked the pouch back beneath his cloak. *This has to be a dream. I know ancient crones on the street who would kill for less cause than this.* "Why should I?"

The guard flushed to the roots of his hair. His fingers slacked and clutched as he fought some internal battle. But when he spoke, his tone sounded almost pleading. "Please. That's two weeks' wages. I've got a wife and three children."

Taziar blinked in astonishment, his sharp retort forgotten in the growing realization that something was terrible wrong. "Aren't you going to arrest me?"

"Were it my decision . . ." The guard's voice remained dangerously flat. ". . . I would stave in your insolent, bloody, little skull." He smiled sweetly, a chilling contrast to his threat. "But the baron has forbidden any of his men to arrest, harm, or even touch you. He says you're working for us. In truth, I liked you better on the other side of the law . . ." He finished from between clenched teeth. ". . . when I could kill you. Fortunately for you, I'd rather starve for two weeks than lose my job."

Taziar went still as death, desperately trying to hide surprise behind a less revealing expression. In silence, he handed the pouch of silver to its owner, adding the six copper ducats from his previous heist in honest apology. When he managed to speak in normal tones, he chose to lie. "The baron asked me to test his men's loyalty to his orders. Forgive my abusive methods, but I wanted to give you fair trial. You passed, of course, with honors." Taziar bowed his head in a gesture of respect, turned, and wandered off down the street before the guard could reply.

Taziar waited only until he had passed beyond sight of

the guard before dropping to his haunches beneath the overhang of the baker's shop. *What now?* The clop of hooves reverberated from a side street, its rhythm soft in Taziar's ears. *There's no way Harriman could know I would try something as crazy as getting myself arrested. Is there?* Taziar slid to one knee, the thought cold and heavy within him. *No,* he answered himself cautiously. *Harriman has other reasons to arrange things so the guards can't act against me. First, it convinces everyone, guards, underground, and street people, that I am, in fact, the informant. Second, the baron cannot interfere with any plans Harriman might have for me.*

Taziar rose, in awe of Harriman's thoroughness despite his need to struggle against it. *The stronger the enemy, the better the fight. If Harriman wants me free, I'll get myself arrested. And, if the guards won't do it, well, sometimes a man has to do these things for himself.*

Aware Harriman might still want him prisoner, Taziar kept to the main thoroughfares where the underground's spies were less likely to prowl. He traveled northward, between the puddled shadows of gables and spires. Through occasional breaks between buildings, Taziar could see that the edge of the sun had scarcely crested the horizon, touching the eastern skyline with glazed semicircles of color. Aside from the merchants, the majority of the townsfolk remained in slumber. Like their baron, most of Cullinsberg's citizens worshiped Aga'arin. By tradition, Aga'arin's followers abandoned routine on his High Holy Day. Instead, they slept until the sessions of prayer which began at high morning on the temple grounds.

Taziar ignored the scattered merchants, trusting his instincts to protect him while he dug knowledge from memory. The layout of the baron's keep was common information, spread throughout the underground as much from curiosity as necessity. No thief ever attempted to rob more than the main corridors near the entrance; those had become appropriately free of grandeur as a result. Since the mansion sported no other inlet, the baron kept his sentries clustered there to prevent any but guards and royalty from penetrating the deeper areas of his keep; there was always enough of the most faithful on duty to prevent a mass bribe. Other routes existed to allow Baron Dietrich and his family an escape in case of emergency, but the underground had discovered that these opened only from the inside and were just as carefully warded.

From rumors in the underground, Taziar had learned that the boulders composing the castle walls had been cut square and polished to shiny smoothness. Between blocks, the builders had layered mortar with an artist's eye for perfection. More than once, friends and strangers had tried to commission the Shadow Climber to obtain items which were in the baron's possession, but Taziar had never found the reasons compelling enough to justify the thefts. The insistence that only the Shadow Climber could scale the castle walls took all challenge from the undertaking; since every member of the underground seemed certain he could succeed, Taziar felt no urge to prove it. He was too busy accomplishing the impossible.

Accompanied only by his own thoughts, Taziar shambled through the streets, uncontested, and soon arrived at the cleared stretch of ground separating the town proper from the wall that enclosed the baron's keep. Tucked into the shadow of a mud-chinked log cottage, Taziar studied the keep from its western side. Lantern light bobbed through windows in the lowest stories, but the upper levels and corner towers remained dark, black arrows silhouetted against the twilit sky.

From remembered description, Taziar located the baron's balcony, which jutted from the fifth floor toward the southern tower. Curtains swirled and flapped in the wind. As they moved, Taziar caught interrupted glimpses of morning's scattered glow sparkling off glasswork. Taziar's position accorded him a flattened view of the southern side of the keep and the seventh story window from which he had escaped the corridor outside the baron's dungeon by plummeting into the moat. *With all my injuries, I would have drowned, too, if Moonbear hadn't pulled me from the water.* Taziar grimaced, recalling that the barbarian prince was also responsible for turning his controlled climb down the wall into a crazed fall. *He meant well. Even so, I've no desire to repeat the maneuver nor force it upon anyone else. And I won't have to so long as Astryd brings the rope.*

The other windows remained mysteries to Taziar. As a member of the underground, he had found the floor plan to the baron's keep so readily available it seemed a waste of time, effort, and brain space for him to memorize it. And, though Taziar hated to begin a caper with less than complete knowledge, he doubted he would need to identify the maze of rooms and passageways defining the baron's keep. The object he sought was on the baron's person. *And right now, I can find the baron's person, almost certainly, in the baron's bed.*

More accustomed to working beneath the unrevealing crescent he called the "thieves' moon," Taziar wanted to start while the sun was still low in the sky. Afraid to tarry too long, he crossed the plain and huddled in the block of shadow cast by the keep and its surrounding wall. Once there, he shinnied up the blocked granite of the wall.

Taziar's elevated position accorded him a perfect view of the keep and its courtyard. Young oak and hickory dotted lush grasses tipped with autumn's brown. Carved from stone blocks or twisted from wrought iron, benches were set at the western and eastern sides of the trees to catch the daily shade or sun. The moat spoiled the grandeur of the scene. Its waters shivered in the breezes, an oily black halo near the base of the keep.

Taziar took in the layout at a glance and turned his attention to the sentries who paced through the twilit gloom. Their movements appeared crisp; apparently their shift had just begun. Even so, Taziar found their patterns indecipherable. He had managed to identify two guards who might cross the straight tract he hoped to take to the baron's window, when a scraping sound on the wall startled him. Taziar flattened to the summit, eyes probing the haze. The noises grew louder, transforming to the unmistakable sound of footsteps on granite. A man became visible walking atop the wall, a colorless, dark shape etched against the dawn.

Taziar scuttled over the edge, climbing partway down the wall toward the courtyard. Something sharp jabbed his back. *A spear?* Taziar froze. When no challenge followed, he rolled his eyes, easing his head around until he saw a spreading oak, its branches stretched to the wall, one pressed into his cloak. Taziar loosed a pent up breath which earned him another poke from the limb. The slap of the wall guard's footsteps passed directly overhead then faded as the man's vigil took him beyond Taziar's hearing.

When I watched from town, I didn't even see the sentry on the wall. Gently, Taziar began extracting himself from the hold of the oak. A branch creaked as he moved. He cringed and further slowed his progress. *That's because I couldn't spend all the time I needed to study things. The only way I could have missed him is if there's only one sentry on the wall.* Taziar pulled himself free of a twig. It broke with a faint snap. Suppressing a curse, Taziar gazed into the courtyard. Apparently oblivious, the nearest sentry continued his march. *Stupid place for a tree, this close to the wall.* Taziar guessed it had been planted as a seed or sapling. *Probably no one considered its branches might eventually grow over the walls and provide access to enemies or that its roots might disrupt the structure of the wall.* Looking down, Taziar saw a haphazard pile of sawed off branches and knew he echoed someone else's concerns. Within the week, this tree would sit in pieces, a neatly stacked pile of seasoning hardwood.

The strain of sideways movement tore at the calluses on Taziar's fingers. He finished his descent, toe groping the dirt for a landing place clear of debris. Finding one, he lowered his feet to the ground and turned toward the castle. Again, he examined the sentries, and, this time, their pattern became obvious to him. They paced in overlapping, cloverleaf figures; the arcs had thrown him off track. But now that Taziar had deciphered their motions, he doubted he would have any difficulty pacing his own activity between them. *Simple.* Sudden realization ruined Taziar's assessment and killed the joy of certain triumph before it even had a chance to rise. *Except for the moat.*

Taziar ducked behind the disarray of branches, hidden from the guards as his thoughts raced. He knew he could swim the brackish waters, but his plan required him to remain dry and only reasonably disheveled. *Somehow, I have to cross over it.* He dug through his pockets while he considered options. *This early, the drawbridge will be up. It's too wide to jump.* Taziar's fingers skipped over crumbs, splinters, and lint. He discovered his utility knife in his right hip pocket along with a striker and a block of flint. The left held only the sailor's sewing needle he had used to rescue Astryd from a locked berth on the ferry boat the day he met her. He had left his other possessions with Silme and

Astryd in anticipation of losing everything to the guards. Now he wished he had at least brought his sword.

Stymied, Taziar picked idly at the bark of a tree branch. Thoughts distant, he glanced down at his fingers and suddenly felt stupid. *The logs.* He looked into the courtyard, watching a sentry complete an arc before him. Selecting a timber heavy enough to serve as a bridge, Taziar tugged. Wood shifted with a muffled thunk. Taziar bit his lip, immediately abandoning his efforts. He chose a different log, examining its length to make certain no other branches lay on top of it. He hefted an end. The sweet, cloying odor of wood lice wafted to him, and he realized the log would prove too heavy for him to do anything more than drag it. Unwilling to risk the sound of rustling grass and the ponderous clumsiness the log would lend to his gait, he chose a thinner limb. Uncertain whether it would serve his purposes, he tucked it beneath his arm, timed a sprint between the sentries' routes, and positioned the branch across the surface of the moat.

A breeze ruffled the stagnant waters into white curls. Leaves skittered across the surface like tiny boats, many caught and anchored in a dense layer of algae. Lit by the diffuse glow of lanterns refracted through the windows of the keep, the branch seemed no thicker than Taziar's wrists and fragile as a stem. But the pattern of the guards did not leave him time for hesitation. He stepped onto the wood. It sagged beneath his weight, but it held, and he crossed with nothing worse than damp boots. He eased the limb into the water. The risk of a splash seemed less worrisome than the guards finding his makeshift overpass. If things went according to plan, he would have no need to escape in the same fashion.

The log slid silently into the water and sank, disrupting the slime in a line that marked its passage. Taziar turned his attention to the wall. The sun still had not passed over the keep to light its western side, but dawn light sheened from the glassy surface of stone. Taziar's heart fell into the familiar cadence that welcomed the coming challenge. He savored the natural elation accompanying it. In the depths of his mind, the memory stirred that he had promised to abandon all emotion, but to ignore the excitement inspired by years of addiction to danger seemed as impossible as a thirsty man refusing water or a man spurning sex an instant before the climax.

Taziar never hesitated. He explored the smoothed surfaces with his fingers, and he discovered tiny flaws in the mortaring that another man might dismiss. To Taziar, they were handholds. He wedged small fingertips into the impressions, hauled his feet into a minuscule cleft and reached for another grip.

Taziar climbed with a careless and practiced strength. Attuned to sounds of discovery, he could spare no attention to his climb. Instead, he relied on the same instincts a swordsman taps when a potential killing stroke comes at him faster than thought. Taziar kept his rhythm steady, a continual cycle of hunting crevices, grasping what his trained fingers deemed solid, and hauling his body along the polished surface of stone. He counted stories by windows, their sills like giants' ledges compared with the stone pocks and mortaring imperfections that served as his other holds.

Absorbed in the pattern of movement, Taziar did not notice the baron's balcony until its shadow fell over him. He heaved upward from a toehold, caught a grip on the supporting bars of a railing painted black to protect it from the elements. He examined the outcropping through the striped view the balustrade allowed. A wooden chair overlooked the courtyard, its seat cushioned with pillows, its feet, handrests, and back intricately crafted and wound through with gold filigree. Yet, despite the elegance, the legs were chipped and the fabric on the upright showed signs of wear.

A favorite chair, Taziar surmised. *Probably too old for the throne room. Rather than repair it, Baron Dietrich had it placed here where courtiers and visitors would never see it.* The thought ignited anger as swiftly as fire set to dry shavings. *The man blithely executed his guard captain on contrived evidence after more than a decade of meritorious service, yet he remains loyal to a piece of furniture.* The logic defied Taziar and brought all morality under question. *I wanted to smother emotion and vulnerability for a cause. Yet to let Harriman change what I am is little different than letting him kill me. It's Harriman against me and all my sentimental weaknesses and strengths. I'll best him or die in the attempt.* Taziar channeled his concentration back to the balcony, but one idea seeped through before he could banish it. *I hope I have the opportunity to apologize to Astryd.*

Beyond the chair, curtains rippled, revealing a glass door. Through the thick, uneven surface, Taziar caught a warped glimpse of another set of curtains just inside. Soothed by the double barrier, Taziar hooked his arm over the top of the rail and pulled himself to the balcony. Time was running short. He would have to move quickly to catch the baron still asleep. Soundlessly skirting the chair as he crossed the balcony, Taziar grasped the door latch and twisted. It resisted his touch.

Taziar hissed his frustration. A closer study of the handle revealed a keyhole beneath it. The locksmith's tools he had described to Silme and Astryd would have proved useful now, but Taziar did not waste time wishing. Retrieving the sewing needle from his pocket, he slid the tip into the hole. He felt the raspy vibrations as the end eased over the mechanism and the jolt as it fell into the groove. He pinned it in place and turned it, rewarded by the click of the lock opening. Gingerly, he inched the door ajar. Silence met him. He spun the needle again, heard the answering snap as the mechanism was thrown back into locked position. Simply shutting the door would restore it to its former, secure state.

Taziar inched through the crack. Foot wedged in the doorway, he peered around the curtain. The material was thick; it lay heavy as sodden wool upon his shoulders. Once pushed aside, it admitted a roar that shook the door frame and set Taziar's teeth on edge. He ducked back behind the fabric, heart pounding, hearing the rush of exhaled air as he moved. *Snoring.* Taziar gave the realization a moment to register. Then he placed the needle against the door frame to prop it so it could not close and lock behind him. Taziar crept around the curtain.

As the curtain dropped back into place, the room fell into a darkness untainted by sunrise. Taziar stared, standing still as his eyes adjusted to a deeper gloom than that he had come from. Soon he could make out a table with widely-splayed, decorative legs which was right in front of him. A cut-crystal carafe occupied its center. A pair of clear wine glasses rested upside down beside it. Relief washed through Taziar as he recognized the disaster narrowly averted by waiting rather than blundering sightlessly forward. Directly across the room, Taziar noted a teak door emblazoned with the baron's crest, a lion's head with mouth wide open. His ears ringing with the baron's raucous breaths, Taziar found the symbol strangely appropriate.

A matched pair of ornately-crafted dressers lined the walls, the curls of their pattern unrecognizable in the lightless interior of the baron's chamber. A recess in the wall held clothing, a blurred collection of silks, brocades, and furs. The baron's bed stood in the direct center of the room. Four pillars sculpted into the forms of shapely women supported a canopy. Beneath it, the baron slept on his side beneath a pile of blankets.

The scene registered instantly. Taziar crossed the room, his boots sinking soundlessly into a plush carpet. He knelt at the baron's head. A snore thundered painfully through his ears, followed by a blast of malodorous breath. Saliva dribbled through the baron's beard. Beneath the tangle of hair, the gold medallion of office hung sideways on the sheets, its chain twisted around the baron's neck.

Like a noose, Taziar thought, and only then, thoughts of murder suddenly burned through him. Violence was not his normal reaction to anything, but the cruelties Baron Dietrich's orders had inflicted upon his family went far beyond what any man should have to tolerate. Taziar paused, fingers clenched, jaw tight, mind filled with the frigid whisper of the wind which had stirred his father's dangling corpse, the grim suffocation of his mother's pride, then her own death in a pool of wine and blood and pain. *Damn.* Almost desperately, Taziar dispelled the images, angered by his lapse. *The baron's just a pawn, a figurehead who shouts orders like a king while other men wield his power.* The idea of killing anyone repulsed Taziar; even his hatred and desire for vengeance had not been enough to make him slay the prime minister who had framed his father and goaded the baron into hanging the captain. The need for haste drove Taziar's bitterness aside, and he knew that even had he carried a weapon, he would have had neither the experience nor the coldness to kill the baron. *And it's just as well. I'm not a killer. And the consequences would be dire. If nothing else, the guards would torture my friends viciously to learn the assassin's name.* Taziar shuddered at the memory of his own prison guard-inflicted agonies. *Talk about betrayal.*

Turning back to his task, Taziar reached around Baron Dietrich's perfumed curls and undid the chain's clasp. He kept both ends between his fingers, not allowing the slightest tickle of movement against the baron's flesh. The routine was familiar to Taziar; once, on a dare, he had stolen three necklaces and an anklet from a dancing girl. But as he eased the last link free of its owner, the pattern of the baron's breathing changed.

Taziar dove to the floor, jabbing the medallion into his pocket as he moved. He heard the rustle of straw as the baron rolled. The snoring dulled to normal breathing, revealing a deep rumbling previously drowned out by the baron's snores. Taziar rose to all fours and found himself staring into the bared teeth of a huge, black mongrel.

CHAPTER 10
Dust and Shadows

The jury, passing on the prisoner's life,
May in the sworn twelve have a thief or two
Guiltier than him they try.

—William Shakespare
Measure for Measure

The baron's snores resumed. Taziar froze, gaze locked on the curled lips and yellowed teeth of the mongrel. He shifted his weight to his feet so slowly that his movement was almost imperceptible. Tearing his stare from the dog, he measured the distance to the table and its fragile burden. A crack of light from beyond the curtain touched the cut-crystal of the carafe, splintering rainbows across the glasses. From the corner of his vision, Taziar saw the mongrel tense to spring.

Taziar dove beneath the table. Snarling, the beast bounded after him. A furry shoulder crashed into a decorative, wooden leg. Taziar sprang free as the table tumbled, then broke into a hunched run. The splash of spilled wine and the chime of splintering glass filled his ears, followed by the dog's surprised yelp. Taziar shouldered open the balcony door. Dashing through, he let the glass panel sweep closed, the click of its locking lost beneath the baron's shout of anger.

Taziar never hesitated. Leaping to the banister, he ran his fingers over the mortaring above his head. Discovering irregularities, he skittered up the final story to the roof. He crouched on the tiles, catching his breath and waiting for his heartbeat to slacken to its normal rate. No sound pursued him. *I don't think the baron saw me.* Taziar peeked over the ledge, studying the curtains stirring in a gentle current of air. He pulled his head beyond sight of the balcony and the guards in the courtyard. *I left the outer door*

*locked, and Baron Dietrich believes his walls "unscalable."
He can't possibly suspect someone slipped in from the outside. Most likely, he'll blame the incident on his dog.* Taziar
frowned, his plan gone dangerously awry. *With his attention
on the mess and the fact that no items were stolen from the
room itself, the baron may not notice his medallion of office
is missing.* Taziar crept toward the northern side of the
keep, aware any guards in the towers would probably watch
over the courtyard rather than the rooftop. *But I can't rely
on chance alone. I have to work fast, before word of my
theft reaches the dungeon guards.*

Taziar pattered around the northwestern tower, confident
that the prison was the last place the sentries would search
for a renegade thief. From experience, he knew guards
filled the hallways nearest the dungeon, on the south side.
So he scooted along the northern edge of the keep, seeking
seventh story windows in the polished stretch of wall. Shutters covered the first two he discovered. He found the third
open, but voices wafted from it, and his plan required that
no one know he had entered through a window.

Taziar continued, rejecting each window with reluctant
necessity. He had nearly reached the northeastern corner
when a tiny, square opening attracted his attention. It appeared too narrow for even a man of Taziar's size to slip
through, but he refused to pass it by without a closer inspection. Clinging to the ledge, he lowered his feet over
the side, defying gravity with only the strength of his fingers. His boots scraped stone as he groped for toeholds,
found them, and lowered himself to the level of the
opening.

A glance across the window revealed an area obscured
by darkness. Aware the rising sun would make it easier for
anyone inside to see him, Taziar peered over the sill with
one eye. The opening admitted only a dim glow of dawn
light. The space beyond seemed oddly-shaped, too long and
thin for a normal-sized chamber. Taziar's angle did not
allow him a glimpse of the floor, but he found no movement or figures to disturb the gloom. He realized he had
squeezed through equally tight spaces, the chimney of
Aga'arin's temple, for example. But he knew he would pay
for such a maneuver with tears in his clothing and skin.

Not wanting to waste time searching for a more suitable

entrance, Taziar accepted the challenge. Clinging with his feet and alternate hands, he worked his cloak off his arms and over his back. Freeing the fabric, he tossed it through the opening, tensed for some reaction from inside. When none came, he descended to a position just below the window, seized the sill in both fists, and poked his head and shoulders through the opening.

Taziar's body blocked out what little light normally penetrated into the area beyond the window. He braced his palms on the inner wall, twisting to allow his chest the widest possible angle, from corner to corner. Unyielding stone wedged his shoulders. He wriggled and pushed despite pain, strengthened by the awareness that the harder he struggled, the sooner he would finish. He stuck fast, feet straining against stone. Then his shoulders popped through, abrading flesh beneath the coarse linen of his tunic. He worked one arm through the opening, creating more room for the other.

Taziar probed for the floor with his left hand, felt wooden planks, and steadied his fingers against them. Allowing his weight to fall forward, he dropped his right hand. It slammed against floor sooner than he expected. Surprised, he examined the area with his fingers. To his right, the level rose in increments. *A staircase.* Taziar worked the remainder of his body through the window, hugging the steps to keep from toppling down them. Once inside, he retrieved his cloak, and flung it across his back to hide the dirt and scrapes.

Taziar trotted up the staircase, making no effort to silence his movements. His shoulders throbbed, and the baron's medallion bounced against his hip with every step. His footfalls echoed hollowly.

Two sentries armed with swords met Taziar at the landing. "Halt!" one challenged. "State your name and your business."

Taziar made a gesture of impatience. "I'm Taziar Medakan, loyal citizen and informant to Baron Dietrich." He used the same contrived facts that had worked against his attempts to become arrested to his own advantage now. "The baron sent me to interrogate the prisoner known as Allerum."

The guard who had spoken shook back a mane of sand-colored curls and glanced at his larger companion. "We know nothing of this. Do you carry a writ?"

"No," Taziar admitted boldly. "Baron Dietrich found this matter of such urgency, he didn't waste time writing. Instead, he gave me this to show you." He plucked the medallion from his pocket and displayed it for the guards.

The sentries exchanged startled looks. The taller one cleared his throat. "This is most irregular. I think we should check with the baron."

Taziar adopted an expression of stern annoyance. He placed his hand on his hip, allowing the golden symbol of office to dangle from his fingers. "Very well. The baron found this matter critical enough to hand over his signet, but if you think it's necessary to delay me with your curiosity, it's your necks. I only hope the baron chooses to forgive as easily as I do." He raised his eyebrows, demanding a response.

The smaller guard's gaze followed the ovoid swing of the medallion. "Come with me." He turned and started down the eastern hallway, the keys at his belt clanging as he moved.

Relief flooded through Taziar. Maintaining a regal stance that implied he expected no other reaction, Taziar followed the leading guard. He heard the second guard fall into step behind him but did not bother to turn.

Closed doors of oak broke the wall to Taziar's right at irregular intervals, some emblazoned with the baron's crest. Another corridor halved the path. Ten uniformed guards with swords and bows milled about this crossway, watching Taziar and his escort as they passed. Aside from memorizing their location, Taziar paid them little heed. At length, the eastern corridor ended at a familiar window and a sharp bend to the right. Through the opening, Taziar watched the colors of dawn disperse as the sun crowned the horizon. An image from the past came, unbidden. Again, Taziar crouched on this sill, the hall guards fanned into a semicircle of drawn bows. The remembrance raised sweat on his temples, and a breeze from the window touched him, drying the moisture with chill air.

Taziar banished the memory as the guards led him around the corner and the window disappeared behind him.

From here, Taziar knew the corridor led directly to the dungeon.

A trio of guards met Taziar and his guides at the steel-barred outer doorway to the prison. "What's going on?" one asked.

The sentry who had ushered Taziar through the passageways removed the keys from his belt. "Baron wants him to question the new prisoner."

The sentries moved aside to allow their companion to unlock the outer door, nudging one another in silent conspiracy. At length, the same man spoke again. "New one's . . . um . . . 'asleep.' "

The guard's emphasis on the last word speared dread through Taziar, and he hoped the guard used sleep as a euphemism for unconsciousness rather than death. He forced contempt into his voice. "So I wake him up. The weasel's a criminal, not a boarder."

The sentry pushed open the door and gestured Taziar through. "Go on."

Taziar stepped inside, just far enough that the sentries could not close it behind him. Turning, he extended a hand, palm up. "The keys, please."

The guard hesitated, two digits looped protectively through the ring.

Taziar wriggled his fingers, impatiently. He raised the baron's symbol with a curt gesture. "I found my first visit here unpleasant. I'm not going in there without assurance I can get back out. If you wish to delay the baron's business . . ."

With a wordless growl of contempt, the sentry dropped the keys into Taziar's palm. He waited only until Taziar pocketed the sigil and keys before slamming and locking the door behind him.

Aware the guards might try to confirm his story and word of the baron's stolen medallion would reach them eventually, Taziar trotted down the pathway. Cells lined the walls; those nearest the outer door lay empty. In the center stood a row of six cages the size of dog kennels. A man occupied each of the smaller cells, their faces blurred by distance.

As Taziar drew closer, he realized two of the larger cells also held prisoners. One was sitting, though all the other occupants of the baron's dungeon sprawled on the granite floor. Taziar approached cautiously, footsteps making raspy echoes through the tomblike interior. The prisoners' silence did not surprise him. Noise carried oddly amidst the metal and stone construction of the baron's dungeon; someone had built it to contain the prisoners' screams and cries, the guards' taunts and curses, and the brutality of torture.

But when Taziar arrived at the first of the middle row of cells, he realized none of the prisoners were moving. He scarcely recognized the man in the closest cage. Fridurik lay on his stomach, face buried in the granite floor of his cell. Sweat spangled his naked torso. In the past, if not for a gentle temperament, Fridurik's robust form would have assured him a warrior's life. Now, tangled red hair tumbled over his shoulders, brittle from starvation. Taziar saw bony prominences through sagging flesh mottled with scars and bruises of varying hues.

Taziar knew the pain of every slash. He recalled the clank of shackles, wrists and ankles rubbed raw from the steel, the malicious smirk of those guards who dared to find pleasure in another man's suffering. His stomach ached in sympathy; and, as he silently paced the cell row, he felt tears press his vision, a hot mix of sorrow, pity, and anger. Beside Fridurik, Amalric lay supine with eyes closed. Excrement stained the remaining tatters of his britches. Even in sleep, he found no peace. He kept his arms tucked defensively across his chest. His breathing remained rapid and uneven, occasionally punctuated by a whimper.

From the next cell, Waldhram's eyes watched Taziar, but they swiveled, dull and lifeless, in gaunt sockets. Taziar returned the stare without expression, awaiting some reaction that would cue him as to how to approach these friends turned prisoners. But Waldhram said nothing. He lay still, giving no sign to indicate he had recognized Taziar. It seemed almost as if his body had died, and his eyes merely followed any movement mechanically.

Taziar shivered, rubbing moisture from his eyes with his fists. *If they've grown weak, I must become strong enough for all of them. I have little enough time to turn them into a fighting force.* The thought seemed ludicrous. Taziar passed Odwulf and Mandel, found them in the same hopeless silence. *Battered, broken, useless.* Taziar shook his head in bleak defeat. *They've been here too long, suffered too much.*

What chance do I have to rouse them? Do they even know I'm not responsible?

As if in answer to his unspoken question, a scratchy voice wafted from the final cell. "Did you come to gloat?"

Taziar whirled, met the strange, violet eyes of Asril the Procurer, and found a faint spark of emotion in their depths. Thrilled at this first trace of vitality, Taziar smiled. A moment later, he recognized the gleam in Asril's eyes as hatred and realized his grin of joy must seem unduly cruel. He immediately suppressed it. A glance at the outer cages revealed the last two prisoners as Shylar and Larson. Seeing no other occupied cells, Taziar suspected that Waldmunt had succumbed to the guard's tortures. The sadness that spiraled through Taziar became lost in the mire of his friends' tragedies. Moments passed in aching quiet before Taziar felt compelled to answer Asril's accusations. "I've come to rescue you." He flashed the keys. "You can't really believe I betrayed you."

Taziar turned toward Shylar as he spoke. She sat with her legs folded. Her dress spread in dirty, rumpled waves around her. Aside from the impression of the fabric's weave on one cheekbone, she seemed untouched by the guards' oppression. Still, her wrinkles had deepened. Shylar's gray-tinged curls appeared to have spread; now the white hairs outnumbered the brown. She had aged ten years in the months since Taziar last saw her. Certain she would defend him, Taziar waited. But, though Shylar met his gaze with crisp, dark eyes, she said nothing. In the cell beside her, Larson sprawled in an awkward heap, unmoving.

Taziar started toward Larson, but Asril's challenge jarred his attention back to the violet-eyed thief. "Even the guards know you informed on us. You conniving, little bastard! Admit it, you came to gloat."

Taziar stared, watched anger restore life to Asril's features, and suddenly Shylar's strategy became clear. *All the "proof" in the world wouldn't turn her against me. But she can't afford to league with me while the others truly believe I informed on them. Her silence leaves me free to use any tactic I need.* He bit his lip. Asril's mistrust hurt like physical pain, but he knew he would have to exploit that hatred to rally his friends. "Gloat?" Taziar forced a sneer. "What the hell do I have to gloat over? All I see here are some half-dead, has-been criminals."

Asril's gaze fell to the floor, but Taziar saw interest spark in Mandel's pale eyes. Encouraged, he pressed on, his voice pitched to slander and incite. "People gloat in triumph, but there's no one here worth besting. I have nothing to gloat over, just pieces of jail room furniture cluttering kennels."

Waldhram climbed to the highest crouch the abnormally low ceiling of his cell allowed. "You snake! You have nothing to gain by insulting us. Go away and leave us alone."

"People have left you alone too long," Taziar shot back. He banged a fist against Odwulf's bars, pleased to see Odwulf and Mandel tense in response. "You're all weak. You've degenerated into garbage. Do you think you're the only people ever thrown in the baron's dungeon? I was here! I got free. Am I that much better than you pitiful pack of whining dogs?"

Asril swept to his knees, eyes blazing. "You had help."

"Sure, a lot of help." Taziar downplayed Moonbear's role out of necessity. "I had a big, stupid barbarian who couldn't spell his own name, let alone pronounce mine. And you're hardly by yourself. Look around, Asril. There're eight of you. Are you waiting for your mother to get you out?"

Scarlet swept Asril's cheeks. He made a grab for Taziar through the bars.

Taziar danced aside with a disdainful laugh. "If you had shown that much fire before, you might not be trapped here now." Suddenly Amalric rolled over to join the argument. Now, only Fridurik and Larson lay still, and Taziar found himself growing more concerned about the latter with every passing second.

Asril growled. "If I was free, I'd rip your evil head off!"

"You want the opportunity?" Taziar played through an array of emotions. *I've roused them. Now all I have to do is keep them from killing me before Astryd arrives.* "I'll let you out. All of you."

"Why?" Waldhram demanded. He sprang forward, but the passion of fury made him careless. His head smacked the cell roof. He hunched back, the pain apparently fueling his rage. "A hanging this evening isn't soon enough for you? You want us killed by guards instead?"

Taziar hesitated. It was too late to change tactics now

without losing the ground he had gained. So far, he had managed to incite without confessing to the crime, without destroying that small shadow of doubt each man must hold within him. The thought of lying to convince his friends he actually did betray them dried Taziar's mouth until he felt incapable of speech. *I can regain their trust but not their lives.* He jabbed a finger at Waldhram, licked his lips, and forced the lie. "Do you really think I got you in here alone? I need to rid myself of my accomplice. I can help you, and you need my help. Later, we can settle scores. But right now, we need each other." Taziar glanced toward the farthest end of the cell row, noticed Fridurik still had not stirred. *He's the biggest and strongest. We need him most of all.*

Asril's fingers curled around the bars. "Who helped?"

Taziar snickered patronizingly. "Oh, you know. Think. Who had most to gain from your imprisonment? Who's in control of the underground now? You don't need a brain to figure it out." He shrugged in dismissal. "Then again, you got caught, so maybe I do have to explain."

From behind Taziar, Shylar's voice sounded calculating. "Of course. It was Harriman, wasn't it? He made me instruct my girls to serve him. He threatened to kill them all if I didn't obey."

Rage caught Taziar. He knew there must be more to Harriman's trickery, but the gist of the story was there. Self-control vanished and, with it, the glib ease with which he taunted and lied to his friends. *Easy,* Taziar cautioned himself. *Shylar's figured out what I'm doing, and she's playing along with my game.* He spun toward her, fathomed the message in her stance warning him not to ruin her cover. He winked for her alone, the gesture betraying the mockery of his words. "Ah, Shylar. So, you're not quite as stupid as the others."

"Not quite," Shylar returned with venom.

"And on the topic of the girls, Harriman's rule hasn't proved pleasant for them." Taziar addressed his next comment for Fridurik's benefit, aware the shambling redhead felt a strong attachment to the one called Galiana. "He's chosen Galiana as his personal 'favorite.'"

Fridurik stirred.

Encouraged, Taziar continued the lie. "He's with her

every night, and the cruelties he's inflicted rival anything I've seen from the guards. I . . ."

The squeak of the outer door resounded through the prison, and six guards filled the entryway.

I've delayed too long. Taziar bounded around the corner, unlocked Larson's cage, and jammed the keys into Shylar's startled grip. "Quick," he whispered. "Free them all. It's too complicated to explain, but if I don't get Allerum up, we're all dead."

Shylar rushed to obey. Taziar jarred open the cell door, caught Larson by the shoulders and yanked. The elf rolled limply to his opposite side, revealing a dark puddle on the stone floor. Blood crusted a gash in Larson's temple, surrounded by a dark halo of bruise. *Dead? Oh, please, not dead.*

"Get them!" The guard's screamed command rose above the click of opening locks.

"Wake up. Allerum, wake up!" Desperately, Taziar jostled Larson, but the elf lolled, dead weight in his arms.

Impatiently, Astryd waited in Cullinsberg's main street while Silme attempted to access Larson's thoughts for what seemed like the thousandth time. A secreted dagger poked at Astryd's forearm, and she plucked at her sleeve to reposition it. The movement earned her a prod from another blade wrapped against her opposite arm. Astryd swore. She lowered her arms. The fabric of her dress and cloak slid over her wrists, and she shook until the four knives along her arms fell into a comfortable alignment. She let her arms dangle, glad for the respite, but unable to shake a feeling that someone was following them.

I'm thinking irrationally. There're few enough people on the streets, so we ought to notice someone spying on us. The scanty traffic in Cullinsberg's streets pleased Astryd, providing fewer people to stare or giggle at her awkward dances. Of course, the absence of merchants caused the problem in the first place. The wares displayed on Aga'arin's holiday consisted almost entirely of necessities: food, firewood, and bottled remedies. Attaining the name of a weaponer had required a bribe. Another payment had convinced the man to open his shop, but Silme's and Astryd's desperation doubled his prices. A rope, twelve daggers, and one sword of dubious quality had depleted their resources beyond even the ability to purchase a bag to carry the supplies. The sight of a woman armed with two swords, Taziar's and the purchased one, drew odd looks from the few people they passed. Astryd had hidden the daggers on her person so as not to alarm the guards on Cullinsberg's market thoroughfares.

Silme rose, grim and silent. Without explanation, she hefted the packs. Astryd followed her, not bothering to question; Silme's expression told the story. Larson remained unconscious, and, until he awakened, Astryd was helpless to come to his aid. The discomfort of unseen eyes rose again, but she hid her fears from Silme. *I'm just not used to working under time constraints. Silme's worried enough without my adding imaginary ghosts to her concerns.*

The knives secured to Astryd's legs chafed and itched as she moved, turning her usually graceful walk into an arrhythmic, limping shuffle. Silme's willowy elegance made Astryd appear even more ridiculous, and concern for Larson and Taziar multiplied her discomfort. Though not well-trained or familiar with battle injuries, Astryd surmised that the longer a head injury left a man unconscious, the more potentially fatal it must prove. *When I last saw Shadow, he acted curt and uncaring; Harriman's cruelty may kill the very humanity that attracted me to Shadow.* Astryd ground her teeth at the thought. *And if Allerum doesn't awaken soon, the guards may finish the job.*

Astryd's engrossment in her friends' plight made her careless to her own. She followed Silme past a narrow crossroad, oblivious to its occupants until Harriman's familiar voice confronted her. "There you are, bitch. Who gave you permission to leave for this long?"

Startled, Astryd tensed, and breath hissed raggedly through her nose. Regaining her composure instantly, she turned toward Harriman and found him leaning against the wall at the alley mouth, Larson's katana dangling from a sheath at his hip. Halden and Skereye stood before him; shadows draped their scarred and smirking faces. Astryd considered running, but she knew the slaps and jabs of the daggers would slow her. *And Silme would need to drop the packs and maybe our staves to stay ahead of those two mon-*

sters. We can handle this peacefully. "Didn't the girls tell you? I quit."

"Quit?" Harriman stared at Silme as he spoke, eyes trailing the sorceress' curves with an intensity Astryd found nauseating. "You can't quit. We have an agreement."

"You haven't paid me yet." It occurred to Astryd that, unless Harriman killed her, he could do her no harm. *Once Allerum awakens, I can transport, in Harriman's presence or not. If Allerum awakens,* she reminded herself with a callous but necessary practicality. *But Harriman could trap Silme. Without magic, she can't transport.* "Don't bother to pay me for the work I've done, and I'll consider us even. I appreciate the opportunity to work for you, but I don't feel I can do an adequate job. I quit."

Harriman smiled with calm amusement, attention still fixed, fanatically, on Silme. "Get them both."

Halden and Skereye sprang forward with alarming speed. Before Astryd could think of dodging, Skereye's fingers closed on her forearm. His touch stung her to anger. She thrust a knee into Skereye's groin, jammed her hand into his face, and raked. One finger gouged an eye. "Run!" she screamed to Silme.

Skereye bellowed in rage, and pain drove him into a murderous frenzy. Rather than the release Astryd expected, his grip clamped tight as a vise. His fist crashed against her ear. The force of the blow hurled Astryd to the ground. Dizziness wrung her consciousness to meaningless tatters of reality, and she felt Skereye heft her by the front of her cloak without understanding the danger she was in. She heard a slap. Though she knew no further pain, Astryd cringed. Skereye freed her, and she collapsed to the cobbles, reeling.

Through a curtain of waving patterns, Astryd noticed the red mark on Skereye's cheek and realized the berserk had taken the blow she heard. Harriman's reprimand blurred beneath the ringing in Astryd's ears. "Damn you, Skereye! Don't hit the girls, or you'll be nursing worse than bruised privates."

Recalling Mat-hilde's ordeal in the whorehouse, Astryd found Harriman's warning ludicrous. Skereye scowled at his master, fists doubled, and coiled to fight. Light-headed, Astryd struggled to one knee. *Gods, I hope Harriman can control that brute.* Though the thought of praying for Harriman's welfare rankled, Astryd knew if Skereye killed his master, she would become the berserk's next victim. She glanced at Silme, saw her standing, regally dangerous despite Halden's grasp on her arms. Regardless of the awkwardness of Halden's presence, Silme managed to keep the packs balanced on her shoulders, though both dragonstaves lay on the cobbles. That, and the wild disarray of her hair made it clear that she had struggled and lost as well.

Skereye grumbled something unintelligible, seized Astryd's wrist, and hauled her to her feet. He lowered his face to hers. His left eye was tearing from her attack, and a scarlet arc marred the white. He spoke in the Scandinavian tongue, his voice as grating as fingernails scratched across stone. "You little bitch, this isn't over yet. I'll kill you."

Still staggering from Skereye's blow, Astryd managed no reply.

Harriman paid the threat no notice; either he lacked command of the language, or he feigned ignorance. "Take them home." He gestured his guards and their prisoners into the alleyway, stooped to gather the dragonstaves, and followed.

Gradually, Astryd's mind cleared as she traversed deserted back streets. Skereye's tightly-wrapped fingers cut off the circulation to her hands, but she made no mention of the dull throb. She tried to keep her gait as normal as possible, concentrating on the pain in her hands to offset the discomfort of a dozen concealed daggers. Though vindictiveness was not a normal part of Astryd's nature, the vision of all twelve blades buried in Skereye's heart soothed her. The realization that she could summon a dragon and destroy Harriman, the berserks, and a quarter of the city only added to her frustration. *I can't slay innocent townsfolk out of anger, and if I deplete my life energy on vengeance, the guards will kill Shadow and Allerum.* She sighed, enduring the indignity of Skereye's harsh tugs as the price of obligatory patience.

The sun had half-crested the horizon when Harriman and his captives arrived at Shylar's whorehouse. They passed through the double set of doors in a tense hush. The early hour and the religious fervor of the holiday left most of the girls free to lounge and talk. As Harriman entered the chamber, the hum of conversation died. He pointed to the stairway. "Take them to my room." He clarified. "The bedroom. The study has windows. Lock them in and stand guard. I'll join you shortly." He handed the dragonstaves to Halden.

Astryd sought Mat-hilde in the crowd, passed over a myriad of concerned expressions before she discovered the prostitute's familiar features. Skereye met Astryd's hesitation with a vicious jab in the spine. "Get moving."

Astryd trotted toward the stairway. Methodically, she climbed to the landing and into the room Skereye indicated. A moment later, Silme joined her, and the door clacked closed behind them.

To Astryd's relief, Halden and Skereye waited outside the chamber. She threw a quick glance at the Spartan effects of a warrior unused to wealth. The pallet she had seen in her location spell graced one corner, encompassing a quarter of the room, its covers and pillow crisply neat. An unadorned, straight-backed chair slanted against it, and a chest lay at the foot of the bed. A simple table held a lantern full of fat, its wick alight, its illumination broad and gray. *A potential weapon,* Astryd noted, but she realized the two swords and twelve daggers on her person would serve at least as well. From her personal link with her rankstone, she knew Harriman had placed the dragonstaves in a nearby room, but that was the least of her worries. She had little enough life energy stored in the garnet stone, and, should it become necessary, she could retrieve that magic instantly, even from a distance.

"What do we do?" Astryd questioned Silme to discover whether her companion had considered a less formidable plan than her own.

"We have no choice." Silme twisted her head and rolled her eyes in all directions, examining Harriman's chamber in her usual calm manner. "The way Harriman stared, he has no intention of killing me. I can handle myself, but Allerum and Shadow need you."

Silme's composure unnerved Astryd. "The way Harriman stared, he has no intention of ignoring you, either."

Silme met Astryd's gaze. "There's nothing Harriman can do to me worse than allowing Allerum and Shadow to die on the gallows. Now sit there." She stabbed a hand toward

the farthest corner. "Keep trying to contact Allerum. Don't
stop for anything. If you can't catch him awake, you're just
going to have to try to arouse him yourself."

"Arouse him myself?" Astryd repeated, confused. "How?"

"Instead of using a mental probe, you'll have to actually
place your presence into his mind. Dig for some sort of
sleep-wake trigger, and prod until he responds."

Silme's words shocked Astryd; the task sounded years
beyond her abilities. "I've never done anything like that."

Silme shrugged. "Of course, you haven't. How could
you? Allerum's the only person I know without mind
barriers . . . except Harriman." Silme paused, as if considering her own words. "Since thought intrusions don't cost life
energy, you risk nothing other than annoying Allerum."
Silme added belatedly, "And one other, more important
thing."

Astryd fidgeted, uncomfortable with the prospect. "And
that is?"

Silme sat on the chest. "By placing a part of yourself
into Allerum's mind, you make yourself vulnerable to any
sorcerer who tries the same tactic, also to Allerum's defenses. Once, Vidarr and I entered Allerum's mind, and he
accidentally pulled us all into his world, a land of fire and
madness." She shivered at the memory of Vietnam. "Apparently, the god, Vidarr, and the great wolf, Fenrir, held
an actual battle in Allerum's brain. Just remember, you'll
be inside his thoughts, displaced in time, not actually physically with him. You'll need to pull out of his mind before
you can transport." Silme leaned closer. "And be careful.
If you sense another presence, get out as fast as you can."

Though Silme never specified, Astryd knew the only foreign obstacle she could meet was Harriman's master. *My
choosing to stand against a sorcerer of his power would be
as absurd as a wounded sparrow challenging a hawk.* She
pressed into the indicated corner. "I'll do the best I can."
Lowering her head, she thrust her consciousness toward
Larson, trusting Silme to keep Harriman and his guards
occupied.

Astryd's probe met darkness.

Harriman slipped into his workroom and quietly closed
the door behind him, leaning the dragonstaves in the corner

by the panel. Dawn light snaked through the misshapen glass of the window, blurring the desktop and a few curled strips of parchment in glare. Harriman extracted a quill pen from the disarray, idly twirling it in loops between his fingers. Knowing better than to further delay the inevitable contact, he sat in the hard, wooden chair, dropped the pen, and drained his consciousness to a single name. *Bolverkr?*

The sorcerer's probe entered Harriman's mind, its touch chilling. *Did you capture him?*

Harriman hesitated, forcing emotion from his surface thoughts with the same ease as he controlled outward expressions. *Taziar?*

Yes.

No, Harriman admitted. *He got away.*

Tangible anger pervaded Bolverkr's silence.

Harriman waited, not allowing the slightest memory or sentiment to come to the fore.

I told you precisely where to find him.

Indeed, lord. And you were right, as always. Harriman stroked, believing his existence was worth less to Bolverkr than the four men Taziar had stranded on the rooftop. *My underlings failed and paid with their lives for the mistake. Next time, I'll catch Taziar myself.*

Next time? Bolverkr's question emerged passionlessly, but Harriman detected guarded hope. *You know where Taziar is?*

Harriman's surprise leaked through his facade. *Lord, I'd hoped to get that information from you.*

Bolverkr's annoyance pounded at Harriman's mind, and the diplomat knew he had struck a sore point. *I've lost my source. Loki's children, you're leader of the underground! Use your own spies. Get every man and child at your command out on those streets and find Taziar Medakan! No excuses. Every moment that little murderer evades us, he could find a way to undo the fate we've designed for him. Force him to watch his friends die. And when that's finished, I want Taziar hanged as well. Do you understand?*

Completely. Harriman picked up on Bolverkr's frustration, and it confused him. Not since the destruction of Wilsberg had any plan of Bolverkr's gone awry. Accustomed to the ever-changing tides of politics, Harriman accepted the unanticipated easily, and the sorcerer's loss of his arrogant self-control appalled him.

Apparently, Bolverkr noticed Harriman's discomfort. Shortly, Harriman felt the heat of Bolverkr's hatred as his own, and it sparked him to the same reckless fury. *Lord, what would you have me do with the women?*

Women? Bolverkr's composure returned in a rush. *What women?*

Taziar's companions. The sorceresses. I have them locked in my bedroom.

Indeed. Bolverkr hesitated, his manner fully calculating. *I doubt you'll be able to hold Astryd long. The one thing all Dragonrank mages learn to do early and well is escape. The other . . .*

Bolverkr's presence trailed away, and only a faint tingle of pleasure alerted Harriman that his master had not yet broken contact. *Lord?* He concentrated on the link so as not to miss Bolverkr's reply.

Bolverkr's words crashed into Harriman's heightened consciousness. *Force Silme to use her magic. Humiliate her any way you can, and don't quit until she's killed that child.* His message softened. *And Harriman . . .*

Master? Harriman prompted cautiously, unable to recall the last time the sorcerer had called him by name.

. . . have fun doing it. The probe disappeared from Harriman's mind.

Harriman pictured Silme's delicate arcs, firm breasts, and the timeless beauty of her golden features. *I wonder how long it will take to destroy the haughty tilt to her chin and the fierce gleam in those ice blue eyes?* A smile pinched Harriman's face as he accepted Bolverkr's task with glee.

Gradually, the tug and jostle of Silme freeing hidden daggers became familiar to Astryd, and the smaller sorceress directed her full concentration to Larson's mind. Mired in darkness, she dodged and crawled through loops of thought as chaotic as a bramble copse. Harriman's bedroom disappeared from her awareness; Astryd did not know she still lay, limp and silent, in the corner. She kept her mind focused, all too aware that she could die as easily from another presence in Larson's mind as from a slash of Harriman's sword.

Uncertain how much stress threads of thought could stand, Astryd brushed them aside with a gentle caution. She wondered how much of what she found constituted actual anatomy and how much was her magical perception of memory. As the intensity of her search absorbed her completely, the question faded into the infinity of insignificant facts. Catching sight of a spark of light, she ran to it with the fatal devotion of a moth to a flame. She skidded to a stop before it, felt Larson's annoyance as though it were her own. *If . . .*

The idea sputtered feebly, and died. In frustration, Astryd kicked the pathway that had initiated the thought, watched it flare and grow. *If that sonofabitch doesn't stop shaking me, I'm going to kill him!* Several nearby avenues flashed as confusion pervaded Larson's mind. A survival instinct blossomed. She felt Larson tense and crouch, even before he opened his eyes. Then his lids fluttered, and Astryd caught a close up view of Taziar's worried features. "Allerum! Can you hear me?"

Rows of cages slashed across Larson's vision, and Astryd saw guards with swords rushing toward emaciated, scarred men cowering at the barred doors. Without waiting for Larson to interpret the reality of the dungeon, Astryd withdrew. She found herself back in the corner of Harriman's room.

Harriman's heavy bootfalls sounded in the outside corridor.

Too concerned about the men to consider Silme's plight, Astryd hugged the piled daggers and triggered her escape transport. Golden light erupted in a blinding flash.

When Harriman opened the door, all that remained of Astryd was a rolling pulse of oily smoke.

CHAPTER 11
Shadows of the Gallows

Whoever fights monsters should see to it that in the process he does not become a monster. And when you look
long into an abyss, the abyss also looks into you.
— Fredrich Nietzsche
Beyond Good and Evil

Light exploded in the baron's dungeon, shattering Taziar's
vision before he could think to shield his eyes. Larson stiffened, and his sudden movement staggered Taziar into the
cell door. Half-blinded, the Climber clawed for support,
barking his knuckles on iron clotted with rust. The click of
opening locks and the pounding of guards' footfalls gave
way to a shocked silence that seemed to amplify Astryd's
plea. "Shadow, hurry. Harriman has Silme trapped in the
whorehouse!"

Back pressed to the bars and supporting much of Larson's
weight, Taziar twisted awkwardly toward the walkway.
Through a web of shadowed afterimages, he recognized Astryd. A coil of rope lay slung across her shoulder. Two swords
dangled at her side, and she balanced an armload of daggers against her chest. Her beauty seemed so misplaced
amidst the filth and gloom of the baron's dungeon, it took
Taziar a moment to believe she was real.

Larson's bulk eased off Taziar as the elf came fully
awake. Seizing the rope from Astryd, Taziar guided Larson's hand to the swords. "Allerum, keep one and take the
other to the redhead." He gestured to the left pathway
where Fridurik crouched in the cage closest to the exit and
the guards. "Go!"

Accepting the swords, Larson tottered off in the indicated direction.

Sound echoed as sentries and prisoners broke free of the
surprise inspired by Astryd's grand entrance. Desperately,

Taziar caught Astryd's arm. "Distribute those knives as quickly and quietly as you can. Then transport out and wait. We'll need your help against Harriman far more than we do here." He released her with a mild push toward the prisoners and wished he could spare a second for comforting.

The central pens split the baron's dungeon into two lanes with Larson's cell along the back wall. Shylar had chosen to unlock the doors from the left pathway. Hoping for a clear passage to the outer door, Taziar sprinted to the right. "This way!"

Within three running strides, Asril the Procurer darted alongside Taziar. A quick glance over his shoulder revealed that only Shylar and Mandel had followed them. Apparently, the others had taken the parallel walkway. *Including both swordsmen,* Taziar realized in sudden alarm. He tried to decipher the blur of color and movement through the central cells, obscured by the yellow backwash of Astryd's magical departure. *Thank the gods, at least she got out safely.*

A warning touch from Asril slowed Taziar's reckless pace and brought his attention to a pair of guards with drawn swords blocking the pathway. A third tensed behind them.

Taziar cursed silently as he realized the guards had separated to prevent escape down either pathway. Well within sword range, Taziar and Asril skidded to a halt in front of the guards; Shylar and Mandel backpedaled, avoiding a collision.

The sentry before Asril waved his sword threateningly. "Get back to your cells."

Taziar met the guard's gaze, his hand sliding, unobtrusively, for his own dagger. From the corner of his vision, he realized Asril held a knife, expertly couched against his wrist so the guards could not see it. Taziar's heart raced. *The cage row would have blocked Astryd from the guards' view. Depending on her caution and when these guards split off from the others, they may not know we have weapons.* Only then did Taziar recall that Asril was a street fighter, born to a freelance prostitute barely into her teens.

Knife still hidden, Asril made a gesture of surrender. "All right. Don't hurt us." A nervous spring entered his step, and he shuffled backward with a commitment that

fooled even Taziar. Suddenly, Asril sprang at the guard.
The dagger flashed, then disappeared, buried in the sentry's
upper abdomen and angled beneath the breastbone.

The guard gasped in shock and pain. The sword fell from
his hands and crashed to the floor. From the parallel pathway, steel chimed repeatedly, as if in echo. Asril shoved
the dying guard backward as he ripped his blade free, but
the sentry before Taziar responded more swiftly. His sword
whipped for Asril's head.

No time to draw a weapon! Taziar dove with desperate
courage. His shoulder crashed into the sentry's gut, driving
him over backward. The guard twisted as he fell. His left
arm encircled Taziar, wrenching. Taziar struck the ground
sideways, breath dashed from him in a gasp. Recognizing
the helplessness of his position, he grabbed wildly for the
guard's sword hilt. His fingers closed over a fleshy hand.
But with superior strength and leverage, the guard tore free
and jammed his elbows into Taziar's face.

Pain shot through Taziar's nose. The force of the blow
smashed his head against stone, and blood coursed, warm
and salty, on his lips. He saw the sword blade speeding
toward him and knew with grim certainty that he could not
roll in time.

Asril's lithe form sailed over Taziar and plowed into the
guard. Taziar scuttled clear as Asril and the guard tumbled.
This time, Asril landed on top, his arm wrapped around
the sentry's throat. A flick of his wrist drew the blade of
his dagger across the guard's muscled neck. Blood spurted,
splashing Mandel as he darted past Taziar in pursuit of the
third guard who had made a dash for the outer door amidst
the crash and bell of swordplay in the other lane.

Taziar staggered after Mandel. "Stop him!" *We can't let
that guard get around the corner to warn the others.* Taziar
watched in frustration as the sentry outdistanced the weakened Mandel, sprinted through the outer, barred door, and
slammed it behind him. The sentry fumbled with his keys.
Jamming one into the hole, he spun it to the locked position then raised his sword and brought it down, hard,
against the stem. Metal snapped with the sickening finality
of bone. The base of the key clattered to the floor, the
remainder wedged in the lock. The guard raced down the
passageway.

Mandel hit the door with a force that rattled the steel. Grasping the bars, he shook them viciously. The panel resisted his efforts. Muttering a bitter blasphemy, he snaked an arm through the bars and hurled his dagger at the guard's retreating back.

Taziar cringed, aware only deep urgency could have goaded Mandel to disarm himself. To Taziar's surprise, Mandel's aim was true. He heard the thud of the guard's body striking the floor, followed by the soft and haunting moans of the dying.

When Taziar reached the outer door, he peered through the bars. The guard lay on the floor of the passageway, Mandel's dagger protruding from his lower back. Blood soaked the hem of his uniform, and Taziar guessed the blade had nicked a kidney. Apparently too weak to gather breath for a scream, the guard was inching toward his companions.

A glance down the dungeon's parallel lane revealed the other three guards had fallen to the swordsmen, though only Larson's blade was blooded. Fridurik panted; weeks of torture had taken a toll on his endurance, but Taziar was just glad to see the red-haired giant on his feet.

Shylar stabbed the key into the lock. It sank in only partway despite maneuvering, and she shook her head in defeat. "It won't go."

Mandel copied her gesture, his arm limp between the bars. "I can't get it from the other side either."

Slipping his thinner, more finely crafted knife from his pocket, Taziar knelt before the lock. Before he could insert the tip, a sudden, sharp movement caught his attention. He ducked, scuttling aside as Larson's sword smacked into the door, jolting the metal to its hinges. Larson drew back for another blow.

"Allerum, stop," Taziar hissed.

The sword paused.

"I think I can get us out faster and quieter. Let me try."

Larson nodded once and lowered his sword.

Taziar wiped moisture from his eyes with his forearm, and the red stain it left on his sleeve revealed blood, not sweat, marred his vision. *Not again.* Suddenly it struck Taziar how badly his shattered nose throbbed and his head ached. *The others are hurt worse,* he reminded himself, forcing his concentration to his task. *I have no right to complain.* He eased the tip of the blade into the hole and met the resistance of the broken key trapped in the mechanism. He applied gentle pressure, but in the locked position the key would not budge.

Pain faded before the intensity of Taziar's thoughts. He could hear the prisoners shifting around him, the clink of steel as they gathered swords from the dead guards, and their bleak whispers about the steady progress of the injured sentry in the hallway. Knife point tight to the base of the broken key, Taziar banished the noises around him and twisted the blade in a fabricated silence. He felt the key give ever so slightly. *It's going to work.* Hope flared, tempered by the urgency of time dwindling. He rotated the dagger again, felt the impasse barely budge. *But it's not going to happen fast. Still, it's quicker than Allerum beating on solid steel and a lot less likely to draw the other nine guards.*

As the movement of rotation and slippage became routine, thoughts invaded Taziar's private world. He considered the many lives that now lay in his hands, a list far beyond the ragged band of friends trapped before the prison door. He considered the beggars, the aged, crazed, and orphaned who wandered Cullinsberg's streets through no fault of their own. He would not wish their fate upon anyone, yet there was no one special enough, no one so favored by gods and men that he could not wind up in their position. *Not even the son of the baron's loyal guard captain.* He turned the blade, felt the metal shift. *Perhaps not even the baron himself.*

Taziar's thoughts turned to the women in the whorehouse, loyal to Shylar's final command despite Harriman's brutality. He contemplated the violence and paranoia of the street gangs, inspired by Harriman's greed, and the many innocent merchants who would pay with their lives. *The same citizens who would cheer the hangings of the underground leaders would suffer for their deaths.* Taziar imagined the city devoid of Shylar's charity, Mandel's payoffs, and the lotteries Amalric skewed toward families in need of food or shelter. Without fighters like Asril to champion them, the young and the old would succumb to the strong; muggers and assassins would replace children and beggars.

Recalling his encounters in the alleyways, Taziar knew Cullinsberg had already changed. *And it's going to get worse unless we stop it.* He wrestled with the jammed key, quickening his pace.

And then there's Allerum. One last picture filled Taziar's mind. He saw Silme, stately and grimly capable. She had spent her childhood protecting her half-human half-brother, Bramin, from prejudice and then was forced to devote her youth to hunting him down and killing him. She had rescued innocents from vengeances as cruel and inappropriate as those of Harriman's master, yet her best efforts could not keep Bramin from slaying her parents and siblings. Silme had suffered through too much; nothing seemed to daunt her anymore. Everything she did, she had learned to do with infallible skill and without external emotion. *But deep down, she cares. She dared open herself to the pain loving Allerum might cost her. Quick as she made it, the decision to save the baby rather than Allerum must have torn her apart. And there's only one reason she could have made the choice she did: she believes in me. Silme's more certain I can free Allerum than I am myself, and hers is a trust I won't betray.*

Odwulf's alarm cut through Taziar's self-imposed isolation. "He made it around the corner."

Taziar spun the dagger hard, adding his curses to those of his friends. A click heralded the final movement of the wedged piece of key; though muffled, it came sweet as a shout of triumph to Taziar's ears. He poked, and the metal twig slid to the granite floor with a clang that sounded loud in an abrupt and hopeful hush.

Taziar rose. The sudden rush of blood made his legs throb, and he hobbled painfully aside.

Asril hit the heavy door with his shoulder, and it swung open with a shrill of rusted hinges. "Got to get the guard," the street fighter mumbled as he raced down the hallway brandishing a sentry's long sword.

Taziar and Shylar scrambled after Asril, Larson and Fridurik on their heels. Taziar darted as fast as his awakening legs could allow. Behind him, the footsteps of Amalric, Waldhram, Odwulf, and Mandel wafted to him like drumbeats. His shoulder ached from the weight of the rope, and he wished he had thought to set it on the floor while he worked. Each running step jarred a pins and needles sensation through his thighs. Far ahead, Asril reached the ninety degree turn in the passage and skidded around the corner. Across from the corridor Asril had entered, the long, stone-framed window lay open, silken curtains dancing in the autumn breeze.

Almost there. The scene was too familiar to Taziar. Memory overpowered him, and he felt himself stumbling down this same passageway, fighting for consciousness at the heels of a barbarian prince. Then, guards with swords and crossbows had filled the corridor. *The corridor Asril just entered.* Before Taziar could shout a warning, Asril reappeared.

"Guards!" Asril screamed, sliding to a halt at the window ledge. He glanced through the opening, staring wide-eyed at the seven-story drop to the baron's moat. "Mardain's mercy."

Taziar ripped the coil from his shoulder as he overtook Asril. He threw only a casual glance at the guards, still some distance down the corridor, and hunted for some object on which to anchor the rope. Finding nothing, he tossed one end through the window and wrapped the other twice around his own middle. Bracing his feet against the wall beneath the window, he sat. "Climb!" he yelled to Shylar. "Fast. And keep everyone together down there. We're going to need all their help to defeat Harriman."

Shylar tossed a meaningful glance of confirmation at Taziar, then obeyed. He felt the tugs as she descended. Taziar gritted his teeth, adding to himself. *And by the gods Shylar, convince them I'm not the traitor.* He looked up to see Asril gawking at the guards. "Go!" Taziar commanded.

"You can't stay there." Asril glanced rapidly from Taziar to the guard-filled corridor behind him. "You're a target."

"Damn it, go!" Frustration and rising anger added volume to Taziar's voice. "Climb down or get the hell out of everyone else's way!" Taziar pulled the rope more securely around him, aware that if the guards killed him, his corpse would still weigh the rope in place to let the others escape.

Sword bared, Larson sprang between Taziar and the guards. Fridurik took a stance at Larson's side. To Taziar's relief, Asril leaped to the windowsill and clambered down the rope. *Good. Shylar will need a fighter like Asril, and at least some of them will make it back to face Harriman.*

Behind Taziar, steel jammed against steel. He did not bother to turn. Any man who could fight through Larson would prove more than a match for Taziar, especially weaponless and tangled in the rope. *But not all of us will survive.* Taziar lowered his head. There was no doubt in his mind that he and Larson would be among the casualties.

Silme stood to face Harriman, her posture projecting dangerous competence. But beneath a calm and imposing exterior, fear coiled in her gut. The feeling seemed alien, from a distant past before the Dragonrank school trained her to a craft few men could stand against. *With magic, I could best him in my sleep. But the handful of tricks I learned from Gaelinar will scarcely delay a soldier who controls a berserk who already overpowered me.*

To Silme's surprise, Harriman seemed unimpressed by Astryd's disappearance. *A sure sign he knows exactly who and what we are.* The thought grated, intensifying her uneasiness until she felt queasy. She took a step back, never losing her quiet dignity and grace.

A smile creased Harriman's handsome features. His dark eyes seemed as flat and emotionless as his expression, but Silme saw madness lurking in their depths. "Well, Silme. I think we're going to become close friends." His voice lingered on the word "close." He approached, regal as a king in his own castle.

He smelled of sword oil, sweat, and perfume. The combination intensified Silme's nausea. Her stomach heaved, and, for a moment, she lost all pretense and sat on the edge of the bed. She regathered her composure, wondering how much of her illness stemmed from the pregnancy. "I think not." Silme managed to keep her voice steady and even added an edge of threat.

Undeterred, Harriman took a seat close behind Silme. Quick as a striking snake, he placed a hand on her head and smoothed the thick, golden waves.

Revulsion turned to rage. Silme caught Harriman's hand before it slid to her breast. She seized it the way Gaelinar had taught her, with her thumb on Harriman's smallest knuckle.

No grimace of pain or surprise flashed across Harriman's face. With a warrior's training, he latched his free hand onto her grip, yanking with a strength that lanced pain through her arm.

It required Silme's full self-control not to gasp. She released his hand, the image of Harriman writhing in magical flames giving substance to her hatred. Still clinging to her hand, he flung her violently to the coverlet. She twisted, clawing for his face with her opposite hand. Batting the attack aside, Harriman wrenched Silme's trapped arm so suddenly she thought it might break. She rolled back to escape the pain as Harriman pinned her other arm beneath his knee.

Silme felt her bravado slipping. Hot with anger, she was almost overwhelmed by another emotion, one she could not name that scattered her wits and goaded her to fight without direction. "Is it death you seek, Harriman? I can make it cruel." She realized a single gesture and a major expenditure of energy could send him into agonized spasms. Then she could shield or transport away, perhaps create an opening to kill him. The idea of murder soothed Silme, smothering her panic. She fought to free her left hand, but Harriman's knee crushed her wrist.

Harriman laughed, the sound light with calculation and eagerness. "Be cruel, then. I've faced death before, and it doesn't frighten me. I've subdued those two berserks." He said it "bair-sair," the musical, Norse pronunciation sounding out of place amidst his southern accent and clipped, Wilsberg dialect. "I doubt you could do worse, but you're welcome to try."

Silme ignored the taunt, forcing herself to think. *Dare I use magic? Allerum and I could conceive another baby.* The moment of consideration reminded her she still had her utility knife tucked in a pocket of her dress.

Harriman eased the pressure on Silme's hands. "Oh, ach, how cruel." He clutched his throat with his free hand. "How do I bear the anguish?"

Silme knew Harriman mocked her. *He wants me to kill the baby.* She winced, realizing fury had nearly driven her to do exactly what he wanted. Now the idea seemed painfully evil. The child had become a real, a solid part of her she had protected through too much already. *Allerum,*

Taziar, and Astryd might die for this baby. I can suffer through Harriman's indignities for the life of our child.

Harriman blinked in the silence. When Silme gave him no reply, he shifted, his weight smashing her legs to the coverlet. One-handed, he fumbled with the buckle of his sword belt, unfastened it, and tossed it to the floor.

The weapon flew in a wide arc. Silme recognized the black brocade of its hilt and the slim curve of its sheath. *Gaelinar's katana.* The sword whacked against the floor, leather whisking as it slid across granite. Gaelinar had often claimed a man's sword was an extension of his spirit. She had seen the ronin samurai let wounds gape and bleed while he tended a blade dirtied or nicked in battle. Harriman's casualness dishonored Silme's memory of the greatest swordsman in the world, a single-mindedly loyal bodyguard who had also been a respected friend. Fear retreated, leaving only the blinding rage. She struggled wildly against him.

Harriman jarred a backhanded slap across her cheek and jerked her trapped arm so savagely Silme could not keep from screaming. She went limp, waiting for the pain to subside. Tears filled her eyes, transforming Harriman into a blue-white blur. She felt him paw at her dress, heard the jerk and tear of undergarments, followed by the cold touch of air on her exposed thighs. Unable to contain her terror, she sobbed, then bit her lip. *He may be able to humiliate me, but I won't give him the satisfaction of seeing me cry.*

A single, sharp tug at the ties of Silme's bodice bared her breasts. Harriman's speed shocked her. She twisted her gaze to the knife he clutched, splinters of leather still clinging to the blade. *My knife,* Silme realized. *My last chance to fight him.* Her hands and legs had gone numb beneath him. Bile rose, sour in her throat. He clamped a hand, icy and pinching, to her breast, and her flesh crawled beneath his touch. She met his eyes, soft brown, his expression gentle and incongruous with his actions.

"You're mine, Silme." Harriman stated it as simple fact, as if gloating was not a part of his emotional repertoire. "You belong to me now, and I can do anything I want." As if to prove his claim, he arched against her and reached to unfasten his own garments.

Harriman's words were a challenge. *He believes he owns*

me, this damaged creature controlled by another sorcerer.
The thought mobilized Silme, and she cursed herself for
not considering the option sooner. She gathered and
grounded her awareness, burying fear and anger beneath
intensity of will, and thrust her way through the ruins of
Harriman's mind barriers.

Silme's last physical perception was of her body sagging
into the straw mattress. Her sense of Harriman's bedroom,
the understanding of pain, Harriman's skin touching hers
all disappeared as she ducked between the clinging shards
of his mental barrier into a world of thought and memory.
The superficial glimpse her probe had admitted the previous day did not prepare her for the vast plain of slashed,
looped, and knotted pathways, chaotic as tangled harp
strings. Harriman's master had made no attempt to hide
his meddling. But no matter how much time the sorcerer
had had to maim and corrupt, Silme knew his efforts must
prove mediocre, at best. In order to maintain Harriman's
abilities as warrior and diplomat, the experiences that
taught him those skills must remain intact. *The master must
have obliterated the connections between action and emotion.*

Surprise reverberated through Harriman's mind, liberally
mixed with confusion and frustration. Silme caught the
name "Bolverkr" bright as a signal flare, a desperate plea
for help radiating from Harriman's thoughts.

Silme froze. She harbored no doubt Bolverkr was Harriman's master, a sorcerer whose skill and strength she could
not hope to stand against. *I must find some memory terrible
enough to distract Harriman while I escape. And I have to
work fast!* Silme sprang forward and swam through the
thought pathways, experiencing rapid glimpses of Harriman's past realities. She found a life entwined with lies and
deception, hidden ideas and expressions. As if from a great
distance and through Harriman's perception instead of her
own, she felt his body stiffen. Lust died like a candle
snuffed. She heard him howl, a deep echo in his own ears,
heard the click of the doorknob.

Silme delved faster, hurling aside thoughts and memories
like bits of colored string. Recollection sparked and died,
an endless show of fragments. Harriman thudded against
the floor, arms wrapped around his head. Silme felt him
rolling, screaming. Her own cruelty raised guilt. Still she

dug, more gently now, seeking a childhood memory Bolverkr might not have bothered to warp. To her surprise, her pang of regret hammered through Harriman's mind, intensified by receptors apparently set by Bolverkr to relay his emotions as if they were Harriman's own.

And Silme found what she sought. She ignited an ancient memory, nurtured and enhanced it like a spark against kindling. Harriman's shrieks stopped abruptly. He waved off the berserks, then sat on the edge of his bed, his face clapped between his palms, and relived the moment with Silme:

Eight years old, Harriman crouched behind a floor-length curtain of velvet and lace, watching naked bodies entwined on the canopied bed at the center of the room. Silme knew the couple as Harriman did, his mother, a maid, smashed beneath the bulk of the duke. As the duke's bastard, Harriman had free run of the keep except for this bedroom. The lure of the forbidden had drawn him here, and now he attributed his mother's moans to violence inflicted upon her by the duke. The scene should have cut him to the heart, but, oddly, it inspired no reaction. Silme separated her mind from Harriman's, discovered the spliced pathways that should have supplied emotion to the scene. Accepting the burden, she forced herself to look upon the incident as a boy concerned for his mother rather than a woman pitying the recollection of a child.

Carefully, Silme added the anguish, rage, and a glimmer of hatred, felt them blossom and Harriman's answering shudder. Linked with his memory, she watched the child that was Harriman dash aside the curtain and run to the bedside. She heard his scream of outrage, felt his tiny fist pound the duke's tautly-muscled back. The duke twisted. A hand lashed out, caught the child a staggering blow across the mouth. The force flung Harriman against the wall. Fighting for breath, hands wet with blood and tears, the child covered his eyes to block out the scene on the bed.

Harriman supplied the memory, Silme the sensation. Magnified by Bolverkr's handiwork, the combination nearly overwhelmed Silme. Tears of rage and pity burned her eyes. She felt Harriman sobbing, too, and released him from the recollection. Quickly, she backtracked, found the remembrances of the berserks battering Taziar, and forced

Harriman to confront his actions in the cruel light of his own judgment. Mangled by the passion borrowed from Silme, Harriman shuddered, racked with guilt. Encouraged by her success, Silme shouldered aside mercy, steering Harriman's thoughts to his attack against her.

Suddenly, fingers gouged Silme's shoulder. She gasped and felt her shock flash solidly through Harriman's mind. Whirling, she found herself staring at a tall, thin man dressed in a tunic and hose so neutral gray they seemed to have no color at all. He wore a brown cloak, and, above the collar, Silme met blue eyes as cold as the bitterest Scandinavian winter. White hair lay sweat-plastered to his forehead. His face was clean-shaven and eternal as mountains. The life aura surrounding him glimmered, as blindingly brilliant as a roomful of high ranking Dragonmages. His stance seemed casual, but it neatly blocked Silme's escape.

Silme knew she confronted Harriman's master yet, oddly, the realization brought no fear. She could not hope to best him; her powers lay so far beneath his, a fight would prove futile. *If he wanted to kill me, he would have done so already.* The awareness released Silme from the need to plot, freed her from all emotion but curiosity, and no pretenses were necessary. "Bolverkr," she said simply, as if well-met over a glass of wine rather than amidst the tatters of a human mind whose owner lay weeping on a granite floor.

"Silme." Bolverkr nodded with careless respect. He continued as if he had come solely to make conversation. "You nearly destroyed my hard work." He flung a gesture at Harriman's mind.

Silme studied Bolverkr's face, unable to guess his age or fathom his intentions. "That was my objective."

"Indeed." He conceded. "And understandable, I suppose."

Silme's gaze followed the lines of Bolverkr's frame. His body obstructed the exit from Harriman's mind too completely for accident. Confused by his pleasantness, she awaited an attack as abrupt and ruthless as the ones perpetrated against Taziar. "I don't suppose you would stand aside and let me leave."

"No need." Bolverkr shrugged narrow shoulders. "You're Dragonrank. A simple transport escape would take you anywhere you wanted to go."

"Not from inside someone else's mind."

Bolverkr shrugged again, this time in concession. "We could go elsewhere. Some place where you could escape with a transport spell."

"Certainly, but at what price?"

"An insignificant expenditure of energy. The life of an unborn child who should never have been conceived. Nothing more."

Bolverkr's game had worn thin and, with it, Silme's patience. "Sorry, it's my baby. I chose to conceive it, and I choose to bear it. That decision doesn't involve you." Annoyance made her bold. "I don't even know you. What possible interest could you have in my baby?"

Bolverkr shifted but left Silme no opening for escape. "That child is an much as anathema as Loki's own. Allowed to live, it might inflict as much evil as its father."

"Evil? Allerum?" Bolverkr's accusation seemed so ridiculous, Silme had to struggle to keep from laughing. She recalled the features that attracted her to Larson: selfless dedication to friends and causes, an unfamiliarity with her world that allowed him to treat her as someone to be loved rather than feared, the ability to cry, and a guileless, solid morality that drove him to defy Gaelinar at the risk of his own life. "That's nonsense, Bolverkr. Allerum acts tough at times. I admit, he's trained to fight, but he wouldn't hurt anyone or anything without good cause."

Bolverkr placed a hand on Silme's shoulder, his touch patronizing. "I didn't question the elf's intentions. You must realize he's an anachronism. He doesn't belong here. Purposeful or not, his presence disrupts the fragile balance of our world. Just like Geirmagnus."

"Geirmagnus?" Silme repeated, floored by the comparison. "The first Dragonrank Master?" She recalled how Larson had let Taziar describe the men's exploits in the ancient estate of Geirmagnus. At the time, Taziar had mentioned that there was something odd about Larson's knowledge of the ancient Dragonmage's artifacts. But Larson had avoided the subject, passing it off as unimportant. Attributing Larson's reticence to grief for Kensei Gaelinar and reluctance to relive his own near-fatal gunshot wound, Silme had let the matter rest. Now, recalling Larson's tendency to gloss over details of his past that he found too complicated to explain, Silme wished she had pressed him harder for information.

"Geirmagnus wasn't a Dragonrank Master," Bolverkr corrected. "He was the Master of the Dragon Ranks. Doesn't that school of yours teach history? Geirmagnus never had the ability to perform magic. Like Allerum, he came from the future. Geirmagnus used techniques from his era to find potential sorcerers and teach them to channel Chaos. I think he meant well, but he dabbled with the foundations of our world as though they were his personal toys. Because of Geirmagnus, the gods of legend became real and Dragonrank mages can tap power. No doubt, his meddling caused many other changes throughout our world and its past and future history. But forces are made to balance, to keep our world alive; and those forces fought back, Silme. The Chaos Geirmagnus summoned killed him before he could inflict more damage on our world."

"How could you possibly know all that? The school teaches Geirmagnus' history as well as any man or god has learned it, but he died centuries ago."

"One hundred eighty-nine years." Bolverkr met Silme's incredulity with an expression so somber, she did not think to doubt him. "I was there."

"That would make you more than one hundred eighty-nine years old."

"Two hundred seventeen." Bolverkr patted his chest. "Not bad for a man of my age."

Silme said nothing, the joke lost in a wash of bewilderment. She glanced at the shattered barriers of Harriman's mind and shivered with awe at the amount of chaos Bolverkr must command. The Dragonrank school had taught her that the earliest sorcerers wielded more power than modern mages, and Taziar's story confirmed the speculation. But not even the exaggerations of bards and storytellers had prepared her for the boundless energy of the Dragonmage before her.

Bolverkr cleared his throat. "Is Allerum a sorcerer?"

Silme knew lying would prove fruitless. Bolverkr had already explored Larson's mind, and his question could only serve to test her honesty. "Certainly not."

"Is he strong?"

"Not unusually," Silme admitted.

"Is he skilled with weapons?"

"Yes."

"When he first arrived in our world?"

When I met Allerum, I'm not sure he knew which end of the sword to hold. "No," she said aloud. Not wanting Bolverkr to lose his reluctance to challenge Larson directly, she added, "But Gaelinar . . ."

Bolverkr interrupted. "Yet a man without any special abilities killed a god and a Dragonrank Master, restored life to a sorceress and another god. A god, I might add, the gods themselves could not rescue. Can you explain that?"

Bolverkr's words spurred memories within Silme, a grim mixture of joy and sorrow. The tasks had proven difficult beyond compare. Success had required effort, desperation, gods' aid, threats, and a lot of teamwork. Luck played a large role, and victory had been tainted by the death of friends. Still, Silme was more interested in Bolverkr's theory, so she turned the question back to him. "Clearer purpose and a more focused will." She used the words Gaelinar would have chosen. "But I imagine you have a different explanation."

"Allerum doesn't belong here. Something about misplacement in time makes the natural forces more sensitive to his interference, Silme." Bolverkr paused, genuine concern creasing his timeless features. "Gradually, Allerum will destroy our world. That's why we have to kill him now."

"You're mad." Silme took the offensive. "And what you propose is madness. I told you before, Allerum would never harm anyone without provocation."

"No?" Bolverkr's tone became a perfect blend of grief and triumph, as though he made a solid point at the expense of his own happiness. "Let me show you." With an exaggerated gesture of apology, he grabbed Silme's wrist and pulled her through the exit of Harriman's memory.

A flash of light obscured the maze of Harriman's thoughts. Silme's awareness overturned. Flung back into her body, she barely had time to glimpse Harriman's bedroom before she was wrenched into a vortex of Bolverkr's sorcery. She landed on her back amid a wreckage of stone. Autumn wind swirled, chill through the tatters of her dress. A stomach cramp doubled her up. She rolled, clutching at her abdomen, knees and elbows drawn in tight.

After the deep gloom of Harriman's mind, the ruddy light of sunset seemed bright as day. At length, Silme's vision sharpened and her nausea subsided. But where she expected to find farmers scurrying to finish harvest before nightfall, smoke twining from cooking fires, and goats tramping muddy paddocks, she saw crops uprooted and a shattered jumble of thatch and stone. Corpses were tumbled in awkward piles, terror locked on every upturned face. Grief battered at Silme, and the foreignness of its source frightened her as much as its intensity did. The spell Bolverkr had used to bring her to this location defied all logic. *He drew us out of Harriman's mind to cast it, so we must have transported here. Yet no Dragonmage has ever held the power or knowledge to transport another being.* "It's a trick," she said. "An illusion."

"Neither." Bolverkr removed his cloak and spread it across Silme's shoulders. "To make you see something unreal, I would have to access your mind. I would need to do to you what I did to Harriman. I think you know I haven't."

Silme sat up, drawing the cloak over her torn clothing. She winced at the imagined pain of Bolverkr's attack against Harriman. *If Bolverkr holds enough life energy to shatter mind barriers, why couldn't he learn to transport another sorcerer?* Fear clutched at her. *How can I hope to defy a mage with this much power?*

"You're seeing Harriman's last memory of his village and his friends." Bolverkr knelt beside Silme, staring out over the town. His features were etched with pain, but he took the time to answer Silme's unspoken questions. "I created an entrance to this thought so it can be accessed with a transport spell, but, as you can see, I didn't change the memory itself. The sorrow we feel is Harriman's."

The immensity of the tragedy jarred Silme beyond speech. A question came to mind, but Bolverkr answered it before she could put it into words.

"I left Harriman the emotion this scene inspired in order to commit him against the enemies who caused the destruction."

Suddenly, Bolverkr's strategy became clear to Silme. "You want me to believe Allerum and Taziar caused this?"

"Yes." Bolverkr pulled at a fold in his cloak, covering a

rip in the fabric of Silme's dress. "But only because it's the truth."

Silme scowled. "You're lying."

"I'm not. And when I explain how they did it, you'll know I'm not."

Silme shrugged. Beneath a noncommittal exterior, she felt ragged with doubt. "Speak, then. But I'll judge for myself."

"I expected nothing else." Bolverkr tipped his face away, and Silme could see the edge of a bitter smile. "Did Allerum and Taziar tell you they killed a manifestation of Chaos?"

"A dragon." Silme felt the queasiness return. "Yes."

"Not just a dragon. The dragon that killed Geirmagnus and nearly all the original Dragonrank mages." Bolverkr seized Silme's hand. "A dragon composed of enough Chaos to balance the resurrection of a god and a sorceress of your power."

Unnerved by the direction Bolverkr's explanation was taking, Silme jerked her hand free. "They told me. What of it?"

Bolverkr accepted her rebuff without comment. His hand hovered, as if uncertain where to go, then it dropped to his knee. "You and I know Chaos is a force, not a being. The only way to destroy chaos is to slay its living host: a man or a god. Dragons are manifestations of raw chaos, not living beings. When Allerum and Taziar killed the dragon, they dispersed that chaos. Dispersed it, Silme, not destroyed it. And the natural bent of such energy, whether of Order or Chaos, is to find itself a master."

Horror swept through Silme, chipping away the confidence she had known since childhood. "You?" Though unnecessary, the question came naturally to Silme's lips. Bolverkr's life aura gave the answer, still so grand as to obscure hers like a shuttered lantern in full sunlight.

"The one man alive since the conception of magic. A logical choice, I think."

Silme doubted Chaos had the ability to reason. *Still, even mindless things seem drawn to survival. Few other hosts could have lived through the transference of that much energy.* She dodged that line of thought, embarrassed curiosity could usurp concern for Larson and Taziar. "Allerum never meant you any harm. He had no idea the Chaos-force would seek you out and no way to know it would kill people. You can't condemn a man for ignorance."

"Why not?" Bolverkr waved his hands in agitation. "The laws do. Imagine if a foreigner killed and robbed a tavern-master in Cullinsberg. It wouldn't matter to the baron that this was acceptable behavior in the foreigner's kingdom. The murderer would be sentenced and hanged as quickly as any citizen." His voice assumed the practical monotone of a lord passing judgment. "The ignorant should not, must not meddle with the fabric of our world. Allerum and Taziar plunge willingly into impossible tasks *without bothering to consider the consequences.* For their crimes, any regime would condemn them to death."

"No." Silme felt as if something had tightened around her chest. "Have you lost all mercy? Allerum and Taziar would never harm innocents on purpose. Even the strictest king would give them another chance."

"Another chance to destroy the world?" Bolverkr dismissed Silme's argument, his tone underscoring the ridiculousness of her claim. "Don't let love blind you to reality."

"Nor should anger and grief blind you!"

Bolverkr's manner went cautious. "Well taken. Neither of us in a position to judge. However, should we leave the question for our peers, I have no doubt their verdict would be, 'Guilty,' and the execution just. Are you equally certain about your assertion?"

Silme's fingers twined in the fabric of Bolverkr's cloak. She pictured her fellows at the Dragonrank school, recalled the thick aura of arrogance and intolerance that seemed to accompany power. *Bolverkr is right. My peers would condemn Allerum.* A breeze creased the valley between her breasts, and she tugged the cloak impatiently to close the gap between its edges. *And for that, my peers are fools.* Aware she could not convince Bolverkr with this line of reasoning, Silme changed tactics. "Why?"

Bolverkr blinked. He turned his head to meet Silme's gaze. "Didn't I just tell you?"

"I mean," Silme started, gaining confidence, "why are you telling me this? I helped to kill Loki. I was the reason Allerum and Taziar fought the dragon."

"Yes." Bolverkr fidgeted.

Sensing his discomfort, Silme plunged ahead. "And?"

Bolverkr folded his fingers together, their skin smooth, elastic, and well preserved despite his age. He hesitated, as if considering options, then sighed, apparently choosing candor. "When I first saw you, I believed I would have to kill you. And I was prepared to do it."

The pronouncement came as no surprise to Silme. Bolverkr's uneasiness gave her the upper hand, and she savored the moment of control. "But something changed that?"

Bolverkr swung around to face Silme directly. Again, he reached for her hand. When Silme shrank from his touch, he did not press the matter further. "People fear what they do not understand. I came to Wilsberg to escape the whispers, the fawning, the isolation. I traveled south to an area where the existence of sorcerers is attributed to legend, to a farm village where even legend might not pierce. I found acceptance. My friendships seemed genuine until necessity forced me to use magic and the townsfolk realized they aged while I did not appear to grow older. They let me stay, whether from familiarity or dread I don't know. And, over time, their grandchildren learned to care as deeply for me as I did for them. But though I fathered many of them and the babies of many others, there was always an awe in their love which kept me distant. They showed the caring of children for a hero rather than the shared love of partners or friends."

Many platitudes came to Silme's mind, but, having no interest in soothing Bolverkr, she kept them to herself. She had a reasonable idea where Bolverkr was heading, and it bothered her. Still, the topic had off-balanced him so she stuck with it rigidly. "You seem to think I have a solution to your problem."

He squirmed with a restlessness that seemed more appropriate to a courting youth than a two-hundred-year-old sorcerer with skills comparable to a god's. "Silme, you're the most powerful woman in existence. You can understand the pain of people staring while they decide whether to run in fear or try to kill you for the fame. You're driven by the same interest, the same need to create, analyze, and experience. I don't frighten you because you know the source of my ability. It makes sense to you. It's concrete and finite, within the realm of your knowledge and experience." He added belatedly, "You're also quite beautiful."

The compliment was familiar to Silme, the sincerity in Bolverkr's voice less so. She chose the direct approach, hoping to push him further off guard. "Are you trying to say you've fallen in love with me?"

"Does that surprise you?"

I would think Bolverkr would have learned the difference between romance and childish infatuation. Silme buried the thought beneath the need to win a game whose prize might include the lives of herself, her baby, and her friends. The explanation came to her in a rush. *Everything Bolverkr knows of me comes from Allerum's perceptions, love-smoothed, my shortcomings overlooked or dismissed. Bolverkr believed he gathered information, but he obtained much more. The strength of Allerum's affection influenced him in a way words never could.* Silme realized she had hesitated too long to hide her startlement. "Of course, I'm surprised. We've never met before."

"It seems like I've known you for a long time."

No doubt. Uncertain how to address the comment, Silme said nothing aloud. Bolverkr reached for her hands. This time, in an effort to gain his trust, she let him clench her hands between his long, delicate fingers.

Gradually, a feeling of peace settled over Silme, so comforting she did not recognize it as alien. Her aura seemed to swell, lending her a strength beyond anything she had known before. The still life of Harriman's memory, frozen in time, spread before her, every detail solid as reality. More than just aware of her surroundings, she became a part of them. The ruddy glow of the setting sun bore no relation to the dried and spangled blood of the corpses. It seemed as though the spectrum of color had widened to admit a million shades between the ones she knew.

"Silme." Bolverkr's voice seemed a distant distraction. "I want you to marry me."

"What?" Silme stiffened, the word startled from her before she could think. She embraced the heightened sense of awareness, followed every crease of Bolverkr's face to his pale eyes.

Bolverkr's hold tightened. "You can keep the baby. I'll raise it as my own. Only Allerum and Taziar have to die."

No one has to die. Silme glanced beyond the sorcerer to the milk-white aura dwarfing its owner like a soap bubble around a grain of sand. Envy spiraled through her from a source she could not place, and the unfamiliarity of the emotion jolted her back to reality. She tore her hands from Bolverkr's grasp and sprang to her feet. "What did you do to me?"

Bolverkr smiled, indicating his aura with wide sweeps of his arms. "Be calm. I didn't hurt you. Look, there's more than enough life force here for two, and I'm willing to share. I gave you a taste, and already I can tell you want more." He offered his hands. "Here, complete the channel. Open your mind barriers and take as much as you want."

A taste. Chaos. The pleasure Silme had experienced went sour. *The stuff of life, but also the force of destruction.* She knew those who served Chaos, god and man, became whimsical, ruinous, evil. It had always seemed a cruel trick of nature to tie power with spite, to assure that every man endowed with life was also endowed with evil. *This power Bolverkr offers comes from a source external to me. If I can grasp it before it bonds with my own life force, I might be able to tap it without risking the baby.* The whisper of Chaos Bolverkr had shared was gone, leaving Silme with a hunger she could not deny. The Chaos promised a paradise, but she also knew it would claim a price. *If I fail to control it, I will become a slave to it. But, without it, I have no hope of fighting Bolverkr.* Silme closed her eyes, drawing on inner resolve. Slowly, she knelt and reached for Bolverkr's hands.

CHAPTER 12
Shadows of Doubt

Our doubts are traitors,
And make us lose the good we oft might win,
By fearing to attempt.

—William Shakespeare
Measure for Measure

Silme folded her legs beneath her, her fingers resting lightly on Bolverkr's outstretched hands despite the crushing tenderness of his grip. Fear and anticipation wound her nerves into tight coils. She wrestled to lower her mind barriers, aware she would need them open to seize the first thin whisper of Chaos that touched her. *Catch it, tap it, and transport.* The words swirled through her mind like a chant. She lowered her head. Hair spilled into her face, and she peered through the golden curtain at the grass spears around her knees. But her mind barriers resisted her efforts; her tension kept them locked closed reflexively.

Frustration heightened every irritation. Silme flung back the obscuring mane of hair, and viciously shook aside each strand tickling her forehead. She became aware of tiny itches over every part of her body, and the inability to claim her hands fueled her annoyance. Again, she struggled against her own defenses, but the more violent the fight, the harder they opposed her.

"Ready?" Bolverkr asked.

"Not yet," Silme snapped back. A light sheen of sweat appeared on her forehead. She called upon the meditation techniques of the Dragonrank, imagining a meadow warmed by summer sun. Stems bowed and rattled in the breeze, while sparrows darted playfully between them. The scene brought an inner warmth. And while she savored the manufactured peace of her illusion, Chaos stole, unnoticed, through the contact. As Silme built details into the picture, the earliest threads of Chaos seeped in, merged with the substance of her life aura, and magnified her serenity. The weeds muted to the hollow fronds of wheat, tufted with stiff strands of silk and deep, amber seeds. The meadow became a village striped with dirt pathways. Suffused with calm, Silme idly wondered at its immensity. Never before had she achieved such harmony. Pleasure seemed to encompass her, its source lost and lacking a physical center.

The mind barriers. Silme let her imagination lapse, but the bliss remained, strong and comforting within her. Her mental defenses responded, sliding downward a crack. Encouraged, she widened the gap.

Chaos struck with heightened force, collapsing the barrier completely. A rational thought flashed through Silme's mind. *I'm tricked! While I fought my own defenses, Chaos had already bonded.* Then the idea was buried beneath a thunderous avalanche of power. Morality fled before the attack. The imagined scene returned. But, where Silme had constructed waving fields of grain, Chaos showed her the reality of a village in shambles, a wild mix of destruction and death. It twisted revulsion to elation, pity to glee, and laughter rang in Silme's ears.

Savage with anger, Silme's sense of self rose to battle the intruder. But Chaos surrounded her inner being, and her sensibilities fled like shadow before rising flames. Silme saw fires grasping for the heavens, red and golden and glorious. That the blaze ate cities seemed unimportant. They challenged the gods themselves and offered the strength and power of their defiance to Silme.

"No!" Silme's cry seemed to come from elsewhere; it lost meaning before it left her throat. As if from a great abyss, her inner self rebelled, a mouse pinned beneath a lion's paw. It roused memories of Larson wordlessly embracing her while her tears left damp patches on his tunic. But Chaos intervened, stripping emotion as completely as in Harriman's damaged thoughts. Silme gasped, surrendering to the blissful oblivion it offered. Each mighty promise left Silme greedy for the next. Now Chaos no longer needed to come to her; she pursued it. She shuddered. Her grip went murderously tight, and her fingernails burrowed into Bolverkr's flesh.

Bolverkr cried out in pain and surprise. He jerked back

instinctively and tore partially free. In the moment of weakness his actions created, Silme's morality launched its attack. *Don't let it have you! Look what it's done to Bolverkr. He claims Allerum and Taziar deserve to die, yet his cruelty goes far beyond simply executing enemies. No amount of power is worth inflicting torture on the guilty or the innocent.*

Chaos responded with a howling whirlwind of fury. It battered Silme's sense of self, pounding it into a darkened corner of awareness. Her sensibilities died to a spark, but that one snippet of consciousness made its final stand. *Got to rid myself of this Chaos long enough to think.* Though crushed and bruised by a force far more powerful than herself, Silme deflected the energy in the only way she knew how. The world clouded to sapphire blue as she channeled all thought to the rankstone clamped between the claws of her dragonstaff.

Designed to store life aura and attuned to Silme, the stone accepted the energy she fed it, brightening as the power gorged it. She felt the gemstone pulse, bloated with Chaos, as her sense of self seeped slowly back into control. *Got to get away from here. How? I can't transport.* She deflected another wave of Chaos.

Power torrented into the stone. Still in Harriman's study, the sapphire quivered, loaded with more energy than its creator had ever intended. Pain engulfed Silme's senses, stretching and pounding from within her, driving her to the rim of unconsciousness. She struggled to retain awareness, unwilling to surrender to Chaos, feeling sanity slip away as darkness crushed in. Another pulse of Chaos ripped through her and crashed into the shuddering facets of the sapphire.

Suddenly, agony splashed Silme's vision in a flash of blinding light. The rankstone exploded, showering fragments through Harriman's study, a blue spray of sapphire chips rattling from the walls and ceiling. Silme screamed, instinctively tearing free of the contact. All sensation fled her, the anguish dulling to an empty ache. She sank to the ground, exhausted, feeling as cold and shattered as her stone. Then, a thought penetrated her muddled senses. *The Chaos I channeled to my rank stone is free, not dead. It has to go somewhere.* Realization mobilized her. *Not somewhere, to someone.* Her vision slid slowly back into focus and Bolverkr's grizzled face, blank with horror, filled her gaze. *Bolverkr, of course! And I'm right in its path!* She floundered to her feet.

Desperately, Bolverkr raised an arm to cast a transport, his other hand groping for Silme.

Slowed by fatigue, Silme felt his fingers close about the torn fabric of her dress. "No!" she screamed. *Chaos will follow Bolverkr. I can't handle the power. If he takes me with him, it'll destroy me and the baby.* She lurched. Cloth tore. She staggered free of his grasp, tripped and sprawled to the dirt.

A storm of Chaos howled toward them.

Bolverkr shouted in frustration and fear. As he transported to the shelter of his fortress, his magic knifed power through Harriman's mind. The chaos-force blinked out as quickly, trailing a suffocating wake of ozone.

Silme choked. Lungs burning, she clung to her life energy and dove for the only sanctuary she knew.

Al Larson crouched at Taziar's back, his gaze locked on four cocked crossbows. "Fire!" The guard's shout sounded thin as smoke beneath the scrambling of Taziar's friends through the window. The bolts sailed over the heads of five kneeling swordsmen. Larson swung as he dodged. One shaft whisked through the air where his chest had been. His blade deflected the other. The bolt snapped, its pieces clattering along the corridor. Suddenly, Gaelinar's throwing rocks at him during training seemed worth the bruises.

Fridurik gasped in pain. Larson glanced to his left. The redhead clasped a bloody hole in his thigh where one of the bolts had penetrated. As the crossbowmen reloaded, two of the swordsmen charged Larson and Fridurik. Though concerned for his companion, Larson was forced to tend to his own defense. As the guardsman rushed down on him, sword swiping for his neck, Larson dropped to one knee. His upstroke sliced open the sentry's abdomen. He shouldered the man aside in time to see Fridurik lock swords with the guardsman's companion. Fridurik's injury made him clumsy. The guard's knee crashed into the thief's gut. Fridurik doubled over, and the guard struck for his unshielded back.

Larson lunged. His blade sheared through the guard's

chest, but the guard's blow landed, too. Both men collapsed, and Larson found himself facing four loaded crossbows alone.

Larson distributed his weight evenly, trying to judge the paths of the bolts in the instant before their release. *Compared with bullets, arrows crawl, and eleventh century bolts move even slower.* Larson gathered solace from the flash of thought. The bolts whipped free. He tensed to dodge. Before he could move, something foreign crashed into his mind with a suddenness that jarred loose a scream. Pained beyond recognition of danger, he caught at his head. The edged steel heads of bolts bit through his left arm and calf, drawing another scream. His sword dropped to the floor.

Larson staggered backward into Taziar. "Allerum!" The Climber broke Larson's fall, though their collision drove him, breathless, to the edge of the window. Dizzied and pain-maddened, Larson could not fathom why Taziar seized him by the hair and jerked him over. The pain of the maneuver seemed a minor annoyance compared with the agony in his skull, and its significance was lost on Larson. But the sensation of falling was not. Wind sang around him as he ripped through air. His composure cracked, his shocked howl vividly betraying fear.

Larson's back hit the moat with a stinging slap. Water smothered him. Dazed and aching, he clawed for the surface. His fingers struck something solid. He grabbed for it, but his frenzied strokes churned it deeper. As the pain in his head died to an ache, sense filtered back into his consciousness. *My god, I'm drowning Shadow.*

Quickly, Larson disentangled from Taziar. His head broke the surface, and he gasped air deep into his lungs. A moment later, Taziar appeared, choking and sputtering, beside him.

"Shit," Larson said. The curse seemed so weak in the wake of near death, that, despite pain, he could not keep himself from laughing in hysteria.

Apparently, Taziar did not find the humor in the scene. He clapped a damp hand over Larson's lips, stifling his laughter. "It's day, and the night sentries will have gone to sleep. But we still have to get by the gate guards." Taziar released his grip and swam toward the far bank with long, steady strokes.

More guards. Larson groaned, following with an ungainly sidestroke that allowed his injured arm and leg to drag. *All this, and it's still not over.* He stared at the wake of blood trailing him through the murky water. His wounds made his limbs ache worse than anything he had known since a college football player put him through a weight training workout in junior high. Then, the ache of tortured muscles had forced him to spend the following morning in bed. He watched Taziar pull himself to shore, shivering as the chill air touched his sodden clothes and skin. *I may not be able to walk, let alone battle through more guards.*

The pain in Larson's head had faded, leaving a foreign presence huddled in a corner of his awareness. It confused him. In the past, when sorcerers and gods had penetrated his thoughts, they had done so without causing him pain. *Except one.* Larson recalled a stroll through a forest in southern Norway when someone or something had entered his thoughts with a violence that left his head throbbing. *Right after it happened, I started recalling sailboating on Cedar Lake, details of the past, and Taziar's stories of Cullinsberg.* Larson reached for the brittle grasses overhanging the bank. *Apparently, the pain comes when the sorcerer breaks in on me at warp speed.* Larson crawled from the water, for the first time sorry his elf form made him impervious to cold. The discomfort might have numbed or, at least, drawn attention from the agony of his crossbow wounds. *Still, despite its desperate entrance, the presence in my mind doesn't appear to be trying to hurt me . . . yet.* It lay unmoving. Larson had discovered he could muster only one form of mental defense against intruders: trapping them in his mind. Quietly, he built a wall around the interloper. *Too much to do now. I'll deal with it later.* Larson ripped strips from the hem of his cloak to serve as bandages.

"Here. Let me do that." Taziar offered his hands to help Larson to his feet. Fearing for his injuries, Larson passed the cloth but waved his friend away. Instead, he clambered to his feet, stiffly guarding the torn, clenched muscles of his arm and calf. With nearly all his weight shifted to the right, he managed to stand.

Taziar knelt. His skilled fingers seemed to fly as he tight-

ened a pressure dressing over the scarlet-smeared hole in
Larson's breeks, then rose and tied another on the elf's arm.

The pain of walking proved tolerable if Larson used a
pronounced limp. "Now what?" he whispered.

Taziar glanced around hurriedly. "It'll take time for the
surviving sentries to get word of our prison break from the
tower to the gate guards." He tapped his fingers on his
knee as he considered. "I have an idea. Allerum, when you
and Silme came to speak with the baron, how many guards
stood at the gate?"

Larson considered. "Two. The gates were open, and a
lot of people milled around the grounds."

"The holiday will keep the peasants away." Taziar traced
some object through the fabric of his hip pocket. "Get
everyone together." He pointed vaguely at the trees,
benches, and gardens of the baron's courtyard, and Larson
noticed the dripping prisoners crouched behind various
plants and ornaments. "Lead them behind that clump of
bushes." Taziar made an arching motion to indicate a huge
copse of grape and berry vines toward the front of the
keep. "Quietly," he warned. "When I yell, have everyone
run through the gate. Tell them to scatter around the city.
We'll meet at the back door of the whorehouse."

Before Larson could question further, Taziar trotted off,
rounding the opposite side of the keep. With a shrug of
resignation, Larson approached the hiding prisoners. Locating Shylar, he repeated the plan, and, with her help, herded
the others behind the brambles. Through a break in the
vines, he watched the guards, standing stiff and solemn before the opened gates. Behind them, the drawbridge over-
passed the moat. Larson saw no sign of Taziar, but he knew
it would take time for the Climber to cover ground.

Clouds formed a thin, pewter layer over the morning sky,
and the day smelled of damp. Larson studied his companions. Of the six survivors, only Shylar and the violet-eyed
thief, Asril, appeared alert enough to run. The mad dash
from the cells, the descent, and the swim across the moat
had taxed the others to the limits of any vitality remaining
after the guards' tortures. Most trembled in the breezes,
naked or clothed in soaking tatters. Though fully clad in
her dress, Shylar kept her arms wrapped to her chest, her

lips blue from cold. Odwulf shivered so hard, his teeth chattered.

Without a weapon, Larson felt as bare as his companions. Aside from Shylar, the other five prisoners clutched swords taken from the dead prison sentries, their blades half-raised or dragging in the dirt. Seeing a chance to arm himself, Larson removed his cloak and offered it to Odwulf. "Here. I'll trade for your sword."

Odwulf looked at the proffered cloak. Though wet, it would certainly offer more protection than uncovered skin, yet Odwulf did not reach for it.

Attributing the thief's hesitation to mistrust, Larson explained. "I have to get out of here, too. I'm trained to fight. Harriman's holding my pregnant wife prisoner, and I'm going to get her back." Speaking the words aloud roused all the anger the need to escape had suppressed. Larson's pain faded before growing desperation.

Odwulf stared at Larson's face, as if to read the thought beyond the emotion. Wordlessly, he handed Larson his sword. Accepting the cloak, he wrapped it tightly over his bruised and sagging shoulders.

Larson slid the sword into the left side of his belt. He peered through the break in the brush just in time to see Taziar race toward the guards, his shout loud and urgent.

"Guards! Quick!" Taziar slid to a halt several yards from the gate and summoned the sentries with frantic waves. The Climber's disheveled appearance made him look even more desperate. "It's an emergency. Over here. We can't be heard."

The guards did not budge. "What's your problem?" one hollered back.

Taziar jabbed an arm into the air. Sunlight struck gold highlights from an object in his fist. Larson gawked, taking several seconds to recognize the medallion the baron had worn in his courtroom. *Now where the hell did Shadow get that?*

Apparently, others recognized the sigil. "I knew Taz leagued with the baron," Waldhram mumbled.

"Don't be a fool," Asril hissed back. "The Shadow Climber could steal teeth from a guard lion."

"Hush," Shylar insisted.

The guards seemed equally impressed. They shifted and exchanged words too softly for Larson to hear.

Taziar's voice went harsh. "I need you." He made a sharp motion with the medallion, allowing the guards to see it was real. "I command you in the baron's name. Get over here. We haven't time to waste."

Caught up in Taziar's exigency, a guard replied with the same rapid speech. "Wait. We don't understand. We can't leave our posts."

"I don't have time to deal with idiots!" Taziar's tone threatened punishment, and even Larson cringed at the Climber's ferocity. "Your incompetence may cost the baron his life."

Taziar's words mobilized the guards. Hesitantly, they approached him, and Larson had to strain to hear the exchange that followed.

Taziar shoved the sigil into a sentry's hand. "Protect this with your lives. It's more important than any of us. The ultimate fate of Cullinsberg is at stake. You must deliver it to the baron immediately." Taziar shouted. "Now! Go!" He glanced toward the berry copse, raising his voice still further. "RUN!"

Suddenly realizing Taziar's command was intended as much for him as for the guards, Larson rose. "Run!" he repeated. He hobbled toward the gate, the thieves swiftly outdistancing him.

The walls muffled Taziar's words beyond Larson's ability to decipher them. Unwilling to abandon his friend, Larson pressed his back to the wall and waited for the pain of movement to subside. The thieves had darted off so quickly he had not even seen which directions they had taken. *Without Shadow, I might not even find the whorehouse.*

A moment later, Taziar sprinted through the gate, caught sight of Larson, and ground to a halt beside him. He yanked at Larson's sleeve. "Are you well? Can you walk?"

Larson studied Taziar's small form, thinking his fragile elf frame looked gigantic in comparison. *And if I can't, will you carry me?* Pain made Larson irritable, but he realized with alarm this was not the time for sarcasm. "Come on." Seizing Taziar's arm, he shared the weight of his inured side with the Climber. Together, they managed an awkward lope across the cleared ground and into the town proper.

As Taziar had predicted, Aga'arin's High Holy Day kept the streets empty. Larson felt as if he ran through a crude, western ghost town. Dodging a guard's patrol, they rounded a cottage, sending an old cart horse skittering and bucking like a colt around its pasture. A faltering sprint through Panogya Street frightened a flock of doves into flight, their wing beats thunderous between the buildings. A few steps farther, a stalking cat lashed its tail in anger at their interference. Oblivious, Larson and Taziar skidded around the corner and found that every escaped prisoner had beaten them to the door.

Astryd pushed through the battered leaders of the underground and embraced Taziar. Loosed from the Climber's support, Larson came down hard on his wounded leg. Gasping, he gripped the wall stones, noticing for the first time that blood soaked the bandages.

Astryd explained quickly. "I transported back here to warn Mat-hilde. She called up as many loyal men as she could in such a short time. We think we have enough to fight off any of Harriman's followers who try to get up the stairs." Her tone went apologetic as she addressed Taziar. "It was difficult enough convincing them the prisoners would be freed. We couldn't tell them about you."

"That's all right." Astryd's cloak muffled Taziar's reply. "So long as the leaders don't attack me, I doubt any of the others will."

The sensitive tone of Taziar's words made it clear that he was lying to comfort Astryd, but a more urgent matter pushed aside all of Larson's concern for the Climber. "Silme," he managed through his pain.

"Trapped upstairs." Astryd let go of Taziar. "After two transports, I didn't dare try to confront Harriman and his berserks alone."

Rage snapped Larson's control. The thought of Harriman touching Silme made him crazy with hatred. He ripped the sword from its sheath so abruptly, the leaders skittered from his path. "Let's go!"

"Wait!" Taziar dodged beneath Larson's blade. "You can't take Harriman and his berserks by yourself. You'll need my help, at least. Someone give me a weapon." He reached out a hand.

No one responded.

Larson knew even the leaders still did not trust Taziar. Every second Silme remained in Harriman's hands tore at Larson's sensibilities, and he could not spare the time convincing them of Taziar's innocence might take. "I don't need your help! You fight like a girl." He shoved past. "Get the hell out of my way."

Astryd gave a light rap on the door, and it swung open. Without hesitation, Larson charged through the gap into a sparse crowd of prostitutes and armed men. He raised his sword, prepared to fight anyone who challenged him.

Behind him, Astryd and Shylar warned the crowd. "Stand aside! He's with us!"

To Larson's relief, the people scampered from his path, leaving him a clear trail through another heavy door, across the kitchen, to the stairway. Larson hurtled up the wooden steps to the landing, and only a few scattered footfalls followed him. His hatred for Harriman grew beyond all boundaries. This close, a fortress could not keep him from championing Silme, and outrage inspired adrenaline that masked his pain.

Larson pounded down the hallway. Only one door was closed. Catching the knob, he wrenched and kicked. The panel flew open. Larson caught a glimpse of a single figure, hunched on the bed. Against the walls, on either side of a corner, the berserks crouched. They started to their feet as Larson raced forward and struck with an animal cry of rage.

Larson's blade caught Halden across the ear and cleaved halfway through his head. The berserk fell dead before he realized his danger. Skereye leaped to his feet, catching Larson's sword arm with his left hand. His right slammed into Larson's chin. The berserk's fingernails raked Larson's face, and the force of the blow sprawled him over backward. Still buried in Halden's skull, the sword was wrenched from Larson's grip. Larson crashed to the floor, pain flashing along his spine.

Skereye dove on Larson. A huge arm snaked around Larson's neck. Larson reacted with the training of his high school wrestling coach. *Got to get off my back.* Seizing Skereye's elbow, Larson drew up his knees and dropped his chest. Skereye barrel-rolled over Larson's shoulder. His choke hold twisted free, and Larson spun away.

The fall had reopened Larson's wounds. Blood drenched

the bandages, seeping through the frayed arrow holes in his britches and shirt and trickling into his boot. He fought to stand, but his injured leg buckled. He slid back to the ground for another effort as Skereye gained his feet.

Desperate, Larson gritted his teeth, forcing himself beyond pain. His head buzzed as he clambered up. Through blurred vision, he saw Taziar rush Skereye's back, watched in horror as the berserk turned to meet the attack. Skereye hit Taziar's right wrist hard enough to send the dagger skittering across the floorboards. An uppercut caught Taziar in the chin, hurling him into the air. He struck the wall and slid, awkwardly, to the floor. Skereye whirled to face Larson. The berserk's sword whisked free of its sheath as he charged.

Larson cursed. Taziar's offensive had gained Larson the time he needed to stand yet might have cost the little thief his life. Larson wanted to watch for some sign of movement from his friend, but he was forced to tend the more immediate danger of Skereye's sword. The blade whipped for Larson's head. Larson ducked and backstepped. The stroke whistled over his head, the backcut inches before his face. Dizziness crushed in on Larson, and he realized he needed to change tactics before dodging sword blows drove him to exhaustion.

This time, Skereye slammed a downstroke for Larson's head. Twisting, Larson blocked the sword at its hilt. The impact hammered his left arm to the shoulder, further tearing his wound. Blood ran freely. He screamed in anguish, completing his defense purely from habit. His right fist jolted into Skereye's face.

Pain had sapped Larson's anger, but it fueled Skereye's. His muscled arms shook with fury, and he lunged for Larson with redoubled vigor. Now, Skereye kept his off-hand before him as if to seize Larson and hold him in place for the sword stroke. The first grab fell short. The sword sliced air, gashing the fingers Larson threw up in defense.

Dizzied by blood loss and pain, Larson retreated blindly. He locked his gaze on Skereye's leading hand. Skereye swept forward. Larson caught Skereye's wrist and wrenched it in a drag that spun the berserk toward him. Larson's open right hand slammed Skereye's hilt hard enough to

break the berserk's thumb. The sword thumped to the
floor.

Larson staggered, too dazed to veer aside. Skereye bellowed in rage. His arms encircled Larson's chest and tensed,
crushing. Larson's breath broke, dashed from his lungs. He
shuddered, gasping for air, but managed to inhale only a
whistling trickle. He felt his consciousness slipping. Panicked, Larson struggled. His fists pounded Skereye's back.
His knee slammed into the berserk's groin.

But pain only angered Skereye more. His grip tightened
convulsively. Ribs snapped, the sound sharp beneath the
ringing in Larson's ears. Bone stabbed Larson's lungs. A
growing numbness dulled the pain. Unconsciousness beckoned, promising respite from the agony of his injuries, and
Larson had to force his thoughts to the fight. *He's got his
balance forward now. Use it!* Larson slid his right leg forward, pushing against Skereye, then let his injured leg collapse beneath him.

Skereye's weight and pressure took them both down.
Larson had intended to curl and let Skereye roll over his
head, but the injuries made Larson clumsy. He landed flat
on his back, Skereye atop him. A deep breath filled his
lungs but jabbed agony through his chest. Again, Larson
worked to his stomach, wrestling mechanically. Skereye
clung, driving his fist repeatedly into the back of Larson's
head. A sharp twist knocked Skereye to his back and tore
Larson from the hold. He staggered to his feet and tensed
to run, his only thought for escape.

Skereye sprang to his feet. Larson's retreat gained the
berserk the opportunity to scoop his fallen sword form
the floor.

"Allerum!" Astryd screamed in warning.

Larson spun as the blade sped for his head. He blocked,
catching Skereye's sword hand in both of his own. Aware
he could not hope to overpower the berserk, Larson used
the leverage of his entire body against Skereye's grip. He
stepped to Skereye's side, pivoted with his arms circling
over his head, and leaned back toward the berserk. The
maneuver whipped the sword to Skereye's back, his arms
raised clumsily above his head. And, suddenly, Larson had
control of the sword in his left hand, his right still locked

to the berserk's wrist. Larson sliced, the blade skimming across Skereye's gut. Larson sprang aside.

Larson naturally passed the hilt to his right hand, certain the blow he'd just dealt was fatal. The incision in Skereye's abdomen gaped open, spilling blood, and pink loops of intestine poked through. Yet, somehow, Skereye remained standing. He stared at the wound, threw back his head in a howl that echoed through the hallway, and charged Larson like an angered bull. Shocked and sickened, Larson scarcely had time to react. He swung the sword for Skereye's neck. The blade slashed flesh and through bone, neatly decapitating Skereye. And this time the berserk collapsed.

It's over. The realization clouded Larson's mind, freeing him from the desperation that had allowed him to fight beyond his endurance. He sank to the floor beside the corpse, feeling no pain. Far below him, the battle between Shylar's faithful masses and Harriman's strongarm men faded to indecipherable noise. Larson's body had gone numb. He could feel Taziar tugging at his calf as the Climber wrapped another pressure bandage. But the efforts seemed remote, a distant glimpse of someone else's leg. *I'm going to die now.* The thought came, unaccompanied by emotion. Larson closed his eyes, surrendering to an inner peace.

Something shook Larson's shoulders. Serenity fled before a nagging tingle of pain, and the tiny measure of strength that touched him seemed foreign. He opened his lids, met Astryd's eyes, the color of faded jeans, her whites marred by crisscrossing lines of red. "Silme," she said.

The single word lanced concern through Larson. He rolled to his hands and knees, the movement ripping his arm from Taziar's grip. Seizing Larson's wrist, Taziar finished his bandage. "Will he . . ." Taziar started, but an unseen gesture from Astryd silenced him.

"Silme," Astryd repeated. "Where's Silme?"

Silme. Larson picked up the urgency of Astryd's question. His gaze swung to the bed. Harriman sat, watching Larson with dull, disinterested eyes. Asril's blade hovered at the nobleman's throat. "Silme." Larson staggered toward Harriman but managed only to sag to his knees at the bedside, one hand looped over the coverlet. "Where's Silme?" Though hoarse and tremulous, his tone conveyed threat.

Harriman blinked in silence. His eyes rolled downward to stare at Larson.

"Where . . . is . . . Silme?" Larson wanted to hit Harriman, to beat the answer from him. But he had to satisfy himself with imagining the blow.

Harriman's voice emerged as broken as Larson's own. "Bolverkr has her. Ripped from my mind."

The explanation made no sense to Larson. He let the words swirl through his thoughts, trying to concentrate on each individual syllable.

Astryd pressed. "Bolverkr's your mast . . ." She amended. "A sorcerer?"

Larson guessed that Astryd received some confirmation from Harriman because she abandoned her inquiry and sat, cross-legged, on the floor. Harriman quivered as she searched his thoughts. A moment later, Astryd leaped to her feet. "They're gone from his mind," she said sorrowfully. "Someone used magic. I still find traces of it. Silme could be anywhere."

Larson struggled for awareness. Deep inside, he knew he held an answer, but he could not quite grasp the question. *Sorcerer. Mind. Ripped.* Abruptly, everything fell together. "Astryd. I think I may know where Bolverkr is."

Astryd whirled toward Larson.

Painfully, word by word, Larson described the presence that had assailed his mind in the seventh-story tower of the baron's keep. "I think it's still there."

Gently, Astryd knelt at Larson's side. She stroked his hair, brushing tangled strands from his face. Stripped of sensation, Larson could not feel Astryd's touch nor the caring she intended to convey. "Allerum, I don't think you trapped Bolverkr, but I do believe we may have found Silme. With your permission, I'm going to enter your mind and check."

Anything for Silme. Larson nodded his consent, but Astryd braced her hand against his head to stop the movement.

"I want you to understand what you're agreeing to. It could be a trap. It may not be Silme. If I encounter Bolverkr, he'll certainly kill us both."

Death no longer frightened Larson. "Try."

This time, it was Taziar who looked stricken.

CHAPTER 13
Shadowed Corners of the Mind

If you love your friends, you must hate the enemies who
seek to destroy them.
　　　　　　　　　　　　—Captain Taziar Medakan, senior

Trusting Asril and Taziar to control Harriman, Astryd
thrust her consciousness into Larson's mind. She entered a
world as gray as tarnished silver. Dull and mostly spent,
her life aura supplied no illumination. Eyes squinted, she
stumbled through patterns of thought, tripped over a stray
loop, and crashed into a tangled tapestry of memory. Astryd winced, awaiting the inevitable wild flashes of reaction.

But Larson's mind lay still as a sea becalmed. Astryd
disentangled, glad her clumsiness had not cost him the pain
of sins or fears remembered. Abruptly, she realized his lack
of response could only stem from the severity of his injuries, and relief gave way to a sorrow that warred with guilt.
*Maybe if I'd used magic in the prison, I might have spared
Allerum some of that beating.* She reviewed her reasoning,
picking her way deeper into Larson's mind. *Weakened by
two transports, I doubt I could have cast any spell strong
enough to influence the fight. And I was so certain rescuing
Silme would require magic, I didn't dare waste it.*

Astryd caught a glimpse of a faint glow in the distance
and steered toward it. Despite her rationalization, she still
felt responsible for Larson's infirmity. *I tried to heal him.*
The memory surfaced. She had channeled most of her remaining life energy into a spell to mend his injuries, but
that had scarcely gained him the strength to open his eyes
and verbally challenge Harriman. *It wasn't enough. And,
now, I'm afraid Allerum is going to die.* A lump filled her
throat and tears burned her eyes. She banished them with
resolve. *If I'm not careful now, we'll both die.*

As Astryd approached, the illumination assumed the

shape of walls, paper thin and translucent, unlike the unyielding steel of natural, mental barriers. The radiance
shone from beyond them. Tentatively, Astryd extended a
finger and poked Larson's defenses. The substance yielded
to her touch, fine as silk, then crumbled to dust. Light
blazed through, its source a hovering speck.

Astryd sprang back in surprise. This went beyond the
realm of her experience. The shimmering fragment seemed
harmless, easily dismissed if not for the overwhelming
gloom of Larson's mind. "Silme?" Astryd tried.

"Allerum?" The reply touched Astryd's ears, more like
a presence than a sound. Despite the strangeness of its
sending, the voice belonged, unmistakably, to Silme.

Astryd exhaled in relief, and only then realized she had
been holding her breath. "Astryd," she corrected. "Silme,
I don't understand. Are you here or not?"

"It's a probe," Silme explained. "A thought extension
of me."

Astryd shook her head to indicate ignorance.

Apparently, Silme misinterpreted Astryd's silence. "Astryd, are you still there?" The odd form of communication
relayed Silme's concern as well as her words.

"You can't see me?"

"No. Through a probe I can only read Allerum's current
concentration and send or receive mental messages. Nothing more."

Many questions came to Astryd's mind, but she knew
most could wait. For now, she needed to know how to bring
Silme back to the whorehouse. "You can't leave with me?"

"No." Sorrow touched Silme's reply. "Unlike you, my
actual presence is elsewhere. I would need to use a transport escape."

Astryd considered. Realizing Silme could not read her
silences, she explained, "I'm thinking." Unable to suppress
curiosity, she questioned. "While you were here, why didn't
you communicate with Allerum? It would have saved us
all grief wondering where to look for you."

"I tried. He walled me in. Usually, he can't detect
probes, but I was desperate. I brought all my life energy
with me and the baby's. I think I hit Allerum too fast
and hard."

"Walled you in?" Astryd stared at the scattered powder

remaining from Larson's conjured barriers. "That thing you call a wall fell apart when I touched it."

"A probe has no physical form," Silme reminded.

Larson's mind dimmed as he slipped farther from awareness. *If Allerum dies, I'll lose contact with Silme.* A more desperate thought gripped her. *I'm in his mind. If he dies, I go with him. And Silme, too.* Aware Silme could not know about Larson's injuries, Astryd tried to keep alarm from her voice. "Silme, how do we get to you? Where do we find you?"

Apparently, Astryd's distress trickled through, because Silme's reply betrayed suspicion. "Is something wrong?"

"Yes." Astryd did not want to burden Silme with additional concerns. If nothing else, urgency would increase the cost in life energy of any spell she might need to cast. "You're in trouble, and I want to help. How do we get to you?"

"You can't. Bolverkr created an isolated location in Harriman's memories and transported me to it. I'm displaced in space and time. You can't transport somewhere you've never seen. Even if you could, you would have no way to get me out." The dejection that slipped through Silme's contact unnerved Astryd. She had never known Silme to surrender to a dilemma. "I'll just have to cast a transport of my own."

Raw fear edged Astryd's voice. "That would kill the baby!"

"What choice do I have?" Silme's grief and desperation wafted clearly to Astryd. "I've given this baby every chance I can, but it apparently wasn't meant to be born. Allerum and I will just have to make another. It might be fun," Silme quipped, but the probe betrayed her attempt at humor as false bravado.

Allerum. Terror crushed in on Astryd, and she had to fight for every breath. *By the time Silme returns, that unborn baby may be the only thing left of the man she loves. I can't let her destroy it.* A million possible replies came to Astryd at once, but she forced herself to remain unspeaking until she had full control over her emotions. "Silme," she said with admirable composure, "we'll find another way."

"What?" Silme said with surprise, rather than as a challenge.

Larson's mind went black as he faded into unconsciousness. Astryd stiffened, and desperation jarred loose a memory of her own. The conversation had occurred only a day earlier, but it seemed like months ago. "Silme, I have an idea! Do you remember when we tried to figure out why a Dragonrank mage would want to kill Taziar, and we talked about spell mergers?"

"Vaguely." Silme sounded guarded. "What are you thinking?"

Astryd was excited now. "Could you tap my life energy through your probe?"

A pause followed. Though short, it seemed interminable to Astryd. "Possibly," Silme said. "I've never tried before. You'd have to be at full strength for me to risk it."

Astryd cringed. The transports and Allerum's healing had tapped her so low she did not hold enough power to transport herself. *But Silme must use less life force than I do for a transport. I have enough for her, I think.*

Silme continued. "There's no way for me to feel how much life energy you have nor for you to guess how much I might tap. Once I start the spell, it'll claim as much life force as it needs. If I tap you to nothing, you'll die as surely as if you miscalculated yourself."

Astryd realized that, soon enough, all three of them might die. She had moments to free Silme and less time to make her decision. Urgency made her curt. "I know that."

"Your life is more important to me than any unborn baby. Even my own."

Astryd hesitated. She could not afford to tell Silme about Larson; nervous energy would increase the amount of life force needed for any spell, and Astryd had little enough to spare. *The decision is mine alone.* "I'm at full strength." The lie came with surprising ease. "Tap as much as you need, and come to Harriman's bedroom."

"Astryd . . . ?" Silme started.

"Just do it!" Astryd snapped, aware they could not waste time for platitudes or good-byes. "Please," she softened the command as if in afterthought.

To Astryd's relief, Silme fell silent.

A moment later, Astryd's strength drained from her, and her awareness plunged into nothingness.

*   *   *

Bolverkr awakened pinned beneath the shattered remnants of a fortress turret. Bruises hammered and throbbed through his body. He tensed to shift, but the blocks and chips of stone held him in place. Agony flashed along his spine, and he gritted his teeth against the pain. He sank back into place, his ragged, gray aura flickering over the granite, like a living thing.

Bolverkr had long ago drained his own life force battling the very Chaos that kept feeding him the energy to continue a fight he could never hope to win. The cycle had seemed like endless nightmare to Bolverkr. Unwilling to surrender, he had had no choice but to draw on Chaos to battle Chaos until his citadel toppled into ruin, taking his consciousness and his identity with it. Then, the Chaos-force had done its job, battering the last of Bolverkr's sense of self into oblivion, destroying even the deepest bindings of morality, leaving only a great and ancient intellect to direct its evil.

Now, Bolverkr channeled energy to himself, directing it into a spell that sent boulders sliding down his person and tumbling down the hilltop. Gingerly, aching, he rose to a sitting position, tapping a shred of Chaos to counter the pain of every injury. Chunks of stone, wood, and fabric littered the hilltop. A few jagged columns of wall clung stubbornly to existence, devoid of their protecting magics, the last remains of Bolverkr's mighty fortress.

Not again! No sorrow accompanied Bolverkr's thought, only a savage, crimson fury that sapped life force like a vortex. He sprang to his feet, clutching the remains of the Chaos-force to him, feeling the weakness of it and knowing its vast potential would return only with time and rest. A cry strangled in his throat, and he quenched rage with vengeful promises against the man, elf, and woman who had ruined him. *To attack in anger is simply stupid. I'm too weak to deal with them now. I need to rebuild. Then I'll lure them to me, force them to fight on my home ground.*

Bolverkr took a step forward. A triangular fragment of stone turned beneath his foot, and he staggered into a short stretch of wall that rose to the level of his chest. He grabbed it for support. *I want them dead. And I want them to suffer NOW.* Frustration speared through him, and he embraced the structure as tightly as a father would a crying child. *Patience has won more wars than skill* Another thought wound a crooked smile across his lips. *There is still one thing I can do without endangering myself.*

Gathering a mental probe, Bolverkr thrust for Harriman's mind.

A brilliant starburst of light snapped open the darkness of Harriman's bedroom. Shocked, Asril the Procurer leaped to his feet, the sword at Harriman's throat fumbling from his grip. Astryd collapsed to the floor. Before Taziar Medakan could identify Silme in the dispersing radiance of her magics, a movement caught his eye. Back in Bolverkr's control, Harriman dove for an object on the floor. Dazzled by the pulse of light, it took Taziar several seconds to recognize Harriman's target.

Gaelinar's sword! Taziar made a wild charge for Harriman. The nobleman dodged, left hand supporting the sheath, right clamped to the hilt. Taziar swept past Harriman. Swearing, the Climber whirled and dove. His outstretched hands slammed into the diplomat's side as Harriman pulled to free the blade. Drawn crookedly, the katana sheared through the wooden scabbard, taking Harriman's fingers with it.

With a scream of pain and outrage, Harriman caught at his mangled hand. Blood-splashed and nearly as shocked as Harriman, Taziar scarcely sprang out of the way before Asril's sword stabbed through the nobleman's chest. Harriman fell dead without a whimper. The katana bounced to the floor and spun toward the bed, stopping a hand's breadth from Larson's limp fingers.

It's almost as if the sword knew Gaelinar wanted Allerum to wield it. Taziar knew Larson was Harriman's likely target and momentum would logically draw the sword in that direction, but the coincidence still seemed eerie. *Just a few months ago, I would have denied the existence of gods and magic, too.* Taziar shifted the thought, aware he was dwelling on nonsense to avoid the reality of Astryd's collapse. Unable to deny it any longer, Taziar approached Silme where she knelt at Astryd's side.

"She lied to me." Silme's tone went beyond anger toward hysteria.

Clutched by sudden terror, Taziar dared not check life signs for himself. "Silme, is Astryd . . . ?"

"Why would she do something this stupid?" Silme raged, ignoring Taziar's unfinished question. "How could she defy her own teacher? Have I taught her nothing?"

"Silme!" Frantic with concern, Taziar gripped Silme's shoulder in both hands. "No lectures. Just tell me if she's . . ." Words failed him. "If she's . . ."

Astryd rolled to her side with a groan of reluctance, as if awakened from deep sleep after a long and arduous day. "If she's what?" Silme prodded impatiently.

Joy displaced Taziar's distress in a wild rush. Releasing his hold on Silme, he hunched beside her and gave Astryd's ankle an affectionate squeeze. "Will she be all right?"

"This time," Silme said, and Taziar recognized the same merciless attention to technique that Gaelinar had always displayed. "Next reckless act of stupidity the Fates might not prove so kind. I'm going to have to take her back to glass-rank lessons."

Taziar smoothed Astryd's rumpled skirt, amused by Silme's anger. "I don't know what Astryd did, and we haven't the time to discuss it yet. But I have no doubt you would have done the same for her." He borrowed Larson's odd mixture of English and Norwegian. "Like one philosopher said, 'Buddies do for each other.' "

Silme's sharp gasp of horror warned Taziar his comment had been callous. He looked up as Silme scrambled to Larson's side, apparently just noticing his limp form half-sprawled across the side of Harriman's bed.

Taziar waited while Silme searched furiously for a pulse. Even from a distance, he could see Larson breathing with the strange, seesaw chest motions his broken ribs allowed. "Silme, did you incapacitate this Bolverkr in some way?"

Silme tucked her hands beneath Larson's armpits and inclined her head toward his legs. "Not exactly. Why?"

Taziar trotted over to help. "Do you think he'll follow you here?" He grasped Larson's ankles.

Together, Taziar and Silme hoisted Larson into Harriman's bed. The elf lolled, unresponsive even to the pain of movement. Silme yanked at the coverlet. Though tears brimmed in her eyes, she kept enough presence to answer Taziar's query completely and without faltering. "Not

likely. Right now, he has his own problems to deal with."
She jerked the coverlet free of Larson's weight, then spread
it neatly over him. "Besides, Bolverkr made a mistake. He
opened me a channel to his own power. I tapped it once,
and I can do so again." Her gaze never left Larson, and
she stroked his arm through the blanket as gently as she
would a newborn kitten. "Bolverkr will have to spend some
time second-guessing me and plotting strategy. A person as
old as he is learns patience. He won't attack a group as
dangerous as us in a hurry."

Behind Silme, Asril made a gesture to indicate he was
leaving. Reminded of other responsibilities, Taziar stayed
him with a raised hand. "Silme, do whatever you can for
Allerum. He'll need more comforting than I can supply."
He smiled, trying to downplay the severity of Larson's condition. "Maybe you can slip into his brain and remind the
jerk we need him." Taziar headed toward the door, and
Asril met him halfway. "Asril and I will let the others
downstairs know what's happened here."

Taziar and Asril trotted down the corridor. At the top
of the staircase, an unruly clamor of conversation wafted
to them. Men clogged the base of the stairwell and the area
just inside the front door. The prostitutes clustered around
Shylar on the benches and chairs of the holding area. Taziar
saw no sign of Harriman's strong-arm men, but splashes of
blood on walls and some of the men's clothing made it
clear the matter had been dispatched. The other rescued
prisoners were nowhere in sight; apparently they had gone
to some sanctuary to rest and recover.

The discussions died to a buzz as Taziar and Asril descended. The crowd pressed forward. Taziar paused on the
last step and announced, "Harriman and his berserks are
dead."

Shouts of joy emanated from the women. The men took
the news in silence. Suddenly, a hand seized Taziar's arm
and ripped him from the step. Taziar stumbled into the
masses. Someone gave him a violent shove, and another
set of fingers crushed his opposite forearm. He found himself staring into a snarl of chest hair through the lacing of
a linen shirt and followed the shoulders and neck up to see
Gerwalt, an aging street tough. Hemmed in by a towering
forest of men, Taziar's mind raced as he tried to devise an

escape, aware he might die at the hands of the very men he had come to help. *Astryd warned me they all still believe I'm the traitor, but I walked right into them.* He cringed, recalling how he had even confessed to the crime while mobilizing leaders in the baron's dungeon. *What in Karana's hell was I thinking?*

"Good. Don't let the little worm get away." Gerwalt ordered. The hold on Taziar's arms tightened, pinning them behind him.

"Hanging's too good for him," someone shouted.

"You can't possibly really believe I . . ." Taziar started, but he stopped, realizing his words were lost beneath the hubbub.

Shylar leaped to a stool. Her voice cut above the noise. "What are you doing? Let Shadow go! He's—"

Gerwalt interrupted, even more commanding. "Listen, you mother of harlots!"

Angered gasps erupted from the women. Some of the men shifted nervously, and the grip on Taziar eased slightly.

Gerwalt continued inciting. "You've had a soft spot in your heart for this little weasel the whole time. He might have confused you and deceived you, but I'm smart enough to see through his lies. I'm not going to let you let us make the same mistake again." His gesture encompassed everyone in the whorehouse.

Taziar had never seen Shylar so furious. Her fists clutched whitely at the fabric of her dress, and her words confirmed that she had abandoned all restraint. "You stupid, worthless, arrogant bastard!"

Asril sprang from the stairs, brushing aside men like furniture. At Gerwalt's side, he stopped, adopting an indisputable fighting pose, his weight spread evenly, his hand prominent on his sword hilt. He spoke in a low growl, but in the tense hush that fell over the room his threat emerged loud enough. "She may have a soft spot in her heart, but you have one in your brain. I don't know who you think you are. I don't know what authority you mistakenly believe you have, and I don't know how much of Harriman's violent idiocy has worn off on you all. First, no one speaks to Shylar that way. And anyone stupid enough to think Taziar is the informant after all that's happened deserves to be hanged himself. Taz freed us from the dungeon after you left us for dead. And do you know why?''

No one hazarded an answer. The grip on Taziar's arms went warm as sweat leeched through the sleeves.

"He did it to help a friend. Do you really think he'd risk his life and everything he has to help one friend after informing on the others? Just how stupid are you?''

"Taz has confused you, too.'' Gerwalt went taut, his hand sliding to his own hilt. "I hate Harriman as much as anyone. I'm loyal to the underground and its leaders. The other leaders told me Taz admitted turning them in, and that he helped Harriman take control.''

"Gerwalt, you're an idiot.'' The crowd fidgeted, the buzz of their exchanges soft beneath Asril's insult. "None of the other leaders really feels that way. Do you see any of them here clamoring for Taziar's blood? The only two prisoners here now are me and Shylar, and both of us are calling you stupid. Consider this a friendly warning. Before I let you do anything to Taziar, I'll slit your ugly throat.''

The group thinned as men slipped quietly beyond sword range. Gerwalt went defensive, his tone losing some of its brash confidence. "Asril, why are you bullying me?''

"Because you're dangerous.''

"*I'm* dangerous?'' Gerwalt glanced about the room, belittling Asril's comment. "Taz is the traitor.''

Asril's sword left its sheath, as soundless and quick as a springing cat. "Taz is not a traitor. He's honest and loyal to his friends, exactly the kind of person we need to keep the underground alive. You're swayed by every slick-talking animal with enough connections to back up his lies. You act without knowledge. You're dangerous. If there's any threat to us here, it's you, not him.''

Guiltily, the hands fell away from Taziar's arms. Gerwalt's gaze jumped from man to man, seeking support. Apparently finding none, he moved his hands away from his sword to indicate surrender. When Asril lowered his blade, Gerwalt whirled and ran for the door. Mercifully, everyone stood aside and let him leave.

Shylar hopped to the floor, the flush fading from her cheeks, but her voice still tense with annoyance. "Nicely spoken, Asril. You had me worried back there in the prison. You sounded as bad there as this idiot here." She pointed at the door slamming closed behind Gerwalt.

Asril sheathed his weapon mechanically. "Stupidity strikes the best of us. But the way Taziar and Allerum stuck together convinced me. They were both willing to fight and die for each other. Someone who treats his friends that way doesn't change." He slapped Taziar across the back. The force drove the Climber forward a step. "It took me a while, but I remembered how good a liar Taz was."

"Thanks," Taziar said sarcastically. He stared at Asril, as impressed by the street fighter's loyalty as Asril was by his. "Just to satisfy my curiosity, tell me. Would you really have killed Gerwalt for me?"

Asril whipped a knife from his pocket and picked idly at his thumbnail. "I guess we'll never find out."

Epilogue

Shadows blurred and spun through Al Larson's world. He fought for clarity of mind and met sharp, unfocused pain. His thoughts swam through darkness, pinned by the same lead weight that held his body in place. He tried to roll, but his limbs would not respond. His breaths were rapid and shallow against the agony jabbing his lungs.

Gradually, Larson's senses returned. First came touch, and he realized he lay on a bed. *A hospital?* The indecipherable roar of conversation touched his ears, completing the picture. A childhood memory rose, a remote recollection of awakening amid a sea of white coats and strange faces, the odor of chemicals harsh in his nostrils. *Mom? Dad!* Larson attempted to scream, but not even a whisper of sound emerged. A different recollection floated, unanchored through Larson's consciousness, a female voice, thick with grief, speaking words that made no sense to him then or now: "I've done all I can to stabilize him until my life energy returns, but it's not enough. The only thing that can save him now is his own stubborn force of will."

Other memories, descended upon Larson now, the smells of excrement, gasoline, and death, muzzle flashes and the scream of jets. *The war. My god, I was injured in the war!* Larson remembered a desperate charge intro the waiting AK-47s of a Viet Cong patrol. *Jesus Christ! Don't tell me some gung ho surgeon sewed the pieces back together.*

Alarmed by what he might find, Larson gathered enough strength to wrench his eyes open. The pale glow of a lantern blinded him after the dark depths of his unconsciousness; its light revealed a group of people sitting on the floor in a circle as ragged and imperfect as a young child's drawing. Slowly, Larson's vision adjusted, and he identified them. Astryd, Silme, and Shylar kept their backs to him. Taziar's position gave him a sideways view of the bed. Only

Asril faced Larson directly. The violet-eyed thief was picking at a splinter in the floorboards, and no one seemed to notice Larson had awakened.

Larson allowed his lids to sink closed, and, finally, Shylar's words became clear to him. ". . . never in any danger from the guards in the prison. You can't believe how much respect my position commands. Harriman may have had the higher ups' ears, but I had their privates. And where men are concerned, the latter is more important."

A wave of polite laughter followed Shylar's pronouncement.

Astryd pressed further. "But if you hold so much power, how did Harriman get you arrested?"

"Even more power and connections. Harriman was the bastard of the duke as well as a competent diplomat. He'd had dealings with the baron for decades, and he learned how to arrange things so people always felt they got the best of any bargain. Once he wrested control of the girls from me, he had everything. But it's not going to happen again. I don't think it could."

Larson recognized Taziar's voice. "What about you, Asril? Shylar's probably safe, but the guards will double patrols looking for you and the others."

Larson opened his eyes in time to see Asril shrug. "It wouldn't be the first time we've gone into hiding." He threw the question back to Taziar. "What about you? Are you staying?" He added hastily. "You know your friends are welcome, too."

Shylar nodded in silent agreement.

Taziar shook his head. "Much as I'd like to, no. We still have a fight to face. Harriman was only a pawn. Our real enemy is a sorcerer willing to destroy people and things to hurt me."

Hopelessness touched Larson. The voices dulled, and darkness clotted his vision.

Asril's reply was shrill. "Are you telling me this person almost got *me* hanged because he was mad at *you*." He did not wait for affirmation. "Taz, forget what I said about hiding. I'm going to kill the bastard!"

"No." Silme's voice lulled Larson. Pain faded, replaced by a comforting void, and he slowly began to give himself over to the darkness. "Asril, you don't understand. We're not going against some farmer. Bolverkr has power you can't begin to understand. We have no choice except to oppose him, but it may prove impossible . . ."

Taziar glanced toward the bed. Larson let his eyes sag fully closed, but not before he saw the Climber make an abrupt gesture that silenced Silme. "We'd welcome your sword arm, Asril, but we don't need it. Of course, Bolverkr's a challenge. Everything's impossible until someone accomplishes it. They said no one could escape the baron's dungeon, but I've done it. Twice. And I'm just a little thief who *fights like a girl. A jerk. A creep. A swimmer who drowns in his own damned city!*"

Taziar's shout cut through the buzzing in Larson's skull. He anchored his senses on Taziar's words.

Taziar leaped to his feet. "Allerum killed a Dragonrank Master after the finest swordsman in the world failed. As if that wasn't enough, he went on to slay a god in the same afternoon. With Allerum on our side, we can't lose. In fact, Asril, maybe you should join Bolverkr. He's the one who needs help!"

Larson fought aside the numbness clutching at his senses. A whisper of vitality returned, awakening the agony he had tried to escape. But now, Larson savored the pain and the life that accompanied it. He struggled to one elbow, his eyes open and alert. "We'll kick Bolverkr's ass!"

"What?" Taziar asked in confusion. Every gaze spun toward the bed.

Larson managed a shaky smile. "Never mind," he said.

By Chaos Cursed

To Nigel Ray,
for a lot

ACKNOWLEDGMENTS

Special thanks to the following people for their help with difficult, frustrating, and bizarre research (the facts are theirs, the mistakes my own): Police Captain Donald Strand, Meyer and Florine Elkin (New Yorkers), Chris Mortika (magician), Arthur Bailey-Murray (SCA), Rockwell Williams (VA psychologist), SPC Ted Meyer, John Stitely (lawyer, martial artist), several unnameable thieves and a gang of New York street montes, who taught me to cheat at cards.

I would also like to thank the rest of "the group": Eleanor, Susan, the Lauras, Beth, Roxanne, Bill, Wendy, and Anastasia for teaching me to like Mondays.

And, as always, to Dave Hartlage, Sheila Gilbert, Jonathan Matson, and Richard Hescox for their repeated help and contributions.

Prologue

Vidarr ambled across a meadow on the god-world of Asgard, pleased by the way the omnipresent sun sparkled off each grass blade as if from a plain of emerald knives. Yet, sharp as the highlights made them seem, the blades tickled harmlessly between the bindings of the sandal on Vidarr's left foot. Constructed from the mismatched scraps of a thousand mortal cobblers, the boot on Vidarr's right foot crushed ovals in the grassland, the blades springing back to attention as he moved. A breeze ruffled golden hair twisted into war braids. His face was fair, handsome, and timeless in the near-perfect way only the gods could achieve. His cloak shimmered, interwoven with silver threads.

Unhurriedly, Vidarr continued his walk, far from the gates of Valhalla, the Bifrost Bridge, and the citadels of his colleagues. Taciturn in the extreme, Vidarr had learned to radiate his emotions in lieu of words, but he preferred the more complete silence that could only come with solitude. Let the other gods argue over the quality of the wine or who deserved the honor of sitting beside beautiful Freyja. A seeker of wisdom and truth could speak with Vidarr's father, Odin. For tales of strength and courage, no one could match Vidarr's brother, Thor; and, for polite and attractive company, Vidarr's other brother, Baldur, recently raised from Hel's underworld, was the ideal. For scintillating conversation, a god could do worse than seek out Freyja's brother, Freyr. Still, it was not bitterness that sent the Silent God tramping the fields of Asgard. Quiet, demure Vidarr simply preferred to be alone.

A patch of aqua and gold wildflowers seized Vidarr's attention, and he swerved toward it. Two long-legged strides brought him to a patch of singed foliage before the flower bed. He froze, suddenly assailed by memory. He recalled a day nearly a year ago, an eye blink to the time sense of a god. Deeply etched remembrance rose, painful in its clarity. Vidarr recalled marching across this same field. Then, he had had a companion. Radiant as a new bride and nearly as handsome as Baldur, Loki the Trickster had matched Vidarr stride for stride, verbally goading the Silent One to interest in the new sword at his hip.

Aware Loki would one day betray the gods, Vidarr cared little for his walking mate. As did all the gods, he knew Loki's destiny was to lead the giants and the souls of the dead against them in a bloody war, called Ragnarok, which would kill all but a handful of the Norse deities. But Vidarr also believed he had nothing to fear. The time for war had not come yet, and, of them all, Vidarr was to be the war's hero, the only god every legend named certain to survive the Ragnarok.

As vividly as if it had been yesterday, light slashed Vidarr's vision, and the explosion of Loki's magics thundered through his ears. Pain slammed his chest with the force of a galloping stallion. Bowled to the ground, he was caught in a whirling vortex of sorcery that stole all sense of time, place, and existence. The recognition of flesh and self disappeared, replaced by a perfect prison of cold, solid iron. Vidarr vaguely recalled the high-pitched fear of his own scream ringing across his hearing through an eternity of otherwise unbroken, silent darkness.

Now, Vidarr shivered at the thought. Trapped within a block of metal, he had fought for a glimpse of light, a whisper of sound, a taste or a touch. As one eternity seemed to pass to the next, he came to believe himself forgotten, lost in an endless void of imprisonment. No external battle gained him so much as a flash of sight, so he strove for a madness that would not come. In this, mankind had surpassed the gods. The knowledge of their own mortality gave men a bent toward insanity that allowed them to surrender to it when other options seemed worse. Vidarr simply suffered, never knowing how hard Freyr tried to reach him through the iron nor how the god of elves and the sun had the dark elves craft Vidarr's prison into a sword.

Freyr had then searched the world for a man without the natural mental barriers that prevented gods and sorcerers from intruding on people's thoughts and dreams or warping their perceptions. Finding no one, Freyr had turned to alternative times, the magic involved costing him volumes in time, health, and valuables. And the answer had come in the finding that future civilizations had no sorcerers and no Balance of Law and Chaos. Unused and unneeded, the mental barriers had evolved away, and Freyr had found his hero/victim in the person of an American soldier in Vietnam, a twenty-year-old private named Al Larson who, against all propriety of his era, called upon Freyr himself as the enemies' machine guns took his life.

The details of the transfer went beyond Vidarr's knowledge. The other gods made only distant mention of the permanent damage to Freyr's magic and his mental stability. Larson had lost his human body, replaced by that of an elf follower of Freyr.

And Vidarr's first glimpse of reality had come through the eyes of his wielder, perceptions warped by battle fatigue, flashbacks, confusion, and gross ignorance. Struggling to sort reality from madness, Vidarr had forged a bond with his human wielder stronger than any ties to the gods. With the help of Larson's Freyr-chosen companions, a powerful Dragonrank sorceress named Silme and her ronin bodyguard, Kensei Gaelinar, Vidarr finally pieced together the means to break Loki's spell, a solution that had required the death, and ultimately the complete destruction, of Loki and the Chaos he harbored. In the process, Vidarr learned details about human nature he could never have guessed.

Now, before the hole of brown, curled grasses burned by Loki's magic, a smile twitched across Vidarr's lips. Unlike the humans of this era who fawned and groveled at the feet of the pantheon, Larson had little respect for anyone or anything. Through him, Vidarr learned that mortality made humans' existence more, not less, precious than the gods'. Each day held the value of a deity's decade. Lives so short and death so complete gave honor and glory to any life voluntarily sacrificed for the good of others. And Vidarr learned one thing more.

Intolerant of untruths, even among themselves, a god's word was always held to be inviolate, unquestionable authority on man's world of Midgard. Morality used to seem simple to Vidarr. What was right was simply right. But mankind, and especially Al Larson, knew a spectrum of behavior in shades of gray that Vidarr would never have hypothesized or understood without having tangled himself so deeply in a mortal's mind. It was Al Larson who taught Vidarr to lie and to deceive and, appropriately, Al Larson who was the victim of that betrayal.

Killed centuries earlier by Loki's treachery, Vidarr's brother, Baldur, had spent his time in the dank, dark, malodorous halls of Hel, comforted by the knowledge that he was destined to live again after the Ragnarok. But Loki's death meant that Ragnarok would never occur. Concerned for his brother, Vidarr had used trickery to commit Larson, Gaelinar, and a quick-witted thief named Taziar the Shadow Climber to a quest long considered impossible. As a result, they were forced to battle unmatched volumes of Chaos-energy in its natural form: as a dragon. The quest had cost Gaelinar his life, but it had brought enough Chaos into the world to balance the resurrections of two powerful keepers of Law, Baldur and Silme, and to replace the permanent loss of Loki.

The reminiscence roused Vidarr's curiosity. Larson had come out of that quest gut-shot by a rifle as out of time as himself and clinging to the meticulously-crafted katana that had belonged to his beloved and respected Kensei swordmaster. Aware that Taziar's Dragonrank girlfriend, Astryd, had some knowledge of magical healing, Vidarr had left Larson, Taziar, Silme, and Astryd to their own devices. *I wonder how they're doing?* Vidarr considered. Larson had made it clear that he resented the gods' intrusions into his mind. Through effort, the elf had learned to wall trespassers into pockets of memory. Vidarr had learned the danger of that tactic when Larson had trapped him and an enemy in the Vietnamese jungles, their only escape, back through Larson's mind, neatly blocked by its owner.

Still, Larson had never found a means to detect the presence of a gentle probe. Through it, Vidarr could communicate and read the elf-man's superficial thoughts. *I'll read his mood without him ever knowing I was there. If he's relaxed, I'll say my hellos. So long as I don't play with his thoughts, he shouldn't mind.* With that idea, Vidarr thrust a probe for Larson's mind.

Vidarr's search met nothing. Shocked, he withdrew and tried again. Once again, he met only darkness.

Vidarr slid to the grass, sitting cross-legged, his fingers to his temples. Never before had it cost energy or effort to explore Larson's mind. Vidarr lowered his head, putting his full concentration into the task. Again, his mental probe met no resistance. *Dead? He's dead?* Surprise and concern sharpened his focus. Gradually, words, images, and the snarl of looping thought pathways took shape, black against near-black, like the outline of sun glazed through thunderheads, viewed as much from his knowledge of its necessary presence as reality. *Not dead,* Vidarr realized, gaining little solace from the realization. *But nearly so. How?* For now, the reason did not matter. Vidarr rooted through the darkness for a single spark of life.

For some time, the search frustrated Vidarr. Apparently, Al Larson still lived, otherwise he would have no memories at all, not even the vague, smeared images obscured by the hovering fog of death. Vidarr drew fully into Larson's mind, forcing himself to evaluate the quality of each shadow, following a subtle and scattered trail that was more "less dark" than light. Gradually, he discovered a single, cold pinpoint of light, rapidly fading.

A thought struck through Vidarr. *If he dies before I get out of here, we're both dead.* Gently, he fanned the glow. It sputtered, frayed like ancient string. For an instant, Vidarr thought he had blown it out. Fear gripped him as the spark sputtered, then grew ever so slightly. He felt a survival instinct shift, erratic as a rusted hinge, then cringe back into hiding from pain.

You bastard! Since when has pain ever stopped you from doing anything? He kicked the wire-thin pathway that housed the instinct. Agony sparked through Larson's mind, but this time the survival instinct hovered, uncertain, tenuous.

Vidarr held his breath.

In Larson's head, a hand clamped onto Vidarr's shoulder.

Shock wrenched a gasp from Vidarr, the strength of the emotion splashing insight through Larson's mind. Heart pounding, Vidarr snapped back to Asgard. He could feel the other presence flash out with him.

After the crushing darkness of Larson's mind, the hovering fire of Asgard's sun blinded Vidarr. He whirled, slashing an arm up instinctively. His forearm crashed against a wrist, breaking the grip, and he found himself facing Freyr.

Freyr stood with arms crossed in judgment, and his pale eyes shone like the sun that was his charge. "What are you doing?"

Vidarr rarely used words. Over time, he had become adept at communication only by radiating his primary emotions. Now, as surprised waned, he stared dispassionately at Freyr.

"Allerum." Freyr used the name Larson had won through an inadvertent spell of stuttering during his original introduction to his friends. "You were healing Allerum."

That being self-evident, Vidarr mimicked Freyr's outraged stance without a reply.

"You can't do that." Freyr made a brisk gesture with his arm that set his clothes shimmering colorfully.

Still, Vidarr waited, not bothering to contradict an obvious fallacy. Freyr's commanding manner was starting to annoy the Silent God, but he kept the first stirrings of irritation from his disclosure and his manner.

Apparently recognizing the ludicrousness of his own claim, Freyr amended. "Well, of course, I suppose you can heal Allerum, but you shouldn't. Vidarr, it would be bad."

Vidarr cocked his brows, demanding explanation. If not for Al Larson's courage and his willingness to fight against Loki, Vidarr knew he would still be trapped within a lightless, soundless void. Loki would still live to lead the hordes of Hel and giants against the gods and men. Without Vidarr to slay the Fenris Wolf, the beast would have survived to aid its loathsome father, Loki. Instead of the prophesied Ragnarok that would have ended with a few gods and men still intact, Loki and his followers would have torn the worlds asunder with a limitless Chaos of slaughter. Wives killing husbands. Fathers raping daughters.

The images wound through Vidarr's mind, bringing a chill that the sun-filled Asgard meadow could not touch. *Averted, all averted, thanks to Allerum. I owe him my life as do all the gods. And he paid a price we should never have asked of anyone.* Vidarr cringed, recalling how moments before the sword stroke that took Loki's life, the Evil One had reminded Larson that destroying him would prevent Ragnarok. Without the war, the Norse gods would reign through eternity, never replaced by the Christian religion Larson embraced. Larson, his family, his friends, and his world would never exist.

Freyr's voice became fatherly. Apparently partially guessing Vidarr's concern, he rationalized. "I know you think you owe something to Allerum, but you don't. Men are pawns, meant to serve us. The opportunity to do so is all the reward they deserve."

"I used to believe that," said Vidarr quietly, his voice a mellow tenor.

Caught off-guard by Vidarr's switch to speech, Freyr stared.

"Before I spent so much time in Allerum's head."

Freyr recovered with a snort. "You can't judge all men by Allerum. He was addled by a war without glory, and he's a product of his time and place. His god chooses to fade into the background, leaving men to make their own decisions and mistakes. I passed over hundreds of loud-mouthed, disrespectful future Americans before I discovered Allerum."

Vidarr did not bother to argue. Natural mind barriers prevented the gods from reading the thoughts and intentions of mortals, so neither side of the discussion could be corroborated by fact. Vidarr extrapolated from the only model he could access: Al Larson. And, having learned how sincerely humans voiced their lies, he had to guess that most of the gods' pawns hid their grudging acceptance of the position behind an artificial enthusiasm. Vidarr let impatience sift through his facade, making it clear he considered Larson's life more important than a discussion on human motivation.

Accepting the cue, Freyr came to the heart of his explanation. "You are familiar with the Balance." It was a statement, not a question.

Vidarr nodded. The Balance between Law and Chaos was eternal, since long before the gods entered the nine worlds. The natural forces seemed to keep themselves in line without need for a guardian. Minor inequalities had no effect upon the worlds and their inhabitants. The deaths of strong proponents of one side were always naturally compensated by equal deaths for the opposite cause.

"Then," Freyr continued, "you must also know the effect Allerum has had on that Balance."

Vidarr lowered his head, feeling responsible. Freed from his imprisonment, joy had made him careless. He had left Loki's corpse where it had collapsed near Hvergelmir's waterfall, never guessing Larson would hurl the body into the cascade that destroyed all things. Annihilated, body and soul, Loki's harbored Chaos disappeared, leaving a gap no one could fill. *Chaos.* Vidarr shook his head. *The stuff of life.* It seemed odd that the very substance defining existence also poisoned it, so that corruption naturally accompanied power. The world's only mortal sorcerers, the Dragonrank, drew their powers from tapping their own internal chaos known as life force. Therefore, those who served Chaos were always more powerful than their counterparts, and there were always larger numbers of Law abiding souls in the world to compensate.

"Allerum destroyed Loki," Freyr explained, anyway. "Then he raised Silme from the dead, balancing her resurrection with an equally powerful servant of Chaos. . . ."

Vidarr nodded smugly, but this perfect example of Larson's concern for the Balance was crushed by Freyr's next description.

". . . whom Allerum later killed, thereby skewing the Balance dangerously further in the direction of Law." Freyr sat in the grass, hugging his knees to his chest. Thin, white-blond hair tumbled about his shoulders. "Then there was that Geirmagnus' rod quest. . . ."

"That's not fair!" Vidarr interrupted. "It wasn't Allerum's idea. In fact, he fought against it so hard I had to lie and cheat to make him finish it. My father forced me to send Allerum on that quest. He couldn't bear the thought of his most beautiful and gracious son rotting in Hel for eternity. . . ."

Freyr raised his hand to stop Vidarr's uncharacteristic flow of words. "I never said it was Allerum's idea, only that no one else could have succeeded. As it was, Allerum, Taziar, and the Kensei resurrected Baldur." Freyr added quickly, "Don't misunderstand. I'm as glad to have Baldur back as anyone. But the rift in the Balance would have been enough to destroy the world. If not for the dragon."

Vidarr nodded. He had seen the beast through Larson's eyes, a towering manifestation of raw Chaos energy imprisoned by the first leader of the Dragonrank sorcerers at a time when the Balance had tipped dangerously in the other direction. Again, he saw the house-sized creature bank and glide on its leathery wings, maneuverable as a falcon. He knew Larson's fear as teeth long and sharp as daggers gashed his arm, and Vidarr also knew the tearing depth of grief when Kensei Gaelinar goaded the beast through a coil of razor wire, sacrificing his own life in the process. Dragons were conglomerates of unmastered Chaos-force; slaying it dispersed rather than destroyed its power. Here, Vidarr believed, was how the Balance had been put right.

But the expression of outrage on Freyr's face cued Vidarr to the fact that there was knowledge he did not yet have. Freyr cleared his throat. "You have no idea how Allerum came to be as near to death as he is. Do you?"

Vidarr shook his head, hoping the gesture made it clear it did not matter. Regardless of the cause, he owed Larson his loyalty. *Don't I?* Doubt seeped silently into his awareness. Feeling weak, he sat beside Freyr.

The lord of elves plucked at grass spears, avoiding Vidarr's stare. "Raw Chaos can't be destroyed, only disbanded. To destroy it, you must destroy its host."

Vidarr waited, aware Freyr had started with the obvious in order to make a more serious point.

"Chaos-force is nonintelligent, geared only toward survival and the Balance. It knows only that it must find a strong host, one capable of surviving its transfer and its demands for cruelty, mayhem, and disorder. Once freed from dragon form, that raw Chaos-energy raged across the Kattegat to a farm town called Wilsberg. There, it struck with a storm that slaughtered every citizen *except its new master.*"

Freyr's words stunned Vidarr into an awed silence. *All of that Chaos into one man?* The thought was madness. Until now, he had assumed the Chaos would disseminate, that every man, woman, and child in Midgard would become a trace more evil. *No one could have survived the transfer of so much Chaos energy.*

"A Dragonrank sorcerer named Bolverkr." Freyr answered the unspoken question. "He came from the earliest days of the Dragonrank when the mages drew reams of raw Chaos to themselves rather than using life energy, ignorant of the cost to the Balance." Freyr paused, leaving time for the words to sink in, waiting to see whether Vidarr would make the obvious connection without further hints.

Vidarr remained stunned.

Freyr met and held Vidarr's gaze. "Chaos hunted out the strongest possible master on the nine worlds."

Suddenly, understanding radiated from Vidarr. *It went to Bolverkr, not me or Freyr or Odin.* The natural conclusion was too enormous to contemplate. *This Bolverkr apparently wields more power than any single god.* He shuddered at the observation.

Freyr concurred. "Frightening, isn't it?"

Vidarr nodded.

Freyr rose, brushing pollen and grass spears from his leggings. "Bolverkr knows Allerum and Taziar loosed the Chaos that destroyed the town and the people he loved, his pregnant wife and his fortress, and turned him into a puppet of Chaos, contaminated beyond redemption. He's sworn to be avenged, but he isn't stupid, either. He knows Allerum and Taziar have already defeated the Chaos-force that is his power, and now they have the Dragonmages, Silme and Astryd, as partners in love and war. He's playing it careful and well. Allerum's current condition demonstrates Bolverkr's skill." Again, Freyr held Vidarr's pale gaze. "And now I think you understand why you can't rouse Allerum."

Vidarr beetled his brows, missing the connection.

Seeing Vidarr's confusion, Freyr explained. "Allerum is an anachronism and Silme, by all rights, should still be dead. Taziar and Astryd are small enough in power that their deaths would not severely affect the balance. But, should Bolverkr die, wielding as much Chaos-force as he does, the Balance would overturn. The world might be destroyed, all men, elves, and gods with it. Or, perhaps, his death would need to be matched with equal amounts of supporters of Law. All the mortal followers of Law might not prove enough. Gods would die, Vidarr. Perhaps you and I? Odin? Thor and Baldur? For the sake of the world, Allerum and his companions must lose this feud. You'll have to undo anything you've done and *let Allerum die.*"

Vidarr bit his lip, pained by Freyr's words. He understood the necessity. The Balance and the lives of gods had to take precedence over one soldier, no matter how much good he had done for Vidarr. The idea of leaving Allerum to his own devices seemed difficult enough. *But what's done is done. To snuff the slight spark I encouraged would be murder.*

Freyr tried to soften his command. "You have to remember, Allerum was as good as dead when I plucked him from the battlefield. We gave him life, if only for a few extra months. If not for me, he'd be a bloody corpse lying in an empty riverbed in Vietnam."

Vidarr said nothing.

Freyr sighed. He clasped Vidarr's shoulder comfortingly. "Do what you have to do." Without further encouragement, Freyr started back across the meadow, his boots crushing foliage in huge patches, his eight foot frame still visible against the sun long after he passed beyond hearing distance of Vidarr.

For some time, Vidarr remained seated without moving. Then, dreading the inevitable, he maneuvered a probe into Larson's mind.

This time, Vidarr met a diffuse grayness that revealed the tangled tapestry of Larson's thoughts as vague sculptures in shadow. He thrust farther, drawing himself directly into Larson's mind. Pain assailed him, wholly Larson's, and the god focused instead on the ring of companions whose words wafted clearly to Larson.

Taziar was speaking, "Everything's impossible until someone accomplishes it. They said no one could escape the baron's dungeon, but I've done it. Twice . . ."

The words droned on, reaching a crescendo, but Vidarr lost his thoughts in a different conversation. He recalled a time when the Fenris Wolf had penetrated Larson's mind, intending to torture the elf with manipulation of his memories. Then, Vidarr's sudden appearance in Larson's mind had startled the Wolf into leaving.

Later, facing Larson's anger rather than gratitude, Vidarr remembered his own words and the frustration that had suffused him at Larson's stubbornness. ". . . And you seem to have forgotten that Freyr rescued you from death to bring you here, at no small risk to his own life . . . Freyr pulled you from a hellish war . . ."

Parts of Larson's reply returned clearly. ". . . to place me into another hellish war. Into Hel itself even! I'm sup-

posed to feel grateful that Freyr ripped me from a world
of technological miracles and dumped me into the body of
a ninety-eight pound weakling?''

"Technological miracles or not. You were dead.''

"Dead or not, I was free. I'm no slave. If I am to serve
gods, I shall do so willingly or not at all. Otherwise, you
can kill me right now.''

The memory slipped from Vidarr's thoughts, driven away
by the growing light of Larson's mind as the dying elf responded to Taziar's rallying speech.

Vidarr cursed, groping for the flaring glow of life before
it could fill Larson's being. He seized its stalk, aware he
would need to retreat as he cut or else die along with Larson. Beneath his grip, he could feel Larson fighting aside
the hovering numbness and peace that death offered. Some
subconscious portion of Larson's mind must have sensed
Vidarr's presence because his thoughts brought another
memory vividly to life:

Larson lay, again near death, on the grounds of Geirmagnus' estate, trying to keep Vidarr's telepathic words in
focus.

". . . I always knew any or all of you might die, but I
had no other choice . . . I care for Baldur very deeply. I
did not enjoy the deception any more than you, but I saw
no other way. I plead the cause of brotherly love and hope
you can find it in yourself to forgive me.''

Then, Larson had fallen unconscious before he could
delve an answer. Now, Vidarr could see that Larson had
added an addendum to the memory, a selfless acceptance
of the apology and an offer of friendship.

Vidarr stared, not daring to believe what he saw. His
fingers slipped from the stalk. Larson's will flared, sparking
thoughts throughout his mind, and Vidarr withdrew.

*If Allerum is to die, let him do so honestly and by his
own doing. I won't have a hand in his murder.*

In the vast meadow of Asgard, a songbird twittered in a
minor key.

CHAPTER 1
Chaos Madness

Chaos of thought and passion, all confused;
Still by himself abused, or disabused;
Created half to rise, and half to fall;
Great lord of all things, yet a prey to all;
Sole judge of truth, in endless error hurled;
The glory, jest, and riddle of the world.
   —Alexander Pope, *An Essay on Man*

A sliver of moon hovered over the Barony of Cullinsberg, revealing the rows of buildings along Panogya Street as familiar blocks of shadow. Taziar Medakan, the Shadow Climber, had chosen the moon's phase from habit; years of work beneath crescents that shed only enough light to etch landmarks had given him cause to call this phase the "thieves' moon" and to consider it a friend. The cobbled roadway felt familiar through the thin, flexible soles of his boots. More times than he cared to remember, he had stalked the thoroughfares and alleyways of Cullinsberg dressed, as now, in tough, black linens. A comma of hair as dark as his clothing spilled from beneath his hood and into his eyes, a familiar annoyance he could not seem to avoid no matter how carefully he cut the straight, fine locks.

As a child, Taziar had memorized every corner of Cullinsberg in order to survive. Later, unable to pass up any task labeled impossible, he had learned the intricacies that came with detailed study of the city's most magnificent defenses, most of which he had thwarted simply for the challenge. But tonight Taziar had no interest in Cullinsberg's secrets and challenges. Beyond the imposing stone walls of the baron's city, Taziar knew a Dragonrank sorcerer named Bolverkr plotted torture and cruel deaths for Taziar and his closest friends. And the Shadow Climber was determined to assess this enemy with his own eyes, to ascertain just how imminently the coming battle loomed.

Taziar caught handholds in the stone and mortar wall of the slaughterhouse and shinnied to its rooftop with the ease that had earned him his alias. He crouched, though even upright he stood half a head shorter than an average woman. Sounds wafted to him, a dull mixture of high-pitched insect shrills, a fox call, distantly answered, the rasp of garbage blowing through an alleyway, and the creak of wood in perfect rhythm with the wind. Taziar sifted through the routine medley of city night. Beneath it all, he heard the steady thump of footsteps, strong and competent, unlike the intermittent shuffle and halt of street people hunting food or the quiet caution of orphan gangs or thieves.

Guards. Taziar verified his guess by a cautious peek into Panogya Street. A half dozen soldiers in the barony's red and black uniforms paced toward the town's central thoroughfare. During the fifteen and a half years that Taziar's father had served as their captain, the patrols had filled young Taziar with pride. But that respect had withered to loathing the day the baron hanged Taziar's father based on evidence contrived by a crooked politician. Taziar's own capture and torture at the hands of sadistic, corrupt guardsmen had destroyed any vestige of deference toward Cullinsberg's defenders.

Taziar lowered himself flat to the roof tiles, intent on the patrol. Usually, the guardsmen prowled in groups of twos and threes. The baron would only have doubled his night watches for a purpose. And, since Taziar had masterminded and commanded Cullinsberg's only prison break just three days earlier, freeing the seven key leaders of the underground, he had every reason to believe the baron wanted him.

Concerned for Al Larson, barely rescued from the brink of death; for Larson's pregnant, sorceress wife, Silme; and for his own girlfriend, Astryd, who spent her days draining her life energy casting spells to enhance and hasten Larson's healing, Taziar had found his attention singularly focused on the Chaos-driven Dragonrank sorcerer who had sworn vengeance against them. In the shadow of Bolverkr's power, Cullinsberg's guard force had paled to an insignificant threat unworthy of Taziar's worry. Yet, now Taziar realized that if he was run through by a guardsman's spear, sword, or crossbow bolt, he would be as dead as if Bolverkr's magics had done the deed.

Taziar smiled, intrigued by the mundane challenge offered by Cullinsberg's guardsmen. Days without the rush of natural stimulants his body produced in times of stress had made him as twitchy as an addict. Sleep had become impossible. Restlessness had driven him to sneak away from his friends, where they hid and recovered in Shylar's whorehouse, in the care of the best comforters and providers the underground could offer. Taziar knew Larson, Silme, and Astryd would chide him for not acting like what Larson called a "team player." The twentieth-century English phrase seemed ridiculously out of place in Taziar's thoughts. But to ignore an enemy as powerful and competent as Bolverkr, trusting luck to hold him at bay until they became strong enough to strike back was insanity, not a strategy.

Days ago, Bolverkr had captured Silme. Attempting to jettison some of the Chaos that warped him, he had tricked her into opening a link to the source of his Chaos-power. Silme had managed to break that contact, freeing the Chaos he had shared with her and causing it to backlash to its master. Silme seemed to believe the shock force of that rebound would keep Bolverkr busy rebuilding his sense of self and his keep, but Taziar felt less certain of Silme's reassurance and more confident of Bolverkr's strength. *I have to see for myself just how badly the Chaos injured Bolverkr and his fortress. And I have to delay his next attack a little longer if I can.*

Taziar watched the gloom swallow the patrol as their footsteps receded to clicks, then disappeared. *But first, I have to get past the sentries.* Taziar rose to a crouch, skittered across the slaughterhouse roof and into a zigzagging series of alleyways. *Which means I need to get a feel for the new patterns of the watch.* Skirting scattered scraps of wood, cloth, and food, feasting rats and rotting crates, Taziar crossed the thready branchways without a sound. His keen, blue eyes measured the depth of every silhouette and shadow, guiding him always to the ones that hid him best. His walks and sprints were steady, sinuous as a cat's, without the jerky impetuousness that draws the attention of predators: hunters, soldiers, and thieves.

Padding southward, Taziar came to Mardain's temple, a towering, seven-story structure of mortared stone. Aside from the baron's keep and Aga'arin's church, both closely guarded even in the most peaceful times, Mardain's temple stood taller than any building in Cullinsberg. Acutely aware of the lack of handholds in its smoothly-chinked lower story, Taziar sprinted down the byway, fingers scraping the temple's masonry. Nearly at the far corner, he hurled himself toward the wall. Momentum carried him to the second story where he ferreted out the familiar handholds and clambered to the rooftop.

The sky spread above Taziar, stars gleaming silver like scales in a fisherman's net. Below him stretched the familiar patterns of the city of Cullinsberg. Safe in his domain high above the citizenry, Taziar felt like a king surveying his realm. To the south, Cullinsberg's gates lay open, as always. Though too distant to discern, Taziar knew guards paced the walls. Usually, people could enter and exit the town without challenge, but Taziar guessed the guards now questioned anyone passing out through the gates, especially at night.

The looming shape of the gallows in the town square unnerved Taziar, so he chose to look another way. To the west, a dozen guards huddled in conference on the main thoroughfare. As he watched, they split into three equal groups, one marching down Panogya Street and each of the others tramping a parallel route in the alleyways on either side.

Taziar held his breath, aware that a few moments earlier that maneuver might have seen him surrounded. *Of course, I still could have escaped by climbing.* He considered this flaw in the guards' tactics. Taziar's capture months ago had lost him the cover of his alias. *They know who I am and that I climb buildings.* The last was gross understatement. Taziar had scaled heights and surfaces that mountaineers would have dismissed as impossible. Though he had never been given the opportunity, he believed he could climb a vertical pane of ice, and those who had seen him in action never challenged the claim.

Intrigued by the guards' formation, Taziar watched the

closest set of men as they passed between the smokehouse and Cullinsberg's inn. The sentries wove through the alley. One always stayed in the lead, apparently watching for movement. Two bobbed their heads, following the sweep of each wall to its ceiling. The last glanced behind rain barrels and garbage, using a torch to peer into any crack large enough to fit a rat.

It seemed only natural for Taziar to anticipate his reactions had the guards, in fact, intercepted him in the alleyway. *I would have slipped ahead and climbed.* He tracked his potential route to a series of shops and cottages closest to the eastern wall enclosing the city. His eyes narrowed suspiciously. *They must have some strategy in mind. Why would they flush me toward the wall? They know I could scale it. Then I'd be free.* Squinting, he studied the eastern wall, wondering if the baron had packed it with sentries. If so, it seemed a foolish mistake that would require him to skimp on guardsmen for the other three walls. *Why short defenses on three sides of the city for one? What would make him that certain I'd go eastward?*

Darkness glazed the outer wall to a blur. Taziar blinked, for the first time cursing the limits of vision imposed by the "thieves' moon." He tensed for a better look, and his movement brought a glint of metal to view. *Too near to be from the catwalk.* Taziar froze, staring. The object flashed away. *Too high to be from a sentry on the ground. Has to be some sort of steel fitting or object on a rooftop.* Discomfort jangled within Taziar, its source not quite able to slip from instinct to understanding. Taziar considered, twisting his head until he found the glitter of metal again. This time, the answer came. *It disappeared even though I didn't move.* Since the moon could not have shifted that abruptly, it had to be the metal that had changed position.

Taziar contemplated the significance of his observation. *Either it's a loose edge of something being blown by wind, or someone is on that rooftop.* The second possibility would have seemed ludicrous under ordinary circumstances, but the guardsmen's behavior in the alleyway clinched it. *The baron stationed sentries on the rooftops for me?* Taziar followed the natural extensions of the strategy. *The patrols weren't trying to drive me eastward, just toward any wall at all. They probably figured I'd know to dodge sentries on the walls, but I'd run right into the ones hiding on the roofs.*

Now the baron's scheme made perfect sense, and Taziar tried to rework it to his advantage. *I can't go through the main gate. I have no choice but to climb the walls.* One alternative presented itself to Taziar. When he had escaped the baron's dungeons months ago, he and his barbarian companion had crept from the city through the sewer system. Now, that option appealed less to Taziar than battling through the guards, though he carried no sword. If not for Moonbear's strength, they would never have hammered free the grating that kept attackers from using the same means to enter the city. *A grating that may have been replaced,* Taziar realized, remembering that Moonbear's quick reflexes had also kept the Climber from drowning when he fell into a depression in the riverbed. *Forget the sewers. I'm just going to have to avoid the outer circle of rooftops and slip over the wall between sentries.* Decision made, Taziar waited until the patrol again turned westward, then clambered down the east side of Mardain's temple, dropping from the second story into the alley.

Back pressed to the wall, Taziar glanced into a connecting east-west roadway. The backs of three retreating guardsmen loomed to the west. Eastward, the path lay open. Quietly, huddled in pooled darkness, he rushed toward the eastern wall and freedom. Flitting past a row of cottages, he slowed as he approached a well-known crosswalk leading to a statue-crowned basin where much of the populace drew its drinking water. Edging forward, Taziar peered around the corner.

He found himself face-to-face with a guardsman urinating on the stone and sod of the candlemaker's shop.

Taziar back-stepped.

The guard's expression went from startled to urgent. Without bothering to fix his britches, he lunged for a spear leaning against the wall. "Here! Shadow Climber. Southeast. Candlemaker's!"

Taziar groaned at the·crisp efficiency of the signal; evidently, the guards had organized precisely for the cause of his capture. Spared only the moment it took the guard to jab his spear, Taziar reacted from long habit. Seizing handholds in the wall, he scurried to the roof. Too late, he realized his mistake. As his head came over the ledge, he caught a split-second glimpse of guardsmen rushing toward him and cold steel whipping for his face.

Momentum overrode Taziar's instinct to duck. Instead, he flung himself to the rooftop. The sentry's sword tore the hood from his head, close enough to ruffle a breeze across his scalp. The backswing caught the Climber nearly at the hilt, a clouting stroke that sent him reeling across the tiles. Head ringing, he dropped to one knee, twisting to face his attackers. One rushed him, catching a tenuous grip on Taziar's sleeve. Taziar jerked backward, and a more solid pair of hands seized him from the opposite side.

"I had him first." A knife flashed in the first guard's hand.

The second recoiled with a gasp of pain. "You bastard!" Blood splashed Taziar's cheek.

The words slurred through Taziar's spinning consciousness. Reflex had him up and halfway to the northern edge of the roof, tearing free of the fingers entwined in his sleeve, before logic took over. He judged the gap between buildings; a leap across a narrow alley would take him onto a cottage roof. He had tensed to spring before sense seeped fully back into his numbed mind, and he recognized the shapes on the reinforced thatch roof as guardsmen with drawn bows. *Karana's hell.* Taziar flinched back, hoping his nearness to the other guards would force the bowmen to hold their fire.

The twang of bowstrings sounded almost simultaneously. Taziar ducked and rolled. Steel heads clattered to the tiles. One guardsman cried out, apparently pierced by a companion's arrow. Others swore, scrabbling for cover. In the confusion, Taziar sprang from the rooftop toward the now empty alley where he had stumbled upon the indisposed guard. He skimmed his fingers and toes along the wall to slow his descent without bothering to catch secure holds. Baron Dietrich's mistake seemed obvious; apparently, the baron had offered an individual reward or bonus to the guard who killed the Shadow Climber. While it encouraged alertness, morale, and healthy competition, it also stretched the already marginal cooperativeness of the guards.

Perhaps, Taziar thought as he crossed the byway and hauled himself up a warehouse wall to a slated, second-story rooftop that came to a central point, *the baron doesn't care how many men he loses, so long as he gets me.* The idea seemed morbid, but not beneath the morality of a leader whose control by Aga'arin's priests had driven him to hang his faithful captain. *If the bowmen aren't afraid to kill their own, how can I possibly survive their barrages?*

Taziar dodged to the northern side of the roof, boots scrabbling on the slanted surface. Arrows thunked into sod or tile; more clicked or snapped against stone. Other noises wafted to him beneath the muffled shouts and curses: scraping, the hollow clunk of wood hitting wood, and the louder impact as heavy objects struck tile. The roof shook beneath his hold. *What?* Needing to understand this new threat, Taziar risked craning his neck around the corner.

The bowmen on the cottage roof had abandoned their attack to place a sturdy board from the lip of their rooftop to Taziar's, spanning the byway the Climber had run across. Farther south, the swordsmen on the neighboring roof had placed a similar passage to the row of cottages next to Taziar's current location.

Taziar jerked his head back around. *They're prepared this time. Those makeshift bridges can get them across roadways too wide for me to jump.* Taziar worked his way to the western side of his roof, considering in which situations the guards' preparation gave them the advantage and how he might turn it against them. *The boards will slow them down. So long as I stay on buildings set closely enough for me to jump across them, I'll be faster.* Taziar frowned, listening to the pound of footsteps as the guards crossed the bridges. *They'll expect me to stay high. That's my style. So, at some point, I'll have to go to the streets.* Taziar leapt from the slanted rooftop, over a narrow alley, to the flower shop, gathering momentum from the story of difference in height. *I need to draw them away from the rooftops near the outer wall.*

Disguising his voice, Taziar shouted, "Here! Shadow Climber. Southeast. Slant-roofed warehouse!" He was rewarded by the clatter of movement as guardsmen on-high all along the eastern wall joined the chase. *All right. I've got them away from the wall. Now how am I going to get them away from me?* No ready answers came.

The patrol on the cottages rounded the slant-roofed

warehouse. Atop the warehouse itself, the archers swore. Tile pattered down the slope and into the street. One screamed as his footing tore free, and he toppled to the packed dirt road below.

Taziar shinnied into the street. Ignoring the moaning guardsman, he sprinted across the roadway and scrambled to the roof of the L-shaped cobbler shop. Behind him, he could hear the scratch of wood dragged along tile. Footsteps thundered across the slaughterhouse roof.

Taziar measured the distance to the smokehouse, then sneaked a peek in the direction of the pursuing guardsmen. It would be a race to the smokehouse. *If I don't leap across, they'll meet me.* The space between buildings gaped. Not daring to contemplate it for too long, Taziar sprinted across the long limb of the L-shaped roof and dove for the smokehouse. He hit with his shoulder, rolling in a crooked arc that saved his life. Arrows rebounded from sun-baked stone and tile, every one taking the straighter path he should have taken.

Once on the smokehouse roof, Taziar wasted no time. He half-leapt, half-climbed into Panogya Street. He twisted his head as he fell, gaining a momentary semicircle of view. Guardsmen clustered on the cottages west of the slant-roofed warehouse, the cobbler shop, smokehouse, slaughterhouse, and the roof of Shylar's whorehouse. Quick as a squirrel, Taziar whisked up the wall of the butcher's shop even as soldiers in black and red uniforms slapped boards into place from Shylar's whorehouse.

Too close. Taziar's heart pounded. His lungs felt as if their linings had been gasped away, leaving them raw and bleeding. *Think. Have to think. A trick.* He knew this side of town well; as a young teen, he had spent much of his time here, filching food for himself and his friends through the baker's third-story window. Running westward, he sprang the short gap between the butcher's shop and the cooper's, then leapt down into the cross street, grabbing a handful of stones from the roadway as he ran.

"Shadow Climber!" someone yelled behind him. "Northeast. Cobbler's!"

Taziar jammed his fingers into cracks of the building that housed the baker's huge ovens. The stone felt warm beneath his hands, and he clambered toward the top without glancing back. He kept himself tightened into the smallest target possible, feeling the wary prickle that came with known enemies at his back. But, apparently, the guardsmen were preoccupied with angling their boards from the single story of the cobbler's shop to the three-story structure that housed the baker's ovens.

Taziar darted across the oven building to the attached baker's shop. There, he paused, his fingers on the westernmost ledge of the baker's shop, overlooking the main thoroughfare, waiting for the guardsmen to come back into sight.

As the first guardsman appeared, Taziar swung down over the side, clinging to the lip of the rooftop as if to drop into the main thoroughfare. At the last moment, he swung his legs and hooked through the baker's window. He landed silently on the floor, turned and hurled the stones he had gathered through the window and into the main street, hoping the mild thump of their landing simulated a small man rolling onto the cobbles with enough accuracy to fool the sentries. Drawing back into the darkness of the baker's shop, Taziar waited.

Shortly, a cry broke the night. "Shadow Climber just entered the northwest quad. Jeweler."

Taziar smiled. The main market thoroughfare onto which the front gates opened ran north and south while Cullinsberg's second largest street, Panogya, ran east and west, dividing the city into four sections. The sentry's misidentification revealed that they believed the Climber had crossed the main thoroughfare.

Cautiously, Taziar avoided the tables, ledges, and tray racks that, before sunup, would hold cooling cakes, pies, and breads. Not wanting to risk waking the baker and his family on the second floor, Taziar padded down both flights of steps to the shop level. Ignoring the front exit onto the main street, he pushed open the heavier, unlocked panel leading into the oven building. Finding the hearth cold, he ducked into the chimney, braced his back and feet against the stone, and edged upward.

Dirt coated Taziar's limbs and face. Soot wedged beneath his fingernails and blackened the tips. He choked on ash, hating the taste, suppressing a cough with effort. At length, he came to the roof. Peering out, he saw no evidence of guards. Relieved, Taziar pulled himself to the tiles. *Ought to charge the baker for the chimney sweeping.* Taziar could not raise a grin for his feeble joke. *Maybe that'll pay him back for some of the bread I stole as a child.* Lowering himself over the ledge, he climbed back into Panogya Street.

In the wake of the guards' chase, the city seemed eerily quiet. Taziar slunk with a graceful speed that brought him swiftly to the eastern side of the outer wall. He waited until the soft slap of footsteps on the upper walk wafted clearly to him. Then, as the sound receded, he shinnied up the stone, scuttled across the top, and lowered himself to the fire-cleared plain that surrounded the city of Cullinsberg. *Done.* Excitement ebbed, replaced by the cold sweat with which Taziar had become all too familiar. The euphoria inspired by action had disappeared, yet the feeling of satisfaction that accompanied outwitting the baron's guardsmen felt twice as sweet for the period of idleness that had preceded it. *It's not over yet. I still have to find out what Bolverkr's doing. And sneak back in.*

Taziar knew the latter would prove simple enough. Once the guards realized he had outwitted them, they would believe he had escaped the city. There was no reason to expect him to return, so the patrols would likely become lax. The last time the baron had sent soldiers beyond the city limits in pursuit of Taziar, he had lost a strong faction of his army, a captain, and a prime minister in a fiasco that nearly reignited the Barbarian Wars. Taziar doubted the baron would risk his men that way again.

Taziar darted across the open stretch of ground to the woodlands that enclosed most of northern Europe. Born and raised a city boy, Taziar had not cared much for forests with their lack of roads, sudden dead ends, and crisp leaves and sticks that revealed his location with every step. But during his several months' stay among Moonbear's barbarian tribe in Sweden, Taziar had learned to anticipate and circle deadfalls and areas of thickest brush. They had taught him to sweep through copses and branches and over the natural carpeting with almost as little noise as on cobbled roadways or tiled rooftops.

Hidden among the trees, Taziar turned southward. Silme had told him that Bolverkr's fortress perched on a hill in the ruins of the town of Wilsberg. The Shadow Climber moved quickly, needing to return to Cullinsberg before daylight. Without the "thieves' moon" to hide him, his black climbing outfit would look conspicuous amid the brighter colors worn by Cullinsberg's townsfolk.

Once encased in forest, Taziar fell into a pattern of cautious movement. No matter how seriously injured Bolverkr was, he still wielded enough Chaos-energy to keep his defenses raised against enemies. Taziar recalled the teachings of a Dragonrank sorcerer who had mistaken him for a low level mage the day Taziar sneaked into the Dragonrank school, defying its "impenetrable" defenses: "The wards become visible if you don't look directly at them." Taziar had gotten his share of practice at finding wards that day, including the one he had accidentally triggered to an explosion that seared his arm and chest, sapping him of consciousness. Now, in the forests south of Cullinsberg, Taziar winced at the memory, focusing on Astryd's explanation: "Magic, by its nature, functions best against creations and users of magic. The ward which harmed you might have killed a low rank Dragonmage. And most of our spells work only when used for or against sorcerers."

I'm the best one to spy on Bolverkr's fortifications. Any defenses Bolverkr created will prove far more dangerous to Silme and Astryd, and possibly to Allerum, too, since elves might be considered creations of magic. Taziar considered this new thought, wondering why he was rationalizing a scouting mission that needed no justification. *Because I know my friends will be furious when they find out I left without telling them.* He continued through the woodlands. *And they'll be right. I'd be mad if one of them went off alone, too.* Taziar shook the black strands from his eyes. *This is stupid. Of course I'd be mad at them. I'm the only one who knows Cullinsberg, and scouting is what I do.*

Still, Taziar could not banish guilt. In his days as the Shadow Climber, his feats had put no one but himself in danger. Since he had climbed the Bifrost Bridge on a dare and accidentally loosed the Fenrir Wolf on a world unequipped to handle it, his love for impossible tasks had placed others in jeopardy as well. *Mostly Allerum, Astryd, and Silme, the people I care about.* He considered how Bolverkr had drawn him and his companions to Cullinsberg by threatening to destroy Shylar, the underground, the street orphans and beggars, the men and women Taziar had helped establish and learned to love. *Maybe it's time to stop accepting every impossible task for the challenge and start considering consequences. I am, after all, a "team player" now.*

Taziar's first warning that something might be amiss came in the form of three dead rabbits and a sparrow. He stopped, head cocked, gaze perpendicular to the line created by the corpses. His off-center glance gave him a perfect view of magics twisted into shimmering, parallel bands that arched into the woods as far as he could see. The lowest braid hovered at ankle level. Nine higher ones rose in increments, the upper one at twice Taziar's meager height. They were spaced widely enough that Taziar considered trying to slip between them. He traced the lines with his vision, suspecting each made a perfect ring. A walk around the perimeter confirmed his guess.

Whether or not I can slip through here, I know Silme and Allerum don't have a chance. Silme was tall for a woman and, though still slim this early in her pregnancy, carried a third again Taziar's weight. Larson stood a half head taller than his wife, and Astryd, though a bit smaller than Taziar, had little experience wriggling through tight spaces. No matter how lightly, touching the wards meant triggering them, and Bolverkr wielded more than enough power to make his sorceries fatal.

Choosing a sturdy oak with branches that overhung Bolverkr's defense, Taziar climbed. Seated in the V formed by trunk and branch, he examined the magics again. His aerial view allowed him to see something missed on first inspection, a second row of wards circling within the first. He nodded at the genius of Bolverkr's arrangement. Had Taziar used any less caution, he might have slipped through or over the outer wards and skidded or fallen into the inner ones. Cued, Taziar scanned for a third ring of magics. Seeing none, he edged out onto the branch. Passing over and beyond the wards, he sprang to the ground, thoughts on his companions. He imagined they could all jump from the tree without injury, though he made a mental note to bring rope just in case.

Now on Bolverkr's territory, Taziar discovered a random array of protective wards. He moved slowly, twisting his head in all directions before each step, zigzagging his way toward the center of the circle where he expected to find Bolverkr's citadel. Though abundant, the spells gave Taziar little difficulty. Wiry and agile, he slipped between magics that Bolverkr needed to place to accommodate his own larger frame and bolder gait. Certainly, no one ignorant of the ways of viewing magic could take more than a few steps without triggering one of the wards. But, as soon as Larson was taught the trick of indirect sighting, Taziar believed all of his companions would have the necessary training and dexterity to maneuver past Bolverkr's obstacle course. *So long as we don't have to do it too fast.*

When Taziar judged he had crossed half the radius of Bolverkr's circle, he paused to climb a tree. The "thieves' moon" drew a glittering line along Bolverkr's catwalk. Leering gargoyles lined the outer wall of the keep, meticulously cleaned though the castle they protected lay in a state of disrepair. Jagged breaks gashed three corners, and crumbled piles of stone, once towers, lay at the base. The fourth tower pointed arrow-straight at the sky, though rubble on the ground below it revealed that it had once been destroyed as well. The design confused Taziar. It seemed odd that Bolverkr had taken the time to completely renovate one full tower while the others gaped open, admitting rain. Glancing at shattered stonework before the outer wall to the keep, Taziar realized Bolverkr had also chosen to repair the decorative masonry and statuettes before working on the major structures of the castle.

As Taziar stared, a figure emerged onto the wall. Moonlight revealed fine, white hair that had once been blond and a stale gray tunic and breeks covered by a darkly-colored cloak. Tall and slender to the point of frailness, the man paced the stones with a brash, solid tread that belied the apparent fragility of his frame.

Bolverkr? Taziar watched, intrigued, certain this could be no one else.

Yet, the way the man on the wall moved seemed somehow alien. On the streets, Taziar had obtained much of his food money through con games, pickpocketing, and entertaining the masses. His survival had depended upon his ability to read wealth, motivation, and intention through word and action. Bolverkr's movements, though fluid, fit

no human pattern Taziar could define. It inspired the same
deep discomfort that he felt in the presence of the most
unstable lunatics, from the type who might stand in a state
of statuelike quiet and stillness one moment then lash out
in violent frenzy the next, to those who slaughtered in the
name of imaginary voices, or the kind who muttered half-
interpretable nonsense while violating every social convention.

Suddenly, Bolverkr froze. He whirled to face a gargoyle
that rose to the height of his knee and shouted a garbled
word, unrecognizable to Taziar.

The gargoyle jumped, torn from its granite foundation,
then shattered in a fountain of chips. Stone fragments
rained into the courtyard.

Bolverkr resumed pacing as if nothing had happened.

Taziar stiffened, wrung through with chills. The sorcerer's
casual power shocked him, and he could not help imagining
himself in the gargoyle's place.

"Who am I?" Pain tainted Bolverkr's shout, but it still
rang with power.

Taziar was so caught up in the display that Bolverkr's
voice startled him. He stiffened, slipping sideways on the
limb. An abrupt grab spared him a fall, and he clutched
the branch tightly enough to gouge bark into his palms.
Balance regained, he watched in awe as Bolverkr stilled,
head tipped to catch the echoes, as though he expected
them to give him an answer.

The Dragonrank mage lowered his head. His hands
twitched, as if he carried on a conversation with himself,
but Taziar's perch was too far away for him to see if the
sorcerer's lips were moving.

Taziar gauged the distance between himself and the sorcerer, wondering if he could kill Bolverkr with a well-
placed arrow. *Assuming I had a bow. Or knew how to use
it.* Taziar had become a mediocre swordsman only because
teaching Taz swordplay had seemed so important to his
father. Pleased enough to get his tiny son practicing any
weapon at all, the elder Medakan had never pressed him
to learn to shoot, and the thought of doing so on his own
had never occurred to Taziar. *Bad enough killing a man
who can defend himself. What need do I have to learn long-
distance slaughter?* Taziar shivered at the thought. Grief-

mad after her husband's hanging, Taziar's mother had forced her only son to assist in her suicide. The experience had so crippled Taziar's conscience that he had found himself unable to take a life, even to save his own. Circumstances had forced him to overcome this limitation enough to kill enemies in defense of innocents or friends, but only at times of grave necessity.

Bolverkr raised his face heavenward. The wind whipped his locks to an ivory tangle. "Who . . . am . . . I?"

Each syllable shocked dread through Taziar. There was something eerily inhuman about the call, though the words emerged plainly enough in the language of Cullinsberg's barony and colored by a clipped Wilsberg accent. The urge to leave as quickly as possible seized Taziar. Studying the ground for glints of magic, he descended with caution, creeping silently back toward the northern forest.

Bolverkr's laughter shuddered between the trunks.

CHAPTER 2
Chaos Dreams

Deep into that darkness peering, long I stood
  there wondering, fearing,
Doubting, dreaming dreams no mortal ever dared
  to dream before.
                    —Edgar Allen Poe *The Raven*

The dream assailed Silme in the deepest part of her sleeping cycle; yet it seemed distant, the trickling backwash of another's nightmare borne on a thread of shared Chaos. Sated with health and life power, she paced the walled defenses of a fortress. But the life aura she had always known as a friend, an integral part of herself, had became a stranger, an enemy crushing, tearing, and stripping her of identity. A scream cycled through her mind: "Who am I?" No answer came but echoes. Still, the reverberation of her familiar voice soothed, bringing snatches of memory. She knew a humble childhood as the third son of a farmer, the dusty, green perfume of new-mown hay, the milk-breath of spotted cows, and the tickle of piled straw while roughhousing in the barn before the cows trooped inside. A brother's laughter rang in her ears.

As each remembrance blossomed, Chaos rose to meet it, battering it to pale outline. Anguish hammered Silme, and she twisted in her sleep, unable to comprehend life energy revolting against its master nor why she would fight the chaos defining her own life. Again, the cry cut above the struggle: "Who am I?" New memories whisked by, veiled in white, now of Dragonrank training beneath the original master, Geirmagnus. She remembered, too, a wife named Magan and a fetus destroyed in the Chaos-storm. She felt the cold bite of winds carrying thatch, stone, and corpses, its swish as cruel and mocking as laughter.

A fetus. Silme anchored her reason on her own growing

baby. Always before, she had received only a hint of its presence; its tiny life aura became blended and lost in the vastness of her own chaos. Now, she felt a strong sense of its aliveness within her. It seemed to have tripled in power overnight. Its energy wove intimately into her own: vital, hovering, wailing. Conscious of the changes within her, Silme slid toward waking far enough to realize that the remembrances of farm and storm and training were never her own. Now removed from the struggle between lord and Chaos, she explored both sides with a clarity of thought that could only come with impartiality.

Still ensconced in sleep, Silme saw only a man battling his own life aura, a war he could never win. Without knowledge of the vision's source, she somehow understand that if it bested him, he would lose whatever identity he still clung to, the snatches of memory Silme had just shared in dream. But to destroy his own life aura, the stuff of life itself, could bring only death.

Silme had dedicated her life to helping the innocent. Sleep stole logic and caution in the same manner as drink. The oddity of their link obscured any recognition of the man, and Silme's dream-state did not leave room for suspicion or questioning. Concerned for this stranger, Silme did not know him as Bolverkr, a sorcerer more than two centuries old, the man who had ordered her friends and husband killed and nearly succeeded at both. She did not identify the Dragonrank mage who had declared vengeance against Larson and promised to share reams of Chaos with Silme through a contact she had created in ignorance. She saw only a creature in agony, trapped and aching from a battle with a Chaos it did not yet recognize as self. And she tended him like a mother with an injured child.

Silme reached out to help, certain she would meet a physical or mental barrier. But her words slipped effortlessly through the contact. Gently, she reassured him that the Chaos was a part of himself, that he should welcome it without fighting and let it serve him as a life aura must. She felt him soften at her words. The fiery rage within him died, and the Chaos, too, gave up its struggles, settling within him, gradually poisoning Bolverkr's last vestiges of self with its presence. Complacency seeped through the contact, drawing Silme deeper into her slumber. At first, she followed it, every muscle falling into perfect laxity, a comfort beyond any she had ever known. Then, a more primitive portion of her mind kicked in, warning of imminent danger. Suddenly fully awake, Silme sprang to her feet, bashing her head on the shelves above the headboard.

An avalanche of books and fruit thundered to the floor. A bowl shattered, and shards of pottery skittered across the wood.

Startled from his sickbed, Al Larson dove beneath the frame in a tangle of blankets. "Incoming!" he screamed.

Then the room fell silent.

Silme reoriented quickly. She sat on a straw-ticked mattress mounted on a metal frame. A half dozen books lay scattered at her feet amid bruised fruit that had once sat in a bowl whose pieces decorated the floorboards in colored triangles. Across the room and nearer the door, Astryd slept despite the noise, alone in the bed she normally shared with Taziar. Propped against the footboard leaned the familiar dragonstaff that identified Astryd as garnet-rank, a smoothly-sanded pole tipped with a faceted, red stone clamped between four black-nailed, wooden claws. Between her and Silme, the room's single window stood ajar. Autumn breezes stirred the gauzy blue curtains. Beneath it, a dresser held their belongings.

Larson's angular, elf face peered from beneath his bed. His pale eyes swept the room, and he seemed to take time to get his bearing.

"I'm sorry," Silme said, her voice loud in the silence.

Astryd continued to sleep.

Larson hauled himself from beneath the bed. "What happened?"

"Bad dream." It sounded like understatement to Silme, so she qualified. "*Very* bad dream."

Larson frowned, apparently thinking about the nightmares that had beset him since Freyr had dragged him to a Norway centuries before his birth and into the guise of an elf. It had turned out his were not dreams at all but sorcerers and gods entering his thoughts through the openings left by his lack of mind barriers. But they both knew no one could penetrate Silme's mental barriers.

Or could they? Doubt trickled through Silme's thoughts. *I opened my mind barriers to Bolverkr's Chaos before.*

Could he have manipulated that weakness? Silme grimaced. She had walled off that contact with defenses Chaos should not have been able to breach. Yet, it seemed to have done so with an ease that could only come of an invitation. *As if some part of me accepted Chaos willingly.*

The idea frightened Silme, suggesting that, deep down, she supported Chaos' evil or, worse, coveted the power it promised. Again, she clutched the baby's aura to her absently, felt the fullness of life energy that had seemed trivial days ago. And the answer accompanied that touch. *The baby is taking the Chaos-energy offered by Bolverkr.* Fear shuddered through Silme at the realization. She knew the child was not capable of thought, that it was simply being a normal fetus, taking whatever nourishment it could, oblivious to the source. *It needs to grow. Yet, the volume of Chaos-energy to which it's become exposed is immeasurable.* The possible consequences seemed so staggering, Silme dared not consider them yet. She buried her face in her hands.

Apparently attributing Silme's discomfort to her dream, Larson limped to her side and caught her into an embrace. "What happened? Tell me about this nightmare."

Silme wrapped her arms around Larson, feeling him wince as the pressure ignited healing bruises and scars. "It's nothing to worry about." She tried to soothe, but her uncertainty sabotaged the effort. "It's not the dream itself. There's something we need to discuss as a group. Why don't I wake up Astryd and . . ." She trailed off as the realization of what she had seen earlier finally seeped into her consciousness.

Larson's gaze went naturally to his friends' bed where Astryd sprawled alone, a petite, curly-haired blonde nearly lost in a twist of blankets.

"Shadow's gone." Silme stated the obvious needlessly. Larson's attention had already shifted to the open window.

"That stupid, little . . ."

Taziar's head and shoulders appeared over the ledge. ". . . son-of-a-bitch," he finished in English, simulating Larson's Bronx accent. He scurried inside, closing the window behind him.

Larson had unconsciously grasped the finely-crafted Jap-

anese longsword that had belonged to Kensei Gaelinar. He
glared. "That's not what I was going to say."

Taziar made a vague gesture to indicate Larson should
speak freely.

"I was going to say 'obnoxious, fucking *asshole* son-of-
a-bitch.' ''

Taziar bowed his head. "I stand corrected," he said with
mock seriousness.

"And," Larson pulled free of Silme, slipping easily into
the facetious manner of his companion. "I speak your language fluently. How come the only things you've bothered
to learn in mine are swear words?"

It was an unfair question. Some effect of Freyr's transporting magic had given Larson the ability to speak the
period languages naturally, while Taziar could only glean
English phrases from the rare times Larson used them, usually in annoyance or anger. Still, the Shadow Climber found
an answer. "Swear words, are they? I was starting to wonder why the only things with names in your language were
excrement, sex, and animal relatives."

Larson chuckled.

"Actually, though, I have learned a few other words."
Taziar sat on the edge of the bed, turning his head to watch
Astryd roll to a sitting position, the blankets clutched to
her chest.

Silme frowned, recognizing Taziar's attempt to turn the
conversation away from his recent absence.

" 'Jerk' and 'creep' are mild insults."

"Terms of endearment," Larson interrupted with a smile.

"Right." Taziar placed a hand on Astryd's covered knee.
" 'Mac' is a casual thing you call a stranger, 'sir' a more
formal one." Taziar rolled his eyes in consideration.
"There's places: 'New York,' 'America,' 'Vietnam.' Then,
I know 'excuse me' and 'team player.' 'Buddy' means a
trusted friend who holds your life in his hands. 'Gun' de-
scribes an object I've seen once and never want to come
up against again. A 'Buick' is an object large things are
compared to in size." He paused. "Oh, and I've heard 'follow that car.' ''

"Great." Larson winked at Silme, apparently oblivious
to her displeasure, and stretched his legs in front of him.

"You're all set if you ever want to take a transcontinental cab ride in an American-made car."

"Enough!" Silme said, bothered by the men's playful banter. "Stop it, both of you!"

All eyes flicked suddenly to Silme, the expression on every face one of befuddled surprise. Never before had the sorceress become angered by a harmless exchange of gibes.

Silme addressed Larson directly. "I understand that you sometimes use humor to release tension, but this isn't the time."

Larson stared, looking hurt. "I was only . . ."

Silme cut him off, fixing her hard, gray eyes on Taziar. "Where were you, Shadow?"

Taziar shifted uncomfortably. His lips framed a feeble smile. "Would you believe enjoying the night air?" He used a small voice that made it clear he was stalling.

Silme's glower deepened, etching wrinkles into her artistically-perfect features. She realized she was acting harsh beyond her nature, perhaps due to the concerns her dream had raised, yet the brusqueness seemed justified. "I'm not kidding, Shadow. Where were you?"

Taziar stared at his feet. "I couldn't sleep. I went scouting."

"You went to Bolverkr's fortress." Silme knew Taziar well enough to guess. "Didn't you?"

Astryd's and Larson's attention whipped to the Shadow Climber.

Taziar nodded grimly. "I found out some information that . . ."

Silme did not allow him to change the subject. "This is all a big game to you, isn't it?"

Taziar went silent. The comma of black hair sagged into his eyes, giving him the look of an unruly child.

"This isn't some interesting challenge someone handed you for fun. Bolverkr commands the largest volume of Chaos-force ever assembled. He's the most powerful creature in existence. Ever. And he wants us dead."

"I'm sorry." Taziar sounded sincere. "I wasn't trying to belittle Bolverkr's power. I was trying to assess it. Know the enemy. It's just good strategy."

Taziar's defensive reply fueled Silme's rage. "You don't even understand what you did wrong! How could you go off alone in the night without telling anyone? If we can stand against Bolverkr, and I'm not at all certain we can, it's going to take all of us working together and at our best. Did it occur to you that you might disturb Bolverkr? Alone, you don't have a chance against him. He could have killed you without bothering to stand. Then, enraged by your interference, he might have come after us. He'd have found us asleep because we had no idea one of our companions had run off recklessly, *stupidly,* into a lion's den."

Larson stroked Silme's long golden locks, trying to appease her. Usually, he respected Silme as the voice of reason, but apparently even he believed she had gone too far. "Shadow made a mistake. He's apologized. No harm done. I think that dream's got you upset. Maybe you should talk about it."

Silme knocked away Larson's caress with the back of her hand. "Don't patronize me, Allerum. I've been fighting Chaos and sorcerers since long before you heard of either." Her fists clenched, her memory gliding back over more than a decade spent protecting innocents from the cruelties of her half-brother, Bramin. Then she had required the aid and protection of the world's greatest swordsman, Kensei Gaelinar. She missed the old ronin's loyalty, his single-minded, predictable code of honor, and the seriousness with which he viewed the world and his role in it. Though crippling at times, Larson's guileless morality had attracted Silme in the same way Taziar's impetuous good intentions had charmed Astryd; but, faced with the most powerful enemy in her life, Silme would have traded man and elf for the Kensei's humorless efficiency. "This isn't the first time Shadow's run off alone without thinking, but it's damned well going to be the last. I'm not going to have my baby, husband, and apprentice endangered by . . ."

Several rapid taps at the door interrupted Silme's tirade.

Larson sighed in relief, rolling his eyes to the ceiling as if to thank some unnamed god.

"Come in," Taziar said, his voice a soft parody of his normal carefree tone and harsh Cullinsberg accent.

Unaccustomed to berating friends, Silme felt a pang of remorse.

The door swung ajar on silent hinges, and Asril the Procurer stood framed in the doorway, backlit by a candle in the hallway. A mop of mouse brown hair crowned knife-scarred cheeks, and his strange, violet gaze swept the room, taking in every sight from long habit. The son of a free-lance prostitute, Asril had won his education and his wounds on the wildest streets of Cullinsberg. Of the seven leaders Taziar had broken out of prison, Asril was the only one who had weathered the guards' tortures well enough to help Larson and Taziar battle Bolverkr's henchman, Harriman, and his berserker bodyguards. "Ah, what a glorious morning and a joy to wake up to friends quibbling. Pressure getting too intense? I don't suppose this means you'll let me help against Bolverkr now?" He bowed with feigned deference. "Lords, ladies, my sword arm is at your service." He winked at Taziar. "I owe you the favor, partner. Won't you let me repay it?"

Silme knew Taziar's caution with his friends' lives would force him to refuse the offer, so it surprised her when he looked to her for guidance before answering. She tightened her lips to a blanched line, shaking her head vigorously. *Our survival is tenuous enough. No need to involve anyone else in our affairs.*

Apparently, Silme had given the response Taziar wanted because his features mellowed with relief. "Shylar and the underground need you here. Since when have I needed help to do anything?" Taziar winced. He had obviously meant the words to assuage Asril, then realized they might provoke Silme as well.

Asril the Procurer's interruption had given Silme time to think, and guilt assailed her. *I shouldn't have scolded Shadow so hard. Stupid as his decision seemed to me, he meant well.* Naturally calm and gentle by nature, as well as competent in her judgments, Silme rarely found herself in a position calling for apology. Now she tried to express her regret to Taziar, but the words seemed to die on her tongue. Emotion lumped within her, nameless irritation, smothered excitement, sorrow, and fear, their sources too vague for her to trace. She knew other feelings as well, a protectiveness toward her forming child and the friends she would give her own life to spare, and a distant, veiled realization that some of the sentiments she felt were not consistent with the self she knew.

Oblivious to Silme's turmoil, Asril shrugged. "If you

change your mind, my offer of help stands." He closed long lashes over his violet eyes, then opened them slowly, his full attention on Taziar. "So, how did the enemy seem last night?"

Asril's voice jarred Silme from the brink of an important revelation. The recognition of the alienness of her current mind-set slipped beyond her grasp, and she did not notice the insidious, almost nonexistent trickle of Chaos seeping through the contact with Bolverkr.

In response to Asril's question, Taziar stiffened. He rolled his gaze toward Silme, awaiting reprimand. When none came, he replied softly. "How would I know that?" He made a brisk gesture to silence Asril.

The violet-eyed thief ignored Taziar's apparent discomfort. "When I saw you trying to get over the walls, I just assumed you went to check on Bolverkr."

Taziar spoke hesitantly, as if trying to hide his surprise. "You . . . saw . . . me?"

Larson frowned, Astryd stared at Taziar, and Silme glowered at the realization that the Climber had not only run off alone but had done so sloppily enough to get noticed by friends and potentially by enemies as well.

Asril closed the door and draped his frame casually against it. "Didn't actually see you, but it's hard to miss a hundred clomping guardsmen. And what purpose would they have on the rooftops besides chasing the Shadow Climber?"

Taziar cringed.

Asril grinned, revealing straight rows of yellowed teeth. "I'd have thought the Climber more careful, though that was before I knew he was reckless Taz."

Taziar made an abrupt quieting gesture, far less subtle than the first.

Silme bit her lip, reminding herself that the reprimands had already been spoken. Compared to the risk of facing Bolverkr alone, Taziar's confrontation with Cullinsberg's town guardsmen seemed trivial.

Asril laughed. Pushing off the door with a foot, he approached Taziar, his voice softer but still discernible to Silme. "Clever ruse, whatever it was you did on the baker's roof. I'm relieved to realize you didn't know you put the whole pack of wolves on my tail."

Taziar looked stricken. "I had no idea. I'm sorry."

Asril shrugged off the apology. "It worked out fine. Gave you time to get away. The guards were so busy worrying about you, they didn't even recognize me. Snarled a few words about being out after curfew, then went back after you." He chuckled. "By then, you were long gone, of course."

"Of course," Larson repeated thoughtfully.

Having failed to silence his friend, Taziar tried changing the subject. "I did discover something important about Bolverkr, though. I think he's gone completely insane."

Larson lay back on the mattress, supported by his elbows with his body curled around Silme's stiffly-seated figure. "What do you mean? Chasing down strangers to torture and kill them never seemed all that sane to me to begin with."

Taziar drew his knees to his chest. "He's not just irrationally vengeful anymore. I found him pacing his wall, wasting his magic on statues and rocks, jabbering about not knowing who he is."

The similarity to her dream struck Silme. No longer able to deny the reality of her connection with Bolverkr, she fidgeted.

No one seemed to notice Silme's new uneasiness. Taziar continued. "Mind you, I don't have any experience with Chaos-madness. I don't know how long it'll last." Taziar squirmed, obviously concerned about the suggestion he was about to make. "So far, we've let Bolverkr do all the attacking while we handled his minions and tried to get a feel for his power. Based on the information Silme and I gathered, I think it's time we took the initiative. We need to strike while he's alone and too crazed to think clearly."

Larson nodded soberly. "Good battle strategy. I think I'm feeling up to . . ."

Realizing she might have accidentally helped stabilize Bolverkr in her sleep, Silme blurted, "We'll need to move as quickly as possible."

The impulsive interruption seemed so unlike Silme that her companions went silent and stared in surprise.

Feeling obligated to clarify, the sorceress continued. "Chaos or power generally comes to people in tiny doses based on the balance of the world and life events. For

them, the corruption of personality comes gradually. Bolverkr was forced to contain, in seconds, enough Chaos to
help offset Loki's destruction and the resurrection of a
god." Absorbed in her narration, Silme sat ramrod straight,
her hands clenched in her lap. Though Bolverkr had proved
himself a bitter and dangerous enemy, she could not help
feeling a twinge of sorrow for him. The Bolverkr whose
memories she had shared was a sweet-tempered and gentle
victim of circumstance. "Forced to cope with a sudden,
drastic change in character, Bolverkr's fighting the Chaos,
trying to find the self he used to be."

Larson traced a wrinkle in Silme's gown with his finger.
"You mean he might be able to shake this Chaos? Deep
down, the dirty scum who ordered Shadow's friends killed,
me tortured, the baby destroyed, and you raped is really a
nice guy? Forgive me while I laugh hysterically. I find that
a bit hard to swallow."

Larson's effortless interplay between English slang and
the barony's tongue made his words difficult to understand,
but Silme managed to follow his main point. "Essentially."

More attentive to Larson's native language, Taziar deciphered and replied more directly. "Are you suggesting
Bolverkr might overcome this Chaos? We might not have
to kill him?"

"No. I don't meant that at all." Silme's back muscles
began to cramp in protest of Silme's sitting "at attention"
for far too long. She sagged, absently massaging her lower
spine with a fist. "The Chaos is far too great and strong
for Bolverkr to fight. His only choice is to give in to it, to
incorporate it into himself as part of his life energy. Any
other decision would be folly."

Taziar and Astryd both raised their brows, though neither spoke aloud.

Silme answered the unspoken question. "Because even
Bolverkr isn't powerful enough to win a battle against renegade Chaos of that magnitude. Remember, embodied
Chaos, the chaos inside of a person, is his life force; it dies
when its master is killed. But if a host to renegade Chaos
is destroyed, that Chaos would be free to hunt for another
host. Along the way, it would destroy anything in its path:
people, animals, forests, entire cities." Silme repositioned
herself, crossing her legs on the pallet. "Since this particular

massing of Chaos chose to go to Bolverkr first, it's probable he was the most likely to survive its linking. If Bolverkr was killed before he merged with his new Chaos, it would try to find another lord. Most probably, no one else could survive the merger. It would kill its next host, and each subsequent attempt would bring it against weaker and weaker hosts. It wouldn't quit until every sentient creature in the world was killed." Silme shivered at the impact of her own words.

Taziar twisted his fine features in thought, brushing the hair from his forehead. "So we have to time this carefully. The only way to destroy this Chaos is to wait for Bolverkr to completely assimilate it, taking it as his life force. Then we kill him." Taziar shook his head, obviously displeased with the concept.

Silme knew Taziar well enough to understand that he cared little for killing, especially pawns. The method did not appeal to her either, but she could see beyond murder to the practical necessity. Bolverkr was too dangerous to everyone to live. "The timing doesn't matter any more. If Bolverkr's still alive when we reach his keep, he'll have certainly surrendered to Chaos. He's at too critical a juncture not to have made the decision last night. We should strike as soon as possible, before he gets a firm grasp on what he can do with his new-found power."

Larson rubbed at the sore spot on Silme's back. "You're sure?"

"Of course I'm sure," she said, irritability rising from a source she did not bother to name. She wanted to detail her dream, to explain that she knew Bolverkr's struggle had reached its climax because she had shared it with him, knew he had surrendered to Chaos because she had pressed him to the concession. But a part of her understood the wrongness of admitting to such a thing. It led her to believe detailing her dream would accomplish nothing except to undermine her companions' morale, and, though her silence seemed as wrong as Taziar's impetuous spying, she clung to it. "Shadow described the situation accurately. Are you well enough to fight today?"

"I'm not at my best," Larson admitted honestly. "But if it's urgent, what choice do I have?" His hand fell away from Silme and to the brocaded hilt of Gaelinar's katana. He smiled. "I'll be fine."

Silme knew Larson gained courage from touching his teacher's katana. In the way of the samurai, the Kensei had always considered his swords an extension of his spirit. As such, he had treated them with more respect than any person, letting his own wounds gape and bleed until he had cleaned, sheathed, and accorded the blades their proper respect. Composed of joined layers of hard and soft steel folded hundreds of times, the katana could cut through armor as if it did not exist or cleanly decapitate a man with a single stroke.

Astryd raised a practical issue in her usual soft-spoken, deferential manner. "I'm years and multiple ranks below you in training, Silme, so you know things I don't. But doesn't the death of a powerful creature of Chaos have to be balanced by one of Law?"

Taziar seized on Astryd's question. "Like Fenrir?"

The reference confused Silme. "Fenrir? The Great Wolf?"

"Right." Taziar went on excitedly, his gaze probing Larson. "Remember back before we fought the Chaos dragon, when Fenrir was our most dangerous enemy. He said we couldn't possibly kill him because it would upset the balance of the world."

Larson remembered. "We never did kill him, either. We captured him." He stroked his hairless, elven chin, following the conversation to its natural, if unnerving, conclusion. "Are you saying it might be literally impossible to kill Bolverkr?"

Astryd shrugged, and Larson touched Silme's thigh to turn the question back to the more experienced, sapphire-rank sorceress.

"I don't know. Nothing like this has ever happened before, as far as I'm aware." Silme inclined her head toward Taziar. "Since I met Shadow, impossible doesn't have a lot of meaning for me anymore. If someone had asked a year ago, I would have said destroying Loki was impossible. Certainly, killing Bolverkr will be the most difficult challenge any of us has ever faced. Impossible? Maybe. I don't know."

Taziar still clung to the chance of a peaceful solution.

"Silme, is there any way to siphon off Chaos from Bolverkr and distribute it around in small, harmless parcels?"

Silme considered. Taziar's idea had not occurred to her before. "By reopening the connection Bolverkr allowed me to create between us, theoretically, yes. I could take Chaos from him. In practice, I don't see how it could work. First, Bolverkr might oppose me. Then we'd have to fight under less than ideal circumstances, on his terms. Second, there's a near certain possibility that I might misjudge and become corrupted myself. Third, in order to spread the Chaos thin enough not to seriously poison each new host, I'd need hundreds or, more likely, thousands of willing volunteers. Each one would need to fight down his mind barriers for me to make the transfer."

Larson finished sarcastically. "By the time you finished, Bolverkr would have died of old age."

Silme shrugged. The only survivor of the original Dragonrank sorcerers, Bolverkr had had access to the earlier, more powerful spells, before the mages had learned the danger of summoning renegade Chaos. Already two hundred and seventeen years old, Bolverkr still seemed spry and agile to Silme, and she had no way to judge his potential life span. Still, Larson's point regarding time seemed valid. "Bolverkr's certain to confront us long before I could muster the necessary volunteers, assuming I could even find people inclined to let me infuse them with Chaos. Having dedicated my life to protecting innocents from Chaos, I don't feel comfortable with the idea, either."

Asril the Procurer rested a sandaled foot on the edge of Astryd's bed, near the garnet-tipped dragonstaff. "So it's settled. You have to kill Bolverkr, and the sooner the better."

"One other thing." Larson glanced at Astryd and Taziar for support, raising a topic they had apparently already discussed in Silme's absence. "You're not coming with us." He caressed Silme's side as he spoke.

Silme twisted toward Larson in disbelief. "You'd better be talking to Asril."

"I'm talking," Larson said firmly, "to you."

Outrage welled within Silme, quickly snuffed by knowledge. *It's not me they're overprotecting, it's the baby.* Instinctively, she clutched the tiny aura to her, felt the edges of its life energy blur into her own. She could not separate the two. Any spell she threw would sap its life force as well as hers, and, once emptied of chaos, the child would die. Thoughts of the coming battle and the risks to the baby had haunted Silme throughout Larson's recovery. When the war against Bolverkr had seemed a distant threat, the decision had come easily. Now, the lives of her friends and husband had to take precedence over that of an unborn child. "That's nonsense, Allerum. You won't have a chance against Bolverkr without a Dragonrank magc." As she spoke, memories tortured Silme. She recalled the hands of Bolverkr's minion tearing at her clothes and person while she wrestled with the realization that Larson, Taziar, and Astryd battled dozens of prison guards, though a few simple spells and a dead fetus could rescue them all from humiliation and death.

"We'll have Astryd." Taziar gave Larson his full support, unaware Silme's thoughts had wandered far beyond her protest. "With you or not, we're not going to be able to best Bolverkr with magic. He's too powerful. It's going to have to be by surprise and luck."

Astryd spoke next, as if to demonstrate that she had thought the subject through as well. "Of us all, you're the only one Bolverkr won't hunt down. We have nothing to lose by fighting him. If we don't, he'll kill us anyway. But you, he'll let live. And the baby." Astryd's loyalty to and excitement about the baby had been unwavering since its conception. Though a mediocre sorceress compared with Silme, she had taken over the magical needs of the group. When Bolverkr's sorcery had trapped Silme in an alternate dimension, escapable only by magic, Astryd had allowed Silme to tap her life aura, a rare process that had nearly resulted in Astryd's death. "By killing Loki, Allerum assured that our Norse gods would endure through eternity. The White Christ will never come, and Allerum's friends and family, his entire world, will never come about. This baby is the only proof that the nine worlds will ever have that Lord Allerum the Godslayer ever existed."

Silme closed her eyes, allowing Astryd's words to seep into her soul, dragging the burden of grief with it. Though not directly spoken, Astryd's words brought home the realization that the task her companions were going to undertake this day was nearly or completely impossible and almost certainly fatal. To die with them was folly. Yet she could not shake the fact that, even though far weaker than Bolverkr, she could add power to her friends' attack. The understanding that she had inadvertently stabilized Bolverkr in her dream, losing her friends the days or weeks they might otherwise have had to prepare, saturated the realization with guilt. "At least let me come along. I'll only use magic if the situation becomes desperate."

"No!" Larson sat up and pounded a fist onto the shelf hard enough to send the last few books tumbling to the floor. "The situation is desperate already. The last time you helped me fight a Dragonrank Master, you forced me to kill you. I won't do it again. I swear it, Silme. I'll let Bolverkr destroy me and everyone else in the world before I'll take your life again."

Silme remembered as vividly as if it had happened the previous day. Before Larson had fought Loki, he had had to face her half-brother, Bramin. In order to neutralize Bramin's magic, Silme had linked her life aura to his, and Larson's sword had killed them both. To restore Silme's life, Larson and Gaelinar had been forced to barter with the goddess Hel, an insane task that had made them enemies among the gods and had ultimately resulted in Bolverkr's tragedy and crazed hunt for vengeance. "But even without magic, I could distract . . ." she began.

Larson interrupted with a crisp wave of dismissal. "The only person you're going to distract is me. You and the baby would be just one more thing to occupy my mind when all I should be thinking about is killing Bolverkr. I don't want you there, and you're not going to be there. Case closed."

Anger boiled up inside Silme, but she bit it back. In her mind, the case was far from closed, but the time for arguing had ended. She saw no need to aggravate Larson just before what might well prove the final battle for them all.

Larson sprang to his feet. "Let's get this over with." He strode toward the door.

Taziar intercepted Larson, hooking his sleeve with a finger. "Not so fast, *buddy*." His harsh, German accent mangled the American slang. "Don't be in such a hurry to die. We can't fight Bolverkr unless we can make it to Bolverkr."

Larson studied Taziar blankly.

"The baron's guards think I escaped. They probably won't be quite so alert and numerous as before, but they do know you came to Cullinsberg with me. The baron's offered a generous enough bounty to make the guards willing to slaughter one another. They're not going to let you walk through the front gates without a thorough questioning." Taziar placed the emphasis on the last few words, obviously intending the expression as a euphemism for torture.

Asril the Procurer laughed. Rising, he stretched like a cat, then leapt lightly between Larson and the door. "You concentrate on Bolverkr and leave the baron's imbeciles to me. With the help of a few dozen thieves, con men, and street gangs, I'm sure I can divert Cullinsberg's red and black long enough for you to get over the south wall. Deal?"

Silme's gaze went naturally to Taziar. She saw the familiar sparkle in his blue eyes that accompanied the opportunity to work against impossible odds. Yet the dullness of his other features belied the excitement. Beneath it all, Taziar knew he no longer belonged in the city of his birth, the place he had called home for all but the last half year. And it pained him.

A deep silence ensued.

A moment later, Silme found herself enwrapped in Larson's arms. His fine white hair felt like silk against her cheeks, smelling pleasantly of soap. His elven frame appeared delicate, but there was nothing fragile about the arms that crushed her to him.

Tears filled Silme's eyes, and she knew with grim certainty that the only man she had ever loved enough to marry would almost certainly be lost to her forever.

CHAPTER 3
Chaos War

A still small voice spake unto me,
"Thou art so full of misery,
Were it not better not to be?"
—Alfred, Lord Tennyson
The Two Voices

The pine and hickory forest beyond the walls of Cullinsberg seemed to close in on Al Larson. He trailed Taziar in silence, trying to focus his thoughts on Bolverkr. But other concerns crowded in, unable to be banished. The tight, damp foliage dragged up memories of suffocating Vietnamese jungles, the reek of blood, gasoline, and excrement, death screams, the echoing shrieks of macaws, and the distant chop of helicopter blades. Through it all, he could not shake a feeling of enemies prowling silently behind him. Every few steps, he stopped abruptly, straining his hearing for the rustle of movement at his back. Occasionally, the rattle of brush or a twig snap answered his efforts, increasing his discomfort though he knew the noise had to come from Taziar, Astryd, or his own hyperactive imagination.

"Here. Stop." Taziar whispered suddenly. Though soft, his voice shattered a long and oppressive quiet.

Larson pushed past Astryd to Taziar's side.

Taziar halted Larson with an extended hand. "Remember what I told you about seeing magic?"

Larson nodded, staring ahead indirectly as the others had shown him. Now he could see the braid of Bolverkr's ward, as tangled and forbidding as a perimeter of concertina wire. "I see it." His voice sounded strained, even to his own ears. Only then did he realize he was gripping Gaelinar's sword's hilt so tightly that his hand had blanched and the brocade had left impressions in his palm. Bothered by his paranoia, he freed his hand and shook it to restore the circulation.

"There's another circle of magic just inside the first."
Taziar rested a palm against the trunk of a sturdy oak with
several jutting branches. "Careful now. Follow me." He
shinnied to a high limb with an ease and quickness Larson
could never hope to copy.

"Yeah, right," Larson mumbled. Turning, he motioned
Astryd over to the base. Cupping his hands, he created a
step for her. "Put your foot here. I'll give you a boost."

Astryd looked doubtfully from Larson's fingers to the
wards while Taziar watched with nervous expectation. Duti-
fully, Astryd passed her dragonstaff to Taziar, then placed
her booted foot on Larson's hands.

Short even compared with Taziar's five foot nothing, Astryd seemed nearly weightless to Larson. He hoisted her
without difficulty, waiting until she caught a solid grip on
a higher branch before lowering his hands. Though agile,
Astryd looked as awkward as a growing adolescent compared with Taziar's practiced grace. Sighing, Larson seized
the trunk and followed her, the rough bark scratching his
hands.

Taziar waited only until Larson had reached the branch
on which he and Astryd perched before tossing the garnet
dragonstaff safely over the wards. He leapt in a gentle arc
to the ground, then signaled for Astryd to jump.

Astryd hesitated while Larson waited, clinging to the
branch with one hand, the other braced against the trunk.
She lowered herself over the limb, dangling by her hands
to lessen the distance to the ground, then let go. She plummeted dangerously close to the wards. Larson held his
breath, scrambling to a position that might allow him to
make a desperate dive for her. Before he could leap, Taziar
stepped between Astryd and the barrier, catching a slender
arm and hauling her to safety.

Larson clambered to the branch, heaving a sigh of relief.
He waved Astryd and Taziar out of his way, not liking the
distance of the jump. In junior high school, a lesser fall had
broken Larson's arm. Edging to the end of the branch, he
sprang to the ground, hit, and rolled to his feet, unharmed.

"That's the hardest part," Taziar said. "The rest is just
dodging around wards. Take your time, don't get sloppy,
and you should do fine."

Larson clapped dirt from his palms. He took little solace

from Taziar's words. Accustomed to judging obstacles by
his own ability to surmount them, Taziar's idea of "sloppy"
rarely gibed with Larson's. A high school soccer player,
weight lifter, and college boxer, Larson had always considered himself fit, but Taziar's nimbleness made the American feel clumsy. Worse, thrown onto an unfamiliar body,
Larson had been forced to relearn coordination, a competence rapidly acquired and sorely tested by Gaelinar's
sword lessons as well as Bramin's and Loki's attacks.

Without further warning, Taziar headed off, soundlessly
weaving through the brush. Astryd followed. Larson darted
glances in all directions, locating the splayed pattern of
magical glints, memorizing positions and trying to trace Astryd's footsteps. Yearly deer hunts in the New Hampshire
forests had accustomed Larson to pine forests and moving
quietly over twigs and brush, and months in Vietnamese
jungle had made him oversensitive to the sounds of rustling
foliage. Again, he thought he heard a distant noise behind
them. His palms went slick, and sweat dampened the
leather-wrapped hilt of Gaelinar's katana. Larson cursed
himself. *Keep your mind on the wards. There's nothing behind you. And even if there is, it can't possibly be as dangerous as what's ahead.*

The uppermost branches of oak caught the dawn light,
silhouetting the autumn leaves red and gold against pink.
Taziar frowned, and Larson understood his discomfort. Accustomed to working in near darkness, night gave the little
Climber an advantage. Daylight would turn the odds even
further in Bolverkr's favor.

At length, Taziar stopped, motioning to Larson and Astryd to stand in place. Without turning to see if they had
complied, Taziar went on alone. Within seconds, he had
disappeared between the trees.

Wind shivered through the branches, sending the pines
into a bowing dance. Larson lowered his head. In a safe
position between the wards, he went deathly still. Something brushed his hand, and he glanced up at Astryd. She
held a stance of defiance, yet fear glazed her eyes. Larson
took her hand, squeezing encouragingly. He had faced
death enough times to know that the trick to succeeding at
a suicide mission was to concentrate wholly on the goal
and forget the consequences. To think about a future with-

out himself, Taziar, and Astryd, to know fear instead of certainty, even for a moment, might jeopardize the success of their attempt. So Larson pushed failure out of his mind.

But Astryd had lived her first fifteen years as a ship-builder's daughter and the last six protected and isolated from the world on the grounds of the Dragonrank school. She had not yet learned to accept her own death. Larson pitied her, sympathizing with her struggle against innocence, yet he knew he could do nothing except understand.

Taziar returned, dodging through the wards once again. "Bolverkr's still pacing the curtain wall. Any suggestions?"

Larson stated the obvious strategy. "We need to hit him fast and hard, preferably from more than one side. Our only chance is to catch him by surprise and strike before he can retaliate."

Taziar nodded in agreement. "I can get us onto the ramparts." He patted his side to indicate a coil of rope he carried beneath his cloak.

Larson frowned, wondering why Taziar had not produced the rope when they'd been maneuvering over Bolverkr's magical perimeter. *Apparently, he didn't see the need. Or he didn't think we could spare the time.* Larson found it difficult to fault a tactic that had worked. *We made it over. That's all that matters.*

Apparently recognizing Astryd's discomfort, Taziar took her other hand. "The wards get thicker the closer we get to the keep. Pay attention. Don't get too eager or distracted. Insane or not, Bolverkr's not stupid. The only safe path to the wall is on the side where he's pacing."

Larson dropped Astryd's hand, leaving her solace to Taziar. They all knew Bolverkr's retribution was aimed specifically against the men who had loosed Chaos against him; if Larson and Taziar were killed, Bolverkr had no further need of Astryd. They had already discussed the contingency; if their attack failed, the Dragonrank sorceress was to use any means at her disposal to return to Silme, accepting the men's deaths without consideration of revenge.

Alert to the urgency of time and the necessity for quiet, Taziar gave Astryd a fond but quick embrace unaccompanied by verbal explanations or platitudes. Pulling away, he knelt, seized a fallen twig amid the underbrush, and cleared a patch of dirt. Using the tip of the branch as a stylus, he drew a series of curved and tangled lines on the ground. "This is the pattern through the wards from the edge of the forest to the curtain wall. We may have to run through it. Can you do that?" He glanced up at his companions.

Larson frowned, uncertain. He had experience with obstacle courses, but none so hair-trigger deadly as a Dragon-rank sorcerer's magic.

Apparently, Taziar intended his last question to remain rhetorical, because he did not wait for an answer before pushing silently through the brush.

Astryd and Larson trailed Taziar. Branches parted before them, leaves brushing quietly against linen and leather. Larson kept his head tilted, his concentration fully on the glittering traces of sorcery, though he could see them only indirectly. Taziar's words haunted him. The idea of racing, almost blindly, through a mine field brought memories of a corporal named Steve, severed at the waist by a V.C. trap, still breathing as his life's blood colored the jungle clay a deeper red. A chill rushed through Larson, and it took an effort of will to keep from seizing Astryd and heading home.

The trees thinned, granting Larson distant glimpses of wall through ragged, dawn-gray holes in the brush. Taziar stopped, allowing his companions to draw up to his side as closely as the tightly bunched wards allowed. He pointed ahead.

Larson shifted until he found a gap wide enough to accord him an unobstructed view of what had once been a farming village called Wilsberg. Shattered stone littered land that rose gradually to a central hill, the carnage interspersed with an occasional jutting foundation of a cottage or fountain. Magics of varying hues reflected the twilight in wild patterns, their otherworldliness enhanced by the need to view them from the corners of his vision. It seemed only natural to Larson to glean details by direct focusing, and the disappearance of the wards whenever he tried to study them drove him into fits of silent but vicious swearing.

On the summit of the hill, Bolverkr's ten foot curtain wall rose squarely around a crumbled ruin of a keep. A man marched along the closest rampart. Though tall and slender, Bolverkr walked with a stomping gait, his fists clenched, his white hair streaming behind him in a snarled mane. He seemed to take no notice of the three hidden spies in his forest, to Larson's intense relief. He traced Bolverkr's straight path across the top of the wall to its farthest corner. There, the sorcerer paused. His hands snapped to chest level, and light blossomed into a ball between his fingers.

"Now," Taziar whispered. He sprinted toward the wall, dodging through the narrow ribbon of safe pathway surrounded by Bolverkr's wards.

Astryd chased Taziar.

Riveted on the sorcerer, Larson all but missed the signal. He raced after Astryd, taking the first several steps by mimicking the location of her footfalls before he remembered the method to seeing wards. The procedure required him to lose sight of the enemy above him, a lapse that sent his survival instinct jangling and wound his nerves to knots.

Larson heard an explosive crash, followed by a woody crack that reverberated from the forest canopy. He stumbled, dropping flat to the ground from habit, his head jerking toward the noise. His left arm scraped a ward, and the magic burned a slash from wrist to elbow. Pain drove a scream from his lungs. He choked it back into a gasp, aware that drawing Bolverkr's attention would be sure suicide, gaining strength from the memory of a young private with his chest flayed by a grenade who had managed to bite back the moans of agony that would have revealed his companions. *I'm not hurt that badly.*

Taziar stood with his back pressed tightly to the base of the curtain wall, directly beneath Bolverkr's line of vision. Even through dawn's copper-pink and gray, Larson could see the concerned expression on the Climber's face. Astryd had nearly reached Taziar. Bolverkr still stood at the farthest end of his walkway, his back toward Larson. On the ground before him, an oak lay beside its smoking, splintered stump. Leaves whipped and tumbled in a multicolored wash. Bolverkr started to turn.

Larson scrambled to his feet, aware he had to cover the three yards to Taziar and Astryd before Bolverkr completed his about-face. *Shit!* Larson sprang for safety.

Astryd gasped.

Larson jerked his head toward her, and a ward appeared

in vivid relief, directly before him at waist level. He jolted backward in midair, all but grazing it as he landed.

Taziar cringed, gaze whipping to Bolverkr.

No time to get fancy. Larson hurled himself over the ward. Landing on his shoulder, he rolled to Taziar's feet, then scuttled in a wild crawl to the base of the curtain wall. He rose and pressed against the wall. The granite felt cold and solid through the sweat-dampened fabric of his tunic. His heart hammered, and his skin itched with a sense of imminent peril. He could almost feel the tear of Bolverkr's magic through his flesh. His injured arm dangled, throbbing without mercy, and he drew some solace from the realization that the injury from Bolverkr's sorcery could have proved far more critical. *It could have killed me. I was lucky. It was weak or old, or perhaps I only grazed it.*

Beside Larson, Astryd stood still as a statue, her back crushed to the wall. Overhead, Bolverkr's footfalls grew louder as he approached.

Larson held his breath, praying to any god who might listen that Bolverkr had not seen him.

The footsteps stopped for several moments, directly overhead. Larson suppressed the urge to look up. If Bolverkr had seen him, it was already too late; movement could only draw the Dragonrank sorcerer's attention.

The silence dragged into an eternity. Larson's lungs ached, and his muscles cramped. Each second seemed too long, and he forced himself through every one individually, trying not to contemplate the next.

Bolverkr's pacing resumed.

Cued by the sorcerer's footfalls, Taziar began a hunched run, his spine just shy of the curtain wall, drawing himself into as narrow a target as possible. Astryd sidled after him.

Gaze off-centered on the wards, Larson understood the Climber's caution. The wards closed in on the wall, hopelessly intertwined, leaving them only a narrow lane around the granite to maneuver.

A series of side steps brought Taziar, Astryd, and Larson around the first corner of the curtain wall. Now, Larson released his pent up breath, allowing himself several deep inhalations of damp, autumn air. It seemed impossible that a sorcerer of Bolverkr's power had not seen the intruders near his citadel. Yet magic often seemed illogical to Larson.

Spells he would have considered simple, like disguises or locating people and objects, often proved difficult; thought readings and illusions were impossible. Others that seemed grandiose, like Astryd's dragon summonings and wards that burned flesh, required far less life energy.

As Larson inched around the surrounding wall, following in Astryd's footsteps, he viewed the town from varying angles. Dawn light reflected from scattered and jagged stone in bloody highlights. Strands of thatch fluttered from between wedged granite. All other evidence that these structures had once been cottages had dispersed to the winds. Over the carnage, spells glinted in tortuous bands, like the webs of a thousand spiders, adding madness to the art of Chaos' destruction.

Larson turned the second corner. Now against the south wall and directly opposite Bolverkr, Taziar drew halfway along its length before stopping. He turned, studying the granite for some time with his head cocked at varying angles. Apparently satisfied, he jammed his fingers between stones that looked seamless to Larson's untrained eyes and clambered to the top. From there, Taziar gazed into the courtyard for a time before scrambling down the far side of the wall and out of Larson's sight.

Uncertain of Taziar's motive, Larson looked to Astryd, who shrugged her ignorance. Kensei Gaelinar had often claimed that a warrior decided his strategies in the instant between sword strokes, but Larson had still not grown accustomed to fighting enemies without making a coherent plan in advance.

Shortly, Taziar reappeared at the top of the wall and tossed the end of a rope over the side. He gestured at his companions to join him.

Now Taziar's intentions became clear to Larson. *He must have secured the other end to something stable in the courtyard.* Larson watched Astryd brace her feet against the granite. Using the rope for support, she clambered to the top of the wall. Larson waited until Taziar helped her to the ramparts before following.

Once the three companions were perched safely on the ramparts, Taziar whispered. "You go that way." He indicated the clockwise direction. "Astryd and I will come around the other. We'll try to surprise Bolverkr from both sides." Taziar trotted off in the opposite direction without pausing for a reply or sign of agreement.

Astryd followed.

Turning on his heel, Larson started around the other way. Alone except for the almost inaudible scrape of his boots against granite, he felt like a child playing army on a real battlefield. *Surely Bolverkr won't fall prey to a simple flanking maneuver.* Yet Larson failed to find a flaw in Taziar's plan. *Often the simplest tactic works the best, and Bolverkr seems ignorant of our presence so far.* The idea that the Dragonrank sorcerer might know they were there and not care seized Larson with frightening abruptness. His step faltered. Concerned the hesitation might throw off his timing from Astryd's and Taziar's, Larson dragged onward, forcing the thought aside. *If our presence means that little to Bolverkr, there's no sense worrying about it. We've just got to do the best we can.*

Larson rounded the first corner and started along the western wall. Bolverkr's single, fully standing tower blocked Larson's view of the north wall completely. Ignorance of Bolverkr's position made him wary, though he gained solace from the realization that the tower would obstruct Bolverkr's view of his own approach as well. He continued on, straining his hearing for some evidence that the Chaos-racked sorcerer still paced his curtain wall.

As the final corner came into sight, Larson drew Gaelinar's katana from its scabbard. The haft filled his grip, already warm from an unconscious series of touches to its hilt. A sense of calmness accompanied the unsheathing. Time seemed to strip away. For a moment, Kensei Gaelinar crouched beside his only student, his every movement crisply precise, each sword stroke flawless in its arc and timing. Competence radiated from him like physical light. His casual confidence remained, a reassuring constant in Larson's mind. He could still hear the Kensei's guttural voice suggesting that they travel to Hel to retrieve Silme's soul, speaking of the impossible as if it were trivial, suggesting Larson defy Vidarr because the Silent One was, "after all, just another god." A weight lifted from Larson's shoulders. The battle with Bolverkr seemed like just another task, scarcely different than the ones before. With Gaelinar at his side, he could do anything.

Sword readied, Larson whipped around the final corner, taking in the situation at a glance. Bolverkr stood three quarters of the way to the opposite side of the rampart, his back to Larson. Beyond him, Taziar stood braced before Astryd, sword bared, while the sorceress shaped a spindle of orange light between her fingers.

Even as Astryd shaped her spell, a white starburst of magic flashed in Bolverkr's hands, dwarfing Astryd's power. She shouted. Her arm snapped out. Her sorceries arched toward Bolverkr.

The sorcerer hurled his own spell. Orange met white in a wild splash of sparks. The darker winked out, the white sputtering a savage backlash in the trail of Astryd's spell. For an instant, the sorceress seemed bathed in milky light. Suddenly, she went limp, collapsing from the ramparts like a rag doll.

Taziar screamed in anguish and rage. Sword raised, he rushed Bolverkr.

Larson charged from behind.

A single laugh rumbled from Bolverkr's throat, rich with ancient evil, a sound so primitive it raised the hair on the nape of Larson's neck. The sorcerer flicked a hand. Lightning flashed from a cloudless sky, lancing toward Taziar like a blue-white arrow.

No! Larson all but shrieked aloud.

Less than half a second elapsed between the time Bolverkr moved and his deadly bolt struck. Electricity crackled against stone. Light flared, wrung through with a thunderclap that set Larson's ears ringing. Blinded and deafened, Larson did not pause to mourn his companions. The katana rose, then crashed down on the spot where Larson last recalled Bolverkr standing. The blade met resistance. Razorhoned, it bit into Bolverkr's shoulder, sheared through his ribs and into his abdomen.

Bolverkr loosed a single cry, as eerie and high-pitched as the scream of a dying rabbit, then collapsed to the ramparts.

Larson tore his sword free, knowing with perfect certainty that the blow he had dealt was fatal. As his vision returned, he caught a glimpse of bone, lung, and heart through the cut; that sight and the odor of blood made his stomach heave. Stepping over Bolverkr, he dropped to his

knees, vomiting into the courtyard. He staggered to his feet
and threw up again, a thin bile. Horror and grief trembled
through him. It required an effort of will to shuffle the last
few steps to where he had last seen Taziar. Once there, he
stared at Gaelinar's katana, mesmerized, trying to gather
the strength to see how little of the Climber remained.

Ozone gorged Larson's nose, overpowering the stench of
blood. Static sizzled the air. A circle of burnt stone met his
glance. Beside it, something moved.

Larson shifted his gaze in shocked disbelief. Taziar lay
prone on the ramparts, his head raised, eyes blinking rapidly as if to clear his vision.

Joy thrilled through Larson. Apparently, the little Climber's quick reflexes had allowed him to backpedal before the
lightning hit. Larson harbored no doubt a direct blast would
have killed him.

"Shadow." Larson caught Taziar by both arms and
hefted the smaller man to his feet. "Are you all right?"

Taziar nodded, floundering as Larson allowed him to
handle some of his own weight. The blue eyes flicked open,
then widened in horror at some sight over Larson's shoulder. "Allerum! Look out!"

Larson whirled, dropping Taziar, who fell to one knee.

Steeped in blood, Bolverkr again stood upon the ramparts. The unequivocally-lethal wound Larson had inflicted
had disappeared as if it never existed.

Holy shit! Shock froze Larson. *How?*

Light blazed to life between Bolverkr's hands.

Mobilized, Larson charged, katana raised for another
death blow. *This time, I take off his fucking head!*

Larson managed only a single step before Bolverkr's
magic burst in a spray of multicolored pinpoints. Larson
crouched as he ran. Bits of magic rained across his back,
every speck as hot as molten lead. Pain all but incapacitated
him. Days in a sickbed had taken their toll on his endurance, but his will to survive remained strong. He sprang
forward.

A blast of magic caught Larson squarely in the chest,
dashing the breath from his lungs. He toppled over backward. The katana crashed against stone. Struck from the
opposite side by sorceries as solid as the granite, the blade
snapped. Its tip gashed Larson's wrist. Stone sheered skin

from his arms and side. A sideways view of grass filled his vision as he teetered on the edge of the catwalk. Rolling, he scrambled to his hands and knees, catching the katana's hilt in his grip. A hand's length of cleanly fractured blade jutted from it.

Horror tore through Larson with a violence that made him scream. The agony of his wounds faded beneath a savage avalanche of grief. *Gaelinar!*

Bolverkr towered, regal as a king before a groveling subject, but Larson's vision failed him. He saw only the aging, Oriental features of his teacher, dark eyes glazing in death. Larson felt the Kensei's touch, the thrust of the katana's hilt into his own scarred hand. The old man's final, whispered words echoed in Larson's ears, "It begins again. Carry on," then faded to an ominous and permanent silence. Now, on Bolverkr's ramparts, something died within Larson. He felt weak and flaccid, unprepared to face even the simplest of challenges. He clenched the hilt to his chest, feeling the leather-wrapped steel gouge painfully into his breastbone. *Astryd's dead. In a moment, Taziar and I will join her. It's over.*

Bolverkr chuckled joyously, his triumph beyond that of simply winning a battle.

The Dragonrank sorcerer's laughter stung Larson. Sorrow parted before a deep courage that had lain dormant since he had charged a circle of AK-47s, Freyr's name on his lips and his buddies' deaths haunting his mind. *If I'm going to die again, it won't be crawling.* Determination spiraled through Larson. Lurching to his feet, he brandished the damaged sword and rushed down on Bolverkr.

A snort escaped Bolverkr. He made an effortless gesture of contempt, and a stone from a shattered gargoyle rolled beneath Larson's feet.

The granite caught Larson across the shins. He tripped, sailing over the boulder. Twisting, he landed on his side, suppressing the urge to roll before it sent him tumbling over the ramparts. His hand tightened on the haft violently; brocade scored his palm. Tears of frustration blurred his vision as Bolverkr stole his chance to at least die with dignity. Anger flared. Larson clambered to his feet, swearing, and raced toward Bolverkr once more.

Again, Bolverkr's arm raised. A sliver of magic glittered

in his palm. Suddenly, with a sound like thunder, it erupted to a blood-red ball that seemed to throb in Bolverkr's hand. Back light washed the creased cheeks, making him seem like an evil parody of a grandfather. He tensed to throw.

Larson sprang forward, realizing as he did that he could never hope to beat Bolverkr's spell.

From the grounds beyond the keep, a stone shot through the air. It crashed against Bolverkr's ear, staggering him. Surprise crossed the pale features. His sorceries exploded in his fist. Sparks splattered to the granite, fizzling onto stone. Bolverkr whirled to face this new threat, just as a second stone whisked through air and slammed into his cheek.

Larson bounded forward, whipping the broken katana for Bolverkr's neck. The sorcerer dodged, slipped, and toppled into his courtyard.

Larson's blow cut air. Momentum sent him tumbling after Bolverkr.

"Allerum!" Taziar shouted in alarm, running to his friend's aid.

Desperately, Larson twisted, flailing. One hand raked granite. He clamped his fist onto the ledge. His fall jarred to an abrupt halt that strained the muscles of his forearm and shot pain through a partially healed tear in his shoulder. Blood soaked his sleeve. He flexed against the agony, clawing for a grip with his other hand.

Taziar's small fingers surrounded Larson's wrist, supporting his mad scramble to the wall top. Once there, the elf glanced down at Bolverkr.

Apparently dazed and injured by the fall, the sorcerer had barely managed to stagger far enough to get beyond range of heavy objects shoved from the ramparts. Light flickered around the sorcerer.

Enraged, Larson flung the remains of Gaelinar's katana at Bolverkr's head. His aim was true, but, inches from its target, the haft bounced from an invisible shield and pitched into the grass. Larson swore, grabbing for Taziar's sword. "Run. I'll finish the bastard right now!"

But Taziar caught Larson's hand, jamming the blade into its sheath instead. "He's too strong. Let's go. Fast!" Taziar bounded from the ramparts, hauling Larson with him.

Dragged into another fall, Larson was forced to concentrate on landing. He touched down feet first. Taziar jerked Larson's arm then let go, sending the elf into a roll. Unhurt, Larson spun to his feet. He glanced first at the wall. Seeing no one on the ramparts, his attention shifted naturally to the direction from which the rocks had come. Silme stood partway up the hillside, another stone clasped in a hand white with strain.

Silme? Larson took a protective step toward her. Then, concerned for Taziar and Astryd, he turned back toward the keep.

Taziar had hefted Astryd. She lay draped across his arms, her limbs dangling and her head lolling. Yet Taziar's expression mingled relief with concern.

She's alive, Larson guessed. *Thank God.* Rushing to Taziar's side, he grasped Astryd's limp figure and hauled it over one shoulder.

Taziar hefted Astryd's dragonstaff, looking distressed. Whether Taziar's unhappiness came from fear for Astryd or disappointment that his slight stature made help necessary, Larson did not bother to consider.

"You lead." Larson gestured at the ruins. "Get Silme away as fast as you can. I won't have as much chance to locate magics, so I'll try to follow in your steps."

Taziar drew his sword and handed it to Larson. Without explanation, he ran toward Wilsberg, maneuvering the maze of wards with deft shifts in direction. Silme whirled and headed away from the keep, to Larson's relief.

Larson followed more ponderously, tracing Taziar's footsteps without wasting time identifying wards. The idea of leaving an enemy at his back pained him, yet Larson understood the necessity of a strategic retreat. His body felt as if it were on fire, every sinew tensed in anticipation of an exploding ward or a spell hurled from behind. Death hovered, drawing in on him, tightening until he scarcely dared to breathe. The feeling had grown familiar since the day his plane had touched down in Vietnam, and he had only managed to shake it a month ago. Now, it returned, a hyper-alertness that would preclude dreamless sleep, that made him certain an enemy hovered behind every rock and tree.

Memories pressed Larson, quick glimpses of a past he thought he had suppressed. Vivid as reality, he watched his friend, Bill Charnin, flip an NVA body, watched the "corpse" empty a pistol clip into the G.I.'s face before Larson could think to shout a warning. He remembered how, forced to tend half a dozen NVA prisoners, Charnin had bound them using detonation cord. Again, the explosion rang through Larson's ears along with Charnin's growled explanation. "Now *that* is how you take prisoners."

Larson continued dodging between the wards, memorizing Taziar's path with meticulous devotion to detail. *Not now. Please, God, no flashbacks now.* He forced memory away using the control he had only recently learned with Vidarr's aid. Remembrance faded, leaving only one set of words to haunt Larson as he ran: "It begins again."

CHAPTER 4
Chaos Link

The sick are the greatest danger for the healthy;
it is not from the strongest that harm comes
to the strong, but from the weakest.
                              —Friedrich Wilhelm Nietzsche
                              Genealogy of Morals

The Dragonmage, Bolverkr, banished pain with a muttered
word and a broad sweep of directed Chaos. Once the agony
had faded enough for him to concentrate, he mentally explored his body for damage. He discovered a fractured left
hip and arm as well as a ruptured spleen and a bruise that
ran the length of his side. Calmly, he tapped his life energy,
performing the sequence of mental exercises that healed
each injury. The glow of his aura faded from its usual fiery
white to pewter. Curative spells cost dearly, and he had
already tapped considerable life force for a gaping wound,
inflicted by Larson's sword, that would have killed a
lesser man.

Bolverkr rose, drawing another sliver of the Chaos-energy
that raged within him for a transport spell. The effort
brought him to his lookout perch on the main curtain wall.
From there, he watched Al Larson maneuver the familiar
pattern of wards, Astryd's limp body bouncing on his shoulder. Ahead, the black-clothed shape of Taziar Medakan
dodged along the trail with an effortlessness that made it
look like child's play, the garnet on Astryd's staff bobbing
like a tiny, red sun above his head. Nearly at the forest's
edge, Silme ran in the lead. Her fine blue dress flapped about
perfect curves. Her hair streamed in a soft fan, reflecting the
sun in highlights that glittered golden through the yellow.
Bolverkr filled in the details from memory: high cheekbones chiseled about a straight, aristocratic nose, vast blue
eyes, and firm ample breasts.

Desire burned through Bolverkr, grown far beyond simple lust. Silme's flawlessness went deeper than beauty. Though sorely outmatched, she had once faced Bolverkr with no weapon except her own defiance. Unable to cast spells without harming her developing baby, she had resorted to wit to incapacitate him. *Strong, intelligent, competent, and beautiful. What more could a man want?* Yet there was one more thing. The most powerful living Dragonrank sorceress, Silme had already proven herself capable of understanding and sympathizing with Bolverkr's situation, if only in her dreams. She could comprehend the loneliness that came of being one of the rare mages in a world where most men believed in sorcerers only as mother's stories to scare children or as demon spawn to be reviled or feared.

Bolverkr gathered power to him, reveling in the energy roiling through his veins; a Chaos that had once attacked him as an enemy and had now become an integral part of himself. A paralyzing spell came to mind, forming so quickly it might have shaped itself. He aimed it for Larson's bounding figure. Once stilled, Larson and Astryd could be killed at Bolverkr's leisure. He knew from past experience that Taziar would come to his friends' aid, opening himself to any slaying spell Bolverkr might choose.

Yet Bolverkr hesitated, the paralyzation magics locked in limbo. It was not mercy that froze him. Mercy, like belief in the sanctity of life, was an arbitrary construct of man and Law. What stopped Bolverkr was the realization that, to slaughter Larson, Astryd, and Taziar now, while Silme still believed she loved them, would ingrain a hatred so profound even Chaos might not overcome it. *They're running. I can't claim self-defense any longer.* Curiosity goaded him to check the slow leak of Chaos between himself and Silme, but he resisted. To draw her attention to its presence might spark her to struggle against its influence. *The unborn baby Silme's friends insist on protecting will become the means of Silme's betrayal and their own destruction.*

Bolverkr chuckled, releasing his spell and letting his quarry reach the sanctity of the forest without persecution. Once, concern for the foursome's power had made him cautious. Now he knew they could never stand against him. *They attacked me while I was surprised and crazed, and still I bested them.* He thought of Larson's broken sword, the beautiful randomness of its destruction, the symbolic slaying of Gaelinar's soul and the splintering of Larson's morale. "I am all powerful! I am king!" He had not intended to speak aloud, yet his words knifed through Wilsberg's ruins, reverberating mournfully back from the huddled forest.

And Bolverkr's own Chaos rose to answer. *To kill you would annihilate too much Chaos for the Balance to remain. It would destroy the nine worlds and every living creature in them. The Fates, the gods, eternity will work to keep you alive. You are invincible!*

Despite having drained a relative avalanche of life energy, enough to have killed him three times over before the Chaos-bond, Bolverkr felt vigor shift through him, as restless and powerful as the tides. He felt giddy, seized by a desire to shape the world to his needs. The creatures of Law served the gods and mankind, but Bolverkr served the older, more primitive power of nature. He knew an elegance that only the finest artists learned, that beauty breeds not from order but from its lack. Chaos' asymmetry and unpredictability inspired Bolverkr to its tenets: hatred, destruction, pain, and subversion. He knew the pleasure that accompanied a scattered array of fragmented rock and corpses, the music inherent in a panicked scream.

Bolverkr stared out over the ruins of Wilsberg, entwined in a raw blaze of wards. Selecting a tree at the edge of the forest, he called down a blast of lightning from the sky's only cloud. The bolt lanced from the heavens and slammed into the trunk. A crack filled the air, soft but impending as a snake's rattle. Split near the base, the tree toppled, its limbs raking through its neighbors in a chorus of swishes and rattles. Branches and smaller trees broke beneath its weight, adding a wild series of snaps to the cacophony. Leaves billowed out in all directions, still floating long after the noise died to silence. Gradually, the odor of charred bark and ozone drifted to Bolverkr's nostrils, a perfume that bore the name Chaos.

Surrounded by his art, Bolverkr laughed, wondering why he had ever bothered to fight the Chaos within him.

Once beyond the outer circle of Bolverkr's ward, Larson followed his companions blindly between trunks, and through brush and deadfalls. His shoulder cramped beneath Astryd's weight, and his brain had gone equally numb. He felt as if the world had crushed in on him, stealing everything worthwhile, revealing Al Larson to be a hopeless incompetent. *What possessed me to think I could take the place of the world's greatest swordsman? That I deserved Silme's love or Astryd's and Taziar's trust?* Larson straggled onward, accepting the pain of his burden as appropriate punishment for his stupidity.

Deep in an unfamiliar part of the woodlands, Taziar called the retreat to a halt. "Let's rest. I think we've gone far enough."

"There's a clearing," Silme said from in front of him. "With some downed trees to sit on."

Taziar glanced at Larson, apparently seeking confirmation or opinion, but Larson stared at his feet, avoiding Taziar's gaze. The Climber narrowed his eyes, studying Larson as if to read his silence. "Be right there," the smaller man told Silme. Shrugging, he pushed through a set of low branches to the clearing.

Larson ducked beneath the foliage, protecting Astryd from the whipping branches, and followed Taziar quietly.

Silme perched on a deadfall, one leg drawn to her chest, the other dangling over the leaf-strewn forest floor. Her hair fell about and into her face in a frizzy tangle, which did not in the least diminish her beauty. Taziar watched Larson's approach, gaze fixed on Astryd.

Larson entered the clearing slowly, shifted Astryd to his arms, and gently lowered her to the ground. For all her stillness, she felt warm and alive. Apparently, her limpness as she fell had protected her from injury in the same way a drunkard survives a car accident more often than his victim. This new line of thought made Larson bitter. He had lost his father to an inebriated driver, and his mother's subsequent financial hardship had forced Larson's sister Pam into a bad marriage and him to enlist for the war in Vietnam.

A faint crackle of leaves behind Larson sent him spinning into a crouch, sword drawn, gaze tearing through autumn-brown weeds. A bushy tail whisked to the opposite side of a broad oak, another squirrel close on its heels. *Calm, Al.*

Calm. Jumping at little, furry animals isn't going to help anyone. He resheathed the sword.

Ignoring Larson, Taziar knelt beside Astryd, checking frantically for life signs, though her chest rose and fell in deep, sluggish breaths.

"Make her as comfortable as you can." Silme hitched forward on the deadfall. "She'll come around."

Taziar sat cross-legged, sliding his lap beneath Astryd's head to serve as a pillow. He stroked her short, feathered locks, brushing strands from her face, without bothering to question Silme's knowledge.

Larson scowled. Standing, he regarded Silme through the speckled shadows of the forest. "How do you know that?"

Silme shrugged. "Dragonrank mages have a visible measure of life energy, an aura that only other sorcerers can see. Astryd's has a bit of fraying around the edges, probably caused by the spell she tried to throw." Silme's gaze settled on Astryd's inert form. "Life aura reflects a state of health, whether it's drained by spells, emotional states, injury, or illness. Other than the border, her aura looks bright."

Silme's calmness dispelled Larson's concern for Astryd, allowing frustration to flood in on him. Failure made him curt. "I thought we decided you were supposed to stay in Cullinsberg."

"You decided." Silme remained calm, driving Larson to fury. "I never agreed."

"You followed us, didn't you?" Larson did not pause for an answer. "You didn't say you'd follow us. Where I come from, that's agreement." It was a half-truth at best, but Larson did not consider his statement too carefully. None of his companions knew enough about twentieth-century America to contradict him.

Taziar continued soothing Astryd, wisely avoiding the argument.

"Without my rocks, you would have been killed. I bought you the time to retreat."

Larson was shouting now. "If you hadn't come, I wouldn't have worried about retreating. I would have killed Bolverkr."

"Bolverkr would have killed you."

Though Silme spoke the truth, her words infuriated Larson. "I would have fought until one of us was dead, not worried about getting you and the baby safely away."

Silme's face reddened, echoing Larson's anger. "Nor, apparently, about leaving Shadow, Astryd, and me to face Bolverkr without you."

"Stop it!" Taziar screamed over the bickering. "We've got an enemy at our backs. We can handle him, but only if we work together."

Larson's rage died to annoyance. The hopelessness of the situation, Bolverkr's seemingly infinite power, and the destruction of Gaelinar's soul would not leave his thoughts long enough to dispel his irritability. "Christ, Shadow. I damn near cleaved the guy in half. Ten minutes later, he's fully healed, throwing magical grenades and directing lightning bolts like he was playing tiddledywinks. Surely he's healed the bumps and bruises from his fall by now. He can transport anywhere instantly. He has perfect access to our location through my thoughts. If he's not here now, slaughtering us like cattle, it's because he chooses not to be. How can we fight against that?"

Ignoring the sprinkling of English words in Larson's tirade, Taziar broke into hysterical laughter.

The humor was lost on Larson. "What's so damned funny?"

"This list of doom from the one who just argued that he would have killed Bolverkr if Silme hadn't shown up." Taziar ran a finger along Astryd's closed eyelids. "The same one, I might add, who killed Loki and helped destroy the Chaos-dragon that slaughtered the original Dragonrank Master and his followers. We can handle this. Everything is impossible until someone proves it otherwise. You know that."

Larson listened dully. In the past, Taziar's enthusiasm and confidence had roused him from despair and rallied him to the most difficult of tasks. But this time, even the little thief's certainty could not penetrate the pall of dread hanging over Larson. Seeing no reason to puncture whatever morale his companions might still harbor, Larson forced a weak smile.

"I think, Allerum," Silme began, her gaze focused on a forested edge of the clearing, "it might be best if you went home."

Larson stared, so stunned it took several seconds to realize moisture glazed Silme's gray eyes. "Home?" He shifted to her side, reaching for her protectively. "What do you mean by home? I haven't stopped traveling since I came to your world. Home's a series of forest floors, farm cottages, and primitive inns. I haven't had a home since I went to Vietnam. I . . ."

Silme dodged Larson's words and his embrace. "That's exactly what I mean."

Larson broke off, blinking. Comprehension seeped in slowly. "What are you saying?"

Silme stared off into the woodlands, her back to her companions. "When I talked to Bolverkr, he said something I can't get out of my mind."

"What!" Larson's exclamation expressed startlement and disbelief that Silme would contemplate the opinions of an enemy, but Silme accepted it as a question.

"He said you were an anachronism. And an anathema."

Larson watched Silme's back, not certain what he was hearing. "Okay. I'll give you anachronism. That just means I'm in the wrong time, right? The other thing, I don't even know what it is."

"A cursed being," Taziar explained. "An anathema."

Larson whipped his attention to his small companion.

"You asked." Taziar shrugged, covering quickly, "Bolverkr was wrong, of course."

Silme ignored the exchange. "He said that something about your misplacement in time makes the natural forces of our worlds more sensitive to your interference. He said that, eventually, you would destroy it."

Tired of addressing Silme's back, Larson drew to her side, caught her arm, and turned her toward him. "Of course, you told him that was nonsense."

Silme returned his gaze, the first tears dripping from her eyes. "That's what I told him, but I'm not sure any more. How else can you explain one man, untrained in magic and barely versed in swordcraft, slaying a god, freeing a soul from Hel, and destroying a Chaos-dragon?"

Stunned, Larson scarcely found his voice. He recalled how each of those successes had cost him months of harried persecution, injury, and plaguing flashbacks. The first had claimed Silme's life, the second Gaelinar's hand and his morale, and the third the Kensei's life and nearly Taziar's and Larson's as well. "You were there the first time. I had help from one of the highest ranking sorceresses . . ." He gestured at Silme. ". . . also the world's best swordsman and at least one god."

"I explain those things," Taziar interrupted softly, "the same way I explain one sapphire-rank Dragonmage protecting the nine worlds from a diamond-rank master." He referred to Silme's dedication of her life and learning to shield innocents from her half-brother's cruelties. "The same way I explain a single, tiny Climber breaking into the Dragonrank's stronghold and bypassing its defenses alone. Careful planning, competent execution, and, in Allerum's case, courageous fighting."

Silme's voice remained steady despite the tears. "No matter how you explain it, the fact remains. Until Allerum came to our world, the Balance simply was. We didn't have trouble with huge shifts tipping the world toward destruction."

Many thoughts converged on Larson. He wanted to scream in frustration, to remind Silme that he had not asked to come to her world. He wanted to tell her that the gods had dragged him from death because of a difficulty with the Balance, and the only solution had been to slide the Balance too far the opposite way. But his mind shifted to new and terrible thoughts. His love for Silme ached within him, tortured by a disapproval he dared not believe he had earned. His vision washed to the red blindness of a tracer round ignited too close. "This is crazy. There's no way back to my world. Hell, Loki said my world doesn't even exist any more!" Larson's grip tightened on Silme's arm. Receiving no answer, he finished his tirade. "Gary Mannix, the original Dragonrank Master, the one you call Geirmagnus. He came from a future even later than mine. He's the one who started this whole mess with the Balance in the first place. He discovered the Dragonrank mages and created the gods hoping they could find a way to take him back to his own time. He failed, damn it! How do you expect me to do it?"

Silme blinked, splashing tears from her lashes, and wiped away another glistening on her cheek. "I know you can get back. You took me there once."

Larson winced. In a time when Vidarr's only link with the world outside his sword-prison was Larson's thoughts, Silme had entered Larson's mind in order to confer with Vidarr. In the process, sorceress and silent god had accidentally sparked flashbacks of Vietnam so vivid they had become reality. Another time, Vidarr and Silme's half-brother had battled in Larson's mind, instigating rapid-fire flashes of memory until, dizzied, sickened, and confused, Larson had clung to one, dashing the combatants into a wild, twentieth-century firefight. "This is crazy! I didn't take you to 'Nam on purpose. I can't help it if I don't have mind barriers and the war drove me nuts. I didn't ask Freyr for my life. I only asked him to let me take lots of V.C. with me when I died."

Larson dropped logic for gut emotion. He slammed a fist into his palm. "Damn it, Silme. I served my time. I'm not going back to 'Nam. For God's sake, I'm dead there." Other thoughts converged on him, a chaotic jumble he had no way to interpret. *The future I once knew doesn't exist. I destroyed it.* Yet events had proven otherwise; some of the sojourns into memory had occurred after Loki's death. *I've been there. And, every time, I've brought others with me and back.* He recalled how Vidarr had taken a bullet from a V.C. rifle, and the wound had returned with him to Midgard.

The world of my future has to exist. Another idea followed naturally. *But maybe only in my mind.* That sparked a new train of thought. *If so, can I control it? Does that make me God?* The possibilities seemed endless, yet they were unsupported by facts. The only control Larson could recall having over the trips into memory was the ability to block the exit in his mind, preventing his companions from going home without his permission. And, though he always popped into the memory exactly as he recalled it, any events transpiring from that point seemed random, related to the actions of himself, his companions, and anyone else in the scene, rather than the events that had taken place the first time he had lived the situation.

The scope became too awesome for Larson to ponder. He had no choice but to assume his world still existed in some form, and that he could go there. He tried a different tack, no longer able to hold back his tears. "I love you,

Silme. I once swore worlds would never keep us apart, and I rescued you from Hel to prove that. How could you suggest we part now?"

Silme buried her face in her palms.

Taziar claimed the argument, his voice calmly rational, unaffected by their recent battle, impending danger, and his concerns for Astryd. "Silme, I can't imagine why you'd trust the words of an enemy. But let's say Bolverkr spoke the truth, and Allerum has some mystical effect on the Balance. So what? That just means we need to be aware of it and use it well rather than foolishly."

Larson stared at Taziar, glad his small companion had a habit of cutting through the bullshit and approaching problems head on.

Taziar's features crinkled thoughtfully. "Allerum leaving can only make the rest of us that much weaker against Bolverkr. But you've given me another idea."

Now Silme also regarded Taziar.

"You've already proven you can take people from this world to yours. In fact, from what you've told me, you may *only* be able to go back when you *do* take someone with you."

Larson nodded encouragingly, eager to hear the rest of Taziar's idea.

"And Geirmagnus has shown that even the most powerful Dragonrank mages can't throw spells that bridge time. So, it follows that if you take us to your world, we're completely safe from Bolverkr. We can plan, prepare, perhaps gather weapons, all in relative safety."

Stunned by the idea, Larson took several seconds to discover its obvious flaws. "It won't work."

"Why not?" Silme asked.

Larson returned to the deadfall and sat. "A bunch of reasons. First, only sorcerers and gods can enter my mind. That means I can't take Shadow." He addressed Taziar directly. "You'd be stuck here to face Bolverkr alone."

Taziar's shoulders rose and fell in resigned acceptance.

"Second, the lapses into memory aren't something I control. They just happen when I'm stressed. I usually return to some horrible, traumatic place and time, too. Third, there's bomps, traps, V.C., and North Vietnam Army soldiers where I'd take you. Not to mention fire-breathing dragon-like things we call jets." Larson recalled how Silme had attacked a phantom with magics that had sent it exploding in a rain of twisted metal and turned Larson's own war buddies against them.

"Fourth, we have reason to believe my world has become nothing more than a figment of my imagination. And last, as far as I can tell, whenever I return to 'Nam, I'm thrown back into my other body. This . . ." He outlined his delicate elf form with both hands. ". . . stays here, unconscious. If it's killed . . ." He trailed off, lacking the knowledge to finish the sentence but naturally assuming the worst. The events in his memory seemed real enough, yet he could not discount the possibility that it all took place inside the brain of this elf body, that death for Allerum the elf meant death for Al Larson the man as well as anyone harbored in his thoughts. At best, he felt certain that death for his elf body meant he could never return to Midgard, trapped in the meaningless violence of the Vietnam conflict, forced to live in terror until the familiar death, riddled by V.C. assault rifles. *Or, perhaps Freyr will rescue me again, and I'll get caught in some asinine, Twilight Zone-ish time loop.*

Taziar's hands went still on Astryd's forehead while he considered Larson's words. "I'm sure you didn't spend your whole life in this 'Nam place. If you concentrate hard enough, I'm willing to bet you could take Silme and Astryd to a safe memory. It doesn't have to really exist. You'll be coming back eventually."

Larson waited, thin brows arched, hoping Taziar had the answer to his other points.

Taziar sighed, as if in answer. "As to leaving me and your body. Naturally, I'd protect both as best as I can." He hesitated, then, apparently seeing no way around the difficulties, he finished lamely. "Fine. So it wasn't a perfect plan. At least keep it in mind if things get desperate."

Larson banished the idea to the back of his thoughts. *I won't abandon Taziar or experiment with Silme's and Astryd's lives. Besides, dwelling on the thought will only give Bolverkr access to it.* Larson knew that because of his lack of mind barriers, sorcerers could read his superficial thoughts without his knowledge. To delve more deeply, though, required the reader to physically enter his mind. Larson had learned to detect and defend against presences and deeper probes, and he doubted Bolverkr would attempt such a thing, except as a full-scale attack.

Astryd's eyes fluttered open. Her body stiffened.

Taziar knelt, pressing a hand to her forehead to keep her from moving too quickly. "Lie still. You're safe."

Taziar's reassurance sounded ridiculous to Larson, and he bit his cheeks to keep from laughing in hysteria. *Safe, that is, except for one lunatic, all-powerful wizard out for our blood who could be anywhere preparing our doom.* He did not speak aloud.

"Bolverkr," Astryd managed.

"We ran," Taziar admitted. "Silme . . ."

Larson tuned out the conversation, not wanting to be reminded of the rout and its consequences. Rising, he approached Silme, catching her in an embrace.

At first, Silme went rigid. Then, slowly, her arms circled him, and she pulled him closer.

"I'm sorry," Larson whispered into Silme's hair. "I don't want to fight. I love you so much."

Silme tilted her face toward his. Something flashed in the depths of her eyes, and Larson felt certain she would impart a message or distant thought of ultimate importance. "I . . ." she started and stopped. "I . . ." The look faded into the vast grayness of her eyes. ". . . love you, too," she finished.

And though it did not seem like the urgent message she had needed to convey, right now, for Al Larson, it was enough.

That night, Silme awakened to the shrill of night insects and the unhurried, regular breaths of her companions. She was uncertain what had awakened her, aware only that it had happened abruptly, like a poke in the ribs by a sleeping companion. But Larson had rolled beyond reach, one hand clamped to the hilt of Taziar's sword, the other arm draped across his face. Taziar and Astryd lay further away, curled together in slumber. The circle of wards Astryd had placed had dwindled to a pale ghost in the night. Moonlight flittered through the branches, diffusing night's ink to gray.

Needing to relieve her bladder, Silme rose with silent grace and pushed through Astryd's fading magic, suffering only a mild sting for her recklessness. Not wanting to wander too far from her friends, she wove between a clump of tightly-packed oaks to a narrow clearing. She fumbled with her dress.

Suddenly, light shattered the darkness.

Silme gasped, straggling backward. She crashed against the line of oaks hard enough to shoot pain along her spine.

A dark figure took shape, clearly outlined in brilliant white. She recognized Bolverkr at once, his eternal features becoming familiar beneath soft, blue-gray eyes. He kept his hands outstretched in a gesture of peace and parlay. His sorceries dispersed around him, plunging the woods back into night's gloom.

Blinded, Silme blinked aside afterimages, drawing breath to scream.

"Please, don't call out." Bolverkr's voice sounded gentle as wind. "I won't hurt you. I promise. We just need to talk."

Silme hesitated, lips still parted but no sound emerging. Usually, emotion tempered her logic only slightly, but now she found herself lost, unable to differentiate the two. She knew Bolverkr had drawn most of his images of her through his searches of Larson's emotions: a young, intense love blind to her flaws. Bolverkr had had the opportunity to kill her before and had chosen only to talk. *I'm in no danger, but if I draw my companions, Bolverkr may kill them. Maybe I can calm him, talk him out of this mindless vengeance.*

Silme stared at the tall, slender wizard, watched the wind feather his milk-white hair and send his brown cloak into a serene dance. His life aura hovered in a glow that dwarfed her own, though hers was vital and untapped and his still tarnished by the battle. Her mouth closed. Her thoughts drifted to a curiosity and hunger she could not deny. The Dragonrank school had taught her that mages were born with all the life energy they would ever possess, that strength came of honing skills until it took less internal chaos to cast any particular spell. Yet Bolverkr's power beckoned, teased her imagination until she needed to understand. Before she knew it, she had taken a step toward him.

Bolverkr smiled, revealing straight teeth. "Come with

me. I told you before, there's enough for us both, and I'm willing to share."

Silme paused. It seemed so simple to follow, to forget the cares she had just left behind in the clearing. Yet something jarred.

"Come." Bolverkr stretched his hand toward her. "I offer power beyond anything you've known, mastery over wind, wave, and fire, the beauty of nature and her art. Why should one of your potential stay with companions so insignificant their presence or absence takes no accounting on the world's balance?"

Silme listened without trying to formulate a reply. She knew Bolverkr spoke the truth. Only Dragonrank sorcerers and gods wielded enough significance, whether for Law or Chaos, to seriously affect the Balance. Of her companions, only Astryd's demise would require compensation in the guise of equal deaths on the side of Chaos. And, at garnet rank, her life could be easily repaid. Still, Silme realized that, though accurate, Bolverkr's point carried no importance. "I've dedicated my life to protecting the innocent. Their effect on the Balance doesn't matter."

Bolverkr's eyebrows arched, smoothing some of the creases from his features. "Doesn't matter? But of course it matters, Silme. It's nature's way to destroy the weak and see that the strong live on to create a better, more vital and significant world. Food, time, and space are wasted on the weak. The mediocre drag us all under, prevent us from becoming the best we can. Come with me, Silme. We'll make the nine worlds perfect."

Bolverkr's philosophy seemed vaguely familiar to Silme. She followed the memory to its source, the dark-skinned diamond-rank master who had been her half-brother, Bramin. She recalled his wanton destruction and deadly rages, the dragons he called down upon villages on a whim. She remembered the great beasts swooping, gouting fire on innocent townsmen and their cottages, their screams wound through with Bramin's laughter.

Another image filled Silme's mind. She thought of the hovel that had served as her only home for ten years, then, later as a blessed vacation from her training at the Dragon-rank school. But her last vision of the cottage pained. Her mother's broken body sprawled on the floor of the main room, her arms gashed from defending herself from her own son's knife. The corpse of Silme's younger brother dangled, decapitated, from the loft stairs. She had found her sister lifeless in her bed, and even the baby was not spared. Silme discovered her youngest sibling chopped in the cooking pot, as if prepared for some hideous stew. Every one had died at Bramin's hand to fulfill some ghastly, Chaos-inspired vengeance against Silme's interference, as if the dark sorcerer had forgotten this family had once nurtured him as well.

"Go away!" Silme shrank from Bolverkr. "Don't you know what Chaos does to people? It robs them of mercy, of kindness and forgiveness."

Bolverkr dropped his hand. "Chaos brings only vitality and power. You may choose to do as you wish with that power."

Silme shook her head, aware her arguments would prove fruitless. The Chaos had poisoned Bolverkr beyond retrieval. *And my insistence, in the dream, that he surrender is the cause.* "Go away. I'm not interested in what you offer, and my friends never meant you any harm. Can't you just leave us alone?"

Bolverkr's cheeks turned scarlet, and his face lapsed into angry creases. "Your friends destroyed a legacy I spent my life building. They killed my wife and my unborn child, shredded my home, slaughtered every person I loved. That crime can only be paid in blood."

Silme bit her lip.

Bolverkr's patient tenderness vanished. "You, my dear Silme, have a choice. You know I can kill your so-called friends any time I choose. You can come with me, share my love and power, or you can die with them. That, my lady, would be a waste and a pity." Bolverkr turned away. A moment later, his magics crackled through the glade, trailing a wake of gray-white smoke. Bolverkr was gone.

Silme sagged to the ground, feeling spent and queasy, though her aura filled the clearing with a vibrant blue glow. She clutched the fetus to her protectively. Its aura hovered within her, more alert and vigorous than ever before. *It's so real, so alive. I can't let it die.* Yet, Silme knew Bolverkr had spoken the truth. *He could kill us at his leisure. Our only hope lies in my using my magic against Bolverkr. Even*

I'm not powerful enough to stand against him, but if we all work together, it just might be possible. Silme let the thought trail, afraid to contemplate the possibilities and consequences. It had become her way to compute the odds, to determine even her most spontaneous courses of action by the probability of success and the way that harmed the fewest innocents. It had made her suggestions intelligent and reasonable, the kind that others accepted with due seriousness. Now, she felt muddled and confused, not wanting to assess Bolverkr's abilities because it might drag her morale deeper into the quagmire.

One course of action permeated Silme's thoughts. *I could take the Chaos Bolverkr offers, then turn that power against him while it's still renegade and not yet assimilated to me and the baby.* Logic interceded. *I tried that before, and it didn't work. Even infused slowly, the Chaos binds too quickly.* Silme recalled the contact she had created with Bolverkr, her intention then to take just enough Chaos to allow her to transport. But the smallest taste of that renegade power had made her crazy for more. Only her last rebelling spark of morality had allowed her to rechannel that Chaos to her rankstone. Its sheer volume had shattered her sapphire irrevocably, returning the Chaos to Bolverkr. *If I accept his gift of Chaos, it will destroy me. Our only chance is to fight with what we have.* Yet the thought of killing her baby seemed more evil and alien than attempting to tap Bolverkr's Chaos again.

Silme buried her face in her arms. *I can't tell the others about Bolverkr's visit. It would destroy them.* Silme justified her silence by recalling the dark atmosphere of depression that seemed to surround her friends since their defeat. *Nothing bad has come of it, no need for them to know.*

Deep within her, the Chaos that had become Silme's supported the decision.

CHAPTER 5
Chaos Destruction

By foreign hands thy dying eyes were closed,
By foreign hands thy decent limbs composed,
By foreign hands thy humble grave adorned,
By strangers honored, and by strangers mourned!
        —Alexander Pope
            Elegy to the Memory of an Unfortunate Lady

Taziar Medakan threaded through the forest east of Cullinsberg, attuned to the nearly inaudible rustle of woodland
creatures fleeing ahead and the louder sounds of his companions behind him. *They're right, of course. There's no
need or reason to return to Cullinsberg. Ever.* Sorrow
crushed in on him, heavy and densely suffocating. It was
the second time he had run from his home city, a bounty
on his head and grief filling his heart. Yet, before, he had
always harbored a spark of hope that he would return, that
the baron would forget the transgressions of one small thief
for graver matters in the city of Cullinsberg. Now, a bleak
sense of permanency hung over the exodus, like a lead
weight dangling from Taziar's shoulders. It held the dark,
unalterable hopelessness accompanying thoughts of death.
The city of Taziar's birth, loves, hopes, and friendships had
become a city of deaths, imprisonments, and torture. *It's
over.* Taziar's perspective had always been one of begin-
nings, an acceptance of changes and hardships as challenges
to be met with enthusiasm. But the baron's city of Cullinsberg had always remained his single anchoring focus, a place
he knew by rote, a home that had outlasted his family.

Taziar pressed through a stand of pine, pausing to let his
companions catch up. Silme came first, her mouth in a grim
line that revealed thoughts as stormy as his own. Astryd
followed, swept into the lengthy silence. Her shoulders
sagged, she kept her gaze rolled toward the needle-covered

ground, and she carried her garnet-tipped dragonstaff in a
carelessly loose grip. Behind her, Larson stopped, drew the
sword Taziar had given him, and examined the flat and
edges with a scowl that appeared indelibly etched onto his
features. It seemed to Taziar as if the elf would spend the
rest of his life comparing a weapon Taziar had purchased
from a roadside stand to the life-culminating labor of a
Japanese swordsmith.

Guilt flickered through Taziar. *Here I am bemoaning the
loss of a childhood village while my friends need comforting.*
Repeatedly, Taziar's rallying speeches had kindled his
friends to their best efforts, making the impossible seem
merely difficult. But Taziar had played all his cards. His
friends had grown numb to the reminders of past prowess
and successes, and the rout at Bolverkr's castle cast a pall
over every previous accomplishment. This time, even Taziar
did not have the answers. *But I have to do something to
raise my friends' spirits.*

Taziar considered, shoving aside his own sadness and discomfort for the cause of his friends' morale. He kept his
voice cheerful and his tone optimistic. "You'll love Mittlerstadt. It's got the area's finest blacksmith, and the Thirsty
Stallion makes a great meal, not to mention a decent glass
of beer . . ." Taziar turned and pressed onward, threading
through the trees, touting a village he had never visited
with half-truths gleaned from friends or outright lies. His
companions knew he had spent most of his life in Cullinsberg, yet they had no way of knowing he had never left its
walls until after his twenty-first birthday, and then only with
the baron's guardsmen at his heels. Aside from merchants
and messengers, few people left the city's comforts for a
cold, lonely ride through desolate woodlands.

Taziar glanced over his shoulder as he detoured around
a tight grouping of trees with vine-choked lower branches.
". . . the typical friendly hospitality of a farm town. . . ."
Taziar's words seemed to have little effect on his companions. Silme shuffled after him mechanically. Larson had
sheathed the sword in order to facilitate movement through
brush, but he kept his fist clutched to the hilt, as if to
memorize it by feel. The flight of each songbird sent him
skittering into a tense defense. Astryd kept her hands near

her face, hiding her emotions from friends too absorbed with their own concerns to take notice of hers anyway.

The forest grew sparser. Ancient oaks and towering pines gave way to fragile, young locusts and poplars. Gradually, the trees disappeared, replaced by fields of broken, brown stalks and unrecognizable tangles of harvested vines. Taziar quieted, mulling new tactics to bolster confidence. Simple, happy conversation did not seem to be having a noticeable effect. Recently, humor seemed to enrage rather than soothe Silme; yet Taziar considered resorting to gibes and jokes because they seemed to improve Larson's mood, at least. The Climber had finally settled on a direct, confrontational approach when a subtle change in the patterns of the fields drew his attention.

Taziar discarded his current abstraction to study the area for the source of his discomfort. Behind him, the forest loomed. In front of him, the sun hung over lifeless fields, sprinkling golden highlights amid a flatland of brown earth and vegetation. In the distance, the village of Mittlerstadt huddled, a black spot on the horizon. Smoke twined from the town, the narrow stalks of gray diffusing among the clouds. *Cook fires,* Taziar guessed. His gait grew more cautious as he focused on his other senses. Wind ruffled the standing stalks, and Taziar sorted the shuffles of his companions' feet from habit. No other sound met his hearing. He would have expected to have disturbed red deer grazing the few dried grains missed at harvest or for some noises to drift over the open fields from the town, but the relative quiet did not seem significant enough to have caught his notice.

Still, Taziar's sense of alarm grew stronger as he dismissed potential causes, rather than bringing the reassurance he would have expected. He stopped, casting a sideways glance at his companions, not wanting to worry them with vague and nameless concerns. Silme drew up beside him. Astryd remained self-absorbed. Larson walked with stiff caution, eyes slitted and nostrils widened.

Cued by Larson's manner, Taziar sniffed the air, concentrating on the mingled odors that had grown familiar so gradually he had dismissed them. He discovered an acrid tinge too strong for hearths and a stench beneath it that he recognized as the root of his growing discomfort. He turned to face Larson and Astryd. "Do you smell . . . ?" He broke off, not quite certain how to describe it.

"Death," Larson finished. "Yes. What . . . ?"

"Dragon!" Silme screamed.

Taziar whirled. A huge, green-black shape hurtled toward them from the village. Its leathery wings skimmed air, its scaled body rippled gracefully, and its mouth gaped open in a triangular head.

Silme's hand lashed upward. From instinct or concern, she was preparing to cast a spell.

The baby. "Silme, no!" Taziar sprang for Silme. He crashed into her side, dashing breath from her lungs in a frenzied shriek of broken spell words. They toppled in a snarl of limbs. Silme cursed. Something sharp slashed Taziar's cheek. Pain sapped his vision to white spots, and he recoiled, tearing himself away from Silme. Hand clenched to his face, Taziar rolled to a crouch. His sight cleared enough to show him Silme, now standing, with a scarlet-stained utility knife in her fist. Blood trickled between Taziar's fingers.

She cut me. The realization seemed so alien, Taziar could only stare at Silme.

Silme glanced at the blade in her fist as if it belonged to a stranger. Her gaze whipped to Taziar, her expression mingling horror, desperation, and rage.

The exchange lasted only a second. Silme's motivations could wait. For now Taziar turned his attention to the more immediate danger. The dragon hovered in a nearly vertical position, its head reared back and its claws splayed. Another dragon shot toward it, copper-gold in the sunlight.

Two dragons. Fear clutched Taziar. He glanced at Larson who hunched in a perfect battle position, too far beneath the dragons to strike. Astryd knelt among the weeds, her eyes locked on the creatures.

Suddenly, the darker dragon's head lunged forward. Its jaw unhinged, and flame gouted from its mouth. The other dragon twisted, spiraling upward. But the blast caught it full in the chest. It screeched, the sound painful in Taziar's ears. Tongues of the fire struck and bounced groundward. Larson sprang sideways, barely missed by a flame that singed the ground where he had stood. Sparks bounced from scales like armor, raining downward, fiery pinpoints that stung Taziar's skin. Astryd remained still.

Astryd. Understanding struck Taziar, making him feel foolish. *She called the yellow dragon, and she's directing its attack.*

The green-black dragon whipped after the gold. Now above the other, Astryd's creation straightened, then plunged for its foe like a living arrow. But the darker dragon changed its course, ripping to the left, then swerving directly toward Larson. Smoke billowed from its nostrils, followed by a spout of red-orange fire.

"Allerum!" Taziar shouted.

The warning was unnecessary. Larson dove aside. Though spared the main blast, he did not move quickly enough. Cinders hissed against the back of his tunic, igniting to flames. He turned the leap into a wild, lurching roll, snuffing the fire against dirt and dry stems.

The copper-gold dragon plummeted, evening sunlight glazing its wings like molten fire. The dark one banked for another pass, dodging too late. The yellow dragon crashed into its side, digging golden claws into the base of a wing. The force of the attack sent the green-black dragon pitching toward the ground.

Larson leapt to his feet, charging the grounded beast. He slashed with enough force to overbalance himself. His blade sliced the opposite wing like paper.

The dragon screamed. Blood splattered over Larson, Astryd, and Taziar, and the great beast whirled on its attacker. Larson fought to change the direction of his momentum, but his foot mired on a dirt clod.

Weaponless, Taziar sprang for the dragon's head. His hip crashed into a scaled head immobile as granite, but one hand plunged into a moist eye. The beast roared. Its teeth clicked closed on empty air. Larson twisted out of its path.

Astryd's dragon circled, unable to strike against its enemy without endangering Larson and Taziar. Its bulk blotted the sun, thrusting the battle into swirling shadow. Blindly, the green-black dragon snapped at Taziar. Its bite fell short, but the force of the movement sent Taziar stumbling into a scaled shoulder. The great mouth twisted toward him, opened for another blast of fiery breath.

Pinned between the dragon's neck and foot, Taziar scrabbled for a hold on its leg. Blood slicked his fingers. The tips slipped from sticky scales. *It's got me.* Unable to climb, he hurled himself flat to the ground, hoping to avoid some of the flame, braced for pain.

A great shudder racked the beast, pinching Taziar's arm between its foot and shin. Then, the green-black dragon went limp. Its head flopped to the ground with an impact that shook the field. Its mangled wings sank, sending dust devils skittering across the dirt.

Taziar looked up. Larson's sword jutted from the corpse's opposite eye, buried nearly to the hilt. Heaving a relieved sigh, Taziar clambered over its muzzle.

Larson walked around the beast and offered a hand.

Taziar accepted, grasping Larson's wrist and using it to steady his ascent over the blood-wet scales. He dropped lightly to the ground. "Thanks."

Larson chuckled at the irony of being thanked for the simple act of helping Taziar climb, after saving his life went unacknowledged. "Hey, pal, no problem. Any time you need a hand getting off a dead dragon, you just call me, okay?" He studied Taziar, and his smile wilted. Pulling a handkerchief from his pocket, he removed his waterskin and drenched the fabric. Replacing the skin, he dabbed at the gash on Taziar's cheek. "Jesus, how'd you get that?"

Astryd's dragon faded. The world seemed to brighten as evening light gaped through the place where it had hovered.

Taziar turned a glance toward Silme. She stood in the same spot where he had left her, though she no longer clutched her knife. She said nothing.

Taziar knew Silme must have injured him by accident. At the Dragonrank school, she had balanced her repertoire of magic toward defenses against her half-brother's cruelties. One such spell allowed her to destroy dragons. *Apparently, she tried to cast it intuitively. Concerned for us, she forgot the baby. Then I dove on her unexpectedly, and she naturally defended herself.* Not wanting Silme to feel any worse than she already must, Taziar answer vaguely. "Just a war wound I picked up in the fight."

Larson examined the clean, straight cut doubtfully, but he did not challenge Taziar's claim. "Well, here. You hold pressure against it. I'm not your mother." He pressed the dampened cloth to the wound, waiting until Taziar raised his hand before letting go.

As Larson turned, Taziar assessed his companion. The elf's leather vest had absorbed most of the damage from the fire. A gap had burned into the center, the area around it darkly singed, and fingertip-sized holes lay scattered over the fabric of his tunic.

Larson ripped his sword from the dragon, using another handkerchief to clean the steel. "Can't believe I look and smell like I've spent a month in a downtown bar, and I didn't even get a damned cigarette."

Uncertain of Larson's reference, Taziar turned his attention to the sorceresses. Astryd and Silme still seemed tense, casting about near the woods as if searching for something.

Handkerchief still clamped to his cheek, Taziar approached Astryd. "What are you looking for?"

"Bolverkr." Astryd poked the brass-bound base of her staff at a clump of vines.

"What?" Taziar hoped he had misheard.

This time, Silme replied. "Bolverkr. We're watching for Bolverkr. Dragons aren't natural. They have to be created and controlled by sorcerers."

"Shit." Larson wandered over, still polishing the sword. "Are you sure? It doesn't make sense. If Bolverkr's here, what's he waiting for? He's got spells that can kill almost instantly. Why's he mucking around with dragons?"

Silme stiffened. "Come on. We'd better check the town." Whirling toward Mittlerstadt, she ran across the furrowed field.

The others caught up to Silme within a few strides. "What are you thinking?" Larson asked the question on all their minds.

Silme did not slow. "Against four people, especially ones who can fight, a dragon *doesn't* make sense. But against an entire town. . . ." She trailed off, the conclusion of her statement obvious.

Taziar cringed. "You think he may have attacked the townsfolk? But why?"

Larson clung to a previous unanswered question. "And, if Bolverkr's here, why hasn't he tried anything besides the dragon?"

"Why, why, why?" Silme flung back her head, setting her golden hair streaming. "How should I know? Do I look like Bolverkr's adviser to you?" She finished with a gasp,

halting so suddenly, Taziar had to take a side step to keep
from running into her.

Larson spun, and Taziar drew to Silme's side to see what
had upset her. A twisted, male body lay in a pile of charred
weeds, its clothing and much of its flesh seared away. Insects crawled over the remains.

Taziar's stomach lurched, and he turned away.

Astryd pointed toward the town. "Look!"

Glad of another place to turn his attention, Taziar
glanced in the indicated direction. Heat haze shimmered
around the dark hulk of Mittlerstadt. Taziar could now see
that the trails of smoke came not from hearth fires, but
from random locations around the streets. The cottages appeared as broken as the newfound corpse. "Oh, no."

Shivers racked Taziar, and fear froze him. Concerned for
what he might find, his mind conjured a thousand excuses
to avoid the town of Mittlerstadt. But he also knew he
might find injured survivors needing aid.

Larson and Silme seemed unperturbed. Grabbing the
corpse by its hands and feet, they hefted it and set it gently
and neatly on the open ground. Familiar with Taziar's discomfort with killing and death, Larson pointed at the field.
"Shadow, why don't you start digging and watch for Bolverkr.
Silme and I can check for survivors and gather bodies for
burial. Astryd, you see if you can find supplies in the town."
Larson turned back to Taziar and offered the sword, hilt first.
"If Bolverkr shows up, you'll need this. I'll get another."

Taziar accepted the sword reluctantly, aware Larson
could find another weapon, though it would take some time
and diligent searching. Farmers rarely had need of blades
longer than a utility knife, and the ones who owned swords
were usually veterans mustered by Cullinsberg's baron for
the old Barbarian Wars. Guilt descended on Taziar at the
thought that his friends would protect him from having to
see the corpses, then send Astryd into the thick of the
town. But, before he could protest, Astryd trotted off, followed by Silme and Larson. *It's probably for the best anyway. I'd rather I met Bolverkr alone than that Astryd did.*

Using the tip of his sword as a shovel, Taziar set to work.

Night descended over the gutted town of Mittlerstadt,
plunging the world into new moon darkness. Unable to sleep,

Silme chose first watch, lost in the arrhythmic harmony of insects as she sat guard over her sprawled companions. Silme recalled the havoc her half-brother had wreaked across the towns of Norway, the trail of slaughter she had followed, the cries and pleas of the villagers, the skewed Dragonrank education she had chosen in order to balance Bramin's malice. *It begins again.* Yet Silme saw other things this time. Bolverkr's destruction seemed far more directed and thorough. He had not left a single survivor in the town of Mittlerstadt nor a bite of food or drop of water for Silme and her companions to find. He had even diverted the primitive sewage system directly into the river that supplied the town.

Silme's mind reconjured the images of corpses heaped in shallow graves and Taziar's hurried, mass eulogies. The Shadow Climber had cried unabashedly. Later, Astryd and Larson had joined his laments. But Silme had not shed a tear. She had seen innocents die too many times to mourn the loss of a few more strangers. And, this time, the sight of the scattered, half-charred corpses had raised emotions she'd never recognized before. She found a rhythm and beauty to nature's completed cycle: birth, life, and death. She saw artistry in the shattered and crumbled randomness of the city and its ghosts. The baby's life aura flickered within her, alternately invader and miracle.

Distantly, light sparked through the trees, a brilliant blast of triggered magics. A fox sprang to vivid relief. Caught suddenly in light, it froze, then twined back into gathered shadow.

Bolverkr's magic. Anger seethed through Silme, faded to concern, then died. She glanced at her companions. Larson slept tensely, curled like a fetus around his sword. Taziar lay on his back. Astryd sprawled nearby, her hand outflung near her dragonstaff and her head cradled on Taziar's thigh.

Silme looked back toward the light. It had withered to a fuzzy glow through branches. *This is a charade. My watch means nothing. Bolverkr could transport right next to us and kill at least one of us before the others came fully awake.* She rose, aware Bolverkr could have only one reason for making his presence known without attacking. *He wants to talk. And talking may be the only way to end this feud without more bloodshed.*

Silme craned her neck, staring at her sleeping companions over one shoulder. Her conscience nudged her to

awaken at least one, and deep down, she knew it was reckless to leave them unguarded. But another thought rose to
smother the first. *No scavenger will harm them with so
many corpses so shallowly buried. Our only enemy is Bolverkr, and I'll be watching him directly. They're tired and
hungry. Better to let them sleep.* Again, Silme turned her
attention on the hovering gleam visible beyond the forest's
trunks. Without further debate, she slipped from the field
and into the woodlands.

Bolverkr met Silme just beyond hearing range of her
companions. He wore a shirt and breeches of matching tailored silk, black trimmed with blue. An azure cape, draped
majestically over his narrow shoulders. Neatly combed,
white hair fell to his collar. He looked more like a politician
or a prince than a sorcerer hell-bent on bloody vengeance,
and the tender glance he gave Silme completed the picture.
"Hello," he said, with the bland affection of a friend seen
only the previous day.

Silme frowned, not bothering to return the greeting.

"You've decided to join me?" Bolverkr did not wait for
an answer to his question. He took a step toward her,
reaching for the satin gold waves of her hair. "A wise
choice. One you won't regret."

Silme sidled, avoiding Bolverkr's touch. "I came to talk."
She added carefully in a voice designed to make her point
clear without inciting, "Only to talk."

Bolverkr lowered his hand with a resigned shrug. "Very
well. Talk." He leaned against a gnarled pine, watching
Silme expectantly.

Having anticipated that Bolverkr would begin the conversation, Silme felt unprepared. She rose to the occasion,
keeping accusation from her tone. "The dragon we met
outside the town. . . ." Silme paused to consider her
wording.

Bolverkr smiled. "Pretty, wasn't he?"

Silme's hand curled at her side, a habit acquired when
she used to carry a dragonstaff. Since her sapphire rankstone had exploded, she could no longer store spell energy
and saw no reason to lug the container around. "So, I can,
in fact, presume *you* sent the dragon after us."

"Do you know of any other Dragonrank mages this far
south?" Bolverkr's pale eyes sparkled, and the grin remained.

"Actually, though, I sent the creature after the village. You and the others arrived conveniently." He added quickly. "Though, of course, I kept it from hurting you."

"So you were there controlling it?" Though it seemed obvious, Silme asked anyway. Summonings had never become a part of her repertoire, but she knew from learning defenses against dragons that, once called, a dragon could be given a single command, such as to attack a specific individual, group, or village.

"Yes," Bolverkr admitted freely. "I was there."

Silme plucked at a fold in her dress. She met Bolverkr's gaze directly, gray eyes glaring into blue. "But when we killed your dragon, you didn't attack."

"Ah." Bolverkr chuckled, folding his arms across his chest. "So you noticed my gift to you."

"Gift?"

Bolverkr pushed off the pine trunk, straightening. "Freyr and the Fates threw you together with a group of fools, and your wonderful sense of loyalty makes you believe you need to protect them for eternity." He shrugged, his rugged, timeless face betraying no emotion.

A fox call whirred through the night, answered by a distant bark, like an echo.

Bolverkr continued, "No matter that these companions consist of an overprotected sorceress of insignificant level, a thief, and a crazed anachronism who, by all natural right, should be dead." Bolverkr crinkled his nose in disgust. "An elf, too. A magical creation of less consequence than the dragons you've killed as beasts."

"I love Allerum," Silme blurted. "And I care about my friends." Her words came without need for thought.

"Why?"

The question caught Silme off her guard. "What?"

"Why do you love Allerum? Why do you care about your friends?"

"I—" Silme considered. "I don't need a reason to love my husband or my friends."

"True." A puff of wind lifted Bolverkr's cloak, revealing silks that clearly outlined a slender but well-proportioned body. "But blind loyalty only works for lemmings. I would never fault anyone for dedicating himself to a cause he believes in. On the other hand, to devote your life and sacrifice a chance at happiness and total power for a love you can't justify is stupid and wasteful."

"Just because I can't justify my love to you doesn't mean it doesn't exist."

"Agreed," Bolverkr conceded. "But you should be able to justify it to yourself. When's the last time you took stock of your feelings? Do you really love these inferiors, or are you just reacting out of habit? Look deep inside yourself, Silme. I think your heart might tell you something different than your mind."

"I think not." Silme tried to redirect the conversation, but Bolverkr interrupted.

"How else can you explain knifing Taziar?"

Silme gasped, not wanting to be reminded of her blunder. She tried to believe she had reacted out of desperation, using the tenets gleaned from her travels with Kensei Gaelinar. Yet she could not forget the rage that had flashed through her at Taziar's interference. She could not escape the memory of a warm glow of self-righteous justice when the blade had struck home, though guilt had followed on its heels. "An accident," she grumbled vaguely. "A stupid accident."

Bolverkr smiled again, in amusement. He did not have to say that the process of drawing a knife and cutting a friend was too complicated and deliberate to pass for accident. It was obvious. "Do as you will. In time, you'll realize what your heart already knows. The irrelevant companions you call friends have become an annoyance."

Silme folded her arms, stung to irritation. Recently, everyone and everything seemed to have become an annoyance, and she did feel as if she needed to sequence her priorities. Normally, the ability came naturally. Now, her wits constantly seemed in a scramble. Compulsive action had replaced her usually thoughtful, ordered plans.

Bolverkr's manner softened. "When that time comes, remember a sorcerer loves you and wants to share his power and his life with you. I'll be there." His voice faded to silence beneath the insect chorus. The fox calls became cyclical, the nearer more distant and the farther closer as the creatures sought one another in the darkness.

Bolverkr's sincerity touched Silme. Trying to read his deeper intentions, she met his gaze. Candor radiated from his eyes and expression, mature emotions that went far beyond Larson's adolescent passion. Her thoughts unwound like those of a stranger, detailing a life with Bolverkr and the Chaos he offered. Logic showed her a man of great consequence, powerfully tender as well as savagely vengeful. She knew he could understand her devotion to the highest causes and her frustration at having the same townsfolk she had rescued from Bramin's magic make signs of warding evil when they realized she was Dragonrank as well. He could teach her about things she never knew existed: the earliest years of the Dragonrank mages, spells her dedication to defense had forced her to forsake, the creation of gods and elves. And he could give her the power to practice them without draining out her life energy.

Silme's life aura gleamed, brighter than she ever remembered it in the past. Unaware of Bolverkr's methodical Chaos-transfer, she attributed its brilliance to the baby's linked aura and having gone longer than ever before without tapping life force. Still, beside Bolverkr's fiery glory, her aura was dwarfed like a lantern in sunlight. For a moment, Bolverkr's vast potential and the inherent common sense of their coupling took precedence over raw emotion. Then an image of Larson seeped into her thoughts, his angular features strangely handsome, his fragile frame and delicately-pointed ears belying a human mind weighted with morality and none of the elves' capriciousness. Yet, somehow, the virtues Silme had embraced since childhood seemed distant and insignificant, their importance erased by experience and time.

I love Allerum. Silme did not allow her thoughts to stray, grounding her reason on the single fact. To contemplate too long might throw her into a frenzy of ideas she did not understand. "Go away." Her words emerged softly and with too little punch to convince even herself of their sincerity.

Still, Bolverkr honored her request. Light cracked open the hovering darkness of moonless night, and the sorcerer disappeared, leaving a trailing pulse of oily smoke.

The forest seemed to close in on Silme. Suddenly wholly alone, battered from without and within, she began to cry.

CHAPTER 6
Chaos' Massacre

Religion, blushing veils her sacred fires,
And unawares Morality expires
Nor public flame, nor private, dares to shine;
Nor human spark is left, nor glimpse divine!
Lo! thy dread empire Chaos! is restored:
Light dies before thy uncreating word;
Thy hand, great Anarch! lets the curtain fall,
And universal darkness buries all.
>   —Alexander Pope
>   *Thoughts on Various Subjects*

A gentle shake awakened Al Larson. He tensed, eyes flicking open to Astryd's tiny face and china doll features. Beyond her, darkness blurred the forest to hulking bands of black and gray. Silme curled some distance away. Larson could not see Taziar. Presumably, the Shadow Climber lay behind him.

My turn on watch. The constant click of insects and the bantered calls of foxes waxed from dismissed subconscious to wakeful background. Larson yawned, stretching to work the cramps from his muscles. He mouthed the word "thanks," not wanting to awaken Silme and Taziar by speaking aloud. Silme always slept on the barest edge of awakening, and Taziar rested nearly as lightly.

Astryd shook her head. She gestured at Larson and herself, then pointed behind him into the woods.

Larson stiffened. His hand tightened on the sword hilt. Slowly he turned, seeing only a broad stretch of shadowed woodland. Taziar was nowhere in sight. "Where?" Larson started.

Astryd's fingers gouged Larson's arm in warning.

Breaking off, Larson turned back to Astryd, not understanding.

Astryd made a grabbing motion in front of her lips, a plea for silence. Again, she pointed deeper into the forest. Curving her fingers so the tips touched her thumb, she placed the hand by her mouth. Opening and closing her fingers rapidly, she simulated lips and the need to talk. Though crisp, her gestures lacked the urgency that would have cued Larson to danger.

Assuming Astryd wanted to converse in private, Larson nodded his understanding. He inclined his head toward Silme.

Astryd shook her head.

Larson bit his lip. The idea of leaving Silme asleep and alone pained him. He whispered, "We can't—"

Astryd clamped a hand to Larson's mouth, shaking her head more vigorously. She waited until he quieted before removing her hand.

Silme did not stir. The patterns of her breathing remained the same.

Turning, Astryd headed off into the forest, crooking a finger over her shoulder for Larson to follow.

Against his better judgment, Al Larson trailed Astryd through autumn-brown undergrowth encased in crumbled leaves. They veered between pine and around copses, ducking beneath a fallen, rotting trunk whose upper end had wedged against a neighbor. Slipping between a pair of narrow hickories, Larson discovered Taziar standing with his foot braced on a deadfall. Astryd sat on the downed trunk.

Larson crouched, his back against a towering oak, awaiting an explanation.

"I'm sorry to call you away in such a strange way." Astryd scuffed at a pile of pine needles. "I didn't want to wake Silme."

Larson frowned, acutely aware that they had not only not awakened Silme, but they had left her unprotected.

Astryd went straight to the point. "There's something wrong with Silme."

Freshly awakened from sleep and immediately reminded of his troubles, Larson did not try to hide his annoyance. "What cued you in? Her griping at Shadow or her suggesting I go back to hell?"

Astryd seemed to take no notice of Larson's sarcasm. "Neither." She looked up. "And both, I suppose. Do you remember how I linked my magic with Silme's so she could tap my life energy to transport without risking the baby?''

Larson nodded. At the time, he had lain unconscious and inches from death, but he saw no need for a detailed description of the process. "What of it?"

"It's a dangerous link, and not well understood. I think there's some . . . well . . . residual.''

Taziar leaned forward, watching Astryd curiously. "What do you mean by residual?''

"It's hard to explain." Astryd kicked needles from one boot to the other. "It's as if there's an invisible, intangible thread tying her aura to mine. Every so often, a trickle of emotion slips through the contact.''

Larson blinked, gathering his thoughts. Magic made little enough sense without complicating it with links and contacts. "So you can read her mind? And you see something bad?''

"No. That's not it at all." Astryd fidgeted, apparently having difficulty finding the words needed to describe a process she did not fully understand herself. "I'm not getting thoughts, just occasional glimpses of emotion. And I'm not trying to read them, either. They just sort of, well, slip through now and again." She sighed heavily, aware she still had not clarified the issue well enough. "I've tried tracing the thread to Silme by using a gentle probe. But she snapped closed the contact so violently, it hurt." Astryd winced at the memory. "Maybe she thought I was Bolverkr.''

Taziar stepped behind Astryd and massaged her shoulders through the heavy fabric of her dress. "Don't you think you should discuss this with Silme?''

Astryd nodded, still looking at Larson. "I will. I just haven't had a chance. Her mood . . .'' She trailed off. "Her mood is why I wanted to talk with the two of you first.''

Larson raised his brows encouragingly.

"This may sound stupid." Astryd spoke slowly, as if considering each word. "But she seems to feel as if she's being invaded. From within.''

Larson froze, the expression sounding familiar in his ears. Then, finding the proper memory, he laughed. "You've never been pregnant, have you, Astryd?''

Taziar's fingers stilled on Astryd's shoulders.

"No," Astryd confessed. She regarded Larson more directly. "And I'd venture to guess you haven't either."

Taziar smiled.

Larson conceded the point. "Do you have younger brothers and sisters?"

"Older," Astryd admitted. "I'm the baby. Why?"

"I just remember when my mother was pregnant with my little brother. She used to call him 'that little alien in my stomach' and talk about how he danced on her bladder and sucked up artichokes." Remote images of his mother standing before the kitchen window warmed Larson's memory, sparking others. The details of his parents' Bronx home seemed faded, another man's life. Nearby, cranes banged and huffed, building city blocks of skyscrapers that would be called Co-op City. He remembered sneaking out at night with his best friend, Tom Jeffers, to clamber over the machinery and skeletal frames, while his brother collected sugar packets and near-empty paste tubes that the work crews had left behind.

Bitterness tinged the memory. Jeffers had died in Vietnam even before Larson had enlisted. Not wanting to contemplate his friend's death, Larson tore himself from reminiscing just in time to hear Astryd's question.

"Artichokes?"

Jarred back to the conversation, Larson nodded. "My mother craved artichokes, white chocolate, and kosher dills all through the pregnancy. And she never used to like pickles."

Astryd swiveled her gaze toward Taziar, and they both shrugged in ignorance.

Larson got to the point. "I'm just saying pregnant women do feel like there's an invader inside." He recalled his mother's temper flaring at the slightest provocation and his father cutting dinner table arguments short with a humble, "yes, dear." "And some of them get snappy and irritable, too. It's hormones." Now, Larson felt pleased Astryd had drawn him away to talk. It gave a name and explanation to Silme's raw-tempered, uncharacteristic behavior.

Several moments passed in silence before Larson noticed Astryd and Taziar were staring at him, apparently awaiting an explanation. He addressed the Shadow Climber. "You were a youngest child, too?"

"*Only* child." Taziar resumed his massage. "I've seen enough women with child to know some do act strangely. But what, exactly, is a hormone?"

The question reminded Larson of an ancient gag: "How do you make a hormone? Don't pay her." Having spent weeks recovering in Shylar's whorehouse, Larson found the joke appropriate, wishing the pun would translate into Old Scandinavian. *If it did, I could technically be the first person to ever tell it.* "Hormones are chemicals the body makes." He searched for a comparison his companions might understand. "It's like the excitement you have long after you've finished doing something stupid." Staring at Taziar, he smiled, "I mean, something *dangerous.*"

"That's funny," Taziar said, though he did not smile.

"Anyway," Larson finished, "this hormone floats around in your blood, making you feel good. Pregnancy hormones make women weepy and testy."

"That doesn't seem fair," Astryd said.

Larson shrugged, not fully certain he had his facts correct, but aware it did not matter. "It evens out. Women make adrenaline, too. And men get violent and flaky around too much male hormones. They just don't get pregnant."

Taziar fingered his cut cheek.

Astryd nodded. Her tension faded, and she seemed satisfied with Larson's explanation of Silme's behavior. "Imagine how she must feel. All this hormony stuff poisoning her blood. Then she's got the baby to worry about. And every time we run into Bolverkr, she has to decide between killing her child and possibly letting her friends die." Astryd winced. "Oh, poor Silme."

Larson frowned, concerned with pressures of his own. The battle at Bolverkr's keep had left him feeling helpless and trivial, a man exposed to a thousand years of science yet unable to stand against a single, primitive man. *Gaelinar gave me his sword, the vehicle of his soul, because he believed I would take care of it. I failed him. I failed myself. And, now, my failure will kill my wife and child as well as my friends.* The image of Bolverkr collapsing, half-cleaved, to the ramparts filled Larson's memory. He swore. *I should never have turned my back on an enemy until I knew he was dead.* For now, Larson conveniently forgot that he had seen heart and lungs through a wound no man could have survived longer than a few seconds. *I can't believe I didn't lop off his head while I had the chance. That mistake may cost all our lives.*

Astryd rose. "We need to let Silme know without doubt that we want her to save the baby over any of us. We need to rescue her from the choice."

Taziar took Astryd's hand, his gaze on Larson. "Good idea, but I think the approach is wrong. No matter what we say, Silme will put our lives before the unborn baby's. Our protests to the contrary would only make our sacrifice seem more noble; it would look as if we were more dedicated to her than she to us."

Taziar's words confused Larson. Not wanting to sit through the justification again, he pressed for the solution. "What do you think we should do?"

An updraft whipped through the pines, dropping a shower of needles onto Taziar and Astryd. Absently, Taziar brushed needles from Astryd's hair. "We need to show Silme some confidence, to make her truly believe we're capable of handling Bolverkr."

Larson snorted.

Taziar raised his hand. "Let me finish."

Larson nodded grudgingly.

"If Silme thinks we can kill Bolverkr, she can stop worrying about us and focus on the baby. If one of us is slain then, it will seem like an error in logic. She'll have misjudged our competence rather than made a conscious choice to save the baby and let us die."

Astryd shivered.

Larson had become accustomed to discussing his own death. Taziar seemed to speak of it openly enough, but Larson did not feel certain the Shadow Climber had fully considered the implications of his words. Astryd seemed all too aware of her mortality, enough to make her unpredictable in combat. Inwardly, Larson groaned. *We're facing the most dangerous enemy in the world, and our army consists of an incompetent twentieth-century soldier, a witch in a hormonal storm, a midget adrenaline addict with few combat skills, and a sorceress' apprentice.* Despair winched tighter. "You know, there is something else to consider."

Apparently cued by an atypical soberness in Larson's tone, Astryd and Taziar regarded their companion intently.

"It's one thing for me to decide my baby takes precedence over my life. It's another for my friends to make the same sacrifice. Neither Silme nor I expect either of you to put the baby's life over your own. That would be unreasonable." Larson considered the situation from another perspective. "Given a choice between rescuing Silme or the baby, I'd have to save Silme. I can hardly blame either of you for making the same decision about the one you love."

Taziar neatly skirted the issue. "No one has to die."

Larson heaved a sigh. Taziar's eternal optimism in the face of hopeless odds had become familiar and annoying. "And the world's oceans could dry up in seconds, leaving us an endless supply of fish. Bolverkr's not going to quit until he or we are dead."

Taziar shook his head, tossing the needles from his hair and sending the sliding comma into his eyes. "I know you're the soldier, and I'm just street scum." He used an English insult Larson had once hurled in anger. "So correct me if I say something wrong." He combed black strands into place with his fingers. "It seems to me that in battle there's rarely a clear-cut choice between one companion's life and another's. You attack the enemy and assist whoever needs help at the moment. I'm not planning to let Bolverkr place me in a situation where I have to choose between helping Astryd rather than Silme, or the baby rather than you. If it happens, there's likely to be too many extenuating circumstances for me to have made the decision in advance anyway."

The simple logic of Taziar's statement struck Larson dumb. *He's absolutely right, and I should have thought of it first.* Despondency had colored his thoughts until they seemed a hopeless blur. *Bolverkr's got me shaken. I'm not thinking clearly.*

Astryd scratched a pine needle free of her collar. "Silme might still have to make the decision to use magic to rescue one of us. For her, that's a likely and constant dilemma."

Taziar turned the conversation full circle. "Which is why we have to reassure and remind her of our competence. If she killed the baby out of necessity, to save one or all of us, it would be sad. If she killed the baby needlessly, out of doubt over our abilities, it would be a senseless tragedy."

Now Taziar's explanation became perfectly obvious to Larson. "Agreed. And as long as we're gathered here, we've got another problem to discuss."

"Food," Astryd guessed.

Al Larson winced. He had hoped he would turn out to be the only one who had carried less than a day's provisions to Bolverkr's keep. "I figured that, if we survived the fight, we'd go back to Cullinsberg to get Silme, and we'd have a chance to pack rations then. I didn't expect her to follow us."

Taziar bobbed his head in understanding. "And why weigh ourselves down with gear when we had wards to avoid and a battle to win? I brought nothing but weapons and a change of clothes. Had to share Astryd's dinner tonight. At worst, I figured we'd buy food in Mittlerstadt."

"Shit." Larson's head began a dull, painful throb. "It's too cold for berries, and there's not a bow between us." He glanced at the sorceress. "Wait a second. Astryd, you've got to be able to make food or zap little animals or something."

"Make food?" Astryd stared, eyes wide with incredulity. "Dragonrank mages haven't been able to make objects out of nothing since they started tapping internal chaos sources. That was long before my birth."

Larson clamped the heel of one hand to his temple, trying to think through the headache. "For God's sake! You can make dragons out of nothing."

Astryd snorted in exasperation. "I've told you before. Dragons are the natural, material form of Chaos. All I have to do is summon a dragon is release some life energy. The hard part is controlling it."

"Damn it!" Frustration and pain made Larson curt. Suddenly, every wound he had taken seemed to spring to the forefront of his attention simultaneously. The burn from Bolverkr's ward stung. The impact of the sorcerer's spell had left a pounding bruise across Larson's chest, and his shoulder ached. "What about magical hunting?"

Astryd shook her head sadly. "If I could cast slaying spells, do you think Bolverkr would still be alive? I paralyzed someone once. It just about drained out my life energy, and that would kill me. At the least, I'd be unconscious and no use against Bolverkr. It's not worth the price for one rabbit.''

Larson threw up his hands in frustration, and the abrupt gesture sparked pain through his injured shoulder. "Shit!" he cried again, this time in agony. "What the hell good is it to have a sorceress who can't cast spells?"

Taziar cut in. "Allerum, back off. She knows what she's doing, and she's doing it the best she can. Don't blame Astryd for the laws of magic."

Astryd closed her eyes but not quickly enough to hide the brimming tears.

Taziar caught Astryd to him, stroking her hair, her face buried in his tough, linen climbing skirt.

Remorse assailed Larson, compounding his irritation. "Look, I'm sorry," he apologized with inappropriate gruffness. "I'm just frustrated and upset. I didn't mean to take it out on Astryd."

Astryd's back quivered.

Despite its seeming insincerity, Taziar accepted Larson's explanation. "We're all on edge. But finding food is no big deal. There's another town about two days' travel from here. I've got money."

"I'm sorry," Larson repeated, this time managing to soften his tone a bit. He knew he was acting viciously toward friends he had come to love like family. Al Larson realized the pressure had touched them all in ways it never had before. Despite her relative inexperience, Astryd had always proven strong and capable under fire; her crying seemed incongruous. Silme had turned into a creature Larson would just as soon avoid. Even Taziar, usually the honey-tongued arbitrator, had snapped at Larson's verbal attack on Astryd, compounding the offense. *Not that I blame him. It's just not like him.*

Larson bit his lip, aware this situation with Bolverkr went beyond any previous challenge. Always before, hope, enthusiasm, and need had brought him through impossible tasks. And always before in the direst circumstances, he had clung to the knowledge that he was dead in Vietnam by all rights, that the time he had in Old Norway was borrowed. Now he had a wife and child to live for, friends whose company he wanted to enjoy for years to come. Yet Bolverkr chose his strategies well, destroying his enemies from within as well as without. All the wounds Larson had suffered seemed minimal, lost beneath a suffocating blanket of grief, fear, and impotent rage. *How can I fight an enemy I can't see, one who can pop in with deadly guerrilla tactics, then disappear before I can strike? How can I protect my wife, child, and friends against a sorcerer of nearly unlimited power? How can I hope to kill a man who can heal lethal wounds?*

Larson whirled, slamming his fist into an oak. The blow ached through his fingers, but he ignored the pain, pounding again and again until the bark scraped skin from his knuckles and he left bloody prints on the trunk. Turning, he headed back toward Silme, not bothering to see if his companions followed.

That morning, clouds pulsed a gray curtain across the sky. Once in place, they remained unmoving in a windless sky, as if they had come to stay forever. The trees formed black skeletons against the vast grayness of the heavens, their leaves and smaller branches fanning into an intertwining network.

Al Larson stared through the branches. His thoughts seemed as drab as the sky. The last of his rations sat like lead in his stomach, and he wished he had saved the food for a time when hunger might have made him less conscious of the stale rubberiness of the cheese. The meal had passed in silence. As they strapped on their packs and prepared to travel toward the nearest city, the only sound came from droplets pattering on colored clusters of leaves and needles. The rain seemed to have driven even the birds and insects to seek shelter.

As the day progressed, the rain pitched harder. Droplets slanted between gaps in the foliage, striking in icy pinpoints through Larson's tunic and breeks. His elf form made him impervious to cold, but the dampness and ceaseless rattle and ooze irritated him to a scowling quiet that warned his friends to let him keep his own company. Finally, fully soaked, Larson no longer cared about the rain. Then, as if on cue, it dropped to a trickle and the wind rose, cutting like daggers beneath his cloak. Concerned for Silme, Larson paused beneath a shielding tangle of branches, opening his pack to offer dry clothing.

At that moment, the clouds heaved rain with redoubled fury. Above Larson, a basket of leaves succumbed to the assault, spewing a gallon of stored water onto Larson's head. Water sloshed into his opened pack. Drenched, along with everything he owned, Larson swore until his voice cracked, then accidentally inhaled saliva and lapsed into a fit of coughing.

Larson caught his breath, glaring at his companions, daring any of them to laugh. But Silme had pressed ahead, apparently too preoccupied with her own worries to bother with Larson's. Astryd waited politely but did not make a move to help. Only Taziar thought to address the obvious concern. As Larson's last cough subsided, Taziar asked with sincere interest, "Can I help? Are you well?"

"Just . . ." Larson took a rattling gasp. ". . . fucking fine." Without bothering to check to see if any of his gear had escaped the soaking, he lashed the pack closed violently and headed after Silme.

Dark, rainy day became dark, rainy night. Images of Bolverkr chased Larson through his nightmares. Repeatedly, he awakened with his muscles so rigid they ached, and it took every relaxation technique he knew to settle back into restless, dream-haunted sleep. He spent his watch stiffly waiting, hearing enemies approaching in the rustle of the leaves and the constant pounding of the rain.

The storm continued into the next day and still showed no sign of abating. No one mentioned food. They all just hefted packs and headed deeper into the woodlands, brushing through branches that showered the next person in line. For a time, Taziar whistled a tune to the rhythm of the rain, but the condemning scowls of his companions silenced even the little Climber. Larson's belly felt pinched and empty. Hoping to forget the pain, he drew up beside Silme and gave her a heartfelt and encouraging squeeze.

Silme caught Larson by the wrist. Spinning, she hurled his arm away. "I'm tired enough. Don't hang on me."

Stung by Silme's rebuff, Larson opened his mouth to protest. Then, recalling the decision to humor Silme, he lowered his head. "I'm sorry." As hard as he tried, he was unable to keep a twinge of defensiveness from entering his voice.

Silme did not seem to notice. She whirled with an aloof briskness that sent her hair whipping into Larson's face, then stomped off toward a break in the foliage.

Grumbling epithets about women and hormones, Larson followed. A hand clasped his shoulder.

Alert to the edge of paranoia, Larson spun, crouching, his sword half free before he identified the touch as Taziar's.

Taziar leapt backward, a look of surprise on his face and his hands hovering before him in a gesture of surrender.

Larson sheathed the sword. "Sorry. I'm a bit tense."

Taziar smiled, the expression misplaced in the gloom of the forest. "A bit tense?" He laughed. "A bit tense would be the fabric of Astryd's dress with a tall, fat man stuffed into it. You would qualify as a . . ." He borrowed an English idiom. ". . . coiled spring." He dropped to a rigid hunch, imitating Larson's startled defense.

Larson chuckled, the noise sounding eerily out of place in the crushing grayness and lingering silence. The need for a snappy comeback cracked the tension. "Yeah, well, you moved pretty quick yourself." He flexed to copy Taziar's harried retreat.

But before Larson could move, Silme reappeared through the brush. Her eyes were slitted and shadowed beneath drawn brows. Larson had seen that expression only once, on the face of a Cullinsbergen guardsman just before he and his companions had pounded Larson to oblivion.

"Don't start with the jokes," Silme's tone precluded argument. "This isn't the time or place, and I'm not in the mood. Now, Shadow, there's a road up ahead. You're the only one who knows the way. Will it take us to a town?"

Taziar darted past Larson, delivering a painless kick to the elf's shin as he passed.

Aware Taziar moved too gracefully for the kick to have been an accident, Larson made a playful grab for his companion. *You bastard.* His lunge fell short, but not far enough to escape Silme's notice.

Silme glared at the antics. Saying nothing, she stomped after Taziar.

Larson trailed them both. Taziar's banter had lifted the veil of depression briefly, but Silme's condemnation slammed it back into place. He could not recall pregnancy affecting his mother so early or so severely, though he had only been a child at the time. *And Mom didn't have death, Chaos, and starvation stalking her across the continent.* Still, one thing seemed clear. *I can't take seven months of this.*

A short brush through the foliage brought Larson to the packed earth pathway Silme had called a road. Exposed to two straight days of rain, the trail should have mired to mud. But the ground only looked damp, packed to stony hardness by years of foot, horse, and cart traffic. He was about to remark on his unusual finding when Taziar spoke, interrupting Larson's train of thought.

"This is the way," Taziar said with exaggerated enthusiasm.

Larson snorted, fairly sure Taziar had no more idea where he was going than anyone else. It only made sense that a well-traveled road would lead to civilization, and if Taziar knew the route, Larson doubted Silme would have needed to stumble upon the pathway. Larson kept these thoughts to himself, aware Taziar was doing his best to lift their spirits, a noble cause that Larson had already dismissed as hopeless. They all headed in the indicated direction. *Eastward,* Larson guessed, though two days without sun or starlight made navigation uncertain.

Taziar, Astryd, and Silme walked near the forested edges of the pathway, partially protected by an umbrella of interwoven branches. Already sodden and oblivious to cold, Larson varied his position, feeling most secure when slinking through the shadows of the trunks. As his companions again sank into the quagmire of their own personal contemplations, Larson fell prey to an oppressive paranoia. He saw flashes of Bolverkr behind every tree, heard the sorcerer's footfalls between the patter of each raindrop, and nearly attacked a deer when it fled into his path, apparently spooked from sleep by something ahead. His sword wound up in his hand so often, he took to carrying it unsheathed. Oddities seized his attention. Though the rain never slackened, the roadway did not seem to absorb the water. Each new step brought Larson over earth scarcely damp, as if they traveled always in the rain's leading edge, as the storm never passed them, and they seemed unable to move ahead of it.

Over time, the trees again thinned to first growth. Ropy

brown vines and berryless copses strung between the trunks. Larson hacked through the brush with more force than necessary, gaining a perverse satisfaction from the slivers flying around his blade. Channeling his frustration into action felt good, easing cramps from his muscles and diverting tension from an unconscious tooth grinding that left his jaw aching.

Suddenly, Astryd screamed. "Look out! Look out! Look out!" Each repetition emerged at a higher pitch.

Confused by the vagueness of her warning, Larson dove forward and down. Astryd's shoulder crashed into his side, knocking him askew. He rolled to his feet awkwardly, sword readied, scanning the woodlands for danger like a cornered animal. "What is it? Where?"

Rising to one knee, Astryd pointed directly to the place Larson had nearly cleared.

Larson followed the direction of her finger, seeing nothing out of the ordinary.

"Spell," Astryd explained.

Clued, Larson stared beyond the spot. He could make out a colored pattern of interlocking glitters, silvered with clinging raindrops. "Bolverkr's?" The answer seemed so obvious as to make the question stupid. Larson did not await a reply before asking, "But how could he know I'd step right there?" He inclined his head toward the ward.

"Hmmm." Taziar scratched his head in a gesture mocking deep thought. "How could Bolverkr know we'd take the natural extension of a road to the village. Hmmm." He looked up suddenly. "Maybe he read your—" He broke off abruptly, though not quickly enough to keep anyone from mentally finishing his sentence with the word "mind." "I didn't mean . . ." he started.

Larson waved Taziar silent, understanding that the Climber had intended his words as a joke, not to remind Larson of his inadequacy. Still, Larson could not keep bleak frustration from accompanying the thought. "You may think he's psychic. But I think he's fucking psycho."

"Bolverkr didn't need to know where you'd be walking. Look around." Astryd waved in a semicircle around the boundary where the woodland path met farm fields.

Larson examined the area from the corner of his eye. Now, he could discern several glints of magic in a random arrangement. Hunger goaded him to wonder why no forest animals had fallen prey to the trap. *More likely, Bolverkr cleared the bodies hoping we'd starve.*

"Look!" Taziar jabbed a finger toward the center of the field.

Larson obeyed. At the distant border of his vision, red and orange flickered through the dullness, and smoke wreathed upward. "The village?"

Astryd made a pained noise. "Thor! Not again."

As one, they sprinted toward the fire. Larson remained alert for glimpses of magic, harvested stalks rattling against his ankles and crunching beneath his boots. A mad dash brought them across the farmer's fields. There, a village smaller than Mittlerstadt lay in ruins. Burned and bloated bodies were scattered amid cottages pounded to rubble. Raindrops sizzled against dying clumps of flame.

Taziar froze. Astryd slammed the base of her staff into the mud. Slowly, she slid down its length, collapsing in a heap at its base, her body racked with sobs. Taziar curled protectively around her, rocking soothingly, his own anguish clearly etched on his features.

Sadness enfolded Larson. But, more accustomed to senseless, wholesale slaughter, he maintained his composure.

Silme simply stared as if rooted. No emotion scored her expression. She might have been examining a Picasso in the New York Museum of Modern Art, studying lines and symmetry, seeking subtleties in tone and pattern.

"Silme?" Alarmed, Larson touched Silme's arm. She had always seemed so strong, he could not imagine her shattered by one setback. Still, they had all weathered so much in such a short space. *Everyone has a breaking point.*

Larson shook Silme's arm gently. "Silme?"

Silme's cheeks twisted. Her eyes closed deliberately, and she tightened the expression until creases ringed her nose. Then her lids flicked open, revealing turbulent, gray irises reflecting an internal struggle, a decision she could not quite reach.

Larson could only guess that she still wrestled with the choice between friends and baby. Pained by her sorrow, he swept her into a reassuring hug.

Silme did not return the embrace but neither did she pull away. She stood, stiff and silent in Larson's arms.

"I love you," he said.

Silme made no reply.

Larson pulled away. "You stay here with Astryd and Shadow. I'm going to look for food and a weapon for Shadow. If I can't find a sword this time, I'll get him an ax, a pick, a shovel. It doesn't matter." *Bolverkr's ass is mine.*

Taziar looked up. "I'll come with you."

"No." Larson rolled his gaze from Silme to Astryd, trying to indicate that they needed watching without offending them. Under ordinary circumstances, he would have chosen either sorceress to back him over any man he had ever met. But Astryd's inexperience seemed to have finally caught up with her, and Silme had become as unpredictable as death.

Apparently catching Larson's hint, Taziar returned to comforting Astryd.

Leaving his pack, Larson headed for the town proper. He discovered the first corpses at the edges of the village, a woman and three children, a bad beginning to a mission he would rather have forgotten. They lay half-buried beneath charred thatch and wood frame, eyes glazed, faces locked in terror. Steeling himself, Larson searched dispassionately, not allowing himself to speculate about their pasts or their shattered futures. They were dead and he was not. They no longer had need of food and weapons; his friends needed both.

As Larson leaned over the bodies, the strange, subtle odor of flayed muscle appeared beneath the stronger smells of blood and fire. Too familiar, it no longer bothered him. The recognition of Caucasian features, blue and green irises among the staring, sightless eyes pained more. He had known several Oriental friends before the war, and he had respected his Japanese swordmaster more than any man in his life. Still, the war had taught him to notice the differences between himself and enemies. The ruins reminded him of a walk with his buddies toward a town in the Mekong Delta, the shrill whine of phantom jets overhead, and the almost instantaneous explosion. Tight to the ground before he could recall moving, he had watched grass huts and villagers dissolve into a raging column of flame.

Now Larson wove quietly amidst tumbled stone, burning thatch, and twisted, leering corpses. Instead of the overwhelming gasoline reek of napalm, he knew the acrid smell of cleaner fires, damp earth, and death. In Vietnam, he could justify the devastation by concentrating on almond-shaped eyes, hair black as ink and sticky with blood, and olive-toned skin, ignoring the arms, legs, bodies, and heads, the hearts that once held hopes and dreams so like his own. Here in the eleventh century, in a part of Europe Larson could only guess was Germany, he could no longer ground his sanity on the racial differences between himself and his enemies. His imagination reconstructed the scorched faces. Every young boy bore the features of his little brother Timmy. Each teenaged girl became his sister Pam. The adults resembled so many friends and relatives from his past, an endless parade of memory that haunted him until he no longer knew who he was mourning.

Overstimulated, Larson's mind numbed the sea of corpses and rubble to a blur, and he checked the bodies with the same indifference as he did the broken remains of their dwellings. Bolverkr had done his job as thoroughly as before. Larson uncovered rakes and hoes, myriad scraps of clothing, dolls with stuffing strewn across the wreckage like the organs of their young owners. He found the ruins of a healer's cottage, some of the vials of salve and powder still intact, useless to the dead. Yet Larson did not discover a single crust of bread. Stored foods had burnt to ash, along with their barrels. And though Larson found the remains of pastures, not one corpse belonged to an animal. Once again, Bolverkr had diverted the sewage into the fountain, but that seemed less of a problem. The constant rain provided a source of water. It held an odd, metallic taste Larson could not explain, but it quenched his thirst.

As the chaos around Larson grew familiar, the odors faded into background, and the vision of death lost its sting. Even the patter of rain seemed to disappear into a dark, empty vacuum of silence and apathy. Larson had seen enough death that the bodies no longer interested him, even as morbid curiosities. He already knew human liver looked the same color and texture as the dinner table liver he had refused as a child, that kidneys were shaped like kidney beans, and that medical science had a reason for calling brains "gray matter." Aside from checking for possessions and life signs, the bodies might have become mannequins for all they mattered to Larson; each funeral ground became just one more place to look for food and weaponry. The quiet grew peaceful beneath the rain's drumbeat, a welcome relief from Silme's nagging and the despondent, unnatural silences of his companions.

Larson's exploration did not go wholly unrewarded. He came away with a pocketful of copper coins, several crude knives, and scraps of cloth that could serve as bandages. A crevice in the road had gathered enough rain to allow him to fill a skin with muddy but untainted water. Pleased with these small gains, Larson pushed into a dwelling on the far edge of town that seemed to have been spared the worst of the dragon's attack.

A hole in the thatch roof supplied enough light for Larson to get a clear view of the furnishings. The loft had collapsed, filling the main room with splintered logs and mattress tickings. A table lay shattered beneath the rubble. In the corner, near the door, a body sprawled. Dark hair fell about shoulders well-muscled from a lifetime of farming. A thick back tapered to a narrow waist. A sword belt cinched crookedly around his girth, the empty, twisted leather of a sheath peeking from beneath one hip.

A sword. Excited by his discovery, Larson bounded toward the figure. As he approached, he could see bone jutting from a bloody hole in the man's thigh. A soft groan escaped the body.

Larson froze. *Alive?* It seemed only natural that someone might survive the carnage. Yet, after several hundred pulse checks, Larson had developed a healthy respect for Bolverkr's precision. He approached cautiously, not wanting to frighten the farmer. "I won't hurt you. My name's Al. I'm a friend." He used the language of Cullinsberg's barony.

The stranger responded with a moan. He remained still.

Larson approached and knelt at the man's side. He pressed his finger to the corded neck, feeling a pulse thump solidly against his fingers. *Good. He's got a chance.* He glanced upward. *Must have taken a bad fall.* "What's your name?"

A long pause followed. The stranger took a shuddering breath. "Will-a-" He took another shallow gasp. "-perht." A thick dialect made it sound more like Wil-burt. "Leg broken. Hurts to breathe. Back . . ." He paused. "Not sure."

A medic in Vietnam had once taught Larson to misname the injured to keep them oriented and focused on something other than the pain. "Listen, Wolfgang. Just lie still. I'm going to get some help moving you."

"Willaperht," the man corrected.

Larson headed for the door. Reminded of Bolverkr's thoroughness, he paused. *How many chances am I going to get to find a sword? Willaperht can't use it for a while, and we're all safer if Shadow's armed as soon as possible.* "Hey, Wildwood, do you mind if I borrow your sword?"

"Willaperht. Don't know where it is."

Larson smiled, shaking his head. "That's all right. Don't bother to get up. I'll find it."

Willaperht moaned in anguish.

Larson returned to Willaperht's side, rubbing the man's shoulder comfortingly as he began his search. *Keep him distracted.* "You a soldier, Willy?"

This time, Willaperht did not bother to correct Larson. "Farmer. Taught myself sword to protect my family. My wife . . . ?"

Larson groped under the fallen rubble, seeing no sign of the sword. The sheath lay flaccid and empty on Willaperht's belt.

"My wife?" the farmer repeated.

It took Larson several seconds to realize Willaperht was asking a question. This did not seem the proper time to tell the injured man he was the town's only survivor. "I don't know. There're too many people, and they're all strangers to me. For now, let's just worry about you." Larson scowled, trying to decide where to look next.

Suddenly, from the opposite end of the cottage, light tore away the gloom. Fear slammed Larson. He dropped to his belly as if his legs had given out on him, then instantly realized that his trained reaction might cost him his life. He whirled, rising to a crouch. His sword whipped free.

Bolverkr stood on the opposite side of the cottage, leaning casually against the wall, one foot propped on the splintered remnants of the loft. "Looking for this, *Allerum?*" He raised a long sword, clutched in one fist.

Larson sprang. He covered the intervening space in a single leap and cut for Bolverkr's neck with all the power he could force into the stroke.

A hand's breadth in front of Bolverkr, Larson's blade rang against an invisible barrier. The unexpected impact staggered Larson. His fingers throbbed. The wound in his shoulder tore open, spilling blood.

Bolverkr remained calmly still, smiling.

Larson's pain transformed to rage. Howling, he slashed at the sorcerer again and again, his sword crashing repeatedly against defenses solid as a mountain.

Bolverkr waited with amused patience.

Larson's arms ached. He retreated, panting, studying Bolverkr with a glare of hatred. "Coward! I'm sick to death of your hit and run tactics. If you want a fight, let's fight. You and I. Right now. Weapon to weapon." He goaded Bolverkr, circling on the balls of his feet, anticipating a strike in anger.

Bolverkr watched Larson, a slight smile on his lips, like an adult watching someone else's child throw a tantrum. Abruptly, he lunged from the rubble.

Larson rushed forward to meet the attack. The invisible barrier caught him in the face. Pain flashed through his nose. The combined force of their charges sent him reeling. His foot came down on a broken table leg. He fell backward, twisting to avoid Willaperht, and came down hard on the farmer's wounded leg.

Willaperht screamed.

Larson cursed into the stone, cheeks stinging and ankle throbbing. Fist still tight around his sword hilt, he scurried to his feet, braced for Bolverkr's magic.

Larson expected a physical attack, so the probe Bolverkr jabbed into his mind caught him completely off guard. White hot agony speared his thoughts, scattering them, and bounced like echoes through his head. He heard himself scream as if from a great distance. Consciousness hovered, blackness pressing in from all sides.

"No!" Larson's voice emerged as a dull croak. Spots prickled and rang through his head, and it ached as if it might explode. *Wall. Got to build a wall.* The world faded around Larson as he threw his full concentration into the vision of a brick tower enclosing the intruder in his thoughts.

The pain subsided. Larson caught a bleary glance of the place where Bolverkr had stood, now empty. The distraction caused the walls to blur.

In Larson's mind, Bolverkr's laughter rang hollowly through the imagined tower.

Dizzied and sickened, Larson clawed through his pain for a coherent strategy. He knew from experience that Bolverkr could spark any memory Larson had inadvertently enclosed within the walls to a vividness that could incapacitate him. He steadied his consciousness, prepared for the inevitable cruel stab of remembrance, the waves of physical or emotional pain, the complete disruption of time, place, and person. *Only one thing to try.* Larson did not consider the tactic too carefully, aware he might falter. Bravely, he waited for his first flashing image of the Vietnam War, prepared to hurl every ounce of his concentration onto that moment, hoping to throw himself into flashback and drag Bolverkr with him. The other two times he had fallen through breeches in his memory, it had happened accidentally. Now, bolstered by Taziar's suggestions to try to enter his own world, he prepared to ground his reason on the hellish war that had driven him to madness. *All right, Bolverkr, let's see how you fare against AK-47s.*

"I've shattered real mind barriers." Though enmeshed in looping coils of Larson's thoughts and memories, Bolverkr fixed his attention on Larson's conjured walls. "Do you think your makeshift defenses can hold me?"

Cued by Bolverkr's words, Larson abandoned his idea. Even the diamond-rank master, Bramin, and the god, Vidarr, had found Larson's created walls too difficult to battle. Both had chosen to assault his memories instead, aware the walls came of Larson's thoughts, and a loss of concentration would cause his barriers to crumble.

Bolverkr snapped a wrist. Fire splashed the tower's wall, flinging burning sparks through Larson's mind. The brick shattered. Chunks of rock pounded Larson's thoughts like physical pain. He started to scream. Anguish pounded him to oblivion, cutting the sound midway. Larson collapsed into darkness.

Bolverkr extracted himself from the dark void of Larson's mind. The elf sprawled on a floor littered with chaotic jumbles of singed thatch, smashed beams and furniture, and fragmented stone. Still clutching Willaperht's sword, Bolverkr studied the base of Larson's skull. *So easy.* He raised the blade. But instead of Larson's neck, Bolverkr shoved it through Willaperht's.

The farmer tensed, shuddered once, then went still.

"You're spared this time," he told Larson's unconscious body. Bracing his foot on Willaperht's spine, Bolverkr withdrew the blade. "For Silme. Once she becomes mine, I'll kill your child. And when you have nothing left but your life, I'll take that, too."

Bolverkr turned, raising the sword. Willaperht's blood trickled down the steel onto the crossguard, striping Bolverkr's knuckles. He watched the scarlet rivulets fill irregularities in the knurling, a bright, beautiful contrast to the brown leather and silvered steel. "And you might as well have this." Bolverkr jammed the point between piled stones and twisted until the steel gave. The broken blade rattled into the crevice.

Bolverkr hurled the hilt at Larson's back. It struck a shoulder blade, sliding into a fold of the elf's cloak. Blood washed from Willaperht's wound, staining Larson's sleeve.

Tapping an insignificant amount of life chaos, Bolverkr triggered an escape transport. White light filled the tiny cottage, then winked out, plummeting the two still forms into a wash of gray smoke.

CHAPTER 7
Chaos of Thought and Passion

Soldier, rest! thy warfare o'er,
Sleep the sleep that knows no breaking
Dream of battled fields no more,
Days of danger, nights of waking.
—Sir Walter Scott
The Lady of the Lake

Al Larson sat beneath a patchwork canopy of branches, ignoring the ceaseless drip of rain, though a stream of droplets pattered on his head. Water plastered long, white-blond hair to his high-set cheekbones, revealing the delicate points of his ears. Yet despite the annoyance of rivulets running from his bangs into his eyes, he did not bother to find a drier seat. Despair rode him, familiar as a childhood playmate. And though his companions were around him, Larson might just as well have been alone. His thoughts carried him beyond the incomplete sanctity of the forest clearing to the tattered, charred corpses of innocents killed in his name, to the body of a young man named Willaperht who might still live if Larson had gone for help immediately rather than wasting time searching for a sword.

Larson buried his chin in his palms, swiveling his gaze to the right where Taziar practiced fighting maneuvers with a branch carved into a shaft. Astryd stood nearby, leaning against her garnet-tipped staff, calling inane suggestions that seemed to have little effect on Taziar's style. Though quick and graceful, Taziar's strokes lacked power. Accustomed to swords, he occasionally used thrusting gestures that, in combat, would accomplish nothing more than giving his enemy a chance to seize the weapon and disarm him. He also tended to lead with one side, as if the staff held an edge.

Larson turned away, discouraged by Taziar's lack of combat skill but unable to gather the momentum needed to teach. He had little enough training with any weapon other than single-edged sword, deer rifle, pistol, and M-16, just a natural eye for technique. And it was obvious Taziar had no technique at all.

Wind rattled through the trees, revealing endlessly gray sky through shifting gaps. A shower of leaf-held rain splashed down on Larson, unnoticed. In Vietnam, he had been told to befriend every companion, yet to hold each at a distance. Though his life might depend on any one of them, he could not afford to let their deaths cripple him. Then, he had tried this method with little success. Now, he found it even more difficult. Never before had his enemies slaughtered women and children as a personal affront to him. Never before did he have to weigh the lives of his beloved wife and forming child in the balance. The animal-like cunning and stealth of the Viet Cong had turned his nights into frenzied firefights or left him curled, shivering despite the heat, sleeping on the heart-pounding, razor's edge of waking. Yet never before had Al Larson felt so helpless and openly flayed before an enemy. In 'Nam, youth, inexperience, and lack of responsibilities made him certain of his permanence. But now he was all too aware of his mortality. Silme and the baby gave that mortality meaning even as Bolverkr's easy victories tainted its significance.

A shadow fell over Larson. Chin sunk into his palms, he glanced up at Silme. The sorceress towered over him, her golden hair shimmering and her cheeks rosy despite the rain. Her pregnancy enhanced beauty Larson had already used as his definition for perfection. But the coldness in her gray eyes marred the effect.

Alerted to the possibility of an argument, Larson lowered his gaze. His belly felt hollow. His conscience ached with the burden of hundreds of blameless deaths, all the murders committed in the name of keeping him from obtaining food or weaponry. Larson could not banish searing guilt and sorrow over the shattering of Gaelinar's sword, the "vehicle of the soul," though once the displaced American would have dismissed such a feeling as superstitious nonsense.

Taziar's staff crashed against an oak trunk used as a target.

"Why do you love me?" Silme's commanding tone turned an innocent question into a demand.

Larson did not bother to raise his head. "Silme, please. I need to be alone for a while."

Another crack sounded from Taziar's direction.

Silme shuffled her feet, kicking up soggy pine needles. "And I need to know why you love me."

Ire flashed through Larson. *Easy,* he cautioned himself. *She's going through a rough time, too. You promised to support her.* He kept his voice level, resorting to monotone to keep himself from provoking conflict. "I went to Hel to retrieve you from death. I blackmailed a god into telling me the secret to raising you. I bartered and fought with Hel's goddess and Hel's hound. With Gaelinar's help, I captured the Dragonrank sorceress who was Hel's guardian." Larson hesitated, mind suddenly filled with the battle. He and Kensei Gaelinar had fought the sorceress, Modgudr, on the bridge spanning the river, Gjoll. Modgudr had hidden behind a shielding spell, similar to the one Bolverkr had created in Willaperht's cottage. She had used the shield to defend against Gaelinar's strokes as well as to drive the Kensei toward Gjoll's fatal currents. *I struck her unexpectedly from behind, and my blow fell. Apparently, either the force field doesn't completely surround the mage or he can only use it to protect against enemies he sees.* A spark of hope flared, quickly dashed by Silme's next affront.

"I didn't ask *if* you love me. That's clear enough. I want to know why."

Taziar's staff drummed repeatedly against the oak.

Larson met Silme's gaze. The distance of his thoughts and the hostility in her expression unsettled him. He spoke from habit rather than his heart. "Because you're beautiful. You're the most beautiful woman I've ever met. I love you." He reached for her, urging her to sit beside him.

Silme back-stepped beyond Larson's reach. "So you love me just because of the way I look."

Realizing his mistake, Larson clarified. "No, not just because of the way you look."

"Then why?" Silme snapped. She folded her arms across her chest, glaring at Larson through narrowed eyes.

Frustration and the ludicrousness of Silme's behavior ignited Larson's anger again. "Cut it out, Silme. I know you're in a weird emotional state. But this isn't a god-damned quiz show, and I'm not in the mood. I've got more important things on my mind."

The noise of Taziar's striking staff disappeared.

The idea that he might have an audience further fueled Larson's annoyance.

Silme's cheeks flushed in scarlet contrast to the grim, white line of her lips. "There are things more important than our love? Is that what you're saying?"

"For the moment, yes." Larson leapt to his feet, control slipping. "Trying to keep my friends and family from starving to death or getting aced by some warped bastard of a warlock takes precedence over the exact reasons why I love my wife." He added with unconcealed sarcasm, "Is that okey-dokey with you?"

"No. That's not O-kee-doe-kee with me." Silme struggled with the slang, apparently guessing its intention from previous conversations. "If you loved me for legitimate reasons, you'd know why."

"That's nonsense!" Larson was shouting now. "That's not how love works. . . ."

"And if you really loved me, you'd go back to your own world."

The track of Larson's thoughts collapsed beneath him, and he found himself scrabbling for ideas as well as words. Rage inspired him. "Damn it, Silme! We're not talking about a subway ride here. I've crossed time once, and you've seen the results. Mythology as reality. Magic. We're supposed to be in historical ninth or tenth century Germany, for Christ's sake. You're not supposed to have elves or wizards or talking wolf-gods. You're not even supposed to have potatoes. Or a barony called Cullinsberg. And what the hell kind of a name is Tazz-ee-ar?"

"Hey!" Taziar edged closer to the argument, Astryd at his heels. He spoke with a soft gentleness designed to soothe. "It was my father's name, okey-dokey? Now why don't you two . . ."

Silme interrupted as if Taziar had not started. "That damage has already been done. I'm trying to protect my world from more of your interference."

"*My* interference!" Larson balled his fists, looking for something safe to hit. "I'm sick and tired of getting blamed for Freyr's magic. Despite what you think, shit happened before I arrived, and shit's still going to happen if I leave. I'm not taking the blame for every crummy, stupid, insignificant thing that goes wrong in this whole fucking world."

Taziar caught Larson's forearm. "Allerum, calm down."

Larson jerked his arm free, sending Taziar stumbling sideways. Whirling, Larson slammed his fist into a tree trunk. Pain lanced through his fingers, and water showered his already sodden figure. "I'm not going back to 'Nam." He punched the oak. "I'm not going back to vicious enemies and ungrateful allies." He struck again. "I'm not going to watch women and children dismembered in the name of peace." He buried his face in his sleeve, the blows becoming less violent and directed. "I'm not going to live like a hunted animal, in constant fear." The significance of his words seeped through the hot blanket of anger. *What's the difference between Bolverkr and NVA artillery? Why should I care less about the scattered corpses in tenth century Germany than the scattered corpses in Saigon?* Madness descended upon him, stealing his vision and filling his ears with a wordless buzzing.

A comforting hand touched Larson's shoulder blade.

Larson shrank away. "Leave me alone. Just leave me the hell alone."

"Fine. I will." Silme's voice scarcely penetrated Larson's fog. "And don't try to follow me."

As Silme's looming presence disappeared, the air around Larson seemed to lighten.

Behind Larson, Astryd's voice settled to an accusing growl. "You know the state she's in. How could you upset her like that?"

Silence hovered. Larson kept his face hidden, his throbbing fist sagging at his side.

Astryd whirled, crashing through the brush, her steps rapidly growing more distant.

Larson waited, the persistent contact on his shoulder the only indication that Taziar had remained. Silent tears glided from Larson's eyes, mingling with the dripping rainwater.

"Allerum." Taziar's composure sounded out of place after the savagery of the argument and the wild chaos of Larson's emotions. "I'll talk to Silme. Will you be all right alone?"

Larson nodded slightly, wanting nothing more than the solace of being by himself. He fingered his hilt. Aware he should say something, he turned, but Taziar was already gone.

Alone. Larson could not shake the crushing feeling of abandonment. *Nothing left.* The idea of death no longer bothered him. It beckoned, welcoming. *But I'll be damned if I'll give that Dragonrank bastard the pleasure of becoming my executioner.* Larson's emotions flickered, flip-flopping him repeatedly from despair to rage. Finally, depression collapsed beneath wild, driving anger. *Bolverkr, I've played your game. Now it's time to use my baseball and my rules.*

Aware Bolverkr could read his thoughts, Larson let the events of the last few days cycle through his mind, fanning his frenzy with each pass. His actions became automatic, lacking the motivations and experience Bolverkr would need to understand them.

Larson returned to the decimated town, steeling himself against the sight of corpses his mind's defenses turned to statues. He worked mechanically, recalling the location of every tool from his recent, minute search of the damaged town.

First, Larson gathered clay crockery and metal cooking pots. Next, he returned to the pastures, scooping up heaps of nitrogen-rich soil. Burned timbers abounded in the dragon-decimated town. Larson collected a hefty pile along with dried twigs, branches, and intact timbers for fuel. He filled several pots with water from the contaminated river. Digging through the ruins of the healer's cottage, Larson uncovered his final ingredient, a single vial of yellow powder. Uncorked, it gave off the unmistakable, rotten egg odor of sulfur. He added a candle and some unraveled, linen thread to the pile.

Saltpeter, charcoal, and sulfur. Larson crowded his raw ingredients onto a space of ground on the boundary of what had once been a village. The formula was one Larson felt certain every man of his era learned as a toddler. *Gunpowder.* He surveyed the piled items, aware he needed one more thing. *A solid container that will allow pressure to build before shattering.* His gaze fell on a nearby corpse, and he hated the source that came naturally to his thoughts. *Bone.*

The idea of disarticulating human femurs made Larson queasy, dispelling some of the anger that had driven him for the past several minutes. The realization of what he planned to do struck him as hard as a physical blow. *Gunpowder.* Memory flooded his mind, of an early autumn day in tenth-century Norway. Bramin crouched before Larson and Taziar, a rifle clutched in his grip. The gun had come from America in the late 1980s, brought by a one-way time traveler named Gary Mannix and called Geirmagnus, the first Dragonrank Master. But it was Larson's war memories that had taught Silme's half-brother to wield the gun.

Larson's remembrance brought a vivid image of Taziar, sprawled on the grass, gaping at a ragged hole in his thigh. The Climber's shocky-white face made a striking contrast to Bramin's inky skin and half dark elven features. The rifle barrel hovered, aimed at Larson's chest, and his own admonishment rang in his ears, bringing a measure of guilt. *Bramin, if you put guns into your world, you open the way for any weak coward to kill you before you see him coming. . . . Once you bring guns into your world, there is no more glory in war.*

The memory faded, leaving Larson awash in questions. He had intended his argument simply to distract Bramin, but the morality had seeped far deeper. Once having won the conflict, Larson had carried that rifle miles to Hvergelmir, the Helspring waterfall that destroys all things in its cascade. He had tossed the gun into the wild braid of waters, hoping to delay the invention to its appropriate time or later, symbolically annihilating his year in the Vietnam War as well.

Doubt assailed Larson. He thought of Silme and how pregnancy and the pressures of combat had wrung her to a cruel, sullen core. He considered Astryd. The less experienced sorceress had withdrawn into her loyalty to Silme, forgetting the debts she owed Taziar and Larson as well. Only the little Climber seemed unaffected by Bolverkr's constant threat. Taziar appeared more distressed by his companions' bickering than the fear of death.

Larson's fall from Bolverkr's wall filled his mind again. Repeatedly, he relived the crash of magics into his chest, the twisting stumble that had driven Gaelinar's blade into the granite, the resisting, reversed-direction force of Bolverkr's next spell striking the steel simultaneously. Then Larson's mind leapt forward to his mental battle in the farm town. Fresh rage burned through him. *It's time I started playing smart, not fair. Magic was discovered by a twentieth-century parapsychologist named Gary Mannix. If Bolverkr can use post-modern technology, then, damn it, so can I.*

Al Larson cast aside guilt and indecision almost as quickly as they arose. *To use anything less than all the weapons I can create would be stupid. Bolverkr, let me introduce you to grenades.* Larson headed off to find suitable thighbones.

The sun swung westward, casting stripes through gaps in the clouds. Rain-smeared light settled over Al Larson where he hunched amid covered crocks, vials, and bones, extracting his third filtered crystallization of saltpeter. Firelight glazed the clearing to a hazy red. A pot dangled over the flames, heat waves dancing over a mixture of powder and boiling water. Larson's limbs had cramped hours ago, but, intent on his work, he did not notice the pain. Winding strips of cloth about his hands to protect them from the heat, he removed the pot from the fire, strained the contents through finely-woven cloth and divided the remaining saltpeter into crocks to cool and crystallize. He shook off the pot holders. Gathering thread and candle, he lit the wick from the flames, sat, and set to interweaving linen with wax.

A presence glided into Larson's brain.

Bolverkr. Larson went rigid, dropping the makeshift wick in order to channel his concentration to this new threat. Mental walls slammed into place, surrounding the intruder. *Damn! Just a few more minutes and I would have had a real weapon.* Frustrated and enraged by the interruption, Larson blasted notions at the being who had invaded his mind. *Bolverkr, you fucking, cheating coward! You want to fight, come on out and fight like a man. Sword to sword! Fist to fist! I'm sick of this mind game shit!*

No verbal answer followed, but the intruder radiated an aura of promised peace and friendship.

"Fuck it, Bolverkr." Larson sprang to his feet, dumping the partially melted candle from his lap. "How stupid do you think I am?" He tightened the conjured barriers. "I'm not going to fall for some ridiculous promise of parlay. Get the hell out here, or I'm coming in after you."

I'm afraid that would be impossible. The soft reply whispered in Larson's mind.

Larson hesitated, recognizing the voice, yet not quite placing it, knowing for certain the intruder was not Bolverkr.

The other fell equally silent.

Expecting further explanation and a chance to identify the presence, Larson found the quiet unnerving. Still, the decision to speak as little as possible identified the being in a way his voice had not. *Vidarr?*

The presence strengthened, then returned to normal.

Driven to impatience by the morning's events and the effort of holding his mental barriers, Larson sighed loudly. "Can the crap, Vidarr. That emotion stuff may work for your god friends, but I'm just a regular guy. I need words. Okay?"

Vidarr's presence tingled with warning.

Larson granted no quarter. "What are you going to do? Kill me for asking you to communicate like a normal human being?"

I've told you before, just think what you wish to say. And I'm not a normal human being.

So I've noticed. Larson tried to keep insult and sarcasm from sweeping to the forefront of his consciousness along with the words. He dropped the mental walls. *Look, I don't mean to be disrespectful, but . . .*

. . . you are, Vidarr finished.

I don't mean to be disrespectful, Larson started again, *but I'm trying to fight Bolverkr, and I don't have time to waste discussing my bad attitude with a mute god. If you've come to help, I'm grateful. If not, I haven't got time for one-way chatter.*

I can't help you.

Then go away. Realizing that antagonizing a god, even one so familiar, might have consequences, Larson softened the command. *Please.* No longer needing to concentrate on holding walls, he sat, gathering the thread and wax.

Apology wove through Vidarr's words. *You have to understand. Bolverkr is the prime source of Chaos in this world. His death would affect the gods.*

Affect the gods? Affect the gods! Galled, Larson abandoned caution. He inhaled a sharp breath in a mock noise of horror, no longer trying to hold back the sarcasm. *Well, excuse me if my self-defense interferes with your comfort. Bolverkr's death may inconvenience the gods. My death would inconvenience me. As would the rape of my wife, the slaughter of my child, and the torture of my friends.*

It's not that simple.

No. Larson's fingers clenched around the wick. *I can see where a life of omnipotent idleness could get rough.*

Stop this nonsense, Allerum! Annoyance flowed freely from Vidarr. *I came to help. Don't incite me. You won't like the results.*

Anger churned inside Larson, driving him beyond fear of consequences or vague threats. *Wake up, Vidarr. You're a god of Law. There's nothing you can do to me that Bolverkr hasn't already considered. I've got nothing left to lose.*

Except Silme.

Suddenly attentive, Larson turned his focus fully inward. *What do you mean?*

Wake up, Allerum. Vidarr borrowed Larson's idiom. *Don't you see what Bolverkr's doing?*

If I could see Bolverkr, one of us would be dead by now. Now wanting to banter words, Larson clung to the point. *What does Bolverkr have to do with Silme?*

Vidarr's presence hovered, no emotion radiating from him. *I don't know for certain. You're the only one without mind barriers. I can't read anyone else's thoughts.*

THE POINT, VIDARR!

Vidarr cringed at the intensity and volume of Larson's mental reply. *Silme's acting wrong.*

Larson snorted. *Tell me something I don't know. This pregnancy's got her hormones in an upheaval.*

Her hor—, what?

The proximity of the name Silme and the syllable "hor" bothered Larson. He made a gesture of dismissal, though Vidarr could not see it from within his mind. *Never mind. This pregnancy and the pressure's made her crazy.*

Is that what you think?

Obviously. The implications of the question struck Larson. *Are you saying there's something else going on?*

You mean besides the fact that you're all acting bizarre and irritable?

Yeah. Besides that.

I recognize the influence of Chaos when I see it.

Frustration rattled through Larson. *You're not making any sense.*

I know Silme as well as I know my brothers. That woman you were traveling with may have looked like Silme and talked like Silme. But she's not acting like Silme. Vidarr shifted, carefully avoiding the tangled tapestry of Larson's memories. *Carrying a baby isn't enough to explain a drastic change in personality. I've seen Silme pressured before. I've known only a few, gods included, as graceful when stressed.*

Larson licked his lips, understanding the words but not quite able to form the conclusion. *Are you trying to say Bolverkr might have kidnapped Silme and replaced her with someone who looks like her?*

Amusement fluttered through Larson's brain. *Not a chance.*

I didn't think so.

Someone or something is intentionally driving a wedge between you and Silme. It seems only natural to blame Bolverkr. I don't know what he's doing, but I'm willing to gamble my immortality that he's doing something.

Larson suddenly felt cold. *Like what? What might he be doing? Give me some possibilities or examples.*

I can't.

The short fuse on Larson's temper flared again. *You can't? Or you won't?*

I can't, Vidarr repeated. *You know I'm not one of the gods who uses sorcery directly. I have to guess based on observation. From what I've seen, I can't think of anything Bolverkr could use to change a personality. Her mind barriers would stop him. It just doesn't make sense.*

Gripping fear replaced Larson's anger. He recalled Silme's description of Bolverkr's follower. Apparently, Harriman had been a diplomat before Bolverkr's magic shattered his mind barriers, providing access for Bolverkr to manipulate Harriman's thoughts. Larson tried to put his concern into words.

Vidarr responded to the idea, without waiting for a coherent question. *No, Allerum. As far as I can tell, Silme's mind barriers remain intact.*

Relief rose, and hope followed. *Maybe one of the gods who does use magic might understand what's going on. Couldn't you ask?*

No. Vidarr fidgeted. His back struck a coil of thought, sparking the familiar and unique odor of damp, jungle clay.

Larson cringed, willing the god to remain still.

If the others knew I was here helping you, they'd chain me to a rock and beat me till I bled.

Larson found sympathy impossible. *If it makes you feel any better, I'd be happy to tell them you were no help at all.*

Very funny.

Larson picked up one of the hollowed thighbones and threaded the fuse through the tiny hole once served by a nutrient artery. Finished, he placed the bone aside and started on the next. *Seriously, if you're not allowed to help me because Bolverkr's death might affect the gods, and if just talking to me might cause them to hurt you, why are you here wasting my time?*

You want the truth?

It seems likely. I can make up my own lies.

The truth is, I don't know.

Larson smiled, certain he knew the justification. Vidarr had reasons to feel indebted to the man who had broken Loki's spell and freed Vidarr from a lengthy imprisonment in a sword. Vidarr's repayment, an attempt to stabilize Larson's mental state against reliving traumatic experiences in times of new stress, against wildly irrational startle responses, and against night terrors, had proven only partially successful. And Vidarr's coercing Larson to complete a second task against his will had shifted the balance of favors in Larson's direction.

Though Larson did not qualify in specific words, Vidarr caught the gist of his thoughts. *I'm a god. I owe you nothing.*

Larson struck home. *If you really believed that, you wouldn't be here.*

Sullen silence.

Larson continued positioning his wick.

Vidarr's brooding turned to thoughtful goodwill.

Refusing to acknowledge any nonverbal communication, Larson ignored the Silent God.

You're ungrateful, Vidarr said at length.

Oh. So the pot's calling the kettle black. Larson set aside the second bone. Fumbling the vial of sulfur from his pocket, he slid a pair of empty crocks toward him. *I rescued you from imprisonment, and how did you thank me? You sent me on a task you knew was impossible, lying to me along the way.*

I apologized.

Oh, well. That makes it okay, then. Angered anew by the memories, Larson dumped half of the yellow powder into each crock. He reached for the charcoal, bitterness oozing into his mental communication. *Kensei Gaelinar died for your brother. Spare me the "I'm a god, you're a measly mortal" speeches. I wielded you. That changes our relationship.* Larson measured out the charcoal, turning his thoughts momentarily to his work. *Four saltpeter to one charcoal to one sulfur.* He poured, returning to the conversation. *Don't get me wrong. I'd appreciate your company. If you've come to help, I'm grateful. Really. In fact, it hurts to think about such a thing, but your aid against Bolverkr might even put* me *in* your *debt again.*

Larson harvested the cooled crystals of saltpeter, mixing them into the two crocks in the proper proportion. He continued. *But if you've only come to whine about how you can't help me because Bolverkr's death might affect the gods, you can leave now. Don't waste my time with excuses.*

Vidarr sighed, the sound echoing through Larson's head. *You don't understand. Bolverkr is ultrapowerful. The other gods have the right to kill me for interfering.*

Vidarr's words sparked an idea too intriguing for Larson to suppress. Aware Vidarr could read his motivations and not wanting to seem as if he were plotting, he sent the message in direct words. *You're a powerful being of Law. Perhaps your death could balance Bolverkr's?*

Stunned rage radiated from Vidarr. *Is that a threat?*

Just an observation. Larson turned his full concentration on Vidarr, alert for evidence of attack. *If I was scheming against you, why would I warn you? On the other hand, if the gods did kill you, I can't deny I'd use the opening in the Balance to slaughter Bolverkr.*

Vidarr's fury turned to calculated understanding. *Don't get too hooked on the idea. My death wouldn't open the Balance nearly enough to compensate for Bolverkr's death.*

The confession startled Larson. *You're saying Bolverkr's more powerful than you?*

Far more.

"Shit." Larson stirred his concoction methodically. *No wonder Bolverkr seems invincible. What would it take to balance him? Every god on Olympus?*

Olympus?

Larson scooped powder into one of the thighbones, packing it tightly. *Oops, wrong pantheon. Sorry. What's the name of the gods' world again?*

Asgard.

Yeah. That's it.

I can usually get that right.

Once powder filled the bone, Larson jammed a stone into the opening, maneuvering until he felt certain he had a seal. *Sarcasm doesn't become you.*

Nor you, Vidarr replied. *But I've been putting up with yours since you got here.*

Touché.

What?

Never mind. Larson set to work on the second thighbone, mind racing. *Vidarr, I have an idea. You can't help me fight Bolverkr directly, right?* He did not wait for an answer. *Could you do something for me that wouldn't affect Bolverkr at all?*

Possibly. Guarded interest slipped from Vidarr.

Larson struggled with a second stone. *I'm hoping it won't happen. But if things get desperate, I promised Shadow I'd take Silme and Astryd to my world. If it comes to that, would you take care of my elf body here?*

A long silence followed. Not a trace of emotion tainted the pause.

Larson finished setting the second stone. He considered asking Vidarr the myriad questions that plagued him about reality and the existence of the world he once knew as the future. However, from past experience, he felt certain Vidarr would not have the answers. *Or if he does, I won't need to ask; he'll tell me.* Carefully, Larson rose, checking his pockets for a block of flint and his dagger. His heart pounded, revealing the trepidations he kept out of his thoughts.

Just as it seemed as if Vidarr had left without answering, the god's soft voice recurred. *Yes. I'll do this for you. I'll take care of your elf body if it becomes necessary.*

Larson read something discomforting beneath the god's promise. Before he could press the issue, Vidarr changed the subject.

What are those things you're working on? Lamps?

Just evening the odds a bit. Larson retrieved the bones from the ground. *Bolverkr's got magic I don't understand, and now I've got magic he won't understand.* He could not help adding to himself, *If we're going to play without rules, we'll just see who fucking loses.*

Vidarr's presence faded, leaving a final warning so gently distant, Larson was uncertain it was intended for him at all. *Let's just try to see to it we don't all lose.*

CHAPTER 8
Chaos-Controlled

Nature, with equal mind,
Sees all her sons at play;
Sees man control the wind,
The wind sweep man away.
—Matthew Arnold
Empedocles on Etna

The rain ceased with the same unnatural abruptness with which it had begun, settling the world into a deep silence that set Larson's every nerve jangling. Sitting in the gutted town, amid his gathered crocks and powders, he saw nothing move. No sound touched his senses, only a quiet, horrible certainty that something was about to happen. He crouched, clutching his makeshift bombs, feeling the drumming solo of his heartbeat against an otherwise overpowering stillness.

Suddenly, light snapped open the evening haze, silhouetting the ruins black against startling brilliance. A distant scream followed, mixing fear and rage.

Larson recognized the voice. *Astryd!* His breath seemed to freeze in his chest. He staggered to his feet, galloping from the village before he even realized he had moved. The clouds unraveled with abnormal speed. Twilight glared through, its grayness bright after days of veiled sun. The magical flash faded. As if it were a signal, a grotesque shadow blotted out his glimpse of sunlight.

Larson glanced upward as he ran, anguish clawing at him like a living thing. A dragon knifed through the air, its wings flapping whirlwinds through muddy fields. Its scales glinted gold in the sparse light of evening. Ignoring Larson, it speared over his head, veering south at a downward angle.

My friends are in trouble, forced to fight Bolverkr without me. How could I let that happen? Larson quickened his pace. Using the dragon as a guide, he sprinted, his momentum thrown so far forward he all but sprawled in the dirt. His hands clenched whitely about the gunpowder-filled bones.

The slap of the dragon's wings beat against Larson's ears. Beneath it, he heard Astryd's cry of outrage. Bolverkr's answer blurred to incomprehensibility, growing louder and clearer as Larson approached. ". . . helpless . . . to . . . dragon . . . down on me. . . ."

Larson darted over a rise, suddenly gaining a distant but perfect view of the battle. Near the forest's edge, Bolverkr stood on a ridge hedged by piled stones, his stance regally upright and unconcerned. Taziar hammered at the sorcerer with his staff; each blow fell short of its target. Behind Taziar, Astryd kept her gaze glued to the dragon. She made a stabbing gesture toward Bolverkr. Silme waited in a silent stillness, her lip blanched between her teeth, her features crinkled in confusion.

Silme! What has he done to Silme? Larson's instincts drove him to rush recklessly to Silme's defense. But common sense stopped him cold. *We'll win this by careful strategy or not at all.* Larson ducked behind a row of stones, forcing himself to think. *Bolverkr's shielded. I need to approach unseen or from behind to get through his magic barrier.*

Calm as a giant playing with children, Bolverkr ignored Taziar's attacks. The dragon screamed toward the sorcerer, obviously in Astryd's control.

Quietly, Larson crawled around a circling ledge of stone and brush, catching shifting glimpses of the combatants.

The dragon plummeted toward Bolverkr.

The sorcerer laughed. He made an abrupt chopping motion. Sparks sprayed from his fingertips, forming a gentle arc. The magics coalesced, exploding into a ball of white that streamed toward Astryd with all the inhuman speed of her dragon.

"No!" Too late, Taziar dove into the path of the spell. The magics shrieked over his head, slamming into Astryd's face. His staff crashed down on Bolverkr's invisible shield. The wood cracked, hurling splinters.

Astryd staggered and fell to one knee.

No longer controlled, the dragon spun crazily. Its form

blurred to a pale outline, wavered as if to disappear. Then, gradually, it resolidified. Suddenly, it whirled toward Taziar.

Silme remained still, watching impassively.

Though driven to action, Larson forced himself to stay hidden. *No way to know if Bolverkr's shield can repel explosives. I can't attack until I'm behind him.* He quickened his crawl.

"See, Silme, I can kill your friends any time. Watch!" Bolverkr's words flowed past Larson unheard. Larson stared in horror as the great, golden beast dipped toward Taziar. The Climber ran in sharp patterns, but the dragon maneuvered with hawklike finesse. It sped downward. One black-nailed claw clouted Taziar's scalp, bowling him across stone and grass. The dragon backpedaled, leaping into the sky.

Bolverkr laughed again. "Still, I've got no reason to kill them. They're nothing to me. They can't hurt us. But Allerum is an anachronism. His influence will destroy our worlds! Will you pay for your love with the lives of gods and innocents?"

"But you destroy innocents, too." Silme's voice sounded strange, faltering.

Concerned for Taziar and intent on his own emplacement, Larson scarcely heard the exchange.

The dragon circled, swooping down on Astryd. Taziar screamed, darting toward the Dragonrank sorceress, the splayed remains of his staff still clamped in his fist.

"I destroyed two villages," Bolverkr confessed. "I killed those townsfolk so you might understand, so we might save the nine worlds. I killed two villages. Allerum's technology will kill thousands!"

The dragon hovered over Astryd. Her eyes went wide, wild, blue orbs of fear and desperation.

Silme rallied against Bolverkr. "You're wrong," she shouted. "Allerum doesn't want to harm anyone. He wouldn't use his knowledge to . . ."

Silme's defense was suffocated beneath Astryd's screeched spell words. Yellow light grew, outlining her tiny form. The dragon's mouth hinged open as it prepared to breathe its fire.

Too late! Though not yet behind Bolverkr, Larson lit the first wick, knowing the attack would reveal him, yet unwilling to let the dragon kill Astryd as the price for his positioning.

Taziar lunged. His wiry form arched through the air and thumped to a landing beside Astryd. He scrambled over her, shielding her with his body.

Caught by surprise, Astryd gasped. Her spell shattered, collapsing to harmless, fizzling pinpoints. The first tongue of flame issued from the dragon's mouth.

Larson hurled his makeshift bomb. The bone thudded against the scaled side. The dragon twisted as it gouted flame, its fires splashing slightly off target. "Get out of the way!" Larson warned his companions. "Now!"

Taziar staggered a few steps, dragging Astryd, his clothes alight.

The Climber's movements seemed ponderous. Larson willed his friend to move faster.

The dragon hesitated.

The wick flame flickered, then seemed to disappear. Larson cursed his failure just as the bone exploded. Brown-white fragments pierced the reptilian hide. The beast roared, then winked out as if it had never existed. The blast's concussion slammed Taziar to the ground. He and Astryd lay still, flaccid as death, oblivious to the flames licking at their clothing.

Bolverkr whirled toward Larson, composure lost, shock and urgency etched clearly on his face. A blinding ball of light snapped to life in his fingers.

Larson fumbled with flint and steel, awkwardly igniting the other wick. *God, please let this penetrate his shield.* He drew back to throw even as Bolverkr's magics left his fingers, blazing a screaming, silver trail.

"No!" Silme did not move, yet a tendril of her consciousness stabbed into Larson's thoughts with enough force to incapacitate him. He collapsed, writhing in pain, blind to the spell that whizzed over his head. The bone tumbled from his grip, clicking against the flint and dagger as it fell. The clearing disappeared, replaced by another, more familiar battleground . . .

"Incoming!" The cry rang around Larson in a dozen different voices. "Incoming!" He woke in a cold sweat, rolling from bed to floor, painfully rigid and alert. Grabbing his

M-16, he clutched it like a favorite doll, half-running, half-crawling for the exit of his wood-framed, bamboo hooch. One of his companions made a dive for the door at the same time. Struck in the ear by a flailing elbow, Larson tumbled into the oppressive, damp heat and darkness of the jungle night. Footsteps pounded around him. Guns coughed and chattered, muzzle flashes cutting the blackness in random spots, densest near the perimeter.

Tracers streaked the night red, and a mortar round thudded to earth, loud despite distance. Gunfire churned dirt that rattled from the tin-roofed shelters. Fear threatened to overwhelm Al Larson. The instinct to run nearly overpowered him, balanced only by the terrible realization that there was nowhere safe to go. He froze, watching illumination rounds glaring whitely, seeing dark forms running, rolling, and low-crawling on both sides of the coiled concertina wire perimeter.

"Mommy!" someone screamed in frantic, mindless agony. "Oh, Mommy, Mommy."

An explosion stifled the sound, close enough to rain dirt over Larson. . . .

. . . A curse reverberated through Larson's head in a foreign tongue he could not quite place, Silme's voice wildly out of place.

The fire support base wavered, smothered suddenly in darkness. The wet, closed heat snapped open to admit New Hampshire breezes. The gun clenched to his chest became a .30/.30 rifle; the white slashes across his vision transformed to the pond-reflected glimmer of dawn light through pine. The chaotic scramble of men vanished as abruptly as a cleaver cut, leaving a peace so complete Larson felt certain he had died.

Carl Larson's whisper rattled in his son's ear. "Al, ease up. Don't strangle the gun."

The voice seemed so familiar yet so wrong. *Dad's dead.* The thought intruded from a later, less innocent age. Panic descended upon Larson. He whirled, needing to see the father who had taught him to hunt deer, scarcely remembering to keep the barrel aimed at the ground.

The father watched his son impassively, eyes gray in the

twilight. Shadows played across wide features, and he ran
a meaty hand through close-cropped hair.

Rounder of face, eyes half-hidden beneath a blond mop,
Larson studied his father as if for the first time. Every taut-
ened nerve in his body screamed of danger and distortion.
Dad's dead. He's dead. The paradox unsettled Larson. He
dove for reality, grounding his sanity on a flash of memory.
Dragon! Taziar and Astryd need my help.

An image of the golden-scaled beast filled Larson's mind.
Still in his head, Silme shouted, pummeling his thoughts
aside. The dragon shimmered and melted, replaced by a
creature every bit as large. It stood on four legs, each one
wide as a tree trunk. Plates rose rigidly from its back. But,
unlike the graceful, slender-necked dragons, its triangular
head jutted from a short bulbous neck, low to the ground.
Larson recoiled, screaming. Around him, a crowd parted
hurriedly, and a vast myriad of conversations and comments swallowed the noise. *It's just wax. A stegosaurus. '64
World's Fair.*

Even as Larson identified his surroundings, he was hurled
into a savage vortex of memories. Bombarded by images,
he lost all sense of place and time. Perceptions passed, too
quickly for him to anchor his reason: turgid, ghost-white
bodies muted to tight couples flinging their arms and hair
in wild dances. Then his sense overturned beneath a pile
of young male day campers. Flowers spun past, followed
by a coffin. *Tom Jeffers' coffin.* Even as Larson identified
it, his mind conjured its contents, though the closed casket
ceremony had never forced him to recognize his friend.
Soft, dark eyes bulged from a face half torn away, revealing
bone streaked scarlet.

Grief struck Larson with a fullness that promised sanctuary. He lunged for its stability. Silme's scream slammed
through his mind. He felt himself falling, spiraling through
madness, clawing desperately for any reality. The collage
of the past shattered. He jarred to a sudden halt, blinking
to get his bearings . . .

A hearse zigzagged between tended plots, cars trailing it
like links in a chain, distant but drawing closer. Al Larson
leaned against a boulder in front of seemingly endless rows

of headstones in lines as straight and proud as soldiers. Beside him, his younger brother, Timmy, huddled, clinging to Larson's T-shirt. Sandy hair framed brown eyes and a freckled face above a too-thin body. *Timmy.* Larson went motionless and silent, trying not to get too involved with the scene in case insanity closed in on him again.

But Timmy's grip felt warm through the cotton. Though quavering, his voice sounded near and real. "Why? Why did Daddy have to die? Why would he go to heaven and leave us?"

Larson forgot to breathe. The words he had meant to speak, that he *had* spoken the first time he lived this same incident vanished. Unable to gather the air needed for speech, Larson grabbed his brother in a crushing, welcoming embrace. "Timmy. God, Timmy."

The boy's arms looped around his brother, tightening.

Timmy's closeness soothed Larson. The sound of the child's heart remained a reassuring constant that precluded concern for groundings and other reality. *Timmy. It's really Timmy. If this is illusion, please, God, let it last.*

Suddenly, Timmy's grip went lax. He struggled. Bracing a hand on Larson's arm, he tried to push away.

Surprised and distressed by the change, Larson released his brother.

"Ow!" Timmy brushed at wrinkles, straightening the New York University symbol on the shirt Larson had gotten during his single semester. "Al, cut it out! Don't squish me."

Scarcely daring to believe excitement had caused him to brutalize his brother, Larson stared at his own muscular forearms in shocked disbelief. Accustomed to the slender appendages that matched his elf form, his weight-trained, human limbs appeared massive, strong as an ox's and nearly as awkward. His blue jeans felt comfortable compared to scratchy wool and homespun, the knees patched with sewn flowers. His black and white tennis shoes looked odd after months of leather boots. He raked back thick blond locks, missing the baby fine hair that had hung to his elven shoulders.

The funeral procession glided to a halt about two hundred yards to Larson's left, another family's problem on a neighboring plot.

Larson opened his mouth, but no words emerged. He had no idea where to start. *I've got Timmy back.* He recalled telling his brother about going to war, Vietnam's distant challenge as enticing as it was frightening, his optimism and youthful confidence not yet poisoned by reality. He remembered, too, the hollow glare of hatred in Timmy's eyes, the boy's refusal to say "good-bye" to his only brother. When Larson had stepped onto the bus that took him to his first army base, he left that silence unbroken, haunted by his brother's betrayal and hostility, feeling sorry for himself. Only much later did he come to realize the hurt he had inflicted on Timmy.

First Dad, then me. One by one, the child's loved ones abandoned him. *I have a chance to say something here and now, to make everything right for Timmy. How often in life do we get a second chance?* Caught up in the moment, other realities slipped from Larson's thoughts. For now, he forgot that he stood in a future he was destined to obliterate from existence, forgot that a semipermanent anchoring in the past meant that he had to have dragged a sorcerer with him to St. Raymond's Cemetery.

"Timmy." Larson put a hand on his brother's wrist, using the other to tousle the sandy hair. "Dad's death was a horrible accident. He didn't want to leave us. He didn't mean to leave us. He loved us dearly, the same way we loved him, and the same way I love you." The words would have been impossible for the nineteen-year-old Al Larson whose body huddled against a boulder in a graveyard. But the mentality that filled it now knew death as a personal enemy. He had tasted fear, been stung to action by desperation, and had slaughtered with his own hands. Still, the words came only with great difficulty. He agonized over each one, certain he could have chosen better ones, yet calmed by the realization that just talking was better than the way he had left Timmy the last time. Al Larson pressed his back against the boulder, now facing the funeral, his attention partially diverted by the procession.

The car doors opened. A couple emerged from the second vehicle, clinging to one another like lost children. Even from a distance, Larson guessed they were in their early forties, about his mother's age. And while he and Timmy

mourned a father, these strangers were, undoubtedly, burying a son.

Timmy shifted closer to his brother.

"With Dad gone, Mom can't afford to take care of us
all. I'm going to have to go to the war." The explanation
pained Larson, trebling in difficulty as a huddled group of
pallbearers hefted a flag-draped coffin. Muffled noises
drifted to Larson's ears, the words a distorted mosaic of
grief.

Larson wiped his palms on his jeans, fighting the denial
that rose within him. *What if I'm here to stay? I'm not
going back to war. They can't make me serve twice.* "It's
not something I want to do. It's something I have to do.
We don't have the money for me to go back to college. If
I don't go voluntarily, the Army will drag me there. Understand, I want to stay with you. If it's at all possible, I'll be
back in a year." Larson felt Timmy trembling against him
and realized he was shaking at least as much. Unable to
look at his brother, he watched as five men in army uniforms emerged from the next car in the procession, three
carrying rifles. Mourners exited the remaining vehicles from
both sides, forming a growing, dark cloud of suits and
dresses.

Larson shivered, his thoughts sliding naturally to his own
death in Vietnam. *Is this where they buried me?* Recalling
his placement in time meant his human persona had another year to live, he amended. *Is this where they will bury
me?* Memories surfaced, of the other members of his patrol
killed, one by one, in the jungle depths, of his own crazed
suicide run amid the blatter of enemy guns. *Missing in action, no doubt. Likely, they never found . . . will never
find . . . the body. This body. My body.* Larson studied
his jeans and sneaker clad form protectively. Suddenly fear
nearly crippled him. *I'm going to die. I even know when.
And how.* He clutched at the boulder, forcing aside the
savage maelstrom of thought for Timmy's benefit. "I love
you." He reached for the boy.

Timmy dodged so abruptly, he nearly fell from the boulder. "You're lying! Why are you lying?" he screamed in
tearful hysteria.

Larson had never seen his brother so unhinged.
"Timmy?"

Crying coarsened Timmy's voice. Sudden frenzied rage and fear turned it into a shrill parody. "You're going to die there! You're going to die in Vietnam, and you know it! You're lying! You already know you're going to die!"

"Timmy, quiet. Please." Larson glanced toward the funeral, relieved to find no one looking their way. Apparently, distance had obliterated Timmy's tirade. Still, Larson knew his brother well. This was not a simple childish outburst, grounded only on fear. The certainty of Timmy's voice was unmistakable. *He knows. How could he possibly know?* Only one source presented itself. *Someone entered his mind and told him. Some Dragonrank sorcerer. But who? And why?* Larson whirled. His father's headstone caught his eye, skewing his attention from his search just long enough for the words and dates to register:

R.I.P.
Carl Larson
Born: February 12, 1926
Died: May 5, 1968

Silme's voice broke the stillness, her presence confirming what Larson had already divined. "Allerum! You killed them!" She spoke in ancient Scandinavian, her tone combining fury and hatred, the accusation etched with venom.

Larson dropped to a crouch, scanning the rows of graves. Silme stared with narrowed eyes, one booted foot propped against a headstone. She wore the same red and gold robes as in tenth-century Europe. Casually, she glanced at the funeral group behind her. Then, apparently finding them occupied and nonthreatening, she turned her full attention to Al and Tim Larson.

Timmy's fingers gouged Larson's shoulder, trembling.

Larson wanted to comfort his little brother but could not tear his gaze from Silme's aggressive stance. He used the same language. "What did you tell Timmy? Why would you torture a child?" Then, as Silme's words penetrated past his alarm for Timmy, he asked, "Killed who? What are you talking about?"

"Taz and Astryd," Silme hissed. "You killed them."

"No." Uncertainly took all vigor from Larson's denial. If his bone bomb had not killed Taziar and Astryd, it might have prevented them from escaping the dragon's flames. Urgency whipped through him. "Silme, we have to get back. We may still be able to save them." He glanced at Timmy, saw confusion and horror on the child's features. Yet Larson knew his responsibilities waited in tenth-century Germany where his friends lay at the mercy of a Chaos-crazed sorcerer. *What's happened has happened. I can't change the past.* Realization struck. *Or can I?*

"You killed them." Silme lowered her foot. "And now I'm going to kill you."

"Kill me? Have you gone mad?" Ideas crawled through Larson's mind. He tried to stall, fighting a paralyzing wave of emotions. "Vidarr was right."

"Right about what?" Silme asked sullenly, despite herself. She had served the god faithfully for years, and, even now, paused long enough to hear him out.

Larson kept his gaze fixed on Silme, trying to read changes in her disposition. "He said you'd succumbed to Chaos. That Bolverkr had done something terrible to you."

Silme's expression became one of cruel amusement. "Bolverkr did nothing but open my eyes to the truth. He made me realize our marriage was based on desperation and convenience. And that you and Vidarr aren't worthy of my time."

Silme's words fell like a slap. *I can't believe I attributed her mood swings to the pregnancy. How stupid could I be?* Silme's loyalty to innocents and her religion had never fallen into question before. "Silme, what are you saying? Now you abuse children? You no longer believe in the god you've served for years. And you're going to kill your own husband and your baby? Can't you see how strange and ridiculous this is? Bolverkr's influenced you somehow. For God's sake, fight him! Remember who you were."

The military men sorted themselves out from the cluster of relatives and friends. Larson envied their rifles, though surely they carried only blanks.

"I was a fool." Silme raised a hand in sudden threat. "You're an anachronism and a menace to the Balance. And now, I destroy you."

Larson shrank back against the stone, shielding Timmy. "Wait, Silme! You can't cast spells. You'll kill the baby. It's your own flesh and blood." Larson groped around the boulder for a weapon, finding nothing. Once Silme called upon her life chaos, the baby would be killed; and, unless Larson moved quickly, he would die with it.

Timmy clutched at Larson.

Silme hesitated, but she did not lower her arm.

Larson measured the distance to her, saw the huge amount of ground he would need to cover faster than her spell, and knew despair. "Silme, if you kill me, you have no way to get back to your own world." He mentally traced the route to the cemetery entrance, beyond the funeral party. *If I can get the bystanders between me and her, surely she won't cast.* He had to hope her long dedication to innocents would keep her from endangering them, even if her morality no longer did. *But how can I buy the time to run that far?* He continued, trying to distract her with speech until a coherent strategy formed. "You're as much an anachronism here as I am there." Larson looped an arm around his brother, drawing the child closer. "Will you have to destroy yourself?" He lifted his pain-filled gaze to her eyes, seeing the perfect beauty that had stolen his love.

Again, Silme paused.

Behind her, three guns roared simultaneously, the first shot of the triple salute. Silme stiffened, spinning to face this new danger.

Now! Larson seized the opening. Shoving Timmy toward the procession, he sprang for Silme. He covered the distance between them in three running strides, raising his clasped hands to strike.

Silme whirled, back-stepping.

Larson tried to redirect his charge but momentum overbalanced him, and he sprawled to the ground at her feet. Scuttling backward, he tried to stand.

The toe of Silme's boot caught Larson square in the ribs, driving the breath from his lungs. She muttered the first harsh syllable of a spell word.

The second gunshot rang through the graveyard.

No! Ignoring his pain, Larson lunged, catching her foot as it retreated. He wrenched.

Silme's incantation broke to a gasp of enraged frustration. No light or sparks accompanied the change, no evidence that she had delved life energy for sorcery. She twisted, falling to her hands and knees. She fumbled for something in her cloak.

The third shot split the air. In its wake, Timmy called frantically, "Al! Al!"

Larson launched himself at Silme, wishing she had spent less time with his ronin swordmaster. "Run, Timmy. Get out of here. Go!"

Silme leapt for Larson at the same time. A glint of sunlight off metal in her fist warned him. Larson lurched sideways, grabbing for her wrist. His attack fell short, but the movement saved him. The knife sliced open a belt loop on his jeans, sparing his flesh. Her knee plunged into his thigh, missing his groin by inches.

Shit. Stunned by the ferocity of Silme's attack, Larson crouched. His fingers knotted, burrowing up handfuls of dirt. He could no longer doubt that she intended to kill him. Still, the idea of harming Silme seemed baser than the vilest evil. *But I don't need to hurt her. I only need time to run. And to think.*

Silme charged again, jabbing the knife expertly. Kensei Gaelinar had taught his lessons well.

Larson dodged, dropping his training for crude, street-fighting techniques. He ducked beneath Silme's guard, hurling both fistfuls of sand into her eyes.

Silme's aim went wild. She skittered backward, avoiding a blow that never came.

Larson did not press the attack, instead using the time gained to cover as much ground as possible. *She can't cast if she can't see.* He darted toward the funeral, and the exit, catching Timmy within four strides. He grabbed the child in mid-run.

Suddenly upended, Timmy yelped, then settled into Larson's arms like a giant rag doll.

Silme made a muffled noise of rage and pain.

Larson sprinted over tended grounds, skirting the funeral at the barest fringes of polite distance before using it as a shield. For now, all he could think about was rescuing Timmy and the baby, though other needs gnawed at the back of his mind.

Once Larson passed the funeral, the wrought iron fencing looked like black thread against the afternoon's silver; it funneled toward the central gate. Larson gained some solace from the realization that most of Silme's spells were defenses learned against Bramin's magic. Although Dragonrank mages could cast any spell, attempting one she had never tried before would cost vast quantities of life energy. And it would take longer and more acute concentration, not the sort of thing she would hurl in a wild situation or blindly. *I hope.* Larson repositioned Timmy over his shoulder, barely noticing the weight but needing to free his hands.

The gate loomed in Larson's vision. He charged for the opening and barreled through it. Setting Timmy down, he whirled, wasting time pulling the gates shut, hoping the technology of its latching would foil Silme, at least temporarily. As the gates creaked closed, too slowly, Larson slammed the bolt home.

"Who is she? What's going on? Why does she want to hurt us?" Timmy barraged his brother with questions.

"Later." Larson grabbed Timmy's hand, breaking back into a run that half-dragged his brother down the sidewalk. *If I stand still and look around, Silme can access my thoughts, locate us, and transport. We've got to keep moving.* Flipping Timmy back into his grip, Larson sprinted around smaller blocks toward the main highway and the hotel district. Cars whizzed along the roadways, seeming absurdly fast after more than a year spent among ox carts and horses.

Larson waited until a break appeared in the traffic, then darted into the street.

A canary yellow taxi careened around the corner, honking a continuous blast at Larsen.

Larsen came to an abrupt stop. Still in the car's path, he swung Timmy to safety.

The cab screeched to a halt inches away from Larson, horn blaring. The driver poked a darkly-bearded head through the window. "Are you deaf and blind or just stupid? I could have killed you!"

"I need a cab."

The driver glanced at the lit sign on the roof of his vehicle. "Well, surprise. You found one." He made a circular gesture, his smile softening his sarcasm. "Most of my fares come in by the door instead of the windshield."

A driver in a powder blue Dart behind the taxi leaned on his horn.

The cabby made an abrupt, obscene gesture through the window, and a line of vehicles squeezed around his taxi.

Seizing Timmy's hand, Larson sidled to the door, wrenched it open, and slid inside. Timmy took the seat beside him, then pulled the panel shut.

The cab threaded back into traffic.

Larson sank into a vinyl seat rank with cigarette smoke. He gasped for breath, only now realizing how much his lungs ached. His heart pained him, too. *I love Silme so much. How could I let this happen?* A worse thought filled his mind. *What if I have to hurt her?* Horror tightened its hold. *What if I have to kill her? Or she kills Timmy?*

Timmy touched his brother's hand in question.

The cabby cleared his throat. "You want to go any place in particular or just ride in circles?"

"Manhattan," Larson said at random. Shaken back to reality, it occurred to him that he might have no money except rude gold and silver coins. He reached into his back pocket, reassured by the bulge of a wallet. Removing it, he flipped it open, discovering more than enough bills to afford the trip from the Bronx to anywhere in Manhattan. His driver's license met his gaze, and he thumbed it free. The smudged photo seemed familiar yet distantly alien, the man he used to be.

"You from I-o-way, kid?"

"What?" Drawn from his reverie, Larson looked up.

"Manhattan's a big town. You want to go any place in particular?"

Larson knew only that he had to keep moving, had to lead Silme away from his family's home in the Bronx village of Baychester. *She can read my thoughts. I can't even think about home or she'll find Mom and Pam. She might hurt them or use them to lure me into a trap.* "Broadway Theater." Feeling a strange need to explain his choice, he continued, "Every time one of my out of state relatives calls, they always tell me to give their regards to Broadway. This seems like as good a time as any." Hoping to confuse Silme, he filled his mind with images of Claremont Park, a broad square of Bronx greenery where he used to take

Timmy when his brother was an infant while his mother and sister shopped at Sears.

"Yeah. Right." The cabby shrugged, and in the rearview mirror, Larson could see the man shaking his head.

Larson considered Claremont Park in rapt detail, purposefully diverting his thoughts from his family. Experience told him that sorcerers could only magically transport to places they had studied personally, but Astryd had once entered a prison she had seen only by accessing Larson's thoughts and looking through his eyes. Uncertain whether Silme could transport to a place Larson saw only in his memory, he repeatedly detailed the route from St. Raymond's Cemetery to Claremont Park. *Silme doesn't know about cars. She'll have to assume I walked. If I can get her to walk, too, it'll keep the baby alive a little longer.*

"Al, what's going on?" Timmy sounded frightened. "Why aren't we going home? How come I know you're going to die?" He huddled closer, his tears warm and wet on Larson's arm.

"Just a second, Timmy." Larson put his brother off a little longer, as a new idea disturbed him. *What if this is an alternate reality? The park I remember may not exist.* He addressed the cabby. "Driver, you familiar with Claremont Park?"

"Yeah, just took a couple of kids there this morning, in fact. Boy carrying this duct tape sword with a girl dressed like she come out of a fairy tale." The cabby shook his head at the memory. "There's some sort of group meeting there. Society for Creating Anarchy-ism or some such." He glanced back. "Why? You want to go there instead?"

"No," Larson said quickly, hoping he had not inflicted a Chaos-cursed sorceress on a crowd of college students. *I can't change focus now, or she'll know I'm diverting her. It's a big park. And I don't think she'll harm anyone if she doesn't find me there.* He turned his thoughts back to the route, keeping it always in a conscious pocket of memory.

"Al," Timmy whined.

Larson sighed heavily, aware his tale might better pass for an episode of Star Trek, yet knowing he had to tell the boy something. He wrapped his arm around the child. "Timmy, favorite brother of mine, you're not going to believe this. . . ."

CHAPTER 9
Chaos Transport

Nothing, I am sure, calls forth the
faculties so much as the being obliged
to struggle with the world.
                    —Mary Wollstonecraft
         Thoughts on the Education of Daughters

Taziar Medakan jolted awake. He kept his eyes closed and,
for a moment, he heard and felt nothing. Unable to remember where he was nor how he might have gotten there, he
tried to orient in his mind. Instantly, agony hammered and
squeezed him. His legs throbbed with bruises, his back
stung from burns, and his wrists and ankles felt raw. A soft,
unfamiliar cloak touched the damaged skin on his back
through holes charred in the cloth of his climbing shirt. He
discovered he was kneeling on stone, head sagged to his
chest. It seemed an odd position for sleeping, but pain fore-
stalled curiosity.

A voice tore open Taziar's dark void of pain. "Answer
me, bitch, or I'll tear open your throat and watch you
bleed."

A choked whimper followed, then Astryd replied, her
tone weak and fearful but still vividly conveying frustration.
"I told you I don't know. I just don't know."

Taziar's eyes snapped open. In the center of an unfamiliar room, Bolverkr supported Astryd with an arm wrapped
across her abdomen. Her hands and feet were bound. The
sorcerer's other arm looped around her neck, a dagger
pressed tightly to her throat. Taziar knelt in a corner, opposite a heavy oak and brass door. Otherwise, the room
stood empty.

Taziar lunged at Bolverkr, but his numbed legs did not
obey him. The abrupt movement tore pain through his
hands, and resistance jarred him backward. Only then did

he realize ropes lashed his wrists so tightly that the hemp had abraded them raw. More rope encircled his ankles, tight enough to leave impressions in his boots, though the leather protected his skin. He howled. "Leave Astryd alone! Let her go!" He struggled madly. His efforts sprawled him to his side. He fought the ropes, pain flashing through him until it overcame vision and thought.

Bolverkr laughed. "So the little thief's awake. Things should get interesting now."

Taziar went still, curled against the pain. The ropes chewed into his flesh, and blood trickled across his palms. He rolled a sideways glance at Bolverkr. "Please. Let Astryd go. Free her, and I'll tell you anything you want to know." Briefly Taziar wondered why a sorcerer of such power chose to use brute force as a means of questioning. *And why doesn't Astryd leave magically?* Taziar knew most Dragonrank mages learned transport escapes early, and he had seen Astryd use spells to travel before.

Bolverkr's grip stiffened. The blade grazed Astryd's neck, but she did not seem to notice. Her expression combined desperation with defeat, and fatigue stole the sparkle from her eyes. Her usually feathered blonde locks now hung in limp, sweat-dampened bangs.

She's exhausted, her life energy wrung out. Taziar recalled hazy details of the battle, aware Astryd had spent her aura on a spell that his frantic dive to protect her had dispelled before she could finish its casting. *How ironic. I threw myself in front of her, ready to die to spare her. And she drained her life energy on a spell that was probably intended to protect me.* Answers wove through Taziar's anguish-fogged mind. He knew that, aside from Bolverkr, no Dragonrank mages held enough power to bring other people with them during transports. It would cost Astryd huge volumes of life energy to break Bolverkr's grip. Bolverkr would know that, too, and it explained why he had chosen a physical means of interrogation.

Bolverkr studied Taziar, a grim scowl tracing aged features. "Where did Silme and Allerum go?"

Taziar blinked, stunned by the question. A myriad of emotions swirled through his mind: relief that some of his companions had escaped safely, shock that Bolverkr could not locate the pair with his magic, and grinding terror that the sorcerer demanded information Taziar did not have. *When Bolverkr finds out I can't give him an answer, what will he do to Astryd?*

"Well?" Bolverkr said.

Stalling, Taziar licked his lips, glancing at Astryd's haggard face for some clue. Another thought dazed him deeper into silence. *Gods, what if she does have enough energy to transport but she doesn't want to leave me?* Astryd's obvious exhaustion precluded the possibility, but pain and concern stifled Taziar's ability to think clearly. He wanted to scream at her to save herself, to see to it that at least one of them survived the ordeal, but he needed to address Bolverkr's query first. He tried to sound matter-of-fact and unafraid. "When Astryd and I fell unconscious, Silme and Allerum were still fighting. Neither of us could know where they went."

Bolverkr tensed in rage. The blade bit into Astryd's flesh, and blood beaded down a line across her neck. "Where are they? Damn it, don't play games with me, or I'll hack your woman into pieces and feed them to you. You've got until I count to ten. One, two . . ."

"Wait!" Taziar screamed, needing time to think.

Bolverkr granted no quarter. ". . . three, four, five . . ."

"At least tell me enough to figure out what might have happened!" Taziar shouted over the next three numbers.

". . . nine. . . ." Apparently recognizing the merit of Taziar's question, Bolverkr dropped his count. "Fine. Silme disappeared without transporting. Allerum collapsed before my spell hit him, then disappeared before I could finish him. Now, *where did they go?*"

Taziar covered his joy at his companions' escape with a blank expression of confusion. As a child, he had won some of his food money by con man's tricks and feats of skill, including freeing himself from ropes. He plucked at Bolverkr's knots, drawing the sorcerer's attention away from the attempt by meeting his gaze. "Why don't you just use a locating spell?"

Bolverkr's blue eyes narrowed. "Of course, I tried a location triangle, you little bastard! It didn't work. I couldn't contact Allerum's mind either. It's as if they disappeared from the nine worlds. And *I want to know why!*"

Because they have *disappeared from our nine worlds.* The answer came easily to Taziar, based on his conversation

with Larson after the attack on Bolverkr's keep, but he
preferred to give the enemy as little information as possible. *Astryd was unconscious during that discussion. She
probably really has no idea where they've gone.* "I can't tell
you where Silme and Allerum went. I don't know."

"You don't?" Bolverkr's scowl disappeared, replaced by
calculation. His grip on Astryd's abdomen loosened.
"Strange coincidence. There are things I don't know either.
Like mercy." He drove his fist into her gut.

Astryd stiffened, then sagged in Bolverkr's grip, fighting
for breath. Panic scored her features.

Taziar cringed in sympathetic agony. The knots defied
him. So far he had managed only to draw their opposite
sides deeper into his flesh. "Stop! Bolverkr, please stop.
Let her go, unharmed, and I'll tell you everything I know."

Sweat spangled Astryd's forehead. She gasped in several
lungfuls of air.

"So you *do* know where they've gone?" A slight smile
appeared on Bolverkr's face.

Taziar knew his own survival and Astryd's depended on
Bolverkr's belief that the Climber had information. As his
pain became more familiar, his mind was clearing, allowing
logic to slip to the forefront. *If we convince him we know
nothing, he'll kill us. If he thinks we've told all we know,
he'll kill us. My life lasts only as long as my silence and
only as long as my pleas of ignorance don't convince him.*
Taziar had survived torture before, but this time Astryd's
life and limbs hung in the balance as well. "Maybe I know
where Allerum's gone. And Silme. Don't hurt Astryd. Free
her, and I'll tell you what I know."

Bolverkr paused, apparently taking the deal under serious consideration. "That's fair. I have no feud with her.
Fine, weasel. Talk." He stared at Taziar, aloofly menacing.

"Don't." Astryd wheezed, raising a glimmer of her usual
emotional strength, now sapped by fatigue. "Don't tell
him anything."

Taziar maneuvered back to a kneeling position, prefer-
ring to face Bolverkr as nearly upright as possible. "Let
her go. Then I'll talk."

Bolverkr snorted. "First you say you know nothing. Then
you say you know something. And I'm supposed to believe you

when you say you'll talk? Without Astryd, what's to keep
you from claiming you don't know anything after all?"

Taziar finally managed to work his smallest finger through
one of the knots. "The same thing that will keep you from
killing Astryd after I talk," Taziar admitted. "Nothing. But
it's a lot more likely you can get me to talk than that I can
get you to release Astryd. Let her go, and I promise to tell
you where I believe Allerum and Silme have gone." Taziar
did not bother to contemplate too long. He had no idea
what he would tell Bolverkr, only that he needed to stall
as long as possible in the hope that he could free himself
or that Astryd would regain enough power to transport.

Bolverkr continued holding Astryd just as solidly. "But,
you see, I'm not in a position where I have to bargain. I've
agreed to let Astryd go when I could have simply promised
to kill her quickly and without torture." No emotion radiated from Bolverkr. His expression went grave, matching
the straightforward seriousness of his tone. "Here's the
deal. There will be no other. I'm going to count to ten
again. If you haven't told me everything about where Silme
and Allerum are by that time, I'll cut off Astryd's head and
throw it to you. Then I'll smash a gaping hole in your mind
barriers and extract the information myself."

Taziar went rigid. Sweat trickled from every pore, and
his mouth went so dry he doubted he could speak. His
every instinct told him that Bolverkr would not threaten
idly, and he knew the Dragonrank mage was capable of
fulfilling his promise. The only being in history with enough
power to rupture the natural mind barrier of any man,
Bolverkr had gained his previous lackey, Harriman, by that
method. Taziar picked more desperately at the knots. Their
stiffness gave him almost no room to work, and his own
blood slicked the coils, making a grip nearly impossible.

"One, two, three . . ."

Broken at last, Astryd began to cry.

". . . four, five . . ." The razor edge of knife blade turned
the scrape at Astryd's throat into a welling line of blood.
". . . six . . ."

The ropes continued to defy Taziar. Hot tears of frustration blurred his vision. *Why does it matter whether I tell
Bolverkr where I think they are? He can't get to them anyway.* A thought flitted past. *But if they went to Allerum's*

world, why did his elf body disappear? Taziar discarded the latter question for more dire concerns.

". . . seven, eight. . . ."

Out of time. Fingers still entangled in the biting ropes, Taziar blurted. "They went to Allerum's world. Now let Astryd go."

"Allerum's world? What do you mean?" Bolverkr interrupted his count to ask.

Astryd shivered in his grip, her eyes clenched shut.

Taziar cleared his throat, speaking slowly, trying to use the opportunity to gain more time. "Well . . . um . . . you see. The truth is that I know that Allerum isn't really an elf. He—"

Bolverkr cut Taziar off. "I know all that! But he's displaced in time. No one can transcend time. How could they get to Allerum's world?"

"Well," Taziar started again. He feigned a coughing fit.

Bolverkr shifted from foot to foot. His glare warned Taziar he would take little more of his stalling.

"Well, I don't really know. I mean, I'm no sorcerer. . . ." Taziar trailed off, but Bolverkr was no longer listening.

The old sorcerer's eyes rolled back. His grip on Astryd's abdomen cinched, though the knife retreated slightly. His face lapsed into wrinkles.

"What's he doing?" Taziar redoubled his efforts at the ropes with little more success.

"I don't know," Astryd whispered, her voice a pale ghost of its usual resonance.

Bolverkr appeared to pay no attention to the exchange, so Taziar took a chance. "Listen, Astryd. Get yourself out of here. There's nothing you can do for me, except maybe to get some help."

Astryd swallowed hard. "I know. But I only have a shred of life energy left. It's all I can do to stay awake. Casting anything would be sure death." Her voice went tremulous. Just the effort of speaking drained her.

"Don't waste your power talking," Taziar said.

Astryd widened her eyes to indicate need. "It'll be half a day or longer before I gain enough energy to do anything else, and you have to know this now. To take control of my dragon, Bolverkr broke into my mind barriers. . . ."

"Gods, no."

Astryd continued, "I don't believe he's manipulated anything yet, but he's got access. Don't trust me. If I start acting strangely, it means he's rearranged my thought processes. Whatever I might do, remember it's not really me. I love you so much."

Taziar caught and held Astryd's urgent gaze. "I love you, too." Still wrestling with his first knot, he turned his attention to Bolverkr. "I'll get you out of this. You know I will."

"I know," Astryd said, without a trace of doubt. "Listen, though. The spell Bolverkr used against my barriers. It drained more life force than I would have believed anyone had. I'm not sure he's got enough left to do it again soon. Even if he does, I doubt he'd take a chance on letting his aura drop that low, especially when he doesn't know where his enemies are. I don't think he'll carry through on his threat to use the same spell on you."

Now you tell me. Taziar tried to think of soothing words, but before he could speak them, he found Bolverkr returning his stare.

The Dragonrank mage's lips twitched into a frown of consideration.

"You promised to free Astryd," Taziar reminded.

"Yes, I did." Bolverkr spoke in a thoughtful monotone. "I lied. Are you surprised?" He did not give Taziar a chance to respond before addressing Astryd. "Silme once opened her mind barriers to me. I checked that link. It's not quite strong enough to let me transport to her. But she opened herself to you once, too. Didn't she?"

"No!" Astryd's denial came too quickly, and she huddled, looking even smaller.

"Let her go!" Taziar hurled himself at Bolverkr, no longer caring about his bonds. The ropes burned across flesh, and Taziar tumbled to the floor at Astryd's feet. Rolling, he rose to the most graceful crouch his tied ankles allowed. "Let her go! You promised to *let her go!*" Though Taziar knew appealing to Bolverkr's conscience would prove hopeless, desperation pressed him to try. "You said you had nothing against her."

"But I do have something against her." Bolverkr's voice went soft, his expression pensive yet amused. "It seems she has very poor taste in friends." Still clutching Astryd by the waist, he sheathed the dagger. Curving and opening the index finger of his now free hand, he gestured Taziar toward him.

Taziar hesitated. "What do you want from me?"

"Come here, and I'll bring you with us."

Taziar frowned, seeing no reason to trust Bolverkr's explanation. It seemed more likely that, once Taziar came within Bolverkr's reach, the sorcerer would kill him. *What possible reason would he have for bringing me along?*

"Come, now." This time, Bolverkr gestured with his entire hand, easily judging Taziar's reluctance. "If I wanted to kill you, I could do it from here. Bound, I doubt you could dodge my lightning."

Astryd remained still. Her eyes flickered from Bolverkr to Taziar.

Guessing Astryd was about to attempt escape, Taziar tried to seize Bolverkr's attention. "Why would you take me along? That doesn't make any sense." Taziar caught and held Bolverkr's gaze, not liking the idea of talking an enemy out of an action that would prolong his life, yet seeing the need to keep Bolverkr occupied.

Keen, blue eyes studied Taziar from features as craggy and timeless as stone. "I'm hardly obligated to reveal my motives to you." He sneered contemptuously. "But it's worth it if it'll make you cooperate. I don't like fighting on someone else's territory. Allerum may have the advantage of familiarity with place and time, but let's see him throw fire bones at me when I've got his closest friend tied at my side. We'll just call you indemnity against. . . ."

Astryd made a sudden, wild twist that broke Bolverkr's hold on her waist. She thrust a knee into his groin.

Bolverkr's expression flashed from derisive to pained. He swore, hunching and staggering backward.

Astryd lurched toward the door. The ropes around her ankles tripped her, and she sprawled on her face.

Equally crippled by his bonds, Taziar rolled toward her.

Bolverkr spoke a harsh, magical syllable, then broke into ugly laughter. Straightening, he trotted toward Taziar. "Astryd, you stupid bitch, don't you see? Run as far as you want, but you can't escape me. I can enter your mind from *anywhere.*" His fingers closed on Taziar's arm.

Taziar stiffened, whirling toward Bolverkr, prepared to battle to the death to gain Astryd a few steps.

Long, slender fingers gouged through Taziar's sleeve. As the Climber launched himself at Bolverkr, the sorcerer shouted a stream of spell words as sharp as Larson's American curses. Something unseen slammed Taziar, and he spun into a dark, whirling vortex of magic. Dazed and dizzied, he clawed for focus. The ropes chafed, and Bolverkr's nails dug deeper into his flesh. Cut off from his other senses, Taziar focused on the pain. His being upended, suspended from any orientation to up or down, time or place. Only the pain remained constant.

Astryd's scream shattered the silent, lightless void, sounding muffled and far too close. Taziar's world flared open. He found himself amid neatly ordered stripes of harpstringlike thought pathways. Light flashed and sputtered across them. Bolverkr stood beside him, eyes darting as he searched for something.

"Astryd!" Taziar shouted in agony. "Where are you? Astryd!"

Ow! Stop shouting. It hurts. Astryd's words came at him from all directions with the deep, enthralling delivery of a god. Her fear was tangible.

Shocked silent, Taziar listened to the echoes of his own voice.

You're in my mind, Astryd explained. *Careful.*

Taziar had heard Astryd and Silme's descriptions of Larson's mind as a snarled tangle of thought and memory full of blind loops and frayed pathways. Astryd's mind seemed militarily well organized in comparison.

"This way." With magically enhanced strength, Bolverkr dragged Taziar around a woven tapestry of thought, toward a corner of Astryd's mind.

Taziar followed docilely, his bound ankles turning his gait into a shuffle. His thoughts raced in a wheel of futile plotting. Usually, delicate situations enhanced his clarity of mind. Now, ignorance left too many gaps for coherent, logical strategy. *How do I get out? How can I resist? If I fight, will I injure Astryd?*

Anchored on his dilemma and concerned for Astryd, Taziar never saw Bolverkr's foot lash toward him. The sorcerer's boot crashed against the side of Taziar's knee. Pain radiated through his leg. He toppled, his tied arms flailing uselessly for balance; he managed only to guide his fall so he landed on his shoulder rather than his head. The impact shuddered through Astryd's mind.

Astryd groaned.

Oblivious, Bolverkr planted his boot in the small of Taziar's back, pinning him to the floor. He raised a hand, chanting magical syllables.

A faint glow rose in the darkened corner of Astryd's mind. Gradually, it intensified, revealing a seemingly endless, thready corridor trailing off into black obscurity. "There," Bolverkr said in soft triumph.

Taziar wriggled, fighting the pressure of Bolverkr's foot.

Astryd's discomfort and uncertainty filled her mind in waves.

Again, Taziar entwined his fingers in the stiff tangle of ropes at his wrist, loosening a knot. *Got to get free. Got to do something. Anything. And fast.*

Bolverkr ground his heel into Taziar's spine to discourage struggling as well as to indicate his words were intended for the Climber. "I'm going to try to keep a solid grip on you. Understand this. If you fight your way free, you'll be lost outside the fabric of time. Dead. And no one, not the entire pantheon of gods, not every Dragonrank sorcerer who ever lived, could rescue you from oblivion."

Astryd added tremulously. *Shadow, nothing like this has ever been attempted before. I don't know for sure, but my training leads me to guess he's telling the truth. Be careful. I love you.* Sorrow permeated her words, pure and unfiltered by distance, facial expression, or consideration. Her emotions came to Taziar directly from their source.

"I love you," he whispered, afraid to cause her anguish by talking too loudly. "I—"

Bolverkr seized Taziar's wrists and wrenched the little Climber to his feet. Pain cut the discussion short. Bolverkr raised his free hand.

A sensation of pins and needles tingled through Taziar, then exploded to a savage rush of magic. His being seemed to swell, pulsing until he thought his skin would tear open, spilling his insides through Astryd's mind. Then, suddenly, the force became external. He surged forward, whipping through a dark tunnel a thousand times faster than a hunter's arrow. Wind rushed past, icy and painful to his ears. He screamed. But he never heard the noise, as if it remained in place while he charged ever onward at a speed sound could never match.

As unnatural as the motion seemed, time accustomed Taziar to it enough to concentrate on other details. Bolverkr's grip remained tight enough to numb Taziar's forearm to the fingers. The sorcerer's closeness became a reassuring constant, despite its potential for evil. Glitters of magic popped and sputtered through the otherwise unbroken darkness, carrying an aura of Chaos-power Taziar knew originated from Bolverkr with a certainty far beyond common sense. Yet, soon, Taziar detected another presence amid the sorceries, an almost inaudible whisper entwined with the raging, near-omnipotent bellows of power issuing from Bolverkr. *Astryd.* Taziar twisted, seeking some tangible evidence of Astryd's presence.

Bolverkr's hold tightened convulsively.

Suddenly, Astryd's power guttered like a windswept candle flame. Panic spiked through Taziar, from an outside source that could only be Astryd, a terror so powerful and wholesome it scattered his wits. Taziar screamed, clawing blindly at Bolverkr.

The Dragonrank sorcerer swore, the sound piercing in Taziar's ear until the wind swirled it away. Bolverkr's other arm whipped around Taziar's waist, crushing the Climber against him.

The mind-shattering aura of terror snapped out, leaving no trace of Astryd's presence.

Astryd! Before Taziar could gather breath to scream again, he jolted to a sudden stop. Stunned by the impact, he scarcely noticed as his momentum resumed, this time, straight downward. Unconsciousness pressed at him. He tore at the rope, needing pain to revive himself. The knots gave, shearing skin from his hands with an agony that awakened but also incapacitated him.

Bolverkr shouted something incomprehensible, his rage, horror, and desperation filling the darkness with the gripping, monster-sated reality of a child's nightmare. The certainty of death touched Taziar.

"No!" Bolverkr shouted, adding reckless courage to the boil of his projected emotion. Black nothingness snapped open, splintered to sudden light. Taziar landed on his feet with enough force to jar pain from soles to hips. He fell, rolling from habit, his hands free but smeared with blood, his lungs empty.

"Astryd?" Taziar said, his voice a choked hiss. Legs still tied, he slithered to a sitting position, gaze skimming wildly over his surroundings.

Taziar lay on a thick patch of grass behind a pair of tawny tents. Bolverkr crouched beside him, hands balled, tensed for action. In front of him, Silme stared, wide-eyed. The thud of steel on padding echoed from beyond the tents.

For several tense moments, nothing happened. Taziar gasped for breath, trying to assuage his throat and lungs before moving. His fingers edged toward the bindings on his ankles.

"Silme," Bolverkr said. A grin quivered across otherwise shaken features.

Silme glided toward Bolverkr tentatively. "How. . . ?" she started. "Why. . . ?" Then she hurled herself into his arms.

Shocked, Taziar watched the two embrace, certain Silme must be distracting Bolverkr to give her friend time to work his way free. He struggled with the ropes.

Distantly, steel chimed against steel. A crowd's roar followed.

Head cradled against Bolverkr's shoulder, Silme fixed her gaze directly on Taziar. "Taz! Put your hands on your head and leave them there, or I'll crush you like a gourd."

Startled by Silme's unbridled hostility, Taziar obeyed.

Bolverkr released Silme, catching her hands. Though he addressed her, he watched Taziar. "Why did you come here?"

Silme shook back waves of golden hair. "When I saw Allerum using his technology against the dragon, I knew you'd been right about him all along. He didn't even care if he killed his own friends." She gestured at Taziar vaguely. "You got me thinking about how Allerum never belonged to our world. How he needed not just to die, since his soul might remain on one of our nine worlds. He needed to die in his own time."

Taziar let one hand slide toward his neck. *This can't be real. Silme would never turn against us. Never. No body chemical in the world could make her do that.*

Silme glared in warning.

Taziar returned his hand.

Apparently satisfied, Silme continued. "Then I saw Allerum about to throw one of those . . ." She crinkled her nose in disgust. ". . . things at you. I saw a way to stop him. Fast. I took it."

Bolverkr smiled in hopeful triumph. "Allerum's dead, then, too?"

The same question plagued Taziar, but it was Bolverkr's use of the word "too" that speared dread through him. He dared not make much of it yet, aware Silme would also want clarification. His chest squeezed closed, and breathing became a fully conscious process.

"No," Silme admitted calmly. "I acted on impulse. Allerum caught me unprepared. It's been a long time since I've used any spell, and I've never used many for attack." She paused thoughtfully, rubbing at her eyes, and Taziar saw her other hand flex around Bolverkr's fingers then loosen again. "From today, that's going to change."

Beyond the tents, something thunked against hollow metal, followed by smatterings of laughter and applause.

Finally, Silme anchored on the final word in Bolverkr's question. "Too? Where's Astryd?"

"Dead," Bolverkr confirmed matter-of-factly. "Drained out her life energy getting us here. Almost got us all trapped outside reality and time. . . ."

Taziar caught nothing more of Bolverkr's explanation. Grief snuffed his hearing to high-pitched ringing, and he saw Silme through a curtain of spots. Years of living on the streets had taught him to read motivations through expressions. He thought he saw a fleeting glimmer of horror on Silme's face, but it disappeared so quickly he could not tell whether her emotion or his imagination had conjured the image.

Astryd's dead. Astryd is dead! Without her corpse to confirm it, the certainty could not register. Taziar had suspected Astryd's death from the instant panic had overtaken her and her presence had disappeared from her own mind. So far, he had concentrated on his own peril, shoving the realization of Astryd's death from his mind, dismissing it as a misinterpretation of magical events he had no way of truly understanding. Now he could no longer deny it. *Astryd is dead. Her body is lost in the fabric of time. Bolverkr*

killed her, and I sat back and watched it happen. His promise reverberated through his ears, a vow so easily shattered
by circumstance. Repeatedly, he heard himself say, "I'll get
you out of this. You know I will," followed by Astryd's
confident, "I know" in a voice he would never hear again.
Astryd. He sank to the ground in a hopeless fit of apathy,
not caring if Silme killed him for the transgression.

Gradually, Taziar's iron will kicked in, reminding him of
responsibilities he needed to attend to before he could
allow sorrow to paralyze him completely. *I can't surrender.
There's too much at stake.* He listened to the indecipherable
hubbub of voices beyond the tents, interspersed with the
thump and chime of swords against padding or metal.
*There's another world here, hordes of people helpless against
Bolverkr's magic and mental manipulations. If what Allerum
has said is true, there's more innocents in New York City
than in my entire world, and every one of them lacks the
mind barriers to protect themselves from Bolverkr.* Taziar
shoved aside his own sense of loss for concern over the
millions of people occupying Larson's era. *I can grieve later,
but I'll dishonor Astryd's memory if I let sadness conquer
me. For her and her causes, I have to fight.*

Despite his bold attempt to wad the realization of Astryd's death into the depths of remembrance, Taziar's will
felt raw, his heart like a granite boulder in his chest. But
the deafening ringing became familiar enough for him to
listen through it, and Silme's muffled voice wafted to him.

". . . strangest thing. It seems to be some sort of fighting
tournament. But their weapons are crude and unedged.
Their style is ponderous. And I've never seen two soldiers
battle so fairly. Not a single kick, no strikes to the head.
It's weird." Silme shrugged, rolling her eyes at the oddity
of it all. "Their dress looks a lot like our own, though I've
never seen such clean, tiny weave and straight stitching. I
guess this is the rich side of the world."

"Their army?" Bolverkr guessed.

Silme frowned, shaking her head. "No. I've seen war in
Allerum's world. This just doesn't fit. From probing minds,
I've gathered this is some sort of recreational group. Their
language seems to be an unpolished derivative of several
tongues, mixed with bizarre idioms and slang. I've been

ignoring words and gathering meaning through light mind probes."

Taziar curled like a fetus, pretending to be fully unmanned by grief, quietly inching his hands almost imperceptibly toward the ropes around his ankles.

This time, Silme did not seem to notice. "This particular group called themselves 'Sca' which seems to translate nearly into 'play group with imagination that supports anachronisms.' Something like that."

Bolverkr's jaw fell, revealing a straight row of teeth. "They have entire organizations to stand behind time traveling world wreckers?"

"I don't think so." Silme's gaze went solidly to Taziar, and she examined him with suspicion. "As far as I can tell, their mission isn't to protect anything. It seems to have more to do with recreating and romanticizing the past." Silme added pensively, "Our time. And later." Her tone softened, and uncertainly tainted her usual strident confidence. "We don't belong here."

Taziar froze.

"Yes." Bolverkr released Silme's hands. His arms dropped to his sides, fingers twitching with anticipation. "That's why we need to take care of our business and get out of here." He clasped his hands, as if to still them.

Silme turned her attention back to Bolverkr. "So you know a way to get us back?"

Bolverkr hesitated, apparently caught off guard by the question. His brow crinkled.

Taziar seized the moment to pull his hands to his lower legs.

"I came through Allerum's mind. That route won't exist any longer. You say you used a double link from our world to me. Now that we're both in the same place, we can't use that either, especially now that Astryd's dead."

"We'll find a way," Bolverkr said with the same vague assurance Taziar had used to comfort Astryd. "And even if we don't, why would it matter? There's no Balance to worry about, no other sorcerers or gods to stop us. Think of the possibilities, Silme. Two Dragonrank mages sharing ultimate authority in a world without mind barriers. I promised you power. I can deliver the world!"

The enormity of Bolverkr's suggestion struck Taziar.

Horror filled him, quickly replaced by relief. *I know Silme too well. She'll never go along with such a thing. Whatever hold Bolverkr has over her, he'll lose from greed and arrogance.*

But Silme's smile revealed genuine pleasure. She stood in rapt attention as Bolverkr rattled vivid descriptions of buildings crumbling to rubble, people fleeing in blind, bloody panic, and forests shattered to splintered, charred ruin.

And Taziar plucked at knots drawn to unbearable tightness by his struggles in Astryd's mind. Dried blood chipped from his fingers as he worked, trying not to draw attention.

Bolverkr finished with charged promises of a rulership too strong to challenge. "All I need, Silme, is a simple indication that you're truly on my side now. I need you to show that you've overcome this irrational love for a group of insignificant and ignorant strangers, something to seal the alliance."

Abruptly aware all eyes would fall on him, Taziar quit his attempts to free the ropes. He rolled his gaze to Bolverkr and Silme.

Silme's merciless, gray eyes met Taziar's stare without flinching. "If I killed Shadow. Would that be enough?"

Taziar's blood seemed to frost over in his veins. *Too slow again, Medakan. And now it's over.* His heart quickened to a flutter. Still, he could not quite comprehend the changes in Silme. *She wouldn't really kill me? Would she?*

"Yes." Bolverkr grinned like a child with a rare but favorite treat. "Killing Taz Medakan would be enough. That was my reason for bringing him." He let the statement linger, giving Taziar plenty of time to understand the significance before letting him off the hook. "But with Astryd dead, I need the little weasel for barter against Allerum."

Taziar's heart rate slowed, though the knowledge that Bolverkr was about to suggest some equally evil course of action kept him from relaxing even slightly.

Silme, too, said nothing, apparently waiting for the other shoe to fall.

"Destroy Allerum's baby," Bolverkr said.

Silme hesitated, still unspeaking.

"It has no purpose anymore," the sorcerer continued, the words meaning more than Taziar could guess. "Evil spawns

evil. Allerum's child has as much potential for evil as its
father. Kill the baby, and it'll free you to use your magic
the way nature intended. Later, we can make another."

A smile twitched across Silme's lips, looking foreign and
cruel on beautiful features that had once represented beautiful morals as well. She glanced into the heavens, as if
seeking divine guidance. Then her head sank to her chest.
Her hands rose.

Spellbound, Taziar watched, fumbling blindly with his
bonds at the same time. Finding the knot, he gouged at it
with his nails.

A curtain of sparkling buttons wove into the air before
Silme, interwoven with multicolored threads of enchant-
ment. Each spot caught and reflected the evening light like
a perfect diamond from the setting of a ring, a glittering
funeral shroud for an infant who would never be born.

Bolverkr laughed, his joy triumphant, evil, and nearly
tangible.

Sorrow tightened over Taziar. The death of the fetus sad-
dened him, but the loss paled before the knowledge of Astryd's demise and Silme's betrayal. He plucked at the knot,
not daring to contemplate too hard.

Suddenly, Silme's expression became pained. Her arms
collapsed limply to her sides. The elegant curtain of magics
dissolved to a gray net of outline, tarry smoke streaming
from its remains. She gazed directly at Taziar, her eyes as
wide as a frightened child's awakening from nightmare. Her
lower lip uncurled, as if she wanted to speak but could not
find the words. Her hands clenched at her lower abdomen.
All color drained from her features, and she slumped to
the ground.

Bolverkr's grin disappeared. He whirled to face Silme
directly, his hands clamped to her arms. "Silme? What's
happening?"

"Pain," she gasped. "The baby. Gods, it hurts." Her
words garbled into a high-pitched whine of agony.

Taziar continued his struggle with the ropes. The knot
inched open. He knew Bolverkr could see him; at any moment, his magics could tear through Taziar with the same
quiet apathy as Silme had used to kill her own child.

But, fully absorbed in Silme, Bolverkr paid Taziar no
heed. "Silme?" he said with alarm. He caught her close,

harsh, magical syllables of healing rushing from his throat. As with Silme's spell, black chaos-smoke billowed from his sorceries, unlike anything Taziar had seen in his own world.

The knot fell free. Taziar's heart quickened.

Silme's breathing grew more comfortable. She kept her eyes closed against dispersing pain.

Swiftly, Taziar untangled the ropes from his ankles. He measured the distance to the tents, starting a cautious crawl. The dispersing smoke settled over him, bringing an alien sensation of hatred and cruelty, goading him to an evil so far beyond his nature it frightened him.

Bolverkr cried out, jerking away suddenly. "The Chaos I used for the spell. It's gone."

Silme's hands fell away from her abdomen. Still, she made no move to rise, and her voice retained the hesitant, breathy quality that comes with tears. "What do you mean, it's gone? Of course, it's gone. You used it."

"You don't understand." Bolverkr drew Silme closer.

Taziar ignored the corrupt stirrings within him, recognizing them as foreign rather than self, certain they came from the sorcerers. He felt the fog roll over him, heading toward the crowd beyond the tents.

Bolverkr continued, his voice growing more distant. "The Chaos I used is gone. Forever. I can tell I can't get it back."

From beyond the tents, steel crashed against steel. Someone screamed, followed by a collective gasp from the audience.

Realizing the noise would draw Bolverkr's attention, Taziar rose and ran.

From the unseen gathering, a strong male voice cried out a command. Then a string of familiar English swear words erupted from the ranks, followed by a heated argument Taziar could not decipher.

The Shadow Climber dodged between the tents. *The Chaos has touched them, too. Bolverkr's right. It's diffusing, fouling the air like a poison.*

Bolverkr howled a spell word. The snap of wood and the flutter of canvas filled Taziar's ears. The tent to his left collapsed, flames licking across the fabric. Taziar saw an open, grassy lot spotted with tents, pole shelters, and occasional young, spindly trees. A crowd of people surrounded a rectangle staked out with ropes and poles. The spectators wore an odd array of colors and clothing, some in belted silk dresses and tunics, others in crude sacks, and still more in strangely sewn fabrics Taziar did not recognize. Inside the rectangle, one man towered over another who knelt on one knee, looking dazed. Both wore thickly padded cloth, wound and tied around waist, chest, arms, and legs, partially hidden beneath hauberks of chain mail constructed of the most perfect rings Taziar had ever seen. The grounded man wore a hopelessly thin, steel helmet with a huge dent hammered into one side. Both held hilted sticks encased in a shiny, fabric-like substance.

Taziar took in the scene at a glance, more concerned with the wide open lot than with the crowd of screeching spectators. As every gaze whirled toward the mangled tent, Taziar plunged into the masses, at first hoping the sorcerers would hold their deadly spells around innocents, then cursing himself for the danger he placed these strangers in by making a ridiculous assumption not supported by facts. *Bolverkr's destroyed entire villages. Why would I think he would hesitate to murder a few bystanders?* More accustomed to guardsmen's tactics, Taziar had reacted from habit. *I have to get away from this crowd.*

Taziar floundered into a young blonde, her hair bunched into a long braid. She gave him a shove that sent him staggering into a hefty man. The collision jarred Taziar to his knees. Fleeing the ruined tent, a woman tripped over him, accidentally ramming a slippered foot into his ribs. Her consort's boot ground Taziar's hand into the dirt as he passed.

The pain scarcely registered beneath the throb of Taziar's bruises and the constant agony of his mangled wrists. Desperation and cordoned grief robbed all meaning from physical pain. As the throng parted, Taziar scrambled to his feet, racing toward the farther edge of the grassy lot, wishing for cover. He listened for Bolverkr's or Silme's voice beneath the mingled and unfamiliar language and accents of the crowd. No magical syllables touched his ears. No brilliant splashes of sorcery split the afternoon. A strange smell filled the air, the mingled reek of smoke, chemicals, and garbage, but Taziar did not find the ozone odor of killing spells.

Still, Taziar ran. Soon the cushion of grass was replaced

by a tan walkway composed of perfect, giant squares of flat stone. A black ribbon of pathway stretched as far as Taziar could see, hedged by buildings taller than any mountain. People swarmed the lighter-colored walkways bordering the black surface, dressed in a wider variety of colors, patterns, and fabrics than Taziar had ever imagined.

But as varied as the clothing seemed, the spectrum of the human beings who wore them shocked Taziar far more. The split second glimpses he caught winding through the crowds were enough to reveal dark-skinned men and women with hair in tight curls or wild, bushlike arrangements. Some people waddled on legs thick as tree trunks, their bodies more bulbous than the richest royalty. These intermingled freely with others as skeletal as starving beggars. Most fell between the extremes. A curvaceous woman swayed her hips, each step flipping an indecently short skirt farther up her thigh. A willowy man in a loose-fitting shirt and sandals walked beside her, his honey-colored hair and beard dangling nearly to his navel.

Despite the teeming mass of people, Taziar never slowed. He wove and darted, ignoring the shouted warnings he did not understand and the muttered obscenities that he did. Most of the people parted around him. Those who stood firm or did not see him coming, he dodged. The buildings confused him. Lean, endless towers sandwiched squat hovels with grimy signs he could not read. To Taziar's left, a red light flashed. He skittered sideways, crashing into a stout woman so suddenly that she dropped an armload of packages. A bag tore, strewing gauzy fabric across the sidewalk.

"You clumsy idiot!" she shrieked, followed by an accusatory sentence Taziar did not understand.

Ignoring her, Taziar crouched, fixated on the light, expecting Bolverkr's attack. But the scarlet flashes simply outlined a series of runes on a building sign. Shortly, they disappeared and flashed on again.

The crowd parted around the heavy woman as she stuffed her purchases back into the ruined bag. Tossing a parting glare at Taziar, she huffed back down the street.

The pattern of the masses shifted slightly as it milled around Taziar where he stood, frozen in awed stillness. Now that the people had become more familiar, other sights and sounds broke through the hovering fog of grief and fear. Lights in red, green, yellow, and white flared and died throughout the city, some curled into letters, others in hovering dots suspended from wires or poles. An ear-splitting wail cut over the ceaseless hubbub of a thousand conversations. Slammed by a noise louder than anything he had ever heard, Taziar bolted in terror. Tearing through the crowd, he slid onto the darker roadway. Brakes squealed. A horn blasted. Something huge whipped by Taziar three times faster than the fleetest horse cart. Then a red metal vehicle fishtailed to an abrupt halt before him. The bumper smashed into Taziar's hip, hurling him to the roadway.

Dazed, Taziar skidded across macadam, the roadway chafing skin from his leg and side. His mind fogged. Agony and darkness closed in on him, and his thoughts churned madly.

"Oh, my God!" the driver shouted. His car door sprang open. The crowd converged on Taziar.

As the masses drew closer, panic assailed Taziar. Lurching to his feet, he sprinted the rest of the way across the street and darted across the walkway. Another high-pitched blare of noise slammed his hearing. Brakes screamed again, but this time, Taziar gained the sidewalk. Voices chased him.

Taziar fled in blind hysteria, unable to make sense of the sounds and sights around him, uncertain how to avoid the impossibly gigantic, metal objects that swooped down on him faster than he could see them coming. His world narrowed to a strip of vision surrounded by fabricated darkness. He flailed through the press of people, whipping across roads, between buildings, and along alleyways with no knowledge of location or direction.

Finally, pain crushed in on Taziar. His legs ached. His lungs labored for every breath, lancing anguish through his ribs. His hip throbbed worse than any bruise he had gained in the battle. Deep in an alley, he pressed his back to a brick wall and slid slowly to the walkway. His vision returned, revealing darkness to his left and a sea of passing legs on the sidewalk to his right. Tears sprang to his eyes, and he did not bother to wipe them away. Gradually, grief stole all meaning from time, place, and pain, and Taziar surrendered to oblivion.

CHAPTER 10
Chaos Coupled

He that wrestles with us strengthens
our nerves and sharpens our skill.
Our antagonist is our helper.
— Edmund Burke
Reflections on the Revolution in France

The yellow taxi threaded through afternoon traffic on the Major Deegan Expressway. Jouncing with his brother in the back seat, Al Larson studied the patterns of cars, trucks, and buses, cringing each time the cabby whipped into an opening scarcely large enough for a pedestrian. The ceaseless rattle and bump of the cab emphasized its speed until Larson felt like a hillbilly locked in a phantom jet. He wished he had chosen a vehicle with working shocks as his reinitiation to twentieth-century American technology.

"So." Timmy stared at Larson with a wide-eyed innocence bordering on hero worship. "That lady's a witch who can read minds and make you think stuff and use magic and junk like that?"

Phrased by a child, the explanation sounded like a rambling rehash of a Disney animated feature. Larson sighed. "Sort of like that." Defining the present danger seemed enough for now. He had not attempted to explain that he had died, then wound up in a warped, mythological version of ancient Europe in the guise of an elf. So far, Timmy seemed to have accepted his brother's story with guileless simplicity, and Larson did not want to press the limits of even a child's credibility.

"Cool." Timmy bounced against the backrest, twisting to get a better view out the side window.

Still rattled by his run-in with Silme, Larson smiled at his brother's resilience. *One moment in a panicked frenzy, the next cool as a cucumber and ready to play cowboys and*

Indians with a Dragonrank mage. His grin wilted. *Of course, it's all a game to Timmy. He trusts his big brother to keep him safe. And he has no way of knowing how dangerous Silme really is.*

Larson looped his arm protectively about Timmy. No longer directly threatened, he gathered enough composure to realize that the stakes had grown critical. *There's nothing I can do for Shadow and Astryd. If my bomb and the dragon didn't kill them, Bolverkr has had more than enough time to finish the deed.* Fighting down a wave of grief and guilt, he forced his thoughts to his present situation. *I love Silme. But I won't let her torture my family and friends or seven and a half million innocent people.* As readily as his morality rose to the challenge, doubt accompanied it. *I can't hurt Silme. Can I?* Larson wrestled with the dilemma, wishing he had paid more attention to Silme's descriptions of magic and Chaos as renegade or bonded to life energy. For now, it all seemed a blur.

Timmy's questions scarcely penetrated Al Larson's fog of emotion and speculation. "How're you gonna get this witch? Does she make things disappear? Can she throw fire and make stuff dance and ride a broom?" Timmy plunked back down onto the seat, studying Larson with sparkling brown eyes. "When are we going home? I wish Dad was here. Dad would know what to do. . . ."

The word "home" triggered a new direction of thought. Larson waved his brother silent. "Hush up, Timmy. I'm trying to think." *I have to keep Timmy and myself from concentrating on home and family. Otherwise, Silme can get that information from his mind.* Realization came with frightening intensity. *Shit. She might get it anyway. She can't delve too deeply into my thoughts because I know how to tell she's there and build defenses. But she could search Timmy's mind to its core.* Larson went rigid. "Turn around!" he instructed the driver.

The cabby glanced at Larson over his shoulder. "You talking to me?"

Larson simulated a U-turn with his hand. "Turn around. Take us to Freedom Land."

The cabby blinked. "You want to go back to the Bronx?"

Through the windshield, Larson watched the taxi roar

dangerously close to a silver sedan. He sucked in a sharp breath, slamming down his foot on an imaginary brake.

Calmly turning his gaze back to the road, the cabby slowed. "Hey, man. I'll take you wherever you want to go. But you probably ought to know Freedom Land closed down five-six years ago. They're building these new rent-controlled apartments. . . ."

". . . Co-op City," Larson finished. "Yes, I know. Take us there."

Timmy stared, silenced by the urgency in Larson's voice.

The cabby shrugged, tossing his blond head. "You're the boss. But, you know, you were only a few blocks from there when I picked you up." He flicked on the blinker, zipping across two lanes of traffic to an exit.

Someone leaned on a car horn.

Larson stiffened, watching the traffic miraculously part before them. "I changed my mind, all right?" he said between gritted teeth.

"Hey, no problem." The cabby sped down the ramp. "It's your bread, man." He met Larson's eyes in the rear-view mirror. Then his gaze played over the reflection of honey-blond hair just long enough to annoy Larson's father, the sweat-dampened T-shirt, and patched blue jeans. The cabby's features squinted suspiciously. "Say, you ain't one of those hippy types that's gonna try to pay me with peace, love, and happiness, are ya, pal? 'Cause I ain't taking nothing but American dollars and cents."

"I've got money," Larson said quietly, wishing the driver would keep his attention on the road. Just the normal highway speed made him nervous enough without the added concern about whether the cabby might cause a fifty car pileup. "If you take me to a drugstore on the way, I'll double your tip."

"You're the boss." The cabby maneuvered back onto the Major Deegan Expressway, now traveling northward.

Taziar Medakan awakened, sprawled alone in a dark alleyway. Afternoon light slanted between impossibly tall buildings, making Taziar realize that he had not slept long. His head pounded, making thought nearly impossible, over-shadowing the grinding chorus of cuts, abrasions, and bruises. The gashes in his wrists had settled to a dull throb.

Taziar savored a moment of disorientation before reality intruded. Gradually he remembered deeper, more horrible pains. *Astryd and the baby are dead. Silme's joined Bolverkr. And I think I've found Karana's hell. What now?* Only one answer came. *I have to find Allerum.* Common sense seeped into thoughts nearly emptied by pain and panic. *Since Silme came here through Allerum's mind, they must have arrived together. She killed the baby in my presence. She couldn't have cast a transport spell until then or the baby would already have died. That means she didn't magically leave Allerum. He can't be far.* Ignorant of planes, subways, and automobiles, Taziar could not see the flaw in his logic. *If I search the city, I'm certain to find him.*

Buoyed by these new thoughts, Taziar tended to his disheveled appearance. First, he removed the cloak that Bolverkr had thrown over his damaged climbing garb, using brisk strokes and a bandage dampened in a puddle to scrub away the most obvious grass stains and dirt. He combed back sweat-plastered, black hair with his fingers. Spitting on his hands, he washed away dried blood, then drew down his sleeves to cover the gashes from the ropes. Rising, he brushed away dirt and flattened the wrinkles from his dark linen shirt and britches. Then he donned the cloak, arranging it over the fire and road burns and belting it at the waist. The cloak hung to his ankles, the hem tattered into fringe, and he had to roll back the sleeves. But it did hide the worst of his injuries.

The normalcy of the routine soothed Taziar. Usually, panic was a stranger to him. The most dire circumstances only fueled his imagination, sending him into a flurry of thoughtful plotting. But Astryd's death unhinged him, and his new surroundings gave him nothing understandable or familiar on which to ground his reason. Cued to the reality of onrushing traffic, hordes of people, towering structures, and winking lights, Taziar's wits settled into a more manageable pattern.

Where do I start my search for Allerum? Taziar crept toward the mouth of the alleyway, reluctant to plunge back into the clustered human traffic. A wash of voices filled his ears. He had grown accustomed to the bizarre hubbub of English, an incomprehensible jumble of foreign words and accents that fused into a dull roar of background. One voice rose above the others, pitched grandly, apparently to draw attention. *Someone selling wares?* Taziar guessed, though his previous experience on New York City's sidewalks had revealed no street vendors.

Taziar poked his head around the corner.

An elderly woman shied from Taziar's sudden, partial emergence from an alleyway. Others glared, giving him a wide berth.

"Sorry," Taziar mumbled in his own language. Glancing along the sidewalk, he saw a small crowd gathered near the mouth of a parallel alley. At its center, a dynamic black monte shuffled a trio of playing cards folded into tents over a table constructed of cinder blocks and a board. A pimply white teenager stood on the opposite side of the table, garbed in a crisply neat, button-down shirt and dress trousers.

Drawn by the familiarity of a con game in a world that otherwise seemed hostile, Taziar crept closer, studying the scene through gaps in the gathering. The monte revealed the front of the cards with a showman's flourish: a red female with two heads and torsos, one upside down; and a not quite matched pair of black cards. One held a pattern of clovers in rows of two, the other a similar arrangement with single leaves. The monte flipped each card to its back. The reverse sides looked impossibly alike, a complicated series of blue circles, squares, and loops. Taziar watched as the black youth gathered the cards, two in one hand, one in the other, then tossed them back down in a different arrangement.

Though alert for sleights of hand and substitutions of cards, Taziar saw no trickery. The pock-faced player laid a handful of uniform, green papers on the table before the card Taziar knew was the red one.

The monte flicked the card to its opposite side, revealing the queen.

Applause splattered through the spectators. The winner shouted in excited triumph, drawing even more spectators.

The monte said something loudly that sent twitters of laughter through the crowd and included the words "son of a bitch." He drew a packet of folded, green papers from his pocket, counted off several bills and handed them to the player with a composure that could only have been rehearsed.

Taziar nodded sagely, guessing the setup. Obviously, the youths on either side of the table were working together. If so, Taziar knew the player's next move would be to feign difficulty finding enough money for his next attempt. He would talk one of the spectators into covering part or all of a huge bet, one he would promptly lose, along with the other man's contribution.

Despite language and technological barriers, other things seemed obvious. Apparently, this green paper possessed some value. It seemed odd to Taziar, but he accepted it with no way to question. Clearly, the object of the game was for the bettor to pick out the odd card based on watching the shuffle. The one card in three odds of selecting the correct card by random chance did not seem to bother the audience. By nature, people trusted their eyesight and ability to outwit scams as surely as the monte believed in his skill at deception.

As Taziar suspected, the pimple-faced teenager turned to a nearby man, speaking quickly and earnestly in low tones while the monte shifted from foot to foot with mock impatience. Taziar scanned the crowd for evidence of other shills. A petite brunette in an indecently short skirt watched with an expression and stance that revealed more than casual interest. From long practice, Taziar picked out the last two members of the monte's gang. A densely-muscled, black youth and a wiry Hispanic studied the proceedings with feigned indifference, occasionally measuring the crowd with glances. Of them all, Taziar felt most certain about the loyalties of his last find. The Hispanic teen carried a deck of cards in his jeans pocket, one back clearly visible above the stitched edge. The pattern matched the cards on the dealer's table.

As Taziar scrutinized the crowd, he also discovered a schemer unrelated to the gang. A nondescript, middle-aged man moved adeptly through the masses. Paunchy and balding, he was small, barely the height of an average woman, though he still towered nearly a full head over Taziar. Attracted by the same inconspicuousness that made the rest of the spectators ignore the stranger, Taziar watched him approach a jovial man clutching the hand of a young boy.

As the thief maneuvered past the father, he deftly flicked a leather billfold from the father's back pocket. Stashing it in his own hip pocket, he barely paused before gliding toward his next victim.

Ordinarily, Taziar would have let the heist pass without comment or action. But the thief's bulging gut and carefully tailored clothes led Taziar to believe that he was not stealing from need. Drawn to the conclusion that father and son could make better use of the money, Taziar considered his options. *I have to find Allerum. Now isn't the time to get involved in conflicts that could get me into trouble.* Still, the simple challenge offered by the situation sent his heart into the familiar, calm cadence that preceded action. *I'll handle the bizarre things happening around me better if I'm composed. What could possibly lull me faster than the chance to match wits with a thief?* Decision made, Taziar closed on the pickpocket.

A collective sigh rose from the audience as the pimple-faced teen and his victim lost their money to the monte's sleight of hand.

While the crowd's attention was on the exchange of bills, the pickpocket swiped another wallet. Taziar moved simultaneously. Even as the thief stuffed the new cache into his pocket, Taziar relieved him of the father's wallet, along with a fat wad of loose bills.

Apparently oblivious, the pickpocket waded into the pedestrian traffic on the sidewalk and wandered out of sight.

A warm sense of accomplishment filled Taziar. Grinning, he approached the father and son, aware a slip now would turn a good deed into a fatal error. Briefly, he considered openly returning the man's property but discarded the idea as quickly. *Allerum said the people in his city tended to mistrust strangers. I've got no words to explain the truth if this man blames me for the theft.* Taziar held the wallet in his palm. To free his hands, he stuffed the additional, loose packet of bills into one of the inner pockets lining his shirt.

The father shifted for a better view. As Taziar slipped behind the man, the boy glanced around, a finger drilling into one nostril.

Taziar smiled at the child.

Apparently recognizing Taziar as a small adult rather

than another child, the boy lost interest. He tugged at his father's sleeve.

The man looked down. A brief exchange followed from which Taziar managed to glean only a few prepositions and definite articles. The man hefted the boy, placing the child on his shoulders.

As the man moved, his attention fully focused on his son. Taziar tapped the wallet back into its proper pocket. The Climber hesitated, practiced at looking casual, aware a mad scramble from the site, though tempting, would draw attention. With appropriate nonchalance, he sauntered back into the milling crowd.

The ease of the maneuver disappointed Taziar, and he missed the exhilarating rush that usually accompanied danger. *Too simple. A blind beginner could have returned that purse.* He searched for a more interesting target. His gaze fell on the Hispanic member of the monte's gang. The deck of cards outlined against the hip pocket of his jeans beckoned, a challenge worthy of a master thief. Taziar took a step toward the stranger. Then, logic caught up with his runaway thoughts. *What am I doing? I've got two Chaos-warped sorcerers chasing me and a friend to locate. Why am I looking for more trouble?*

The answer came more easily than Taziar expected. Trapped in a world and time that seemed less ordered than Bolverkr's Chaos, Taziar was clinging to the only familiar situation he had found. The chance to match wits with future hustlers and thieves, sharks with years of others' experience to draw on, intrigued him; and the familiarity of the challenge soothed. Whatever technology the future brought, people apparently were still people, constantly seeking a fast and easy means to make their money. And it seemed there would always be other people willing to prey upon this basic flaw in human nature, sating the same flaw in themselves.

Now understanding his motivations, Taziar forced aside his curiosity. He turned to leave, tossing one last glance at the monte game. At the table, a small, oval-faced woman pulled a bill from her pocketbook.

Astryd! Taziar stared, not daring to question, afraid he might lose her again. *Astryd!* He shoved through the crowd, skidding to a stop beside her.

As Taziar drew up near the woman, he realized his mistake. She stood slightly shorter than he, but there all resemblance to Astryd ended. Dark hair fell to her shoulders. Her muddy-green eyes followed the monte's movements with a precision and concentration even Taziar's sudden appearance could not shake.

Hope vanished in an instant, dashed beneath a rush of disappointment. Unaccustomed to sudden, impetuous actions, Taziar froze, uncertain of his next move. Concerned that grief could shake his judgment so completely that he could mistake another woman for Astryd, he concentrated on the game, hoping to ground his sanity.

The monte talked continuously as he shuffled. Taziar managed to pluck a few catch phrases from the pitch, by their repetition, the resemblance to his own language, and Larson's hints. The phrase, "find the lady" seemed to recur with the greatest frequency.

The woman slapped her bill down before the center card. The monte frowned, apparently displeased by the paltriness of her wager. He paused, as if waiting for her or someone else to increase the bet. When no one did, he revealed her chosen card as a black six. Collecting the money, he then showed her the queen as the leftmost card and another six on the right. He gathered the cards, a six tented in his left hand, the other six in his right with the queen beneath it. With a smooth, practiced sweep, he flicked the black card over the red and let it drop to the table. All eyes in the crowd then followed the displaced six as he rearranged them on the table.

Simple single substitution. Taziar assessed the method naturally, hardly daring to believe such an easy maneuver could fool a crowd. Yet he had already watched several people lose their money to it. Trained to observe every subtlety, he had no difficulty following the exchange. The queen sat in the middle, the decoy to her right.

The woman hesitated, her hand in her purse.

The monte continued his pitch, his words uninterpretable but his voice wheedling encouragements.

Taziar could not help liking this woman. He wanted to point out the correct card but realized she had no reason to trust him. *Besides, if it seems too easy, it probably is. I could be missing something, and I'd hate to steer her wrong.*

The woman sighed. She hauled a crumpled bill from her purse. Her hand hovered, her gaze shifting from card to card.

The crowd waited patiently, the monte less so. He said something that sent a ripple of laughter through the masses, making an undulating gesture with his hand to hurry the woman.

She placed the bill before the decoy.

The monte flipped it, revealing the six. He took her money then turned the other cards, gathering them for the next round.

The woman backed away, disappointment traced vividly across her features.

Before she could leave, Taziar touched her arm. He held up a finger, indicating she should wait, then closed in to win back her money, glad for the excuse to play.

The monte turned his attention to Taziar, gaze flicking over the dirty, overlarge cloak and the healing slash on his cheek.

Taziar plucked the stolen bankroll from his pocket.

Interest flashed across the monte's face, disappearing beneath a mask of professional indifference, but not quickly enough. Apparently, the sight of money allowed him to dismiss his player's battle-scarred appearance. The patter began again.

Taziar peeled through several, identical outer bills until he reached ones that looked like those the woman had played. He slipped two from the stack, then rifled through the others, gauging their value from the expressions on the faces of the monte's gang. Apparently, the pickpocket had arranged the wad with the least valuable bills outside in a gradual progression toward the center. Accustomed to rapid-fire assessments of objects and human reactions, Taziar noted that the two different types of outer bills, including the ones he had pulled out, had single digits in the corners. He found three types of double digit bills as well as four identical bills with triple digits. And the gang's interest told Taziar he carried enough money to mark him as a target.

The woman waited, watching.

The monte's patience seemed to have increased exponentially. He waited until Taziar looked up before launching into the usual shuffle and banter.

Taziar remained silent, easily following the original switch and the subsequent arrangement of the cards. The brunette in the miniskirt, whom Taziar had pegged as a gang member, drifted toward the game.

Not wanting to reveal himself as other than a curious passerby, Taziar hesitated, looking over the cards as if confused. He liked this woman who reminded him of Astryd and saw no reason to let her know he was as crooked as any monte. He dropped his two bills before the center card, trying to make the selection look casual and random.

Instantly, the long-legged brunette tossed a pair of double digit bills before the decoy card.

The monte looked at Taziar apologetically and said something the Shadow Climber guessed to mean that only one bet was allowed per round. The monte managed to indicate that, since both wagers were placed at once, he would have to accept the more valuable one. Returning Taziar's two fives, he concentrated on the female gang member's money instead.

Annoyance gripped Taziar, though he hid it behind a pall of bland disappointment. He doubted anyone else in the crowd recognized the woman as a shill, so he alone identified the scam. *There's no way to win this game. If the sleight of hand doesn't fool the player, he uses the gang to cheat.* In his youth as a con man, Taziar had always relied on complex, showy tricks, believing the audience deserved entertainment in exchange for their gold. When hunger drove him to simple trickery or thievery, he always played fairly, preying only on the rich and sharing his spoils. There was an honor even among swindlers; unwritten rules specified that if one con outwitted another's scam, the lesson learned outvalued the money lost. Now, suddenly, the stakes changed. The challenge escalated from a good deed designed to help a pretty woman to a temptation too difficult to resist. *There's got to be a way to win.* Reclaiming his bills, Taziar handed them to the woman he had mistaken for Astryd to replace the ones she had lost in the previous round.

Features twisted in confusion, the small woman tried to

return the bills, speaking in sentences Taziar could only identify as questions.

Taziar shook his head, refusing the fives, then turned his attention back to the monte who was revealing the decoy as a six. The monte collected the brunette gang member's money as well as the cards, pausing only long enough to demonstrate that the central one was indeed the queen.

The monte gestured at Taziar with both hands, encouraging him to try again.

Taziar examined the youth more closely. His pants pockets bulged with money. He wore an open dress shirt over a white undershirt. His breast pocket contained a partially crushed box of white paper sticks, and the remainder of the deck of cards. He asked Taziar an uninterpretable question.

Taziar shrugged. "I don't understand your language," he said in the tongue of Cullinsberg's barony.

The wiry Hispanic gang member moved in. He leaned past Taziar, talking with the monte in low tones. As close as the youth stood, Taziar could scarcely hear him. Yet, coincidentally, he chose words Larson had taught Taziar. "The little guy's a foreigner."

The monte's reply emerged equally comprehensible and pitched too softly for the crowd to hear. "Who fucking cares? The ratty little dirtball's got money."

Taziar made no pretext of understanding. As the game ground to a halt, bystanders drifted away. The deck of cards in the Hispanic's pocket hovered, temptingly close to Taziar's reach. *I saw the rest of the leader's cards in his pocket. That can only mean this man carries an unrelated deck of his own.* Grasping the opportunity, Taziar calmly edged the cards from the teen's pocket and stashed them in his own.

A moment later, the gang member sidestepped, returning to his position. The monte spun the queen, face up, on the table. His speech became loud, slow, and broken, addressed directly at Taziar. "You play?" He made grand gestures at the table. "You find the lady?"

Taziar drew the folded stack of bills from his pocket again. He glanced thoughtfully from the money to the cards.

The banter grew more urgent, the motions more beckoning. "Come on. It's fun. You'll . . ." The rest of his sentence was unfamiliar. ". . . find the lady." He tapped a fingertip on the red card and shouted something obviously for the benefit of the crowd, a showman to the core.

Apparently lured by high stakes, a new crowd formed. The youngsters Taziar had identified as gang members merged into the new group, and the pickpocket returned as well.

Taziar nodded to indicate interest. Then he looked deep into the crowd, as if at someone. Raising a finger to indicate that he would return, he wove into the masses. Once beyond sight, he ducked into an alleyway. Behind him, he heard the din of conversation, pierced by the monte's charismatic baritone. Taziar heard something about a winner, knowing it had to be a member of the gang pretending to win in order to draw the attention of players who believed that if one person beat the odds, so could they.

Taziar flashed through the deck, studying the cards in the hazy light filtering into the alley. Plucking the queen of diamonds and a black six from the deck, he folded them into tents that matched the cards on the table. Shoving the remainder of the deck back into his pocket, he palmed the queen in his left hand, clutching the money in his right.

As Taziar worked his way back to the gaming table, the monte smiled in welcome. Unable to communicate with Taziar, he addressed the crowd in warm, congenial tones, turning the cards to reveal every face. The monte waited until Taziar stared at the cards. "Ready?" the black man said.

Taziar nodded.

The monte jumbled cards, talking the entire time.

Taziar ignored even those words he understood, following the double substitution as easily as he had the previous single exchanges. When the monte finished moving cards, Taziar knew the queen sat at the rightmost end of the table with the sixes central and to the left. Still clutching his own queen, Taziar opened the stack of bills and peeled from the middle, placing three hundreds in front of the center card. He let the fourth hundred slip from his fingers. It floated to the sidewalk.

Every eye followed the fluttering bill.

Taziar knelt to retrieve the fallen hundred dollar bill, dropping his left hand to the table as if to steady himself.

With smooth and practiced dexterity, he replaced the central six with his queen. Now palming a six, he placed the last hundred with the others.

The monte grinned broadly. He tossed over the middle card, revealing Taziar's queen. "Sorry, sir. . . ." His smile wilted to a shocked grimace, and his words trailed into oblivion. The attention of every gang member riveted on the card, the diversion so engrossing that Taziar might as well have had a year to switch the monte's queen with the palmed six.

Gasps startled through the crowd, followed by a smattering of applause that strengthened and rose to cheers.

The monte flipped the rightmost card, revealing the replaced six. He stared. Then, regaining his composure, he huffed out a strained laugh. Plucking bills from his pocket, he flicked fifties and twenties onto Taziar's stack, the crowd loudly counting each bill with him.

As the monte tallied, he glanced meaningfully at the thickly-muscled gang member who had, so far, remained quiet and still. The large man's hand slid into his pocket. There was no mistaking the gesture. Taziar guessed that if he left without losing all the cash he had won, he would meet with a horrible accident in some alley.

As the last bill landed on the stack, Taziar reached for it. The monte's hand touched his, pressing the money to the table. "Play some more?"

Taziar shook his head.

The monte's hand retreated, and Taziar put the bills in his pocket.

The monte asked another question, this one unfamiliar.

Again, Taziar shook his head, followed by a shrug to convey ignorance. He knew he was acting foolishly. He had no need for money. He could not even understand its relative value. But he cared little for the methods of this particular gang and felt certain he could find a more worthy cause.

Taziar also realized he would need a distraction if he wanted to leave the area alive. *As long as I stay in the crowd, I'm safe. If they threaten me here, I'm not only their last winner, I become their last player ever.* He put the extra queen into his pocket, retrieving the folded six from the purloined deck.

The largest gang member shifted his weight, causally watching Taziar.

Taziar remained near the table, feigning engrossment in the next player. His huge win had brought a surge of people who pressed eagerly toward the makeshift table, certain they could match the feats of an ignorant, little foreigner who could not even understand English. Each hoped to win large sums of money with minimal effort, and Taziar realized human nature would refill the gang's coffers, with overflow. *In that respect, I actually aided their scam.*

The monte returned to his pitch. He turned over the cards, mixing them, his usual prattle sounding like a thin, shaken whisper after his previous, strident bellows. As the last card fell, a heavyset man slapped down a fifty with such enthusiasm that he sent the cards scuttling. As the monte straightened them, Taziar seized the moment to replace the queen with his six, leaving three black cards on the table and no red. Pocketing the second queen, Taziar turned, squeezing into the stream of sidewalk traffic. A casual glance over his shoulder revealed that the muscled hoodlum was following him. The wiry Hispanic teenager also disengaged from the crowd.

Taziar broke into a trot. A quick look backward showed him that his pursuer had quickened his pace as well.

Unaccustomed to the volume of traffic that filled New York City's streets, Taziar misjudged. The moment he took to check the hoodlum's position sent him careening into a slender redhead dressed in a multihued T-shirt, jeans nearly as tattered as Taziar's britches, and a string of beads. She fell with a gasp, flailing so wildly she took a nearby black businessman down with her. The man's foot crashed into Taziar's shin, sprawling him. A dive and twist saved Taziar from landing on the woman, but he hit the pavement instead. The passersby parted around the collision.

Taziar scrambled to his feet. The brawny hoodlum had almost closed the gap. The Hispanic youth was nowhere Taziar could see.

The familiar excitement of the chase made Taziar giddy. Suddenly, the strangeness of the city seemed to fade to insignificance. He might have been back in Cullinsberg, dodging through alleyways and scaling buildings with the guard force at his heels. The exotic city and its streets only added to the challenge. His grief disappeared, forgotten beneath more urgent need, and its release freed him to think logically. He felt joyful and unfettered for the first time in weeks, though he realized the youth might carry a gun or other unguessable technology that would enable him to quickly end Taziar's life.

Taziar wove into a clustered knot of citizens on the edge of the sidewalk closest to the buildings. As they passed an alleyway, he glided inside, hoping to decoy the gang member into following the masses. Pigeons much like the ones in Cullinsberg fluttered skyward, their wing beats slapping echoes between the buildings; their cooing filled the alley. Metal ash cans and plastic bags lined the walls of the buildings.

Unfooled, the hoodlum whipped around the corner, now only a few arm's lengths behind Taziar. He growled a command, from which Taziar deciphered only the terminating swear word. A patterned sequence of whistles followed.

Taziar picked his way swiftly and carefully through the garbage. Recognizing the high-pitched noises as a signal, he suddenly wished he knew the exact location of the muscled teen's Hispanic companion. As Taziar moved, he eyeballed the walls on either side. Though well-mortared, the perfect bricks composing the walls would supply regular, if tiny, handholds.

The rumble of the crowds faded. A click reverberated through the alley, and a blade appeared, glinting in the gang member's hand. A new set of footsteps pattered from in front of Taziar. *That answers the question of where his friend went.* Taziar eased his back against the wall, fingers groping the brick for handholds, finding more than enough for a climb. Some distance directly above him, a metallic platform jutted from the building. Steps rose from it, zigzagging to several similar decks, each set a story higher than the previous one.

Now Taziar could see both youths, closing in on him from either side. Whirling, he fitted his fingers into miniscule ledges and clambered to the platform. Catching hold of the metal, he ducked through a space in the railing, landing lightly on the deck.

Beneath Taziar, the two gang members hesitated. The larger one swore, his tone mingling frustration and surprise.

The Hispanic leapt to a trash can, using the height it gained him to catch the lowest rung of the fire escape. Carefully drawing himself up, he charged after Taziar. His companion followed, rattling the entire structure with his footfalls.

Taziar sprang back to the railing, aware a climb up the bricks, though taxing, would give him a more direct route to the rooftop. As the hoodlums charged toward him, he flattened to the side of the building and scrambled easily upward.

"Shit," the brawnier gang youth said, awe clearly evident in the expletive. He continued to pound up the stairways.

"Look at the little son-of-a-bitch go." His sinewy companion seemed equally impressed. "How. . . ?"

The rest of the question blurred to nonsense in Taziar's ears. Still, their amazement made one thing clear. Apparently, despite the contrived regularity of handholds, climbing buildings was as unusual here as in his own time and city.

Catching the ledge, Taziar flung himself to the rooftop. Pigeons scattered, some taking to wing, others strutting beyond his reach, their heads bobbing crazily. A grimy metal box sat in a central position, spinning blades visible through its grates. To his left, a shack rose from the floor, latched by a rusted padlock.

Having gained several moments from his straighter climb, Taziar scuttled to the opposite side of the roof. As he passed the shack, a grinding, whirring noise erupted so suddenly that Taziar instinctively dodged.

His pursuers heaved to the rooftop behind him, panting, red-faced, and obviously annoyed.

Taziar gauged the distance to the neighboring buildings, and realized the strangeness and unusual height of the structures had caused him to miscalculate distances. The alley between this storefront and the next gaped like an open wound, too wide to jump even with a running start. Taziar looked down, measuring the distance to the alley below. His elevated position gave him a wide view of the street, including the location where the monte game had taken place. There, he could see a fight had broken out, presumably over the missing queen. People surged, a mad chaos of bodies. "Look!" Taziar said in accented English. He pointed.

The hoodlums closed, hunched and with wary delibera-
tion. Taziar's effortless climb made it clear he was no normal immigrant. Either they worried that Taziar might have
more unexpected tricks to use against them or, he hoped,
they just wanted their money back without sending their
victim tumbling to his death.

"Look!" Taziar said again, jabbing his finger toward the
crowd. Having spent many of his early years in a gang, he
understood the need for loyalty. *That card shuffler could
be the only family these men have.* Desperate to communicate, he struggled with the language. "Summa bitch! Ex-
kyuse-me." Running out of relevant expressions, he chose
at random, trying to get his message across with wild gestures and a dire tone. "Buick. Follow that car!"

Apparently impressed by Taziar's urgency, if not his
words, the robust youth took a careful glance over the
edge. He remained partially twisted toward Taziar, as if
concerned the Shadow Climber might rush him.

Taziar inched backward, away from the teenagers and
the building's edge.

"Fuck!" the heavier hoodlum shouted. Ignoring Taziar,
he charged back toward the fire escape, calling something
sharply to his companion as he ran.

The wiry Hispanic studied Taziar for a moment. He
pointed, addressing Taziar in a threatening manner before
whirling to follow his friend.

Though unable to understand, Taziar guessed he had received a lecture on luck. He waited until both youngsters
disappeared over the side before breaking into laughter.
Moving back toward the edge, he tried to identify Al Larson in the milling crowds below him.

CHAPTER 11
Chaos at the Tower

When bad men combine, the good must associate; else they will fall one by one, an unpitied sacrifice in a contemptible struggle.
—Edmund Burke
Thoughts on the Cause of the Present Discontents

Al Larson hated himself for an evil he saw no way to avoid. Crouched against the Jeffers' wooden house, he watched flames of gold and red engulf the dwelling he had called home for more than fifteen years. Heat blackened white-painted shingles. Yellow trim disappeared beneath fire that crackled and capered like demons. And Al Larson lamented that, if the war had taught him nothing else, it had shown him how to build a successful pyre, to overcome the protestations of his conscience, and to destroy even those things he loved.

Timmy clutched his older brother's waist, tears rolling down cherubic cheeks.

Though concerned for the child, Larson kept his eyes locked on the burning house. Soon, neighbors would mobilize. Someone would call the fire department, and Larson knew he and Timmy had best disappear long before that happened. Still, he waited, wanting to make certain his mother and sister escaped unharmed.

Timmy said nothing. He did not question Larson's wisdom.

But Larson was questioning enough for both of them. *What am I doing? What the hell am I doing? There has to be another way to protect Mom and Pam.* Larson sighed, knowing the luxury of time might have given him a better strategy, but he had been unable to conjure one from the swirl of thoughts and emotions besieging him. *Silme never met Mom or Pam, so she can't enter their minds to find them. But she could use Timmy's thoughts or mine to locate this house. I had no choice. I have to force the women to leave until this is settled, to move someplace without Timmy or me knowing where.* The rationalization did not quiet his guilt. *One more crisis. Just what Mom and Pam needed. First Dad's death, then Timmy's and my disappearance. And now I'm burning down my own goddamned house.*

The wind shifted, funneling ash and smoke into Larson's lungs. He coughed. *I've waited long enough. Perhaps too long.* Grabbing Timmy, he followed a line of trees toward the road.

A screen door slammed. Someone screamed, and the village of Baychester awakened sluggishly to danger.

Larson broke into a run, hoping no one had spotted him. *Please let Mom and Pam get out safely. Please, God, let them not be home.* Larson had never thought much of religion; his jokingly forsaking Christianity for the warlike Norse pantheon just before his death in Vietnam had resulted in his being dragged into ancient history. But now he could not stop himself from appealing to a higher source.

Lawns and rows of closely-placed houses disappeared behind Larson and Timmy, replaced by streets. The wail of a siren floated over the village like an accusing scream. Every instinct told Larson to stay, to check on his mother's and sister's safety and keep looters from pillaging his family's belongings, the familiar, beloved objects that were all that remained of Carl Larson and the house in Baychester. But Al Larson knew he could not afford to see his family; to give Silme even a distant glimpse of his mother's current looks or plans would be folly. He believed the Dragonrank sorceress could glean some details from his or Timmy's memories, but he hoped those would prove distant enough that they would only allow her to recognize the women if she found them by random chance. *In a city this size. Think of the odds.*

Now outside the village, Larson slowed, not wanting his haste to draw attention. To get hauled in by the police, even just for questioning, meant remaining in one place long enough for Silme to locate him. *Sure suicide.* It also brought the possibility of being forced to confront his mother. Releasing Timmy's hand, Larson kept his pace brisk, trying for an air of casual disinterest with little success. He could only hope the oddities of New York City would keep Silme busy until he could devise a coherent strategy against her.

Larson's walk brought him to the enormous tract of dirt that had once been Freedom Land and would soon become Co-op City. Bulldozers and cranes huffed over the single street, adding beams to a towering skeleton of steel that, when finished, would loom over the double-story dwellings in Baychester. Construction workers scurried around the machinery, their white undershirts dampened in wide, semi-circular patches at the neck and armpits. One lounged near the marked perimeter of the hard hat area, munching an apple and sipping coffee from a styrofoam cup. A radio near his feet blasted the news through a wash of static.

As Larson passed by, one of the other workers approached the man on break and flopped down beside him.

Timmy gasped for air.

Larson paused, giving the boy a chance to catch his breath.

The new worker removed his yellow hard hat to rub sweat from his forehead with the back of his hand. "What's the word on that lady jumper?"

The first worker spoke around a mouthful of apple. "Don't think it's a lady anymore. They're saying it's a real small guy now. And he ain't maybe jumping. Actually climbed higher, straight up the goddamned wall."

The other man grunted, scratching at a hairy beer gut beneath his shirt. "Little guy in black and gray crawling up a building? Gotta be a publicity stunt. Some company's showing off new mountain climbing gear or looking for free advertising."

Larson froze, images of Taziar rising to his mind, though he knew it was impossible. Still, he eavesdropped, aware that with a Dragonrank sorceress loose in the city, he had to pay attention to any reports of weird happenings.

The first man shrugged. "Yeah, well. That was my thought, too, man. But if they're looking for publicity, why's he climbing Sears and Roebuck? Why not the Empire State Building or some real skyscraper in Manhattan? Besides, they're sayin' now they don't think he understands English. Jabbered back at them in some sort of French or

German. What kind of advertising you going to get when the guy can't even say nothing about no product?"

A short silence fell. Larson ran their conversation repeatedly through his mind, unable to shake the certainty. *A little man who doesn't speak English climbing a twelve-story building. Who the hell else could it be?*

"So, you hear anything from your son?"

"Not since last week when they moved him to Mai Lai. . . ."

Larson pressed on, concerned for the climber and not wanting to hear war tales. "Come on." Seizing Timmy's hand, he rushed the child across the lot, fumbling in his pocket for a dime. Near St. Raymond's Parish Cemetery, where the population clustered, he had had no difficulty finding an independent cab. Here, in this section of town empty except for construction, he would need to call for a ride.

Timmy stumbled.

Larson stopped, reached to carry the child, and caught his first clear glimpse of his brother's features since burning down the house. Tears glazed the freckled, doll-like face. His brown eyes looked hollow and haunted.

Larson had seen the same expression in the visage of a Vietnamese girl after one of his companions raped and killed her mother. He shivered, barraged with pain. Then, he had walked away, sickened. And although he had not participated, his failure to put an end to the torture made him equally guilty by his conscience's judgment. Since that first time, he had seen the hopeless agony of surrender in the eyes of too many children, had watched innocence die in the split second it took for a blow or bullet to slaughter loved ones, had wondered what the future held for those children and their morality. The comparison ached through him. *Not Timmy. Please, not Timmy.*

Larson hated the idea of stopping long enough to give Silme a transport site or of delaying his aid to a man who might be Taziar, but both seemed preferable to letting Timmy succumb to despair. He knelt, catching Timmy's forearms, losing himself in the child's eyes.

"I want to go home." Timmy burst into sobs. "I want to be with Mommy and Pam. And Dad. I want to go home."

Larson clutched Timmy to his chest, waiting for the child

to calm down enough to understand his words. Timmy's grip went convulsively tight around his brother.

Larson whispered soothingly, despising each second that ticked by, yet understanding the need.

The child's hold loosened, but his face remained buried in Larson's T-shirt.

Larson stroked his brother's sandy locks. "Timmy, do you trust me?"

Timmy's head bobbed beneath Larson's hand.

"I had to burn the house. The witch can read our minds because she's met us. I had to get Mom and Pam to leave so we don't know where they are. Do you understand that?"

Timmy hesitated. His voice was muffled almost to incomprehensibility, but Larson managed to catch the main idea. The boy wanted to know why Larson had not simply told the women to relocate.

Larson chewed his lip, trying to decide how to explain. He pictured himself attempting to talk his mother and sister into abandoning their home. *Well, you see, Mom, there's this sorceress who followed me from ancient Norway. I'm an elf there, you see.* He shook his head, on the verge of hysterical laughter. *They'd think Dad's death drove me over the edge. They'd probably have me committed, and Silme would have all the time in the world to identify them.* "Listen, Timmy. You're just going to have to believe me. That was the only way to keep Mom and Pam safe."

Timmy nodded again, still clinging.

"This is kind of like the first ten minutes of a *Mission: Impossible* episode. Lots of bad things are going to happen over the next few hours or days. *If we last that long.* He kept the thought to himself. "Silme's got magic bombs and bazookas and dragons and what-not. I may have to find a gun and shoot her." Larson shivered at the thought. "People. . . ." His voice cracked, and he paused to gather his composure before continuing. *It won't help Timmy if I get overwrought.* "People may die. Even me."

Timmy looked up, a grimace of horror covering his features.

Larson wanted to support Timmy, but lies and false reassurances would only lead to later betrayals. "If that happens, I want you to run to the nearest policeman as fast as you can. Can you handle that?"

Timmy lowered and raised his head once in an uncertain nod. "I don't want you to die. Are you going to die?"

"I don't want to die, either. I'm going to do everything I can to keep that from happening. But I brought Silme here. She's my responsibility." He tousled Timmy's bangs. "We can't go back to Mom and Pam until Silme's taken care of." *I wish I could have gotten Timmy elsewhere, too.* Larson shook his head in frustration. *But Silme's already entered his mind once. She can find him anywhere.* Only one solution came to the forefront of his thoughts. "Timmy, I can try to get the police to put you in protective custody." *God only knows what I'd say. In their place, I sure as hell wouldn't believe my story.*

Timmy went rigid. "I want to stay with you."

Larson considered, understanding the child's motives. Having lost his father, sister, and mother, he was clinging desperately to his only remaining family member, the brother he had always emulated as the ideal of masculine cool. "All right. Fine. But there's going to have to be some rules."

Timmy whipped his head up and down in a frenzied promise.

"First, you have to trust me. Bad things are going to happen. No matter what, you have to believe I'm doing my best to be the good guy. Second, if I'm killed, you run. Third, you have to do whatever I tell you, no matter how weird it sounds." Larson rose. Placing an arm across Timmy's shoulders, he steered the boy across the lot. "I love you, you little turd."

Timmy stuck out his lip. The hunted look disappeared from his features. "Yah. You big jerk." He ducked under Larson's hold.

"Creep," Larson returned, flipping Timmy's hair into his eyes.

"Dumbhead." Timmy shook his locks back.

"Jerkface."

"Retard."

Larson laughed, hardly daring to believe he had discussed his death only three breaths back, and now he was exchanging insults with an eight-year-old. He took Timmy's hand as they came to the lot's end and crossed the street toward the supermarket. "Listen, this guy who's climbing the building. If it's who I think it is, you'll like him. He's kind of an Errol Flynn type."

"Earl who?"

"Robin Hood." Larson pulled open one of the glass doors. He ushered Timmy through, then followed the boy inside. "You remember that movie where the guy steals from the rich and gives to the poor."

Timmy danced in a circle, waving an imaginary weapon. "You mean he's real fast and jumps around and people can't catch him and he fights good with a sword?"

"Not exactly." Larson approached the pay telephone, grabbing the book dangling from its chain. Only then did it strike him how near Timmy's description had actually come to the truth. "But real close." Larson flipped through the yellow pages to the Taxicab section, seeing no reason to tell Timmy that his older brother could beat Taziar in any sword spar, even with one hand tied behind his back.

Finding a number, Larson dropped his dime into the slot and dialed.

When Larson's cab approached the corner of Webster and Fordham, they discovered a snarl of traffic behind a milling horde of gawking pedestrians. Patting Timmy's knee reassuringly, Larson leaned over the seat to address the driver. "I'm going to get out here. Take my brother to Marion and 193rd and wait there with the meter running. I'll be back."

Timmy opened his mouth to protest, but Larson cut him short.

"I'll return as soon as I can. Hopefully with Taz. Remember what I told you about listening to me." Freeing his wallet from his pants pocket, Larson fished through the bill section, finding only a ten and four ones remaining. Though only two dollars and change showed on the meter, he handed over the ten. Then he opened the door and charged out onto the sidewalk.

Behind him, the cab backed into the jam.

Larson hated leaving Timmy with no protection other than a strange cabby, yet he knew the boy's presence would make rescuing Taziar even more impossible than it already seemed. *If it's even Shadow doing the climbing. This is crazy. There's no possible way he could have gotten here.* Still, the description fit too well. Despite logic's contradiction, Larson's intuition told him the climber could be no one else.

The crowd pressed in on Larson. Panic clutched him, with a claustrophobia he had never experienced before Vietnam. Every instinct told him to flee, and the resolve he raised to combat impulse also brought determined rage. He elbowed through the masses, ignoring curses, shouts, and jabs.

A man grabbed Larson by the front of his shirt. Larson glared into a pair of eyes recessed in a fat, red face. The stranger's gaze traveled up Larson's brawny, six foot frame to his hard, ice-blue eyes. Backing down, the man faded into the crowd.

Larson scarcely hesitated. He rushed and shoved the spectators, clearing a path like a bulldozer through a herd of sheep. He saw police and fire vehicles and the flashing lights of Emergency Rescue Teams. Uniformed men perched atop the cars with binoculars. Police on foot or horseback cordoned the sidewalk, some ushering people leaving the building to safety beyond the barricades. A patrol supervisor with a bullhorn peered upward, his head cocked, listening to the radio at his belt. Other officers waited nearby. One elderly man in civilian clothes talked urgently with the supervisor.

Larson glanced upward. Men hung out most of the fifth floor windows, hurriedly trying to assemble a net. Several stories above them, a lone figure clung to the bricks with one hand. He used the other to shield his eyes from the sun as he scanned the crowd.

"Jump!" someone yelled nearby, his voice snapping clear over the hubbub. "Jump!"

Larson was seized by a sudden urge to rip out the stranger's lungs without benefit of anesthesia. Instead, he rammed through the crowd with a violence and determination that many cursed but no one challenged.

As Larson reached the edge of the cordoned boundary, Taziar Medakan's familiar voice wafted from beneath a blast of radio static. A louder voice followed in a Brooklyn accent so thick it sounded like a parody. "Did the translator get that, Captain?"

The supervisor glanced at the aging civilian, who wrung his manicured hands. "It's gibberish. The accent's German, but the words don't mean a damned thing."

"Gibberish my ass!" Larson shouted. "I heard him clear as day."

The translator and the supervisor whirled. The elderly man flushed. The policeman looked skeptical and frustrated, but hopeful.

"Listen, young man." The translator jabbed a finger at Larson. "I speak six languages. . . ."

Larson ignored the translator, locking an urgent, sincere expression on his face and addressing the policeman directly. "The jumper said 'I'm sorry . . .'" He left out the expletive. "'. . . but I don't speak your language.'"

The translator snorted.

The supervisor shifted from foot to foot. A tense, crowd-drawing situation always dragged out the crazies, and he had to suspect Larson was fabricating. Yet the police officer seemed near his wits' end. "What language is he speaking?"

Larson opened his mouth, instantly realizing archaic German would not work for an answer. Inadvertently, he hesitated just long enough to put his integrity into question. "He's speaking perfect Perkanian."

"Perkanian?" The translator threw up his hands. "What kind of nonsense. . . ? There's no place called . . ."

"Perkania." Larson continued to hold the policeman's gaze, trying to sound confident and matter-of-fact. "It's a tiny country near Estonia." The lie came easily.

Another policeman trotted to the supervisor's side. "Captain, I've got Bellevue on the line."

The captain waved his subordinate silent, but the translator seized the moment. "Captain, this man is wasting your time. Anyone could make up what the jumper might have said. And there's no country called Perkania."

Larson could no longer control his temper. "Look," he snapped. "If you never learned your geography, that's your own fucking problem. There's a man up there who might slip and fall twelve stories if we don't get him down. If you can't talk him in, then move your fat butt aside and let someone do it who can." Larson softened his tone, his focus returning to the captain. "May I try, sir?" He extended a hand for the radio.

Taziar's voice crackled through the static again. "I'm looking for an elf named Allerum, or rather a man named Allerum."

Oh, my God. Realization smacked Larson. *He climbed the freaking building hoping to pick me out of seven and a half million people.* Larson choked back a laugh, turning it into a feigned sneeze. In tenth-century Germany, the strategy made sense. *From the roof of the tallest building in Cullinsberg, Shadow could probably view his city end to end.*

Taziar hesitated in frustration, then finished in English so heavily accented, Larson felt certain he alone recognized the words. "Team player. Buddy Allerum. Stupid son of a bitch."

Larson thumbed the button. "Shadow," he said in the tongue of Cullinsberg's barony. "It's me. Allerum."

"Mardain's mercy." Taziar swung around so suddenly, the crowd loosed a collective gasp. "How come I can hear you, but I can't see you? Where are you?"

"I'm on the ground. I'll explain later."

"I'm coming down."

"No, wait. Stay there. Whatever you do, don't move."

The supervisor made a gesture of impatience. "What's he saying?"

Larson addressed Taziar first. "Hang on, buddy." He turned to the policeman, suddenly recognizing the unintentional pun of his own words. He returned to English, knowing he could not relay the actual conversation without cornering himself into an unbelievable story. *I've got to get Shadow down and out of here without committing either of us to the loony bin.* "He said his name is Taz, and he has some demands. First, he wants me up there to talk to him directly. Through the window."

The supervisor frowned. "Are you willing to do that?"

"Yes. Of course. A man's life is at stake." Larson handed back the radio, then ducked beneath the barricade.

The translator waved his hands wildly. "I can't believe you're wasting time with this imposter."

The Brooklyn accent came over the radio again. "Captain?"

"Hang on Dixson," the patrol supervisor said. He looked at Larson. "What's your name, kid?"

"Al," Larson started. Then, recognizing the danger of his mother hearing his name on television or radio news, he caught himself. "Smith. Al Smith." *Oh, good going, Larson. Why didn't you just say John Doe?* He changed the subject immediately. "And if it'll make him feel better . . ." He jerked a thumb at the translator. ". . . I can prove I'm really talking with this climber." He reached for the speaker again.

The captain passed the radio.

Larson thumbed it on. "Dixson?"

"Yeah."

"I'm going to tell your jumper to nod twice. Tell us when he does."

"All right."

Larson switched to archaic, dialectal German. "Shadow, listen. You can't come down because the place is crawling with . . ." The word "police" had no translation, so Larson used the closest one he could find. ". . . city guardsmen. Climbing buildings is illegal here. They'll arrest you if you come down. Don't do anything elusive, or I'll never find you again. Just hold tight, and I'll be up to get you." *Somehow.* "Now, don't ask any questions. Just nod your head two times."

"He's nodding," Dixson confirmed. "Twice."

The translator fell silent, utterly speechless.

"Come on." The captain placed an arm around Larson's shoulders and steered him across the concrete. "You got any experience talking down jumpers?"

None whatsoever, but I won't need any. Larson thought it better to lie. "Used to work a suicide hotline in high school."

The patrol supervisor glanced upward, past Taziar's clinging form, and silently mouthed, "Praise the Lord."

A trio of uniformed policemen herded a dozen gawking office personnel out the front door; they filed through the cordoned area and into the crowd. While the supervisor waited for them to pass, Larson took a closer look at his surroundings. The ropes, barricades, and emergency vehicles formed a semicircle extending from the front of the building, directly beneath Taziar. The danger area included a single street around which mounted police diverted traffic. The back exit and at least one side door remained clear for shoppers to enter and leave Sears and Roebuck.

The patrol supervisor waved at a group of uniformed officers. "McCloskey. Johnston."

A husky, middle-aged redhead and a willowy brunet disengaged from the others and obediently trotted over.

The captain took the two aside, talking in hushed tones.

Unable to hear the conversation, Larson continued to study the area. Cops and emergency personnel scurried in efficient patterns, exchanging messages and controlling the crowd with masterful cooperation. Taziar clung at the level of the tenth floor, his attention now turned toward the window. Apparently, he was staring at the policeman called Dixson.

"Mr. Smith." The redhead touched Larson's arm. His tone made it clear he had tried to get Larson's attention at least once before.

Larson glanced up into a wide face with friendly, blue eyes.

"Mr. Smith, we're going to accompany you upstairs to talk to the jumper and to help you decide what to say." The redhead smiled, gesturing Larson through the door ahead of him. "Don't worry. You're not alone."

That's what worries me. Larson smiled nervously.

The policemen near the door moved aside to let Larson and his escort through it.

"Just call me Al." Larson entered the building and waited for the officers to take the lead. His thoughts were spinning, and he saw no reason to further complicate the matter by needing to learn a new name. *I had enough trouble remembering to answer to Allerum. And that starts with Al.*

The door opened onto a squat entryway. Ahead, another set of steel-framed, glass doors led into the main store. To the left, a pair of elevators graced the wall. Directly opposite loomed a dark, metal door with a "1" stenciled on it in white paint.

Larson followed the policemen through the lobby to the elevator bank.

The redhead framed a wipe-lipped smile. "John McCloskey," he said. "The quiet guy is Phil Johnston."

"Ha ha." Johnston punched the "up" elevator button. Resting a hand against the frame of the leftmost elevator, he turned to face Larson and McCloskey.

Larson watched the milling shoppers in Sears and Roebuck.

"What language did you say this jumper was speaking?" Johnston asked.

Larson drew a blank. The invented country near Estonia seemed to have disappeared from his mind as quickly as it had come. "What language is he speaking?" He stalled. "Um, he's speaking, um. . . ."

The door ground open, revealing a drab, two-toned car and a row of black push buttons. Johnston stepped inside, trailed by Larson and McCloskey. The door rattled shut.

The seconds of reprieve gave Larson the time he needed to untangle his lies. "Perkanian." *That's it.* "He's speaking Perkanian."

Johnston pressed "10." "Never heard of it."

"Small country." Larson shrugged.

McCloskey kept his chin tilted upward, watching the floor numbers light on the overhead monitor. "Not to be a wise guy or nothing, Al. But Perkanian doesn't strike me as the type of language they teach in high school."

Larson sighed, trying to concentrate on his next move and bothered by the need to make petty conversation. "My grandparents came from Perkania." *Or Queens. One of the two.* "They used to talk Perkanian with my old man when they didn't want me to understand what they were talking about. Things like sex and Christmas presents. Stuff like that. I've got a thing for picking up languages." The ab-lib seemed plausible, and Larson impressed himself with his own quick alibi. Then another thought made him frown. *Great. I'm becoming a good liar. Something to be proud of.*

"Yeah?" McCloskey glanced away from the advancing numbers to look at Larson. "I had enough trouble just getting past 'Oy Maddamoysal.'" His Bronx accent mangled the French.

It took Larson a moment to decipher. "I think you mean 'Oui, Mademoiselle.'" Larson developed a sudden appreciation for freshman French. "I've got some advice for you, McCloskey. If you ever go to France, don't go alone."

The officers chuckled.

Larson stared at his feet, aware he had to get Taziar down without turning him over to the police, his head empty of ideas. It was too late for truth. Even if he could have convinced the police about a Chaos-crazed sorceress and a thief from ancient Germany, he would first have to admit to creating Perkania and using an alias. *Knowing I lied once, why would they believe me? At best, they'd haul us both into the station. Or Bellevue. And every second Silme has to accustom herself to the city, locate us, and plot, the more dangerous she becomes.* Larson shook his head, panicky about the only solution that sprang to mind. *We've got to escape cleanly and quickly. Which means I have to ditch the escort.*

The elevator pinged, slowing before it ground to a halt. Still uncertain, but aware he had to make a fast decision, Larson ushered the policemen ahead of him.

They stepped into the hallway.

Larson followed, taking an instant to get his bearings. Across from the elevators, the stairwell was marked with a painted "10." The hallway led off to the left and right, broken only by doors, a water fountain, and the occasional recessed fire extinguishers. From his memory of Taziar's position, Larson guessed Dixson and his team were stationed down the left hallway and inside one of the front offices.

As if to confirm Larson's guess, McCloskey and Johnston turned left.

Here goes nothing. Calling on his boxing and martial arts training, Larson slammed the side of his hand into the back of McCloskey's neck.

The redhead toppled without a sound.

Johnston whirled. "What the. . . ?"

Larson plunged a fist into Johnston's face.

The cop crumpled, crashing awkwardly to the corridor.

Shit. Larson nursed his knuckles, cursing himself, and hating what urgency had forced him to do. Whirling, he ran to the stairwell, aware his attack would only buy him a few minutes. Shoving through the door, he took the concrete steps two at a time. *I punched out a pair of cops. If Nam and Gaelinar taught me nothing else, they made me one hell of a dirty fighter. I can't believe I sucker-punched a cop.* Oddly, his attack against New York City's finest raised more doubt and guilt than shooting soldiers in the jungle or slaughtering guardsmen in Cullinsberg's streets. There was something sacred, something magically innocent about the world of his childhood, a memory-protected sanctuary from the hard, cold realities thrust at him since the day his plane had touched down in Vietnam. Still, for all its familiarity, New York City had changed. The events that had once composed his life faded to trivia beneath the atrocities of war and the threat of a Dragonrank mage. Even with live mythology, dragons, and wizards, the warped ancient Europe he'd just come from seemed less of a fantasy world than the New York City he used to know.

At the next landing, Larson burst through the door. He raced down the left hallway, nearly trampling a young secretary juggling three styrofoam cups. She gasped, dodging so abruptly she sent coffee sloshing over herself and Larson.

Without wasting time on apologies, Larson sprinted past. Finding an office he believed was directly above Taziar, he shoved through the door without knocking. He found himself facing a wide, wooden desk with a matching leather chair. There was no one in the room. *Thank God.* Larson careened around the desk to the window beyond it. He slammed his hands against the frame. The window jolted ajar, one pane shattering beneath the blow. Larson crammed his head through the opening just in time to see glass rain down on Taziar. *Shit. Still don't know my own strength.* Larson ducked back inside hating the seconds lost but knowing the sprinkle of glass on pavement would draw every eye. He counted to himself, wasting a full twenty seconds for the shards to land and the crowd to glance up, see no one, and refocus on Taziar.

Larson eased the window farther open, poked his face through it, and glanced downward. He caught a solid glimpse of Taziar's black mop of hair and small, callused hands. The Climber gripped the bricks with a lax ease. "Shadow," Larson whispered.

Taziar did not move.

Larson raised his voice slightly. "Shadow."

Taziar looked up, staring blankly.

Expecting a welcoming grin and not receiving so much as a glimmer of recognition from his friend, Larson hesitated. Then he remembered how different he looked from the tall, skinny elf Taziar Medakan had come to know. "It's Allerum." He gestured Taziar to him.

The Shadow Climber remained still, clearly doubtful.

Those cops will be awake and alerting everyone any moment. Larson's patience evaporated. "Taz, you stupid little bastard! Get the hell up here!"

Apparently, the words and voice were enough identification for Taziar. He scrambled to the ledge.

Larson retreated, leaving Taziar space to clamber inside. Taziar leapt lightly to the floor, studying this friend in the body of a stranger. "Allerum, you've changed."

"Hurry!" Larson whirled, charging for the door. His hip struck a corner of the desk, jarring pain through his leg and knocking the desk askew. Papers scattered to the floor, spiraling in the breeze from the window. "We've got to get out of here, and we can't get grabbed."

"Relax." Taziar caught up to Larson at the door. "I do this for a living, remember?"

Larson grabbed Taziar by the arms. "No, listen. You don't understand. I don't do this climb, dodge, and leap around buildings thing. If we get separated, we'll never find each other again."

"It's not a problem."

Larson blinked, stunned. "There's seven and a half million people in New York. Finding one would be like finding a needle in a haystack. A *big* haystack."

"I found you this time, didn't I?"

Larson groaned, unwilling to go into a long explanation now. "Luck. If we get separated, I'll meet you. . . ." He trailed off, realizing he could never explain city blocks and taxicabs in a reasonable amount of time. "Never mind. Just stay with me." Releasing Taziar, he pulled open the door, emerging into an empty hallway. Contradicting his last command, he raised a hand to still Taziar. "Wait right here. I need to check something." Larson crept down the hallway to the right, retracing his earlier route.

Seconds ticked by in silence while Larson's mind raced, trying to relate the corridors to his memory of the building's outside.

Suddenly, pounding footsteps echoed from the stairwell. The elevator whirred. Its display clicked from "3" to "4."

Here they come. Larson spun back toward Taziar. Even as he moved, an ear-piercing hiss split the air, followed by a crash that shook the hallway.

Larson's heart leapt. He dove for cover, rolling flat against the wall.

A fire extinguisher rocked hollowly on the floor. A pool of white powder settled around Taziar's feet. Dust swam crazily through air.

The stairwell door clicked.

"What are you doing? What the hell are you doing?" Larson ran. Grabbing Taziar as he passed, he bolted up the corridor, skidding around a corner into a perpendicular hallway.

"This way!" someone shouted. Footfalls thudded through the hall they had just left.

"What . . . were you doing?" Larson whispered as he ran.

"Just looking for something to help us get away." Taziar kept pace, his arm mashed in Larson's desperate grasp.

"That wasn't it. That only works on fires." Larson careened around the next corner, coming suddenly upon a second bank of elevators. He hammered at the down button. The numbers changed with maddening slowness. The footsteps drew closer.

Larson slammed the button repeatedly with his fist. "You better know this. Silme's trying to kill me."

Taziar studied the chemical residue on his hand. "I know. I saw her league with Bolverkr."

"Bolverkr? Oh, shit! He's here, too?" Suddenly, running from the cops seemed a miniscule annoyance.

The pursuit grew louder. Larson could pick out at least six separate sets of footsteps. *Damn it! That elevator's going to get here just in time for them to use it. Nice work, Larson.* "Come on." He charged for the stairwell, turning the knob with one hand while his shoulder struck the door at a dead run.

The panel swung open, revealing concrete steps. Larson shoved Taziar, sending the Climber hurtling down the stairs, the little man's agility all that saved him from a fatal fall. Not bothering to silence the door, Larson plunged after his companion. "Move! Move! Move!"

Taziar and Larson whipped headlong down several flights. On the seventh floor landing, Larson ripped open

the metal door. "Follow me." Surging through, he fled back
in the direction they had come, now four floors lower.

As they whipped around the corner, Larson and Taziar
discovered a cluster of four milling, chatting office personnel in the center of the corridor.

Larson did not slow.

The group scattered to the walls. Larson raced through,
Taziar swerving between the people behind him. "Excuse
me," he said in heavily accented English.

Without looking back, Larson tore around the next corner. Finding the stairwell across from the elevators that he
and his police escort had used, he again hit the door, running and turning the knob simultaneously. Taziar balked,
apparently not wanting to get thrown down the steps again.
But this time, Larson did not hesitate. He galloped down
the concrete steps, hearing no sound beneath the slap of
his own sneakers, yet certain Taziar had followed.

As Larson rounded the third floor landing, he heard the
click of a door opening below. *Uh-oh!* Leaping the last half
flight to the landing, he ripped open the door and exited
onto the second floor. Finding the corridor empty, he
waited for Taziar to dart in, then took the time to ease the
door closed quietly. *Letting them know our location after
all that maneuvering would be stupid.*

Taziar waited, breathing softly but deeply.

Larson realized he was panting and tried to control each
breath. He made a throwing motion to indicate the need
to travel up the corridor and back around the first corner.
There, he knew from his memory of Sears and Roebuck,
they would find a set of escalators. *Hopefully unguarded.*
Larson shook his head, aware New York City's police force
would mobilize swiftly. *But it's only been a few minutes
since I punched the cops. Most of what's out there is rescue
forces and crowd controllers. They had no reason to expect
violence, especially from a translator.* Larson headed for the
corner at a brisk walk.

"What now?" Taziar said in the barony's tongue, pawing
his hair from his eyes and pulling his cloak more securely
over his mangled climbing outfit.

Larson answered in the same language. "We're going to
join the crowd in the shop. Try to blend in as best as you

can, but be ready to turn and leave if the area's crawling with . . . city guardsmen. Follow my lead."

Braced for action, Larson started around the corner. The area opened into a central lobby with soda and candy machines. Several people lounged on chairs arranged in clusters, smoking, talking, and eating. They paid no heed as Taziar and Larson walked past and onto the down escalator.

Taziar stared at his feet, hands well away from the conveyor belt railings.

"It's an escalator," Larson explained, gaze playing over the people in the store below, trying to pick out police officers. "Careful when we get to the bottom. The steps sort of disappear, and you have to watch your balance."

Taziar cast his glance to the bottom of the flight. "Are we safe now?"

"I wish." Larson searched his memory for the location of the men's rest room. *I need a secure place to think.* "We've got to get out of the building, at least. Even then, they'll hunt us all over the city."

"Mardain," Taziar muttered a curt blasphemy. "I never would have guessed climbing was that serious an offense."

Larson flushed, anticipating the end of the escalator ride, still seeing no policemen in the store. "Climbing's not that serious. Just a city ordinance thing. A misdemeanor probably." He stepped down, turning to help Taziar do the same. But the Climber took the sudden flattening of the mechanical steps in stride.

"Unfortunately, assault and battery is a felony. It's me they'll mostly be chasing." Through the doorway to the main entryway, Larson could see milling policemen. He slipped through the aisles in the opposite direction. "All right, we have to sneak out of here without being seen. Or at least without being recognized."

Taziar gawked at the rows and shelves of merchandise.

"Most of them won't know you." Larson thought aloud. "Some of them had binoculars. But most of those people were probably the fire rescue crew, not cops."

Taziar shrugged. "I'm not understanding you."

Larson switched to the barony's tongue. "I'm just saying you were too high for many of the city guards to get a good look at you. You might be able to walk out right under their noses." Larson studied Taziar doubtfully. "If you weren't wearing that burned, shredded, crudely-sewn, centuries out of date, black outfit that practically has 'weirdo' stitched in neon."

Taziar fell easily into Larson's sarcastic rhythm. "Oh, well. Excuse me for not dressing for the occasion. What is the proper attire for being attacked by a dragon, hit by an exploding bone, tortured, and flung through time?"

Larson continued toward the rest room.

Taziar asked the obvious. "Why don't we just change clothes?"

"Don't be ridiculous." Larson discarded the idea, threading through the sporting goods section. "I'm a foot taller than you and twice your weight. We couldn't switch."

"Switch? Who said anything about switch?" Taziar stared at the equipment, gaze sweeping up to the fluorescent lighting. "Now, I admit I'm a bit confused about your customs, but I do know what to do in a shop. I saw some racks back there that looked like clothes. Why not buy some?"

Larson sighed. "I've got this odd, moral thing about limiting myself to one felony a day. I'm not stealing, and the four dollars in my pocket would barely buy a decent T-shirt."

"I have money."

"You don't understand. The gold and silver you're carrying would probably bring decent money from a coin collector. Here in Sears, they're worse than useless. They'd draw attention."

"Will this?" Taziar displayed a fat roll of bills that stopped Larson in his tracks.

"Where did you get that?"

"I—" Taziar started.

Larson pocketed the money and waved Taziar quiet. "Don't tell me. I'm sure I don't want to know." He led the smaller man around the end of the row and down a short corridor to the men's room. They pushed inside.

Six porcelain urinals lined the walls, and three stalls filled the area beyond them. Sinks and a paper towel dispenser jutted from the opposite wall. A man used the farthest urinal.

Taziar watched with unabashed wonder.

The stranger looked over casually, then glared at the little Climber.

Larson smacked Taziar's shoulder with the back of his hand. "Don't stare. It's impolite." He motioned to a corner.

Taziar wandered to the indicated location. "I'm sorry. I just never saw a man piss in a fountain before."

Larson shook his head in frustration. "I'll explain later. For right now, you stay in one of those with the door closed." He inclined his head toward a stall. "I'll be back. *Please* don't start any trouble."

The New Yorker zipped his pants, throwing Larson and Taziar a hostile glance before leaving.

Probably thinks we're gay. Too harried to see the humor in the situation, Larson headed back into the store without bothering to see if Taziar had obeyed.

CHAPTER 12
Chaos Hunted

Behold! human beings living in an underground den. . . .
Like ourselves . . . they see only their own shadows, or
the shadows of one another, which the fire throws on the
opposite wall of the cave.

—Plato
The Republic

The taxicab crawled through rush hour traffic, cutting
through cracks and openings so tiny that Al Larson felt
like a thread poked repeatedly and recklessly through the
eye of a needle. Timmy sat at Larson's right. To his left,
Taziar Medakan plucked at his own blue jeans, toying with
the first zipper he had ever seen. He also wore a black and
gray shirt and a Dodger's cap pulled low over his eyes.
Wisps of sable hair poked from beneath the brim, making
him look as much like a child as Timmy.

Taziar's disguise, in addition to timing and luck, had gotten them past the police, but Larson knew they had not
seen the last of New York's finest. *They'll forgive Shadow.
Climbing a building, though stupid, seems harmless. But I
laid out two cops, and cops protect their own.* Larson accepted the thought philosophically, without need for judgment. In Vietnam, if someone, even another American, had
assaulted his companions, he also would have sought revenge. And the police had the law on their side as well.
*After I tried to convince Taziar that cops are friends, unlike
Cullinsberg's cruel, thrill-seeking murderers on the take, he
may get a stunning example of police brutality.*

Timmy leaned across Larson, studying Taziar with shame-
less forthrightness. "This is Robin Hood?" He sounded
skeptical.

Larson pushed his thoughts aside. "His name's Taz, Timmy."

Taziar looked up, leaving the zipper in its closed position.

At the least, he seemed to have guessed its use and the proper location for social dignity. "How do you say 'Shadow' in your language?"

Larson pronounced the word for Taziar. It sounded vaguely similar to its ancient German equivalent.

Taziar nodded. "Just wanted to make sure it didn't come out like 'cow dung' or 'idiot' or some swear word. Tell your brother he can call me . . ." He used his best English. ". . . Shadow."

Larson relayed the message.

"This is the Grand Concourse," the cabby said.

Larson located the subway sign and its corresponding concrete steps dragging downward into darkness. "Pull over if you can."

The driver complied, double parking against a row of cars. Behind him, a horn blared, followed by a linear symphony of honks that stretched down the roadway.

Ignoring the noise, Larson ushered his companions onto the sidewalk. Once out of the taxi, he leaned against the driver's window, drew a twenty from his pocket and handed it to the cabby.

The cabby accepted it, his brow furrowed. The previous ten more than covered the fare.

"You keep that. Forget where you took us, and I'll give you another." Larson dangled a twenty between his thumb and first finger.

The man smiled, revealing tobacco-stained teeth. "Make it two, and I never saw any of you in my life."

Larson passed a pair of twenties to the grinning cabby, then joined his companions. "Come on."

Taziar and Timmy spoke simultaneously, their languages markedly different, but their words nearly identical. "Where are we going?"

The taxicab pulled back out into traffic. A single horn wailed, then the noise level died to the normal rush hour hubbub.

Taziar relaxed visibly.

"Subway," Larson said to Timmy. He switched to the barony tongue. "We need a safe place to talk, someplace Silme and Bolverkr won't be able to recognize in a location spell. Down those steps we'll find row after row of connected cars that all look essentially the same. They're moving, too, so by the time the sorcerers could locate us and transport, we'd be elsewhere." He continued toward the steps as he talked. "It's just a temporary solution. We can hardly live on the subway, but it should give us a safe place to exchange information and plan strategy."

Taziar nodded, his gaze flicking among automobiles, buildings, and the hordes of people.

Timmy tugged at his brother's shirt. "It took all those funny words just to say 'subway' to him?"

"Huh?" Larson turned to Timmy, realizing his explanation to Taziar had taken far longer than his answer to Timmy. "They don't have subways where Shadow comes from." *Or three quarters of the things you use every day.* Larson trotted down the steps. "I had to explain it to him."

At the bottom of the flight, Larson pulled out two singles.

Timmy continued to watch Taziar. "When's he going to do something like Robin Hood?"

"Oh, for God's sake."

Apparently recognizing annoyance in Larson's tone, if not his words, Taziar questioned. "What's the matter now?"

"I made the mistake of telling Timmy you're quick and agile. He keeps watching for you to do something . . ." He tried to put the swashbuckler image into words.

". . . quick and agile?" Taziar supplied.

"Right." Larson waved Taziar and Timmy aside. "Wait here and don't move. I need to get us through the turnstile." He added swiftly, "Legally."

Larson walked to the back of the fast moving line. Purchasing three tokens, he returned to find Taziar juggling eight gold barony ducats to Timmy's evident amusement. A small crowd had gathered.

Larson sprang to Taziar's side, snatching a coin out of the air. "What the hell are you doing?"

Taziar caught the other ducats easily, amidst a spattering of applause. "Being quick and agile. For Timmy."

"Well, cut it out." Larson separated bills in his pocket. "The last thing we need now is attention. And don't be flashing money around." Unobtrusively, he handed Taziar a generous third of the currency. "Speaking of which, in case we get separated, you should have some of this."

The cash disappeared in Taziar's grip.

Larson pressed bills into Timmy's hand. "Here. Put this

in your pocket and keep it there. It should get you anywhere in case of emergency. Hopefully, you won't need it,
but it's not worth taking chances." Without awaiting a
reply, he headed for the turnstile. Placing a token in the
slot, he passed through, turned and dropped in tokens for
Timmy and Taziar. They joined the milling crowd on the
platform.

In the pit, subway rails gleamed like stiff, silver snakes.
A wall separated the southbound tracks from the north-
bound side. Businesspeople slouched near where they knew
the cars would stop. Others sat on benches evenly spaced
against the outer wall that separated the platform from the
token booth and stairs. A concession stand interrupted the
array of seats.

Larson addressed his brother. "We may be riding all
night or longer. I'm going to get some survival gear. If the
train comes, don't get on until I'm back. Then, help
Shadow. Remember, he's never seen a subway before."

"Okay." Timmy's face twisted in concentration as he prepared for his job with appropriate seriousness.

Trotting to the booth, Larson purchased several comic
books, two dozen packages of crackers and candy and three
cups of soda. As he turned, a line of subway cars pulled to
the platform, brakes squealing. The familiar, metallic oil
odor blasted through the air.

People funneled onto already packed cars, grabbing
handholds on the poles edging each rattan seat, Larson
grabbed his change and raced on board. Taziar followed
hesitantly, Timmy urging him onward.

The doors hissed closed.

"Hang on tight," Larson warned. Hands full, he braced
himself by looping a foot around a chair leg.

The car accelerated with a halting spasm. Caught by surprise, Taziar jolted into a businessman in front of him,
saved from a fall only by his natural grace.

The stranger turned to glare. Then, apparently mistaking
Taziar for a child, he smiled indulgently instead.

"Excuse me, sir," Taziar managed in passable English.

The car clacked and rattled over the tracks. As its movement stabilized, Larson passed the sodas to Timmy and
Taziar.

Taziar released the pole, staring into his drink doubtfully.

"Sweet beer," Larson explained. "With a lot more fizz and none of the kick. Drink slowly until you get used to it. And, for God's sake, don't spill it on anyone." The subway slowed gradually. "Hang on. There's going to be another hard shock. In fact, we'll be starting and stopping over and over again."

Taziar curled the fingers of his free hand around the pole, this time taking the jerky movements in stride.

The doors wrenched open, and people filed off or on.

"What are you guys talking about?" Timmy asked.

The car started again with another lurch, sloshing cola down the front of Taziar's shirt.

"Timmy," Larson shouted over the rumble of conversations and the squeal of metal wheels against track. "Shadow and I need to talk for a while. Here." He handed over the comic books. "Whenever a seat frees up, take it and read." He turned back to Taziar. "Now, tell me how you got here." He sipped at his drink.

Over the next half hour, Taziar described the sequence of events from the time he had awakened until Silme's decision to slay the baby.

Larson listened with rapt attention and empathy. The deaths of Astryd and the baby tore at his heart, a single, paired grief he did not try to separate. "I'm sorry, Taz. I'm so sorry." The words seemed inadequate. The tears that sprang to his eyes added the sincerity his words could not. He crushed the paper cup in frustration, the only gesture he dared in the crowded car.

Taziar said nothing. He looked away.

Dozens of stops came and went while both men regained their composure. The silence that hung between them seemed so much more meaningful that it overpowered the continuous, surflike roar of half-heard conversations. People loaded and unloaded, the ratio of standing to sitting passengers becoming more equal by tedious increments.

Gradually, Larson shoved aside grief, aware it could wait. For now, plotting had to take precedence. "Did you get any feel for Bolverkr's and Silme's plans?"

"Just that they wanted to slaughter us." Taziar glanced up, eyes bloodshot and shadowed by the brim of his cap. The harsh, German accent sounded ridiculous issuing from this boyish figure.

Larson snickered, barely catching himself before hysterical laughter overtook him.

"Oh, and the usual posturing men do when they want to impress a woman. Bolverkr promised Silme the world."

Larson frowned, staring at the scratched, green walls of the car. "Unfortunately, Bolverkr's powerful enough that he might be able to give it to her."

"I'm not so sure."

The subway ground to another halt. Larson watched people file through the single sliding door to the platform. This time, only three people replaced the exiting crowd. "What do you mean? Vidarr said Bolverkr's even more powerful than the gods."

"In our world, true." Taziar apparently meant "our" to refer to Bolverkr, Silme, and himself. "But when Bolverkr threw that spell, he said something about the Chaos he used never coming back."

The doors closed, and the train continued. Larson stared at Taziar. "What does that mean?"

"I'm not sure." Taziar no longer needed to hold the pole. He finished the last sip of soda and clung to the paper cup as if it was the finest mug. "From what I saw, I'd guess the rules are different here. The Chaos they threw into their spells dispersed, though not without consequence. I felt its evil wash through me. Then it passed over a group of passersby, sending them into a wild argument."

Larson made a vague noise of consideration.

"It seems to me as if every spell drains Chaos permanently, releasing it into the surroundings."

"Chaos is life energy," Larson recalled aloud.

"Right."

"So every spell Bolverkr throws not only makes him weaker magically but physically. Each loss of Chaos takes him one step closer to death."

"Presumably."

A horrible idea followed naturally. "And Silme, too."

"Presumably," Taziar repeated with less vigor. He went quiet a moment, then raised a loophole. "Assuming Chaos and life force are linked in your world the same as in mine." He threw the question back to Larson. "Are they?"

Larson snorted. "How would I know? Sorcerers don't

exist here as far as I know. At least, they didn't before Bolverkr and Silme."

At the next stop, Timmy managed to find a seat on the far side of a row, near a window that overlooked the central wall between tracks.

Taziar worked with the available information. "We can't fight Bolverkr at his current power. That's clear enough. The best strategy seems obvious to me. The more spells he casts and the stronger those spells are, the more equal the fight becomes. If we can survive his magic long enough, he'll eventually weaken enough for us to best him."

Larson said nothing, his thoughts still on Silme.

"At least we know he won't waste his spells. As for Silme, Bolverkr must have found a way to channel Chaos to her. Immediately after she cast that spell and lost some Chaos, there was a moment before pain set in when her loyalties seemed to shift back to me, as if the Chaos lost some of its influence over her."

Hope thrilled through Larson. "You mean if we can drain enough Chaos from Silme . . ." He trailed off, letting Taziar finish the sentence.

Taziar obliged. ". . . we may get her back. Yes. I think it's possible. That is, so long as Bolverkr doesn't keep replacing the Chaos she loses."

For the first time in weeks, Larson's spirits lifted. The odds had gone from hopeless to vaguely possible, and, for now, that seemed more than enough.

Afternoon passed to evening on New York's Independent Line. As rush hour dispersed to quieter times, Larson, Taziar, and Timmy found seats together. Timmy slept, his sandy head propped against the window. Beside him, Taziar munched at a peanut butter cracker, occasionally adding inspiration to the clouded phantom plans taking shape in Larson's mind. The general strategy seemed obvious, guerrilla attacks that drained Bolverkr's Chaos followed by sudden retreats. However, the practical mechanics of such a scheme eluded Larson. And Taziar's ignorance of the city made his input little more than useless.

Larson glanced around the subway car, at the double row of parallel seats and the aisle between them. A stout, dark-haired man sat in the last seat of the opposite row beside a curvaceous, but moon-faced, bleached blonde in a fur coat. She wore a large diamond on her left hand. In front of the couple, three teenagers discussed rock and roll, dressed in tie-dyed T-shirts and bell-bottom jeans with fringe. Six businessmen in suits reposed in various locations around the car. Two women in gray skirts and suit coats sat, chatting softly together.

The subway ground to another stop, the halt and start up having grown so familiar in the last few hours that Larson no longer noticed it. But, this time, the three men who boarded drew his attention. They wore matching black T-shirts displaying rearing cobras and tucked into grimy jeans. One, tanned and blond, wore a leather jacket that fell to his knees, and Larson could tell the youth carried something beneath its folds. The jacketed stranger walked to the door between their car and the one ahead of it, steadying himself against the door frame. The largest of the three braced himself between the seat directly in front of Larson and its neighbor. He was a dark-haired, scar-faced man a few years older than Larson and obviously the leader of the trio. The last, a redhead, took a position at the back of the car.

The door slid shut. The subway lurched.

As if it were a signal, the blond at the front whipped a sawed-off shotgun from beneath his coat. Scarface raised a .45 Colt army sidearm, and the redhead drew a .38 special. "Don't scream," the leader said. "Do what I say, and no one gets hurt." All three moved as lightly as cats, covering every person in the car. They had the routine down well.

Larson stiffened.

The leader grabbed one of the teenagers by a tie-dyed sleeve and shoved a plastic drawstring bag into the youth's quivering hand. "Go around the car. I want wallets and jewelry. I don't want trouble."

The car went deathly still. Larson could hear his heart hammering, and the almost inaudible sound of the shotgun's safety clicking off. *No big deal. It's just money. One blast from that 12 gauge will blow us all to kingdom come.* He bit his lip, recalling how safe the subways had always seemed before Vietnam, wondering if this could be part of the spreading effects from Bolverkr's and Silme's Chaos.

The teenager obeyed, opening the bag for a businessman on Larson's side of the car. The people in the seats in front of Larson, Taziar, and Timmy gave up their possessions without hesitation, keeping their heads low and their movements nonthreatening.

Concerned for Taziar's ignorance and his tendency to embrace challenges and fight injustice, Larson whispered. "Give them your money. Don't start any trouble."

"Shut up!" The leader swung around, the .45 aimed at Larson's head. "Say another word and I'll blow you away!"

Larson went silent, gaze locked on the man's hands.

The teen with the bag waited until the gun retreated before shuffling between the scar-faced hoodlum and Larson.

Larson dumped his money, watch, and wallet into the bag, relieved to see his friend and brother surrender their bills also. *It's not worth dying over.*

No longer the direct focus of the leader's attention, Larson took a surreptitious glance around the car. Several people seemed rattled, shivering or clinging with white knuckles to the seat backs. One of the businessmen kept a hand clenched across his mouth. The bleached blond sat still as a statue, but her fiancé's gaze kept rolling between the gunmen. His hands twitched, and his arms tensed and loosened.

Larson willed the man still. *Don't be a hero, you dumb ass. You'll get us all killed.*

Timmy curled like a fetus against the window. Taziar remained still, following Larson's lead.

The shotgun and .38 special remained leveled and steady. The bagman finished Larson's row and started toward the couple.

Larson mentally prepared himself for trouble, careful to give no outward sign of his tension. The man dropped his wallet into the bag, the natural action soothing Larson's raw-edged nerves. Then the man stopped.

The teen took a hesitant step forward.

"Watch and ring, too." The leader swung his .45 toward the hefty man.

With a twisted glare, the man removed and tossed in his watch. "The ring doesn't come off." He indicated the diamond on his fiancée's hand.

Larson suppressed a groan.

"The ring, too!" Scarface said. "Now!"

The tension in the car increased visibly. Tears coursed down the face of one of the well-dressed women.

"Look," the man said. "It's too tight. It doesn't come off."

Don't do it, man. Don't do it. Larson tried to send a mental message.

The teen looked nervously between the guns.

The leader made a subtle gesture with his head, addressing the hippie with the bag. "Take the ring off her finger. I don't care if you have to take the fucking finger with it!"

The teen reached toward the woman. Outraged, the hefty man sprang to his feet.

The .45 blasted, its roar deafening, sending Larson's ears into aching ringing. The hefty man collapsed back into his seat, his pale eyes staring.

The bleached blonde gasped. Scream after scream shuddered from her throat.

"Shut up!" The gun swung toward her. "Shut the hell up!" The leader's hand tensed.

Larson sprang. He slammed one arm around the leader's throat, the other groping for the gun. Cartilage cracked beneath Larson's wrist. The gun fired, and the bullet went wild, punching a hole in the ceiling. Screams echoed through the car. Larson wrenched the .45 from the leader's hand.

The shotgun. Using the gasping leader as a shield, Larson whirled and fired. The bullet tore through the blond hoodlum's chest, driving him into the door frame. Larson spun again, his mind blandly registering that his prisoner was no longer struggling.

The redhead had a perfect bead on Larson. For an instant, he hesitated. Then, apparently realizing the leader Larson was using as a shield was already dead, the redhead pulled the trigger.

The subway car jolted to a sudden stop.

The redhead stumbled. His shot pinged through a mental pole, winging one of the businessmen, who shrieked. Larson returned fire as the car's momentum shifted backward. His slug blasted a hole in the hoodlum's head.

Terrified screams ripped from half a dozen throats. Other passengers dove for cover beneath the seats. The doors jogged open.

The noise drew Larson. Every combat instinct aroused, he swung the gun toward the sound, still clutching the leader's corpse.

A half dozen men in uniforms graced the platform, pistols drawn. "Put down the gun! Now!"

Larson hesitated less than a second. Before he could think to lower his weapon, a bullet tore through his upper left arm. Pain shocked through him. His legs seemed to give out, and he collapsed to the floor, his right hand clinging naturally to the wound, his vision a swirl of scarlet.

"Al!" Timmy's hysterical cry sounded thousands of miles away.

A louder voice filled Larson's ringing ears. "Roll over." Someone kicked him. "Roll over now!"

An alarm shrilled through the subway car. Footsteps pounded around Larson. Voices, high-pitched and frenzied, cut through Larson's fog, their words meaningless. He looked up to a gun clenched in two white fists the barrel pointed at his head. "Roll over!"

Guarding his injured shoulder, Larson scrambled until he lay facedown on the dirty, tile floor.

"Al! Al! Leave him alone! Leave my brother alone!" Timmy's shrieks emerged, recognizable over the confusion of words and noises.

"Put your right arm behind you," the commanding voice instructed.

Larson moved his hand to the small of his back. Immediately, a man's weight dropped onto his spine. A metal cuff slapped around his wrist. A sweaty hand seized his injured arm, jerking it behind him with an abruptness that stabbed agony through his wound. He loosed a sharp moan.

The cop snorted, snapping the second handcuff into place. "Yeah, I feel sorry for you, punk. Get up." He yanked Larson to his feet. "You're under arrest. You have the right to remain silent. . . ."

The policeman's words registered only as a familiar rhythm from every television cop show Larson had ever seen. His world buckled and spun. He caught a bleary, shock-glazed glance at the other passengers, huddled in a corner, ringed by Transit Authorities, and all talking at once. One policeman clutched Timmy, who clawed and kicked in the uniformed arms.

After a while, the subway sputtered and sped away. The four corpses lay heaped on the concrete. The handful of recently alighted passengers formed a gawking semicircle on the platform. Larson did not see Taziar among the others.

Despite multiple simultaneous conversations, Larson picked one of the softer ones from the clamor. ". . . found the shotgun and a .38. We searched the whole car. No sign of the gun he was holding. Finally just had to let the train go . . ."

"Timmy," Larson gasped. "He's only eight. He thinks policemen are his friends. . . ."

"Shut up!" The policeman snarled in Larson's face. He broke off his reading of the rights. "You should have thought of that before you started killing people." His tone reverted to its gruff monotone. "You have the right to an attorney . . ."

Larson went silent, catching another piece of the conversation on which he had been eavesdropping. ". . . Check the kid first. Sometimes these guys'll hand off their weapons to a child, thinking we won't think to search 'em. Then . . ." He broke off abruptly. "Hey!" He ran toward the tracks. "Hey, you! Stop!"

Every head whipped toward the tracks. Larson caught a glimpse of a pale form dashing through the pit. *Shadow!*

The conclusion to Larson's rights was obscured by a warning shout. "Halt! Police! Halt, or we'll shoot!"

Larson gasped.

A grumble emerged, barely audible beneath the wild cacophony of shouts and suggestions. "Speak for yourself, Murph. I ain't shooting no little kid."

"He doesn't speak English!" Larson screamed.

The policeman at Larson's side yanked at the cuffs, shooting pain through his injured arm. The agony went deep, the incessant, screaming grind of a toothache.

Larson finished despite the pain. "He's scared. Please, don't shoot him. Please. Please don't shoot." Fear for Taziar brought tears to Larson's eyes. He had only known the Shadow Climber a few months, yet the image of the thief's tiny body bleeding on the rails, crushed beneath the metal wheels like a crow-picked road kill made him grief-crazy in a way even his unborn baby's death had not.

"Hey," someone shouted. "Don't touch that. . . ."

Third rail. Larson cringed as his mind finished the sentence for him. *It'll fry him. I have to warn him. In his language.* "Shadow, don't touch the steel—"

"Shut up!" The man who had handcuffed Larson lashed a hand across his face.

The blow staggered Larson. He fell to his knees, dizziness crushing his world to a gray blank. He tried to catch his balance, the natural movements seeming slowed and outside reality. He collapsed to the concrete, feeling no pain.

Timmy screamed.

"Shit," someone unidentifiable said. Gasps shuddered through the crowd.

A closer voice addressed the cop standing over Larson. "Easy on that guy, Gaets. That woman says he saved her life. Jumped the punk that shot her boyfriend."

Gaets grunted, the sound uninterpretable without the accompanying facial expression.

Larson rolled, fighting for understanding. Awareness returned in a rush, unconsciousness fading behind him in a crackle of pinpoints and sparks. "Timmy," he managed. "Timmy, don't fight. I'm all right. Do whatever they say."

A subway screeched to a halt on the opposite track.

Larson's mind kicked into overdrive. His glance toward the rail pit had revealed that this was one of the many stations without a wall separating the inbound and outbound trains. *That means Shadow might have run onto the other track! Right under the wheels of that subway.* "Shadow," he said hoarsely. "Is Shadow okay?"

"He got away," Timmy answered excitedly from across the platform. "He runned and leaped and climbed right up the wall. Just like Robin Hood."

Larson never remembered Robin Hood dodging through subway pits. Relief flooded him. *At least one thing went right.*

Gaets helped Larson to his feet, his grip still firm, but his manner gentler.

"Meat wagon's on the way. Think we should get this kid to a hospital, too?"

"Naw," Gaets replied. "It's a clean shot through the arm.

We've already lost one possible accomplice. I say we get him down to the station, ASAP."

Gaets nudged Larson toward the stairway, the Transit Authority clearing a pathway through the spectators.

Several other policemen joined the group clustered around Larson.

"What kind of story you getting?" Gaets asked one of the newcomers.

"Most of them didn't see nothing. A few willing to come in and give a statement, though they each saw something different. The blonde lady seems to have the most coherent story, when she's not crying hysterically. The little boy says he's this guy's brother." He pointed at Larson. "At least two witnesses are saying this guy killed one of the gunmen with his bare hands."

"Shit," one said.

Docilely, Larson let himself be led away, adding nothing to the exchange. Knowing Taziar had escaped alive freed his mind to concentrate on other matters, and the policeman's description struck home. *I did kill someone with my bare hands.* He felt no remorse for the slaying. *The man was a murderer. If I hadn't taken him, he would have become a mass murderer, if he wasn't already.* But Gaelinar's lessons had penetrated deep. *I killed him accidentally, because I don't know my own body and my own strength well enough. I lost control. And, without control of myself, I have nothing.* A sudden thought shivered terror through him. *What if I hit those cops back at Sears harder than I intended, too? What if I'm a cop-killer?*

Larson's insides felt as if they had melted within him, and self-loathing hammered at the back of his mind. Torn by emotional pain, the physical ramifications seeped into his thoughts more slowly. His taste of brutality had, so far, been mild, a slap on the wrist compared to the broken skulls reported during protests and college campus demonstrations. *If I killed either of those cops, I'll never make it to trial.* And the most frightening thing of all was that Larson knew from his war experience that, if he was the policeman and someone else Al Larson, he would stand back and let his companions beat the cop-killer to death.

CHAPTER 13
Chaos Justice

At the height of their madness
The night winds pause
Recollecting themselves;
But no lull in these wars.
  —Herman Melville
   The Armies of the Wilderness

Taziar Medakan huddled against the wall of a building just beyond the subway station, muddled by the flashing lights and the sudden blatters of sound, metallic voices surrounded by fizzles and crackles. Ignorance made a plan of action impossible, yet Larson's descriptions and his own scant experience gave him a few usable facts. *The guards caught Allerum and Timmy, presumably to torture them in some dungeon. This time, Allerum can't find me. He says the city's too big to search, and with those car vehicles, they could take him far away and anywhere. I've got to find Allerum again. And, this time, I can't let him out of my sight.*

Taziar sighed, ignoring the myriad aches of abrasions and bruises, hoping he had chosen the correct location from which to observe. His position in the building's shadow gave him a clear view of both inbound and outbound subway exits, and he hoped that would prove enough. Except for the trains, Taziar had seen no other ways to leave the station. *And, if the guards planned to use the underground vehicles, why did they make everybody leave the car?* Taziar sighed again, certain he was overlooking something. It seemed to be taking far too long for the city guards to pound Larson and Timmy unconscious and drag them from the concrete bowels of New York City. *There's just too much I don't understand.*

Still, Taziar had some tricks of his own. Gingerly, he touched the .45 in his pocket. Having seen the damage the pistol could create, he held a healthy respect for the weapon. The observation had given him a reasonable idea of which end the projectiles came from, though he had little grasp of the mechanisms and procedures involved in activating it. Once, in ancient Norway, Silme's half-brother had shot Taziar, but the time-displaced rifle bore little resemblance to the dense chunk of carbon steel he now carried.

Taziar jabbed his fingers into his jeans' pocket, patting the crumpled wad of currency, his other ace in the hole. On the train, he had pretended to shuffle the bills into the gunmen's bag, palming more than twice as many as he dropped. It had proven easier than the trick he had used against the monte gang. Cards needed to remain crisp, while paper money wadded into neat balls that could be straightened. Taziar frowned. Larson's casual folding of the bills had led him to believe creases and rumples did not deflate their value. Now, he hoped he would not need to test that theory.

A chunky, middle-aged woman sat on a bench across the street from the subway and the blinking bank of police cars. Her cheeks looked flushed, her lips unnaturally red. Thin, black lines circled her eyes. Her lashes seemed impossibly long, curving around lids discolored blue. Despite the need to plan, Taziar could not help staring. *Did she paint dyes on her face? Or was she just normally ugly?*

Before Taziar could answer the question, even in his own mind, several members of the town guard emerged from the subway. Others followed, Larson between them, his hands manacled behind him. Still more guards appeared. They headed toward the row of flashing cars.

Taziar flattened to the stone, certain of only one thing. *If they ride away in those vehicles, I'll never find Allerum again.* He watched, heart pounding, as the uniformed men ushered Larson into the back seat of one of the squad cars.

Desperate for a solution, Taziar glanced around. A taxicab turned the corner, identical to the one he, Timmy, and Larson had used to escape the Sears building. The woman rose to greet it, and the cab decelerated.

The squad car doors slammed. The guardsmen climbed into the front seat, then closed their doors, too. The vehicle hummed to life.

Taziar recalled a day in another world. Larson's sarcasm came back to him verbatim, though riddled with English phrases: "You're all set if you ever want to take a transcontinental cab ride in an American made car." Waiting until the policemen were all involved with Larson and one another, Taziar darted across the street to the taxicab. Seizing a rear car handle, he worked the mechanism. The door swung open.

Taziar sprang into the back seat just as the woman edged in from the other side. He pulled his door closed.

The woman stared, blinking her color-enhanced eyes repeatedly. Then her face lapsed into angry creases, and she shouted at Taziar, waving her arms wildly. Not a single word was comprehensible.

The first police car roared away from the curb. The others began to follow.

Taziar ignored the woman, leaning forward. A man stared back from the driver's seat, his olive-skinned face fuzzed with three days' growth of beard. He waved a hand, calling calmly over the woman's tirade.

The car with Larson in it glided down the roadway.

Taziar chose the only universal language he knew. Digging into his pocket, he emerged with a random handful of currency and hurled it into the front seat. Ones, twenties, and fifties fluttered, churning through the air, then fell to the vinyl. "Follow that car!" he screamed in his best English. He jabbed a finger at the squad car. "Follow that *damned* car!"

The woman lapsed into shocked silence.

A sparkle appeared in the cabby's eyes as he stared at the money. "You want me to chase down a police car?"

The squad car turned a corner.

Taziar could not catch all the cabby's words, but he recognized police as the term Larson used for guards. "Police. Yeah. Follow that car!" He crooked his finger to indicate the turn. "Okeydokey?"

The driver glanced at the money strewn across his seat. "Sure. Okeydokey, man. You got it." He addressed the woman.

She shouted something back at him, flinging her arms frantically.

The cabby spoke, his voice becoming menacing.

The woman pursed her lips, then clambered back outside. She slammed the door hard enough to shake the entire vehicle.

The taxicab maneuvered into the road on the trail of the squad cars.

A short circuit in the overhead socket caused the light bulb to flicker and sputter, dancing shadows over the four men in the police interrogation room. Seated in a folding chair, Al Larson kept his right hand clamped over the hastily bandaged gunshot wound in his shoulder. Across a metal and wooden table, a white-haired detective named Harrison tented his fingers over a sheaf of papers. A telephone graced the corner near his left elbow, and he sat in a cushioned swivel chair that seemed far more comfortable than the seats of Larson and his two police escorts.

At least they took off the handcuffs. Larson knotted his free hand, keeping it draped in his lap. *I hope that means they're willing to listen.*

"What's your name, kid?" Detective Harrison asked, staring at the papers as if to read and talk at the same time.

Larson presumed they had recovered his wallet from the subway. If so, lying could only get him deeper into trouble. "Larson."

The detective glanced over at one of the officers who nodded almost imperceptibly.

Satisfied, Harrison looked back at his papers. "First name?"

"Al," Larson said.

"Al?" The detective shuffled a page from the stack. "Al, what?"

"Al, *sir.*" Larson supplied naturally.

Detective Harrison looked directly at Larson for the first time. He squinted, apparently trying to read his captive's intentions. Then, satisfied Larson was not trying to sound intentionally flippant, he clarified. "No, I meant Al-*len,* Al-*bert,* Al-*exander*?"

"Just Al, sir."

A thoughtful silence fell. Harrison looked at the officer. This time, the patrolman shrugged.

Larson felt a need to clarify. "My father didn't like nicknames. He thought people should be named what they're

called. Hence my sister Pam, not Pamela, and my brother
Tim, not Timothy." He added quickly, "Though we do call
Tim, 'Timmy.' "

"Right." Detective Harrison flipped the paper across the
desk. "If you're going to answer any more questions, you'll
have to sign this first."

The page slid in front of Larson. Reaching out, he
straightened it. A quick glance revealed it as a waiver, stat-
ing his constitutional rights. At the bottom, he was given
the option of whether to sign it, thus proving he understood
that he did not have to submit to questioning and had chosen to do so willingly.

Harrison offered a black ballpoint.

Taking it, Larson signed. He passed pen and waiver back
to the detective.

"You can read, I presume, Mr. Larson?"

"Yes, sir." Larson said.

"You understand you are still under arrest. Nothing you
say is going to change that. Even in extenuating circumstances, we can't . . . um . . . 'unarrest' you until the District
Attorney asks for a dismissal. You will go to jail until your
appearance before a magistrate."

Larson bit his lip, not liking the sound of the detective's
explanation. "I'm willing to cooperate any way I can." *Anything else would be folly, an admission of guilt. Right now,
that's the last thing I need.*

"Very well, Mr. Larson. Your story of what happened
this evening on the subway." Harrison pocketed the pen
and swept the waiver aside. He made a broad gesture indicating Larson should begin.

Al Larson launched into his tale, starting with the moment the gunmen entered the train and ending with his
arrest. He avoided all mention of Taziar or of their original
purpose for taking the subway. He kept his tone casual,
not daring to overplay his hand in the rescue of innocent
passengers.

As he spoke the last word, the interview room fell back
into an unnerving hush. The patrol officer nearest the door
fidgeted, chewing at a thumbnail. The other watched Larson.

Detective Harrison leaned forward, fingers laced on the
tabletop. "Mr. Larson, how many shots did you fire?"

"Two, sir."

"And are you aware where each of those bullets went?"

"Yes, sir." Larson wondered where the line of questioning was leading.

"Mr. Larson." A hard edge entered Harrison's tone. He met and held Larson's gaze. "Are you also aware we took four corpses off that train?"

"It doesn't surprise me," Larson admitted. He added belatedly, "Sir."

The detective's cheek twitched, and Larson guessed he had come to a significant question. "Mr. Larson, how many of those men did you kill?"

"Three, I think, sir."

"Three men, Mr. Larson. With two bullets."

"Right."

"How do you explain that?" Detective Harrison leaned back into his chair, his hands still threaded and clenched.

Larson blinked, unable to guess what Harrison wanted. "I already told you the story. I accidentally crushed one guy's windpipe." Once spoken, the words sounded bad, and Larson felt the need to add, "While wrestling free a gun he was using to shoot down passengers."

The light splayed shadows over Harrison's face, making him look camouflage-painted. "How's exactly, Mr. Larson, does one *accidentally* crush a man's windpipe?"

Oh, for Christ's sake. The repetition and unwarranted suspicion wore at Larson's patience. His shoulder ached, and his head throbbed. Every wasted second pulsed at his sensitivities. *Surely Silme and Bolverkr have located us by now. I hope Timmy's okay. And Shadow.* "Look, Detective Harrison. I was scared. Things happened fast. Innocents were getting killed. I did what I thought was right. Stress can do some pretty impressive things to the human body, especially when loved ones are in danger. My baby brother was in that subway."

The patrolmen exchanged knowing glances. Detective Harrison frowned. "We'll get back to your brother in a moment, Mr. Larson. I admit, I've heard of mothers lifting cars off their children. But panic doesn't turn a nineteen-year-old college student into a crack marksman. Mr. Larson, where did you learn to shoot?"

You've obviously managed to obtain some information about me already. You tell me. Larson choked back the words but did not manage to fully contain his sarcasm. "I was trained in the 101st anti-squirrel division."

Harrison's frown deepened. His knuckles blanched. "What are you saying, Mr. Larson?"

"I'm a hunter." Larson wrestled down his temper, aware angering policemen could only hurt his case. "My father's taken me to New Hampshire every deer season since I was legal to hold a gun."

"You hunted game with a handgun?"

"Of course not." Larson glanced between the uniformed officers, hoping to get some support against this lunacy. But the patrolmen kept their expressions unreadable. "But a gun is a gun. Once you've learned to quick-draw a rifle on a distant, moving target, how much training does it take to pull a trigger?"

"Mr. Larson, you want me to believe you've never handled a handgun? Yet you fired only two shots, one through a man's heart and the other through a man's brain. Two bullets. Two perfect, lethal shots. How do you explain that, Mr. Larson?"

Impressed with his own targeting, Larson took a moment to respond. When he did, it sounded lame. "Luck?"

Harrison jerked his head forward, flinging his face completely into darkness. "Luck, Mr. Larson? Is that the best you can do? Do you expect me to believe you attacked a gang of gunmen, unarmed, fired two shots, and killed three people without any training except matching wits with Thumper and Bambi?"

Larson's control broke. "Damn it, Detective Harrison. I'm not trying to 'get you to believe' anything. I'm just telling the goddamned truth. What you choose to believe is your own business." Fuming, he could not help adding, "And can the 'Mr. Larson stuff. I know my name." He clutched the arms of the chair, tensed to rise.

Detective Harrison retreated. The light strengthened, revealing flushed cheeks and narrowed eyes. "Mr. Larson, stay seated or we'll have to cuff you again. And please calm down. I'm just trying to put the stories together."

Larson remained rigid. "There must have been a dozen witnesses. Surely they've told you the same thing I did."

"There's a blonde woman who claims you saved her

life," Harrison admitted. "There's others who give a story similar to yours."

Larson said nothing, waiting for the other shoe to fall.

"Some are saying you were part of the gang. At least one claims you boarded the subway with the gunmen."

"That's ludicrous!" Larson burrowed his nails into the chair seat. "Timmy and I were on that train for hours." As soon as Larson spoke the words, he realized his mistake.

"For hours, Mr. Larson? For hours?" Harrison stared without blinking. "Do you realize how weird that is? What were you doing on the subway for hours?"

Larson shrugged. Finding no ready answer, he invented a lame one. "Cheap amusement. My little brother digs trains, okay?"

"Ah, back to your brother." Harrison unclasped his hands, removed the pen from his pocket, and twiddled it. "To hear him tell it, you're a cross between Elliot Ness and God Almighty. The kid needs to get away from the TV set. He kept babbling about witches and Robin Hood."

Larson groaned. "What happens now?"

"Well, I've still got some details to work out." Harrison flipped the pen, catching it by the cap. "I know you have an accomplice who made a break for it. We think he took the gun. That's suspicious." He stared at Larson.

Larson saw no need to answer a statement. *How the hell am I going to explain Shadow?* A more bewildering thought struck home. *His climbing Sears and Roebuck made the news. Surely, if we discuss the little sewer rat for long, they'll connect this incident with the other. And my ass is toast.*

Harrison continued, "If I can get enough answers to satisfy me, I'll get you to the night court magistrate for an initial appearance tonight. Judge Stoffer's fair. If we decide it's self-defense, he might let you off on your own recognizance. If we decide it's manslaughter, he'll probably have you post bond. But if we draw up a first-degree murder charge, you're in jail till the trial."

Larson stiffened further, aware his life, his friends', and seven and a half million strangers' might depend on how well he answered Harrison's questions.

Apparently misinterpreting Larson's discomfort, Harrison softened. "Don't get too hyped up. You may never hit lockup. I'm guessing it'll be a lesser charge. If Stoffer's got a full docket, he might well clear it by giving you a choice between jail and the army."

Larson felt as if an iced dagger had been thrust between his ribs.

The detective continued, apparently missing Larson's sudden, deadly-coiled stillness. "I mean, war's hell, but it's better than a jail cell. As easily as you shot those punks and as little remorse as you've shown, I can't imagine you're a Conscientious Ob—"

Roused from his initial shock, Larson sprang to his feet. "No!" His fist crashed against the desktop. "I'm not going to Vietnam." The telephone jumped, its bell clanging dully. "I'm not going back to 'Nam!"

As suddenly, light blasted through the interrogation room, aching through Larson's eyes. Shadows spun, then fled like spiders. The patrol officers dove behind the desk, while the detective froze in blind confusion. In between Harrison and Larson, Silme and Bolverkr appeared in a misty wash of smoke.

Bolverkr's arm arched. Lightning flashed down from the ceiling, striking the chair where Larson had sat a moment before. The seat splintered. The metal glowed, then warped into a twisted outline of legs and frame.

Bolverkr swore. He whirled toward Larson.

An officer peered over the desk, his handgun aimed at Bolverkr. "Police! Stand where you are!"

Larson snatched up another chair.

Gleaming strands of magic formed between Bolverkr's hands.

Larson ducked, hurling the chair at the sorcerer. Wood shattered against an invisible shield, but the impact drove barrier and Dragonrank mage a step backward. The spell misfired to glittering slivers in his hand.

A gun roared as Larson leapt for the door. Without bothering to see the consequences, he seized the handle and wrenched.

Bolverkr cursed. "Don't waste spells."

A probe speared through Larson's mind with an abruptness that sent him sprawling through the doorway. Silme's voice filled his head. "You're dead now, Allerum. You're dead." Her presence slammed into his skull.

Desperately, Larson threw up a mental wall. Magic

crashed against the conjured barrier. For an instant, the imagined bricks wavered. Then the spell exploded to sparks, scattering in a backlash that again lit the room like day.

Silme screamed.

Larson staggered to his feet, taking in the outer room at a glance. Policemen huddled behind overturned desks and chairs, guns drawn. The precinct lockup facility contained a single drunkard who cowered in its farthest corner. Still dazed by Silme's attack and weakened by his wound, Larson lurched against the bars, seizing the cold metal to steady himself.

"Don't move!" one of the cops hollered. "Don't anybody move."

Ignoring the warning, Larson whirled. Bolverkr was now only a few steps away from him.

"Shit!" Larson tried to dodge the sorcerer's charge, but Bolverkr's shield slammed into his gut, driving him back against the bars. His skull banged into the steel. Consciousness receded before a rush of rising darkness. Larson struggled in blind panic.

Bolverkr pressed in, his shield crushing Larson against the cage. The bars branded impressions into Larson's back, the pressure on his ribs quickly growing unbearable. He tried to drop to the floor, but Bolverkr pinned him like a moth beneath a cat's paw. All breath was compressed from his lungs. His head felt as if it would rupture between the bars. Air-starved, Larson felt the darkness deepen, scarcely noticing Silme's frantic search through his mind. His near unconsciousness gave her nothing concrete to manipulate.

Silme retreated. A moment later, a bullet bounced from Bolverkr's shield, inches from Larson's head. Realization penetrated Larson's numb and dizzied mind. *Silme's taken control of a cop. She's making him fire at me.* Larson rallied. Bracing against the bars, he tried to fling Bolverkr backward.

Pain shuddered through Larson's body. His empty lungs forced him to gasp in wild, uncontrollable bursts.

Another gunshot sounded. Then another.

Two more bullets ricocheted from Bolverkr's magics. Then a slug passed through the unprotected back of his shield, tearing a line along his side.

Bolverkr shrieked in anguish. His face a scarlet mask of fury, he whirled toward the policemen, sorceries snapping between his fingers.

The pressure on Larson disappeared. He sucked a dire lungful of air, then leapt for the sorcerer's unshielded back.

Fire erupted from Bolverkr's fingers, a storm of savage flame as ugly as his rage swirled through with black smoke. Furniture and men disappeared, boiled away in the rush of magics. Stunned by the sudden loss of a huge volume of Chaos, Bolverkr pitched a step backward.

Abruptly closer to his target than anticipated, Larson struck Bolverkr's back with his forearms instead of his fists.

Without bothering to assess the threat behind him, Bolverkr grabbed Silme and waved an arm. The air snapped open, swallowing the mages, leaving only an oily smoke that paled against the streaming, tarry residue of Bolverkr's magical fire.

The room fell horribly quiet. Lacy black smoke veiled Larson's vision. Evil drummed at his sensibilities, goading him to vengeance and violence. For an instant, the idea seized him to find the startled survivors and slaughter them one by one. But morality rose to beat the thought aside. *It's Chaos. It's the damned Chaos.* He coughed, choking on smoke and the dusty heat of cinders. *Got to get out of here while it's still possible.* He dropped, crawling to the front door.

Larson had just reached the panel when a sound clicked through the smoky darkness. A hand reached out of nowhere and wrapped around his neck. A gun's barrel gouged into his temple.

Larson froze, heart thumping. "Don't shoot," he rasped. "Please, don't shoot."

No reply. The gun remained in place.

Slowly, without threat, Larson rolled his eyes to a soot-and sweat-streaked face. Hazel eyes stared wildly back at him from beneath a patrolman's cap.

"Easy." Larson spoke soothingly, resorting to horror film clichés to make his point. "That smoke is a . . . an evil being possessing you. Think about what you're doing. Think, buddy, think!"

The arm tightened around Larson's throat. The gun dug into his scalp.

Larson's mind raced. *Gotta fight.* He gritted his teeth. *But I can't outmaneuver a bullet.*

The officer tensed suddenly.

Understanding flashed through Larson's mind. *He's going to shoot me whether I move or not.* Without time for strategy, he let his body go limp, collapsing suddenly to the ground.

The gun blast shattered Larson's hearing. Pain tore through his scalp.

Shot in the head. He shot me in the goddamned head. I'm dead. Larson rolled onto concrete, the paradox of his movement reviving a survival instinct that seemed ridiculous and impossible.

The gun roared again, the sound muffled to Larson's near-deafened ears. Chips of floor tile stung his arm and face.

Catching a moving, sideways glimpse of the officer's legs, Larson dove for them. His shoulder crashed against a knee. His fingers curled around a shin, yanking.

The cop tumbled, his gun careening into the raging inferno behind them. He clawed for Larson, driving an elbow into his face.

Larson fought through pain. Sweat trickled into his eyes, thickened with blood. Half-blinded, he wrapped his fingers around the officer's neck, driving his thumbs into the man's windpipe.

Now the policeman's struggles became more violent and less directed. He heaved at Larson's chest, arching to get his feet beneath him.

Larson released his choke hold with one hand. He drove his fist into the other man's forehead. The officer's head slammed against tile, and he went limp beneath Larson.

Larson clambered to his feet, not daring to check for a pulse. Sound filtered back to his ears, the whoosh of passing traffic and the distant blast of a car horn. He wiped his eyes with the back of his hand, smearing blood across his brow. Snatching the unconscious officer's hat, he ducked through the door. Once outside, he prodded the wound in his scalp with a finger. The touch hurt, and sweat stung the wound; but he felt certain the bullet had only grazed him.

Stars winked down at Larson through a thin blanket of smog, broken in patches by the New York skyline. A stubby yard of grass surrounded the three-story precinct, interrupted by a concrete path leading from the front door to a sidewalk parallel to the street. Another stripe of tree-lined yard separated the walk from the road.

Though tainted with factory contaminants, the cool, crisp air seemed a welcome relief after the heated smoke and rank discharge of Chaos. Still, the change in atmosphere came with a suddenness Larson's lungs could not accept. He coughed twice, then doubled over into a racking fit.

A hand dropped to Larson's shoulder.

Gripped by sudden panic, Larson whirled, striking at the presence. His arm swirled through air. The abruptness of his movement sent him into another bout of coughing. "Still a little excitable, I see." Taziar crouched just beyond Larson's reach, near the building's corner.

"Shit." Larson managed between coughs, his voice strained. "Don't sneak up on me." He loosed another series of rasping coughs. "I might hurt you."

Taziar's blue eyes caught the light from an upper window, twinkling with childish mischief. "You'd never catch me." He handed Larson a bandage from his jeans pocket.

Larson ignored the crack, his voice wheezy. "Silme and Bolverkr were here." Meticulously, he mopped blood and sweat from his forehead before twisting the strip of cloth into a tight knot around his head, staunching the bleeding. Covering it with the policeman's cap, he scooted around the corner of the building. The pain in his head had nearly disappeared, but the arm wound still throbbed with a deep, dull agony, sapping him of strength.

"Obviously they were here. The air is foul with Chaos. I hope that means you forced them to cast some draining spells."

Larson replied in a voice more closely approximating his normal one. "I don't know that I can take all the credit. But Bolverkr cast the most spectacular spell I've ever seen." Larson exhaled through pursed lips. "I'm glad he didn't use that against us at his castle." He considered aloud. "I wonder why not?"

Taziar shrugged. "Hard to say. Guess it's the same reason a soldier doesn't always use the best maneuver in a fight. He didn't think of it under pressure. Remember, too, he was crazed then. Or maybe he didn't want to waste the life energy."

"Doesn't make a difference." Larson dismissed the question for more urgent matters. "In the future, we need to be prepared for fire. That was the spell, some sort of wave of flame. And we need to find Timmy. Fast."

"I know. . . ."

"Let's go." Larson started along the building, uncertain where to begin his search.

"Wait." Taziar caught Larson's forearm.

Larson shook free. "You don't understand. We need to move quickly. For all I know, Timmy might be within the area of the fire."

"He's not."

Larson turned.

"You didn't let me finish." Taziar drew up beside Larson. "I was trying to say, 'I know where Timmy is.' I got here shortly after you did. What do you think I've been doing all evening?"

"What?"

Taziar paused, apparently surprised by the question. "I just told you. Looking for Timmy. And you, too." He smiled. "I started high and worked down. Timmy's on the second floor. He's fine. For you, I just followed the fighting noises." He brushed aside the hem of his shirt, revealing the Colt .45. "Oh, and here. Can you use this?" He pulled the pistol from his belt, clutching it upside down with a finger looped behind the trigger and the barrel facing his own abdomen.

Larson winced. "Better than you can, I'm sure." He took the gun, pausing to check the cartridge. *Four shots left.* He chambered the gun, placing it in the cocked and locked position for hip defense. He tucked it into his waistband, disliking the cold touch of carbon steel against his skin. "Now tell me about Timmy." He placed his back to the wall, crouched in the shadow of the precinct building.

"He's on the second floor in a room." Taziar rubbed his side, looking relieved to have disposed of the gun. "There's a woman with him."

"A policewoman?"

Taziar's eyes widened. "You have female city guards?"

"A few." Larson rearranged the gun to a more comfortable position. *Bleeding, armed, and wearing a cop cap. We've got to keep out of sight. This would be impossible to explain.*

"I don't know. How do you tell?"

"A uniform? A gun?"

Taziar's mouth formed a grim line. "I didn't see either."

"Go on."

"There's a man who enters and leaves at intervals. He does have a uniform. Gun, too, I think."

Larson frowned. "How did you see all this?"

"Through the window. The rooms to either side have windows, too."

"Open window or closed?"

Taziar did not hesitate. "Half opened. The rooms to either side are empty. All three rooms lead to the same hall-way. There're long bars along the hall ceiling that make light. The rooms are lit by flasks hanging from a metal stalk."

Fluorescent and overhead lighting. Larson chuckled inwardly at Taziar's focus on the technologies he could not understand. "You did your homework."

"Excuse me?"

"You did a good job scouting the area." Larson rephrased his comment in words Taziar could comprehend.

"Thank you." Taziar accepted the compliment off-handedly. "It's what I do. Remember? It's kind of nice not to get scolded about it for a change." A slight smile and a friendly gaze stole all bitterness from the comment.

Larson grunted. "Yeah. Well, I guess sneaking off half-cocked has its place. Though remind me to tell you about third rails sometime." He changed the subject. "Let's get moving. Where is this room Timmy's in anyway?"

Taziar inclined his head, indicating the back of the precinct.

Larson inched toward the corner. "Listen, you've been up there clambering around already, right?"

Taziar followed closely. He made no verbal reply.

Larson swiveled his neck to look over his shoulder, catching the end of Taziar's affirmative nod. "You think it's climbable?"

Taziar stared. He imitated the tone Larson used when

voicing sarcasm. "No. It's impossible. I made up that whole story about Timmy and the rooms."

Larson loosed a snorting laugh, only then realizing how silly his question must have seemed to a man who had scaled a skyscraper. "No. I meant do you think I could climb it."

Taziar studied Larson's sturdy, human frame. "I haven't seen you in this form all that much. I'd guess you could."

"Good. Let's go." Larson continued around the building, Taziar behind him. "I have an idea."

CHAPTER 14
Chaos Stand

One God, one Law, one element,
And one far-off divine event,
To which the whole creation moves.
                    —Alfred, Lord Tennyson
                    In Memoriam, Conclusion

Still wearing the policeman's cap, Al Larson crept over
checkered patterns of black and white tile and around the
simple furnishings of the police office, cautious as a thief.
A metal desk was set near one corner, lusterless despite
the glow from the overhead lighting. Mismatched chairs
formed a semicircle around the front of the desk, with one
chair on rollers behind it. A telephone graced the right
corner of the desktop, amid framed pictures and lopsided
stacks of paper. Exhaustion rode Larson. Despite Taziar's
boost, the single-story climb had made his injured arm ache,
and only concern for Timmy's safety kept him alert despite
fatigue and pain.

The now-open window that Larson had used as his entrance riffled air through the office. Directly across the
room, the door stood ajar.

A sudden gust of wind whipped through the confines.
The door flapped opened, then thrashed back toward its
closed position.

Realizing the panel would bang against its frame, Larson
sprang to quiet it. He skidded across the room, just in time
to shove his fingers between jamb and door. The wood
bruised his knuckles painfully, and he sublimated the urge
to scream with a string of mental swear words. Catching
the knob with his other hand, he levered the door off his
fingers without opening it.

Footfalls rang from the hallway beyond.

Larson froze, hand straying to the Colt .45 sidearm. He

hoped he would not need to use it for anything worse than intimidation. *I can't leave Timmy. My brother's life is worth too much, and it's obvious the cops can't protect him against Bolverkr and Silme.*

The footsteps tracked past Larson's door and on to the next, the room where Timmy waited with a female stranger. The hall went silent as the walker paused before the door. Hinges creaked, then the door clicked closed without latching.

Larson peeked out into the hallway. Doors interrupted the walls on both sides, the one to Timmy's room resting, unlatched, against its jamb. No living creature moved through the corridor. Apparently, most of the men had run to the defense of their colleagues downstairs. *Which means anyone left up here's going to be trigger-twitchy as hell.* The .45 slipped naturally into his fist.

Quickly, Larson exited his room, twisting the knob and closing it silently behind him. Two strides brought him to the room in which Taziar had seen Timmy.

A gruff, male voice wafted through the crack. ". . . tracked down your mother. She was looking for you. Real worried. She's coming to get you. . . ."

The news shocked Larson. *Oh, no. Why did we have to hear that? Now we know where Mom will be at a given time. And Silme will probably search Timmy's mind for the information.* The concern that he had burned down his home for no good reason wrestled with the need for his full concentration.

Timmy's alto lifted through the door. "But Al said we shouldn't be with her now. That we shouldn't know where she's at."

The man snorted. "Your brother slaughtered—"

The woman interrupted. "Timmy, I'm sure Al had a good reason for giving you that advice. But things are different now. You understand. Don't you want to go home with your mother?"

Timmy gave no verbal reply, but Larson guessed the boy must have nodded, because no one pressed him further.

"Your mother's staying with . . ." the man started.

Recognizing the danger of learning that piece of information, Larson grasped the knob and pounded on the door. "There's violence in the main office! We need every man!"

He ran farther down the hallway, hammering in a linear pattern of urgency. Then, he darted quietly to a position on the farther side of the door to Timmy's room, back flattened to the wall.

A moment later, the door creaked partway open. A slender policeman appeared in the doorway, leading with his handgun. He faced the direction Larson had taken, decoyed by footfalls and unaware that Larson now stood behind him. Seeing no one, he started to turn.

Swinging his gun, Larson clouted the policeman against the temple, remembering, at the last moment, to pull the blow. *Tired as I am, I'm still stronger than I'm used to.* The cop's .38 clattered to the floor. He crumpled into Larson's arms.

Though small, the senseless man felt like a lead weight in Larson's crippled grip. Prodding the door open with his knee, he dragged the man back into the room, aiming the .45 from beneath one sagging armpit.

Timmy hunched in a plush chair. A plump, handsome woman in her thirties sat beside him. *A social worker,* Larson guessed. Beyond them, the window edged open silently, as if of its own accord.

The woman gasped, gaze locked on the gun. Timmy went still, eyes wide, utterly speechless.

"Freeze! Hands up!" Larson tried to sound desperate, but his tone emerged more tired than anything else. He dropped the policeman; the still form flopped to the floor.

Taziar clambered through the window. With the woman and Timmy focusing their attention on Larson's weapon, the Shadow Climber went unnoticed.

Larson kept his eyes on the woman, watching the remainder of the room only through peripheral vision.

The social worker's mouth opened.

Afraid she might scream, Larson pointed the .45 directly at her chest. "Lady, shut up. You scream, I kill you. And don't move, please." Larson kept the gun in place, using neither it nor his hand to gesture. *Please? Did I just say please?* The incongruity of the propriety struck him. *Wouldn't want to be impolite while threatening her life.*

The social worker raised her arms, glancing protectively at Timmy, fear etched like a grisly mask across her features.

Just inside the doorway, Larson pinned the policeman's

.38 beneath his shoe and dragged it into the room. He kicked the door closed behind him, then, circumventing the woman, used the ball of his foot to send the gun skittering across the room to Taziar. "Cover her," he said in English for the woman's benefit, aware his other-world companion would have no idea what he meant. He adopted a perfect Weaver stance.

The woman twisted her head toward Taziar. She started to shake. Timmy opened his mouth, presumably to greet his brother.

Before he could speak, Taziar clamped a hand over Timmy's lips. He spun the boy, gesturing him to silence before removing the restraining hand. Catching Timmy's wrist, Taziar led the child to a position beside the window. Releasing his hold, the Climber picked up the gun.

"Please," the social worker said soothingly, voice faltering, tears glazing her eyes and her face drained of color. "Don't hurt the boy."

"Just stay quiet and still, and we won't hurt anyone." Larson switched to the barony tongue to address Taziar. "Keep the thing pointed at her and pretend you know what you're doing."

Taziar positioned himself between Timmy and the social worker, the gun leveled in both hands, finger well back from the trigger, his posture a poor imitation of Larson's earlier pose. He only succeeded in looking as if he wanted the Police Special as far away from himself as possible.

It'll have to do. Larson jammed the .45 back into his pocket, aware that, to a person on the wrong end of a gun, even a .22 seemed like a naval cannon, no matter how incompetent the wielder. He glanced at the policeman. *We have to work fast, before this guy wakes up.* Kneeling, he set to work stripping the man of shirt and undershirt.

Abruptly, the radio at the policeman's belt crackled. A voice emerged, uninterpretable beneath the static.

Startled, Larson jumped, naturally bringing the .45 up to cover his only threat.

The woman shuddered back into the chair, biting off a scream midway through, then clamping a hand over her mouth to stifle the sound. Timmy's head flicked repeatedly from her to Taziar to Larson.

The policeman on the floor groaned.

Larson swore. Seeing that Taziar still held the woman captive, he returned his own gun to his pants and set to work knotting the clothing together. The need for speed made him feel slow and clumsy. *Can't afford to hit this guy again. I don't want to kill him.* Finishing the tie, he bounded across the room to Timmy's side, hoping the other men in the precinct were too involved with the fires to hear or answer the broken scream.

"Go! Out!" Larson commanded Taziar in his language. Without waiting to see if the Climber obeyed, he turned to the social worker. "Give me your jacket."

"W-what?"

"Give me the damn jacket now! Move!" Larson made a threatening gesture with a muscled arm, not wanting to waste the time to draw his gun again. The need for action so soon after his gunshot wound was making him nauseated and dizzy.

The woman removed her pants suit jacket in nervous, jerky motions that, to Larson's heightened senses, seemed to progress in slow motion. She hurled the polyester jacket toward him.

The policeman stiffened, eyes fluttering open.

Larson snatched the garment from midair, the brisk gesture aching through his shoulder. Hastily attaching the jacket to the shirts, he grabbed Timmy and laced the string of clothing through the boy's belt. Taziar was nowhere to be seen.

"Hey!" The cop scrambled to an awkward crouch. Then, apparently realizing Larson had a gun and he did not, he fast-crawled behind a chair.

Seizing both ends of his makeshift rope, Larson eased Timmy to the windowsill. "Careful," he whispered through gritted teeth. "You'll be all right. Shadow'll be there to catch you." He forced his thoughts away from Taziar's slight stature. *A guy who climbs buildings with stolen objects and no support has to be strong, no matter how small.* Scrambling onto the ledge, he lowered the boy as far as possible before letting go. Whirling, Larson prepared to climb.

"Hey!" the policeman shouted again. "You! Freeze!" Footfalls thumped across the floor toward Larson. The social worker screamed, long, loud, and unstifled.

Larson skittered down the wall, the effort of supporting his weight tearing at the wound in his shoulder. Halfway down, his strength gave out. He plummeted, the penetrating, driving ache in his arm overwhelming his other senses. He did not feel Taziar's steadying hands, helping him through an instinctive roll. The pain of impact brought tears to his eyes. The police cap tumbled from his head, revealing the bloody headband.

Timmy made a high-pitched noise of distress.

Al Larson managed to stagger to his feet. As he rose, he found himself staring into Taziar Medakan's face. Timmy stood, watching in horror.

"Quick." The Shadow Climber said. He crammed his Dodger's cap on Larson's head. Too tight, it squeezed the wound, but the pain seemed minimal compared with the deeper ache of his shoulder.

Bulling through agony with will alone, Larson grabbed Timmy with his good arm and swung the boy to his uninjured shoulder. "Hang on. We're out of here." He ran. Scarcely able to see through the darkness, Larson kept to the grass, tracing brightly lit sidewalks. Though he could not see or hear Taziar, he trusted that his companion sprinted along beside him.

From his perch, Timmy prattled excitedly. "He is Robin Hood. Shadow really *is* Robin Hood. You should have seen him crawl all over the wall. Outta sight! Did you really point a gun at that lady? I can't believe the way you decked out that cop." He made several sound effects to mimic punches.

Larson let Timmy ramble on, afraid to let his last words to his brother become "shut up." *Silme and Bolverkr will return and soon. There's nothing left but to make a stand, someplace where no more innocents can get injured.* Larson gritted his teeth until his jaw hurt nearly as much as his arm. *We're going to need food. And ammunition.* He channeled his mind to practical issues, aware he could never hope to defeat two high-ranking Dragonrank sorcerers. *God, I hope Shadow's swiped some cash from somewhere. What a time for shopping.* If he had felt any less battered and harried, he might have found the observation funny. He clutched Taziar's cap to his head with his free hand. *Can't afford to lose the hat. Dirt won't bother anyone, and*

*half the young adult population in New York wears clothing
as tattered as mine. But blood's gonna draw attention.*

Larson shifted to a more sobering thought. *There's got
to be a way to keep Timmy safe.* He drew a blank, and his
attempts tore memory to the forefront. He could not help
but recall the last time he had dealt with a loved one Timmy's age, a half-breed, bumbling boy named Brendor who
had served as Silme's apprentice. He recalled leaving the
child with Silme's friends in a village, hoping to keep
Brendor secure until they defeated Bramin and returned
for the child.

The remembrances came, rapid-fire, between each of
Larson's running steps and panting breaths. Vivid as yesterday, he saw Brendor's savage rush, felt the boy crush him
to the ground with magically enhanced strength. He relived
the brilliant yellow spears of Silme's sorcery as they tore
through the last remnants of Brendor, a corpse killed and
animated by Bramin.

*Silme can track Timmy through his mind. As dangerous
as it seems, Timmy is safer with me.* Larson put the thought
of his mother heading toward the station from his mind.
*We'll just have to start the battle before Mom arrives. And
hope Silme and Bolverkr take the bait.*

Larson and Taziar ran on.

Cobwebs choked the abandoned warehouse on 6th
Street, dividing its single room into triangles with gossamer
walls. Al Larson crouched on a floor thick with dust and
the scattered, unidentifiable shards that had fallen from objects long ago moved. Timmy huddled in a corner, his
grime-smeared features angelic in sleep. Taziar sat beside
a fire extinguisher and behind the bags of rations they had
bought with what little of his money remained. He chewed
on a ham and cheese sandwich, pausing after every bite to
stare at the unfamiliar arrangement of meat and bread. He
offered the next taste to Larson.

Larson shook his head, frowning. He knew he should eat,
yet he dared not do so. Anxiety kept hunger at bay, and he
felt certain he could not keep food down for long. Images of
Silme paraded through his mind: the smile that seemed to
touch deep into his soul, her warm, silky skin pressed up
against him in desire, the soft look in her gray eyes when

he made a comment only she could understand. His mind seemed incapable of capturing her beauty; every glance he took showed facets he had forgotten, the perfect shape of her features, the cascade of golden hair, the firm, slender curves he could never tire of seeing. Thoughts of her brought a whirlwind of grief and hope. *We can get her back. We have to be able to free her from Chaos.* He could not abandon that hope, yet reality intruded. *I have to fight against her. I might have to kill her.* His hand fell on the .45. It felt heavy and dragging, out of place at his side. "I can't do it."

Taziar looked up. "Excuse me?"

"I can't hurt Silme. I just can't."

Taziar set his sandwich on the bag of canned goods and jerky sticks. "I know. That's why you need to focus your attention on Bolverkr. I'll handle Silme."

Doubt assailed Larson. "Handle her? What does that mean, handle her? Kill her?"

Taziar scooted around to face Larson, sitting cross-legged, the fire extinguisher against his knee. "If that's what it takes, yes." He brushed away the comma of hair that continually slipped down his forehead. Though routine, the gesture seemed contrived, not quite hiding his nervousness.

Larson knew just the idea of killing anyone sickened Taziar, that the little Climber tended to freeze in combat, even when his life or his friends' lives lay in the balance. Still, Larson's love for Silme drove him to discard this knowledge and assume the worst. "I know she may have to die. I've accepted that. But you won't kill her if you see another way?"

Taziar said nothing.

Larson's concern quadrupled in an instant. "Right?"

Taziar brushed crumbs from his lap.

"Answer me, damn it!"

Larson's shout awakened Timmy. The boy opened one eye, then rolled over and relaxed again.

"Allerum," Taziar said mildly. "It is fair to assume I have a plan. Silme and Bolverkr can read your mind. Therefore, if I told you anything, I'd be an idiot." He shrugged. "Despite Bolverkr's opinion, I'm not an idiot."

"But . . ." Larson started. He stopped, uncertain what to say. If he needed to steal an elephant from seven hundred armed guards on the topmost floor of the Empire State Building, he would consult Taziar. But for combat strategy, Taziar's eye for guesswork and detail had proven worse than blind in the past. Still, Taziar had made an effective point. The best plot in the world became far more dangerous than the lousiest once it fell into enemy hands. "At least tell me what you want with that?" He pointed to the fire extinguisher that Taziar had pilfered on the way out of the grocery store.

"Sure." Taziar patted the canister, his fingers thudding hollowly against it. "You told me it fights fires."

"Right," Larson agreed.

"And you told me Bolverkr has a spectacular fire spell that we should prepare against."

"Ri-ight." Larson blinked, the pieces falling together slowly. "You brought it to put out Bolverkr's fire spell?"

"Ri-ight," Taziar imitated Larson's thoughtful stretching of the syllable.

Larson closed his eyes, his fingers on the blood-smeared headband, shaking his head at the craziness of the idea. "Shadow, if Bolverkr hits us with that spell, we'll be cooked before you could even think to use the extinguisher."

"Maybe." Taziar shrugged. "Maybe not. No one's supposed to be able to dodge those magical lightning flashes either, but I've done it several times."

Larson pursed his lips in consideration. He recognized his challenging and irritation as a reaction to fear for Silme. Once identified, he could not disperse it, but he did find it easier to think around the concern. "Actually, that's not a bad idea. From what I remember from Silme and Astryd talking, Dragonrank magic doesn't work all that well against nonmagical objects and beings, like us. If there was a spell that could shatter a man's heart instantly or could heat the air around us all to a bazillion degrees or could create a giant blend-o-matic, I'm sure Bolverkr would have used it against us already. I've seen single spells destroy dragons and 'living corpses,' but the worst I've experienced is a spell that paralyzed me and the lightning that missed you."

Taziar retrieved his sandwich, not bothering to voice the obvious. They both remembered how Bramin's paralyzing spell had once left Larson helpless, that Bramin would have stabbed Larson to death if not for Taziar's unexpected interference. Both knew Taziar had dodged the lightning with a skill and speed Larson could never hope to match. Even then, the concussion had left the little Climber unconscious on Bolverkr's ramparts.

Larson's words died to hopeless silence.

"We can handle this," Taziar said with cheerful certainty. "Remember, as powerful as he seems, Bolverkr's Chaos isn't infinite. If it was, he could make up any spell he wanted, even that blend-o-whatever-you said. The bulk of Silme's power comes from him, so, in that respect, her presence weakens him. They can throw twice as many spells against us at once, but with Bolverkr's Chaos-energy curtailed by the sharing and by whatever he's lost permanently in your world, he's not likely to try some newly invented, complicated, mass-slaughtering spell."

Larson considered, but took little comfort from Taziar's explanation. *Right. So all we have to worry about is being burned, electrocuted, mentally tortured, chased by a dragon, or paralyzed, unable to move but fully aware of our defenselessness. Great. How comforting.*

Taziar took another bite of sandwich, ignoring Larson's turmoil. He chewed carefully, then swallowed before speaking. "I was thinking. Since I didn't save enough money to buy more bullets, would it help if you kept this?" He held out the policeman's gun, casually pointing the barrel toward Larson.

Having been taught since childhood to treat every gun as if it were loaded and lacking a safety, Larson cringed out of the line of fire. "Careful with that!"

Taziar lowered the weapon.

"You want me to hold both guns?" Larson knew it made more sense to spread their fire, yet he had no time for a crash course in marksmanship. He realized a quick and dirty "aim and shoot" technique would only take a few minutes to explain to Taziar; but, with himself, Silme, and Timmy in the room, wild shooting would prove far more dangerous than none at all. "All right." Larson took the second gun. "But what will you use for a weapon?"

"This." Taziar pulled out his utility knife. "And this." He patted the fire extinguisher. "I'm not much good with any weapon. If you're capable enough with yours, I shouldn't need one. I've seen and felt what guns can do."

"Not against Bolverkr." Another wave of frustration struck Larson. "Those magical shields of his deflect bullets, too. And I'm not shooting Silme unless I have to."

"Nor would I expect you to. I don't want to harm Silme, either." Taziar looked away, his food forgotten.

Only then it occurred to Larson how callous his attitude must seem. *Here I am going on about how I don't want to hurt Silme, even though she was indirectly the cause of Astryd's death. He understands how I feel about Silme. He's not going to do anything foolish. And he cares for her, too.* "Look, Shadow. I'm sorry. I'm just sick and tired, frustrated, annoyed . . ." He paused, hardly daring to admit it to himself. ". . . and scared. I'm also damned scared."

"Good," Taziar said.

"Yeah. What's so good about it?"

"It's just good to see something normal in all this chaos. Now get some sleep."

"Sleep?" The suggestion startled Larson. "How am I supposed to sleep?"

"I don't know, but you can't afford not to." Taziar glanced at Timmy. "We can't go to Bolverkr. We have to wait until he comes to us. If I were him, I'd be thrilled to know my opponents had decided to exhaust themselves by staying awake forever. So I figured we'd work shifts, one of us up during the day, the other at night. There'll be some overlap for exchanging ideas." He waved at the darkening confines of the warehouse. "I'm guessing I'm more used to a night schedule than you. Besides, you're more injured. So you sleep now."

"Here." Larson rummaged through the bags, emerging with a flashlight and a package of batteries. Placing the batteries into the stem, he switched on the light and handed it to Taziar. "Not the best lantern in the world, but it'll have to do."

Taziar accepted the flashlight, staring at it curiously.

Larson crawled over to Timmy. Catching a shoulder, he shook the boy.

"Hmmn?" Timmy rolled toward Larson.

"Timmy, sorry to wake you, but this is important."

"Uhn-huhn." Timmy sighed, opening one eye reluctantly.

Certain Timmy was awake enough to hear, Larson continued. "At any time, the witch and an evil sorcerer named

Bolverkr may appear here. No matter what happens, I want you to stay in this corner and away from the fight. Do you understand that?"

"Uhn-huh."

"Don't do anything else unless I tell you to. Or unless I'm killed. Then, you run away. Got that?"

"Uhn-huh."

Larson frowned, believing Timmy had received the message, but wishing he could make sure. "All right, go back to sleep."

"Okay," the boy murmured.

Larson moved away, hoping a sudden spell against him would not strike Timmy as well. He curled against the wall, barraged by worries and tension. His muscles cramped. He closed his eyes against a burning discomfort, certain he would never fall asleep. Yet fatigue overtook him in minutes.

Larson awakened to Taziar's warning shout. Instantly alert, he sprang to a crouch, and his eyes snapped open to blinding light. A grim sense of evil engulfed him, and he caught a dull, retinal impression of a brilliant flash against the painful glare. Taziar crashed against him, bowling him into a concrete corner that bruised his leg and sent pain shocking through his wounded shoulder. Something struck the stone where he had lain. Electricity raised the hair along the back of his neck, and a thunderstorm odor permeated the air.

A second later, Taziar's weight disappeared. Again, Larson leapt to a crouch, blinking wildly as the flare of magics faded to a darkness pierced only by the flashlight's beam on the floor. Taziar had scuttled along the wall, and was now several feet from Larson. The Shadow Climber clutched the fire extinguisher as if it were a baby. Bolverkr's dark form towered in the room's center. Silme stood some distance behind him, her arm flexed in menace, her fingers clenched around a glowing sphere of readied sorcery.

Larson seized the .45, firing a quick-draw hip shot. The bullet struck Bolverkr's shield, whining off into the darkness. Impact staggered the Dragonrank sorcerer back a step, and Larson stole the second it gained him to dart around for Bolverkr's unshielded back.

"Al!" Timmy shouted from the corner, now behind Larson. "Watch out! The witch!"

Larson ducked as he fired. His shot pinged off at an angle, defining the edge of Bolverkr's shield.

A deafening hiss reverberated through the room so abruptly that even Larson jumped, though this time he recognized the sound of the fire extinguisher.

Silme screamed. Her spell splintered to glimmering fragments around her. White powder coated her dress.

Apparently equally startled, Bolverkr ripped both his arms downward. Magic pulsed through the room, chokingly thick with Chaos smoke, and he disappeared.

"Bolverkr!" Silme shouted, suddenly without an ally. Gathering her composure, she began another spell.

Larson spun crazily, trying to relocate Bolverkr. *Only two bullets left in this gun. Got to make them count.* He felt for the .38 and found it tucked in his belt, its presence reassuring.

Awkwardly, Taziar backed away from Silme, still gripping the fire extinguisher.

Light tented between Silme's fingertips, chaotic as a spider's web, its glow intensifying with each new strand. Suddenly, she tensed.

Again, the fire extinguisher boomed, blasting some of its contents over Silme.

For the second time, Silme's unfinished spell fizzled to harmless sparks. "You little bastard!" she shrieked. "You *insect!*" She began to charge Taziar, then retreated, hurriedly forming another spell. Chaos in the form of tarry smoke undulated from her, gorging the room with a foul-smelling, translucent mist.

Bolverkr! Where the fuck is Bolverkr? Larson wished his eyes could adjust fully to the wavering darkness, afraid to concentrate on Silme for fear of missing Bolverkr. *Shadow knows what he's doing.* Taziar's plan seemed clear now. *He's trying to force her to keep casting, to drain enough Chaos for her identity to come through.* Larson tried not to contemplate the situation too hard. *Guess this is where we find out whether Chaos and life energy are the same thing here.*

"Allerum!" Taziar screamed. "Behind you!"

Even as the warning came, Larson heard rushing footfalls at his back. *Bolverkr!* He whirled, firing as he moved.

But the person who charged was not a sorcerer hellbent on vengeance, just a boy under his influence. The bullet tore through Timmy's abdomen. He collapsed, screaming in agony and terror.

Timmy. A thousand emotions paralyzed Larson. The .45 fell from his fingers, the sound of its landing lost beneath another blast from the extinguisher. Larson could not know that Bolverkr had drawn illusions in his brother's mind, warping Larson's form to look like Bolverkr's own. Nor could he know that Bolverkr had imitated Al Larson's voice, desperately commanding the boy to battle. Larson knew only that he had sent his eight-year-old brother into an unbearable anguish that could only end in death.

"Timmy." Larson's voice rose to a hysterical shriek. "Timmy! Timmy!"

Behind Larson, light flared and snapped, slashing ricocheting bands through the confines of the warehouse.

Larson could not gather enough interest to turn, but his instincts betrayed him. He spun, apathy transforming the movement to an awkward stumbling. Silme's magic silhouetted Taziar in blue, revealing an expression of stark realization through air smoky as a barroom's.

Suddenly, the Shadow Climber collapsed. The fire extinguisher crashed down on his abdomen, driving breath between clenched teeth. The magics faded to a sultry afterimage. He lay still, eyes open and staring, blood trickling from the corner of his mouth.

Timmy's screams fell silent.

Larson's muscles all seemed to give out at once. He dropped to his knees, no longer caring whether he lived or died. Tears streamed from his eyes, and he crawled toward the still form of his brother, dragging himself with an effort that seemed heroic. He reached for a pulse. His hand hovered over the boy's neck, the ragged, scarlet hole in Timmy's shirt mesmerizing him, a solid fact in his consciousness that he tried to drive away but could not. He willed his hand forward. It disobeyed him, hanging in midair like a thing disconnected. Until Larson touched Timmy, he could presume the boy lived.

Even as Larson waited, poised between fantasy and

knowledge, a grimmer reality intruded. *Silme's still alive. And she's planning to destroy my world.* His hand retreated from Timmy, closing over the Police Special instead. *My best friend is dead. My brother is dead. And I'm dead, too. But I'm going to take my enemies with me.* Slowly, he twisted, raising the gun.

Haze swirled through the warehouse, turning Silme into distant shadow. She stood over Taziar, her expression as blank as the Climber's. She did not seem to notice the threat behind her.

Larson drew a perfect bead on Silme's spine at the level of her chest. His hand tensed. The gun trembled in his grip. Despite all that had happened, he could still feel her warmth against him, still remember the concerns of the world that she repeatedly, unselfishly took upon herself. *She's not Silme anymore. She's the Chaos-warped stranger who killed Taziar.* Rage rose in Larson like fire, and he gathered the courage to shoot.

Suddenly, shadows leapt, broken like glass, as light erupted in the middle of the room. Bolverkr appeared between Larson and Silme, black smoke trailing from his figure.

Aim destroyed, Larson pulled his shot. He whipped the gun toward Bolverkr.

The Dragonrank mage laughed. Sorcery glazed eddying mist, and the air seemed as tense and impending as a predator coiled to spring. A ball of white-hot magics flared into his hands with the suddenness of a gas jet.

Larson fired. The shot struck Bolverkr's shield at the level of his heart, then bounced into the shadows. Chaos-smoke leeched from Bolverkr's spell. He tensed to throw, then went suddenly rigid. Light danced and died in his grip. He whirled toward Silme, the threat behind him abruptly forgotten. "Bitch! What are you doing? What the hell are you doing?" He used a commanding tone, yet a hint of frenzy betrayed him.

His back. No shield. Even as Larson reaimed, Bolverkr lurched out of the firing line. Smoke boiled from him.

"The power is mine," Silme chanted, invisible in the thick wash of dispersing Chaos. "You gave it to me. It's mine!" Her voice was almost unrecognizable. *"And I want it all!"*

Dense as grease, the Chaos-smoke roiled through the room. Larson's lungs ached, and his eyes burned. The air became rancid, suffocating him toward the brink of unconsciousness. He sank to the floor. The world blurred to two dark figures who pirouetted like dancers or like demons capering through the ruins of hell.

"Silme, I said I'd share. There's enough for us both." Bolverkr pitched backward with an abruptness that all but sprawled him over Larson.

Silme's answer was a shriek that combined pain and fury. "It's mine! All mine! Give it to me!"

Larson scrambled for consciousness, desperate to gather the shards of his composure. Dizziness battered him, upending him through a smoky swirl of vertigo. *They're fighting through the link. They're battling over the same ugly, evil Chaos that turned Bolverkr into a monster and Silme into an enemy.* With effort, Larson raked his limbs toward him, trying to regain enough balance to rise, forcing his focus to his own snarl of pain and grief. The handle of the pistol gouged his palm. He forced memory for a solid grounding. *Timmy's dying.* The thought flooded Larson with grief, numbing him. The gun slipped from quivering fingers.

Silme and Bolverkr tore back and forth, limbs jerking as if in a seizure. Though no physical blows fell, sweat sheened their hands and faces, haloing features strained with mental effort. The smoke thickened.

Timmy . . . is . . . dying. Larson gritted his teeth, demanding a rage that would not come. His vision all but disappeared beneath the hovering blanket of Chaos darkness. *His killer is here. I can avenge him.* A dribble of anger suffused Larson, crushed by a voice from within. *You, Al Larson, you are Timmy's slayer.* And the swirling Chaos dragged satisfaction into the thought. *Slaughter. Destruction. Chaos ruin.*

Larson fought the battering tide of Chaos' smoke. Again, he raised the gun. But the darkness slammed his sight to nothing. Even movement was lost, and only the muffled exchange of the Dragonrank mages' curses told Larson the battle continued.

But, where his own efforts to spark fury had failed, the strain of fighting Chaos succeeded. Larson surged to his feet, the gun clamped in both fists, desperately scanning the fog for his target. *Bolverkr. You're going to die, you son of a bitch.* Larson stumbled toward the noises of the war.

Even as Larson moved, Bolverkr jerked backward with the sudden triumph of a tug of war.

Silme gasped in frustration.

Larson sprang for the sorcerer. The gun's barrel drove against the back of Bolverkr's skull. And Larson pulled the trigger in a red fog of anger. "Die, you bastard!"

An explosion rang through the room. Bolverkr toppled, Larson atop him, his body twisted, but the gun still clamped to the Dragonrank mage's head.

Silme screamed. Slammed suddenly with all the remaining Chaos, she crumpled.

"Let's see you heal this." Larson fired at Bolverkr again, point-blank. Blood splattered Larson's face. The Chaos seethed around him like a living thing. Perceptions struck him, distant and not his own. He knew a familiar war in Vietnam, escalating, fed by Chaos from another era. He saw trains and subway cars scrawled black with graffiti, children with knives battling in alleyways and concrete parks, intolerance of skin color, ideas, and religion sparking to a violence justified by warped, self-righteous moralities, a New York Larson no longer knew as home. The gun spoke repeatedly, until it dry fired, its wielder's finger still spasming on the trigger.

Now, the anger Larson had needed for action became a curse. He slammed the gun down on the remains of Bolverkr's head. Bone gashed his palm, and impact resonated through his fingers. Torn from his hands by force, the gun bounced into the darkness.

Chaos. Larson staggered to his feet, nudging through anger for a semblance of sanity and self. *Silme has it all. It'll warp her like Bolverkr. There's no choice any longer. I have to kill her.* Rationality seeped through, bringing an important memory. *The .45. There's still one bullet left.*

Dropping back to his hands and knees, Larson fished through the darkness, scarcely noticing that the blackness had died back to an opaque haze and he could breathe more freely. A glint of metal met his gaze, and he crept toward it. His hand closed over the .45.

Larson could again discern shapes through the haze of

Chaos. All four bodies lay still, Timmy at one end of the room, Taziar at the other, Silme and Bolverkr between them. Larson crept to Silme's side. The Chaos smoke grew progressively lighter, and it seemed to take Larson's fury with it. The emotion unraveled, leaving nothing in its place.

Now beside Silme, Larson crouched at her head. Tentatively, he extended a finger, tracing a winding highlight through the gold of her hair. Even sweat-slicked and clammy, she seemed the epitome of beauty, her warmth so real and alive. "I love you, Silme," he said, the words deafening in the silence. "I love you so much. And I'm sorry." He pressed the gun against her temple, wishing he had just one more bullet. One more bullet. For himself.

A perception touched Larson's consciousness, an alien idea that took the form of concept rather than words. *Don't do it, Allerum. It's not necessary.* The presence did not actually call him by a name. Rather, it seemed to appeal to the portion of his being that had been an elf in Midgard.

Startled, Larson glanced around. The darkness had faded to a maddeningly shifting gray. All the bodies lay where he had left them, but a new figure stood near the door. He towered over Larson, easily eight feet tall. White hair hung around comely features, and the gray eyes held the color and timelessness of mountains. Divinity fairly radiated from the being, a depth of sensation Larson had not known, even in the presence of Norway's gods.

Larson blinked. *I've finally gone irreversibly over the edge.* He drew some comfort from the thought. *At least the pain will be gone. Thank God for small favors.*

You're welcome, the other sent, again in concepts. Though voiceless, Larson discovered something familiar in the tone.

"Vidarr?" Larson shook his head, knowing he must be mistaken. If this was Vidarr, he had aged a thousand years. *Aged a thousand years? Christ, could this be a future Vidarr?*

Vidarr confirmed the identification.

"But you're . . ." Larson started. "How could . . ." The theological implications because too staggering, and philosophy seemed far too secondary to discuss when Silme's life hung in the balance. "What did you mean when you implied Silme's death wasn't necessary?"

Vidarr responded in the same complex, nonverbal manner. *Chaos doesn't bind or assimilate in your world. It only goads.* He waved a hand through the air, as if gathering something, and the room brightened again. *When Silme cast the spell that paralyzed Taziar, she lost enough of her bound Chaos to release her from its influence. She went after Bolverkr's power not because she wanted it, but to save you from his spells.*

"Oh, no." Larson dropped the gun and hugged Silme to him, stroking the damp locks. "Is she going to be okay?"

She was knocked unconscious by the sheer volume of Chaos she pulled to herself. She's starting to come around now.

Larson drew Silme closer. "What about Timmy? Is he. . . ?" He let the question hang.

He's alive. The concept of a tenuous link to life came clearly with the words. *For now. So is Taziar. But say good-bye. Neither will survive more than a few minutes longer.*

Silme trembled in Larson's arms, her lids flickering.

"Can't you do something for them? You must be able to do something?"

I could, Vidarr admitted. *But I won't. If I've learned nothing else over the last ten centuries, it's not to interfere. You mortals make your own histories and cause your own ends.*

"Cut it out!" Frustration drove Larson to shout. "Don't give me that Silent God and noninterference bullshit! I know you too well."

You don't know me at all. Not anymore.

"Damn it!" Larson could almost feel the seconds ticking away, stealing his brother's final breath. "I don't have time for this. You want me to beg. Fine, I'll beg. Please, Vidarr, save my brother and my friend. We'll discuss the implications later. You can always change your mind and kill them again. I'll do anything! Anything, Vidarr."

I'm sorry. There was no trace of compromise.

You bastard! Hot tears entered Larson's eyes, and it was all he could do to keep from rushing Vidarr. "You have to do something!"

*On the contrary. I don't have to do anything at all. Ex-

cept return this Chaos. Vidarr arched his arm once more. *And take Bolverkr's body and Silme back where they belong.*

"Take Silme? You're going to take Silme, too?" Terror battered at Larson's remaining reason. "You're going to leave me with nothing?" Another thought surfaced, without Vidarr's input. "Or will I simply die in Vietnam, never rescued by Freyr?"

All that has gone before has gone before. Your history from this moment is open. You have to chart your own waters.

This time, the concepts seemed more vague. "Chart my own waters? What the hell is that supposed to mean? You're starting to sound like Gaelinar." Larson imitated his swordmaster; hysteria allowed him to joke about the Kensei for the first time since his death. "Ah so, hero. It's not the weapon that cuts, it's the intention of the wielder." He returned to his normal voice. "I'm having enough trouble keeping my sanity. Damn it, use a language I can understand!"

Vidarr remained patient. *Just as alternate events have occurred since you returned to the graveyard, so will they continue. No mortal should know when he's going to die. From now on, whatever happens happens, unrelated to the future you remember.*

Silme sat up, clutching at Larson's hand.

Larson glanced at her, and her smile sparked hope. "You're saying I can make my own choices."

Correct.

"Then I choose to return to Midgard with Silme."

You can't.

"Why not?"

I destroyed your elf body.

"What!" Larson's voice roared through the room. He leapt to his feet. "You promised to protect it! You lied! You fucking traitor! How could you swear to protect it then destroy it? I thought gods didn't lie."

I didn't lie. I promised only to take care of the body as I saw fit. Vidarr ignored the advancing human. *I saw fit to destroy it.*

"You arrogant son-of-a. . . ."

God, Vidarr finished, this time in straight words. *I'm a god. And the son of a god. Don't ever forget that.* He switched back to instant conceptualizations. *Now let me explain.*

Silme drifted toward Taziar's still form, as if in a trance.

Vidarr continued, *When Bolverkr left our world, it was instantly hurled too far in the direction of Law. Only one of two things could happen: either the world could shatter into nothingness, or we had to kill several powerful, Lawful creatures quickly. Our world had only one group of beings powerful enough to balance Bolverkr's disappearance.*

"Gods," Larson said, the word as much an expletive as an answer.

Ragnarok. The fated war that destroyed the gods. All but one god. Me. One God. Your God, Allerum.

"No." Larson rallied for a last, desperate protest. "No. My God is merciful. You're mean, spiteful, and deceitful. Like Bolverkr, you would take everything I love from me. But, in one way, you're worse. Bolverkr had the decency to claim my life as well, but you're stupid enough to believe I would draw solace from living on, haunted by my brother's slaying, and the loss of my best friend, my baby, and my wife."

Check the Bible, Allerum. Your God is no stranger to meanness or spite.

Larson fell into a deep, mournful silence. There was nothing left to live for, and nothing left to say.

Silme cleared her throat. "My Lord, may I speak?"

Of course.

Silme used the edge of her skirt to wipe the blood from Taziar's cheek. The expression on her face mixed grief and guilt. "There's no Balance in this world of Allerum's. Is that correct?"

Correct.

"Well, since this is supposedly a future time from mine, I have to assume my absence hasn't caused Midgard to collapse."

Actually, even after Ragnarok, the world remains dangerously tipped toward Law. It is only because I return this mass of Chaos to the past that the world still exists.

Silme rolled the fire extinguisher from Taziar, her voice level. "Since you've gathered the dispersed Chaos, can I assume the Chaos you take back doesn't necessarily need to be bound to any individual?''

Correct. You're asking if I can take the Chaos you wield and leave you behind.

Silme nodded.

Larson held his breath. His heart pounded, but he dared not raise too much hope for fear it would come crashing down around him again.

That would require you to cast out every bit of Chaos you hold. You would no longer be a sorceress, Silme. You would be trapped in a world whose language you don't speak and whose technology you don't understand. Is that what you want?

"No," Silme admitted.

Larson lowered his head.

"I want Allerum. I love him. He's made sacrifices for me, and now it's time for me to make a few for him. I have no reason to return to Midgard. My family's dead. My loved ones are here. And I'm not stupid. If I return to Midgard with as much Chaos as I carry now, I'll become as corrupted and terrible as my brother ever was. But if you take my Chaos unbound, you can distribute it more evenly. No individual needs to be wholly evil."

A silence followed Silme's speech. To Larson, it seemed to last an eternity.

At last, Vidarr replied. *Very well. You can stay, on the condition that you drain yourself of all Chaos before leaving this room. Once I gather that Chaos, you will never see or hear from me again. You must accept the consequences of your decision and your actions, and they are yours to suffer.*

"I do," Silme said, certainly unaware of the irony in her choice of phrase. She glanced from Taziar to Timmy, a worried frown creasing her features. "And I think I know exactly what to do with all this magic."

Larson recalled how Bolverkr had used his sorcery to heal his own fatal wound. For the first time in as long as he could remember, Al Larson smiled.

Epilogue

Al Larson perched on the edge of his hotel bed, staring at the clock's hash marks of hands and numbers glowing through the darkness. *One in the afternoon.* Larson estimated he had been awake for thirty hours.

After Silme had healed Timmy and Taziar, they had all headed back to the police station. Larson had sent Silme and Timmy with his mother and sister, to an uncle's house in New Jersey. Then, the most intense questioning in Larson's life had begun.

Policemen from two precincts had fired challenges at Al Larson until exhaustion rode them all. Seven separate interpreters had failed to find a means to communicate with Taziar. The police had forced Larson to relay multiple, complex commands to the Climber before reluctantly accepting that Taziar's language was, in fact, a language, and allowing Larson to do the translating.

Larson smiled weakly at the remembrance, not quite distant enough to find it humorous yet. He glanced over to the other bed. Taziar slept, curled beneath the bedspread, looking as fragile and insubstantial as a battered child. It had seemed easier for Larson to answer those questions the cops had aimed at the Shadow Climber. So, instead of translating, Larson had used the exchanges in barony tongue to explain the progress of the questioning, then he'd given the police the best and most consistent responses he could muster. Once, to lighten the mood, he had told Taziar a joke. That technique backfired when Taziar could not hold back a chuckle at what should have been a gruelingly serious query.

By the end of the precinct night shift, everyone appeared to have tired of the whole affair, eager to finish as soon as possible. The witnesses to the subway crime corroborated Larson's story, hailing him as a hero. From then on, the

cops' manner softened. They became more willing to give
Larson the benefit of the doubt on other matters as well.
The murder and resisting arrest charges were dismissed. A
kidnapping case dissolved when Mrs. Larson failed to press
charges against her son or Taziar. And, with their own officers babbling about sorcerers and evil possessions, the
precinct glossed over Larson's earlier escape.

Now, immersed in memory, Larson drew a knee to his
chest. With the shades drawn and the lights turned off, the
hotel furnishings looked like ghostly black silhouettes in
the darkness. He had brought Taziar here, too tired to
make the longer drive to New Jersey until after a rest. Still,
something nagged at the edges of Larson's consciousness.
Some small thing he had placed on hold kept sleep at bay.

Larson sighed, searching his memory. Some of the other
charges had proven more difficult to dodge. His previously
clean police record, a semester of college, and a history of
participation in high school athletics had helped emphasize
his upstanding image. To his surprise, the two officers he
had attacked in Sears and Roebuck dropped the assault
charges. McCloskey apparently believed Larson's story:
that he tripped over the elevator door slot and accidentally
knocked the shambling redhead unconscious. Though more
skeptical, Johnston grunted when Larson said he had then
panicked and hit his other escort. Still, the quieter policeman did not push the issue either.

Larson stretched his legs, jabbing his hands into his jeans'
pockets. A crumpled envelope met his touch, and he pulled
it free. His mother had handed it to him just before the
questioning, without explanation, and he had promptly forgotten it in the confusion. He held the envelope in both
hands, certain it was the object that bothered him and believing, without the need to look, that it held bad news. He
folded it, delaying, letting his thoughts wander back to the
ordeal in the police station.

Avoiding the miscellaneous weapons charges had required more finesse. Larson had claimed Bolverkr as a
stranger who had been chasing him for some time, demanding money and threatening his life; in the process,
Larson implied that Carl Larson might have gotten himself
indebted to a mob-tied loan shark. And, though he knew
he should try to avoid bitterness, Larson could not help

feeling a modicum of satisfaction that his story might cast suspicion on the drunken driver who had killed his father. A roomful of officers confirmed Larson's understatement that Bolverkr was dangerous and eager to murder, and that affirmation led naturally to the gunfight in the 6th Street warehouse.

Perhaps because of the confusion and swirling fog of Chaos, most of the officers who had survived Bolverkr's and Silme's attack remembered the Dragonrank sorcerer's accomplice as a man. In the end, Larson claimed that Bolverkr had lured him, Timmy, and Taziar to the warehouse where the sorcerer attacked and wounded them. Larson confessed to having shot Bolverkr, aware the police would uncover bullets as well as traces of Taziar's, Timmy's, and Bolverkr's blood, though they could never find the body.

Larson sighed more deeply, clenching the letter in both hands, listening to the rustle of stiff paper bending in his grip. It was not over yet. He knew the police would be sorting questions and answers for a long time, that he would still go to trial, perhaps even serve some time in jail. Still, when it was all over, he had reached the hotel room in reasonably good spirits, despite exhaustion. He had Silme, Taziar, and his family, far more than he had a right to expect. *I'm surrounded by people I love and who love me. For the first time in more than a year, my life is on the right track. Aside from Astryd and my father, I have everything. What more could I ask for?*

Buoyed by the thought, Larson rose and crept to the window. Pulling one curtain a few inches aside, he let the exposed beam of sunlight fall across the paper in his hands. Without glancing at the return address, he drew the letter free. He read only one word, the first: "Greetings. . . ."

Larson stood frozen for a full minute. His gaze locked on the word, and he was unable to continue.

Gradually, helplessness suffused Larson. *Greetings.* He wadded the letter in his fist, his mood shattered. *Greetings. And welcome to your new future, Al Larson.* He hurled the letter across the room, watched it bounce from door to lamp to television before landing at the foot of Taziar's bed. *Greetings. Welcome back to Vietnam.* He held his breath for a moment, as if the mere act of tossing the letter away might make it disappear, along with everything for which it stood. *Back to shallow graves and body counts. Back to maggots and leeches, the constant odor of excrement and death. Back to sleepless nights and desperate days, warm blood, the screams of the injured and fear hovering always like a too familiar friend.*

A million possibilities came to Larson's mind at once, each crazier than the one before. He sorted and discarded every one. *This is no dream. If I ignore it, the government won't just forget about it. And I'm not running.* Grief turned to frustration then flared to rage. *Finally, things were going right.* He slammed his hand against the window hard enough to rattle the pane. *And now, NOW, I'm going to die.* "Damn it." His fist crashed against the glass again. "Damn it, damn it, *damn it*!" He shouted, emphasizing each word with another blow to the window. With the last strike, the glass exploded, raining shards to the street below with a musical sprinkle of sound.

"Allerum, calm down." Taziar's voice wafted from behind Larson. "What's wrong with you?"

Larson whirled.

The little Climber watched him through widened, concerned eyes, keeping the bed safely between them.

Anger waned beneath an onrush of self-pity. Larson stared at his hand, rivulets of his own blood twining between his fingers. "I've been drafted." The words sounded strange, impossible. "I've been fucking drafted."

Taziar said nothing, not understanding the English word.

Larson did not bother to explain. "Last time, I only enlisted this week. I knew they'd have to draft me this time. I figured I had a year, at least. I can't believe this is happening. Just when I thought things were working out."

Apparently, Taziar put the pieces together. "Don't panic, Allerum. You told me Vidarr said this would be a different future. Maybe this time things will go better."

"Better?" Larson shouted. "Better! The only way it could be better is if I'd die in my first firefight instead of a month shy of leaving hell. We're talking about 'Nam, Shadow. Viet-fucking-nam. The place that drove me mad, stole every shred of compassion I ever had, then took my life as an afterthought!"

Taziar crawled across the bed to Larson's side. "Calm down. We'll work this out."

"No." Larson sat on the edge of the bed, feeling weak and rubbery in the wake of his fury. His head sank to his chest. Blood seeped into the coverlet, unnoticed. "The first time, I had all my wits about me and I still died. I've been getting flashes of war memory in your world. What's going to happen when I'm back, stressed by similar circumstances to the ones that caused the insanity?" Larson did not wait for Taziar to respond to a mostly rhetorical question. "I'll get confused, maybe panic. I'll get not just myself but every member of my platoon killed. And, if I survive, and any of them do, too, they'd be stupid not to shoot me dead."

Taziar placed a hand on Larson's shoulder. "You're saying you're a danger to the other soldiers."

"Yeah. That's what I'm saying."

"Maybe if you explained that? Maybe they wouldn't want you?"

"How could I possibly explain?"

"The way you just did to me," Taziar suggested with simple logic.

Larson placed his chin into cupped palms. "It won't work. They'll have no record of me enlisting or going to Vietnam. They'll think I'm just scared, just like everyone else." He looked up. "Shadow, I believe in fighting for my country. I really do. But, damn it, I've already served my time, and no one should have to go through hell twice. I may inhabit the same body, but I'm not the same person I was. I can't be."

Taziar rubbed Larson's shoulder reassuringly. "What if I went with you?"

"What?" Larson raised his head, twisting to confront Taziar directly.

Taziar withdrew, sitting cross-legged on the coverlet. "What if I went with you? I can keep you on task. I think we work pretty well together. We've handled Bramin and Fenrir and Bolverkr. . . ."

"Whoa, Taz! I'm not talking about a romp in the park or protecting loved ones from crazed enemies. I'm talking about running around in a steamy, smelly jungle, killing guys you don't know, kids in their early teens. Meanwhile, they're sneaking around slaughtering you and your buddies."

Taziar hesitated, an unnameable emotion sparking in his usually friendly eyes, now reddened and swollen from a previous session of crying. "You do what you have to do."

There was a determined tinge to Taziar's voice that shocked Larson past anger and exhaustion to rationality. "First of all, the army would never let you in. Even if we could forge the paperwork to make you a citizen, you couldn't pass the height and weight requirements. Second, even if we joined together, they'd separate us right after Basic. And, third, it's not like you to give up on a problem this way." Larson remembered how he had felt when he believed he had to kill Silme, how he had wished for the means to take his own life as well. "You once told me how you became reckless right after your father was hanged as a way to avoid confronting problems, and that after his murderer's death you learned to love action for its own sake. Well, if you're thinking of running off and getting killed so you don't have to mourn Astryd, you'd better think again. You're going to stay here, live, and suffer grief like the rest of us!"

Taziar recoiled, startled. Slowly, a lopsided grin wriggled across his features. "Well, I see your point. Wouldn't want death to go cheating me out of a good cry." The smile became more natural. "But I'm worried about you. There's got to be a way to get you out of this war."

Larson shrugged, becoming calmer and more fatalistic himself. "Maybe this is the best thing. I mean, the future I remember didn't actually happen. It's my duty as much as anyone else's to fight this war." He spoke easily, hiding a stifling fear and hatred from Taziar.

"What about putting your buddies in danger?" Taziar reminded.

"Yeah. There's still that."

Silence followed. Blood soaked into the flowered pattern of the coverlet.

"What are you going to do?" Taziar asked at length.

"I think," Larson said carefully, "I'm going to take your advice. For once, I'm going to tell the truth. And see where it gets me."

Two months later, Larson sat on a rigid, wooden bench, dressing amid a swarm of inductees. A familiar day of examination, paperwork, and questioning had passed in a dark blur of depression. The room hummed with conversations, none of which Larson heard. And, even the sound of his own name did not disrupt the mechanical donning of his jeans.

"Larson! Al!" A voice boomed again, louder, now directly behind him.

Startled, Larson jumped, diving to safety behind the bench. He peered over the edge, his heart pounding, strangers' laughter echoing around him.

A tall, muscular man stared at him impassively, hands clenched to hips. Young men in various stages of dress chuckled merrily until a gesture from the newcomer silenced them.

Larson flushed and rose. "You scared me, sir," he said by way of apology, clutching a hand to his chest.

Some of the inductees snickered, but the man ignored them as well as Larson's comment. "You're Larson, I presume."

Larson nodded.

"Come with me." Without further explanation, he exited the dressing room.

Hurriedly, Larson buttoned and zippered his fly, grabbing his shoes without bothering to put them on. He trotted after the burly man who was now most of the way down a long hall. Even as Larson watched, the other man turned a corner.

Larson had to trot to keep up with the man's huge strides. He caught up halfway down the next hallway. *What's going on? Why was I singled out?* He glanced over his shoulder to affirm that no one had followed. By the time he looked back, the larger man had whipped around another bend in the corridor.

Larson raced around the corner so quickly, he nearly banged into the stranger's back. "Where are we going?" he asked.

"Here." The man stopped, pointing at a plain, wooden door.

Larson halted beside him.

"Well, go ahead, Larson. Go on in."

Larson caught the knob, uncertain what to expect. His mind conjured a thousand impossible explanations, from a horror film version of hell to a Twilight Zonish image of other worlds. *This is insane. Vidarr said he wouldn't inter-*

fere, and I believe that. They singled me out for a logical, routine reason. Larson twisted and pushed.

The door swung open to reveal a squat office painted olive drab. A paunchy, balding man sat behind a government-issue desk. Wire-rimmed glasses perched on an amicable face. A handful of manila folders and a pen covered the desk's surface. One file lay open. *Mine.* Larson guessed. A lone, wooden chair faced the desk.

The door closed behind Larson. The man behind the desk picked up the pen and twirled it between his fingers. "Al Larson?"

"Yes, sir." Larson listened to his escort's footsteps retreating down the corridor.

"I'm Dr. Millson. I'm a psychiatrist." He paused, studying Larson for a reaction.

Larson narrowed his eyes in confusion. He set his shoes on the floor by his chair.

"Do you know why you're here?"

"Yes, sir," Larson said. "I'm being inducted into the United States Army."

"How does that make you feel?"

Larson shrugged, too uncomfortable and puzzled to give an emotional response. "I had already enlisted before my draft letter came," he said vaguely, not wholly certain whether he spoke the truth.

Dr. Millson sat back, still playing with the pen, seeming a bit disconcerted himself. "When I asked about knowing why you're here, I meant 'do you know why you're here *in my office* at this time?' "

"No, sir." Larson sank deeper into confusion. *I haven't done anything weird that I know about.*

"Do you remember taking a written test for us?"

Larson nodded. "Sure."

Millson leaned forward, pencil still weaving between his fingers. "Al, what was your state of mind at that time?"

Larson shrugged, trying to remember if he had written anything bizarre. "Regular, I guess, sir. Why?"

In characteristic fashion, the psychiatrist threw the question back. "Why do you think, Al?"

"I honestly don't know." Larson guessed some of his responses seemed unusual for a man of his age, either due to his experiences or his grief for Astryd, the baby, and his father. "I didn't get called before a psychiatrist the last time I was inducted." He looked up, soberly awaiting Millson's response to his reference, remembering his promise to tell the truth.

Millson's gaze fell to the file. His eyes rolled back up to meet Larson's. "You've been inducted before?"

Larson kept his tone level, allowing no emotion to leach through. "Of course. I spent almost a year in Vietnam."

The pen stopped moving, then dropped to the paper. Millson scribbled something. "When was this?"

"November 16, 1968 through September 8, 1969."

Millson glanced up, frown scoring his features. "Are you sure of those dates, Al?"

"Yes, sir. Particularly the second one. That was the day I died."

Millson put the pen aside and leaned forward, his chin on his hands, his full concentration focused on Larson. "Do you know today's date?"

Larson nodded, still keeping his expression rigid and unreadable. "Yes, sir, I do. August 3, 1968."

"Doesn't something strike you as odd in the comparison of those dates?"

"Yes, sir. It's because I wound up in a sort of time loop."

"A time loop, Al?"

"Yes, sir."

"Tell me more." Millson looked openly skeptical.

Larson ignored Millson's manner. He explained with the composed matter-of-factness that could only accompany truth. "The Norse god, Freyr, rescued me from death and put me into another body. An elf's body." He added, "Mine was pretty torn up, I guess."

Millson retrieved his pen. "And why do you think this god . . ." He paused, squinting over the rim of his glasses. ". . . Fred, was it?"

"Freyr." Larson restored the name, adding its Old Norse inflection.

"Why did Freyr do this favor for you?"

Larson met Millson's gaze without flinching. "It was hardly a favor. Freyr needed a man from our century because we don't have mind barriers and the people in his time do. He needed someone to wield a sword that could only communicate with an unshielded mind."

"I see." A light seemed to dawn behind Millson's dark eyes. He wound the pen between his fingers again. "Al, has anything like this ever happened to you before?"

"Of course not."

"Do you ever hear voices in your head?"

"Well, yes, sir," Larson admitted. "But only when there's a sorcerer or god who wants to talk to me."

"And what do these sorcerers and gods say to you?"

Larson shrugged. "It depends on the sorcerer or god. Bramin and the Fenris Wolf mostly just threatened. Sometimes, they forced me to remember things from the war."

"The Vietnam War."

"Right."

"What about Freyr?"

Larson continued, still holding his voice to a monotone. "Freyr stayed sort of aloof. Vidarr. . . ." He clarified, "That was the sword. See, he was a god, too." He considered. "Still is. Anyway, Vidarr used to argue with me a lot, though he always meant well. He thought I was too sarcastic."

The speed of the pen increased, lashing between the stubby fingers like the tail of a riled cat. Millson sighed into a long silence. "Al, tell me. Who's the president of the United States?"

"Lyndon Baines Johnson. At least until September."

"And before him?"

"Kennedy."

"And before him?"

"Eisenhower. Dwight."

Millson frowned, apparently not receiving the responses he expected. "Classic," he muttered.

Larson said nothing, not daring to believe other men might have told Dr. Millson stories about dying, Old Norway, and gods. A strange thought struck him. *Perhaps my return has changed history as well as the future. Maybe I got those presidents wrong.* Suddenly, he needed to know. "Did I make a mistake?"

"Huh?"

"The presidents. Did I miss one?"

"Oh." Millson seemed startled by the question. "No. No. Your *memory* works just fine. No evidence of an organic brain lesion."

Larson blinked, uncertain what to make of the statement. By declaring one aspect of Larson's mental functioning normal, he seemed to imply others were faulty. *Not surprising after the story I just told.* "Is that good?"

"Well, yes. Of course." Millson set aside the pen. "Al, have you ever been hospitalized for mental illness?"

"No." The psychiatrist's intention came through clearly. "Are you suggesting I should be?"

Millson dodged the question. He gathered the papers on his desk, shoving them into the manila envelope. "You stay here. I'll be back shortly." He scurried out of the office with little decorum, as if he needed to put distance between himself and Larson.

Al Larson folded his hands in his lap. And waited.

Silme met Al Larson at the outer door, looking stunningly beautiful in curve-hugging blue jeans and a T-shirt that left little to the imagination. The comparison to the conservative, loose-fitting garments she had worn in Old Norway staggered Larson. He stared, studying the golden waves of hair, his eyes tracking down breasts and thighs with a pleasure that almost allowed him to forget a day of needles, doctors' cold hands, and corridors full of young men in their underwear.

"Gosh," Larson said at last. He tried to say more, but was overcome by incoherent stammering.

Silme laughed. She caught his hand, leading him onto the sidewalk. "So how did it go?" She used English, colored with her melodious accent.

"They didn't take me." Larson placed an arm around Silme's narrow waist. "They did recommend a good psychiatrist, though." He waited. Although Silme could no longer cast spells, she had retained her ability to explore superficial thoughts, a process that had never cost her life energy in the past. Now she was using the procedure to help her learn English, slang and connotation as well as denotation.

"They think you're crazy?" Silme tested her newly gained knowledge.

"Right."

"You're not going to see the doctor. Are you?"

Larson retrieved the psychiatrist's card from his pocket. "Actually, I was thinking I might." He corrected quickly,

"Not because I'm insane for talking to sorceresses and gods, though. I'm just thinking he might be able to help with the war memories."

"I hope so," Silme said. "You know, I love you."

"I love you, too." Larson gave Silme a vigorous hug. "And you know why?"

Silme embraced him with nearly as much force. "No, why?"

"No reason at all. Does that bother you?"

Silme hesitated, her grip loosening. Then she laughed. "Not this time. Not in the least."

Larson released Silme, taking her hand and continuing the walk along the roadway. Now, fully drawn into his joy, the induction process faded, allowing other thoughts to intrude. "Shadow didn't feel up to coming along?" Astryd's death had taken its toll on the little Climber. And, though understandable, it hurt Larson to see the friend who had kept his spirits through so much pain now fade into a quagmire of despair no one could broach. Over the last two months, Taziar had made obvious and conscious efforts not to inflict his grief on anyone else, even those who had known Astryd and shared his sorrow. He had even learned some new English phrases.

Silme stopped at a four-way intersection, waiting for the walk sign to light, watching the cars trickle past. "Shadow came along. He's just down the road here, helping a woman who locked her keys in the. . . ." Silme trailed off, apparently trying to remember the correct English word.

"Car?" Larson supplied.

People joined Larson and Silme in clusters of two and three, gathering to wait for the light.

"Correct." Silme pointed to a row of cars parked along the curb ahead. "He's right there."

Larson craned his neck around the crowd. Taziar crouched on the hood of a red Mustang, concentrating on some unrecognizable object in his hand. He wore a black dress shirt tucked into pants equally dark, looking like a tiny but dashing villain. A woman leaned against the bumper, watching him intently. She was small. Larson guessed she would stand only a few inches taller than Taziar. Copper highlights wound through sandy curls, defying the current long, straight style. Her body went against the trend as well, stocky and muscled like an athlete's, squarish in an era of tall, willowy women.

The walk sign lit, and Larson and Silme crossed with the group. Apprehension struck Larson. *Shadow doesn't know a damned thing about modern locks. What if he breaks something?*

As if to enhance Larson's concern, a policeman wandered over to the car just as Larson and Silme arrived. The remainder of the crowd passed with no more than a disinterested glimpse.

Taziar looked up. "How'd it go?" he asked in barony tongue.

Closer, Larson identified the object in Taziar's hand as a piece of wood carved to the shape of a key. The Climber clutched tiny tools, using them to scrape shavings from the wood.

"Fine," Larson said. "They didn't take me."

"Great!" Taziar said with genuine enthusiasm, before returning to his work. "Perfect."

The officer peered over Larson's shoulder. "What's he doing?"

The woman poked a finger at the Mustang's driver's window, a fingernail clicking against the glass. "I locked my keys inside. There."

Larson looked in the indicated direction. A ring with three keys lay on the seat, frustratingly beyond the locked doors and closed windows.

The woman's freckled face turned from the policeman to Taziar and back. "He's making a temporary key, I think."

The policeman snorted. "That's stupid. It's not going to work."

Larson nodded, echoing the sentiment.

Taziar sprang from the hood to the ground. "Excuse me," he said in English, pushing past Larson and the officer. "May I, Claire?" He turned his attention to the woman, awaiting permission.

Claire nodded. "Can't hurt. Give it a try."

Taziar placed the makeshift key in the lock. To Larson's surprise, it fit, though when Taziar twisted, nothing happened.

The policeman rolled his eyes.

Larson sighed, sympathizing with his friend's failure.

Taziar put a bit more pressure on the key, then whipped it free. Seizing the handle, he opened the door, ushering Claire inside.

An expression of delight crossed Claire's features in direct contrast to the policeman's shocked stare. Claire snatched up her keys. "Thanks, Taz. Thank you so much."

The policeman took the wooden key from Taziar, examined the complex series of serrations from all sides, then returned it to Claire. "I wouldn't have believed it," he muttered. Shaking his head, he continued on his way.

Larson squeezed Silme's hand.

"Taz, hold on just a minute, would you?" Without awaiting a response, she turned her back, rummaging through her purse. Shortly, she spun around to face Taziar again. She handed him a folded ten dollar bill, then climbed into the car and settled into the driver's seat. She started the engine, then rolled down her window. "Bye! And thanks again." With a final wave, she pulled onto the road and roared away.

Taziar watched the car glide into city traffic, smoothing the bill between his fingers.

Noticing something unusual, Larson reached for the ten. "Can I see that?"

Taziar relinquished it without looking.

Larson studied the bill, discovering numbers hastily scrawled across Alexander Hamilton. "I think she liked you."

Taziar turned. "What do you mean?"

"She left you her telephone number." Larson indicated the handwritten numbers. "Apparently, she wants to see you again."

Taziar made a noncommittal noise. At length, he smiled.

Larson handed back the bill. "At least, you seem to have found your calling. Carving out a working key. I'm impressed." It occurred to Larson just how versatile his companion's skills were. *Even without an education, he could become almost anything. A circus acrobat, a locksmith, a stunt man.* He smiled. *Even a jockey.*

"Just one thing," Taziar said.

Larson nodded, prepared for a discussion on telephones and twentieth-century dating practices and, thus, wholly unprepared for Taziar's question.

"What's this for?" Taziar balanced the policeman's badge on his palm.

Startled speechless, Larson stared, his smile wilting. "I don't believe you did that."

Silme lowered her head, apparently trying to glean the implications from Larson's most shallow thoughts.

"You know I'll give it back."

"I don't believe you did that." Larson found himself unable to find other words, though his mind did conjure the perfect want ad: *For sale: Small, agile lunatic. Slightly used. Guaranteed never a dull moment.*

Taziar met Larson's consternation with laughter. He whirled with a dancer's grace, taking in the skyscrapers, lights, and human and vehicular traffic. "I think I love New York."

Silme chuckled.

Larson knew the year would bring its trials: teaching two other-world companions English, turning them into American citizens, convincing his family he should marry a woman he seemed to have known only a few days. Yet, in the wake of all that had happened, those issues seemed trivial. He joined the laughter, wholeheartedly, though he knew it was aimed at him.

Taziar's mirth died away. Larson followed his gaze to a familiar, rocket-shaped building, the tallest in the world, its spire visible through the smog. The expression of determination on the Shadow Climber's face looked frighteningly unconstrained.

Taziar will get along in this endless, concrete playground. Let's just hope New York City can survive Taziar Medakan. "Come on." Larson grabbed Taziar's arm, offering his other hand to Silme. "Let's go home."

According to Norse Mythology, the end of their religious pantheon would come in the form of a great war, the Ragnarok. The gods' enemies would gain access to Asgard via a rainbow bridge called the Bifrost. One god, Heimdallr, was charged with preventing the giants and Hel's hordes from crossing the Bifrost Bridge. Therefore, Heimdallr's responsibility was to guard the Bifrost in order to prevent Ragnarok and assure that the Norse gods survived and reigned for eternity.

Any organization dedicated to recreating the Old Norse age and beliefs, perhaps a subgroup of the Society for Creative Anachronism, could thus be said to have taken over Heimdallr's job as "Guardian of the Bifrost."

—Astryd Larson,
newsletter
August 1991